"Girl, Colored"
and Other Stories

ALSO BY JUDITH MUSSER
AND FROM MCFARLAND

_____

"Tell It to Us Easy" and Other Stories:
A Complete Short Fiction Anthology of African American
Women Writers in Opportunity *Magazine (1923–1948)* (2008)

"Girl, Colored" and Other Stories

A Complete Short Fiction Anthology of African American Women Writers in The Crisis *Magazine, 1910–2010*

Edited by Judith Musser

McFarland & Company, Inc., Publishers

Jefferson, North Carolina, and London

LIBRARY OF CONGRESS ONLINE CATALOG DATA

"Girl, colored" and other stories : a complete short fiction anthology
of African American women writers in the Crisis magazine,
1910–2010 / edited by Judith Musser.
p.   cm.
Includes bibliographical references and index.

ISBN 978-0-7864-4606-3

softcover : 50# alkaline paper ∞

1. American fiction—African American authors.   2. American
fiction—Women authors.   3. Short stories, American.
4. African American women—Fiction.

PS647.A35 G57   2011   813'.0108928708996073—dc22   2010033897

British Library cataloguing data are available

© 2011 Judith Musser. All rights reserved

Front cover: *Summer Flowers with Two Chairs*, 1944. (Also known as
Love Letter [Summer Flowers]). Oil on fabric, 8½ x 11½ in. Private collection

Manufactured in the United States of America

McFarland & Company, Inc., Publishers
Box 611, Jefferson, North Carolina 28640
www.mcfarlandpub.com

To Kathy, Janie, David, and Missie
and in memory of Becky

ACKNOWLEDGMENTS

There are always many people who help make a project like this happen. First, thank you to La Salle University for their generosity in providing a semester's research leave to work on this book. I also thank Kevin Harty, chair of English, and my other colleagues in the English Department for their advice and support. I am indebted to the library staff at Connelly Library and to Jim who fixed all the microfilm machines. I especially appreciate Thom and Linda for their practical help. Thanks to Sydney for her assistance at the Library of Congress. I am grateful to Diana and Dan for the peace of the Tree House and Janet for the quiet of Truro. Thank you to Beth and Fabrizio for keeping me connected and to Rufus for keeping me grounded.

TABLE OF CONTENTS

INTRODUCTION

The Crisis magazine celebrates 100 years of continuous publication in 2010. It is one of the longest running African American journals in the history of American publishing. This anthology is a complete collection of short stories by African American women that were published during this 100-year period and offers an historical, literary, and cultural perspective on the lives of African American women beginning in the Harlem Renaissance to the present time.

African American women writers of the short story play a significant role in the long history of women's writing in general as well as the development of the genre of the short story. Bill Mullen asserts in his essay "'A Revolutionary Tale': In Search of African American Women's Short Story Writing" that "African American short fiction owes its beginnings to a woman" (192). This woman was Frances Ellen Watkins Harper whose story "The Two Offers" was published in 1859. Ann Allen Schockley writes that Harper was "the bibliographic and historical starting point for the complex yet heretofore unsketched development of the short story by African American women" (58). The appearance of Harper's story, which was published in Thomas Hamilton's short-lived journal *The Anglo-African,* was noteworthy; most of the nineteenth-century magazines, journals and periodicals were dominated by white publishers and editors who rarely encouraged or included the publication of literature from African American writers. Though Harper's story was published in 1859, it would take at least 30 years until short stories became a standard genre of literary output for African American women. Henry Louis Gates notes that more works of fiction by black women between 1890 and 1910 were published than by black men in the previous half-century (cited in Hull xvi.) This change from obscurity to prominence was dramatic, and the stories published in *The Crisis* engendered this progression.

One additional impetus helped to set the stage for African American women's rise to prominence in the genre of short stories. In 1900, Pauline E. Hopkins (her novel *Contending Forces* was published the same year), with the help of Walter W. Wallace and some investors, published the monthly illustrated magazine entitled *Colored American.*[1] Mullen believes that "Hopkins's successful promotion of unheralded black women writers, providing them a credible, uniquely black-owned literary market, as well as her anti-accommodationist stance as editor of *Colored American*, helped inspire W. E. B. Du Bois to establish the magazine that turned the tide of African American literary production forever to include and celebrate short fiction" (196).

W. E. B. Du Bois's magazine was *The Crisis* and it started its publication ten years after *Colored American* began circulation. *The Crisis* also helped cultivate literature in the Harlem Renaissance; African American journals and magazines became the primary channels for literary output during this period of intellectual and creative activity. Writers, editors, literary critics, political leaders and the readers of the journals all became involved in the ongoing debate concerning the purpose of African American literature. The discussion centered on whether Black Art should be judged according to its political and propagandistic merits or its aesthetic value. Writers, in particular African American women writers of the short story, were especially conspicuous in their creative choices and these preferences were revealed in the types of journals to which they submitted their work. The most prominent periodicals were *Opportunity* and *The Crisis*.[2] Those writers who were more concerned with artistic and aesthetic purity tended to publish their fiction under the editorial direction of Charles Johnson in *Opportunity*. Those more dedicated to conveying a political message contributed their work to W. E. B. Du Bois's *The Crisis*.

Theodore Peterson, in a speech given at the editorial seminar of the American Press in 1966, stated the following: "Great magazines are made by great editors [and] express the personalities of the men who edit them" (quoted in Kimbrough). This is most clearly demonstrated in *The Crisis*, for in its pages the debate encompassing literary aesthetic creativity and propaganda creativity is clearly portrayed in its editorials and the literary contributions. In the case of *The Crisis*, as editors changed, so did the number, content, and style of those contributions and this is most markedly demonstrated in the short stories.

As the first editor and founder of *The Crisis*, Du Bois published the journal's objectives clearly in the opening pages of the first edition:

> It will first and foremost be a newspaper: it will record important happenings and movements in the world which bear on the great problem of inter-racial relations, and especially those which affect the Negro-American.
> Secondly, it will be a review of opinion and literature, recording briefly books, articles, and important expressions of opinion in the white and colored press on the race problem.
> Thirdly, it will publish a few short articles.
> Finally, its editorial page will stand for the rights of men, irrespective of color or race, for the highest ideals of American democracy, and for reasonable but earnest and persistent attempt to gain these rights and realize these ideals. The magazine will be the organ of no clique or party and will avoid personal rancor of all sorts. In the absence of proof to the contrary it will assume honesty of purpose on the part of all men, North and South, white and black [November 1910].

Thirteen years later, Charles Johnson, as editor of *Opportunity* magazine, would propose very different goals. As with the objectives, the titles also reflected the differences between the two journals.[3] For example, Johnson encouraged an agenda which would be uplifting and hopeful whereas Du Bois preferred to focus on the "the great problem" of race. *Opportunity* followed the National Urban League's doctrines closely whereas *The Crisis*, though professing to not follow the dictates of a "clique or party," was under the auspices of the National Association for the Advancement of Colored People (NAACP). *Opportunity* openly supported the arts as part of the journal's agenda. As is noted in the objectives quoted above, *The Crisis* did not initially include a direct call for literary submissions. But this would quickly change. Two months after the opening issue in January 1911, poetry appeared. With the rare exception, at least one poem, and sometimes as many as five or six, appeared with every issue of the monthly journal up until the mid 1980s; the inclusion of poetry after the 1980s was sporadic. The first short story to appear in the journal was "The Doll" by Charles Chesnutt in April of 1912.[4] For the next 40 years, an average of five short stories would appear every year. Finally, the most significant difference between the two journals concerns the attention given to articulating a purpose for African American literature. Johnson did not specify his own views. Du Bois, on the other hand, would attempt throughout the 24 years of his editorship to develop a theory which would address the debate between propaganda and art. As will be demonstrated, Du Bois would change his mind often and his varying advice is reflected in the short stories written by women.

In the beginning, Du Bois set a tone for his magazine which, to some readers, was too bitter, satiric, brutal and even depressing; the journal was clearly not to be a source of entertainment. In 1912, some members of the Board of Directors of the NAACP complained that Du Bois was focused too much on the dark side of things. Du Bois responded to their criticism in an editorial entitled "The Gall of Bitterness":

> It may be acknowledged at the outset that *The Crisis* does not try to be funny ... our stock in trade is not jokes. We are in earnest. This is a newspaper. It tries to tell the Truth.... Its whole reason for being is the revelation of the facts of racial antagonism now in the world, and these facts are not humorous....
>
> True it is that this country has had its appetite for facts on the Negro problem spoiled by sweets. In earlier days the Negro minstrel who "jumped Jim Crow" was the typical black man served up to the nation's taste....
>
> In the last fifteen years there has come a new campaign of Joy and Laughter to degrade black folks.... We have had audiences entertained with "nigger" stories, talks of pianos in cabins, and of the general shiftlessness of the freedman, and concerted efforts to make it appear that the wrongs of color prejudice are but incidental and trivial, while the shortcomings of black men are stupendous, if not fatal.
>
> This is the lie which *The Crisis* is here to refute. It is a lie, a miserable and shameful lie [February 1912].

Art and literature, according to Du Bois, should follow this lead. To demonstrate this, six months later in August of 1912, Du Bois announced a short story competition; however, his directions to writers were a bit confusing considering his concern for revealing the "grim awfulness of the bare truth" as prescribed earlier in February. The short story competition resulted in submissions of stories in three groups:

> Didactic stories. Some of these have had good plots, others none, but nearly all have been hurt artistically by the always present desire to instruct the reader. This is a common fault among writers in America. An able critic has said of us: We are preachers, not artists.
>
> Old-time "darky" stories. From the literary viewpoint these have been the best. But the most of them have been too evidently old time, copying a style so well known as to be stereotyped. We want humorous tales, but we would like them in a little less threadbare clothes.
>
> Character sketches. The story that we print below comes under this head.[5] It is slight, but it bears the stamp of sincerity and truth. It shows us a young colored girl from a viewpoint new to many. It interprets for us a bit of human life.
>
> We hope that our readers will send up other stories. We want the good plots well worked out; we want merriment and laughter; we want pictures of the real colored America [August 1912].

A significant number of stories and poems printed during the first ten years of *The Crisis* were exclusively didactic and demonstrated an attempt to not portray the joy and laughter which Du Bois originally saw as degrading. The literary contributions dramatized and exposed discrimination, racial injustice, and the disinherited state of the African American at this time. Most of the short stories written by men introduced and glorified themes of retribution and upheaval. These stories centered around the melodramatic heroism of African American characters who were soldiers or athletes who carried their race's hopes to victory. Du Bois himself contributed some material of this didactic sort. In January of 1912 he wrote an ironic piece called "A Mild Suggestion" proposing, like Swift, the mass murder of all ten million American Negroes as the only equitable and merciful solution to the problem. Du Bois had the mind of an activist and propagandist, and revealed himself as much more interested in the effect a work had on the readers than in a story's intrinsic merits. What he wanted was literature that was "beautiful, alluring, delicate, fine" but more importantly literature "that had ideas" as well (March 1915), that "bore the stamp of sincerity and truth," that "pictured the real colored American" (August 1912) and that did so "with honesty and respect" (March 1911). Judgment was eventually and finally to be made on the basis of a work's practical effects and not on its internal relationships. And perhaps most important, Du Bois believed that literature was to be part of his dedicated campaign to instill in the African American race a dynamic and self-motivating pride that he believed was so essential for the success of the long uphill struggle for racial justice and legal and social equality.

In 1919, Jessie Fauset joined the staff as literary editor and stayed until May 1926. Her editorial influence is demonstrated in two ways. First, she persuaded Du Bois to promote a literary contest for poetry, drama, essays and short stories much like those held in *Opportunity*. The first of the three competitions began in 1925, and each was held annually until 1927. Amy Spingarn sponsored the first two contests with additional contributions made by women's clubs and business organizations. *The Crisis* contests were not as successful as those held by *Opportunity*. Abby Arthur Johnson and Ronald Maberry Johnson suggest that the reasons may be because "Du Bois did a workmanlike job with his competitions. [In contrast], Johnson created an electric excitement ... [and] Johnson offered greater rewards than did Du Bois" (*Propaganda* 54).[6]

Jessie Fauset's subtle influence as literary editor is also revealed in the types of stories published by women in the early 1920s. Fauset's style of writing ran counter to that which had been proposed by Du Bois in his February 1912 editorial. One of her most characteristic pieces, "Double Trouble," published in *The Crisis* and later expanded into her novel *The Chinaberry Tree*, hinted toward the kinds of characters she would create in her later career. They tended to be middle to upper class and educated, and her female characters were typically described as women of extreme beauty. In fact, because these women were both racially mixed and of a higher economic class, they often were able to pass for white. Four stories published in *The Crisis* in the 1920s imitated not only Fauset's melodramatic style, but also her plot development in which coincidental circumstances greatly affected the lives of these upper-class, attractive women. In Marie Louise French's story "There Never Fell a Night So Dark," which won second prize in one of the short story contests, a wealthy, light-colored African American woman on the brink of suicide reunites with her estranged husband on a park bench. In Anita Coleman's "Three Dogs and a Rabbit," another wealthy woman, a widow who passed for being white, radically reveals her true identity. Anna, the young white heroine in Iva L. Cotton's "Anna," convinces a judge that she would be better off with a black identity in a black community. And perhaps the most dramatic story is "In Houses of Glass" in which a young girl, raised to believe that she is white, is told of her mixed heritage and she enthusiastically embraces her African roots. Fauset's editorship ended in 1926 and Du Bois's editorial comments one year earlier may hint at their different philosophies in creative aesthetics. At this time, Du Bois believed that African American art was being strangled by its own cloying sweetness and light. "[We refuse] to contemplate any but handsome heroines and flawless defenders; we insist on being always and everywhere all right and often we ruin our cause by claiming too much and admitting no fault. Here *The Crisis* has sinned with this group" (May 1925). At the end of Fauset's tenure as literary editor in 1926, women's stories began to change.

Ultimately, Du Bois presented the position that all art was propaganda and its products would be judged in terms of their social effects:

> Thus all Art is propaganda and ever must be, despite the wailing of the purists. I stand
> in utter shamelessness and say that whatever art I have for writing has been used always

for propaganda for gaining the right of black folk to love and enjoy. I do not care a damn for any art that is not used for propaganda [October 1926].

Marita Bonner's fiction is probably the best illustration of this emphasis in short fiction which espouses a social and political purpose. Her first three published stories in *The Crisis*, all in 1926, demonstrate this clearly. The first story, "The Prison Bound," portrays the truth of a woman's frustration of living in a greasy, cramped apartment where she feels literally imprisoned. Denny, a young, sensitive black artist in Bonner's "Nothing New" is convicted of murder. Bonner's emphasis on poor working conditions is emphasized in "Drab Rambles." Her fictional characters, such as Madie Frye, are distinctly different from the women characters portrayed in Fauset's short fiction and in other stories published ten years earlier in *The Crisis*.

Du Bois's politically charged statements about art and propaganda also had repercussions ten years later. According to Walter C. Daniel, both *The Crisis* and *Opportunity* magazines were temporarily banned from the approved reading list of the District of Columbia public schools. In 1936, *The Crisis* had been declared "objectionable" reading matter because it "carried militant propaganda" ("*The Crisis*" 205). Daniel suggests that any writing that used the buzzword "propaganda" was the spark that ignited fear, especially during the repressive climate of this time period because of the anxiety of fascist governments in Europe. The proposed banning of the journal was not only based on the strong political prose, but also the vocabulary choices used in the creative fiction. The superintendant of schools was concerned with the "practice of using the opprobrious term 'N-----' in its published stories of Negro life" (quoted in Daniel 206).

The beginning of Du Bois's third decade as editor of *The Crisis* marked another change in his literary criticism from that which he espoused in the first decade. *The Crisis* was declining as a literary power and this was partly due to Du Bois's contentious relationship with the NAACP. In the 1930s, the quest for a separate African America began to dominate Du Bois's thoughts. One of the results of his focus was that the literary submissions to *The Crisis* were judged almost exclusively on the basis of their ability to separate from the negative expectations of white readers. The short stories written by women from 1931 to the end of Du Bois's editorship in 1934 are illustrations of this agenda. One of the common features of these stories is that an African American male character, although often not the main character, represents positive and admirable characteristics. For example, Du Bois comments that Edith Manual Durham's "Deepening Dusk" is "one of the most interesting stories *Crisis* has had the privilege of publishing. You can not afford to miss it" (January 1931). The story is about Vivvie, a mulatto girl, who could easily pass in the white world. She is encouraged by her mother to leave home and live with her white father, but Vivvie prefers to stay and marry Tim, primarily because his skin is very dark. She is steadfast in this decision, even at the risk of her mother's life-threatening physical reaction to her daughter's preference for a black man. Another example is Lillian Beverton Mason's story "Honor" in which an African American male character, "Big Bill Harris," heroically chooses not to deflower a young African American woman and ruin not only her reputation but her chances of attending college. Du Bois wrote the following concerning this story:

> *The Crisis* seeks fiction like this—clear, realistic and frank, and yet fiction which shows the possible if not actual triumph of good and true and beautiful things. We do not want stories which picture Negro blood as a crime calling for lynching or suicide. We are quite fed up with filth and defeatism. Send us stories like this [July 1931].

Other women's stories demonstrate a shift in focus to African American male characters who act heroically and receive their just reward. In "The Greatest Gift," an African American "working man" returns a lost purse intact. A character in Anita Scott Colman's story "Two Old Women A-Shopping Go" professes that "Black men really had tougher sledding than black women." And, like Vivvie in "Deepening Dusk," Marianna in Madelen C. Lane's story "Black Mestiza" ultimately chooses Earl, a black college man, over the possibility of passing as the wife of a Filipino. In each of these stories, there is a clear representation of male characters who defy negative stereotypes that were prevalent in white culture.

Du Bois's position as editor of *The Crisis* ended in 1934. For years, his theories expressed in *The Crisis* had run counter to the philosophy of the NAACP, which was dedicated to the policy of gradually achieving total integration. Du Bois, on the other hand, had come to embrace economic, educational, political and social segregation. This caused a final rift that was emphasized by the growing personal antagonism between Du Bois and the new secretary of NAACP, Walter White. In June of 1934, the Board of Directors accepted Du Bois's resignation which terminated his 24 years of editorship.

Du Bois's legacy as editor was clearly influential; however, the editors who followed Du Bois's regime were less concerned with any debate surrounding literary criticism. Roy Wilkins, who served under Walter White as Assistant Secretary of the NAACP, became the next editor of *The Crisis* from 1934 to 1949. His challenge in the midst of the Great Depression was not to resolve racial issues or to define the purpose of art; it was financial: "The big job was keeping [*The Crisis*] alive.... The new editor's salary was seventy-five dollars a month, five more than was being paid the stenographer.... [We] had no money to pay for articles and pictures; the purchase of a new typewriter was a great triumph" (quoted in Rodriguez 72). Twenty-nine stories by African American women were published during Wilkins's editorship. One change he made that is very helpful to anyone researching some of the more obscure women short story writers was to include a brief biographical note on the contributors in each issue.[7] These biographical notes are significant for two reasons. First, we learn that African American women writers came from varying areas of the country, most notably the Midwest which suggests that the readership of *The Crisis* was indeed country-wide. It also indicates that although Harlem was the publishing capital of the Renaissance, African American women short story writers, through both their locations as well as the setting of their stories, broadened this geographical center. Second, it is noted that for most of these writers, the only biographical information provided is the place where they live. The inclusion of awards, education, other publications, or noteworthy accomplishments is noticeably absent. It is a reminder that many of the stories published in *The Crisis* came from women who were not necessarily prominent writers. Thus, the authors of these short stories offer a rich cultural resource and diversity of personal histories, experiences, and perspectives.

After March 1947, short story publications in *The Crisis* almost vanished. Seven stories by men appeared up until 1952 and no stories by women surfaced until three contributions by African American writers Hazel James in 1975 and Mary Carter Smith in 1978. Ama Ata Aidoo, the noted African writer from Ghana, had one of her stories published in 1998. There are some possible explanations, not least of which is that the focus of the magazine had changed under Roy Wilkins's editorship. As is noted in the following list of editors and their dates, the leadership of the magazine changed hands often; the average length of term for one editor was only five years: James W. Ivy (1950–1966), Henry Lee Moon (1966–1974), Warren Marr III (1974–1981), Maybelle Ward (1984–1985), Fred Beauford (1985–1992), Denise Crittendon (1994–1995), Paul Ruffins (1995–1997), Ida E. Lewis (1998–2000), Victoria Valentine (2001–2007), and currently interim editor Phil W. Petrie (2007–present).[8] These frequent changes of leadership understandably challenge any attempt to create a focus and direction for a magazine, let alone establish an agenda on creative writing. In addition, other venues for women to publish their stories began to emerge. For example, between 1944 and 1946, the bimonthly publication *Negro Story Magazine* appeared. It was edited by two women (Alice C. Browning and Fern Gayden) and is described by Walter Daniel as "a black literary magazine that was almost totally dedicated to publishing the short-story" (*Black* 288). Other magazines began to emphasize literary submissions, specifically short stories by African American women, such as *Phylon*, *Black Fire*, *Ebony*, and *Essence*. In addition, African American women writers began to find success in publishing their own collections of stories in book form. The best example is Alice Walker's ground-breaking 1973 *In Love and Trouble*. Mullen uses Walker's collection as an example of these connections among African American women writers of the early century with writers of the Black Arts Movement: "Walker's extrapolations on Harlem Renaissance short fiction themes, particularly those of Hurston, now energized by black nationalist and black feminist awareness, heralded the revolutionized nature, form and function of contemporary black women's short fiction as it suddenly became not a marginal but a central form in African American women's cultural expression" (201).

As noted earlier, even though *The Crisis* did not set out to be a source for literary publications, it emerged as a strong venue for writers for the first 40 years of its publication. Additionally, *The Crisis* has never been categorized according to gender and thus it is not identified as a ladies' magazine.[9] However, it is clear from looking at the content pages of *The Crisis*, the advertisements, and the literary contributions, that women's issues, women readers, and women's voices were important, directive, and culturally influential in establishing a feminist and racial standard for African American women. I believe there is evidence to demonstrate that *The Crisis* did not merely include women; instead, a case can be made that the political, economic, educational, and social issues that permeated the editorials, news reports, literary contributions, and even the physical layout of the magazine, all demonstrate that women's issues and voices directed and sustained the focus of the journal, and the effects of this focus are still present in *The Crisis* today.

To begin, black womanhood was featured on the covers of the magazine. From the first issue to around the early 1970s, women and children were prominently depicted, either in drawings or in photographs.[10] Usually the identity of the woman was noted on the cover page or the table of contents and the types of individuals ranged widely to include well-known actresses, politicians and wives of politicians, writers, artists, and leaders of women's clubs. Some had familial connections with NAACP personnel. Some were historical figures of which the most notable was Sojourner Truth who is depicted beside Abraham Lincoln. Jean Fagin Yellin notes that this particular issue of *The Crisis* (August 1915) was devoted to women's suffrage and this cover picture "recalls Du Bois' earlier effort to revive the historic alliance between 'women and Negroes'" (370). Often, a college graduate was featured with a notation of her accomplishments during her tenure at a university. Aaron Douglas presented his artistic rendering of the African American woman on the cover with the painting titled "The Burden of Black Womanhood." In other cases, there were news photographs, such as a picture of "Mrs. Gifford Pinshot Organizing Colored Strikers" and a photograph of the first Negro WAVES. There were also examples of nameless generic representations of womanhood, such as "an octoroon," "a quadroon," "Negro womanhood," "a Harlem girl," "A Haitian woman," "Head of a Bethlehem woman," "Madonna," "The Mother," and "Woman of Santa Lucia." Carolyn Kitch writes, "It is likely that these images were empowering for the magazine's audience. Here were faces recognizable as the Christy Girl, the vamp, the flapper—and they were black" (99). Years later, in an essay published in *The Crisis* in which he reminisced on his career, Du Bois would attribute the success of the magazine in part to its inclusion of visual images. "Pictures of colored people were an innovation," he remembers;

those that showed African Americans in a positive light were particularly crucial because "at that time it was the rule of most white papers never to publish a picture of a colored person except as a criminal" ("Editing *The Crisis*" March 1951). The cover photographs, pictures, and drawings of African American women in *The Crisis* served as an important antidote to negative images of African Americans revealed in other publications, advertising, cartoons, and films.

After viewing the cover, the reader would then turn to the table of contents. The items included in this list varied throughout the 100 years of publication, but repeated features can be noted. In particular, there were regular columns which focused on women. For example, in the first 30 years there were repeated features titled "Talks about Women," "Women's Clubs," and biographies of outstanding women in the "mis-named" (Yellin 365) "Men of the Month" series; there was a photographic series entitled "First Ladies of Colored America," and another sequence of features named "Queens of the Colleges." Reports of symposiums were held with topical titles such as "A Suffrage Symposium," "Symposium on Votes for Women," "Intermarriage—A Symposium," and a report on the "International Council of Women" held in Norway.

In addition to these regular features, specific editorials and special articles which related to women's concerns appeared in every issue. The more typical article focused on women in the job market which included factual studies of employment of black women; surveys of wages, hours, and working conditions; and job opportunities. The headlines for these articles were "Employment of Colored Women in Chicago," "The Colored Woman in Industry," "Red Cross Nurses, Camp Grant," "From Housecleaner to Business Executive," "Women Workers in Indianapolis," "Jim Crowing Nurses," "Negro Women in Steel," "Women of the Cotton Fields," and "Negro Army Wives."[11] Some essays were directed towards educational opportunities for women such as "And So Lucille Went to College," "Beta Chapter, Chicago of the Alpha Kappa Alpha Sorority," "Women's Medical College," "Can a Colored Woman Be a Physician?," "Black Beauty and the University," and "She Knocks at the Door of Missouri U."

A large number of articles addressed issues related to mothering and child-rearing. As noted earlier, photographs of both women and children were featured on the cover. Readers were encouraged to send photographs of their children and there were various issues in which pages of the journal were filled with photographs of children and babies, often in groups ranging from 70 to 150 pictures. Patricia A. Turner, one of the commentators on the 1986 Emmy award winning documentary film *Ethnic Notions*, describes the stereotypical caricature of African American children in the late 1800s and early 1900s:

> They're always on the river, on the ground, in a tree, partially clad, dirty, their hair unkempt. This suggests that there was a need to imagine black children as animal-like, as savage. If you do that, if you make that step and say these children are really like little furry animals then it's much easier to rationalize and justify the threat that's embodied in having an alligator pursuing the child.

Anne Carroll, in her essay analyzing the layout of *The Crisis*, points out that Du Bois often used editorials to spell out particular arguments about what these children demonstrate: "In an essay on 'Our Baby Pictures' in October 1914, he emphasizes that the physical attractiveness of these children disproves common racist arguments that African Americans are physically degenerate. His point is confirmed by photographs of African American children scattered across the pages of the essay" (102).

These precious children, the future of the race, needed wise, encouraging, supportive, and health-conscious mothering. *The Crisis* included featured topics with titles such as "A

Message to Colored Mothers," "Keeping Well Babies Well," "Prevention of Children's Handicaps," "Racial Inferiority among Negro Children," and "Reports on Schools for Black, White and Yellows." And *The Crisis* didn't shy away from more controversial women's issues as illustrated in the article titled "The Case for Birth Control."

A final category of articles highlighted topics that related to African American women and the suffrage movement. The September 1912 issue was dedicated to women's suffrage. Du Bois's lead editorial explained to readers why they should be interested in woman's suffrage. He ended his discussion with this argument:

> Finally, votes for women means votes for black women.... The enfranchisement of these women will not be a mere doubling of our vote and voice in the nation; it will tend to stronger and more normal political life, the rapid dethronement of the "heeler" and "grafter" and the making of politics a method of broadest philanthropic race betterment [*The Crisis* September 1912].

What followed in the issue was a symposium on suffrage which included contributions from various women such as Fanny Garrison Villard, Mary Church Terrell, Martha Gruening, and Adella Hunt Logan. In August of 1915, Du Bois devoted another special issue of *The Crisis* to woman's suffrage.[12] Political issues involving women also included the role of women internationally. For example, three articles appeared highlighting women's rights around the world: "Murdering Women in Nigeria," "Women Among the Soviets," and "A Black Woman in Red Russia."

It is important to note that an overview of the current table of contents of *The Crisis* is actually very similar to the original in terms of content related to women. The subject matter of the last ten years of *The Crisis*[13] indicates that the interest in and coverage of women's issues have not diminished. For example, contemporary women of all backgrounds, representations, and abilities are highlighted in various articles such as "Mildred Roxborough," who served the NAACP longer than anyone except Roy Wilkins; "Other Legends of the NAACP"; "Judicial Nominee Justice Janice Rogers Brown"; "Dr. Ruth Simmons," who was the first woman and the first African American to head one of the eight Ivy League schools; a biographical listing of "African American Women College Presidents"; "Wisconsin Representative Gwen Moore, the first African American elected to Congress from her State"; "Shirley Ann Jackson's Groundbreaking Career in Science"; "Marine Capt. Vernice Armour, the Nation's First Black Woman Combat Pilot"; "Lillian Roberts," who at the age of 79 headed the nation's largest labor union; St. Louis lawyer "Margaret Bush Wilson," nearly 90 years old, who struggled for justice during the turbulent civil rights era; Lorraine Miller, who was the "First African American Clerk of the House of Representatives"; and "the Rev. Dr. Vashti Murphy McKenzie" who was elected the AME Church's first female bishop.

In the past ten years, *The Crisis* also included stories about famous historical women such as Lucy Parsons, Madame C. J. Walker, Mrs. Garvey, Mary McLeod Bethune, Mamie "Peanut" Johnson (Negro League pitcher for the Indianapolis Clowns), Mary Seacole, Coretta Scott King, Rosa Parks, and Jo Ann Robinson. Features discuss the role of artists, writers, performers, and musicians, both historical (Sarah Vaughn, Jessie Fauset, Zora Neale Hurston, and Hattie McDonald) and contemporary (Octavia Butler, Sarah Jones, Suzan-Lori Parks, Ruby Dee, Alice Walker). International women are highlighted such as Doras Chirwa's work with black women with AIDS in the U.S. and Zambia; Ellen Johnson Sirleaf, as the new president of Liberia and Africa's first female head-of-state; and Emira Woods's article which describes women leaders in Liberia and other African countries.

The journal continues to cover important national issues that relate to or concern women and the titles demonstrate the complexity and variety of this coverage: "Why Sexism Should

Top the Civil Rights Agenda," "Private Prisons Profiting at the Expense of Women of Color," "Up Front: Black Women in the Military Make Strides," "Black Woman Founds Florida City," "Katie Geneva Cannon on Gender Issues in the Church and Same-Sex Marriage," "Women Leaders are Backbone of the NAACP," "Raising Money to Support Black Female Politicians," "Women Inspired to Transform Mentors of Former Female Prisoners," "The Leading Cause of Death for African American Women between the Ages of 25 and 34," "New Book by the National Council of Negro Women on Women and Aging," "Why Poor Women Put Motherhood Before Marriage," "Black Women in Sport Foundation," and "An Examination of the Dearth of Black Female Coaches." Perhaps one of the most interesting articles demonstrates that W.E.B. Du Bois's ideas are still debated; *The Crisis* conducted a symposium in which ten African American women respond to Du Bois's 1920 essay "Damnation of Women."

As the title of this anthology suggests, the most important contribution that *The Crisis* provided to readers was its century-long record of contributions from African American women writers who were inspired to realistically and creatively present what it means to be female and what it means to be black. Thus, while the magazine placed women on the covers, devoted regular monthly columns to addressing women's's issues, and responded to specific concerns, the strongest expression of being female and being black came from women creative writers. There were other magazines that included poetry, short stories, and drama, but *The Crisis* was the most enduring, the most prolific, the most supportive, and the most diligent in presenting consistent submissions.[14] *The Crisis* has published 206 short stories in its 100 years of publication. Fifty-two percent of those stories (106) were written by women[15]; 48 percent (100) were written by men. *The Crisis* also published drama: between 1918 and 1934, 14 plays were published (9 one-act plays and 5 full-length plays, seven of these written by women and seven written by men.) The largest number of literary contributions were from poets. During the 100 years, more than 900 poems were published; about one third of these poems were written by women. Langston Hughes published more than 100 poems and Georgia Douglas Johnson published more than 40 poems. Thus, while poetry was dominated by men, the short story was the genre of choice for women.

An easy assumption may be that just because a writer's work appeared in a magazine dedicated to uplifting the African American race, to recording the issues affecting people who were African American, and to calling attention to African American names and voices, that this writer was African American. Of the 106 stories written by women, 12 of these stories are by white women. Some of these white women were well known for their activism in the NAACP and thus did not need the editors of *The Crisis* to clarify their race or identity. For example, a story was published by Mary Ovington White[16] who in May of 1910 was appointed to the NAACP as executive secretary and later as chair and served for 38 years total. She also wrote various books and articles, including biographies, histories, anthropological studies, and an anthology for children. Her short story in *The Crisis* was a rare example of her creative fiction. Martha Gruening,[17] another activist white woman, also worked for racial justice and peace while serving as secretary to Herbert Seligmann, the director of public relations for the NAACP.

Other well known white contributors were not directly connected to the NAACP, but were established published writers of fiction. In particular, early 20th-century best-selling author and educational reformer Dorothy Canfield (Fisher)[18] contributed a story and later helped to direct literary tastes by serving as a member of the Book of the Month Club selection committee. Esma Rideout Booth[19] graduated with an MA from the Kennedy School of Missions (a division of the Hartford Theological Seminary), was a missionary in Africa for

40 years, and published various children's books of African stories. Another white writer, perhaps not as well known today, was Maria Moravsky,[20] an immigrant (unknown country of origin) whose stories also appeared in *Harpers Magazine*.

The Crisis also published stories by well-known Jewish women writers. Rose Dorothy Lewin (Franken), award-winning playwright and director, submitted a story.[21] Jessie Bernard, an American sociologist who provided insights into women, sex, marriage, and the interaction of the family and community, wrote her only fictional story in *The Crisis*.[22] Annie Nathan Meyer, one of the founders of Barnard College and a prolific writer, published a story in *The Crisis*.[23] Finally, Babette Stiefel,[24] identified in Michael Rogin's *Blackface, White Noise: Jewish Immigrants in the Hollywood Melting Pot*, wrote the only story by a woman writer in which anti–Semitism is linked with discrimination against blacks.[25]

Finally, there are three stories by white women who were not well known in politics or the literary field. When they submitted their stories for consideration, they identified themselves as white and the editors of *The Crisis* included the revelation of their racial heritage with the story. Mary G. Roessler[26] explains her enthusiasm for *The Crisis* as a "member of the lighter races." And Caroline Stetson Allen[27] inquires of the editors if they "accept any fiction ... unless written by your own people." Maria Wirth's[28] racial identity is noted under the title of her story in the table of contents.

As with the well-known white writers and leaders, racial identity is traceable when the writer is a recognized African American woman. Du Bois's call for a rising of the talented tenth to lead the race is certainly represented through the educational backgrounds, careers, and activism of a talented percentage of the African American women contributors of short stories. The biographies of some of the writers demonstrate high academic achievement. Noted high schools and universities are represented widely, from Boston Latin School for Girls and High School for Girls in Philadelphia, to Bryn Mawr, Cornell, University of Pennsylvania, Straight University, Oberlin College, London School of Economics, Wellesley, New Mexico Teachers College, Fisk University, Radcliffe, Wilberforce, University of Minnesota, and Connecticut College of Pharmacy. After graduation, most of these college educated women became teachers, often in public school, some on the college level. Some were also musicians and artists, and others were fluent in German, French, and Italian. In addition, their contribution of a short story was not their only record of publication. Most published novels, poetry, collections of short stories, and other essays.

The most recognizable of this gifted group, of course, is Jessie Fauset, assistant editor of *The Crisis* and one of the most published of Harlem Renaissance women writers. She contributed six stories to the magazine, but she was not the most prolific short story writer contributor. The highest number of contributions was from two writers who each published nine stories. Marita Bonner, a Radcliffe graduate who studied German and music and was the founder of Radcliffe chapter of Delta Sigma Theta, published most of her entire work (short stories, essays, and drama) in both *The Crisis* and *Opportunity* magazines. The other contributor of nine stories is Octavia Wynbush, whose biography is similar to these other well-known African American women. She was born in the North (Washington, Pennsylvania); she obtained college degrees (BA in German from Oberlin and MA in English from Columbia); she taught at colleges in New Orleans, Louisiana, and Arkansas; and she eventually retired as a high school teacher.

One name in the list of prominent African American women contributors is particularly recognizable—Mrs. Paul Lawrence Dunbar. Although her story was published after her separation from her first husband, poet Paul Laurence Dunbar, and after her marriage to Henry Callis in 1910, she still used her first husband's name, albeit changing the spelling. Her fame as a short story writer was well documented with the publication of two collections in 1895. She then went on to write four novels, two volumes on oration, dramas, newspaper columns, collections of essays and reviews, and poetry.

Another prolific writer was Effie Lee Newsome who was familiar to readers of *The Crisis*. Newsome was a children's poet, short fiction writer, and editor of a literary column for children in *The Crisis* from 1925 to 1929. Under W. E. B. Du Bois's editorship, Newsome established this regular column where she catered to children readers with nature poetry, nonsense verse, and parables about the unique experience of being young and African American.

An additional well-known writer was Ann Petry, who, by training, was a pharmacist; however, she changed careers through the encouragement of an English teacher. Her most popular novel *The Street* was published in 1946 and won the Houghton Mifflin Literary Fellowship. *The Street* was the first book by a black woman writer to sell more than a million copies. Ann Petry contributed four stories to *The Crisis*.

An African American woman did not necessarily have to be a prolific writer to play a part in the up-lifting of the race and to have a short story published in *The Crisis*. The organization of women's clubs began in the 19th century with the aims of self-development and social reform and this movement didn't waver in the early 20th century. Many of the writers of the short stories in this collection were founding and active members of these various clubs. For example, another well-known contributor of two short stories was Leila Amos Pendleton.[29] Her notoriety was gained through local activism. She was the founder (in 1898) of the Alpha Charity Club of Anacostia; she served as the club's president for thirteen years; she founded and was president of the Social Purity Club of Washington; she was the vice-president for the District of Columbia of the Northeastern Federation of Women's Clubs; and she served as secretary of the National Association of Assemblies of the Order of the Golden Circle, Auxiliary to the Scottish Rite of Freemasonry, S. J., U. S. A.

Another activist contributor of a story to *The Crisis* was Mary Church Terrell who was a charter member of the NAACP. Her activity in the feminist movement included helping to integrate the American Association of University Women and founding the Colored Woman's League in Washington in 1892. This organization merged with the National Federation of Afro-American Women in 1896 and adopted the name National Federation of Colored Women. Mary Church Terrell was elected the first president.

Brenda Moryck, another contributor of a short story, began her work as a volunteer in New Jersey working with the Newark Bureau of Charities. She was also an active participant in a variety of reform organizations including the Urban League of Harlem's YWCA and the New York NAACP Women' Auxiliary. Another short story contributor was Ethel Caution (Davis) whose activism centered in the Midwest; while in Kansas, she served on the Executive Committee of Citizen's Forum of the NAACP, and for three years she worked as the Dean of Women at Talladega College. Mary Carter Smith, the writer of the last published short story in this anthology, combined her literary talents with a commitment to promoting and organizing venues and outlets for all storytellers. Her grass-roots efforts include operating as hostess of *Black Is*, a Maryland Public Television program; presenting and producing a Saturday morning show *Griot for the Young and the Young at Heart* on WEAA-FM, Morgan State University; serving as the founding member of Big Sisters International and Arena Players; and co-founding the National Association of Black Storytellers. Among her various awards, Smith has received a Lifetime Achievement Award from the National Storytelling Association.

Three of the contributors of short stories to *The Crisis* also claimed international reputations and careers. After her activism in the U.S., Mary Church Terrell represented colored women on the American delegation to the International Congress of Women at Berlin in 1904 and she was the only women to deliver her address in English, German, and French. In 1919, she received international recognition as a speaker on the program at the Quinquennial International Peace Conference in Zurich, and in 1937 she delivered an address before the International Assembly of the World Fellowship of Faith in London. Ruth Fisher, likewise, ended her career on the international stage at the London School of Economics where she served as the official representative of the Library of Congress in England and where she directed the Rockefeller Grant "Project A" for the copying of materials relating to American history found in the British Museum, the British Public Records Office, the libraries of the House of Lords, House of Commons and Windsor Castle as well as various other private archives.

Thelma Thurston (Gorham)'s international career started from humble beginnings. She was born in Kansas, attended public schools, and moved with her mother to Detroit. It was here that she decided she didn't want to be a maid like her mother and began to apply to colleges. She was denied entrance to the University of Missouri because of her race. She chose not to attend the University of Kansas because African Americans were not allowed in the swimming pool on campus. Instead, she headed to the University of Minnesota where she was initiated into Theta Sigma Phi (the national honorary journalism society) and where she earned a degree in journalism. This began her fast rising career—first as a beat reporter, then editor, and finally as a foreign correspondent for the United Nations Conference of International Organizations.

These 13 highly educated, active, prolific African American women represent one fifth (doubling the one tenth calculated by Du Bois) of the African American women contributors of short stories to *The Crisis*. Because of their fame, their ethnicity is easy to identify; the task of researching the ethnicity of lesser-known writers is more challenging. Elizabeth Ammons, in the introduction to her anthology, *Short Fiction by Black Women, 1900–1920*, suggests that "the likelihood of lesser-known authors in this volume [*Short Fiction by Black Women*] not being African American is very small" (8). I believe the same assumption can be applied to this anthology as well. One of these potentially lesser-known writers, Anita Scott Coleman, has fortunately been raised from obscurity,[30] suggesting the need and call for more rigorous research into the identity of these African American women writers. Anita Scott Coleman grew up on a ranch in New Mexico (which makes her unique as an African American woman writer from the West), acquired an average education, taught school for a few years, married, raised four children, and ran a boardinghouse in California—not the typical biography of the talented tenth. But she was a prolific and talented writer; her total literary output included short stories written while living in New Mexico and California and then, later, two volumes of poetry. She died in relative obscurity.

The majority of writers who contributed stories to *The Crisis* were, likewise, also relatively obscure. Much of the biographical information is limited to the notes provided by *The Crisis* under Wilkins's editorship (see endnote 7). Additional information is sketchy. Mrs. Emma E. Butler may have been the secretary of the board of New England Hospital in Roxbury and a member of the National Black Nurses Association of Massachusetts. There is a photograph of Florence Lewis Bentley in Fanny Jackson Coppin's "Reminiscences of School Life, and Hints on Teaching." De Reath (Irene) Byrd Busey's short story was re-written as a one-act play and performed by the Howard University Players. Ottie B. Graham (Lottie Beatrice Graham) was a choreographer and wrote at least two one-act plays. Ola Calhoun Morehead may have had the distinction of being among the first members of the first historically black sorority founded on the University of Iowa campus and the second chapter of a sorority founded on a traditionally white campus. Annice Calland may be the same writer who published two obscure novels, *Voodoo* (1926) and *Grape with Thorn* (1933). Laura D. Nichols may be the author of several children's books published in the 1880s. Marion Cuthbert probably wrote a 1946 article on the status of black women connected to the YWCA of New York. According to the Chicago 1907 census, Edwina Streeter Dixon was a mulatto with two sisters and a brother and whose father was born in Tennessee. Hazel James was an advisor to an NAACP youth council in Houston, Texas.

Other writers have been included in recent anthologies and the editors of these anthologies indicate that they are African American. Edith Manuel Durham's short story is included in Barbara Foley's *Radical Representations: Politics and Form in U.S. Proletarian Fiction*. Edna May Harrold is cited in Elizabeth Ammons's collection. Maude Irwin Owen may have been an artist and her literary work is included in Shawn Ruff's anthology *Go the Way Your Blood Beats: An Anthology of Lesbian and Gay Fiction by African-American Writers*. Adeline Reis is listed in an anthology entitled *The Unforgetting Heart: An Anthology of Short Stories by African American Women* edited by Asha Kanwar. Marian Minus's story is included in Craig Gable's anthology *Ebony Rising*.

"Girl, Colored" and Other Stories provides a balanced and unedited representation of both the talented fifth, the who's who of African American women, and the not-so-famous women. I believe these women's stories offer a diversity of cultural artifacts which reveal experiences, views, details, and perspectives of what it means to be a woman and to be African American. These stories are perhaps some of the best depictions of what life was like for both the average African American woman and the extra-ordinary African American woman, in both urban and rural settings, among the wealthiest and the poorest of economic environments, in various locations across the country and internationally, and of all ages, occupations, educational backgrounds, and religions. An overview of the themes, characters, and stylistic characteristics of the 94 stories collected in this edition gives evidence of their historic validity and cultural variety.

Most historians locate the beginning of the "black is beautiful" movement in the 1960s. Others suggest that the phrase had roots in a speech by John Sweat Rock in Faneuil Hall in 1858 in which he refuted western standards for beauty.[31] I believe that the truth may lie somewhere in the middle, literally, and that the source of the movement came from African American writers of the short story during the Harlem Renaissance. In the descriptions of their female characters, these writers were meticulous in maintaining, encouraging, substantiating, supporting, and verifying the truth that African American women's hair, skin, eyes, teeth, lips and limbs were specific features of beauty as well as markers uniquely connected to their African heritage. For example, a sampling of the narrative description of women's hair shows how the writers glorified the color and texture. The most common descriptor is "curly"; "black hair that was extremely curly." Other delineations are as follows: "her hair was like coal"; "silvery hair crinkled almost to the point of that natural curliness"; "the kind of curl that no artificial aid so far invented can duplicate"; "black hair all curled up on the end like a nice autumn leaf"; "curling raven's-wing hair"; "black curly hair, soft and silky"; "her hair, coal black like her mother's had deep natural waves"; "blue-black hair sweeping below her waist"; and "gleaming black curls, which framed her delicately-featured face."

African American women writers also carefully described the color, tone and shade of women's skin and always the connotation in the comparison and descriptor was positive: the character's face is "wholesome, brown—a clear brown face"; her skin is "copper colored";

"sepia-tinted"; "like bronze"; "velvety"; "olive"; "satin polished"; "honey colored"; "transparent, light brown showing creamy underneath"; "butter-colored"; "velvet black brown"; and "pale sugar-brown."

Care is taken to emphasize race, even in the description of a heroine's eyes: "her eyes bright black twinkled"; "eyes spaklin' lak black diamonds"; eyes that were "deep black"; "her eyes like dark, melted pansies"; "eyes black like black marble"; her "eyes were extremely heavy-lidded, which is, as you know, a purely Negro attribute"; "pretty black eyes"; "hazel eyes that were sly and coquettish"; "dark brown eyes, like stars peeping thru a sunset sky"; "appealing eyes almost ethereal"; and "flashing, black eyes."

These descriptions are nothing like the distorted images of African Americans often seen in cartoons during this time—characters whose eyes were snow white and bulging, giving a crazed appearance. These grotesque depictions of African Americans not only distorted the person's eyes, but other African features of the face such as overly large lips that looked like pieces of liver, huge mouths made even larger in blackface, and oversized teeth biting into watermelons. African American women described characters with mouths, lips and teeth that were not hideous: "teeth [that] gleamed like pearls between her full, red lips"; "teeth were like the purest snow of the fields of Archangel"; "teeth like sugar"; "straight teeth flashed with glistening whiteness"; "her lips and mouth are gently pushed ... red lips"; "her mouth had a fullness, a ripeness, exceedingly—*African*"; and "little pink mouth with lips the pink of luscious melons."

An African American woman's distinctive features are highlighted and valued in these narratives in sharp contrast to the exaggerated stereotypes often depicted in the popular culture's advertisements, cartoons, product designs, films, and the stage. These characters in the short stories are different from the mammy's, the sambos, the coons, the savage beasts, and the pickaninny children that reinforce the psychology that black is ugly. Thus, readers of *The Crisis* were not only presented with models of beauty on the cover, but also in the creative descriptions of women which emphasized the uniqueness and appeal of racially distinctive features.

It is also noted that the advertising in *The Crisis* reiterated this emphasis on natural beauty. Specifically, women were encouraged to buy products that were for their various skin colors and types, not to lighten the color or to make their features more Nordic, but to enhance their African heritage and, perhaps, to look like the women described in the stories. For example, Mrs. Daisy Tapley, "New York's favorite contralto and vocal instructor," testifies that she finds "Crisis-Maid Face Powder a most valuable toilet accessory."[32] Red Rose Face Powder came in all colors: "Whether the complexion is cream, olive, or brown, we have a tint to match it." Lyda's Red Rose Face Creams provided for various conditions: "Red Rose Cold Cream: for dry faces; Red Rose Vanishing Cream: for oily faces; Red Rose Beauty Cream: for use at night." Lemon Massage Cream guaranteed to provide "a real skin food that cleanses, softens, and preserves. In all seasons, in all weathers, you can have lovely skin. Maintain its dainty softness and smoothness. Cleanse and refresh the skin, beautify and preserve the complexion." Some of the manufacturers emphasized their exoticness in their product names and descriptions: "Don't worry about bad skin. Learn the Kashmir Way. Harmless. A beautiful complexion. The Greatest Charm of All." And as the short story writers noted, African American women had remarkable white teeth, perhaps because they used Dr. Welter's Antiseptic Tooth Powder which promised to polish gold teeth and bleach white teeth.

There were numerous ads for hair care products. The advertisement for S. D. Lyons East Indian Hair Grower provides the best example of the complexities and care associated with African American hair. The ad also reiterates the politics of respectability:[33]

Beauty? No, we cannot all be beautiful but we can be neat and attractive. Let Mrs. Lyons show you how. If your Hair is Dry and Wiry or if you are bothered with Falling Hair, Dandruff, Itching Scalp or any Hair Trouble, We want you to try a jar of EAST INDIA HAIR GROWER. The Remedy contains medical properties that go to the roots of the Hair, stimulate the skin, helping nature do its work. Leaves hair soft and silky. Perfumed with a balm of a thousand flowers. The best known remedy for Heavy and Beautiful Black Eye-Brows. Also restores Gray Hair to its Natural color. Can be used with Hot Iron.

However, the most prominent and successful business woman to manufacture, advertise, and develop a true emporium of beauty products for women was Madam C. J. Walker. Some historians believe she was first African American millionaire as well as the first African American woman millionaire.[34] She provided everything: Wonderful Hair Grower, Vegetable Shampoo, Tetter Salve, Temple Grower, Glossine, Perfume, Rouge, Cold Cream, Dental Cream, Toilet Water, Talcum Powder, Antiseptic Soap, Complexion Cream, Vanishing Cream, Witch Hazel Jelly, Floral Cluster Talcum, Superfine Face Powder (White, Rose-Flesh, Brown).[35]

This emphasis on beauty did not detract the writers from grappling with the political events that were happening in the news and which were covered extensively in the columns of *The Crisis*. As stated earlier, *The Crisis* was not a women's magazine and the African American women short story writers did not ignore Du Bois's directive to write stories "that had ideas" and that "bore the stamp of sincerity and truth." The best illustration of this concerns the topic of lynching. Beginning in 1912, the NAACP kept an independent record of lynchings and these statistics were reported consistently in *The Crisis*. But *The Crisis* did more than report the numbers; there were various editorials, articles, and crusades in opposition to lynching. Some articles were titled as follows: "Do Lynching Pictures Create Race Hatred?," "Can the States Stop Lynching?," "The Lynching Industry," "The National Academy of Lynching," and coverage of the Dyer Anti-Lynching Bill in the House and Senate. George Schuyler, a known satirist, wrote "Scripture for Lynchers." There was a map which indicated the locations of thousands of lynchings in the U.S. There was an art exhibit against lynching, anti-lynching crusades, and an anti-lynching button could be purchased ("Stop Lynching Buttons. Nation-wide Sale by NAACP. Buy a Button—Build Democracy").

But it was the inclusion of photographs of lynchings in *The Crisis* that was most notorious. Du Bois clearly believed that these brutal images were necessary for full coverage of the events. Russ Castronovo, in his article "Beauty along the Color Line: Lynching, Aesthetics, and the *Crisis*," believes that there is an aesthetic theory of social transformation that is derived from Du Bois's particular placement of the pictures and drawings of lynchings. He notes the conjunction of articles portraying examples of "Music and Art" which document the importance of intellectual and aesthetic uplift with the top of the page containing a lynching cartoon; he describes it as follows: "rows of corpses stretch into the distance, the horizon broken only by a corpulent white figure, an allegory of mob 'justice,' who hold fast the ropes that strangle human beings [*The Crisis* 1914]." On the other hand, Anne Carroll describes the danger in this visual depiction of lynching:

> But displaying the bodies of lynching victims nonetheless had troubling implications. Using the bodies of murdered African Americans to stir up opposition to lynching also perpetuated lynching's dehumanization. These photographs reduce the victims' bodies to symbols; showing only their corpses implies that the important fact about these people's lives is how they ended [98].

African American women writers did not shy away from addressing the horror of lynching and its effects on the victims, families and communities. In fact, in some of the stories, the graphic and detailed description of the lynching has the same effect as that of the photographs. The stories presented more than a shocking picture of a person's death; these stories provided context, facts and conditions that created such violence, as well as the human reaction to the event that included more than just the victim. There are 13 stories that include lynching in the plot or history of a character. Perhaps the most representative story depicting a lynching is "Mob Madness" in which the psychosis associated with the white mob carries over to the wife of one of the white men involved in a lynching. The wife kills her daughter and herself in response to the horror she witnesses.

Another subject that occupied the pages of *The Crisis* and the life experiences of its readers was the constant presence of racism and prejudice in employment. Racial discrimination was rampant; the jobs available to African Americans were limited to low-wage positions such as domestic workers, factory employees, and manual labor.[36] Du Bois particularly noted the difficulty of women domestic servants when he stated in his essay "The Servant in the House," "The personal degradation of their work is so great that any white man of decency would rather cut his daughter's throat than let her grow up to such a destiny" (67). Likewise, the reports and articles in *The Crisis* highlighted the causes, conditions, and limitations of the job market and financial institutions as illustrated in articles such as "Colored Interns and Nurses," "Urban Conditions," "Savings Banks, Philadelphia's Building and Loan Associations," "Business Enterprises for Colored People," "Negro Letter Carriers in Alabama," "The Negro and Low Rent Housing," "Negro Farmer," "Equal Salaries for School Teachers," "10 million Sharecroppers," "After College, What?," "Vocational Choices," and "Occupational Choices for Negro High School Boys." But even these articles didn't match the reality of the conditions as presented in African American women's stories. African American women writers paid attention to this issue and the effects of poverty and urban conditions that resulted from these low-wage, low-prestige jobs. In particular, Marita Bonner's stories detail working conditions for women. In "Drab Rambles," she describes the oppression women face while working in a laundry and in "One True Love," a young domestic worker is determined to better herself and go to law school, but with dire consequences. Other writers illustrate spiraling depression for those who work in mundane, repetitive, regressive jobs. "Sunday," by Lucille Boehm, reveals the mind-numbing life of a seamstress and Ann Petry's "Like Winding Sheet" depicts a couple's struggle with violence as a result of their wearisome and unfulfilling work in the night shift at a factory. The title story for this anthology, Marian Minus's "Girl, Colored," addresses how the competition from the non–English speaking immigrant population threatened the employment opportunities for African Americans. Other stories in this collection portray the dehumanization and harsh realities of low-wage jobs and the effects of poverty: children eat out of garbage cans, apartments are described as prisons, women face discrimination by welfare officers, one-room apartments occupied by multi-member families are overcrowded, children are dying in apartment complex fires, and there is the constant sound of screaming babies in the ghetto.

Poverty and poor health were closely related. Various articles in *The Crisis* addressed public health, often under the repeated general headline of "Health of Black Folk." Some articles were more specific such as "Fighting Syphilis." African American women writers presented various characters in their fiction who faced health problems such as pneumonia, syphilis, heart disease, malnutrition, and infant mortality. Tuberculosis, however, was the deadliest and most common disease among African Americans in urban areas during the Harlem Renaissance. Articles targeted the disease, such as "Tuberculosis among Negroes," "New Control of TB," and "Warring against TB in Harlem." For the first half of the 20th century, tuberculosis in African American children was five times the rate in white children

(Byrd 31) and in adults, tuberculosis was four times that of whites ("Congestion").[37] One story, Anne Du Bignon's "The Doctor's Dilemma," not only presents the effects of the disease, but also the discrimination African American patients faced in sanitariums near New York.

Readers of *The Crisis* were also interested in the relationship of the Christian church to the African American's life. In particular, articles appeared which reported on church activity such as "The Negro-American Church," "Catholic Negroes," "The Baptist Controversy," "The Episcopal Church," "The Catholic Church and the Negro Priest," "Leaders of the Young Men's Christian Association," " Organized Religion and Cults," and "Jesus and Wealth." In addition, occasionally sermons by noted church leaders appeared. The church was also a popular topic for African American women short story writers. The theme ranged from an account of a character's personal spiritual journey to the humorous retelling of biblical stories. Octavia B. Wynbush's story "The Conversion of Harvey" tells of the struggle of one soul to express his personal understanding of his relationship with God. Other stories ridicule church leaders; the most memorable are "The Foolish and the Wise: Sallie Runner is Introduced to Socrates" by Leila Amos Pendleton and her follow-up story "The Foolish and the Wise: Sanctum 777 N.S.D.C.O.U. Meets Cleopatra." Finally, a frequent version of the religious theme depicted the tension between mainstream religions and the practice of conjuring and power of witch doctors. Examples of this conflict are found in Ottie Graham's "Blue Aloes," Maude Irwin Owens's "Bathesda of Sinners Run," Annice Calland's "The Papaloi," and Octavia B. Wynbush's "Conjure Man."

The Crisis also tackled the issue of interracial marriage. In particular, one of the more interesting segments originated with a letter addressed to Du Bois. The writer asked for advice because he is "a white man ... in love with a colored girl" (January 1930). Du Bois writes back advising "that if [he] wish[es] to marry the girl and she wishes to marry [him], then get married." Du Bois then invited letters from the readers, "white, black, green, or yellow" to respond "in answer to this letter" (Jan 1930). The result is "Intermarriage: A Symposium" in the March 1930 issue and includes fifteen letters of varying lengths and opinions from men and women around the country and from different racial backgrounds. The topic returns in 1931 with an article on racial intermarriage and then in 1932 with another featured article on miscegenation. The stories from African American women writers, however, do not necessarily espouse the acceptance of miscegenation that Du Bois voices or that of the majority of letter writers on the topic. Interracial couples in the stories appear in three forms and all complicate the issue of miscegenation with that of passing. For example, the only stories that present an interracial marriage are those in which the woman (and only occasionally a man) chooses to pass as white in order to marry a white spouse and reap the economic and social benefits and freedoms. The choice to marry white is not motivated by love and usually the marriage fails. A second approach to presenting interracial marriage is through ignorance: a white woman suddenly discovers that she has a black ancestor and must decide whether to reveal this secret to her white husband or live covertly. There are no characters in these stories in which an African American woman or man purposefully chooses from the single motivation of love to marry someone of a different race.

Slavery was also a common topic; however, it was one theme that was not garnered from the articles and editorial pages of *The Crisis*. The historical institution of slavery, the familial repercussions, and the specific experience of female slaves continued to hold importance for women writers of short fiction. One possible reason may be that most of the precursors for African American fiction writers at the beginning of the 20th century were the slave narratives of women from the previous generation. However, the stories in *The Crisis* do not simply replicate these earlier slave narratives; many offer a twist on the plot line. For example, the traditional figure of the "mammy" is challenged in Adeline F. Ries's story "Mammy," when the loyal female servant surprisingly murders the white family's grandchild. "White Lilacs" by Edith L. Yancy is a haunting story of another mammy figure and her daughter and the mysterious death of the white slave owner.

Stylistically, the most prominent feature in more than half of the stories is the use of dialect in the characters' speech acts.[38] The most prevalent debate about the use of dialect centered on the impression that was created through this idiomatic language; detractors believed that dialect reinforced a negative and stereotypical image of blacks. One of the often cited criticisms of the Harlem Renaissance was that the black artist catered to white audiences in various venues such as nightclubs, movies, music, art, and literature, and that dialect fostered a white audience's expectations of the black character's lack of intelligence or refinement. However, in the context of stories contributed to *The Crisis*, this argument may be qualified. The majority of readers who bought and read *The Crisis* were African American. Thus, African American women submitted their stories to a readership much like themselves and they were eager to have their personal experiences reflected in what they wrote and read. The familiar use of idioms, language, and vernacular in the speech of the characters would not necessarily have been foreign or degrading to these readers. A more interesting approach to this topic is to consider the power that is represented in the orality of the characters' speech acts. In particular, Do Veanna S. Fulton, in her book *Speaking Power: Black Feminist Orality in Women's Narratives of Slavery*, looks at slave narratives and proposes that orality is gendered: "Women's slave narrative emphasizes orality ... which conveys both their sense of identity and familial relationships and some of the ways they resisted oppression and facilitated their freedom" (21–22). Men's slave narratives, she contends, emphasized the written word as a means of empowerment. By using dialect, African American women writers combined this ability to articulate their character's identity through the imitation of the spoken word with the authority of the written word in their published presentations of short fiction.

In the end, this collection of stories does not pretend to uncover any undiscovered gems of artistic quality, but these stories do present a cultural and historical insight into a century of African American women's lives. In August 1912, when Du Bois outlined the stories submitted for the short story contest, he wrote, "We hope that our readers will send up other stories ... we want pictures of real colored America." I believe that women from all walks of life did "send up" their responses and recorded their experiences, their hopes, their observations, and their pictures of what it meant to be a "Girl, Colored."

NOTES

1. For more information on Paula Hopkins and magazine publication, see Hazel V. Carby's *Reconstructing Womanhood: The Emergence of the Afro-American Woman Novelist*.

2. There were other smaller and short-lived magazines published during this time: *Messenger, Saturday Evening Quill, Black Opals, Stylus, Fire!!*, and *Harlem*. See Abby Ann Arthur Johnson and Ronald M. Johnson's article "Forgotten Pages: Black Literary Magazines in the 1920s." For information on the next decade of small periodicals, see Abby Arthur Johnson and Ronald M. Johnson's article "Reform and Reaction: Black Literary Magazines in the 1930s."

3. According to Abby Arthur Johnson and Ronald Maberry Johnson, the name for *The Crisis* was not suggested by Du Bois, but by William Walling who recommended the name after hearing a comment by Mary White Ovington concerning Lowell's poem "The Present Crisis" (*Propaganda* 33).

4. The short sketch entitled "The Coward" appeared in October of 1911, but it was not characterized by *The Crisis* as a short story.

5. The story Du Bois is referring to is Fenton Johnson's "The Servant."

6. For more information on the literary contests, see Addell P. Austin's article "The *Opportunity* and *Crisis* Literary Contests, 1924–27."

7. This information, though limited, does help to identify some of the lesser-known writers. For example, we learn that Violet G. Haywood lived in Baltimore, Maryland; Isabel M. Thompson lived in Kansas City, Kansas; Octavia B. Wynbush lived in Lawrence, Kansas, and later taught English in Lincoln High School in Kansas City, Missouri; Elizabeth Thomas lived in Plainfield, New Jersey; Carol B. Cotton was a member of the faculty of Barber-Scotia College in North Carolina; Marion Cuthbert was employed by the national board of the YWCA and was a member of the board of directors of the NAACP; Edna Quinn lived in Leavenworth, Kansas; and "Joyce Reed," the penname for Marita Bonner, was described as living in Chicago. The editors wrote, "[B]ut *The Crisis* has not been very fortunate in coaxing her manuscripts into its office," a comment which indicates that Wilkins and his editorial staff were actively recruiting manuscripts from creative writers. Marita Bonner is later described in more detail: "[She] lives in Chicago and takes time out between attending to husband and babies to write short stories and plays of Negro life" and her fiction is described as "excellent." Edwinda Streeter Dixon lived in Chicago; Corinne Dean lived and taught school in Puerto Rico before moving to Harlem; Lucille Boehm lived in New York; Marian Minus graduated from Fisk University in 1935, majored in anthropology at the University of Chicago, co-edited *The New Challenge*, and lived in New York; Vera Williams lived in Nashville, Tennessee; Violet C. Haywood, who six years earlier lived in Baltimore, moved to Nashville, Tennessee; and Margaret Williams was the penname of an unknown writer from Denver, Colorado. Ann Petry was formerly employed on the *People's Voice* and lived in New York. Later she is described as a native of Saybrook, Connecticut; a graduate of the Connecticut College of Pharmacy; and after her marriage, moved to New York. Her fiction is also described as "brilliant" and listed "among the distinctive stories of 1944." Gwendolyn Williams lived in Indianapolis, Indiana; Florence McDowell lived in New York City; Teresa O'Hiser lived in Tacoma, Washington; and Mary J. Kyle (Mrs. Earle F. Kyle) lived in Minneapolis, Minnesota.

8. For a summary of biographies of editors up to Ida E. Lewis, see Zina Rodriguez's article "Shaping *The Crisis*."

9. According to Noliwe Rooks, there were nine African American women's magazines from the end of the 19th century to mid 20th century: *Half-Century Magazine* (1916–1923), *Woman's Voice* (1912–1927), *Women and Children* (1888–1891), *Sepia Socialite* (1936–1938), *Africamerican Woman's Journal* (1935–1954), *New York Age* (1911), *Woman's Era* (1894–1897), *Ringwood's Afro-American Journal of Fashion* (May-June 1893, September-October 1893), and *Tan Confessions* (November-December 1950). More contemporary examples are *Essence*, *Ebony* and *O*.

10. Women's cover photographs continued to appear after 1970; however, the percentage of women on the covers was not significantly greater than that of men after 1970.

11. For more information on job opportunities for women, see Stephanie Shaw's *What Women Ought to Be and to Do: Black Professional Women Workers During the Jim Crow Era*.

12. For a more in depth discussion of Du Bois's stand on suffrage, see Jean Fagan Yellin's article "Du Bois' *The Crisis* and Woman's Suffrage."

13. *The Crisis* changed its name to *The New Crisis* in 1997 and then returned to the original title of *The Crisis* in 2003. Other changes occurred throughout the century of publication. *The Crisis* began as a monthly and sold for ten cents a copy, or $1.00 per year. It is now a bi-monthly magazine that sells for $12.00 a year, and is available online.

14. For a comprehensive and detailed account of early African American periodicals, see Penelope L. Bullock's *The Afro-American Periodical Press 1838–1909*.

15. The gender of the writer, as with race, is not always clear. When the writer was unknown, I relied on the first name. When initials were used, I assumed the writer was male.

16. "A Christmas Happening," *The Crisis* 27.2 (December 1923): 60.

17. "The Hoodoo," *The Crisis* 7.4 (February 1914): 195–199.

18. "An American Citizen," *The Crisis* 19.6 (April 1920): 302–308; 20.1 (May 1920): 23–29.

19. "The Rising Sun," *The Crisis* 40.7 (July 1933): 158, 166.

20. "The Black Swan," *The Crisis* 21.6 (April 1921): 255–259, 22.1 (May 1921): 12–17.

21. "A. Fragment," *The Crisis* 12.5 (September 1916): 222 -229.

22. "Alycia's Grandchildren," *The Crisis* 40.10 (October 1933): 225, 238.

23. "The Shoe Pinches Mr. Samuels," *The Crisis* 42.1 (January 1935): 8–9, 24–25.

24. "Look Away, Dixie Land," *The Crisis* 53.7 (July 1946): 207, 217–219.

25. The relationship between Jews and African Americans was often discussed in the editorial pages of *The Crisis*.

26. "Idyll in a Country Graveyard," *The Crisis* 40.10 (October 1931): 339.

27. "Color-Blind: A Story," *The Crisis* 37.7 (July 1930): 231??

28. "Skin-Deep," *The Crisis* 39.4 (April 1932): 126–127.

29. She also published one book, *A Narrative of the Negro*.

30. See three publications: Bruce A. Glasrud and Laurie Champion's "Anita Scott Coleman"; Laurie Champion and Bruce A. Glasrud's *Unfinished Masterpiece*; and Mary E. Young's "Anita Scott Coleman: A Neglected Harlem Renaissance Writer."

31. See C. G Contee's biographical article, "John Sweat Rock, M.D., Esq., 1825–1866."

32. It is unknown if the name of the product is connected to *The Crisis* magazine title.

33. The politics of respectability is discussed in Paisley Jane Harris's article "Gatekeeping and Remaking: The Politics of Respectability in African American Women's History and Black Feminism" and in E. Francis White's book *Dark Continent of Our Bodies: Black Feminism and the Politics of Respectability*.

34. See A'Lelia P. Bundles's book *On Her Own Ground: The Life and Times of Madam C.J. Walker*.

35. According to Paula Giddings, the decade of 1910–1920 "put a beauty parlor in nearly every small town, saw cosmetics grow from a minor business into one with a turnover worth $500 million a year, and created a whole new career for young women, that of the beautician" (185).

36. Mrs. N. F. Mossell's 1908 book lists the following types of jobs held by African American women in the early 1900s: educator (teacher, principal), editor, writer, medicine, mission, stenographer, insurance, secretary, lawyer, State worker, member of State committees and World's Fair committees, the Arts, sculpture, elocution, hoer, raker, cook, washer, chopper, garment maker, quilter, undertaker, dry goods merchant, cateress, milliners, dressmaker, hair dresser, employee in a tonsorial parlor, manager of hotels, ice trader, type writer, book keeper, sales woman, patent writer, hauler of sand, Sunday school teacher, musical composer, dramatist, anti-slavery laborers and organizer, club organizer, and philanthropist.

37. See also David McBride's *From TB to AIDS: Epidemics Among Urban Blacks Since 1900*.

38. In reproducing these stories, punctuation has been edited to conform to modern standards. Obvious typographical errors have been corrected without editorial notation; otherwise, spellings have remained the same including all nuances of dialect.

WORKS CITED

Ammons, Elizabeth, ed. *Short Fiction by Black Women, 1900–1920*. Introduction. New York: Oxford University Press, 1991: 3–20.

Austin, Addell P. "The *Opportunity* and *Crisis* Literary Contests, 1924–27." *CLAJ* 32.2 (1988): 235–246.

Bullock, Penelope L. *The Afro-American Periodical Press 1838–1909*. Baton Rouge: Louisiana State University Press, 1981.

Bundles, A'Leilia P. *On Her Own Ground: The Life and Times of Madam C.J. Walker*. New York: Scribner, 2001.

Byrd, Michael, and Linda A. Clayton. *An American Health Dilemma: A Medical History of African Americans and the Problem of Race*. New York: Routledge, 2000.

Carby, Hazel V. *Reconstructing Womanhood: The Emergence of the Afro-American Woman Novelist*. New York: Oxford University Press, 1987.

Carroll, Anne. "Protest and Affirmation: Composite Texts in the *Crisis*." *American Literature* 76.1 (2004): 89–116.

Castronovo, Russ. "Beauty Along the Color Line: Lynching, Aesthetics, and the *Crisis*." *PMLA* 121.5 (2006): 1443–59.

Champion, Laurie, and Bruce A. Glasrud, eds. *Unfinished Masterpiece: The Harlem Renaissance Fiction of Anita Scott Coleman*. Lubbock: Texas Tech University Press, 2008.

"Congestion Causes High Mortality." *The New York Times*, October 24, 1929.

Contee, C. G. "John Sweat Rock, M.D., Esq., 1825–1866." *Journal of the National Medical Association* 68.3 (May 1976): 237–242.

Coppin, Fanny Jackson. "Reminiscences of School Life, and Hints on Teaching." Philadelphia: A.M.E. Book Concern, 1913. http://docsouth.unc.edu/neh/jacksonc/ill11.html.

Daniel, Walter C. *Black Journals of the United States*. Westport, CT: Greenwood, 1982.

_____. "*The Crisis* and *Opportunity* vs. Washington, D.C., Board of Education." *The Crisis* 85.6 (June/July 1978): 205–207.

Du Bois, W. E. B. "The Servant in the House." *Darkwater: Voices from within the Veil*. [1920]. Mineola, NY: Dover, 1999: 63–69.

Foley, Barbara. *Radical Representations: Politics and Form in U.S. Proletarian Fiction, 1921–1941*. Durham: Duke University Press, 1993.

Fulton, DoVeanna S. *Speaking Power: Black Feminist Orality in Women's Narratives of Slavery*. Albany: SUNY Press, 2006.

Gable, Craig. *Ebony Rising: Short Fiction of the Greater Harlem Renaissance Era*. Bloomington: Indiana University Press, 2004.

Giddings, Paula. *When and Where I Enter: The Impact of Black Women on Race and Sex in America*. New York: Morrow, 1984.

Glasrud, Bruce A., and Laurie Champion. "Anita Scott Coleman." *Twentieth Century American Women Writers, 1900–1945: A Bio-Bibliographical Critical Sourcebook*. Ed. Laurie Champion. Westport, CT: Greenwood, 2000: 77–81.

Harris, Paisley Jane. "Gatekeeping and Remaking: The Politics of Respectability in African American Women's History and Black Feminism." *Journal of Women's History* 15.1 (Spring 2003): 212–200.

Hull, Gloria T., ed. *The Works of Alice Dunbar-Nelson*. Foreword and Introduction. New York: Oxford University Press, 1988: vii–xxii, xxix–liv.

Johnson, Abby Ann Arthur, and Ronald M. Johnson. "Forgotten Pages: Black Literary Magazines in the 1920s." *Journal of American Studies* 8.3 (1974): 363–382.

Johnson, Abby Arthur, and Ronald Maberry Johnson. *Propaganda and Aesthetics: The Literary Politics of Afro-American Magazines in the Twentieth Century*. Amherst: The University of Massachusetts Press, 1979.

Johnson, Abby Arthur, and Ronald M. Johnson. "Reform and Reaction: Black Literary Magazines in the 1930s." *North Dakota Quarterly* 46.1 (1978): 5–18.

Kanwar, Asha. *The Unforgetting Heart: An Anthology of Short Stories by African American Women (1859–1993)*. San Francisco: Aunt Lute Books, 1995.

Kimbrough, Marvin Gordon. "W. E. B. Du Bois as Editor of *The Crisis*." *Dissertation Abstracts: Section A. Humanities and Social Science* 35 (1975): 5332A.

Kitch, Carolyn. *The Girl on the Magazine Cover: The Origins of Visual Stereotypes in American Mass Media*. Chapel Hill: University of North Carolina Press, 2000.

McBride, David. *From TB to AIDS: Epidemics Among Urban Blacks Since 1900*. New York: State University of New York Press, 1991.

Mossell, Mrs. N. F. *The Work of the Afro-American Woman*. [1908]. Reprint. New York: Oxford University Press 1988.

Mullen, Bill. "'A Revolutionary Tale': In Search of African American Women's Short Story Writing." *American Women Short Story Writers: A Collection of Essays*. Ed. Julie Brown. New York: Garland, 1995: 191–207.

Rodriguez, Zina. "Shaping *The Crisis*." *New Crisis* 107.4 (July/August 2000): 72–74.

Rogin, Michael. *Blackface, White Noise: Jewish Immigrants in the Hollywood Melting Pot*. Berkeley: University of California Press, 1998.

Rooks, Noliwe M. *Ladies' Pages: African American Women's Magazines and the Culture That Made Them*. New Brunswick: Rutgers University Press, 2004.

Ruff, Shawn Stewart. *Go the Way Your Blood Beats: An Anthology of Lesbian and Gay Fiction by African-American Writers*. New York: Henry Holt, 1996.

Shaw, Stephanie. *What a Woman Ought to Be and to Do: Black Professional Women Workers During the Jim Crow Era*. Chicago: University of Chicago Press, 1996.

Shockley, Ann Allen. *Afro-American Women Writers, 1746–1933: An Anthology and Critical Guide*. Boston: G.K. Hall, 1990.

Turner, Patricia A. *Ethnic Notions*. Dir. Marlon Riggs. California Newsreel, 1986. VHS.

Walker, Alice. *In Love & Trouble: Stories of Black Women*. San Diego: Harcourt Brace Jovanovich, 1973.

White, E. Francis. *Dark Continent of Our Bodies: Black Feminism and the Politics of Respectability*. Philadelphia: Temple University Press, 2001.

Yellin, Jean Fagan. "Du Bois' *Crisis* and Woman's Suffrage." *Massachusetts Review* 14.2 (Spring 1973): 365–375.

Young, Mary E. "Anita Scott Coleman: A Neglected Harlem Renaissance Writer." *CLA Journal* 40 (1997): 271–287.

EMMY

⧥

by Jessie Fauset

I

"There are five races," said Emmy confidently. "The white or Caucasian, the yellow or Mongolian, the red or Indian, the brown or Malay, and the black or Negro."

"Correct," nodded Miss Wenzel mechanically. "Now to which of the five do you belong?" And then immediately Miss Wenzel reddened.

Emmy hesitated. Not because hers was the only dark face in the crowded schoolroom, but because she was visualizing the pictures with which the geography had illustrated its information. She was not white, she knew that—nor had she almond eyes like the Chinese, nor the feathers which the Indian wore in his hair and which, of course, were to Emmy a racial characteristic. She regarded the color of her slim brown hands with interest—she had never thought of it before. The Malay was a horrid, ugly-looking thing with a ring in his nose. But he was brown, so she was, she supposed, really a Malay.

And yet the Hottentot, chosen with careful nicety to represent the entire Negro race, had on the whole a better appearance.

"I belong," she began tentatively, "to the black or Negro race."

"Yes," said Miss Wenzel with a sigh of relief, for if Emmy had chosen to ally herself with any other race except, of course, the white, how could she, teacher though she was, set her straight without embarrassment? The recess bell rang and she dismissed them with a brief but thankful "You may pass."

Emmy uttered a sigh of relief, too, as she entered the schoolyard. She had been terribly near failing.

"I was so scared," she breathed to little towheaded Mary Holborn. "Did you see what a long time I was answering? Guess Eunice Leeks thought for sure I'd fail and she'd get my place."

"Yes, I guess she didn't," agreed Mary. "I'm so glad you didn't fail—but, oh, Emmy, didn't you mind?"

Emmy looked up in astonishment from the orange she was peeling.

"Mind what? Here, you can have the biggest half. I don't like oranges anyway—sort of remind me of niter. Mind what, Mary?"

"Why, saying you were black and"—she hesitated, her little freckled face getting pinker and pinker—"a Negro, and all that before the class." And then mistaking the look on Emmy's face, she hastened on. "Everybody in Plainville says all the time that you're too nice and smart to be a—er—I mean, to be colored. And your dresses are so pretty, and your hair isn't

23

all funny either." She seized one of Emmy's hands—an exquisite member, all bronze outside, and within a soft pinky white.

"Oh, Emmy, don't you think if you scrubbed real hard you could get some of the brown off?"

"But I don't want to," protested Emmy. "I guess my hands are as nice as yours, Mary Holborn. We're just the same, only you're white and I'm brown. But I don't see any difference. Eunice Lecks' eyes are green and yours are blue, but you can both see."

"Oh, well," said Mary Holborn, "if you don't mind—."

If she didn't mind—but why should she mind?

"Why should I mind, Archie," she asked the faithful squire as they walked home in the afternoon through the pleasant "main" street. Archie had brought her home from school ever since she could remember. He was two years older than she; tall, strong and beautiful, and her final arbiter.

Archie stopped to watch a spider.

"See how he does it, Emmy! See him bring that thread over! Gee, if I could swing a bridge across the pond as easy as that! Oh, I don't guess there's anything for us to mind about. It's white people, they're always minding—I don't know why. If any of the boys in your class say anything to you, you let me know. I licked Bill Jennings the other day for calling me a 'guiney.' Wish I were a good, sure-enough brown like you, and then everybody'd know just what I am."

Archie's clear olive skin and aquiline features made his Negro ancestry difficult of belief.

"But," persisted Emmy, "what difference does it make?"

"Oh, I'll tell you some other time," he returned vaguely. "Can't you ask questions though? Look, it's going to rain. That means uncle won't need me in the field this afternoon. See here, Emmy, bet I can let you run ahead while I count fifteen, and then beat you to your house. Want to try?"

They reached the house none too soon, for the soft spring drizzle soon turned into gusty torrents. Archie was happy—he loved Emmy's house with the long, high rooms and the books and the queer foreign pictures. And Emmy had so many sensible playthings. Of course, a great big fellow of 13 doesn't care for locomotives and blocks in the ordinary way, but when one is trying to work out how a bridge must be built over a lop-sided ravine, such things are by no means to be despised. When Mrs. Carrel, Emmy's mother, sent Céleste to tell the children to come to dinner, they raised such a protest that the kindly French woman finally set them a table in the sitting room and left them to their own devices.

"Don't you love little fresh green peas?" said Emmy ecstatically. "Oh, Archie, won't you tell me now what difference it makes whether you are white or colored?" She peered into the vegetable dish. "Do you suppose Céleste would give us some more peas? There's only about a spoonful left."

"I don't believe she would," returned the boy, evading the important part of her question. "There were lots of them to start with, you know. Look, if you take up each pea separately on your fork—like that—they'll last longer. It's hard to do, too. Bet I can do it better than you."

And in the exciting contest that followed both children forgot all about the "problem."

II

Miss Wenzel sent for Emmy the next day. Gently but insistently, and altogether from a mistaken sense of duty, she tried to make the child see wherein her lot differed from that of her white schoolmates. She felt herself that she hadn't succeeded very well. Emmy, immaculate in a white frock, her bronze elfin face framed in its thick curling black hair, alert to interest, had listened very attentively. She had made no comments till toward the end.

"Then because I'm brown," she had said, "I'm not as good as you." Emmy was at all times severely logical.

"Well, I wouldn't—quite say that," stammered Miss Wenzel miserably. "You're really very nice, you know, especially nice for a colored girl, but—well, you're different."

Emmy listened patiently. "I wish you'd tell me how, Miss Wenzel," she began. "Archie Ferrers is different, too, isn't he? And yet he's lots nicer than almost any of the boys in Plainville. And he's smart, you know. I guess he's pretty poor—I shouldn't like to be that—but my mother isn't poor, and she's handsome. I heard Céleste say so, and she has beautiful clothes. I think, Miss Wenzel, it must be rather nice to be different."

It was at this point that Miss Wenzel had desisted and, tucking a little tissue-wrapped oblong into Emmy's hands, had sent her home.

"I don't think I did any good," she told her sister wonderingly. "I couldn't make her see what being colored meant."

"I don't see why you didn't leave her alone," said Hannah Wenzel testily. "I don't guess she'll meet with much prejudice if she stays here in central Pennsylvania. And if she goes away she'll meet plenty of people who'll make it their business to see that she understands what being colored means. Those things adjust themselves."

"Not always," retorted Miss Wenzel, "and anyway, that child ought to know. She's got to have some of the wind taken out of her sails, some day, anyhow. Look how her mother dresses her. I suppose she does make pretty good money—I've heard that translating pays well. Seems so funny for a colored woman to be able to speak and write a foreign language." She returned to her former complaint.

"Of course it doesn't cost much to live here, but Emmy's clothes! White frocks all last winter, and a long red coat—broadcloth it was Hannah. And big bows on her hair—she has got pretty hair, I must say."

"Oh, well," said Miss Hannah, "I suppose Céleste makes her clothes. I guess colored people want to look nice just as much as anybody else. I heard Mr. Holborn say Mrs. Carrel used to live in France; I suppose that's where she got all her stylish ways."

"Yes, just think of that," resumed Miss Wenzel vigorously, "a colored woman with a French maid. Though if it weren't for her skin you'd never tell by her actions what she was. It's the same way with that Archie Ferrers, too, looking for all the world like some foreigner. I must say I like colored people to look and act like what they are."

She spoke the more bitterly because of her keen sense of failure. What she had meant to do was to show Emmy kindly—oh, very kindly—her proper place, and then, using the object in the little tissue-wrapped parcel as a sort of text, to preach a sermon on humility without aspiration.

The tissue-wrapped oblong proved to Emmy's interested eyes to contain a motto of Robert Louis Stevenson, entitled: "A Task"—the phrase picked out in red and blue and gold, under glass and framed in passepartout. Everybody nowadays has one or more of such mottoes in his house, but the idea was new then to Plainville. The child read it through carefully as she passed by the lilac-scented "front yards." She read well for her age, albeit a trifle uncomprehendingly.

"To be honest, to be kind, to earn a little and to spend a little less;"—"there," thought Emmy, "is a semi-colon—let's see—the semi-colon shows that the thought"—and she went on through the definition Miss Wenzel had given her, and returned happily to her motto:

"To make upon the whole a family happier for his presence"—thus far the lettering was in blue. "To renounce when that shall be necessary and not be embittered"—this phrase was in gold. Then the rest went on in red: "To keep a few friends, but these without capitulation; above all, on the same given condition to keep friends with himself—here is a task for all that a man has of fortitude and delicacy."

"It's all about some man," she thought with a child's literalness. "Wonder why Miss Wenzel gave it to me? That big word, cap-it-u-la-tion"—she divided it off into syllables, doubtfully—"must mean to spell with capitals I guess. I'll say it to Archie some time."

But she thought it very kind of Miss Wenzel. And after she had shown it to her mother, she hung it up in the bay window of her little white room, where the sun struck it every morning.

III

Afterward Emmy always connected the motto with the beginning of her own realization of what color might mean. It took her quite a while to find it out, but by the time she was ready to graduate from the high school she had come to recognize that the occasional impasse which she met now and then might generally be traced to color. This knowledge, however, far from embittering her, simply gave to her life keener zest. Of course she never met with any of the grosser forms of prejudice, and her personality was the kind to win her at least the respect and sometimes the wondering admiration of her schoolmates. For unconsciously she made them see that she was perfectly satisfied with being colored. She could never understand why anyone should think she would want to be white.

One day a girl—Elise Carter—asked her to let her copy her French verbs in the test they were to have later in the day. Emmy, who was both by nature and by necessity independent, refused bluntly.

"Oh, don't be so mean, Emmy," Elise had wailed. She hesitated. "If you'll let me copy them—I'll—I'll tell you what I'll do. I'll see that you get invited to our club spread Friday afternoon."

"Well, I guess you won't," Emmy had retorted. "I'll probably be asked anyway. 'Most everybody else has been invited already."

Elise jeered. "And did you think as a matter of course that we'd ask you? Well, you have got something to learn."

There was no mistaking the "you."

Emmy took the blow pretty calmly for all its unexpectedness. "You mean," she said slowly, the blood showing darkly under the thin brown of her skin, "because I'm colored?"

Elise hedged—she was a little frightened of such directness.

"Oh, well, Emmy, you know colored folks can't expect to have everything we have, or if they do, they must pay extra for it."

"I—I see," said Emmy, stammering a little, as she always did when she was angry. "I begin to see the first time why you think it's so awful to be colored. It's because you think we are willing to be mean and sneaky and"—with a sudden drop to schoolgirl vernacular—"soup-y. Why, Elise Carter, I wouldn't be in your old club with girls like you for worlds." There was no mistaking her sincerity.

"That was the day," she confided to Archie a long time afterward, "that I learned the meaning of making friends 'without capitulation.' Do you remember Miss Wenzel's motto, Archie?"

He assured her he did. "And of course you know, Emmy, you were an awful brick to answer that Carter girl like that. Didn't you really want to go to the spread?"

"Not one bit," she told him vigorously, "after I found out why I hadn't been asked. And look, Archie, isn't it funny, just as soon as she wanted something she didn't care whether I was colored or not."

Archie nodded. "They're all that way," he told her briefly.

"And if I'd gone she'd have believed that all colored people were sort of—well, you know, 'meachin'—just like me. It's so odd the ignorant way in which they draw their conclusions. Why, I remember reading the most interesting article in a magazine—the *Atlantic Monthly* I think it was. A woman had written it and at this point she was condemning universal suffrage. And all of a sudden, without any warning, she spoke of that 'fierce, silly, amiable creature, the uneducated Negro,' and—think of it, Archie—of 'his baser and sillier female.' It made me so angry. I've never forgotten."

Archie whistled. "That was pretty tough," he acknowledged. "I suppose the truth is," he went on smiling at her earnestness, "she has a colored cook who drinks."

"That's just it," she turned emphatically. "She probably has. But, Archie, just think of all the colored people we've both seen here and over in Newton, too; some of them just as poor and ignorant as they can be. But not one of them is fierce or base or silly enough for that to be considered his chief characteristic. I'll wager that woman never spoke to fifty colored people in her life. No, thank you, if that's what it means to belong to the 'superior race,' I'll come back, just as I am, to the fiftieth reincarnation."

Archie sighed. "Oh, well, life is very simple for you. You see, you've never been up against it like I've been. After all, you've had all you wanted practically—those girls even came around finally in the high school and asked you into their clubs and things. While I—" he colored sensitively.

"You see, this plague—er—complexion of mine doesn't tell anybody what I am. At first—and all along, too, if I let them—fellows take me for a foreigner of some kind—Spanish or something, and they take me up hail-fellow-well-met. And then, if I let them know—I hate to feel I'm taking them in, you know, and besides that I can't help being curious to know what's going to happen—"

"What does happen?" interrupted Emmy, all interest.

"Well, all sorts of things. You take that first summer just before I entered preparatory school. You remember I was working at the camp in Cottage City. All the waiters were fellows just like me, working to go to some college or other. At first I was just one of them—swam with them, played cards—oh you know, regularly chummed with them. Well, the cook was a colored man—sure enough, colored you know—and one day one of the boys called him a—of course I couldn't tell you, Emmy, but he swore at him and called him a Nigger. And when I took up for him the fellow said—he was angry, Emmy, and he said it was the worst insult he could think of—'Anybody would think you had black blood in your veins, too.'"

"Anybody would think right," I told him.

"Well?" asked Emmy.

He shrugged his shoulders. "That was all there was to it. The fellows dropped me completely—left me to the company of the cook, who was all right enough as cooks go, I suppose, but he didn't want me any more than I wanted him. And finally the manager came and told me he was sorry, but he guessed I'd have to go." He smiled grimly as at some unpleasant reminiscence.

"What's the joke?" his listener wondered.

"He also told me that I was the blankest kind of a blank fool—oh, you couldn't dream how he swore, Emmy. He said why didn't I leave well enough alone.

"And don't you know that's the thought I've had ever since—why not leave well enough alone?—and not tell people what I am. I guess you're different from me," he broke off wistfully, noting her look of disapproval; "you're so complete and satisfied in yourself. Just being Emilie Carrel seems to be enough for you. But you just wait until color keeps you from the thing you want the most, and you'll see."

"You needn't be so tragic," she commented succinctly. "Outside of that one time at Cottage City, it doesn't seem to have kept you back."

For Archie's progress had been miraculous. In the seven years in which he had been from home, one marvel after another had come his way. He had found lucrative work each summer, he had got through his preparatory school in three years, he had been graduated number six from one of the best technical schools in the country—and now he had a position. He was to work for one of the biggest engineering concerns in Philadelphia.

This last bit of good fortune had dropped out of a clear sky. A guest at one of the hotels one summer had taken an interest in the handsome, willing bellboy and inquired into his history. Archie had hesitated at first, but finally, his eye alert for the first sign of dislike or superiority, he told the man of Negro blood.

"If he turns me down," he said to himself boyishly, "I'll never risk it again."

But Mr. Robert Fallon—young, wealthy and quixotic—had become more interested than ever.

"So, it's all a gamble with you, isn't it? By George! How exciting your life must be—now white and now black—standing between ambition and honor, what? Not that I don't think you're doing the right thing—it's nobody's confounded business anyway. Look here, when you get through look me up. I may be able to put you wise to something. Here's my card. And say, mum's the word, and when you've made your pile you can wake some fine morning and find yourself famous simply by telling what you are. All rot, this beastly prejudice, I say."

And when Archie had graduated, his new friend, true to his word, had gotten for him from his father a letter of introduction to Mr. Nicholas Fields in Philadelphia, and Archie was placed. Young Robert Fallon had gone laughing on his aimless, merry way.

"Be sure you keep your mouth shut, Ferrers," was his only enjoinment.

Archie, who at first had experienced some qualms, had finally completely acquiesced. For the few moments' talk with Mr. Fields had intoxicated him. The vision of work, plenty of it, his own chosen kind—and the opportunity to do it as a man—not an exception, but as a plain ordinary man among other men—was too much for him.

"It was my big chance, Emmy," he told her one day. He was spending his brief vacation in Plainville, and the two, having talked themselves out on other things, had returned to their old absorbing topic. He went on a little pleadingly, for she had protested. "I couldn't resist it. You don't know what it means to me. I don't care about being white in itself any more than you do—but I do care about a white man's chances. Don't let's talk about it any more though; here it's the first week in September and I have to go the 15th. I may not be back till Christmas. I should hate to think that you—you were changed toward me, Emmy."

"I'm not changed, Archie," she assured him gravely, "only somehow it makes me feel that you're different. I can't quite look up to you as I used. I don't like the idea of considering the end justified by the means."

She was silent, watching the falling leaves flutter like golden butterflies against her white dress. As she stood there in the old-fashioned garden, she seemed to the boy's adoring eyes like some beautiful but inflexible bronze goddess.

"I couldn't expect you to look up to me, Emmy, as though I were on a pedestal," he began miserably, "but I do want you to respect me, because—oh, Emmy, don't you see? I love you very much and I hope you will—I want you to—oh, Emmy, couldn't you like me a little? I—I've never thought ever of anyone but you. I didn't mean to tell you all about this now—I meant to wait until I really was successful, and then come and lay it all at your beautiful feet. You're so lovely, Emmy. But if you despise me—" he was very humble.

For once in her calm young life Emmy was completely surprised. But she had to get to the root of things. "You mean," she faltered, "you mean you want"—she couldn't say it.

"I mean I want you to marry me," he said, gaining courage from her confusion. "Oh, have I frightened you, Emmy, dearest—of course you couldn't like me well enough for that all in a heap—it's different with me. I've always loved you, Emmy. But if you'd only think about it."

"Oh," she breathed. "There's Céleste. Oh, Archie, I don't know, it's all so funny. And we're so young. I couldn't really tell anything about my feelings anyway—you know, I've never seen anybody but you." Then as his face clouded—"Oh, well, I guess even if I had I wouldn't like him any better. Yes, Céleste, we're coming in. Archie, mother says you're to have dinner with us every night you're here, if you can."

There was no more said about the secret that Archie was keeping from Mr. Fields. There were too many other things to talk about—reasons why he had always loved Emmy; reasons why she couldn't be sure just yet; reasons why, if she were sure, she couldn't say yes.

Archie hung between high hope and despair, while Emmy, it must be confessed, enjoyed herself, albeit innocently enough, and grew distractingly pretty. On the last day as they sat in the sitting room, gaily recounting childish episodes, Archie suddenly asked her again. He was so grave and serious that she really became frightened.

"Oh, Archie, I couldn't—I don't really want to. It's so lovely just being a girl. I think I do like you—of course I like you lots. But couldn't we just be friends and keep going on—so?"

"No," he told her harshly, his face set and miserable; "no, we can't. And Emmy—I'm not coming back any more—I couldn't stand it." His voice broke, he was fighting to keep back his boyish tears. After all he was only 21. "I'm sorry I troubled you," he said proudly.

She looked at him pitifully. "I don't want you to go away forever, Archie," she said tremulously. She made no effort to keep back the tears. "I've been so lonely this last year since I've been out of school—you can't think."

He was down on his knees, his arms around her. "Emmy, Emmy, look up—are you crying for me, dear? Do you want me to come back—you do—a little." He kissed her slim fingers.

"Are you going to marry me? Look at me, Emmy—you are! Oh, Emmy, do you know I'm—I'm going to kiss you."

The stage came lumbering up not long afterward, and bore him away to the train—triumphant and absolutely happy.

"My heart," sang Emmy rapturously as she ran up the broad, old-fashioned stairs to her room—"my heart is like a singing bird."

IV

The year that followed seemed to her perfection. Archie's letters alone would have made it that. Emmy was quite sure that there had never been any other letters like them. She used to read them aloud to her mother.

Not all of them, though, for some were too precious for any eye but her own. She used to pore over them alone in her room at night, planning to answer them with an abandon equal to his own, but always finally evolving the same shy, almost timid epistle, which never failed to awaken in her lover's breast a sense equally of amusement and reverence. Her shyness seemed to him the most exquisite thing in the world—so exquisite, indeed, that he almost wished it would never vanish, were it not that its very disappearance would be the measure of her trust in him. His own letters showed plainly his adoration.

Only once had a letter of his caused a fleeting pang of misapprehension. He had been speaking of the persistent good fortune which had been his in Philadelphia.

"You can't think how lucky I am anyway," the letter ran on. "The other day I was standing on the corner of fourth and Chestnut Streets at noon—you ought to see Chestnut Street at 12 o'clock, Emmy—and someone came up, looked at me and said: 'Well, if isn't Archie Ferrers!' And guess who it was, Emmy? Do you remember the Higginses who used to live over in Newtown? I don't suppose you ever knew them, only they were so queer looking that you must recall them. They were all sorts of colors from black with 'good' hair to yellow with the red, kinky kind. And then there was Maude, clearly a Higgins, and yet not looking like any of them, you know; perfectly white, with blue eyes and fair hair. Well, this was Maude, and, say, maybe she didn't look good. I couldn't tell you what she had on, but it was all right, and I was glad to take her over to the Reading Terminal and put her on a train to New York.

"I guess you're wondering where my luck is in all this tale, but you wait. Just as we started up the stairs of the depot, whom should we run into but young Peter Fields, my boss's son and heir, you know. Really, I thought I'd faint, and then I remembered that Maude was whiter than he in looks, and that there was nothing to give me away. He wanted to talk to us, but I hurried her off to her train. You know, it's a queer thing, Emmy; some girls are just naturally born stylish. Now there are both you and Maude Higgins, brought up from little things in a tiny inland town, and both of you able to give any of these city girls all sorts of odds in the matter of dressing."

Emmy put the letter down, wondering what had made her grow so cold.

"I wonder," she mused. She turned and looked in the glass to be confronted by a charming vision, slender—and dusky.

"I am black," she thought, "but comely." She laughed to herself happily. "Archie loves you, girl," she said to the face in the glass, and put the little fear behind her. It met her insistently now and then, however, until the next week brought a letter begging her to get her mother to bring her to Philadelphia for a week or so.

"I can't get off till Thanksgiving, dearest, and I'm so lonely and disappointed. You know, I had looked forward so to spending the 15th of September with you—do you remember that date, sweetheart? I wouldn't have you come now in all this heat—you can't imagine how hot Philadelphia is, Emmy—but it's beautiful here in October. You'll love it, Emmy. It's such a big city—miles and miles of long, narrow streets, rather ugly, too, but all so interesting. You'll like Chestnut and Market Streets, where the big shops are, and South Street, teeming with Jews and colored people, though there are more of these last on Lombard Street. You never dreamed of so many colored people, Emmy Carrel—or such kinds.

"And then there are the parks and the theatres, and music and restaurants. And Broad Street late at night, all silent with gold, electric lights beckoning you on for miles and miles. Do you think your mother will let me take you out by yourself, Emmy? You'd be willing, wouldn't you?"

If Emmy needed more reassurance than that she received it when Archie, a month later, met her and her mother at Broad Street station in Philadelphia. The boy was radiant. Mrs.

Carrel, too, put aside her usual reticence, and the three were in fine spirits by the time they reached the rooms which Archie had procured for them on Christian Street. Once ensconced, the older woman announced her intention of taking advantage of the stores.

"I shall be shopping practically all day," she informed them. "I'll be so tired in the afternoons and evenings, Archie, that I'll have to get you to take my daughter off my hands."

Her daughter was delighted, but not more transparently so than her appointed cavalier. He was overjoyed at the thought of playing host and of showing Emmy the delights of city life.

"By the time I've finished showing you one-fifth of what I've planned you'll give up the idea of waiting 'way till next October and marry me Christmas. Say, do it anyway, Emmy, won't you? He waited tensely, but she only shook her head.

"Oh, I couldn't, Archie, and anyway you must show me first your wonderful city."

They did manage to cover a great deal of ground, though their mutual absorption made its impression on them very doubtful. Some things though Emmy never forgot. There was a drive one wonderful, golden October afternoon along the Wissahickon. Emmy, in her perfectly correct gray suit and smart little gray hat, held the reins—in itself a sort of measure of Archie's devotion to her, for he was wild about horses. He sat beside her ecstatic, ringing all the changes from a boy's nonsense of the most mature kind of seriousness. And always he looked at her with his passionate though reverent eyes. They were very happy.

There was some wonderful music, too, at the Academy. That was by accident though. For they had started for the theatre—had reached there in fact. The usher was taking the tickets.

"This way, Emmy," said Archie. The usher looked up aimlessly, then, as his eyes traveled from the seeming young foreigner to the colored girl beside him, he flushed a little.

"Is the young lady with you?" he whispered politely enough. But Emmy, engrossed in a dazzling vision in a pink décolleté gown, would not in any event have heard him.

"She is," responded Archie alertly. "What's the trouble, isn't to-night the 17th?"

The usher passed over this question with another—who had bought the tickets? Archie of course had, and told him so, frankly puzzled.

"I see. Well, I'm sorry," the man said evenly, "but these seats are already occupied, and the rest of the floor is sold out besides. There's a mistake somewhere. Now if you'll take these tickets back to the office I can promise you they'll give you the best seats left in the balcony."

"What's the matter" asked Emmy, tearing her glance from the pink vision at last. "Oh, Archie, you're hurting my arm; don't hold it that tight. Why—why are we going away from the theatre? Oh, Archie, are you sick? You're just as white!"

"There was some mistake about the tickets," he got out, trying to keep his voice steady. "And a fellow in the crowd gave me an awful dig just then; guess that's why I'm pale. I'm so sorry, Emmy—I was so stupid, it's all my fault."

"What was the matter with the tickets?" she asked, incuriously. "That's the Bellevue-Stratford over there, isn't it? Then the Academy of Music must be near here. See how fast I'm learning? Let's go there; I've never heard a symphony concert. And, Archie, I've always heard that the best way to hear big music like that is at a distance, so get gallery tickets."

He obeyed her, fearful that if there were any trouble this time she might hear it. Emmy enjoyed it all thoroughly, wondering a little, however, at his silence. "I guess he's tired," she thought. She would have been amazed to know his thoughts as he sat there staring moodily at the orchestra. "This damnation color business," he kept saying over and over.

That night as they stood in the vestibule of the Christian Street house Emmy, for the first time, volunteered him a kiss. "Such a nice, tired boy," she said gently. Afterward he stood for a long time bareheaded on the steps looking at the closed door. Nothing he felt could crush him as much as that kiss had lifted him up.

V

Not even for lovers can a week last forever. Archie had kept till this last day what he considered his choicest bit of exploring. This was to take Emmy down into old Philadelphia and show her how the city had grown up from the waterfront—and by means of what tortuous self-governing streets. It was a sight at once dear and yet painful to his methodical, mathematical mind. They had explored Dock and Beach Streets, and had got over the Shackamaxon, where he showed her Penn Treaty Park, and they had sat in the little pavilion overlooking the Delaware.

Not many colored people came through this vicinity, and the striking pair caught many a wondering, as well as admiring, glance. They caught, too, the aimless, wandering eye of Mr. Nicholas Fields as he lounged, comfortably smoking, on the rear of a "Gunner's Run" car, on his way to Shackamaxon Ferry. Something in the young fellow's walk seemed vaguely familiar to him, and he leaned way out toward the sidewalk to see who that he knew could be over in this cheerless, forsaken locality.

"Gad!" he said to himself in surprise, "if it isn't young Ferrers, with a lady, too! Hello, why it's a colored woman! Ain't he a rip? Always thought he seemed too proper. Got her dressed to death, too; so that's how his money goes!" He dismissed the matter with a smile and a shrug of his shoulders.

Perhaps he would never have thought of it again had not Archie, rushing into the office a trifle late the next morning, caromed directly into him.

"Oh, it's you," he said, receiving his clerk's smiling apology. "What d'you mean by knocking into anybody like that?" Mr. Fields was facetious with his favorite employees. "Evidently your Shackamaxon trip upset you a little. Where'd you get your black Venus, my boy? I'll bet you don't have one cent to rub against another at the end of a month. Oh, you needn't get red; boys will be boys, and everyone to his taste. Clarkson," he broke off, crossing to his secretary, "if Mr. Hunter calls me up, hold the 'phone and send over the bank for me."

He had gone, and Archie, white now and shaken, entered his own little room. He sat down at the desk and sank his head in his hands. It had taken a moment for the insult to Emmy to sink in, but even when it did the thought of his own false position had held him back. The shame of it bit into him.

"I'm a coward," he said to himself, staring miserably at the familiar wall. "I'm a wretched cad to let him think that of Emmy—Emmy! And she the whitest angel that every lived, purity incarnate." His cowardice made him sick. "I'll go and tell him," he said, and started for the door.

"If you do," whispered common sense, "you'll lose your job and then what would become of you? After all Emmy need never know."

"But I'll always know I didn't defend her," he answered back silently.

"He's gone out to the bank anyhow," went on the inward opposition. "What's the use of rushing in there and telling him before the whole board of directors?"

"Well, then, when he comes back," he capitulated, but he felt himself weaken.

But Mr. Fields didn't come back. When Mr. Hunter called him up, Clarkson connected him with the bank, with the result that Mr. Fields left for Reading in the course of an hour. He didn't come back for a week.

Meanwhile Archie tasted the depths of self-abasement. "But what am I to do?" he groaned to himself at nights. "If I tell him I'm colored he'll kick me out, and if I go anywhere else I'd run the same risk. If I'd only knocked him down! After all she'll never know and I'll make it up to her. I'll be so good to her—dear little Emmy! But how could I know that he would take that view of it—beastly low mind he must have!" He colored up like a girl at the thought of it.

He passed the week thus, alternately reviling and defending himself. He knew now though that he would never have the courage to tell. The economy of the things he decided was at least as important as the principle. And always he wrote to Emmy letters of such passionate adoration that the girl for all her natural steadiness was carried off her feet.

"How he loves me," she thought happily. "If mother is willing I believe—yes, I will—I'll marry him Christmas. But I won't tell him till he comes Thanksgiving."

When Mr. Fields came back he sent immediately for his son Peter. The two held some rather stormy consultations, which were renewed for several days. Peter roomed in town, while his father lived out at Chestnut Hill. Eventually Archie was sent for.

"You're not looking very fit, my boy." Mr. Fields greeted him kindly; "working too hard I suppose over those specifications. Well, here's a tonic for you. This last week has shown me that I need someone younger than myself to take a hand in the business. I'm getting too old or too tired or something. Anyhow I'm played out.

"I've tried to make this young man here,"—with an angry glance at his son—"see that the mantle ought to fall on him, but he won't hear of it. Says the business can stop for all he cares; he's got enough money anyway. Gad, in my day young men liked to work, instead of dabbling around in this filthy social settlement business—with a lot of old maids."

Peter smiled contentedly. "Sally in our alley, what?" he put in diabolically. The older man glared at him, exasperated.

"Now look here, Ferrers," he went on abruptly. "I've had my eye on you ever since you first came. I don't know a thing about you outside of Mr. Fallon's recommendation, but I can see you've got good stuff in you—and what's more, you're a born engineer. If you had some money, I'd take you into partnership at once, but I believe you told me that all you had was your salary." Archie nodded.

"Well, now, I tell you what I'm going to do. I'm going to take you in as a sort of silent partner, teach you the business end of the concern, and in the course of a few years, place the greater part of the management in your hands. You can see you won't lose by it. Of course, I'll still be head, and after I step out Peter will take my place, though only nominally I suppose."

He sighed; his son's business defection was a bitter point with him. But that imperturbable young man only nodded.

"The boss guessed right the very first time," he paraphrased cheerfully. "You bet I'll be head in name only. Young Ferrers, there's just the man for the job. What d'you say, Archie?"

The latter tried to collect himself. "Of course I accept it, Mr. Fields, and I—I don't think you'll ever regret it." He actually stammered. Was there ever such wonderful luck?

"Oh, that's all right," Mr. Fields went on, "you wouldn't be getting this chance if you didn't deserve it. See here, what about your boarding out at Chestnut Hill for a year or two? Then I can lay my hands on you any time, and you can get hold of things that much sooner. You live on Green Street, don't you? Well, give your landlady a month's notice and quit the 1st of December. A young man coming on like you ought to be thinking of a home anyway. Can't find some nice girl to marry you, what?"

Archie, flushing a little, acknowledged his engagement.

"Good, that's fine!" Then with sudden recollection—"Oh, so you're reformed. Well, I thought you'd get over that. Can't settle down too soon. A lot of nice little cottages out there at Chestnut Hill. Peter, your mother says she wished you'd come out to dinner to-night. The youngest Wilton girl is to be there, I believe. Guess that's all for this afternoon, Ferrers."

VI

Archie walked up Chestnut Street on air. "It's better to be born lucky than rich," he reflected. "But I'll be rich, too—and what a lot I can do for Emmy. Glad I didn't tell Mr. Fields now. Wonder what those 'little cottages' out to Chestnut Hill sell for. Emmy—" He stopped short, struck by a sudden realization.

"Why, I must be stark staring crazy," he said to himself, standing still right in the middle of Chestnut Street. A stout gentleman whom his sudden stopping had seriously incommoded gave him, as he passed by, a vicious prod with his elbow. It started him on again.

"If I hadn't clean forgotten all about it. Oh, Lord, what am I to do? Of course Emmy can't go out to Chestnut hill to live—well, that would be a give-away. And he advised me to live out there for a year or two—and he knows I'm engaged, and—now—making more than enough money to marry on."

He turned aimlessly down 19th Street, and spying Rittenhouse Square sat down in it. The cutting November wind swirled brown, crackling leaves right into his face, but he never saw one of them.

When he arose again, long after his dinner hour, he had made his decision. After all Emmy was a sensible girl; she knew he had only his salary to depend on. And, of course, he wouldn't have to stay out in Chestnut Hill forever. They could buy, or perhaps—he smiled proudly—even build now, far out in West Philadelphia, as far as possible away from Mr. Fields. He'd just ask her to postpone their marriage—perhaps for two years. He sighed a little, for he was very much in love.

"It seems funny that prosperity should make a fellow put off his happiness," he thought ruefully, swinging himself aboard a North 19th Street car.

He decided to go to Plainville and tell her about it—he could go up Saturday afternoon. "Let's see, I can get an express to Harrisburg, and a sleeper to Plainville, and come back Sunday afternoon. Emmy'll like a surprise like that." He thought of their improvised trip to the Academy and how she had made him buy gallery seats. "Lucky she has that little saving streak in her. She'll see through the whole thing like a brick." His simile made him smile. As soon as he reached home he scribbled her a note:

"I'm coming Sunday," he said briefly, "and I have something awfully important to ask you. I'll be there only from 3 to 7. 'When Time let's slip one little perfect hour,' that's that Omar thing you're always quoting, isn't it? Well, there'll be four perfect hours this trip."

All the way on the slow poky local from Harrisburg he pictured her surprise. "I guess she won't mind the postponement one bit," he thought with a brief pang. "She never was keen on marrying. Girls certainly are funny. Here she admits she's in love and willing to marry, and yet she's always hung fire about the date." He dozed fitfully.

As a matter of fact Emmy had fixed the date. "Of course," she said to herself happily, "the 'something important' is that he wants me to marry him right away. Well, I'll tell him that I will, Christmas. Dear old Archie coming all this distance to ask me that. I'll let him beg me two or three times first, and then I'll tell him. Won't he be pleased? I shouldn't be a bit surprised if he went down on his knees again." She flushed a little, thinking of that first wonderful time.

"Being in love is just—dandy," she decided. "I guess I'll wear my red dress."

Afterward the sight of that red dress always caused Emmy a pang of actual physical anguish. She never saw it without seeing, too, every detail of that disastrous Sunday afternoon. Archie had come—she had gone to the door to meet him—they had lingered happily in the hall a few moments, and then she had brought him in to her mother and Céleste.

The old French woman had kissed him on both cheeks. "See, then it's thou, my cherished one!" she cried ecstatically. "How long a time it is since thou art here."

Mrs. Carrel's greeting, though not so demonstrative, was no less sincere, and when the two were left to themselves "the cherished one" was radiant.

"My, but your mother can make a fellow feel welcome, Emmy. She doesn't say much but what she does, goes."

Emmy smiled a little absently. The gray mist outside the somber garden, the fire crackling on the hearth and casting ruddy shadows on Archie's hair, the very red of her dress, Archie himself—all this was making for her a picture, which she saw repeated on endless future Sunday afternoons in Philadelphia. She sighed contentedly.

"I've got something to tell you, sweetheart," said Archie.

"It's coming," she thought. "Oh, isn't it lovely! Of all the people in the world—he loves me, loves me!" She almost missed the beginning of his story. For he was telling her of Mr. Fields and his wonderful offer.

When she finally caught the drift of what he was saying she was vaguely disappointed. He was talking business, in which she was really very little interested. The "saving streak" which Archie had attributed to her was merely sporadic, and was due to a nice girl's delicacy at having money spent on her by a man. But, of course, she listened.

"So you see the future is practically settled—there's only one immediate drawback," he said earnestly. She shut her eyes—it was coming after all.

He went on a little puzzled by her silence; "only one drawback, and that is that, of course, we can't be married for at least two years yet."

Her eyes flew open. "Not marry for two years! Why—why ever not?"

Even then he might have saved the situation by telling her first of his own cruel disappointment, for her loveliness, as she sat there, all glowing red and bronze in the fire-lit dusk, smote him very strongly.

But he only floundered on.

"Why, Emmy, of course, you can see—you're so much darker than I—anybody can tell at a glance what you—er—are." He was crude, he knew it, but he couldn't see how to help himself. "And we'd have to live at Chestnut Hill, at first, right there near the Fields,' and there'd be no way with you there to keep people from knowing that I—that—oh, confound it all—Emmy, you must understand! You don't mind, do you? You know you never were keen on marrying anyway. If we were both the same color—why, Emmy, what is it?"

For she had risen and was looking at him as though he were someone entirely strange. Then she turned and gazed unseeingly out the window. So that was it—the "something important"—he was ashamed of her, of her color; he was always talking about a white man's chances. Why, of course, how foolish she'd been all along—how could he be white with her at his side? And she had thought he had come to urge her to marry him at once—the sting of it sent her head up higher. She turned and faced him, her beautiful silhouette distinctly outlined against the gray blur of the window. She wanted to hurt him—she was quite cool now.

"I have something to tell you, too, Archie," she said evenly. "I've been meaning to tell you for some time. It seems I've been making a mistake all along. I don't really love you"— she was surprised dully that the words didn't choke her—"so, of course, I can't marry. I was wondering how I could get out of it—you can't think how tiresome it's all been." She had to stop.

He was standing, frozen, motionless like something carved.

"This seems as good an opportunity as any—oh, here's your ring," she finished, holding it out to him coldly. It was a beautiful diamond, small but flawless—the only thing he'd ever gone into debt for.

The statue came to life. "Emmy, you're crazy," he cried passionately, seizing her by the wrist. "You've got the wrong idea. You think I don't want you to marry me. What a cad you must take me for. I only asked you to postpone it a little while, so we'd be happier afterward. I'm doing it all for you, girl. I never dreamed—it's preposterous, Emmy! And you can't say you don't love me—that's all nonsense!"

But she clung to her lie desperately.

"No, really, Archie, I don't love you one bit; of course I like you awfully—let go my wrist, you can think how strong you are. I should have told you long ago, but I hadn't the heart—and it really was interesting." No grand lady on the stage could have been more detached. He should know, too, how it felt not to be wanted.

He was at her feet now, clutching desperately, as she retreated, at her dress—the red dress she had donned so bravely. He couldn't believe her heartlessness. "You must love me, Emmy, and even if you don't you must marry me anyway. Why, you promised—you don't know what it means to me, Emmy—it's my very life—I've never even dreamed of another woman but you! Take it back, Emmy, you can't mean it."

But she convinced him that she could. "I wish you'd stop, Archie," she said wearily; "this is awfully tiresome. And, anyway, I think you'd better go now if you want to catch your train."

He stumbled to his feet, the life all out of him. In the hall he turned around: "you'll say good-by to your mother for me," he said mechanically. She nodded. He opened the front door. It seemed to close of its own accord behind him.

She came back into the sitting room, wondering why the place had suddenly grown so intolerably hot. She opened a window. From somewhere out of the gray mists came the strains of "Alice, Where Art Thou?" executed with exceeding mournfulness on an organ. The girl listened with a curious detached intentness.

"That must be Willie Holborn," she thought; "no one else could play as wretchedly as that." She crossed heavily to the armchair and flung herself in it. Her mind seemed to go on acting as though it were clockwork and she were watching it.

Once she said: "Now this, I suppose, is what they call a tragedy." And again: "He did get down on his knees."

VII

There was nothing detached or impersonal in Archie's consideration of his plight. All through the trip home, through the long days that followed and the still longer nights, he was in torment. Again and again he went over the scene.

"She was making a plaything out of me," he chafed bitterly. "All these months she's been only fooling. And yet I wonder if she really meant it, if she didn't just do it to make it easier for me to be white. If that's the case what an insufferable cad she must take me for.

No, she couldn't have cared for me, because if she had she'd have seen through it all right away."

By the end of ten days he had worked himself almost into a fever. His burning face and shaking hands made him resolve, as he dressed that morning, to 'phone the office that he was too ill to come to work.

"And I'll stay home and write her a letter that she'll have to answer." For although he had sent her one and sometimes two letters every day ever since his return, there had been no reply.

"She must answer that," he said to himself at length, when the late afternoon shadows were creeping in. He had torn up letter after letter—he had been proud and beseeching by turns. But in this last he had laid his very heart bare.

"And if she doesn't answer it"—it seemed to him he couldn't face the possibility. He was at the writing desk where her picture stood in its little silver frame. It had been there all day. As a rule he kept it locked up, afraid of what it might reveal to his landlady's vigilant eye. He sat there, his head bowed over the picture, wondering dully how he should endure his misery.

Someone touched him on the shoulder.

"Gad, boy," said Mr. Nicholas Fields, "here I thought you were sick in bed, and come here to find you mooning over a picture. What's the matter? Won't the lady have you? Let's see who it is that's been breaking you up so." Archie watched him in fascinated horror, while he picked up the photograph and walked over to the window. As he scanned it his expression changed.

"Oh," he said, with a little puzzled frown and yet laughing, too, "it's your colored lady friend again. Won't she let you go? That's the way with these black women, once they get hold of a white man—bleed 'em to death. I don't see how you can stand them anyway; it's the Spanish in you, I suppose. Better get rid of her before you get married. Hello—" he broke off.

For Archie was standing menacingly over him. "If you say another word about that girl I'll break every rotten bone in your body."

"Oh, come," said Mr. Fields, still pleasant, "isn't that going it a little too strong? Why, what can a woman like that mean to you?"

"She can mean," said the other slowly, "everything that the woman who has promised to be my wife ought to mean." The broken engagement meant nothing in a time like this.

Mr. Fields forgot his composure. "To be your wife! Why, you idiot, you—you'd ruin yourself—marry a Negro—have you lost your senses? Oh, I suppose it's some of your crazy foreign notions. In this country white gentlemen don't marry colored women."

Archie had not expected this loophole. He hesitated, then with a shrug he burnt all his bridges behind him. One by one he saw his ambitions flare up and vanish.

"No, you're right," he rejoined. "White gentlemen don't, but colored men do." Then he waited calmly for the avalanche.

It came. "You mean," said Mr. Nicholas Fields, at first with only wonder and then with growing suspicion in his voice, "you meant that you're colored?" Archie nodded and watched him turn into a maniac.

"Why, you low-lived young blackguard, you—" he swore horribly. "And you've let me think all this time—" He broke off again, hunting for something insulting enough to say. "You Nigger!" he hurled at him. He really felt there was nothing worse, so he repeated it again and again with fresh imprecations.

"I think," said Archie, "that that will do. I shouldn't like to forget myself, and I'm in a pretty reckless mood to-day. You must remember, Mr. Fields, you didn't ask me who I was, and I had no occasion to tell you. Of course I won't come back to the office."

"If you do," said Mr. Fields, white to the lips, "I'll have you locked up if I have to perjure my soul to find a charge against you. I'll show you what a white man can do—you—"

But Archie had taken him by the shoulder and pushed him outside the door.

"And that's all right," he said to himself with a sudden heady sense of liberty. He surveyed himself curiously in the mirror. "Wouldn't anybody think I had changed into some horrible ravening beast. Lord, how that one little word changed him." He ruminated over the injustice—the petty, foolish injustice of the whole thing.

"I don't believe," he said slowly, "it's worth while having a white man's chances if one has to be like that. I see what Emmy used to be driving at now." The thought of her sobered him.

"If it should be on account of my chances that you're letting me go," he assured the picture gravely, "it's all quite unnecessary, for I'll never have another opportunity like that."

In which he was quite right. It even looked as though he couldn't get any work at all along his own line. There was no demand for colored engineers.

"If you keep your mouth shut," one man said, "and not let the other clerks know what you are I might try you for awhile." There was nothing for him to do but accept. At the end of two weeks—the day before Thanksgiving—he found out that the men beside him, doing exactly the same kind of work as his own, were receiving for it five dollars more a week. The old injustice based on color had begun to hedge him in. It seemed to him that his unhappiness and humiliation were more than he could stand.

VIII

But at least his life was occupied. Emmy, on the other hand, saw her own life stretching out through endless vistas of empty, useless days. She grew thin and listless, all the brightness and vividness of living toned down for her into one gray, flat monotony. By Thanksgiving Day the strain showed its effects on her very plainly.

Her mother, who had listened to her usual silence when her daughter told her the cause of the broken engagement, tried to help her.

"Emmy," she said, "you're probably doing Archie an injustice. I don't believe he ever dreamed of being ashamed of you. I think it is your own willful pride that is at fault. You'd better consider carefully—if you are making a mistake you'll regret it to the day of your death. The sorrow of it will never leave you."

Emmy was petulant. "Oh, mother, what can you know about it? Céleste says you married when you were young, even younger than I—married to the man you loved, and you were with him, I suppose, till he died. You couldn't know how I feel." She fell to staring absently out the window. It was a long time before her mother spoke again.

"No, Emmy," she finally began again very gravely, "I wasn't with your father till he died. That is why I'm speaking to you as I am. I had sent him away—we had quarreled—oh, I was passionate enough when I was your age, Emmy. He was jealous—he was a West Indian—I suppose Céleste has told you—and one day he came past the sitting room—it was just like this one, overlooking the garden. Well, as he glanced in the window he saw a man, a white man, put his arms around me and kiss me. When he came in through the side door the man had gone. I was just about to explain—no, tell him—for I didn't know he had seen me when he began." She paused a little, but presently went on in her even, dispassionate voice:

"He was furious, Emmy; oh, he was so angry, and he accused me—oh, my dear! He was almost insane. But it was really because he loved me. And then I became angry and I wouldn't tell him anything. And finally, Emmy, he struck me—you mustn't blame him, child; remember, it was the same spirit showing in both of us, in different ways. I was doing all I could to provoke him by keeping silence and he merely retaliated in his way. The blow wouldn't have harmed a little bird. But—well, Emmy, I think I must have gone crazy. I ordered him from the house—it had been my mother's—and I told him never, never to let me see him again." She smiled drearily.

"I never did see him again. After he left Céleste and I packed up our things and came here to America. You were the littlest thing, Emmy. You can't remember living in France at all, can you? Well, when your father found out where I was he wrote and asked me to forgive him and to let him come back. 'I am on my knees,' the letter said. I wrote and told him yes— I loved him, Emmy; oh, child, you know what love is. If you really loved Archie you'd let him marry you and lock you off, away from all the world, just so long as you were with him.

"I was so happy," she resumed. "I hadn't seen him for two years. Well, he started—he was in Hayti then; he got to New York safely and started here. There was a wreck—just a little one—only five people killed, but he was one of them. He was so badly mangled, they wouldn't even let me see him."

"Oh!" breathed Emmy. "Oh, mother!" After a long time she ventured a question. "Who was the other man, mother?"

"The other man? Oh! That was my father; my mother's guardian, protector, everything, but not her husband. She was a slave, you know, in New Orleans, and he helped her to get away. He took her to Hayti first, and then, afterward, sent her over to France, where I was born. He never ceased in his kindness. After my mother's death, I didn't see him for ten years, not till after I was married. That was the time Emile—you were named for your father, you know—saw him kiss me. Mr. Pechegru, my father, was genuinely attached to my mother, I think, and had come after all these years to make some reparation. It was through him I first began translating for the publishers. You know yourself how my work has grown."

She was quite ordinary and matter of fact again. Suddenly her manner changed.

"I lost him when I was 22. Emmy—think of it—and my life has been nothing ever since. That's why I want you to think—to consider—" She was weeping passionately now.

Her mother in tears! To Emmy it was as though the world lay in ruins about her feet.

IX

As it happened Mrs. Carrel's story only plunged her daughter into deeper gloom.

"It couldn't have happened at all if we hadn't been colored," she told herself moodily. "If grandmother hadn't been colored she wouldn't have been a slave, and if she hadn't been a slave—that's what it is, color—color—it's wrecked mother's life and now it's wrecking mine."

She couldn't get away from the thought of it. Archie's words, said so long ago, came back to her: "Just wait till color keeps you from the thing you want the most," he had told her.

"It must be wonderful to be white," she said to herself, staring absently at the Stevenson motto on the wall of her little room. She went up close and surveyed it unseeingly. "If only I weren't colored," she thought. She checked herself angrily, enveloped by a sudden sense of shame. "It doesn't seem as though I could be the same girl."

A thin ray of cold December sunlight picked out from the motto a little gilded phrase: "To renounce when that shall be necessary and not be embittered." She read it over and over and smiled whimsically.

"I've renounced—there's no question about that," she thought, "but no one could expect me not to be bitter."

If she could just get up strength enough, she reflected, as the days passed by, she would try to be cheerful in her mother's presence. But it was so easy to be melancholy.

About a week before Christmas her mother went to New York. She would see her publishers and do some shopping and would be back Christmas Eve. Emmy was really glad to see her go.

"I'll spend that time in getting myself together," she told herself, "and when mother comes back I'll be all right." Nevertheless, for the first few days she was, if anything, more listless than ever. But Christmas Eve and the prospect of her mother's return gave her a sudden brace.

"Without bitterness," she kept saying to herself, "to renounce without bitterness." Well, she would—she would. When her mother came back she should be astonished. She would even wear the red dress. But the sight of it made her weak; she couldn't put it on. But she did dress herself very carefully in white, remembering how gay she had been last Christmas Eve. She had put mistletoe in her hair and Archie had taken it out.

"I don't have to have mistletoe," he had whispered to her proudly.

In the late afternoon she ran out to Holborn's. As she came back 'round the corner she saw the stage drive away. Her mother, of course, had come. She ran into the sitting room wondering why the door was closed.

"I will be all right," she said to herself, her hand on the knob, and stepped into the room—to walk straight into Archie's arms.

She clung to him as though she could never let him go.

"Oh, Archie, you've come back, you really wanted me."

He strained her closer. "I've never stopped wanting you," he told her, his lips on her hair.

Presently, when they were sitting by the fire, she in the armchair and he at her feet, he began to explain. She would not listen at first, it was all her fault, she said.

"No, indeed," he protested generously, "it was mine. I was so crude; it's a wonder you can care at all about anyone as stupid as I am. And I think I was too ambitious—though in a way it was all for you, Emmy; you must always believe that. But I'm at the bottom rung now, sweetheart; you see, I told Mr. Fields everything and—he put me out."

"Oh, Archie," she praised him, "that was really noble, since you weren't obliged to tell him."

"Well, but in one sense I was obliged to—to keep my self-respect, you know. So there wasn't anything very noble about it after all." He couldn't tell her what had really happened. "I'm genuinely poor now, dearest, but your mother sent for me to come over to New York. She knows some pretty all-right people there—she's a wonderful woman, Emmy—and I'm to go out to the Philippines. Could you—do you think you could come out there, Emmy?"

She could, she assured him, go anywhere. "Only don't let it be too long, Archie—!"

He was ecstatic. "Emmy—you—you don't mean you would be willing to start out there with me, do you? Why, that's only three months off. When—" He stopped, peering out the window. "Who is that coming up the path?"

"It's Willie Holborn," said Emmy. "I suppose Mary sent him around with my present. Wait, I'll let him in."

But it wasn't Willie Holborn, unless he had been suddenly converted into a small and very grubby special-delivery boy.

"Mr. A. Ferrers," he said laconically, thrusting a book out at her. "Sign here."

She took the letter back into the pleasant room, and A Ferrers, scanning the postmark, tore it open. "It's from my landlady; she's the only person in Philadelphia who knows where I am. Wonder what's up?" he said incuriously. "I know I didn't forget to pay her my bill. Hello, what's this?" For within was a yellow envelope—a telegram.

Together they tore it open.

> Don't be a blooming idiot, the governor says come back and receive apologies and accept job. Merry Christmas. PETER FIELDS

"Oh," said Emmy, "isn't it lovely? Why does he say 'receive apologies,' Archie?"

"Oh, I don't know," he quibbled, reflecting that if Peter hadn't said just that his return would have been as impossible as ever. "It's just his queer way of talking. He's the funniest chap! Looks as though I wouldn't have to go to the Philippines after all. But that doesn't alter the main question. How soon do you think you can marry me, Emmy?"

His voice was light, but his eyes—

"Well," said Emmy bravely, "what do you think of Christmas?"

[*The Crisis* 5.2 (December 1912): 79–87; 5.3 (January 1913): 134–142]

MY HOUSE AND A GLIMPSE OF MY LIFE THEREIN

by Jessie Fauset

Far away on the top of a gently sloping hill stands my house. On one side the hill slopes down into a valley, the site of a large country town; on the other it descends into a forest, thick with lofty trees and green, growing things. Here in stately solitude amid such surroundings towers my dwelling; its dull-red brick is barely visible through the thick ivy, but the gleaming tops of its irregular roof and sloping gables catch the day's sunlight and crown it with a crown of gold.

An irregular, rambling building is this house of mine, built on no particular plan, following no order save that of desire and fancy. Peculiarly jutting rooms appear, and unsuspected towers and bay-windows,—the house seems almost to have built itself and to have followed its own will in so doing. If there be any one distinct feature at all, it is that halls long and very broad traverse the various parts of the house, separating a special set of rooms here, making another division there. Splendid halls are these, with fire places and cosy arm-chairs, and delightful, dark corners, and mysterious closets, and broad, shallow stairs. Just the place in winter for a host of young people to gather before the fire-place, and with pop-corn and chestnuts, stories and apples, laugh away the speeding hours while the wind howls without.

The hall on the ground floor has smaller corridors that branch off and lead at their extremity into the garden. Surely, no parterre of the East, perfumed with all the odors of Araby, and peopled with houris, was ever so fair as my garden! Surely, nowhere does the snow lie so pure and smooth and deep, nowhere are the evergreen trees so very tall and stately as in my garden in winter! Most glorious is it in late spring and early June. Out on the green, green sward I sit under the blossoming trees; in sheer delightful idleness I spend my hours, listening to the blending of wind-song with the "sweet jargoning" of little birds. If a shower threatens I flee across my garden's vast expanse, past the gorgeous rosebushes and purple lilacs, and safe within my little summer-house, watch the "straight-falling rain," and think of other days, and sighing wish that Kathleen and I had not parted in anger that far-off morning.

When the shower ceases, I hasten down the broad path, under the shelter of lofty trees, until I reach one of my house's many doors. Once within, but still in idle mood, I perch myself on a window-seat and look toward the town. Tall spires and godly church steeples rise before me; high above all climbs the town clock; farther over in the west, smoke is curling from the foundries. How busy is the life beyond my house! Through the length of the long hall to the window at the opposite side I go, and watch the friendly nodding of tall trees and the tender intercourse of all this beautiful green life. Suddenly the place becomes transformed—this is an enchanted forest, the Forest Morgraunt—in and out among the trees pass valiant knights and distressed ladies. Prosper le Gai rides to the rescue of Isoult la Desirous. Surely, the forest life beyond my house is full of purpose and animation, too.

From the window I roam past the sweet, familiar chambers, to the attic staircase, with its half-hidden angles and crazy old baluster. Up to the top of the house I go, to a dark little store-room under the eaves. I open the trap-door in the middle of the ceiling, haul down a small ladder, mount its deliciously wobbly length, and behold, I am in my chosen domain— a queen come into her very own! If it choose I can convert it into a dread and inaccessible fortress, by drawing up my ladder and showering nutshells and acorns down on the heads of would-be intruders. Safe from all possible invasion, I browse through the store of old, old magazines and quaint books and journals, or wander half-timidly through my infinite unexplored land of mystery, picking my way past heaps of delightful rubbish and strong, secret chests, fancying goblins in the shadowy corners, or watching from the little windows the sunbeams' play on the garden, and the grey-blue mist hanging far-off over the hollow valley.

From such sights and fancies I descend to my library, there to supplement my flitting ideas with the fixed conception of others. Although I love every brick and little bit of mortar in my dwelling, by library is of all portions the very dearest to me. In this part of the house more than any place else, have those irregular rooms been added, to receive my ever-increasing store of books. In the large room,—the library proper,—is a broad, old-fashioned fire-place, and on the rug in front I lie and read, and read again, all the dear simple tales of earlier days, "Mother Goose," "Alice in Wonderland," "The Arabian Nights"; here, too, I revel in modern stories of impossible adventure. But when a storm rises at night, say, and the rain beats and dashes, and all without is raging, I draw a huge, red armchair before the fire and curl into its hospitable depths,

> "And there I sit
>   Reading old things,
> Of knights and lorn damsels
>   While the wind sings—
> Oh, drearily sings!"

Off in one of the little side-rooms stands my desk, covered with books that have caught my special fancy and awakened my thoughts. This is my *living*-room, where I spend my moods of bitterness and misunderstanding, and questioning, and joy, too, I think. Often in the midst of a heap of books, the Rubaiyat and a Bible, Walter Pater's Essays and "Robert Elsmere" and "Aurora Leigh," and books of belief, of insinuation, of open unbelief, I bow my head on my desk in a passion of doubt and ignorance and longing, and ponder, ponder. Here on this desk is a book in which I jot down all the little, beautiful word-wonders, whose meanings are so often unknown to me, but whose very mystery I love. I write, "In Vishnu Land what Avatar?" and "After the red pottage comes the exceedingly bitter cry," and all the other sweet, incomprehensible fragments that haunt my memory so.

High up on many of the shelves in the many rooms are books as yet unread by me, Schopenhauer and Gorky, Petrarch and Sappho, Goethe and Kant and Schelling; much of Ibsen, Plato and Ennius and Firdausi, and Lafcadis Hearn,—a few of these in the original. With such reading in store for me, is not my future rich?

Can such a house as this one of mine be without immediate and vivid impression on its possessor? First and most of all it imbues me with a strong sense of home; banishment from my house would surely be life's most bitter sorrow. It is so eminently and fixedly mine, my very own, that the mere possession of it,—a house not yours or another's, but mine, to lie in as I will,—is very sweet to me. It is absolutely the *chey soi* of my soul's desire. With this sense of ownership, a sense which is deeper than I can express, a sense which is almost a longing for some unknown, unexplainable, entire possession—passionate, spiritual absorption of my swelling—comes a feeling that is almost terror. Is it right to feel thus, to have this vivid, permeating and yet wholly intellectual enjoyment of the material loveliness and attractiveness of my house? May this not be perhaps a sensuality of the mind, whose influence may be more insidious, more pernicious, more powerful to unfit me for the real duties of life than are other lower and yet more open forms of enjoyment? Oh, I pray not! My house is inexpressibly dear to me, but the light of the ideal beyond, "the light that never was on sea or land," is dearer still.

This, then, is my house, and this in measure, is my life in my house. Here, amid my favorite books, and pictures, and fancies, and longings, and sweet mysteries, shall old age come upon me, in fashion most inglorious, but in equal degree most peaceful and happy. *Perhaps*—that is! For after all my house is constructed of dream-fabric, and the place of its building is—*Spain!*

[*The Crisis* 8.3 (July 1914): 143–145]

HIS MOTTO

~~~~⟨⟩~~~~

by Lottie Burrell Dixon

"But I can't leave my business affairs and go off on a fishing trip now."
The friend and specialist who had tricked John Durmont into a confession of physical

bankruptcy, and made him submit to an examination in spite of himself, now sat back with an "I wash my hands of you" gesture.

"Very well, you can either go to Maine, not at once, or you'll go to—well, as I'm only your medical, and not your spiritual advisor, my prognostications as to your ultimate destination would probably have very little weight with you."

"Oh well, if you are so sure, I suppose I can cut loose now, if it comes to a choice like that."

The doctor smiled his satisfaction. "So you prefer to bear the ills of New York than to fly to others you know not of, eh?"

"Oh, have a little mercy on Shakespeare, at least. I'll go."

And thus it was that a week later found Durmont as deep in the Maine woods as he could get and still be within reach of a telegraph wire. And much to his surprise he found he liked it.

As he lay stretched at full length on the soft turf, the breath of the pines filled his lungs, the lure of the lake made him eager to get to his fishing tackle, and he admitted to himself that a man needed just such a holiday as this in order to keep his mental and physical balance.

Returning to the gaily painted frame building, called by courtesy the "Hotel," which nestled among the pines, he met the youthful operator from the near-by station looking for him with a message from his broker. A complicated situation had arisen in Amalgamated Cooper, and an immediate answer was needed. Durmont had heavy investments in copper, though his business was the manufacture of electrical instruments.

He walked back to the office with the operator while pondering the answer, then having written it, handed it to the operator saying, "Tell them to rush answer."

The tall, lank youth, whose every movement was a protest against being hurried, dragged himself over to the telegraph key.

"'S open."

"What's open?"

"Wire."

"Well, is that the only wire you have?"

"Yep."

"What in the dickens am I going to do about this message?"

"Dunno, maybe it'll close bime-by." And the young lightning slinger pulled toward him a lurid tale of the Wild West, and proceeded to enjoy himself.

"And meanwhile, what do you suppose is going to happen to me? thundered Durmont. "Haven't you ambition enough to look around your wire and see if you can find the trouble?"

"Lineman's paid to look up trouble, I ain't," was the surly answer.

Durmont was furious, but what he was about to say was cut off by a quiet voice at his elbow.

"I noticed linemen repairing wires upon the main road, that's where this wire is open. If you have any message you are in a hurry to send, perhaps I can help you out."

Durmont turned to see a colored boy of fifteen whose entrance he had not noticed.

"What can you do about it," he asked contemptuously, "take it into town in an ox team?"

"I can send it by wireless, if that is sufficiently quick."

Durmont turned to the operator at the table.

"Is there a wireless near here?"

"He owns one, you'll have to do business with him on that," said the youth with a grin at Durmont's unconcealed prejudice.

It would be hard to estimate the exact amount of respect, mingled with surprise, with which the city man now looked at the boy whose information he had evidently doubted till confirmed by the white boy.

"Suppose you've got some kind of tom-fool contraption that will take half a day to get a message into the next village. Here I stand to lose several thousands because this blame company runs only one wire down to this camp. Where is this apparatus of yours? Might as well look at it while I'm waiting for this one-wire office to get into commission again."

"It's right up on top of the hill," answered the colored boy. "Here, George, I brought down this wireless book if you want to look it over, it's better worth reading than that stuff you have there," and tossing a book on the table he went out followed by Durmont.

A couple of minutes' walk brought them in sight of the sixty-foot aerial erected on the top of a small shack.

"Not much to look at, but I made it all myself."

"How did you happen to—construct this?" And Durmont really tried to keep the emphasis off the "you."

"Well, I'm interested in all kinds of electrical experiments, and have kept up reading and studying ever since I left school, then when I came out here on my uncle's farm, he let me rig up this wireless, and I can talk to a chum of mine down in the city. And when I saw the wire at the station was gone up, I thought I might possibly get your message to New York through him."

They had entered the one room shack which contained a long table holding a wireless outfit, a couple of chairs and a shelf of books. On the walls were tacked pictures of aviators and drawings of aeroplanes. A three-foot model of a biplane hung in one corner.

"Now if he is only in," said the boy, going over to the table and giving the call.

"He's there," he said eagerly, holding out his hand for the message.

Durmont handed it to him. His face still held the look of doubt and unbelief as he looked at the crude, home-made instruments.

"Suppose I might as well have hired a horse and taken it into town." But the sputtering wire drowned his voice.

"And get on your wheel and go like blazes. Tell 'em to rush answer. This guy here thinks a colored boy is only an animated shoe-blacking outfit; it's up to us to remedy that defect in his education, see!" Thus sang the wires as Durmont paced the floor.

"I said," began the nervous man as the wires became quiet. "I—" again the wire sputtered, and he couldn't hear himself talk. When it was quiet, he tried again, but as soon as he began to grumble, the wire began to sputter. He glanced suspiciously at the boy, but the latter was earnestly watching his instruments.

"Say," shouted Durmont, "does that thing have to keep up that confounded racket all the time?"

"I had to give him some instructions, you know, and also keep in adjustment."

"Well, I'll get out of adjustment myself, if that keeps up."

Durmont resigned himself to silence, and strangely enough, so did the wire. Walking around the room he noticed over the shelf of books a large white card on which was printed in gilt letters: "I WILL STUDY AND MAKE READY, AND MAY BE MY CHANCE WILL COME." —ABRAHAM LINCOLN

Durmont read this, and then looked at the boy as if seeing him for the first time. Again he looked at the words, and far beyond them he saw his own struggling boyhood, climbing daily. Life's slippery path, trying to find some hold by which to pull himself up. And as he watched the brown skinned boy bending over the instruments, instinct told him here was one who would find it still harder to fight his way up, because of caste.

"Ah!"

The exclamation startled him. The boy with fones adjusted was busily writing.

"Well, has that partner of yours got that message down at his end yet?"

"Yes, sir, and here is your answer from New York."

"Why, it's only been half an hour since I wrote it," said Durmont.

"Yes, that horse wouldn't have got into town yet," grinned the boy.

Durmont snatched the paper, read it, threw his cap in the air, exclaiming: "The day is saved. Boy, you're a winner. How much?" putting his hand in his pocket suggestively.

"How much you owe to my help, I don't know," answered the lad sagely. "I offered to help because you needed it, and I was glad of the chance to prove what I believed I could do. I'm satisfied because I succeeded."

Durmont sat down heavily on the other chair; his nerves couldn't stand much more in one afternoon. To find himself threatened with a large financial loss; to have this averted by the help of the scientific knowledge of a colored boy, and that boy rating the fact of his success higher than any pecuniary compensation—he had to pull himself together a bit.

His eyes fell on the motto on the wall. He read it thoughtfully, considered how hard the boy had worked because of that, his hopes of the future based on that; saw the *human* element in him as it had not appealed to him before, and then turning something over in his mind, muttered to himself, "It's nobody's business if I do."

He got up, and walking over to the boy, said: "What's your name?"

"Robert Hilton."

"Well, Robert, that motto you've got up there is a pretty good one to tie to. You certainly have studied; you have made yourself ready as far as your resources will permit, and I'll be hanged if I don't stand for the 'chance.' In the manufacturing of electrical instruments you could have great opportunity for inventive talent, and in my concern you shall have your chance, and go as far as your efficiency will carry you. What do you say, would you care for it?"

"I'd care for it more than for any other thing on earth, and am very grateful for the chance."

"The chance wouldn't be standing here now if you had not had the inclination and the determination to live up those words on the wall."

[*The Crisis* 8.4 (August 1914): 188–190]

HOPE DEFERRED

by Mrs. Paul Lawrence Dunbar

The direct rays of the August sun smote on the pavements of the city and made the soda-water signs in front of the drug stores alluringly suggestive of relief. Women in scant garments, displaying a maximum of form and a minimum of taste, crept along the pavements, their mussy light frocks suggesting a futile disposition on the part of the wearers to keep cool. Traditional looking fat men mopped their faces, and dived frantically into screened doors to emerge redder and more perspiring. The presence of small boys scantily clad and of dusky hue and languid steps marked the city, if not distinctively southern, at least one on the borderland between the North and the South.

Edwards joined the perspiring mob on the hot streets and mopped his face with the rest. His shoes were dusty, his collar wilted. As he caught a glimpse of himself in a mirror of a shop window, he smiled grimly. "Hardly a man to present himself before one of the Lords of Creation to ask a favor," he muttered to himself.

Edwards was young; so young that he had not outgrown his ideals. Rather than allow that to happen, he had chosen one to share them with him, and the man who can find a woman willing to face poverty for her husband's ideals has a treasure far above rubies, and more precious than one with a thorough understanding of domestic science. But ideals do not always supply the immediate wants of the body, and it was the need of the wholly material that drove Edwards wilted, warm and discouraged into the August sunshine.

The man in the office to which the elevator boy directed him looked up impatiently from his desk. The windows of the room were open on a court-yard where green tree tops waved in a humid breeze; an electric fan whirred, and sent forth flashes of coolness; cool looking leather chairs invited the dusty traveler to sink into their depths.

Edwards was not invited to rest, however. Cold gray eyes in an impassive pallid face fixed him with a sneering stare, and a thin icy voice cut in on his half spoken words with a curt dismissal in its tone.

"Sorry, Mr.—Er—, but I shan't be able to grant your request."

His "Good Morning" in response to Edwards' reply as he turned out of the room was of the curtest, and left the impression of decided relief at an unpleasant duty discharged.

"Now where?" He had exhausted every avenue, and this last closed the door of hope with a finality that left no doubt in his mind. He dragged himself down the little side street, which led home, instinctively, as a child draws near to its mother in its trouble.

Margaret met him at the door, and their faces lighted up with the glow that always irradiated them in each other's presence. She drew him into the green shade of the little room, and her eyes asked, though her lips did not frame the question.

"No hope," he made reply to her unspoken words.

She sat down suddenly as one grown weak.

"If I could only just stick it out, little girl," he said, "but we need food, clothes, and only money buys them, you know."

"Perhaps it would have been better if we hadn't married—" she suggested timidly. That thought had been uppermost in her mind for some days lately.

"Because you are tired of poverty?" he queried, the smile on his lips belying his words.

She rose and put her arms about his neck. "You know better than that; but because if you did not have me, you could live on less, and thus have a better chance to hold out until they see your worth."

"I'm afraid they never will." He tried to keep his tones even, but in spite of himself a tremor shook his words. "The man I saw to-day is my last hope; he is the chief clerk, and what he says controls the opinions of others. If I could have gotten past his decision, I might have influenced the senior member of the firm, but he is a man who leaves details to his subordinates, and Mr. Hana was suspicious of me from the first. He isn't sure," he continued with a little laugh, which he tried to make sound spontaneous, "whether I am a stupendous fraud, or an escaped lunatic."

"We can wait; your chance will come," she soothed him with a rare smile.

"But in the meanwhile—" he finished for her and paused himself.

A sheaf of unpaid bills in the afternoon mail, with the curt and wholly unnecessary "Please Remit" in boldly impertinent characters across the bottom of every one drove Edwards out into the wilting sun. He knew the main street from end to end; he could tell how many trolley poles were on its corners; he felt that he almost knew the stones in the buildings, and that the pavements were worn with the constant passing of his feet, so often in the past four months had he walked at first buoyantly, then hopefully, at last wearily up and down its length.

The usual idle crowd jostled around the baseball bulletins. Edwards joined them mechanically. "I can be a side-walk fan, even if I am impecunious." He smiled to himself as he said the words, and then listened idly to a voice at his side, "We are getting metropolitan, see that!"

The "That" was an item above the baseball score. Edwards looked and the letters burned themselves like white fire into his consciousness.

STRIKE SPREADS TO OUR CITY, WAITERS AT ADAMS' WALK OUT AFTER BREAKFAST THIS MORNING

"Good!" he said aloud. The man at his side smiled appreciatively at him; the home team had scored another run, but unheeding that Edwards walked down the street with a lighter step than he had known for days.

The proprietor of Adams' restaurant belied both his name and his vocation. He should have been rubicund, corpulent, American; instead he was wiry, lank, foreign in appearance. His teeth projected over a full lower lip, his eyes set back in his head and were concealed by wrinkles that seemed to have been acquired by years of squinting into men's motives.

"Of course I want waiters," he replied to Edwards' question, "any fool knows that." He paused, drew in his lower lip within the safe confines of his long teeth, squinted his eye intently on Edwards. "But do I want colored waiters? Now, do I?"

"It seems to me there's no choice for you in the matter," said Edwards good-humoredly.

The reply seemed to amuse the restaurant keeper immensely; he slapped the younger man on the back with a familiarity that made him wince both physically and spiritually.

"I guess I'll take you for head waiter." He was inclined to be jocular, even in the face of the disaster which the morning's strike had brought him. "Peel off and go to work. Say, stop!" as Edwards looked around to take is bearings, "What's your name?"

"Louis Edwards."

"Uh huh, had any experience?"

"Yes, some years ago, when I was in school."

"Uh huh, then waiting ain't your general work."

"No."

"Uh huh, what do you do for a living?"

"I'm a civil engineer."

One eye-brow of the saturnine Adams shot up, and he withdrew his lower lip entirely under his teeth.

"Well, say man, if you're an engineer, what you want to be strike-breaking here in a waiter's coat for, eh?"

Edwards' face darkened, and he shrugged his shoulders. "They don't need me, I guess," he replied briefly. It was an effort, and the restaurant keeper saw it, but his wonder overcame his sympathy.

"Don't need you with all that going on at the Monarch works? Why, man, I'd a thought every engineer this side o' hell would be needed out there."

"So did I; that's why I came here, but—"

"Say, kid, I'm sorry for you, I surely am; you go on to work."

"And so," narrated Edwards to Margaret, after midnight, when he had gotten in from his first day's work, "I became at once head waiter, first assistant, all the other waiters, chief boss, steward, and high-muck-a-muck, with all the emoluments and perquisites thereof."

Margaret was silent; with her ready sympathy she knew that no words of hers were needed then, they would only add to the burdens he had to bear. Nothing could be more bitter than this apparent blasting of his lifelong hopes, this seeming lowering of his standard. She said nothing, but the pressure of her slim brown hand in his meant more than words to them both.

"It's hard to keep the vision true," he groaned.

If it was hard that night, it grew doubly so within the next few weeks. Not lightly were the deposed waiters to take their own self-dismissal and supplanting. Daily they menaced the restaurant with their surly attentions, ugly and ominous. Adams shot out his lower lip from the confines of his long teeth and swore in a various language that he'd run his own place if he had to get every nigger in Africa to help him. The three or four men whom he was able to induce to stay with him in the face of missiles of every nature, threatened every day to give up the battle. Edwards was the force that held them together. He used every argument from the purely material one of holding on to the job now that they had it, through the negative one of loyalty to the man in his hour of need, to the altruistic one of keeping the place open for colored men for all time. There were none of them of such value as his own personality, and the fact that he stuck through all the turmoil. He wiped the mud from his face, picked up the putrid vegetables that often strewed the floor, barricaded the doors at night, replaced orders that were destroyed by well-aimed stones, and stood by Adams' side when the fight threatened to grow serious.

Adams was appreciative. "Say, kid, I don't know what I'd a done without you, now that's honest. Take it from me, when you need a friend anywhere on earth, and you can send me a wireless, I'm right there with the goods in answer to your S.O.S."

This was on the afternoon when the patrol, lined up in front of the restaurant, gathered in a few of the most disturbing ones, none of whom, by the way, had ever been employed in the place. "Sympathy" had pervaded the town.

The humid August days melted into the sultry ones of September. The self-dismissed waiters had quieted down, and save from an occasional missile, annoyed Adams and his corps of dark-skinned helpers no longer. Edwards had resigned himself to his temporary discomforts. He felt, with the optimism of the idealist, that it was only for a little while; the fact that he had sought work at his profession for nearly a year had not yet discouraged him. He would explain carefully to Margaret when the day's work was over, that it was only for a little while; he would earn enough at this to enable them to get away, and then in some other place he would be able to stand up with the proud consciousness that all his training had not been in vain.

He was revolving all these plans in his mind one Saturday night. It was at the hour when business was dull, and he leaned against the window and sought entertainment from the crowd on the street. Saturday night, with all the blare and glare and garishness dear to his heart of the middle-class provincial of the smaller cities, was holding court on the city streets. The hot September sun had left humidity and closeness in its wake, and the evening mists had scarce had time to cast coolness over the town. Shop windows glared wares through colored lights, and phonographs shrilled popular tunes from open store doors to attract unwary passersby. Half-grown boys and girls, happy in the license of Saturday night on the crowded streets, jostled one another and pushed in long lines, shouted familiar epithets at other pedestrians with all the abandon of the ill-breeding common to the class. One crowd, in particular, attracted Edwards' attention. The girls were brave in semi-décolleté waists, scant short skirts and exaggerated heads, built up in fanciful designs; the boys with flamboyant red neckties, striking hat-bands, and white trousers. They made a snake line, boys and girls, hands on each others' shoulders, and rushed shouting through the press of shoppers, scattering the inattentive right and left. Edwards' lip curled, "Now, if those were colored boys and girls—"

His reflections were never finished, for a patron moved towards his table, and the critic of human life became once more the deferential waiter.

He did not move a muscle of his face as he placed the glass of water on the table, handing the menu card, and stood at attention waiting for the order, although he had recognized at first glance the half-sneering face of his old hope—Hanan, of the great concern which had no need of him. To Hanan, the man who brought his order was but one of the horde of menials who satisfied his daily wants and soothed his vanity when the cares of the day had ceased pressing on his shoulders. He had not even looked at the man's face, and for this Edwards was grateful.

A new note had crept into the noise on the streets; there was in it now, not so much mirth and ribaldry as menace and anger. Edwards looked outside in slight alarm; he had grown used to that note in the clamor of the streets, particularly on Saturday nights; it meant that the whole restaurant must be prepared to quell a disturbance. The snake line had changed; there were only flamboyant hat-bands in it now, the décolleté shirt waists and scant skirts had taken refuge on another corner. Something in the shouting attracted Hanan's attention, and he looked up wonderingly.

"What are they saying?" he inquired. Edwards did not answer; he was so familiar with the old cry that he thought it unnecessary.

"Yah! Yah! Old Adams hires niggers! Hires niggers!"

"Why, that is so," Hanan looked up at Edwards' dark face for the first time. "This is quite an innovation for Adams' place. How did it happen?"

"We are strike-breakers," replied the waiter quietly, then he grew hot, for a gleam of recognition came into Hanan's eyes.

"Oh, yes, I see. Aren't you the young man who asked me for employment as an engineer at the Monarch works?"

Edwards bowed, he could not answer; hurt pride surged up within him and made his eyes hot and his hands clammy.

"Well, er—I'm glad you've found a place to work; very sensible or you, I'm sure. I should think, too, that it is work for which you would be more fitted than engineering."

Edwards started to reply, but the hot words were checked on his lips. The shouting had reached a shrillness which boded immediate results, and with the precision of a missile from a warship's gun, a stone hurtled through the glass of the long window. It struck Edwards' hand, glanced through the dishes on the tray which he was in the act of setting on the table, and tipped half its contents over Hanan's knee. He sprang to his feet angrily, striving to brush the débris of his dinner from his immaculate clothing, and turned angrily upon Edwards.

"That is criminally careless of you!" he flared, his eyes blazing in his pallid face. "You could have prevented that; you're not even a good waiter, much less an engineer."

And then something snapped in the darker man's head. The long strain of the fruitless summer; the struggle of keeping together the men who worked under him in the restaurant; the heat, and the task of enduring what was to him the humiliation of serving, and this last injustice, all culminated in a blinding flash in his brain. Reason, intelligence, all was obscured, save a man hatred, and a desire to wreak his wrongs on the man, who, for the time being, represented the author of them. He sprang at the white man's throat and bore him to the floor. They wrestled and fought together, struggling, biting, snarling, like brutes in the dèbris of food and the clutter of overturned chairs and tables.

The telephone rang insistently. Adams wiped his hands on a towel, and carefully moved a paint brush out of the way, as he picked up the receiver.

"Hello!" he called. "Yes, this is Adams, the restaurant keeper. Who? Uh huh. Wants to know if I'll go his bail? Say, that nigger's got softening of the brain. Course not, let him serve his time, making all that row in my place; never had no row here before. No, I don't never want to see him again."

He hung up the receiver with a bang, and went back to his painting. He had almost finished his sign, and he smiled as he ended it with a flourish: WAITERS WANTED. NONE BUT WHITE MEN NEED APPLY

Out in the county work-house, Edwards sat on his cot, his head buried in his hands. He wondered what Margaret was doing all this long hot Sunday, if the tears were blinding her sight as they did his; then he started to his feet, as the warden called his name. Margaret stood before him, her arms outstretched, her mouth quivering with tenderness and sympathy, her whole form yearning towards him with a passion of maternal love.

"Margaret! You here, in this place?"

"Aren't you here?" she smiled bravely, and drew his head towards the refuge of her bosom. "Did you think I wouldn't come to see you?"

"To think I should have brought you to this," he moaned.

She stilled his reproaches and heard the story from his lips. Then she murmured with bloodless mouth, "How long will it be?"

"A long time, dearest—and you?"

"I can go home, and work," she answered briefly, "and wait for you, be it ten months or ten years—and then—?"

"And then—" they stared into each other's eyes like frightened children. Suddenly his form straightened up, and the vision of his ideal irradiated his face with hope and happiness.

"And then, Beloved," he cried, "then we will start all over again. Somewhere, I am needed; somewhere in this world there are wanted dark-skinned men like me to dig and blast and build bridges and make straight the roads of the world, and I am going to find that place—with you."

She smiled back trustfully at him. "Only keep true to your ideal, dearest," she whispered, "and you will find the place. Your window faces the south, Louis. Look up and out of it all the while you are here, for it is there, in our own southland, that you will find the realization of your dream."

[*The Crisis* 8.5 (September 1914): 238–242]

THE FAIRY GOOD WILLA

by Minnibell Jones, written when
she was ten years of age

In the good old days when the kind spirits knew that people trusted them, they allowed themselves to be seen, but now there are just a few human beings left who ever remember or believe that a fairy every existed, or rather does exist. For, dear children, no matter how much the older folks tell you that there are no fairies, do not believe them. I am going to tell you now of a dear, good fairy, Goodwilla, who has been under the power of a wicked enchanter called Grafter, for many years.

Goodwilla was once a very happy and contented little fairy. She was a very beautiful fairy; she had a soft brown face and deep brown eyes and slim brown hands and the dearest brown hair that wouldn't stay "put" that you ever saw. She lived in a beautiful wood consisting of fir trees. Her house was made of the finest and whitest drifted snow and was furnished with kind thoughts of children, good words of older people and everything which is beautiful and pleasant. She was always dressed in a white robe with a crown of holly leaves on her head. In her hand she carried a long magic icicle, and whatever she touched with this became very lovely to look upon. Snowdrops always sprang up wherever she stepped, and her dress sparkled with many small stars.

The children loved Goodwilla, and she always welcomed them to her beautiful home where she told them of Knights and Ladies, Kings and Queens, Witches and Ogres and Enchanters. She never told them anything to frighten them and the children were always glad to listen. You must not think that Goodwilla always remained at home and told the children stories, for she was a very busy little fairy. She visited sick rooms where little boys or girls were suffering and laid her cool brown hands on their heads, whispering beautiful words to them. She touched the different articles in the room with her magic icicle and caused them to become lovely. Wherever she stepped her beautiful snowdrops were scattered. At other times she went to homes where the father and mother were unhappy and cross. She was invisible to them, but she touched them without their knowing it and they instantly became kind and cheerful. Other days she spent at home separating the good deeds which she had piled before her, from the bad deeds. So you see with all of these things to do Goodwilla was very busy.

Now, there was an old enchanter who lived in a neighboring wood. He was very wealthy, but people feared him, although they visited him a great deal. His house was set in the midst of many trees, all of golden and silver apples. The house was made of precious metal and the inside was seemingly handsome. But looking closely one could see that the beautiful chairs were very tender and if not handled rightly they would easily break. Music was always being played softly by unseen musicians, but one who truly loved music could hear discords which spoiled the beauty of all. In fact, everything in his palace, although seemingly beautiful, if examined closely, was very wrong. Grafter, which was the enchanter's name, spent all of his time in instructing men how to be prosperous and receive all that they could for nothing. He did not pay much attention to the children, although once in a while a few listened to his evil words. He was always very busy, but somehow he did not at all times get the results he expected. He scratched his head and thought and thought. Finally, one day he cried, "Ah, I have it, there is an insignificant little fairy called Goodwilla who is meddling in my affairs, I'll wager. Let me see how best I can overcome her." The old fellow who could change his appearance at will, now became a handsome young enchanter and looked so fine that it would be almost impossible for the fairy herself to resist him. He made his way to her abode and asked for admittance to her house. She gladly bade him enter, for, although she knew him, she thought she could persuade him to forego his evil ways and win men by fair means.

Now something strange happened. Every chair that Grafter attempted to take became invisible when he started to seat himself and he found nothing but empty air. After this had happened for a long while, he became so angry that he forgot the part he was trying to play and acted very badly indeed. He stormed at poor Goodwilla as if she had been the cause of good deeds and kind words to vanish at his touch. "You, Madam," said he, "are the cause of this, and I know now why I cannot be successful in my work. You fill the children's heads full of nonsense and when I have almost persuaded the fathers to do something which will benefit them as well as their children, these brats come with their prattle and undo all that I have done. Now I have stood it long enough. I shall give you three trials, and if you do not conquer, you shall be under my power for seven hundred years."

The Good Fairy listened and felt very grieved, but she knew that Grafter was stronger than she, as minds of men turned more to his commanding way than they did to hers. Nevertheless she determined to do her best and said, "Very well, Grafter, I shall do as you wish and if I do not succeed I am in your hands, but later everything will be all right and I shall rule over you." Grafter, who had not expected this, now became alarmed and thought by soft words he could perhaps coax her to do his way, but Goodwilla was strong and would not listen to his cajoling and flattering. "Then, Madam," he said, "I shall force you to perform these tasks or be my slave:

"First, you must cause all of the people in the world to help and give to others for the sake of giving and not for what they shall receive in return.

"Secondly, you must cause all of the rich to help the poor instead of taking from them to swell their already fat pocketbooks, and thirdly, you must cause men and women to really love for love's sake and not because of worldly reasons."

The poor little fairy sighed deeply, for she knew that she could not perform these tasks in the three days that Grafter had allowed her. She talked to the children, but they were being dazzled by Grafter since he had become so handsome. Goodwilla continued to work through, and had just commenced to open men's eyes to Grafter as he really was when the three days expired.

She was immediately whisked off by the wicked old fellow, who chuckled with glee. He did not know that there were many people in whose hearts a seed had been planted (which would grow) by this good little fairy and that she herself had a plan for helping all when she was released. Grafter, after having locked her up, departed on his way rejoicing. He has been prosperous for a long, long time, but the seven hundred years are almost up now, and soon Goodwilla will come forth stronger and more beautiful than ever with the children as her soldiers.

[*The Crisis* 8.6 (October 1914): 294–296]

BREAKING THE COLOR-LINE

by Annie McCary

"Coach Hardy has selected for the two-mile relay team to go against Gale, Carter, Pratt, Staunton and Thacker, to run in the order named. Payne, you will 'sub.'"

"Captain Pratt, I certainly object to that nigger's presence on the team. Whom do I mean? Thacker, of course, he's a nigger, and no southern gentleman would compete against or run with a nigger and I—"

"Now, Staunton, none of your southern idiosyncrasies go here," cut in Pratt. "You know we want to win that relay, and Gale is priming her best half-milers for the race and since Thacker can do the half in less than two minutes, take it from me, so long as I'm captain, he runs."

"Then I quit," and red as a beet, Staunton sat down.

"Quit, then, if you want to!" thundered Pratt.

"Hold on, Pratt, we're all white fellows together and there's no need of our having a row over a colored chap. You know, I'm from Texas anyway, and I want to say that here in Starvard we've never had any colored fellows on the track team in the three years I've been here, and I'm hanged if I see why we've got to start now. These niggers are always trying to get out of their place," said Payne, the junior who had been crowded off the team by Thacker.

"Well by Jove, he seems to have pushed you out of *your* place on the team. He's beaten you more than once in the time trials and—"

"Just a minute," a calm voice put in, and Thacker came into the meeting. "I did not hear the beginning of this discussion, but I did hear some remarks and I judge that I am considered objectionable as a member of the relay because of—surely not the color of my skin (for he was a fair as any of the other fellow there) but because I have Negro blood in my veins." Every man was breathless. "Let me say this one thing, that *nigger* or not, I have won the place on the team but rather than cause any discord which might end in Starvard's losing the meet to Gale, I'll quit!" he swung on his heel and strode from the gym.

As the door slammed the storm broke.

"I didn't know he was colored," said one.

"Well, he is," answered Staunton.

"Well, he's whiter than you both in skin and in heart, Phil Staunton," yelled Pratt.

"You are insulting me, you Yank," and Staunton sprang at Pratt. The other men jumped in and held the two apart. Finally, quiet was restored and Payne was replaced on the team.

The meet was to come off a week from the coming Saturday. This was on Wednesday. Saturday, Gale had a dual meet with East Point, and Pratt and the coach, Hardy, went down to look over Gale's two-mile relay team and get a general line on the rest of the men. Silently they watched Gale win 69 to 20. On the return to Wainbridge, Hardy said: "Pratt, you fellows are all sorts of fools to let that man Thacker get off the team. Why, he's the fastest half-miler I've seen. I bet you he walks away with the half—if his heart isn't taken out by this dirty work," he added in an undertone.

"Hardy, you know I did all I could but he stuck out. He's as proud as the deuce, and as for those Southerners, they stuck out, too. They're always trying to make it hard for these colored boys. Oh, they make me sick!"

"Well, he's going to win that half in a walk, although Price ran a pretty race against those soldiers. Well, here's my jumping off place, Pratt," and the coach swung off the trolley.

"Curse the luck! Hardy doesn't want to own it, but we can't beat that Gale team."

The day of the meet came. Gale was down, brimming over with confidence, for the news that the crack half-miler on the relay was not going to run had spread like wild fire. Gale had no opinion, Starvard was divided.

At 1:30 the pistol cracked for the start of the hundred yard dash. Gale took first, but Starvard got second and third. Engle, of Gale, won the 120 hurdles, Wilson and Desmond, of Starvard, second and third. In the broad jump Bates and Hines of Starvard took first and third, but again Gale took first in the hammer throw.

The quarter-mile was next. In a close and exciting race Chalmers of Starvard began to hope. She grew frantic as she landed first in the high jump, although Gale took second and third.

Then came the half mile. The pride of Gale, Price's equal, Simpson, followed by his teammates, Parsons and Terry, sprang out to toe the mark. James and Keele threw off their crimson sweaters and a third Starvard man stepped up. It was Thacker. He was an ideal half-miler, five feet eleven inches, lean of face, broad shouldered, slender waisted, and with great long tapering legs. Simpson was short and stocky with a choppy stride with which he hoped to break Thacker.

All six got off to a good start. Thacker set the pace for the first lap. Then he seemed to slow up and Simpson and Terry drew up. Terry was now two feet ahead of Thacker, and Simpson stride and stride, with Parsons pushing him hard. Keele was out of it. As they turned in the last stretch, pandemonium broke loose in the Gale stands. Starvard cheered on her men. Thacker had seen Staunton leer at him and his heart gave a great jump and his feet responded to the call. His big lead was gone and it would be no easy matter to get in first in the short distance remaining. Teeth set, head back, he began a great sprint. With forty yards to go Terry and Simpson were leading, Terry a good two feet in front of Simpson and Thacker a yard behind. Three great strides and the red and blue jerseys were neck and neck. The stands were hushed. Nothing was heard but the pat-pat-pat of the spikes on the cinders. All three runners were straining every muscle, calling on their reserve strength, holding on by sheer nerve. Five great jumps and Thacker toppled over a winner in 1:58 flat, Simpson dropped a hand's breadth behind, and Terry was all in as he fell across.

Starvard cheered and cheered Thacker. Rooters jumped from the stands to pat Thacker on the back. Hardy drove them off and arm in arm he and Thacker went to see a rub down.

"All out for the 220 high hurdles!" Payne and Gardner showed Starvard's crimson, while Kittredge and Fields wore the Gale blue. Payne was showing an easy first with Gardner and Fields neck and neck, with Kittredge a good third. As Payne took the last hurdle, Starvard's cheers turned to groans, for Payne stumbled and fell. In a flash he was up, just to limp across the finish behind Grander, who was trailing the Gale man. Gloom pervaded the Starvard stands when the news spread that Payne, the anchor man of the two-mile relay was out with a sprained ankle. Second and third in the 120 high hurdles gave Starvard four points to Gale's five. Gale took first and third, in the mile and first in the pole vault.

There was but one event lift on the program—the two-mile relay. In the stands it was figured that Gale was three points to the good: Starvard 48, Gale 51.

"Who's going to take Payne's place?" was the question in the Starvard stands. Then calls for "Thacker! Thacker!" came from the crimson supporters. For if Starvard took the relay, the meet was hers by a scant two points. If Gale won, the meet was *hers*, together with the Eastern championship.

"Hardy, do you suppose Thacker *could* run *another* half against Price, who is perfectly fresh?"

"Pratt, I'd think you fellows would be so ashamed of the dirt you've done Thacker that you'd go hide yourselves. I won't ask him, I'll tell you, but—" here the coach looked straight into Pratt's eyes, "I bet you he'll run, and mark my words, he'll beat Price, if it kills him. Now, go ask him."

Pratt came back looking relieved. "All right, Hardy!"

Carter toed the mark against Steen, the first Gale runner. Crack! went the piston, off they sped.

"Staunton, Thacker takes the baton from you," called Pratt. Staunton looked sullen. Down the home stretch came Carter and Steen, Carter giving Pratt a good five-yard lead which he held and increased by five, and then Staunton took up the running. Archer brought joy to Gale as he cut down Staunton's lead yard by yard. Then he tore down to give Price an eight-yard start. Thacker snatched the baton from Staunton and sped away on a seemingly impossible task.

"Can he catch him? Will he hold out?"

Thacker seemed to be oblivious to the fact that the heat was terrific, of everything indeed, but the eight-yard lead he had to cut down. What difference did it make that his throat was parched, his head was splitting, that Price was the fastest man in the East and this was *his* first year in collegiate circles? He had to win. He had to make good, even under handicaps. Starvard thundered encouragement as he tore after the flying Price. After the first hundred yards, he began a terrific pace. His feet seemed to barely touch the ground. All thoughts of his blood done, Starvard cheered him on: "Keep it up! Thack, old boy, go it! Come on, old man!"

He heard nothing. He thought he had cut down the lead by two yards. He prayed for strength: "Oh, Lord, just let me catch him and I can pass him!" On and on they flew. No cheering now, for the stands had settled down to watch a match between two strong men. The great stadium was silent save for the crunching of the cinders. Thacker was crawling up, foot by foot. Yard after yard was covered at the murderous pace. Around the last turn they sped, Price running easily, Thacker glassy-eyed, hollow-cheeked but still flying. One hundred yards to go—Thacker's breath was coming hot and fast, his knees felt as if they must give way, yet he spurred his failing strength for one last great sprint. He again increased his speed, to the amazement of the stands. Half-way down he seemed almost gone. Forty yards—two more yards to make up on Price, who although tiring was beginning a spurt. Twenty-five yards—he was just behind Price but his chin had dropped to his chest, his mouth hung open, and his eyes were blinded with tears as he felt unable to pass Price, laboring at his side. Eight yards—he was growing weaker stride by stride, but Price had slipped an inch or so behind. Thacker no longer heard the heavy breathing of Price and raised his eyes to see whether he was in front. Nothing in front but that bit of worsted which marked the finish. He threw up his arms and Hardy caught him as he fell unconscious, breasting the tape, and breaking the color-line.   [*The Crisis* 9.4 (February 1915): 193–195]

POLLY'S HACK RIDE

―――∞∞∞―――

by Mrs. Emma E. Butler

Polly Gray had lived six and one-half years without ever having enjoyed the luxury of a hack ride.

The little shanty, merely an apology for a house, in which she lived with her parents, sat in a hollow on the main road in the village, at least fifteen feet below the road; and when Polly sat or stood at the front window up stairs, she watched with envy, the finely dressed ladies and gentlemen riding by on their way to the big red brick building on the hill.

On several occasions her secret longing got the best of her, and she mustered all the self control of which her nature boasted to keep from stealing a ride on behind, as she had seen her brothers do on the ice wagon, but the memory of the warm reception usually awaiting the little male Grays, accompanied by predictions of broken necks, arms, legs, etc. caused her little frame to shiver.

Who then could say that Polly was wanting in sisterly love when she exulted in the fact that she was going to a funeral? What did it matter if Ma Gray was heart-broken, and Pa Gray couldn't eat but six biscuits for his supper when he came home and found the long white fringed sash floating from the cracked door knob?

Polly reviewed the events leading up to her present stage of ecstasy: Ma Gray had sent in hot haste for Aunt Betty Williams, who came with question marks stamped on her face, and when she found Ella, the two-year-old pet of the family in the throes of death she was by far too discreet to say so but advised Ma Gray to put her down. Polly had then become afraid and had run down stairs. She felt it—yes, sir—she felt it 'way down in her "stummik!" Something was going to happen, so when Ma Gray appeared at the head of the stairs with eyes swollen, and still a-swellin,' and told her in a shaky voice to go to school for the children, she knew it had happened.

She started off at break-neck speed but, undecided just as to the proper gait for one bearing a message of such grave importance, she walked mournfully along for a while, then as the vision of a hack and two white horses arose, she skipped and finally ran again until she reached the schoolhouse.

The afternoon session had just begun, as she timidly knocked on the door of the class-room where the two elder Grays were "gettin' their schoolin'"; and when the teacher opened the door, she beheld a very dirty little girl blubbering, "Ella's dead; Mamma's cryin'. Kin Bobby and Sally cum home?"

Master Bobby and Miss Sally were dismissed with the reverence due to the dignity of their bereavement, and on their way home they proceeded to extract such bits of information as they deemed suitable for the occasion: "Were her eyes open or shut? Had she turned black yet? Did Aunt Betty cry too? Did Mamma fall across the bed as the breath was leaving her body?" Whereupon Miss Polly, being a young lady of a rather keen imagination upon which she drew, and drew heavily in times of need, gave them quite a sensational version of the affair, and by the time they reached home they were fully prepared to grieve with a capital "G." Sally ran to Ma Gray and with a shriek, threw both arms around her neck, while Bobby fell on his knees by the deceased Ella, imploring her to come back and be his baby sister once more.

Aunt Betty told her next door neighbor afterwards that she had her hands full and her heart full too, trying to quiet them. And if the smell of fried liver and onions had not reminded Bobby that it was near dinner time, she really couldn't tell how she should have managed them.

As plateful after plateful of liver, onions and mashed potatoes disappeared, the raging storm of grief subsided in the hearts of the young Grays, and by the time dinner was over Bobby was kept busy unpuckering his lips to suppress a whistle, and Sally had tried several bows of black ribbon on her hair to see which one looked best.

After the dishes were cleared away, and Ma Gray was scouring the floor in a solution of concentrated lye, water and tears, Uncle Bangaway, a retired deacon in the Baptist church, stepped in to pay his respects.

Uncle Bangaway was considered a fine singer in his younger days and was quite proud of his accusation, so he proceeded to express his sympathy for Ma Gray in the words of his favorite hymn, kept in reserve for such occasions:

> "Wasn't my Lord mighty good and kind?
>   O Yeah!
> "Wasn't my Lord mighty good and kind?
>   O Yeah!
> "Wasn't my Lord mighty good and kind
> "To take away the child and leave the mother behind?
>   O Yeah! O Yeah! O Yeah!"

When he finished singing Ma Gray stopped crying to smile on him. It seemed that the hymn brought to her mind certain facts that were well worth considering.

On the morning of the day appointed for the funeral, a dark cloud hung over the village when Polly awoke, and her heart sank within her. Oh! if it should rain! Every hack she had ever seen on a rainy day had the curtains down, and there was no use riding in a hack if you had to have the curtains down. Anyhow, she began to dress, and before she was half through, the sun began to peep through the clouds, and finally it shone brightly; and so did Miss Polly's face.

Who, then, could not pardon the cheerful face she brought down stairs where the funeral party was gathered? Dressed in a new black dress, new shoes, new hair ribbon, even new gloves, and a hack ride scheduled for the next two hours, was enough to make her very soul shine.

She hardly heard the minister as he dwelt at length on the innocence of childhood; nor his reference to Him who suffered the little ones to come unto Him; but the closing strains of "Nearer My God To Thee" seemed to awaken her from pleasant dreams.

When the funeral procession started out Polly felt very sad, but the tears wouldn't come and, of course, "you can't make 'em come, if you ain't got no raw onions."

Now, it fell to her lot to sit in the hack with her great uncle, "Uncle Billings" Ma Gray called him, but Polly often wondered why Pa Gray spoke of him as "Uncle Rummy."

One of the many reasons for Polly's aversion to Uncle Billings was because of his prompt appearance before dinner every Sunday, when he would call her mother's attention every time she, Polly, took another doughnut or cookie. So you may be sure her spirits fell when she realized the state of affairs.

On the way to the cemetery neither found much to say to the other, but when they started home Uncle Billings began to lecture Polly concerning her apparent indifference to the family bereavement; during which discourse Polly sat without hearing one word, as her mind was otherwise engaged. She was trying to think of some manner in which to attract the attention of the Higdon girls as she passed the pump; she knew they would be there.

Before her plans were matured, however, the red bonnet of Cecie Higdon loomed up at the corner, and standing right behind her were Bessie and Georgia Higdon and Lucy Matthews.

Now was her chance! Nor or never! So she sprang from her seat, leaned far out of the window, and gave one loud "Whee!" to the girls, waving her black-bordered handkerchief meanwhile.

Uncle Billings had just dropped off in a doze, and Polly's whoop brought him out of it so suddenly that he could find nothing more appropriate to say than, "Hush your noise, gal!" when with a sudden jerk the hack stopped and they were home.

As Polly alighted from the hack, she began to realize how, as a mourner, she had lowered her dignity by yelling from the window like a joy-rider, and she was not a little uneasy as to how Ma Gray would consider the matter should old Rummy inform her. So during supper she cautiously avoided meeting his eye, and as soon as she had finished eating she ran upstairs to change her clothes.

Here her mother found her later, with her head resting on the open Bible, and when she tried to awaken her she said, "Yes'm, just tell him not to drive quite so fast."

[*The Crisis* 12.2 (June 1916): 84–85]

"BITS": A CHRISTMAS STORY

—⊷⊶⊷—

by Helen G. Ricks

The feathery snowflakes came hurrying down simply because it was the day before Christmas and not because there was any intention on their part to remain. It was late afternoon and the holiday bustle had only partially subsided.

Pushing through the crowds at the railway station a young girl emerged, muffled up to the ears in furs, with a girlish face wreathed up to the eyes in smiles. It was very evident with her that Christmas was coming. At the gate entrance she inquired about her train. The *train was gone!* To stand there stupidly gazing at the official who certainly was not responsible helped matters not at all. Of course, it meant a "wire" and a wait until next morning. To a girl who was bent on meeting a bunch of college friends at a house party Christmas morning, the laconic information concerning the means of her transportation came not joyously. The tears which filled her brown eyes were definitely feminine. And then a little smile slipped out from somewhere and she proceeded to the Western Union office.

She was pushing through the door leading out to the busy street when a little brown hand caught at her skirt.

"Evenin' Herald, Lady?"

The girl looked down.

"Why, little fellow, you're crying. I can't let you take my pet indulgence away from me like that. Tell me about things, dear." And she brushed a perfectly good little tear out of the corner of her eye—the one that had refused to be chased when the smile came.

"It's—it's that I've just *got* to sell out tonight. It's—it's oranges for Bits."

By this time the ragged little coat-sleeve was serving wonderfully as a handkerchief.

"Come, come, little lad, stand over here out of the crowd. Somehow I don't understand. Who is Bits?"

"Why, he's all I'm got—that's all."

"Oh, I see! Can't you tell me more about him and your own little self?" Maybe I can *buy you out!*"

The childish face stared up into the girl's with an incredulity that was not at all concealed.

"Mean it, or jes' kiddin'?"

"Yes, dear, I *do* mean it. Tell me."

"It ain't so awful much to tell you 'bout where we live, 'cause we ain't roomin' in any manshun. Bits and Spatch an' me all sleeps on a cot in Mis' Barnery's basement, an' we gets our feed from Greeley's grocery when we *gets* it. Spatch is jes' beany 'bout weenies—swellest little *poor* dog you ever seen. We ain't got no folks but jes' ourselves, an' Spatch. Somehow, though, Bits hits it off with the papers—he's onto *his* job all right. I'm littler than him an' folks lots of time passes me up. We ain't never had *heaps*, but we has allus been happy, 'cause Bits says it's the only way to top off things. He's sick, though, now—he jes' all to oncet took down an' they bustled him off to the hospital. He looked right spruce an' cleaned up in that white bed when I went to see him, but say, he was *some* sick. They told me I could come back tonight, an' I wanted *awful* hard to take him oranges 'cause tomorrer's Christmas. But you see, I'm down to six cents, less'n I sell out. Guess I wasn't a game thoroughbred, like when you saw me cryin'—bet you Bits wouldn't a done it! My name's Rodney, but folks as knows me calls me Pep, 'cause some days I hits it off right spunky—specially when they're hot on—and Spatch's trail—he's one-eyed."

With the ingeniousness of the small boy he related the history of himself, Bits and Spatch. And the girl understood.

"Rodney, I'm going to buy you out and we'll dispose of these Heralds someway. You lead the way because we must get those oranges to Bits. May I go with you, please, to see your brother?"

"Well, I should jes' bet you *can*! It ain't so far, but I spect as how you'll better take the car. I'm only got six cents, but I'll boost you up an' pop the conductor a half dime an' beat it faster than the car an' be *waitin'* for you."

"Thank you, dear, for wishing for me to ride, but oh, I'd love to walk with you. If I may."

"Say, you are *some* great—know it?" And the look of gallant appreciation overspread the boy's face.

"Maybe if you're this good for walkin'—maybe you wouldn't mind cuttin' over two blocks with me. I promised Spatch that *he* could go tonight."

"Certainly! Are you cold, dear?"

"*Should say not*—too excited!"

They were reaching the quarter of the city very unfamiliar to the girl. Faithfully she followed the little figure striding along manfully with a bundle of "Evenin' Heralds" tucked under one arm.

"'Lo, kids!"

They had passed a bunch of little street children.

That's *my* bunch. They was some starin'—huh? Wonderin' bout *you*, I guess."

Finally they had reached a tenement house.

"Can't ast you in, but I'll be right down soon as I untie him. An'—an' shall I leave these papers? She could use them for kindlin'.."

"Oh, yes, by all means! I'll wait for you."

In an incredibly short space of time a boy with a dog was retracing his steps down the street in company with the girl.

"Ain't he a dog for you? Spatch is the cut' off for 'Dispatch'—one of the old papers. We're *pardners!*"

His new friend smiled understandingly.

At the fruit stand they purchased the oranges.

"Say! But you're *some* lady. I'll bet Bits will like you heaps. What made you good to me today?"

"Why, my dear! I just love all the little boys and girls of my race. I just wanted to help you if I could, just a little bit."

They had now reached the hospital. The girl, the small boy and the dog entered the building. It so happened that the lady visitor was not a stranger to the hospital force, consequently Spatch was graciously accorded a permit.

"How is the little lad, nurse?"

"The crisis came four nights ago—he will recover. He's been waiting for his little brother—go right in."

The white hospital cot was near the window and a shaft of light fell across the face which instantly became illumined with a smile when Spatch and Pep uttered their effusive greetings.

"Well, if here ain't the little kid and Pardner! How's business? Sleep cold last night, Pep?"

"*Should say not!* So warm, almost had to hist the window!"

The tail of Spatch wagged perilously near the sack of oranges purposely concealed at the foot of the bed.

Bits smiled, and then his eyes fell on the girl standing a little away from the bed. He turned towards Pep, and in a voice a trifle weak and very much puzzled exclaimed, "Pep, who's the swell in the skirt? She with you?"

"She's *some* lady!" A smile followed his words, absolutely appreciative. "She bought me out an' then come clear here jes' to see you. Can't you shake? She's a—a friend of *mine*."

In the course of a few minutes *she* was irrevocably taken into the partnership with Bits, Pep and Spatch. After the neighborhood news had been imparted and all preliminaries completed, the oranges were presented. The smile from Bits more than paid their real value.

All too soon the nurse came to announce the close of visiting hours.

"Pep, old feller, cover up good tonight. Give Pardner a weenie and please take three of these oranges for yourself—tomorrer's Christmas. Stick it out! I'll be back to the old job soon. They're bully to me here."

The girl bent over the little sick-a-bed laddie.

"Bits, is there a single Christmas wish of yours that I could fulfill, dear? Please let me try."

"Mighty nice of you. I think you've done a heap now. But there is—is something. It's the little kid there. I've heard about juvenile officers an' their doin's. Mebbe *somebody* could get a home for him. He's a smart little chap, Miss, an' deserves a chance. When I get well I'd work to help for his keep. Could you get him in?"

"Yes, dear, I've been thinking of Rodney all the way over here. Fortunately I know the very people to secure him a home. And I have a friend who has charge of a settlement house, and I am going to take him there tonight so he won't be lonesome. It's warm there, and they'll be good to him—they really would be happy to have him come. Plenty of boys there, and games, and a Christmas tree. I'll be there myself for a while. Now, have a good sleep and don't worry about him. Spatch is going too. Good-bye."

As they turned to look back once more at the door, a smile from Bits was following them. Outside Pep hesitated.

"Look here, I've *lied*—yes, I've told a ripper! I was freezin' cold last night—I give the blanket to my Pardner here."

"I understand, laddie. Tomorrow is Christmas. We're going down town on this car and I'm going to fit you out in some real warm clothing for your Christmas present, Rodney. And then tonight you, and Spatch, and I, are going to the settlement house. There, other little colored children are having a Christmas tree, and games, and fun! And there isn't going to be any more paper selling for you, or Bits, but you're going to have a real home and a chance to go to school. I have friends who will help me. Are you willing, dear?"

Two little cold hands ecstatically clasped themselves over one of the girl's, and two little tears of joy made two little tracks on his childish brown face.

"I guess you're the 'Christmas Angel' I heard 'bout oncet. Gee! But you're touchin'!"

The happiness that reigned in his little heart that Christmas eve is not to be described in words. Pep appreciated.

On Christmas morning a car stopped outside the settlement house and the girl bounded out to return leading a small boy, refreshed and happy and followed by a one-eyed canine disciple.

All arrangements had been made and both boys were to be located in a private home with a fair chance. A young doctor, the very dearest friend of the girl's, had consented to look after her charges in her holiday absence. It was he who opened the door of the car as they approached.

"Good morning, little chap! Merry Christmas!"

"Ditto"—this last from Pep, and an exhilarating bark from Spatch.

"Rodney, this is Dr. Weston—our *friend*."

When they reached the ward, one bound and Pep was at the side of the bed.

"Know me, Bits? *Some looker*, ain't I? Had one spludge las' night—too big almost to talk about. She done it all. *She's an angel!* Now, hold your breath while I tell you the biggest ever! She's found a home for you, an' me, an' Spatch, an' we're going to *school*, and'—an' *she means it!*"

The "Christmas Angel" and the doctor came nearer the bed. Professionally he reached for the pulse and all the friendliness possible was in his greeting.

"Well, little friend, I'm in the partnership, too, and we're going to get you well in ten days!"

Bits smiled first at one and then at the other appreciatively.

"You two don't know how I thank you for myself an' the kid! I can't tell you. Just give us the chance—we'll prove the claim!" Determination and gratitude were in his face.

"I'm glad if you're pleased, Bits. You are both going to be my little brothers, and Spatch here (at this opportune moment there was an appreciative tail-wag) is going to be our mascot. I must hurry now to catch the train, for I'm going away for three days. Dr. Weston is going to give Rodney a 'big day,' and I think he has a surprise for Bits. Good-bye, dear!"

There was a kiss left on the warm forehead. A little hand shot out from the covering.

"*You're* the best Christmas I ever had. I—I just wish I could whisper to you, somethin'—"

The girl bent down. Two arms went around her neck, two words from a little heart filled with gratitude slipped out—

"Merry Christmas!" [*The Crisis* 13.2 (December 1916): 64–66]

MAMMY

by Adeline F. Ries

Mammy's heart felt heavy indeed when (the time was now two years past) marriage had borne Shiela, her "white baby," away from the Governor's plantation to the coast. But as the months passed, the old colored nurse became accustomed to the change, until the great joy brought by the news that Shiela had a son, made her reconciliation complete. Besides, had there not always been Lucy, Mammy's own "black baby," to comfort her?

Yes, up to that day there had always been Lucy; but on that very day the young Negress had been sold—sold like common household ware!—and (the irony of it chilled poor Mammy's leaden heart)—she had been sold to Shiela as nurse to the baby whose birth, but four days earlier had caused Mammy so much rejoicing. The poor slave could not believe that it was true, and as she buried her head deeper into the pillows, she prayed that she might wake to find it all a dream.

But a reality it proved and a reality which she dared not attempt to change. For despite the Governor's customary kindness, she knew from experience, that any interference on her part would but result in serious floggings. One morning each week she would go to his study and he would tell her the news from the coast and then with a kindly smile dismiss her.

So for about a year, Mammy feasted her hungering soul with threes meager scraps of news, until one morning, contrary to his wont, the Governor rose as she entered the room, and he bade her sit in a chair close to his own. Placing one of his white hands over her knotted brown ones, he read aloud the letter he held in his other hand:

> "Dear Father:
> "I can hardly write the sad news and can, therefore, fully appreciate how difficult it will be for you to deliver it verbally. Lucy was found lying on the nursery floor yesterday, dead. The physician whom I immediately summoned pronounced her death a case of heart-failure. Break it gently to my dear old mammy, father, and tell her too, that the coach, should she wish to come here before the burial, is at her disposal.
> "Your daughter,
> "Shiela"

While he read, the Governor unconsciously nerved himself to a violent outburst of grief, but none came. Instead, as he finished, Mammy rose, curtsied, and made as if to withdraw. At the door she turned back and requested the coach. "If it weren't asking too much," and then left the room. She did not turn to her cabin; simply stood at the edge of the road until the coach with its horses and driver drew up, and then she entered. From that time and until nightfall she did not once change the upright position she had assumed, nor did her eyelids once droop over her staring eyes. "They took her from me an' she died"—"They took her from an' she died"—over and over she repeated the same sentence.

When early the next morning Mammy reached Shiela's home, Shiela herself came down the road to meet her, ready with words of comfort and love. But as in years gone by, it was Mammy who took the golden head on her breast, and patted it, and bade the girl to dry her tears. As of old, too, it was Mammy who first spoke of other things; she asked to be shown the baby, and Shiela only too willingly led the way to the nursery where in his crib the child lay cooing to itself. Mammy took up the little body and again, and again tossed it up into the air with the old cry, "Up she goes, Shiela," till he laughed aloud.

Suddenly she stopped, and clasping the child close she took a hurried step towards the open window. At a short distance from the house rolled the sea. And Mammy gazed upon it as if fascinated. And as she stared, over and over the words formed themselves; "They took her from me an' she died"—"They took her from me an' she died"—"They took her from me an' she died."From below came the sound of voices, "They're waiting for you, Mammy,"—it was Shiela's soft voice that spoke—"to take Lucy—you understand, dear."

Mammy's eyes remained fixed upon the waves,—"I can't go—go foh me, chile, won't you?" And Shiela thought that she understood the poor woman's feelings and without even pausing to kiss her child she left the room and joined the waiting slaves.

Mammy heard the scraping as of a heavy box upon the gravel below; heard the tramp of departing footsteps as they grew fainter and fainter until they died away. Then and only then, did she turn her eyes from the wild waters and looking down at the child in her arms, she laughed a low, peculiar laugh. She smoothed back the golden ringlets from his forehead, straightened out the little white dress, and then, choosing a light covering for his head, she descended the stairs and passed quietly out of the house.

A short walk brought Mammy and her burden to the lonely beach; at the water's edge she stood still. Then she shifted the child's position until she supported his weight in her hands and with a shrill cry of "Up she goes, Shiela," she lifted him above her head. Suddenly she flung her arms forward, at the same time releasing her hold of his little body. A large breaker caught him in its foam, swept him a few feet towards the shore and retreating, carried him out into the sea—

A few hours later, two slaves in frantic search for the missing child found Mammy on the beach tossing handfuls of sand into the air and uttering loud, incoherent cries. And as they came close, she pointed towards the sea and with the laugh of a mad-woman shouted: "They took her from me an' she died."   [*The Crisis* 13.3 (January 1917): 117–118]

"THERE WAS ONE TIME!": A STORY OF SPRING

by Jessie Fauset

"There was one time," began the freckled-faced boy. Miss Fetter interrupted him with emphasis—"but that is not idiomatic, our expression for *il y avait une fois* is 'once upon a time.' The value of a translation lies in its adequacy." And for the fiftieth time that term she launched into as explanation of the translation of idioms. The class listened with genial composure—the more she talked, the less they could read. She reached her peroration. "Do you understand, Master Reynolds?"

The freckled-faced boy, who had been surreptitiously consulting his vocabulary, turned deftly back to the passage. "Yes'm,' he nodded. "There was one time"—he began again unabashed.

Miss Fetter sighed and passed on to another pupil. Between them all there was evolved in hopelessly unsympathetic English the story of a dainty French shepherdess who growing tired of her placid sheep left them to shift for themselves one gorgeous spring-day, donned her sky-blue dress, traversed the somber forest and came to another country. There she met the prince who, struck with her charm and naiveté, asked her to play with him. So she did until sunset when he escorted her to the edge of the forest where she pursued her way home to her little thatched cottage, with a mind much refreshed and "garlanded with pleasant memories."

The pupils read, as pupils will, with stolid indifference. The fairy-tale was merely so many pages of French to them, as indeed it was to Miss Fetter. That she must teach foreign languages—always her special detestation—seemed to her the final irony of an ironic existence.

"It's all so inadequate," she fumed to herself, pinning on her hat before the tiny mirror in the little stuffy teachers' room. She was old enough to have learned very thoroughly the aphorisms of her day. She believed that all service performed honestly and thoroughly was helpful, but she was still too young to know that such was literally true and her helplessness irked her. See her, then, as she walked home through the ugly streets of Marytown, neither white nor black, of medium height, slim, nose neither good nor bad, mouth beautiful, teeth slightly irregular, but perfect. Altogether, when she graduated at eighteen from the Business High School in Philadelphia she was as much as any one else the typical American girl done over in brown, no fears for the future, no regrets for the past, rather glad to put her schoolbooks down for good and decidedly glad that she was no longer to be a burden on her parents.

Getting a position after all was not so easy. Perhaps for the first time she began to realize the handicap of color. Her grade on graduation had been "meritorious." She had not shone, but neither had she been stupid. She had rarely volunteered to answer questions, being mostly occupied in dreaming, but she could answer when called on. If she had no self-assurance, neither had she a tendency to self-belittlement. Her English, if not remarkable, was at least correct; her typewriting was really irreproachable; her spelling exact; and she had the quota of useless French—or German—vocabulary which the average pupil brings out of the average High School. Perhaps it was because she had lived all her life in a small up-town street in a white neighborhood and played with most of the boys and girls there, perhaps it was because at eighteen one is still idealistic that she answered advertisement after advertisement without apprehension. The result, of course, was always the same; always the faint shock of surprise in the would-be employer's voice, the faint stare, the faint emphasis—"You! Oh no, the position is not open to—er—you." At first she did not understand, but even when she did she kept futilely on—she *could* not, she *would* not teach—and why does one graduate from a Business High School, if one is not to be employed by a business firm?

That summer her father, a silent, black man, died and her decisions against teaching fled. She was not a normal school graduate, so she could not teach in Philadelphia. The young German drummer next door told her of positions to be had in colored schools in the South—perhaps she could teach her favorite stenography or drawing in which she really excelled. Fate at that point took on her most menacing aspect. Nothing that was not menial came her way, excepting work along lines of which she knew nothing. Her mother and she gave up the little house and the two of them went to service. Those two awful years gave Anna her first real taste of the merciless indifference of life. Her mother, a woman of nerveless and, to Anna, enviable stolidity found, as always, a refuge in inapt quotations of Scripture. But Anna lived in a fever of revolt. She spent her days as a waitress and her evenings in night school trying feverishly to learn some of those subjects which she might have taught, had she been properly prepared. At the end of two years the change came carelessly, serenely, just as though it might always have happened. The son-in-law of Mrs. Walton, for whom she worked, passed through town late one night. The family had gone out and for want of something better he had, as he ate his solitary dinner, asked the rather taciturn waitress about her history. She had told him briefly and he had promised her, with equal brevity, a position of drawing teacher at a colored seminary of which he was a trustee. Anna, stunned, went with her mother to Maryville. Just as suddenly as it started, the struggle for existence was over, though, of course, they were still poor. Mrs. Fetter found plenty of plain sewing to do and Anna was appointed. But Fate, with a last malevolence, saw to it that she was appointed to teach History and French, which were just being introduced into the seminary. She thought of this as she opened her mother's gate—the irony of the thing made her sick. "Since my luck was going to change, why couldn't I have been allowed to teach mechanical drawing," she wondered, "or given a chance at social work" But teaching French! "I suppose the reason that little shepherdess neglected her sheep that day was because *they* were French."

II

Still one cannot persist in gloom when it is April and one is twenty-six and looks, as only American girls, whether white or brown, can look, five years younger. Anna, hastening down the street in her best blue serge dress, her pretty slim feet in faultless tan shoes, felt her moodiness, which had almost become habitual, vanish.

The wearing of the blue dress was accidental. She had come down to breakfast in her usual well-worn gray skirt and immaculate shirt-waist in time to hear her small cousin, Theophilus, proclaim his latest enterprise. A boy was going to give him five white mice for his pen-knife and he was going to bring them home right after school and put them in a little cage. Pretty soon there'd be more of them—"they have lots of children, Aunt Emmeline, and I'm going to sell them and buy Sidney Williams' ukulele, and"—

"Indeed you are going to do no such thing," exclaimed Anna, her high good humor vanishing. "Mother, you won't let him bring those nasty things here, I know. As for keeping them in a cage, they'd be all over the house in no time."

But Mrs. Fetter, who loved Theophilus because he was still a little boy and she could baby him, opined that foxes and birds had their nests. "Let's see the cage, Philly dear, maybe they can't get out."

The rest had followed as the night the day. Theophilus, rushing from the table, had knocked Anna's cup of cocoa out of her hand and the brown liquid had run down the front of the immaculate blouse and settled in a comfortable pool in her lap.

"Oh well," her mother had said, unmoved as usual, "run along, Anna, and put on your blue serge dress. It won't do you any harm to wear it this once and if you hurry you'll get to school in time just the same. You didn't go to do it, did you, Philly?"

Theophilus, aghast, had fled to the shelter of his banjo from which he was extracting plaintive strains. He played banjo, guitar and piano with equal and indeed amazing facility, but as his musical tastes were surprisingly eclectic, the results were at times distressing. Anna, hastening out, a real vision now in her pretty frock, and unwanted color in her smooth bronze cheeks, heard him telling his aunt again about the ukulele which Sidney Williams owned but couldn't play. "It's broke. Some folks where his father works gave it to him. Betcher I'll fix it and play it, too, when I get hold of it," his high voice was proclaiming confidently.

"I suppose he will,"—thought his cousin, "I hope that North street won't be hung up this morning. He ought to make a fine musician, but, of course, he won't get a chance at it when he grows up." The memory of her own ironic calling stung her. "He'll probably have to be a farmer just because he'll hate it. I do wish I could walk, it's so lovely. I wish I were that little shepherdess off on a holiday. She was wearing a blue dress, I remember."

Well, her mind leaped up to the thought. Why shouldn't she take a day off? In all these six years she had never been out once, except the time Theophilus had had the measles. The street car came up at this point, waited an infinitesimal second and clanged angrily off, as if provoked at its own politeness. She looked after it with mingled dismay and amusement. "I'd be late anyway," she told herself, "now that I've lost that car. I'll get a magazine and explore the Park; no one will know."

Two hours of leisurely strolling brought her to Hertheimer Park, a small green enclosure at the end of the ugly little town. Anna picked her way past groups of nursemaids and idlers looking in newspapers for occupation which they hoped they would never find. She came at last to the little grove in the far side of the Park where the sun was not quite so high and, seating herself near the fountain, began to feed the squirrels with some of the crackers which she had bought in one of the corner groceries.

Being alive was pretty decent after all, she reflected. Life was the main thing—teaching school, being colored, even being poor were only aspects, her mind went on. If one were just well and comfortable—not even rich or pampered—one could get along; the thing to do was to look at life in the large and not to gaze too closely at the specific interest or activity in hand. Her growing philosophy tickled her sense of humor. "You didn't feel like that when you were at Mrs. Walton's," she told herself bluntly and smiled at her own discomfiture.

"That's right, smile at me," said an oily voice, and she looked up to see one of the idlers leaning over the back of her bench. "You're a right good-lookin' gal. How'd you like to take a walk with me?"

She stared into his evil face, fascinated. Where, where, where were all the people? The nurse-maids had vanished, the readers of newspapers had gone—to buy afternoon editions, perhaps. She felt herself growing icy, paralyzed. "You needn't think I mind your being a nigger," went on the hateful voice, "I ruther like 'em. I hain't what you might call prejudiced."

This was what could happen to you if you were a colored girl who felt like playing at being a French shepherdess. She looked around for help and exactly as though at a cue in a play, as though he had been waiting for that look a young colored man stepped forward, one hand courteously lifting his hat, the other resting carelessly in his hip-pocket.

"Good afternoon, Miss Walker," he said, and his whole bearing exhaled courtesy. "I couldn't be sure it was you until you turned around. I'm sorry I'm late, I hope I haven't kept you waiting. I hope you weren't annoying my friend," he addressed the tramp pleasantly.

But the latter, with one fascinated glance at the hand still immobile in that suggestive hip-pocket, was turning away.

"I was jus' askin' a direction," he muttered. "I'll be going now."

III

The two young colored people stared at each other in silence. Anna spoke first—

"Of course, my name isn't Walker," she murmured inadequately.

They both laughed at that, she nervously and he weakly. The uncertain quality of his laughter made her eye him sharply. "Why, you're trembling—all over," she exclaimed, and then with the faintest curl of her lip, "you'd better sit down if you're as much afraid as all that," her mind ended.

He did sit down, still with that noticeable difference, and, removing his hat, mopped his forehead. His hair was black and curly above a very pleasant brown face, she noted subconsciously, but her conscious self was saying "He was afraid, because he's colored."

He seemed to read her thoughts. "I guess you think I'm a fine rescuer," he smiled at her ruefully. "You see, I'm just beginning to recover from an attack of malarial fever. That is why I pretended to have a gun. I'm afraid I couldn't have tackled him successfully, this plagued fever always leaves me so weak, but I'd have held him off till you had got away. I didn't want him to touch you, you seemed so nice and dainty. I'd been watching you for sometime under the trees, thinking how very American you were and all that sort of thing, and when you smiled it seemed to me such a bit of all right that you should be feeling so fit and self-confident. When I saw the expression on your face change I almost wept to think I hadn't the strength to bash his head in. That was why I waited to catch your eye, because I didn't want to startle you and I didn't have strength for anything but diplomacy."

She nodded, ashamed of her unkindness and interested already in something else. "Aren't you foreign?" she ventured, "You seem different somehow, something in the way you talk made me feel perhaps you weren't American."

"Well I am," he informed her heartily. "I was born, of all places, in Camden, New Jersey, and if that doesn't make me American I don't know what does. But I've been away a long time, I must admit, that's why my accent sounds a little odd, I suppose. My father went to British Guiana when I was ten; but I got the idea that I wanted to see some more foreign countries, so when I was fifteen I ran away to England. You couldn't imagine, a girl like you, all the things I've seen and done, and the kinds of people I've known. I had such an insatiable thirst for adventure, a sort of compelling curiosity."

He paused, plainly reminiscent.

"I've picked up all sorts of trades in England and France—I love France and it was my stay there that made me long so much to get back to America. I kept the idea before me for years. It seemed to me that to live under a republican form of government, with lots of my own people around me, would be the finest existence in the world. I remember I used to tell a crowd of American chaps I was working with in France about it, and they used to be so amused and seemed to have some sort of secret joke."

Anna thought it highly probable.

He looked at her meditating. "Yes, I suppose they had—from their point of view but not from mine. You see," he told her with an oddly boyish air of bestowing a confidence, "life as life is intensely interesting to me. I wake up every morning—except when I have malarial fever"—he interrupted himself whimsically—"wondering what I'll have to overcome during the day. And it's different things in different environments. In this country, it's color, for instance, in another it might be ignorance of the native tongue.

"When I came back to New York I was a little non-plussed, I must confess, at the extraordinary complexes of prejudice. I went to a nice-looking hotel and they didn't want me a bit at first. Well, I pick up the idiom of a language very quickly and I suppose at this point my English accent and expression out–Englished most Englishmen's. After a bit the clerk asked where I hailed from and when I told him Manchester, and displayed my baggage—only I called it luggage—all covered with labels, he said 'oh, that was different,' and gave me a room just as right as you please. Well it struck me so peculiarly idiotic to refuse your own countryman because he is brown, but to take him in, though he hasn't changed a particle, because he hails from another country. But it gave me a clue."

"Yes?" she wondered.

"You see, it made me angry that I had allowed myself to take refuge under my foreign appearance when what I really wanted to do was to wave my hat and shout, 'I'm an American and I've come home. Aren't you glad to see me? If you only knew how proud I am to be here.' The disappointment and the sting of it kept me awake all night And next day I went out and met up with some colored fellows—nice chaps all right—and they got me some rooms up in Harlem. Ever see Harlem?" he asked her,—"most interesting place, America done over in color. Well it was just what I wanted after Europe.

"But it struck me there was a lack of self-esteem, a lack of self-appreciation, and a tendency to measure ourselves by false ideals." He was clearly on his hobby now, his deep-set eyes glowed, his wide, pleasant mouth grew firmer.

"Your average British or French man of color and every Eastern man of color thinks no finer creature than, himself ever existed. I wanted to tell our folks that there is nothing more supremely American than the colored American, nothing more made-in-America, so to speak. There is no supreme court which rules absolutely that white is the handsomest color, that straight hair is the most alluring. If we could just realize the warmth and background which we supply to America, the mellowness, the rhythm, the music. Heavens," he broke off, "where *does* one ever hear such music as some of the most ordinary colored people can bring out of a piano?"

Anna, thinking of Theophilus, smiled.

"And there's something else too," he resumed. "The cold-bloodedness which enables a civilized people to maim and kill in the Congo and on the Putumayo, or to lynch in Georgia, isn't in it with the simple kindliness which we find in almost any civilized colored man. No people has a keener, more rollicking humor, and the music—

"Excuse my ranting," he begged, all apology, "but I get so excited about it all. Did you ever read any Pater?" he asked her abruptly.

"No," she told him shamefacedly—Pater was not included in her High School English and she had read almost no literature since.

He nodded indifferently. "Well, in 'The Child in the House,' the chap says if he had his way he wouldn't give very poor people 'the things men desire most, but the power to realize and taste at will a certain desirable, clear light in the new morning.' That's me." He concluded, too earnest to care about grammar. "I'd give us the power to realize how wonderful and beautiful and enduring we are in the world's scheme of things. I can't help but feel that finally a man is taken at his own estimate."

They were silent a moment, watching a flock of pale, yellow butterflies waver like an aura over a bed of deep golden crocuses.

"Have you told your views to many people?" Anna asked him a trifle shyly. His mood, his experiences, his whole personality seemed so remote from anything she had ever encountered.

"No," he told her dryly. "I haven't done anything. I came from New York down to this town to visit my aunt, my mother's youngest sister—she's as young as I am, by the way, isn't that funny? And I've had the malarial fever ever since. I get it every spring, darn it!" He ended in total disgust.

"You might tell me something of yourself. We'll probably never see each other again," he suggested lingeringly, with just the faintest question-mark in his voice.

But Anna didn't catch it, she was too absorbed in the prospect of having some one with whom to discuss her perplexities. She launched out without a thought for the amazing unconventionality of the whole situation. "And so," she finished, "here I am painfully teaching French. I don't make enough to allow me to go to summer school and I don't seem to make much progress by myself." He seemed so terribly competent that she hated to let him know how stupid she was. Still, it was a relief to admit it.

"I know," he comforted her. "You needn't feel so very bad, there are some things that just don't come to one. I'm a mechanical engineer and I can read any kind of plans but it worries me to death to have to draw them."

"Why, I can draw," she told him—"anything."

Their first constraint fell upon them.

He tried to break it. "If you teach," he asked her, "What are you doing here? Wednesday isn't a holiday, is it?"

She broke out laughing. "No, it's too funny! You wouldn't believe how it all happened"—and she told him the story of the little shepherdess. "And this morning my little cousin split cocoa all over my school clothes and I had to put on my blue dress. It made me think of the little shepherdess and here I am."

He was watching her intently. How charming she was with all that color in her face. Comely, that was the word for her and—wholesome. He was sure of it.

"How did the story end?" he wondered.

She didn't know, she told him, shamefaced anew at her stupidity. "You know it is so hard for me, every year we read a new book and I never get a chance to get used to the vocabulary. And so the night before I just get the lessons out for the next day. I teach six preparations, you see, three in history and three in French. And it takes me such a long time I never read ahead. I simply cannot get the stuff," she explained, much downcast.

"I've tried awfully hard; but you know some people have absolutely no feeling for a foreign language. I'm one of them! As for composition work"—she shook her head miserably, "I have to dig for it so. The only thing is that I *can* feel whether a translation is adequate or not, so I don't mind that part of the work. But when we got that far in this story the head language teacher—crazy thing, she's always changing about—said to lay that aside and finish up all the grammar and then go back and do all the translating. I've never looked at the story since. All I know," she ended thoughtlessly, "is that the shepherdess played and talked with the prince all day and he took her to the edge of the forest at sunset—what's the matter?" she broke off.

"You didn't tell me," he said a trifle breathless, "that she met a prince."

"Didn't I? Well she did—and it's four o'clock and I must go. My mother will be wondering where I am." She held out her ungloved hand, shapely and sizeable and very comely. It took him sometime to shake hands, but perhaps that was one of his foreign ways.

She had gone and he stood staring after her. Then he settled back on the bench again, hat over his eyes, hands in his pockets, long legs stretched out in front of him.

"Of course," he was thinking, "you can't say to a girl like that, 'well, if you're playing shepherdess let me play your prince?' Wasn't she nice, though, so fine and wholesome—and colored. What's that thing Tommy was playing last night with that little Theophilus somebody? Oh yes."—he hummed it melodiously:

"'*I'm for you, brown-skin.*'"

IV

Not until June did Anna encounter the little shepherdess again.

She settled down the night before the lesson was due to read it with a great deal of interest. Her meeting with "the prince," as she always called the strange young man, had left on her a definite impress. She wondered if ever she would meet him again, and wished ardently that she might. Her naiveté and utter lack of self-importance kept her from feeling piqued at his failure to hunt her up. She wondered often if life still seemed interesting to him, found herself borrowing a little of his high ardor. On the whole her attitude toward "the adventure," as she loved to call it, was that of the little shepherdess and she brought back from that day only a mind "garlanded with pleasant memories."

Perhaps, she thought fancifully that Thursday evening,—the shepherdess meets the prince again and he gives her a position as court-artist. And she opened the little text to find out. But that lesson was never prepared, for Theophilus came in at that point with a bleeding gap in his head, caused by falling off a belated ice wagon. The sight of blood always made Mrs. Fetter sick, so Anna had the wound to clean and bind and Theophilus to soothe and get to bed.

So as it happened all she could do was to underline the new words and get their meaning from the vocabulary and trust to the gods that there would be no blind alleys in construction.

Anyone but Anna would have foreseen the end of that fairy-tale. For the prince, with the utter disregard for rank and wealth and training which so much falls to distinguish real princes, sought out the little shepherdess, who had been living most happily and unsuspectingly with her little sheep and her "so pleasant souvenirs" (so said "Miss Selena Morton in translation), and besought her to marry him and live forever in his kingdom by the sea.

"'Oh, sky!' (thus ran Miss Morton's rendition for the French of 'Oh, heavens!') 'Oh, sky!' exclaimed the shepherdess, and she told him she would accompany his all willingly, and when the prince had kissed her on both jaws they went on their way. And if you can find a happier ending of this history it is necessary that you go and tell it to the Pope at Rome." Thus, and not otherwise, did Miss Selena Morton mutilate that exquisite story!

But Miss Fetter was too amazed to care. Moreover, Tommy Reynolds and some of the other pupils had translated very well. Perhaps the work in grammar had been the best thing and perhaps she, too, was becoming a better teacher, she hoped to herself wistfully.

"I'm very much pleased with the work you've done today," she told the class. "It seems to me you've improved greatly particularly Master Reynolds."

And Master Reynolds, who was cleaning the black-boards, smiled inscrutably.

"But just think the first part of the story had come true, why shouldn't the second? Oh, I wish, I wish." She rushed into the "front room," where Theophilus sat, his small broken head bandaged up, picking indefatigably at his banjo, and hugged him tumultuously.

He took her caress unmoved, having long ago decided that all women outside of aunts and mothers were crazy. "Look out, you'll break my new strings," he warned her. And she actually begged his pardon and proffered him fifteen cents towards the still visionary ukulele.

One can't go far on the similarity between one incident in one's life and the promise of a French fairy-tale. "Still, things do happen," she told herself, surprised at her own tenacity. "Think of how Mr. Allen came into Mrs. Walton's that night and changed my whole life." She went to bed in a maze of rapture and anticipation.

Her mother was interested in a bazaar and dinner for the bazaar workers in the Methodist Church, but she had quarreled with one of the sisters and she meant to go and arrange her booth and come back, so she shouldn't have to eat at the same table with the benighted Mrs. Vessels.

"I'd rather eat stalled oxen by myself all my days," she told her daughter Saturday morning, "than share the finest victuals at the same table as Pauline Vessels."

"Oh, mother," Anna had wailed, "how *can* you say such things? 'Stalled oxen' *is* the choice thing, the thing you are supposed to want to eat. You've got it upside down."

"Well, what difference does it make?" her mother had retorted, vexed for once. "I'm sure I shouldn't like the stuff, anyway. They'd probably be tough. Don't you let Philly stir out of this house till I come back, Anna. I don't want him to hurt hisself again. Do you think you can manage everything? I swept all the rooms yesterday but the kitchen. There's only that to scrub and the dusting to do."

Anna nodded. She was glad to be alone, glad to have work to do. She sent Theophilus out to clean up the side yard. She could hear him aimlessly pattering about.

"Ann," he called. She had finished scrubbing and all the dusting, too, except in the "front-room," which her mother *would* keep full of useless odds and ends, sheaves of wheat, silly bric-a-brac or what-nots. Ordinarily she hated it, but to-day—"to be alive"—her mind, not usually given to poetical flights, halted—"to be alive," no, "to be *young*," that was it, "to be young was very heaven." And he *had* said in the queerest way, "you didn't say she met a prince." If she could just find out something about him, who he was, where he lived, who *was* his mother's youngest sister. Why, what had she been thinking about to let two months go by without making any inquiry? True, she didn't know many colored people in Marytown, she had never bothered—she had been so concerned with her own affairs—but her mother knew everybody, positively, and a question here or there! Oh, if he only know how the story ended! She became poetical again—"Would but some winged angel ere too late." She had to smile at that herself. Yet the winged angel was on the way in the person of Theophilus. He couldn't have adopted a more effective disguise.

"Ann," he called again, "C'n I go fishin' now with Tommy Reynolds? I've found all these nice worms in the garden, they'll make grand bait. Aunt (he pronounced it like the name of the humble insect) won't mind. She'd let me go 'n the air 'll be good for my head," he wheedled.

Anna, dusting the big Bible, hardly turned around. "No," she told him vigorously, "you can't go, Philly. You must stay till mother comes—she'll be here pretty soon, and you wash your hands and study your lessons a bit. Your last report was dreadful. Tommy Reynolds is only one year older than you and there he is in the second year of the seminary and you still in the graded schools. He plays, but he gets his lessons, too."

And then Theo began to rustle his wings, but neither he nor his cousin heard them.

"Oh, pshaw!" he retorted in disgust. "Tommy don't get no lessons. Someone around his house's always helpin' him—he don't do nothin'. Why, his mother always does his drawin' for him."

"I don't know about his drawing," retorted his cousin 'but I know he does his French. He had a beautiful lesson yesterday. Don't laugh like that, Theophilus, it gets on my nerves."

For Theophilus was laughing shrilly, which perhaps drowned the still louder rustling of his wings.

"There you go," he jibbed, "there you go. He doesn't do his French at all, his uncle does it for him; he did it Thursday night when I was there. I heard him and ain't tellin' any tales about it, neither," he put in, mistaking the look on her face, "for he said you'd be interested to have him do it for Tommy. He said he'd tell you about it the next time he saw you."

"Theophilus Jackson, you're crazy. I never saw Tommy Reynolds' uncle in my life. I don't even know where they live."

"Well, he's saw you," the child persisted and hesitated and looked puzzled—"though he did ask an awful lot of questions about you as if he didn't know you. Well, I don't know what he meant, but he did Tommy's French for him, I know that!" he ended in defiance.

Some faint prescience must have come to her mind, for she spoke with unwonted alertness. "He asked about me?" she insisted. "Sit down here, Theo, and tell me all about it. Who is his uncle?"

"Oh, I don't know, you needn't hold me so tight. I ain't goin' to go. Uncle Dick, Tommy calls him, Uncle Dick somethin'—oh—Winter—Mr. Richard Winter I heard Mrs. Reynolds call him. 'Now see here, Mr. Richard Winter,' she said to him—and she's his aunt, Anna, ain't that funny?—and he's bigger'n she and older, I guess, 'cause she looks awful young. I though aunts were all old like Aunt Em."

She was sure now, and this miserable little boy had known all along. She alternately longed to shake him and hug him. She restrained both desires, knowing that the indulgence of either would dam the fount interminably.

"Go on, Philly," she begged him. "Maybe I can get Sid Williams to let you have the ukulele right away and you can pay him on the installment plan."

"Well, ain't I tellin' you? Tommy and me, we wanted to go to the movies and his mother said, 'No' he'd got to get all his lessons first, and Tom winked at me and said he had 'em all, and his mother said, 'Not your French,' and Tommy said, 'Well, Uncle Dick's well again now, c'n I ask him tonight?' And just then his uncle walked in and said, 'Hullo, what's it all about?'— he talks so funny, Anna, and Tommy said, 'Please do my translation!' His mother said, 'Not till he's reviewed the first part then, he hasn't seen the part for two months, because he's been studying something else.' And his uncle said, 'All right, hurry up, kid, because I must pack, I've got to go away again to-morrow.' And that was when Tommy's mother said, 'Well, Mr. Richard Winter, do you own the railway? Why don't you stay in one place? You've been here and gone again four times in the last two months!' And he said 'Oh, Nora, I'm looking for something and I can't find it.' And she said, 'Did you lose it here?' and he answered, awful said, 'I think I did.' Why doesn't he buy another one, whatever it is, Cousin Anna?"

"I don't know, dear. Go on—did he say anything else?"

"Uh, huh—my but your face is red! And he said, 'Hit it up, Thomas-kid,' and Tommy opened the book and began to read all the silliest stuff about a lady in a park tending goats in a blue dress, and he said, his uncle did, 'What's that? What's that?' and he snatched the book away and looked at it, and he said in the funniest voice, 'I thought you said you were studyin' German all along. I never realized till this minute. Who's your teacher, Thomas?' And Tommy said *you* was. And he said, 'What does she look like?' Tommy said, 'She's awful cute, I must give her that, but she is too darn strict about her old crazy French.' And I said you was my cousin, and I told him not to get gay when he talked about you and if you was strict he needed it. And Mr. Winter said, 'right-oh!' and asked me a lot of questions, and I said, no, you weren't pretty, but you were awful nice looking and had pretty skin and little feet, and he asked me did I ever spill a cup of cocoa in your lap."

She was on the floor now, her arms around him. "And what else, Philly. Oh, Philly, what else?"

"Lemme go, Ann, ain't I tellin' you?" He wriggled himself free. "Oh, yes, and then he said, 'Where does she live?' I said, 'With me, of course,' and he said, 'Here in Marytown?' and I said, 'Yes, 37 Fortner street, near North,' and he said—oh, he swore, Ann—he said, 'My God, to think she's been here all this time. Here, boy, gimme that book,' and he sat down and started to read the old silly stuff to Tommy, and I ran out and jumped on the ice wagon and got my head busted. And will you get me the ukulele, Anna?"

She would, she assured him, get him anything, and he could go fishing and she would explain to Aunt Emmeline. "And here, take my apron upstairs with you. Why didn't you tell me before, Philly?"

"Well, what was there to tell, Anna?" he asked her, bewildered.

V

As soon as her mother should come in she'd bathe and dress and go out—but where? After all she was a girl, she must stand still, she didn't even know Mrs. Reynolds. But she could go by the house—yes, but he was to go away Friday, Theo said—why he *had* gone. Well, he would come back.

The gate clicked. At least, she could tell her mother. But she was crazy—she had only seen him once—well, so had the shepherdess seen the prince only once. Her mother would *have* to understand. What an age she was talking to one of those old Dorcas society sisters! She ran to the door, and, of course, it was he on the steps, his hand just raised to knock.

Together they entered the room, silent, a little breathless. Even *he* was frightened. As for Anna—

"You knew I was coming," he told her "I didn't find out until Thursday. Somehow I thought you lived in another town. You know you said the shepherdess had come such a long, long way, and I thought that meant you had too, and I was afraid to ask you. Oh, I've hunted, and Tommy, the rascal, told me he was crazy about German because he wanted some illustrated German books he saw in my trunk, and I thought he was studying it," he rushed on breathlessly. "And Thursday night I had to go to New York to be sure about something before I dared to talk to you. And I'm to be a social settlement worker, and I can talk and talk and tell people about all those things," he ended lamely.

Anna stood silent.

"Anna, I thought, I hoped, I wondered"—he stammered. "Oh, do you think you could go with me—I want you so. And don't say you don't know me, we've always known each other, you lovely, brown child." His eyes entreated her.

But she still hung back. "*You* could talk to people about those wonderful things, but I, what could I do?"

"After the war," he explained to her, "we could go back to Europe and I could build bridges and you could draw the plans, and after we had made enough money we could come back and I could preach my gospel—for nothing."

"But, till then?"

"Till then," he whispered, "you could help me live that wonderful fairy-tale. Dear, I love you so"—and he kissed her tenderly, first on one cheek and then on the other.

"On both jaws," she whispered, a bit hysterically.

So then he kissed her on her perfect mouth.

Just then her mother, bidding Sister Pauline Vessels an amicable good-bye at the gate, came up the walk. So, hand in hand, they went to tell her about the happy ending.

[*The Crisis* 13.6 (April 1917): 272–277; 14.1 (May 1917): 11–15]

AUNT CALLINE'S SHEAVES

by Leila Amos Pendleton

No, indeed, chile, I never did believe in taking things frum dead people. You know Aunt Calline Juniper was my mother- in-law and a grander one never hopped, so when she died, me and May Jane Juniper, which married her other son, was awful sorry. We certainly was. As for Uncle John, her husband, he just took on turrible. Everybody loved Aunt Calline and they sent lots of flowers to the funeral and three sheaves of wheat.

Now I never could bear the sight of sheaves of wheat, less they was at the mill, and when all them sheaves come rollin' in to Aunt Calline, I begun to look at 'em cross-eyed. I was in hopes, though, that everybody would forget 'em and they'd be left in the simitary. But no sooner was Aunt Calline covered up than here comes the undertaker with a long face and all three of them sheaves.

Uncle John took 'em very solemn-like, handed one to me and one to May Jane and says, "Chillun, always keep these to 'member Calline. I'll keep one and when I die, Sally, you must take it, as you're the oldest." Ever notice how people are always making you presents of things you hate? "Laws," thinks I to myself, "this is worse than Chrismus." I groaned down in my toes, but didn't say anything outward, and here goes May Jane and me home loaded down with wheat. They was the biggest sheaves I ever seen,—they was small-sized shocks, in fact.

Well, after I got that wheat home, I didn't have a place to put it and everytime I cleaned up, I had it to move. "No, indeed," thinks I to myself, "I'll never have a chance to forgit Aunt Calline." Finally, the thought struck me to have the sheaf framed, because though I never could like it any better, it would at least be out of the way.

And what do you think that man charged to frame it? Ten dollars! Ten whole dollars! It certainly do seem funny to me how folks are always laying to rob bereaved mourners. Seems like they've made up their minds to git all they can out of you while you're kinder unconscious-like. But I wasn't that much of a mourner, so I carries my wheat home without a frame, and then me and that sheaf has it. Every time I went into the settin' room I was either knocking it down or pickin' it up until I was sick and tired of the sight of it.

One day, about six months after Aunt Calline died, just as I was haulin' that sheaf around, May Jane came in. "May Jane," says I, "how do you like your sheaf?" "Don't like it a tall, Sally." "Well." Says I, "I've got a plan, and if you'll stand by me and say nothin'. I think we kin fix Aunt Calline's sheaves." So the day when Uncle John and Georgie, which is my husband, and Samyell, which is May Jane's, went over to Rushtown to the hog-killin,' I sent for May Jane. "M.J.," says I when she got there, "the men are gone for the day and now's our time. Wrap up your sheaf with a plenty of paper and bring it over here."

When May Jane came back, I had my sheaf all bound up so you couldn't tell what it was, and my hat and coat on. "Sally," says May Jane, very solemn, "What on earth are you goin' to do?" Says I, "May Jane, foller me." So out we goes with them great bundles and all the neighbors peepin' through their blinds and wonderin' what we had and where we was goin'.

I led May Jane to the horse-cars and as the line ended at our street we set there a while before the car started, both of us feelin' very funeral-like and neither sayin' a word, though May Jane kept a eyein' me as if she wanted to ask some questions. But I kep' lookin' straight ahead with a long face, so she didn't say nothin'.

All of a sudden the conductor broke out singin' "Bringin' in the Sheaves," and the driver joined in the chorus. I never have known how they happened to strike on that hem, but it was too much for us. We looked, at each other and then we burst out, and we laughed untel we couldn't see. The driver started up his horses and the conductor looked at us as if he thought we was daft, but that did not hender us from laughin'.

As soon as she could speak, May Jane says, "Sally Ann Juniper, you have just got to tell me what you're goin' to do. May Jane," says I, "we air goin' to carry these sheaves right straight to Aunt Calline. That's what. When people gives things to dead people, they wants 'em to have 'em. That's why they gives 'em sheaves and pillers and pams and such instid of pincushions and calendars and postcards, and I believe in lettin' dead people have everything that belongs to 'em." May Jane got pop-eyed but she never said a word.

So we carried that wheat out and laid it on Aunt Calline's grave and I hope she feels satisfied. We do if she don't. But one quare thing about it is that neither Georgie nor Samyell has ever inquired after them tributes. I believe in my soul that they was just as tired of 'em as we was. As for Uncle John, he went to desperate courtin' of that little sixteen-year-old Simmins gal just six weeks after Aunt Calline had been put away. He tried to git Cannie Simmins to accept him as a husband, and his sheaf as a bokay, but she wouldn't have neither, so that wheat offering is still willed to me. But if I should be the longest liver, I mean to see to it that sheaf number three is left in the simitary on top of Uncle John.

[*The Crisis* 14.2 (February 1917): 62–63]

LEONORA'S CONVERSION

by Edna May Harrold

It all started on the day Gaynell, Lenora, and I decided to pay our first visit to Mrs. Holman, whose husband had just been assigned to the pastorate of our church. I had dressed and was waiting when Lenora came with the news that Gaynell was at home with an aching tooth, but that she would join us in an hour's time if she felt better. So Lenora and I prepared to relieve the tedium of waiting with a game of cards, mother being absent. We were just beginning the second game of "Seven Up" when foot-steps sounded on the walk. Discovery was imminent; quickly stuffing the deck of cards into my blouse pocket I seized the morning paper and was reading reports of the cotton and zinc markets to Lenora when mother came in.

An hour had passed and Gaynell had not come. Lenora and I started out to pay our call without her. The Reverend Mr. Holman, himself, answered our ring and ushered us very courteously into the parlor where Mrs. Holman sat knitting. After we had talked awhile, she asked us if we were Christians and seemed pained when we said, "No." Then she asked us if we would not care to give our souls to God. Lenora sighed and murmured something about wishing to do better, but I said nothing because for some reason I was beginning to feel uneasy. Then Mr. Holman spoke: "There is no reason why these dear children should not become soldiers for Christ," he said. "God wants the lambs in His fold. Now is the time to give Him your hearts; now, while they are tender and comparatively free from sin."

"There is no time like the present," said Mrs. Holman, rising. "Reverend, pray that these darling girls' hearts may be touched, and that they may accept the Master now."

So we all knelt down and as the pastor opened his mouth to pray I shifted my position just a little and—luck of the luckless—those cards fell out of my pocket!

Well, as real authors say: "Let us draw a curtain over the painful scene that followed." Somehow I managed to get away from that house, but not before I had been shown several reasons why I, if no one else in town, needed religion badly.

The following Sunday Mr. Holman started a revival. The services lasted a week and on the last night Lenora joined the church. When Mr. Holman asked her to testify, she said she felt so happy and wished her sinful companions would follow her step. Her heart, she said, was too full for words: then she began to sing: "Though Your Sins Be As Scarlet," looking straight at me! Gaynell chuckled right out, but I sat there hating everybody and *especially* that unknown person who invented the first card game.

Lenora's conversion caused much happiness among the older members of the church, but most of her young friends took a different view of the situation. Lenora had always been a jolly girl, popular with nearly everyone, but now her conduct showed a marked change. She shunned all of the girls except Gaynell and myself, and into our unhappy ears she was continually pouring tales of the Joys of Salvation and imploring us to give up the pleasures of this wicked world before it was too late.

"Lenora," I said, one day after she had spent half an hour or more pitying our unsaved state, "you talk like Gaynell and I are simply steeped in sin. I'm not saying a word against you having religion, but I really don't see what we have done that is so very, very sinful."

"You really don't, Belle?" Lenora asked, and her eyes narrowed. "Well, maybe you have forgotten that miserable card episode, but I haven't and never shall."

Of course, that made me furious, and I said: "No, Miss Angel, I haven't forgotten that 'card episode,' as you call it, and I know you haven't. Nor have Mr. Holman and Mrs. Holman forgotten. It didn't make any difference to any of you that I cried myself sick and apologized a dozen times. It seems to me that if you all had so much religion you'd forget it and forgive me, too, instead of always throwing it in my face!"

Gaynell said, "Belle, be careful," but Lenora replied very gently: "I'm only telling you for your own good, and I'll forgive all you have said to me because 'Blessed are ye when men shall revile you,' you know," and she walked off, leaving me too angry for words.

"Gaynell," I said, "I know it's wrong, but I do wish something would happen to bring Lenora down from her pedestal. If Mr. And Mrs. Holman could only see that their idol's feet are made of clay, my cup of joy would overflow."

"I know how you feel," said Gaynell, "but nothing will ever happen to Lenora. She doesn't go any place, but to church." And so we were plunged into despair, forgetting that the darkest hour is just before the dawn.

Then about ten days before school opened, Mrs. Greenway issued invitations to a dance in honor of her son, Henry, who was going away to begin his first term in college. It rained during the whole of the day set for the dance, but when night came the weather cleared and the stars twinkled in the sky and I was glad just to be alive.

Gaynell and I went to the dance together. We didn't say much, but deep in my heart I was thinking of Lenora and I know Gaynell was, too. I remembered how she loved dancing and I couldn't help feeling glad I wasn't converted when I thought of all Lenora was going to miss that evening.

The first ten minutes or so after we arrived at Mrs. Greenway's, we were very busy getting our dance cards filled.

Then the music started and everyone was searching through the crowd for their partner for that dance, when Gaynell clutched my arm.

"For mercy sakes," she whispered, "look, it's Lenora!"

It *was* Lenora.

And even as I looked, amused, I saw Henry Greenway approach her eagerly and whirl her away in the dance.

Lenora's backsliding created as much comment as her conversion. The Reverend Mr. Holman and his wife prayed over their fallen idol and bade her think of the fate of those who set their faces toward the Light and then turned back. Some of the old people said it was a wonder that Lenora had held out as long as she did, considering Gaynell and myself. Others said Lenora didn't have much religion in the first place, or she would not have lost it so easily. I inclined to the last opinion myself, but I said nothing, for I was glad Lenora had ceased trying to be an angel and had become human once more.

[*The Crisis* 15.4 (February 1918): 171–173]

THE LEGEND OF THE BLUE JAY

by Ruth Anna Fisher

It was a hot, sultry day in May and the children in the little school in Virginia were wearily waiting for the gong to free them from lessons for the day. Furtive glances were directed towards the clock. The call of the birds and fields was becoming more and more insistent. Would the hour never strike!

"The Planting of the Apple-tree" had no interest for them. Little attention was given the boy as he read in a sing-song spiritless manner:

> "What plant we in this apple-tree?
> Buds, which the breath of summer days
> Shall lengthen into leafy sprays;
> Boughs where the thrush, with crimson breast,
> Shall haunt and sing and hide her nest."

The teacher, who had long since stopped trying to make the lesson interesting, found herself saying mechanically, "What other birds have their nests in the apple-tree?"

The boy shifted lazily from one foot to the other as he began, "The sparrow, the robin, and wrens, and—and snow-birds, and blue-jays—"

"No, they don't, blue-jays don't have nests," came the excited outburst from some of the children, much to the surprise of the teacher.

When order was restored some of these brown-skinned children, who came from the heart of the Virginia mountains, told this legend of the blue-jay.

Long, long years ago, the devil came to buy the blue-jay's soul, for which he first offered a beautiful golden ear of corn. This the blue-jay liked and wanted, badly, but said, "No, I cannot take it in exchange for my soul." Then the devil came again, this time with a bright red ear of corn which was even more lovely than the golden one.

This, too, the blue-jay refused. At last the devil came to offer him a wonderful blue ear. This one the blue-jay liked best of all, but still was unwilling to part with his soul. Then the devil hung it up in the nest, and the blue-jay found that it exactly matched his own brilliant feathers, and knew at once that he must have it. The payment for that one blue ear of corn each Friday the blue-jay must carry one grain of sand to the devil, and sometimes he gets back on Sunday, but oftener not until Monday.

Very seriously the children added, "And all the bad people are going to burn until the blue-jays have carried all the grains of sand in the ocean to hell."

The teacher must have smiled a little at the legend, for the children cried out again, "It is so. 'Deed it is, for doesn't the black spot on the blue-jay come because he gets his wings scorched, and he doesn't have a nest like other birds."

Then to dispel any further doubts the teacher might have, they asked triumphantly, "You never saw a blue-jay on Friday, did you?"

There was no need to answer, for just then the gong sounded and the children trooped happily out to play.   [*The Crisis* 16.1 (May 1918): 12]

AT THE TURN OF THE ROAD

by Helen G. Ricks

> At the turn of the road,
>   There'll be luck to share;
> At the turn of the road,
>   Silver and gold and a dream to spare,
> And a host of sunny sweet days and fair,
>   And all that you wish for most out there,
> At the turn of the road.

It wasn't Christmas Day, but it was *Christmas* in the heart of Mr. Jimps. There seemed never a time when there wasn't some sort of a smile on his wholesome brown face. Sometimes it was one of those right-up-from-the-heart smiles; sometimes just one of those sudden-willing smiles,—but always a smile.

Many a spring with violets and robins, many a summer with June and summer loveliness;

many an autumn with symphonies in gold and brown; many a winter in snowy whiteness had all come and gone; but each had found Mr. Jimps contented in the little hut at the turn of the road.

Pedestrians of every type through many years had stopped to talk to this village character as they had passed and always had left him filled with a newer zeal and a keener happiness. Mr. Jimps possessed the great gift of human understanding and in his heart there lived nothing but a love for his fellowmen. There was in his kindly face an expression of his own ideals. The encouragement which he had so generously given to individuals all along the way was never to be measured.

On this particular afternoon it was snowing, seemingly with the one thought of preparedness for the Christmas Day, which was only two days distant. The old man sat nodding by an eastern window pipe between his teeth, glasses tilted perilously on his nose, and an open book on his knee. Finally he aroused himself.

"Well, a-neddin' still and a-snowin' still. Fire all low and supper-time. Mr. Jimps, it looks like you had better oust, yourself together smartly-soon."

Busied with the reflections of the duties before him, he had not seen the stranger approaching the hut (struggling up the snow-covered road), and was a little startled when the rap came.

"Howdy, friend. Come in and warm yourself. I'll have a blaze sputtering in a slim few minutes. Are you in a hurry?"

"There is no hurry, my friend," was the laconic reply.

Commonplaces were exchanged during the simple meal, and the stranger rose to go. "I thank you, Mr. Jimps, for your generous hospitality to me, a stranger. Before leaving you, may I ask you a question?"

"As many as you wish, my friend."

"Why do you *always* smile?"

"Because it is the easiest way, I find."

"Perhaps it is better, but how find it easier? I find nothing in all the world worth smiling for."

"What? With Christmas coming!—aye, even with Christmas gone!"

"Mr. Jimps, I have come to the place where the morning of another day is never welcome."

"Sit down, friend. Let me tell you a story."

Outside the flakes of snow descended noiselessly. Inside the hut there was a stillness. Tenderly Mr. Jimps laid down his pipe.

"There came a day into my life when I not only felt the meaning of your words but lived them. It seems to me that when an unhappiness comes, it comes only after some great happiness has just passed. A month before *she* had given me her promise of fidelity and love. I had been saving all along with just a hope—saving for the little home our dreams had built. Young we were and happy. She was a woman wonderful—the greatest gift God ever gave to man. I remember the night of her promise. There were cornflowers,—cornflowers of an unforgettable spring. We do not know what love is—we know it just *is*. But the story!

"I had just finished high school two years before and had been doing all kinds of jobs in the little town, earning the dollars required to pay for the little farm where we were both to be just happy. One particular job was that of janitor in the largest bank. My mother and I lived alone. Returning one night from work I entered my home where officers of the law stood waiting to arrest me. Seven hundred dollars had been stolen from the bank. I was accused. Our home had been searched. My saving budget contained just two hundred dollars. The sentence was fifteen years. During that time my mother died, and the girl—her heart broke first and then she passed away. That was fifty years ago, my friend.

"For years I wandered only with a bitterness burning in my heart,—a bitterness toward man and his injustice. With all the heart-break, there never came a bitterness toward God. Still when birds sang, their songs seemed a mockery to me. The most beautiful of melodies seemed just like little lost tunes too tired to die. Even the sunshine hurt. I hated everything. My life seemed useless,—as useless as a Jimpson weed; I called myself plain Mr. Jimps.

"Then twenty years after my Shadow, sick and heart-sore, I came to a stranger's cabin,—just as you have come to mine. It was two days before Christmas, and, yes,—it was snowing. While we were sitting there a gust of wind blew open the door and blew in the tiniest sprite of a lad, all snow covered, all smiles. 'Hey, Grandpa. It's a booster out there for sure, but I got your tobacco and the other stuff.' And then he noticed me and removed his cap. 'Evenin', sir.' I nodded and spoke to the child in my usual tone. 'Pardon me, mister, but didn't you forget to smile?'"

Mr. Jimps wiped a tear from the corner of his eyes, rememberingly.

"Friend, from that hour on I have been *always* smiling. Why not? There were more heart breaks than my own. After all, it was a love-world; and there could come a peace from simply mending hearts. The friendly comfort of that old man and the radiant cheer from that child-heart, untouched, warmed the littleness of my own worn heart.

"After leaving the shelter of that home I wandered through the snow until I came to this poor hut on Christmas Day. From that day until this have I lived here, my friend—here at the turn of the road. My little garden furnishes my living and my friends of the wayside, who come, furnish me my pleasures. People have wondered how life could slip by me, leaving of its joys and sorrows scarcely a trace. It has been because I have been happy in trying to be happy in smiling at the shadows and the sunshine both. And so each day I sit here waiting patiently for the Joy I feel shall come someday to me—at the turn of the road.

The guest of the roadside hut rose falteringly. "Mr. Jimps, your words have been both a salvation and a happiness. Someday I shall return." The stranger *smiled* his farewell from the door as he trudged on his way.

Christmas morning came in a flurry of snowflakes. Mr. Jimps after clearing away the breakfast dishes spread out the numerous parcels, ribbon-wrapped and otherwise, that had come the day before. Few of his wayside acquaintances and friends from the village had forgotten his roadside cordiality. His old heart was indeed cheered as he viewed these tokens of appreciation.

The last package unopened lay at the end of the table. It was copy of Henry Van Dyke's story of "The Other Wise Man." On the flyleaf was the inscription: "To him, who in his kindly way opened forever the heart of a stranger of yesterday."

Mr. Jimps smiled understandingly as he turned the pages. A few hours later he looked up from his new book and through the eastern window. A figure was plodding faithfully through the snow. The old man opened the door and looked out.

"Hey! Over there," called a fresh young voice. "The turn of this old road has got me fussed *some more!* Know any old guy around here by the name of Jimps?"

"This is the offender. How best can I serve you, this Merry Christmas?"

"Merry Christmas, yourself—here's a 'special.' I've been tracking around here an hour or two. Oh, no, thanks—must be moving on."

The envelope slid to the floor as Mr. Jimps held shakingly the letter from the old attorney's son.

Chelsea, Virginia,
December 17, 1916

James Avery—

Dear Friend:—
For ten years we have sought vainly to locate you. The thief of fifty years ago con-
fessed, exonerating you entirely. In the Citizens Savings Bank ten thousand dollars is
accredited to your name,—a gift from the stockholders and the townspeople. This is not
an effort to make amends—no amends can be made.
We beg you to return to your home and honor its citizens.
Very truly yours,
HOWARD KILTHROP, JR.

Mr. Jimps sat down before the fire. Two tears fell, one on the wrinkled brown hand;
and one on the crumpled white linen sheet. Tenderly he smoothed out the letter and smiled.
"Fifty years! But it came—at the turn of the road."

[*The Crisis* 17.2 (December 1918): 64–66]

A FAIRY STORY

———— ⤫ ————

by Carry S. Bond

Once upon a time—a long, long, time ago, there lived in the wild and hilly country of
Morocco, in a region called the Bled-el, Makhsen, a beautiful little princess. She had cop-
per-colored skin and black hair that was exceedingly curly. When she laughed, her bright
black eyes twinkled and her teeth gleamed like pearls between her full, red lips. Her name
was Ean. She used to play games on the hill-sides of the Atlas Mountains, with the other
children of her father's household.

Sometimes they would pretend that they were mounted Arabs and that they were riding
down upon another village to attack it, and sometimes they would pretend that they were fighting
a neighboring tribe, and then some of them would hide in the thick holes and jump out at the
others as they passed. This last was very dangerous, however, because bears and elephants and
wild bears lurked in these woods and the children were forbidden to go beyond those bushes.

One day while playing here they found a little ostrich that seemed to have been wounded
by a wild animal and left there. The children would have stoned it, but Ean came to its
rescue; she gathered it up in her arms and took it home, and of course, being a princess, the
others dared not interfere.

Now this ostrich was an enchanted prince in disguise, but, of course, the children did
not dream of that. Meantime, every day the gentle little princess would go and feed her new
pet and look after his wounded wing before she went out to play. The other children were
chiefly Berbers and Semites, but Ean's father was a Hamite, and that is why she was gentler
and darker than the others.

She had a little Berber cousin among them named Maga, who was also very pretty. She had very pale olive skin with highly arched eye-brows and a thin nose, with long, straight, black hair, and her face was not as round as Ean's or her lips as full. She did not have as nice a disposition as Ean either. She was a very selfish and quarrelsome little girl and always wanted the best of everything.

When Ean was only twelve years old, her father called her to him one day and told her that it was time for her to become betrothed; that she could no longer play with the children, but must begin to dress herself in a haik and wear golden ear-rings and bracelets of silver coins. A Berber chief in a neighboring town had been selected for her husband, but Ean had never seen him. Of course, she did not want to be married to a man whom she had never seen, although her father said that he was very rich and that she would have a great many slaves. Ean did not care for slaves or lots of money. She much preferred to play with her pet ostrich and gather figs and wild cherries and run about in the fields.

However, her father said that if this chief could not marry her, he would bring war on all their tribe and it would be a great disaster, for he was the most powerful man in Northern Africa. So, of course, Ean loved her father and wanted to save him and was willing to obey him. She was a very sad little girl when she went to bed that night, though, and wished for her mother.

You see, Ean's mother had been dead a long time and Maga's mother ruled everything in the palace. She was very angry, too, that this wonderful wedding was not being planned for her daughter instead of Ean. She thought that riches were the most important things in the world, and began plotting how she could get rid of Ean and substitute Maga in her place for this wedding.

Of course none of them had seen this Berber chief, or they would not have thought it such a wonderful wedding, for he was old and cruel and horribly ugly. He had only one eye and great teeth which protruded like tusks. But they did not know this.

Several weeks passed and the morning of the wedding arrived. Everything was in readiness for the feast. Great jars of Kush-Kush were being prepared and musicians were brought from far and near.

The wicked aunt had ordered the wedding garments to be laid out, then she sent Ean with an old waiting-woman down to a special pool surrounded by holy date palm trees for her bath. On her way there Ean stopped and kissed her ostrich good-bye and petted him a little for she knew that in a very short while she would have to leave him.

Now Maga's mother was planning as soon as Ean went out to dress Maga in the bridal clothes and have her married to the Berber chief in Ean's place. With her face covered with a veil, who would know the difference until afterwards, for were not both girls about the same size? When the Sheik Ean's father found out, it would be too late, and if he were angry, the aunt would go and live with her own daughter, she planned.

However, when the old crone and Ean reached the pool, just before the girl laid aside her garment, a horseman galloped up and stopping at the edge of the cluster of trees called out. Immediately the old woman took her head-cloth and tied it over Ean's mouth and dragged her to the horseman, but when she looked up, to her surprise, she did not see the old servant whom Maga's mother had planned to send, but a handsome young Arab prince on a beautiful white horse. Before the waiting-woman could speak, he had Ean up on his horse and had taken the cloth from her mouth.

Of course, you know that this was the enchanted Prince who had been disguised as an ostrich. He began explaining to Ean, as they galloped away and left the old woman standing there, that all he had needed to break the spell of his enchantment was for some beautiful maiden to kiss him, and this she had done that very morning. He was a very brave and wonderful Prince and Ean fell in love with him at once and was willing to go with him into his land, where they lived happily ever afterwards.

How the wicked aunt was disappointed after she carried out her plans and how Ean's father finally went to live with her—that is another story.

[*The Crisis* 18.6 (October 1919): 290–291]

MARY ELIZABETH

by Jessie Fauset

Mary Elizabeth was late that morning. As a direct result, Roger left for work without telling me goodbye, and I spent most of the day fighting the headache which always comes if I cry.

For I cannot get a breakfast. I can manage a dinner,—one just puts the roast in the oven and takes it out again. And I really excel in getting lunch. There is a good delicatessen near us, and with dainty service and flowers, I get along very nicely. But breakfast! In the first place, it's a meal I neither like nor need. And I never, if I live a thousand years, shall learn to like coffee. I suppose that is why I cannot make it.

"Roger," I faltered, when the awful truth burst upon me and I began to realize that Mary Elizabeth wasn't coming. "Roger, couldn't you get breakfast downtown this morning? You know last time you weren't so satisfied with my coffee."

Roger was hostile. I think he had just cut himself shaving. Anyway, he was horrid.

"No, I can't get my breakfast downtown!" He actually snapped at me. "Really, Sally, I don't believe there's another woman in the world who would send her husband out on a morning like this on an empty stomach. I don't see how you can be so unfeeling."

Well, it wasn't "a morning like this," for it was just the beginning of November. And I had only proposed his doing what I knew he would have to do eventually.

I didn't say anything more, but started on that breakfast. I don't know why I thought I had to have hot cakes! The breakfast really was awful! The cakes were tough and gummy and got cold one second, exactly, after I took them off the stove. And the coffee boiled, or stewed, or scorched, or did whatever the particular thing is that coffee shouldn't do. Roger sawed at one cake, took one mouthful of the dreadful brew, and pushed away his cap.

"It seems to me you might learn to make a decent cup of coffee," he said icily. Then he picked up his hat and flung out of the house.

I think it is stupid of me, too, not to learn how to make coffee. But really, I'm no worse than Roger is about lots of things. Take "Five Hundred." Roger knows I love cards, and with the Cheltons right around the corner from us and as fond of it as I am, we could spend many a pleasant evening. But Roger will not learn. Only the night before, after I had gone through a whole hand with him, with hearts as trumps, I dealt the cards around again to imaginary opponents and we started playing. Clubs were trumps, and spades led. Roger, having no spades, played triumphantly a Jack of Hearts and proceeded to take the trick.

"But Roger," I protested, "you threw off." "Well," he said, deeply injured, "didn't you say hearts were trumps when you were playing before?"

And when I tried to explain, he threw down the cards and wanted to know what difference it made; he'd rather play casino, anyway! I didn't go out and slam the door.

But I couldn't help from crying this particular morning. I not only value Roger's good opinion, but I hate to be considered stupid.

Mary Elizabeth came in about eleven o'clock. She is a small, weazened woman, very dark, somewhat wrinkled, and a model of self-possession. I wish I could make you see her, or that I could reproduce her accent, not that it is especially colored,—Roger's and mine are much more so—but her pronunciation, her way of drawing out her vowels, is so distinctively Mary Elizabethan!

I was ashamed of my red eyes and tried to cover up my embarrassment with sternness.

"Mary Elizabeth," said I, "you are late!" Just as though she didn't know it.

"Yas'm, Mis' Pierson," she said, composedly, taking off her coat. She didn't remove her hat,—she never does until she has been in the house some two or three hours. I can't imagine why. It is a small, black, dusty affair, trimmed with black ribbon, some dingy white roses and a sheaf of wheat. I give Mary Elizabeth a dress and hat now and then but, although I recognize the dress from time to time, I never see any change in the hat. I don't know what she does with my ex-millinery.

"Yas'm," she said again, and looked comprehensively at the untouched breakfast dishes and the awful viands, which were still where Roger had left them.

"Looks as though you'd had to git breakfast yourself," she observed brightly. And went out in the kitchen and ate all those cakes and drank that unspeakable coffee. Really she did and she didn't warm them up either.

I watched her miserably, unable to decide whether Roger was too finicky or Mary Elizabeth a natural born diplomat.

"Mr. Gales led me an awful chase last night," she explained. "When I got home yistiddy evenin', my cousin whut keeps house fer me (!) tole me Mr. Gales went out in the mornin' en hadn't come back."

"Mr. Gales," let me explain is Mary Elizabeth's second husband, an octogenarian, and the most original person, I am convinced, in existence.

"Yas'm," she went on, eating a final cold hot cake, "en I went to look fer 'im, en had the whole perlice station out all night huntin' im.' Look like they wusn't never goin' to find 'im. But I ses, 'Jes' let me look fer enough en long enough en I'll find 'im,' I ses, en I did. Way out Georgy Avenue, with the hat on ole Mis' give 'im. Sent it to 'im all the way fum Chicaga. He's had it fifteen years,—high silk beaver. I knowed he wusn't goin' too fer with that hat on.

"I went up to 'im, settin' by a fence all muddy, holdin' his hat on with both hands. En I ses, 'Look here, man, you come erlong home with me, en let me put you to bed. 'En he come jest as meek! No-o-me, I knowed he wusn't goin' fer with ole Mis' hat on."

"Who was old 'Mis,' Mary Elizabeth?" I asked her.

"Lady I used to work fer in Noo York," she informed me. "Me en Rosy, the cook, lived with her fer years. Ole Mis' was turrible fond of me, though her en Rosy used to querrel all the time. Jes' seemed like they couldn't git erlong. 'Member once Rosy run after her one Sunday with a knife, en I kep 'em apart. Reckon Rosy musta bin right put out with ole Mis' that day. By en by her en Rosy move to Chicaga, en when I married Mr. Gales, she sent 'im that hat. That old white woman shore did like me. It's so late, reckon I'd better put off sweepin' tel termorrer, ma'am."

I acquiesced, following her about from room to room. This was partly to get away from my own doleful thoughts. Roger really had hurt my feelings—but just as much to hear her talk. At first, I used not to believe all she said, but after I investigated once and found her truthful in one amazing statement, I capitulated.

She had been telling me some remarkable tale of her first husband and with the stupefied attention to which she always reduces me. Remember she was speaking of her first husband.

"En I ses to 'im, I ses, 'Mr. Gale,—'"

"Wait a moment, Mary Elizabeth," I interrupted, meanly delighted have caught her for once. "You mean your first husband, don't you?"

"Yas'm," she replied. "En I ses to 'im, Mr. Gale, I ses—'"

"But, Mary Elizabeth," I persisted, "that's your second husband, isn't it,—Mr. Gale?"

She gave me her long drawn "No-o-me! My first husband was Mr. Gale and my second husband is Mr. *Gales*. He spells his name with a Z, I reckon. I ain't never see it writ. Ez I wus sayin', I ses to Mr. Gale—"

And it was true! Since then I have never doubted Mary Elizabeth.

She was loquacious that afternoon. She told me about her sister, "where's got a home in the country and where's she's got eight children." I used to read Lucy Pratt's stories about little Ephraim or Ezekiel, I forget his name, who always said "where's' instead of "who's," but I never believed it really till I heard Mary Elizabeth use it. For some reason or other she never mentions her sister without mentioning the home too. "My sister where's got a home in the country" is her unvarying phrase.

"Mary Elizabeth," I asked her once, "does your sister live in the country, or does she simply own a house there?"

"Yas'm," she told me.

She is fond of her sister. "If Mr. Gales wus to die," she told me complacently, "I'd go to live with her."

"If he should die," I asked her idly, "would you marry again?"

"Oh, no-o-me!" She was emphatic. "Though I don't know why I shouldn't, I'd come by it hones.' My father wus married four times."

That shocked me out of my headache. "Four times, Mary Elizabeth, and you had all those stepmothers!" My mind refused to take it in.

"Oh, no-o-me! I always lived with mamma. She was his first wife."

I hadn't thought of people in the state in which I had instinctively placed Mary Elizabeth's father and mother as indulging in divorce, but as Roger says slangily, "I wouldn't know."

Mary Elizabeth took off the dingy hat. "You see, papa and mamma—" the ineffable pathos of hearing this woman of sixty-four, with a husband of eighty, use the old childish terms!

"Papa and mamma wus slaves, you know, Mis' Pierson, and so of course they wusn't exackly married. White folks wouldn't let 'em. But they wus awf'ly in love with each other. Heard mamma tell erbout it lots of times, and how papa wus the han'somest man! Reckon she wus long erbout sixteen or seventeen then. So they jumped over a broomstick, en they wus jes as happy! But not long after I come erlong, they sold papa down South, and mamma never see him no mo' fer years and years. Thought he was dead. So she married again."

"And he came back to her, Mary Elizabeth?" I was overwhelmed with the woefulness of it.

"Yas'm. After twenty-six years. Me and my sister where's got a home in the country— she's really my half-sister, see Mis' Pierson,—her en mamma en my step-father en me wus all down in Bumpus, Virginia, workin' fer some white folks, and we used to live in a little cabin, had a front stoop to it. En one day an ole cullud man come by, had a lot o' whiskers. I'd saw him lots of times there in Bumpus, lookin' and peerin' into every cullud woman's face. En jes' then my sister she call out, 'Come here, you Ma'y Elizabeth, 'en that old man stopped, en he looked at me en he looked at me, en he ses to me, 'Chile, is yo name Ma'y Elizabeth?'

"You know, Mis' Pierson, I thought he wus jes' bein' fresh, en I ain't paid no 'tention to 'im. I ain't sed nuthin' ontel he spoke to me three or four times, en then I ses to'im, 'Go'way fum here, man, you ain't got no call to be fresh with me. I'm a decent woman. You'd oughta be ashamed of yorself, an ole man like you!'"

Mary Elizabeth stopped and looked hard at the back of her poor wrinkled hands.

"En he says to me, 'Daughter,' he ses jes' like that, 'daughter,' he ses, 'hones' I ain't bein' fresh. Is yo' name shore enough May Elizabeth?'

"En I tole him, 'Yas'r,'

"'Chile,' he ses, 'whar is yo' daddy?'

"'Ain't got no daddy.' I tole him peart-like. 'They done tuk 'im away fum me twenty-six years ago, I wusn't but a mite of a baby. Sol' im down the river. My mother often talks about it.' And oh, Mis' Pierson, you shoulda see the glory come into his face!

"'Yore mother!' he ses, kinda out of breath, 'yore mother! May Elizabeth, whar is your mother?'

"'Back thar on the stoop,' I tole 'im. 'Why, did you know my daddy?'

"But he didn't pay no 'tention to me, jes' turned and walked up the stoop whar mamma wus settin'! She wus feelin' sorta porely that day. En you oughta see me steppin' erlong after 'im.

"He walked right up to her and giv' her one look. 'Oh, Maggie,' he shout out, 'oh Maggie! Ain't you know me? Maggie, ain't you know me?'

"'Mamma look at 'im and riz up outa her cheer. 'Who're you?' she ses kinda trimbly, callin' me Maggie thata way? Who're you?'

"He went up real close to her, then, 'Maggie,' he ses jes' like that, kinda sad 'n tender, 'Maggie!' And hel' out his arms.

"She walked right into them. 'Oh!' she ses, 'it's Cassius! It's Cassius! It's my husban' come back to me! It's Cassius!' They wus like two mad people.

"My sister Minnie and me, we jes' stood and gawped at 'em. There they wus, holding on to each other like two pitiful childrun, en he tuk her hands and kissed 'em.

"'Maggie,' he ses, 'you'll come away with me, won't you? You gona take me back, Maggie? We'll go away, you en Ma'y Elizabeth en me. Won't we Maggie?'

"Reckon my mother clean forgot about my step-father. 'Yes, Cassius,' she ses, 'well go away.' And then she sees Minnie, en it all comes back to her. 'Oh, Cassius,' she ses, 'I cain't go with you, I'm married again, en this time fer real. This here gal's mine and three boys, too, and another chile comin' in November!'"

"But she went with him, Mary Elizabeth," I pleaded. "Surely she went with him after all those years. He really was her husband."

I don't know whether Mary Elizabeth meant to be sarcastic or not. "Oh, no-o-me, mama couldn't a done that. She wus a good woman. Her ole master, whut done sol' my father down river, brung her up too religious fer that, en anyways, papa was married again, too. Had his fourth wife there in Bumpus with 'im."

The unspeakable tragedy of it!

I left her and went up to my room, and hunted out my dark blue serge dress which I had meant to wear again that winter. But I had to give Mary Elizabeth something, so I took the dress down to her.

She was delighted with it. I could tell she was, because she used her rare and untranslatable expletive.

"Haytian!" she said. "My sister where's got a home in the country, got a dress looks somethin' like this but it ain't as good. No-o-me. She got hers to wear at a friend's weddin'—gal she wus riz up with. Thet gal married well, too, lemme tell you; her husband's a Sunday School sup'rintender."

I told her she needn't wait for Mr. Pierson, I would put dinner on the table. So off she went in the gathering dusk, trudging bravely back to her Mr. Gales and his high silk hat.

I watched her from the window till she was out of sight. It had been such a long time since I had thought of slavery. I was born in Pennsylvania, and neither my parents nor grandparents had been slaves; otherwise I might have had the same tale to tell as Mary Elizabeth, or worse yet, Roger and I might have lived in those black days and loved and lost each other and futilely, damnably, met again like Cassius and Maggie.

Whereas it was now, and I had Roger and Roger had me.

How I loved him as I sat there in the hazy dark. I thought of his dear, bronze perfection, his habit of swearing softly in excitement, his blessed stupidity. Just the same I didn't meet him at the door as usual, but pretended to be busy. He came rushing to me with the *Saturday Evening Post*, which is more to me than rubies. I thanked him warmly, but aloofly, if you can get that combination.

We ate dinner almost in silence for my part. But he praised everything,—the cooking, the table, my appearance.

After dinner we went up to the little sitting-room. He hoped I wasn't tired,—couldn't he fix pillows for me. So!

I opened the magazine and the first thing I saw was a picture of a woman gazing in stony despair at the figure of a man disappearing around the bend of the road. It was too much. Suppose that were Roger and I! I'm afraid I sniffled. He was at my side in a moment.

"Dear loveliest! Don't cry. It was all my fault. You aren't any worse about coffee than I am about cards! And anyway, I needn't have slammed the door! Forgive me, Sally. I always told you I was hard to get along with. I've had a horrible day,—don't stay cross with me, dearest."

I held him to me and sobbed outright on his shoulder. "It isn't you, Roger," I told him, "I'm crying about Mary Elizabeth."

I regret to say he let me go then, so great was his dismay. Roger will never be half the diplomat that Mary Elizabeth is.

"Holy smokes!" he groaned. "She isn't going to leave us for good, is she?"

So then I told him about Maggie and Cassius. "And oh, Roger," I ended futilely, "to think that they had to separate after all those years, when he had come back, old and with whiskers!" I didn't mean to be so banal, but I was crying too hard to be coherent.

Roger had got up and was walking the floor, but he stopped then aghast.

"Whiskers!" he moaned. "My hat! Isn't that just like a woman?" He had to clear his throat once or twice before he could go on, and I think he wiped his eyes.

"Wasn't it the—" I really can't say what Roger said here,—"wasn't it the darndest hard luck that when he did find her again, she should be married? She might have waited."

I stared at him astounded. "But, Roger," I reminded him, "he had married three other times, he didn't wait."

"Oh—!" said Roger, unquotable, "married three fiddlesticks! He only did that to try to forget her."

Then he came over and knelt beside me again. "Darling, I do think it is a sensible thing for a poor woman to learn how to cook, but I don't care as long as you love me and we are together. Dear loveliest, if I had been Cassius," he caught my hands so tight that he hurt them,—"and I had married fifty times and had come back and found you married to someone else, I'd have killed you, killed you."

Well, he wasn't logical, but he was certainly convincing. So thus, and not otherwise, Mary Elizabeth healed the breach. [*The Crisis* 19.2 (December 1919): 51–56]

EL TISICO*

by Anita Scott Coleman

"What is patriotism?" shouted O'Brady, the Irish engineer, as peppery as he was good-natured. He was showing signs of his rising choler faster and faster as the heated argument grew in intensity.

He argued that it was a thing men put before their wives, and Tim held that it couldn't be compared with love-making and women.

"Cut it, boys, and listen to this, broke in Sam Dicks, a grizzled old trainman, who had more yarns in his cranium, than a yellow cur has fleas on a zig-zag trail between his left ear and his hind right leg.

"Fire up," roared the crowed of us.

The debate on patriotism had started between O'Brady and Tim Brixtner in the Santa Fé restroom. It was a typical scene,—the long paper-strewn table occupying the center space, and sturdy sons of America—hard-muscled, blue chinned, steady-nerved, rail-road men—lounging around it. Over in the alcove, upon a raised platform, three colored men, who styled themselves, The Black Trio, were resting after their creditable performance. They had given us some of the best string music from banjo, mandolin, and guitar, I have ever heard.

One of them, a big, strapping, ebony fellow, minus an arm, had a baritone voice worth a million, headed under different color. He sang Casey Jones—not a classic—but take it from me, a great one among our kind. He sure sang it....

A colored youngster, whom they carried about with them, had just finished passing the hat. It had been all both hands could do to carry it back to "The Black Trio." I, myself, had flung in five bucks, the price I'd pay, maybe, to go to a swell opera.

The guy who played the banjo was a glowing-eyed, flat-chested fellow with a cough, which he used some frequent.

I lit my pipe, and O'Brady and Brixtner and the rest lit theirs. Sam Dicks was about to begin when the "Trio" showed signs of departing. He left us with, "Wait a bit boys," and went to them. He gave the glad hand to the glowing-eyed, coughing one, with a genuine friendship grip. He came back ready for us.

"In the early nineties I was working with Billy Bartell, the greatest daredevil and the squarest that ever guided a throttle. We made our runs through that portion of the country which is sure God's handiwork, if anything is. It always strikes me as being miraculous to see the tropic weather of old Mex and the temperate weather of our U. S., trying to mix as it does along the border. It gives us a climate you can't beat—but the landscape, sun-baked sand, prairie-dog holes, and cactus with mountains dumped indiscriminately everywhere, all covered by a sky that's a dazzle of blue beauty, is what I call God's handiwork, because it can't be called anything else.

"At one of our stops in one of Mexico's little mud cities, a colored family,—father, mother, and baby—boarded the train. The woman was like one of those little, pearly-grey doves we shoot in New Mexico, from August to November—a little, fluttery thing, all heart and eyes.

"When they got on, their baby was a mere bundle, so no one noticed its illness. But it was soon all aboard that a sick kid was on. He *was* a sick kid, too: so sick that every mother's son on that train felt sorry and wanted to do something.

"The mother's eyes grew brighter and brighter, and the father kept watching his kid and pulling out his big, gold watch. The baby grew worse.

"In some way, as the intimate secrets of our heart sometimes do, it crept out that the family was trying to get over to the U.S. side before the baby died. We still had an eight hour run, and the baby was growing worse, faster than an engine eats up coal.

"The mother's eyes scanned the country for familiar signs. Every time I passed through that coach and saw her, I was minded of the way wounded birds beat their wings on the hard earth in an effort to fly. To all our attempted condolence, she replied with the same words:

"'If he lives until we get home—if he lives till we get home.'

"Billy Bartell always knew who his passengers were. He used to say he didn't believe in hauling whole lots of unknown baggage. So he knew that we carried the sick kid. We passed word to him that the kid was worse, and what his parents were aiming for.

"Well, boys, after that, our train went faster than a whirligig in a Texas cyclone. The landscape—cactus, prairie-dog holes, and mountains, rolled into something compact and smooth as a khaki-colored canvas, and flashed past us like sheets of lightning. We steamed into Nogales. The depot was on the Mexican side, but the coach with the sick kid landed fair and square upon the American sod.

"The little colored woman with her baby in her arms, alighted on good old American turf. She turned in acknowledgment to the kindness she had received, to wave her hand at the engine and its engineer, at the coaches and all the passengers, at everything, because she was so glad.

"If the kid died, it would be in America—at home."

Old Dicks paused a moment before querying, "Boys, did you get it?"

"You bet," spoke up Brixtner. "That's patriotism. Now, Pat O'Brady! "Twasn't no man and woman affair either," he cried, eager to resume their interrupted debate.

"Wait a minute fellows," pleaded Dicks, "wait."

"I want to know, did the kid live?" somebody asked.

"That's what I want to tell," said Dicks.

"Eh, you Tim! Cut it, cut it ..."

"That little banjo picker was the kid whose parents did not want him to die out of sight of the Stars and Stripes."

A long-drawn "phew" fairly split the air,—we were so surprised.

"Yes," said he, "and he has never been well, always sick. He's what the Mexicans call, "el Tisico.'"

"Scat ... He isn't much of a prize!"

"What's he done to back up his parents' sentiments?"

"He sure can't fight." These were the words exploded from one to the other.

"Do you know what "The Black Trio" do with their money?" asked Dicks, pride modulating his voice.

"Well—I—guess—not," drawled someone from among the bunch.

"Every red cent of it is turned into the American Red Cross—do you get me?" And old Dicks unfolded the evening paper and began to read.

"Be Gad, that's patriotism, too," shouted O'Brady. "Can any son-of-a-gun define it?"

[*The Crisis* 19.5 (March 1920): 252–253]

THE SLEEPER WAKES: A NOVELETTE

by Jessie Fauset

Amy recognized the incident as the beginning of one of her phases. Always from a child she had been able to tell when "something was going to happen." She had been standing in Marshall's store, her young eager gaze intent on the lovely little sample dress which was not from Paris, but quite as dainty as anything that Paris could produce. It was not the lines or even the texture that fascinated Amy so much, it was the grouping of colors of shades. She knew the combination was just right for her.

"Let me slip it on, Miss," said the saleswoman suddenly. She had nothing to do just then, and the girl was so evidently charmed and so pretty—it was a pleasure to wait on her.

"Oh, no," Amy had stammered. "I haven't time." She had already wasted two hours at the movies, and she knew at home they were waiting for her.

The saleswoman slipped the dress over the girl's pink blouse, and tucked the linen collar under so as to bring the edge of the dress next to her pretty neck. The dress was apricot-color shading into a shell pink and the shell pink shaded off again into the pearl and pink whiteness of Amy's skin. The saleswoman beamed as Amy, entranced, surveyed herself naively in the tall looking-glass.

Then it was that the incident befell. Two men walking idly through the dress-salon stopped and looked—she made an unbelievable pretty picture. One of them with a short, soft brown beard,—"fuzzy" Amy thought to herself as she caught his glance in the mirror—spoke to his companion.

"Jove, how I'd like to paint her!" But it was the look on the other man's face that caught her and thrilled her. "My God! Can't a girl be beautiful!" he said half to himself. The pair passed on.

Amy stepped out of the dress and thanked the saleswoman half absently. She wanted to get home and think, think to herself about that look. She had seen it before in men's eyes, it had been in the eyes of the men in the moving-pictures which she had seen that afternoon. But she had not thought *she* could cause it. Shut up in her little room she pondered over it.

Her beauty,—she was really good-looking then—she could stir people—men! A girl of seventeen has no psychology, she does not go beneath the surface, she accepts. But she knew she was entering on one of her phases.

She was always living in some sort of story. She had started it when as a child of five she had driven with the tall, proud, white woman to Mrs. Boldin's home. Mrs. Boldin was a bride of one year's standing then. She was slender and very, very comely, with her rich brown skin and her hair that crinkled thick and soft above a low forehead. The house was still redolent of new furniture; Mr. Boldin was spick and span—he, unlike the furniture, remained so for that matter. The white woman had told Amy that this henceforth was to be her home.

Amy was curious, fond of adventure; she did not cry. She did not, of course, realize that she was to stay here indefinitely, but if she had, even at that age she would hardly have shed tears, she was always too eager, too curious to know, to taste what was going to happen next. Still since she had had almost no dealing with colored people and she knew absolutely none of the class to which Mrs. Boldin belonged, she did venture one question.

"Am I going to be colored now?"

The tall white women had flushed and paled. "You—" she began, but the words choked her. "Yes, you are going to be colored now," she ended finally. She was a proud woman, in a moment she had recovered her usual poise. Amy carried with her for many years the memory of that proud head. She never saw her again.

When she was sixteen she asked Mrs. Boldin the question which in the light of that memory had puzzled her always. "Mrs. Boldin, tell me—am I white or colored?"

And Mrs. Boldin had told her and told her truly that she did not know.

"A —a—mee!" Mrs. Boldin's voice mounted on the last syllable in a shrill crescendo. Amy rose and went downstairs.

Down the comfortable, but rather shabby dining-room which the Boldins used after meals to sit in, Mr. Boldin, a tan black man, with aristocratic features, sat practicing on a cornet, and Mrs. Boldin sat rocking. In all of their eyes was the manifestation of the light that Amy loved, but how truly she loved it, she was not to guess till years later.

"Amy," Mrs. Boldin paused in her rocking, "did you get the braid?" Of course she had not, though that was the thing she had gone to Marshall's for. Amy always forgot essentials. If she went on an errand, and she always went willingly, it was for the pure joy of going. Who knew what angels might meet one unawares? Not that Amy thought in biblical or in literary phrases. She was in the High School it is true, but she was simply passing through, "getting by" she would have said carelessly. The only reading that had ever made any impression on her had been fairy tales read to her in those long remote days when she had lived with the tall proud woman; and descriptions in novels or histories of beautiful, stately palaces tenanted by beautiful, stately women. She could pore over such pages for hours, her face flushed, her eyes eager.

At present she cast about for an excuse. She had so meant to get the braid. "There was a dress" she began lamely, she was never deliberately dishonest.

Mr. Boldin cleared his throat and nervously fingered his paper. Cornelius ceased his awful playing and blinked at her shortsightedly through his thick glasses. Both of these, the man and the little boy, loved the beautiful, inconsequent creature with her airy, irresponsible ways. But Mrs. Boldin loved her too and because she loved her she could not scold.

"Of course you forgot," she began chidingly. Then she smiled. "There was a dress that you looked at *perhaps*. But confess, didn't you go to the movies first?"

Yes, Amy confessed she had done just that. "And oh, Mrs. Boldin, it was the most wonderful picture a girl such a pretty one and she was poor, awfully. And somehow she met the most wonderful people and they were so kind to her. And she married a man who was just tremendously rich and he gave her everything. I did so want Cornelius to see it.

"Huh!" said Cornelius who had been listening not because he was interested, but because he wanted to call Amy's attention to his playing as soon as possible. "Huh! I don't want to look at no pretty girl. Did they have anybody looping the loop in an airship?"

"You'd better stop seeing pretty girl pictures, Amy," said Mr. Boldin kindly. "They're not always true to life. Besides, I know where you can see all the pretty girls you want without bothering to pay twenty-five cents for it."

Amy smiled at the implied compliment and went on happily studying her lessons. They were all happy in their own way. Amy because she was sure of their love and admiration, Mr. and Mrs. Boldin because of her beauty and innocence and Cornelius because he knew he had in his foster-sister a listener whom his terrible practicing could never bore. He played brokenly a piece he had found in an old music-book. "*There's an aching void in every heart, brother.*"

"Where *do* you pick up those old things, Neely?" said his mother fretfully. But Amy could not have her favorite's feelings injured.

"I think it's lovely," she announced defensively. "Cornelius, I'll ask Sadie Murray to lend me her brother's book. He's learning the cornet, too, and you can get some new pieces. Oh, isn't it awful to have to go to bed? Good-night, everybody." She smiled her charming, ever ready smile, the mere reflex of youth and beauty and content.

"You do spoil her, Mattie," said Mr. Boldin after she had left the room. "She's only seventeen here, Cornelius, you go to bed but it seems to me she ought to be more dependable about errands. Though she is splendid about some things," he defended her. "Look how willingly she goes off to bed. She'll be asleep before she knows it when most girls of her age would want to be up in the street."

But upstairs Amy was far from asleep. She lit one gas-jet and pulled down the shades. Then she stuffed tissue paper in the keyhole and under the doors, and lit the remaining gas-jets. The light thus thrown on the mirror of the ugly oak dresser was perfect. She slipped off the pink blouse and found two scarfs, a soft yellow and a soft pink,—she had had them in a scarf-dance for a school entertainment. She wound them and draped them about her pretty shoulders and loosened her hair. In the mirror she apostrophized the beautiful, glowing vision of herself.

"There," she said, "I'm like the girl in the picture. She had nothing but her beautiful face-and she did so want to be happy." She sat down on the side of the rather lumpy bed and stretched out her arms. "I want to be happy, too." She intoned it earnestly, almost like an incantation. "I want wonderful clothes, and people around me, men adoring me, and the world before me. I want everything! It will come, it will all come because I want it so." She sat frowning intently as she was apt to do when very much engrossed. "And we'd all be so happy. I'd give Mr. and Mrs. Boldin money! And Cornelius he'd go to college and learn all about his old airships. Oh, if I only knew how to begin!"

Smiling, she turned off the lights and crept to bed.

II

Quite suddenly she knew she was going to run away. That was in October. By December she had accomplished her purpose. Not that she was the least bit unhappy but because she must get out in the world,—she felt caged, imprisoned. "Trenton is stifling me," she would have told you, in her unconsciously adopted "movie" diction. New York she knew was the place for her. She had her plans all made. She had sewed steadily after school for two months—as she frequently did when she wanted to buy her season's wardrobe, so besides her carfare she had $25. She went immediately to a white Y.W.C.A., stayed there two nights, found and answered an advertisement for clerk and waitress in a small confectionery and bakery-shop, was accepted and there she was launched.

Perhaps it was because of her early experience when as a tiny child she was taken from that so different home and left at Mrs. Boldin's, perhaps it was some fault in her own disposition, concentrated and egotistic as she was, but certainly she felt no pangs of separation, no fear of her future. She was cold too,—unfired though so to speak rather than icy,—and fastidious. This last quality kept her safe where morality or religion, of neither of which had she any conscious endowment, would have availed her nothing. Unbelievably then she lived two years in New York, unspoiled, untouched, going to work on the edge of Greenwich Village early and coming back late, knowing almost no one and yet altogether happy in the expectation of something wonderful, which she knew some day must happen.

It was at the end of the second year that she met Zora Harrisson. Zora used to come into lunch with a group of habitués of the place—all of them artists and writers Amy gathered. Mrs. Harrisson (for she was married as Amy later learned) appealed to the girl because she knew so well how to afford the contrast to her blonde, golden beauty. Purple, dark and regal, enveloped in velvets and heavy silks, and strange marine blues she wore, and thus made Amy absolutely happy. Singularly enough, the girl, intent as she was on her own life and experiences, had felt up to this time no yearning to know these strange, happy beings surrounded her. She did miss Cornelius, but otherwise she was never lonely, or if she was she hardly knew it, for she had always lived an inner life to herself. But Mrs. Harrisson magnetized her—she could not keep her eyes from her face, from her wonderful clothes. She made conjectures about her.

The wonderful lady came in late one afternoon—an unusual thing for her. She smiled at Amy invitingly, asked some banal questions and their first conversation began. The acquaintance once struck up progressed rapidly—after a few weeks Mrs. Harrisson invited the girl to come to see her. Amy accepted quietly, unaware that anything extraordinary was happening. Zora noticed this and liked it. She had an apartment in 12th Street in a house inhabited only by artists—she was no mean one herself. Amy was fascinated by the new world into which she found herself ushered; Zora's surroundings were very beautiful and Zora herself was a study. She opened to the girl's amazed vision fields of thought and conjecture, phases of whose existence Amy, who was a builder of phases, had never dreamed. Zora had been a poor girl of good family. She had wanted to study art, she had deliberately married a rich man and as deliberately obtained in the course of four years a divorce, and she was now living in New York studying by means of her alimony and enjoying to its fullest the life she loved. She took Amy on a footing with herself—the girl's refinement, her beauty, her interest in colors (though this in Amy at that time was purely sporadic, never consciously encouraged), all this gave Zora a figure about which to plan and build a romance. Amy had told her the truth, but not all about her coming to New York. She had grown tired of Trenton—her people were all dead—the folks with whom she lived were kind and good but not "inspiring" (she had borrowed the term from Zora and it was true, the Boldins, when one came to think of it, were not "inspiring"), so she had run away.

Zora had gone into raptures. "What an adventure! My dear, the world is yours. Why, with your looks and your birth, for I suppose you really belong to the Kildares who used to live in Philadelphia, I think there was a son who ran off and married an actress or someone—they disowned him I remember,—you can reach any height. You must marry a wealthy man—perhaps someone who is interested in art and who will let you pursue your studies." She insisted always that Amy had run away in order to study art. "But luck like that comes to few," she sighed, remembering her own plight, for Mr. Harrisson had been decidedly unwilling to let her pursue her studies, at least to the extent she wished. "Anyway you must marry wealth,—one can always get a divorce," she ended sagely.

Amy—she came to Zora's every night now—used to listen dazedly at first. She had accepted willingly enough Zora's conjecture about her birth, came to believe it in fact—but she drew back somewhat at such wholesale exploitation of people to suit one's own convenience, still she did not probe too far, into this thought—nor did she grasp at all the infamy of exploitation of self. She ventured one or two objections however, but Zora brushed everything aside.

"Everybody is looking out for himself," she said fairly. "I am interested in you, for instance, not for philanthropy's sake, not because I am lonely, and you are charming and pretty and don't get tired of hearing me talk. You'd better come and live with me awhile, my dear, six months or a year. It doesn't cost any more for two than for one, and you can always leave when we get tired of each other. A girl like you can always get a job. If you are worried about being dependent you can pose for me and design my frocks, and oversee Julienne"—her maid-of-all-work—"I'm sure she's a stupendous robber."

Amy came, not at all overwhelmed by the good luck of it—good luck was around the corner more or less for everyone, she supposed. Moreover, she was beginning to absorb some of Zora's doctrine—she, too, must look out for herself. Zora *was* lonely, she *did* need companionship; Julienne *was* careless about change and old blouses and left-over dainties. Amy had her own sense of honor. She carried out faithfully her share of the bargain, cut down waste, renovated Zora's clothes, posed for her, listened to her endlessly and bore with her fitfulness. Zora was truly grateful for this last. She was temperamental but Amy had good nerves and her strong natural inclination to let people do as they wanted stood her in good stead. She was a little stolid, a little unfeeling under her lovely exterior. Her looks at this time belied her—her perfect ivory-pink face, her deep luminous eyes,—very brown they were with purple depths that made one think of pansies—her charming, rather wide mouth, her whole face set in a frame of very soft, very live, brown hair which grew in wisps and tendrils and curls and waves back from her smooth, young forehead. All this made one look for softness and ingenuousness. The ingenuousness was there, but not the softness—except of her fresh, vibrant loveliness.

On the whole then she progressed famously with Zora. Sometimes the latter's callousness shocked her, as when they would go strolling through the streets south of Washington Square. The children, the people all foreign, all dirty, often very artistic, always immensely human, disgusted Zora except for "local color"—she really could reproduce them wonderfully. But she almost hated them for being what they were.

"Br-r-r, dirty little brats!" she would say to Amy. "Don't let them touch me." She was frequently amazed at her protégée's utter indifference to their appearance, for Amy herself was the pink of daintiness. They were turning from MacDougall into Bleecker Street one day and Amy had patted a child—dirty, but lovely—on the head.

"They are all people just like anybody else, just like you and me, Zora," she said in answer to her friend's protest.

"You are the true democrat," Zora returned with a shrug. But Amy did not understand her.

Not the least of Amy's services was to come between Zora and the too pressing attention of the men who thronged about her.

"Oh, go and talk to Amy," Zora would say, standing slim and gorgeous in some wonderful evening gown. She was an extraordinarily attractive creature, very white and pink, with great ropes of dazzling gold hair, and that look of no-age which only American women possess. As a matter of fact she was thirty-nine, immensely sophisticated and selfish, even, Amy thought, a little cruel. Her present mode of living just suited her; she could not stand any condition that bound her, anything at all *exigeant*. It was useless for anyone to try to influence her. If she did not want to talk, she would not.

The men used to obey her orders and seek Amy sulkily at first, but afterwards with considerably more interest. She was so lovely to look at. But they really, as Zora knew, preferred to talk to the older woman, for while with Zora indifference was a rôle, second nature now but still a rôle—with Amy it was natural and she was also a trifle shallow. She had the admiration she craved, she was comfortable, she asked no more. Moreover she thought the men, with the exception of Stuart James Wynne, rather uninteresting—they were faddists for the most part, crazy not about art or music, but merely about some phase such as cubism or syncopation.

Wynne, who was much older than the other half-dozen men who weekly paid Zora homage—impressed her by his suggestion of power. He was a retired broker, immensely wealthy (Zora, who had known him since childhood, informed her), very set and purposeful and polished. He was perhaps fifty-five, widely traveled, of medium height, very white skin and clear, frosty blue eyes, with sharp, proud features. He liked Amy from the beginning, her childishness touched him. In particular he admired her pliability—not knowing it was really indifference. He had been married twice; one wife had divorced him, the other had died. Both marriages were unsuccessful owing to his dominant, rather unsympathetic nature. But he had softened considerably with years, though he still had decided views, was glad to see that Amy, in spite of Zora's influence, neither smoked nor drank. He liked her shallowness—she fascinated him.

Zora had told him much—just the kind of romantic story to appeal to the rich, powerful man. Here was beauty forlorn, penniless, of splendid birth,—for Zora once having connected Amy with the Philadelphia Kildares never swerved from that belief Amy seemed to Wynne everything a girl should be—he was so unspoiled, so untouched. He asked her to marry him. If she had tried she could not have acted more perfectly. She looked at him with her wonderful eyes.

"But I am poor, ignorant—a nobody," she stammered. "I'm afraid I don't love you either," she went on in her pretty troubled voice, "though I do like you very, very much."

He liked her honesty and her self-depreciation, even her coldness. The fact that she was not flattered seemed to him an extra proof of her native superiority. He, himself, was a representative of one of the South's oldest families, though he had lived abroad lately.

"I have money and influence," he told her gravely, "but I count them nothing without you." And as for love—he would teach her that, he ended, his voice shaking a little. Underneath all his chilly, polished exterior he really cared.

"It seems an unworthy thing to say," he told her wistfully, for she seemed very young beside his experienced fifty-five years, "but anything you wanted in this world could be yours. I could give it to you,—clothes, houses and jewels."

"Don't be an idiot," Zora had said when Amy told her. "Of course, marry him. He'll give you a beautiful home and position. He's probably no harder to get along with than anybody else, and if he is, there is always the divorce court."

It seemed to Amy somehow that she was driving a bargain—how infamous a one she could not suspect. But Zora's teachings had sunk deep. Wynne loved her, and he could secure for her what she wanted. "And after all," she said to herself once, "it really is my dream coming true.

She resolved to marry him. There were two weeks of delirious, blissful shopping. Zora was very generous. It seemed to Amy that the whole world was contributing largely to her happiness. She was to have just what she wanted and as her taste was perfect she afforded almost as much pleasure to the people from whom she bought as to herself. In particular she brought rapture to an exclusive modiste in Forty-second Street who exclaimed at her "so perfect taste."

"Mademoiselle is of a marvelous, of an absolute correctness," she said.

Everything whirled by. After the shopping there was the small, impressive wedding. Amy stumbled somehow through the service, struck by its awful solemnity. Then later there was the journey and the big house waiting them in the small town, fifty miles south of Richmond. Wynne was originally from Georgia, but business and social interests had made it necessary for him to be nearer Washington and New York.

Amy was absolute mistress of himself and his home, he said, his voice losing its coldness. "Ah, my dear, you'll never realize what you mean to me—I don't envy any other man in this world. You are so beautiful, so sweet, so different!"

III

From the very beginning *he* was different from what she had supposed. To start with he was far, far wealthier, and he had, too, a tradition, a family-pride which to Amy was inexplicable. Still more inexplicably he had a race-pride. To his wife this was not only strange but foolish. She was as Zora had once suggested, the true democrat. Not that she preferred the company of her maids, though the reason for this did not lie *per se* in the fact that they were maids. There was simply no common ground. But she was uniformly kind, a trait which had she been older would have irritated her husband. As it was, he saw in it only an additional indication of her freshness, her lack of worldliness which seemed to him the attributes of an inherent refinement and goodness untouched by experience.

He, himself, was intolerant of all people of inferior birth or standing and looked with contempt on foreigners, except the French and English. All the rest were variously "guineys," "niggers," and "wops," and all of them he genuinely despised and hated, and talked of them with the huge intolerant carelessness characteristic of occidental civilization. Amy was never able to understand it. People were always first and last, just people to her. Growing up as the average colored American girl does grow up, surrounded by types of every hue, color and facial configuration she had had no absolute ideal. She was not even aware that there was one. Wynne, who in his grim way had a keen sense of humor, used to be vastly amused at the artlessness with which she let him know that she did not consider him to be good-looking. She never wanted him to wear anything but dark blue, or sombre mixtures always.

"They take away from that awful whiteness of your skin," she used to tell him, "and deepen the blue of your eyes."

In the main she made no attempt to understand him, as indeed she made no attempt to understand anything. The result, of course, was that such ideas as seeped into her mind stayed there, took growth and later bore fruit. But just at this period she was like a well-cared for, sleek, house-pet, delicately nurtured, velvety, content to let her days pass by. She thought almost nothing of her art just now except as her sensibilities were jarred by an occasional disharmony. Likewise, even to herself, she never criticized Wynne, except when some act or attitude of his stung. She could never understand why he, so fastidious, so versed in elegance of word and speech, so careful in his surroundings, even down to the last detail of glass and napery, should take such evident pleasure in literature of a certain prurient type. He fairly reveled in the realistic novels which to her depicted sheer badness. He would get her to read to him, partly because he liked to be read to, mostly because he enjoyed the realism and in a slighter degree because he enjoyed seeing her shocked. Her point of view amused him.

"What funny people," she would say naively, "to do such things." She could not understand the liaisons and intrigues of women in the society novels, such infamy was stupid and silly. If one starved, it was conceivable that one might steal; if one were intentionally injured, one might hit back, even murder; but deliberate nastiness she could not envisage. The stories, after she had read them to him, passed out of her mind as completely as though they had never existed.

Picture the two of them spending three years together with practically no friction. To his dominance and intolerance she opposed a soft and unobtrusive indifference. What she wanted she had, ease, wealth, adoration, love, too, passionate and imperious, but she had never known any other kind. She was growing cleverer also, her knowledge of French was increasing, she was acquiring a knowledge of politics, of commerce and of the big social questions, for Wynne's interests were exhaustive and she did most of his reading for him. Another woman might have yearned for a more youthful companion, but her native coldness kept her content. She did not love him, she had never really loved anybody, but little Cornelius Boldin—he had been such an enchanting, such a darling baby, she remembered,—her heart contracted painfully when she thought as she did very often of his warm softness.

"He must be a big boy now," she would think almost maternally, wondering—once she had been so sure!—if she would ever see him again. But she was very fond of Wynne, and he was crazy over her just as Zora had predicted. He loaded her with gifts, dresses, flowers, jewels—she amused him because none but colored stones appealed to her.

"Diamonds are so hard, so cold, and pearls are dead," she told him. Nothing ever came between them, but his ugliness, his hatefulness to dependents. It hurt her so, for she was naturally kind in her careless, uncomprehending way. True, she had left Mrs. Boldin without a word, but she did not guess how completely Mrs. Boldin loved her. She would have been aghast had she realized how stricken her flight had left them. At twenty-two, Amy was still as good, as unspoiled, as pure as a child. Of course with all this she was too unquestioning, too selfish, too vain, but they were all faults of her lovely, lovely flesh. Wynne's intolerance finally got on her nerves. She used to blush for his unkindness. All the servants were colored, but she had long since ceased to think that perhaps she, too, was colored, except when he, by insult toward an employee, overt, always at least implied, made her realize his contemptuous dislike and disregard for a dark skin or Negro blood.

"Stuart, how can you say such things?" she would expostulate. "You can't expect a man to stand such language as that." And Wynne would sneer, "A man—you don't consider a nigger a man, do you? Oh, Amy, don't be such a fool. You've got to keep them in their places."

Some innate sense of the fitness of things kept her from condoling outspokenly with the servants, but they knew she was ashamed of her husband's ways. Of course, they left— it seemed to Amy that Peter, the butler, was always getting new "help,"—but most of the upper servants stayed, for Wynne paid handsomely and although his orders were meticulous and insistent the retinue of employees was so large that the individual's work was light.

Most of the servants who did stay on in spite of Wynne's occasional insults had a purpose in view. Callie, the cook, Amy found out had two children at Howard University—of course she never came in contact with Wynne—the chauffeur had a crippled sister. Rose, Amy's maid and purveyor of much outside information, was the chief support of the family. About Peter, Amy knew nothing; he was a striking, taciturn man, very competent, who had left the Wynne's service years before and had returned in Amy's third year. Wynne treated him with comparative respect. But Stephen, the new valet, met with entirely different treatment. Amy's heart yearned toward him, he was like Cornelius, with short-sighted, patient eyes, always willing, a little over-eager. Amy recognized him for what he was: a boy of respectable, ambitious parentage, striving for the means for an education; naturally far above his present calling, yet willing to pass through all this as a means to an end. She questioned Rosa about him.

"Oh, Stephen," Rosa told her, "yes'm, he's workin' for fair. He's got a brother at the Howard's and a sister at the Smith's. Yes'm, it do seem a little hard on him, but Stephen, he say, they're both goin' to turn roun' and help him when they get through. That blue silk has a rip in it, Miss Amy, if you was thinkin' of wearin' that. Yes'm, somehow I don't think Steve's very strong, kinda worries like. I guess he's sorta nervous."

Amy told Wynne. "He's such a nice boy, Stuart," she pleaded, "it hurts me to have you so cross with him. Anyway don't call him names." She was both surprised and frightened at the feeling in her that prompted her to interfere. She had held so aloof from other people's interests all these years.

"I *am* colored," she told herself that night. "I feel it inside of me. I must be or I couldn't care so about Stephen. Poor boy, I suppose Cornelius is just like him. I wish Stuart would let him alone. I wonder if all white people are like that. Zora was hard, too, on unfortunate people." She pondered over it a bit. "I wonder what Stuart would say if he knew I was colored?" She lay perfectly still, her smooth brow knitted, thinking hard. "But he loves me," she said to herself still silently. "He'll always love my looks," and she fell to thinking that all the wonderful happenings in her sheltered, pampered life had come to her through her beauty. She reached out an exquisite arm, switched on a light, and picking up a hand-mirror from a dressing-table, fell to studying her face. She was right. It was her chiefest asset. She forgot Stephen and fell asleep.

But in the morning her husband's voice issuing from his dressing-room across the hall, awakened her. She listened drowsily. Stephen, leaving the house the day before, had been met by a boy with a telegram. He had taken it, slipped it into his pocket, (he was just going to the mail-box) and had forgotten to deliver it until now, nearly twenty-four hours later. She could hear Stuart's storm of abuse—it was terrible, made up as it was of oaths and insults to the boy's ancestry. There was a moment's lull. Then she heard him again.

"If your brains are a fair sample of that black wench of a sister of yours—"

She sprang up then thrusting her arms as she ran into her pink dressing-gown. She got there just in time. Stephen, his face quivering, was standing looking straight into Wynne's smoldering eyes. In spite of herself, Amy was glad to see the boy's bearing. But he did not notice her.

"You devil!" he was saying. "You white-faced devil! I'll make you pay for that!" He raised his arm. Wynne did not blench.

With a scream she was between them. "Go, Stephen, go,—get out of the house. Where do you think you are? Don't you know you'll be hanged, lynched, tortured?" Her voice shrilled at him.

Wynne tried to thrust aside her arms that clung and twisted. But she held fast till the door slammed behind the fleeing boy.

"God, let me by, Amy!" As suddenly as she had clasped him she let him go, ran to the door, fastened it and threw the key out the window.

He took her by the arm and shook her. "Are you mad? Didn't you hear him threaten me, me,—a nigger threaten me?" His voice broke with anger, "And you're letting him get away! Why, I'll get him. I'll set bloodhounds on him, I'll have every white man in this town after him! He'll be hanging so high by midnight—" he made for the other door, cursing, half-insane.

How, *how* could she keep him back! She hated her weak arms with their futile beauty! She sprang toward him. "Stuart, wait," she was breathless and sobbing. She said the first thing that came into her head. "Wait, Stuart, you cannot do this thing." She thought of Cornelius—suppose it had been he—"Stephen,—that boy,—he is my brother."

He turned on her. "What!" he said fiercely, then laughed a short laugh of disdain. "You are crazy," he said roughly, "My God, Amy! How can you even in jest associate yourself with these people? Don't you suppose I know a white girl when I see one? There's no use in telling a lie like that."

Well, there was no help for it. There was only one way. He had turned back for a moment, but she must keep him many moments—an hour. Stephen must get out of town.

She caught his arm again. "Yes," she told him, "I did lie. Stephen is not my brother, I never saw him before." The light of relief that crept into his eyes did not escape her, it only nerved her. "But I am colored," she ended.

Before he could stop her she had told him all about the tall white woman. "She took me to Mrs. Boldin's and gave me to her to keep. She would never have taken me to her if I had been white. If you lynch this boy, I'll let the world, your world, know that your wife is a colored woman."

He sat down like a man suddenly stricken old, his face ashen. "Tell me about it again," he commanded. And she obeyed, going mercilessly into every damning detail.

IV

Amazingly her beauty availed her nothing. If she had been an older woman, if she had had Zora's age and experience, she would have been able to gauge exactly her influence over Wynne. Though even then in similar circumstances she would have taken the risk and acted in just the same manner. But she was a little bewildered at her utter miscalculation. She had thought he might not want his friends—his world by which he set such store—to know that she was colored, but she had not dreamed it could make any real difference to him. He had chosen her, poor and ignorant, but of a host of women, and had told her countless times of his love. To herself Amy Wynne was in comparison with Zora for instance, stupid and uninteresting. But his constant, unsolicited iterations had made her accept his idea.

She was just the same woman she told herself, she had not changed, she was still beautiful, still charming, still "different." Perhaps, that very difference had its being in the fact of her mixed blood. She had been his wife—there were memories—she could not see how he could give her up. The suddenness of the divorce carried her off her feet. Dazedly she left him—though almost without a pang for she had only liked him. She had been perfectly honest about this, and he, although consumed by the fierceness of his emotion toward her, had gradually forced himself to be content, for at least she had never made him jealous.

She was to live in a small house of his in New York, up town in the 80's. Peter was in charge and there was a new maid and a cook. The servants, of course, knew of the separation, but nobody guessed why. She was living on a much smaller basis than the one to which she had become so accustomed in the last three years. But she was very comfortable. She felt, at any rate she manifested, no qualms at receiving alimony from Wynne. That was the way things happened, she supposed when she thought of it at all. Moreover, it seemed to her perfectly in keeping with Wynne's former attitude toward her; she did not see how he could do less. She expected people to be consistent. That was why she was so amazed that he in spite of his oft iterated love, could let her go. If she had felt half the love for him which he had professed for her, she would not have sent him away if he had been a leper.

"Why I'd stay with him," she told herself, 'if he were one, even as I feel now."

She was lonely in New York. Perhaps it was the first time in her life that she had felt so. Zora had gone to Paris the first year of her marriage and had not come back.

The days dragged on emptily. One thing helped her. She had gone one day to the modiste from whom she had bought her trousseau. The woman remembered her perfectly—"The lady with the exquisite taste for colors—ah, madame, but you have the rare gift." Amy was grateful to be taken out of her thoughts. She bought one or two daring but altogether lovely creations and let fall a few suggestions:

"That brown frock, Madame,—you say it has been on your hands a long time? Yes? But no wonder. See, instead of that, dead white you should have a shade of ivory, that white cheapens it." Deftly she caught up a bit of ivory satin and worked out her idea. Madame was ravished.

"But yes, Madame Ween is correct,—as always. Oh, what a pity that the Madame is so wealthy. If she were only a poor girl—Mlle. Antoine with the best eye for color in the place has just left, gone back to France to nurse her brother—this World War is of such a horror! If someone like Madame, now, could be found, to take the little Antoine's place!"

Some obscure impulse drove Amy to accept the half proposal: "Oh! I don't know, I have nothing to do just now. My husband is abroad." Wynne had left her with that impression. "I could contribute the money to the Red Cross or to charity."

The work was the best thing in the world for her. It kept her from becoming too introspective, though even then she did more serious, connected thinking than she had done in all the years of her varied life.

She missed Wynne definitely, chiefly as a guiding influence for she had rarely planned even her own amusements. Her dependence on him had been absolute. She used to picture him to herself as he was before the trouble—and his changing expressions as he looked at her, of amusement, interest, pride, a certain little teasing quality that used to come into his eyes, which always made her adopt her "spoiled child air," as he used to call it. It was the way he liked her best. Then last, there was that look he had given her the morning she had told him she was colored—it had depicted so many emotions, various and yet distinct. There were dismay, disbelief, coldness, a final aloofness.

There was another expression, too, that she thought of sometimes—the look on the face of Mr. Packard, Wynne's lawyer. She, herself, had attempted no defense.

"For God's sake why did you tell him, Mrs. Wynne?" Packard asked her. His curiosity got the better of him. "You couldn't have been in love with that yellow rascal," he blurted out. "She's too cold really, to love anybody," he told himself. "If you didn't care about the boy why should you have told?"

She defended herself feebly. "He looked so like little Cornelius Boldin," she replied vaguely, "and he couldn't help being colored." A clerk came in then and Packard said no more. But into his eyes had crept a certain reluctant respect. She remembered the look, but could not define it.

She was so sorry about the trouble now, she wished it had never happened. Still if she had it to repeat she would act in the same way again. "There was nothing else for me to do," she used to tell herself.

But she missed Wynne unbelievably.

If it had not been for Peter, her life would have been almost that of a nun. But Peter, who read the papers and kept abreast of times, constantly called her attention, with all due respect, to the meetings, the plays, the sights which she ought to attend or see. She was truly grateful to him. She was very kind to all three of the servants. They had the easiest "places" in New York, the maids used to tell their friends. As she never entertained, and frequently dined out, they had a great deal of time off.

She had been separated from Wynne for ten months before she began to make any definite plans for her future. Of course, she could not go on like this always. It came to her suddenly that probably she would go to Paris and live there—why or how she did not know. Only Zora was there and lately she had begun to think that her life was to be like Zora's. They had been amazingly parallel up to this time. Of course she would have to wait until after the war.

She sat musing about it one day in the big sitting-room which she had had fitted over into a luxurious studio. There was a sewing-room off to the side from which Peter used to wheel into the room waxen figures of all colorings and contours so that she could drape the various fabrics about them to be sure of the best results. But today she was working out a scheme for one of Madame's customers, who was of her own color and size and she was her own lay-figure. She sat in front of the huge pier glass, a wonderful soft yellow silk draped about her radiant loveliness.

"I could do some serious work in Paris," she said half aloud to herself. "I suppose if I really wanted to, I could be very successful along this line."

Somewhere downstairs an electric bell buzzed, at first softly, then after a slight pause, louder, and more insistently.

"If Madame sends me that lace today," she was thinking, idly, "I could finish this and start on the pink. I wonder why Peter doesn't answer the bell."

She remembered then that Peter had gone to New Rochelle on business and she had sent Ellen to Altman's to find a certain rare velvet and had allowed Mary to go with her. She would dine out, she told them, so they need not hurry. Evidently she was alone in the house.

Well she could answer the bell. She had done it often enough in the old days at Mrs. Boldin's. Of course it was the lace. She smiled a bit as she went downstairs thinking how surprised the delivery-boy would be to see her arrayed thus early in the afternoon. She hoped he wouldn't go. She could see him through the long, thick panels of glass in the vestibule and front door. He was just turning about as she opened the door.

This was no delivery-boy, this man whose gaze fell on her hungry and avid. This was Wynne. She stood for a second leaning against the door-jamb, a strange figure surely in the sharp November weather. Some leaves—brown, skeleton shapes—rose and swirled unnoticed about her head. A passing letter-carrier looked at them curiously.

"What are you doing answering the door?" Wynne asked her roughly. "Where is Peter? Go in, you'll catch cold."

She was glad to see him. She took him into the drawing room—a wonderful study in browns—and looked at him and looked at him.

"Well," he asked her, his voice eager in spite of the commonplace words, "are you glad to see me? Tell me what you do with yourself."

She could not talk fast enough, her eyes clinging to his face. Once it struck her that he had changed in some indefinable way. Was it a slight coarsening of that refined aristocratic aspect? Even in her sub-consciousness she denied it.

He had come back to her.

"So I design for Madame when I feel like it, and send the money to the Red Cross and wonder when you are coming back to me." For the first time in their acquaintanceship she was conscious deliberately of trying to attract, to hold him. She put on her spoiled child air which had once been so successful.

"It took you long enough to get here," she pouted. She was certain of him now. His mere presence assured her.

They sat silent a moment, the late November sun bathing her head in an austere glow of chilly gold. As she sat there in the big brown chair she was, in her yellow dress, like some mysterious emanation, some wraith-like aura developed from the tone of her surroundings.

He rose and came toward her, still silent. She grew nervous, and talked incessantly with sudden unusual gestures. "Oh, Stuart, let me give you tea. It's right there in the pantry off the dining-room. I can wheel the table in." She rose, a lovely creature in her yellow robe. He watched her intently.

"Wait," he bade her.

She paused almost on tiptoe, a dainty golden butterfly.

"You are coming back to live with me?" he asked her hoarsely.

For the first time in her life she loved him.

"Of course I am coming back," she told him softly. "Aren't you glad? Haven't you missed me? I didn't see how you could stay away. Oh! Stuart, what a wonderful ring!"

For he had slipped on her finger a heavy dull gold band, with an immense sapphire in an oval setting—a beautiful thing of Italian workmanship.

"It is so like you to remember," she told him gratefully. "I love colored stones." She admired it, turning it around and around on her slender finger.

How silent he was, standing there watching her with his somber yet eager gaze. It made her troubled, uneasy. She cast about for something to say.

"You can't think how I've improved since I saw you, Stuart. I've read all sorts of books— Oh! I'm learned," she smiled at him. "And Stuart," she went a little closer to him, twisting the button on his perfect coat, "I'm so sorry about it all,—about Stephen, that boy, you know. I just couldn't help interfering. But when we're married again, if you'll just remember how it hurts me to have you so cross—"

He interrupted her. "I wasn't aware that I spoke of our marrying again," he told her, his voice steady, his blue eyes cold.

She thought he was teasing. "Why you just asked me to. You said 'aren't you coming back to live with me—'"

Still she didn't comprehend. "But what do you mean?" she asked bewildered.

"What do you suppose a man means?" he returned deliberately, "when he asks a woman to live with him but not to marry him?"

She sat down heavily in the brown chair, all glowing ivory and yellow against its sombre depths.

"Like the women in those awful novels?" she whispered. "Not like those women!—Oh Stuart! you don't mean it!" Her very heart was numb.

"But you must care a little—" she was amazed at her own depth of feeling. "Why I care—there are all those memories back of us—you must want me really—"

"I do want you," he told her tensely. "I want you damnably. But—well—I might as well out with it—A white man like me simply doesn't marry a colored woman. After all what difference need it make to you? We'll live abroad—you'll travel, have all the things you love. Many a white woman would envy you." He stretched out an eager hand.

She evaded it, holding herself aloof as though his touch were contaminating. Her movement angered him.

"Oh, hell!" he snarled at her roughly. "Why don't you stop posing? What do you think you are anyway? Do you suppose I'd take you for my wife—what do you think can happen to you? What man of your own race could give you what you want? You don't suppose I am going to support you this way forever, do you? The court imposed no alimony. You've got to come to it sooner or later—you're bound to fall to some white man. What's the matter—I'm not rich enough?"

Her face flamed at that—"As though it were *that* that mattered!"

He gave her a deadly look. "Well, isn't it? Ah, my girl, you forget you told me you didn't love me when you married me. You sold yourself to me then. Haven't I reason to suppose you are waiting for a higher bidder?"

At these words something in her died forever, her youth, her illusions, her happy, happy blindness. She saw life leering mercilessly in her face. It seemed to her that she would give all her future to stamp out, to kill the contempt in his frosty insolent eyes. In a sudden rush of savagery she struck him, struck him across his hateful sneering mouth with the hand which wore his ring.

As *she* fell, reeling under the fearful impact of his brutal but involuntary blow, her mind caught at, registered two things. A little thin stream of blood was trickling across his chin. She had cut him with the ring, she realized with a certain savage satisfaction. And there was something else which she must remember, which she *would* remember if only she could fight her way out of this dreadful clinging blackness, which was bearing down upon her—closing her in.

When she came to she sat up holding her bruised, aching head in her palms, trying to recall what it was that had impressed her so.

Oh yes, her very mind ached with the realization. She lay back again on the floor, prone, anything to relieve that intolerable pain. But her memory, her thoughts went on.

"Nigger," he had called her as she fell, "nigger, nigger," and again, "nigger."

"He despised me absolutely," she said to herself wonderingly, "because I was colored. And yet he wanted me."

V

Somehow she reached her room. Long after the servants had come in, she lay face downward across her bed, thinking. How she hated Wynne, how she hated herself! And for ten months she had been living off his money although in no way had she a claim on him. Her whole body burned with the shame of it.

In the morning she rang for Peter. She faced him, white and haggard, but if the man noticed her condition, he made no sign. He was, if possible, more imperturbable than ever.

"Peter," she told him, her eyes and voice very steady, "I am leaving this house today and shall never come back."

"Yes, Miss."

"And, Peter, I am very poor now and shall have no money besides what I can make for myself."

"Yes, Miss."

Would nothing surprise him, she wondered dully. She went on. "I don't know whether you knew it or not, Peter, but I am colored, and hereafter I mean to live among my own people. Do you think you could find a little house or little cottage not too far from New York?"

He had a little place in New Rochelle, he told her, his manner altering not one whit, or better yet his sister had a four-room house in Orange, with a garden, if he remembered correctly. Yes, he was sure there was a garden. It would be just the thing for Mrs. Wynne.

She had four hundred dollars of her very own which she had earned by designing for Madame. She paid the maids a month in advance—they were to stay as long as Peter needed them. She, herself, went to a small hotel in Twenty-eighth Street, and here Peter came for her at the end of ten days, with the acknowledgement of the keys and receipts from Mr. Packard. Then he accompanied her to Orange and installed her in her new home.

"I wish I could afford to keep you, Peter," she said a little wistfully, "but I am very poor. I am heavily in debt and I must get that off my shoulders at once."

Mrs. Wynne was very kind, he was sure; he could think of no one with whom he would prefer to work. Furthermore, he often ran down from New Rochelle to see his sister; he would come in from time to time, and in the spring would plant the garden if she wished.

She hated to see him go, but she did not dwell long on that. Her only thought was to work and work and work and save until she could pay Wynne back. She had not lived very extravagantly during those ten months and Peter was a perfect manager—in spite of her remonstrances he had given her every month an account of his expenses. She had made arrangements with Madame to be her regular designer. The French woman guessing that more than whim was behind this move drove a very shrewd bargain, but even then the pay was excellent. With care, she told herself, she could be free within two years, three at most.

She lived a dull enough existence now, going to work steadily every morning and getting home late at night. Almost it was like those early days when she had first left Mrs. Boldin, except that now she had no high sense of adventure, no expectation of great things to come, which might buoy her up. She no longer thought of phases and the proper setting for her beauty. Once indeed catching sight of her face late one night in the mirror in her tiny work-room in Orange, she stopped and scanned herself, loathing what she saw there.

"You *thing*!" she said to the image in the glass, "if you hadn't been so vain, so shallow!" And she had struck herself violently again and again across the face until her head ached.

But such fits of passion were rare. She had a curious sense of freedom in these days, a feeling that at last her brain, her senses were liberated from some hateful clinging thralldom. Her thoughts were always busy. She used to go over that last scene with Wynne again and again trying to probe the inscrutable mystery which she felt was at the bottom of the affair. She groped her way toward a solution, but always something stopped her. Her impulse to strike, she realized, and his brutal rejoinder had been actuated by something more than mere sex antagonism, there was race antagonism there—two elements clashing. That much she could fathom. But that he despising her, hating her for not being white should yet desire her! It seemed to her that his attitude toward her—hate and yet desire, was the attitude in microcosm of the whole white world toward her own, toward that world to which those few possible strains of black blood so tenuously and yet so tenaciously linked her.

Once she got hold of a big thought. Perhaps there was some root, some racial distinction woven in with the stuff of which she was formed which made her persistently kind and unexacting. And perhaps in the same way this difference, helplessly, inevitably operated in making Wynne and his kind, cruel or at best indifferent. Her reading for Wynne reacted to her thought—she remembered the grating insolence of white exploiters in foreign lands, the wrecking of African villages, the destruction of homes in Tasmania. She couldn't imagine where Tasmania was, but wherever it was, it had been the realest thing in the world to its crude inhabitants.

Gradually she reached a decision. There were two divisions of people in the world—on the one hand insatiable desire for power; keenness, mentality; a vast and cruel pride. On the other there was ambition, it is true, but modified, a certain humble sweetness, too much inclination to trust, an unthinking, unswerving loyalty. All the advantages in the world accrued to the first division. But without bitterness she chose the second. She wanted to be colored, she hoped she was colored. She wished even that she did not have to take advantage of her appearance to earn a living. But that was to meet an end. After all she had contracted her debt with a white man, she would pay him with a white man's money.

The years slipped by—four of them. One day a letter came from Mr. Packard. Mrs. Wynne had sent him the last penny of the sum received from Mr. Wynne from February to November, 1914. Mr. Wynne had refused to touch the money, it was and would be indefinitely at Mrs. Wynne's disposal.

She never even answered the letter. Instead she dismissed the whole incident,—Wynne and all,—from her mind and began to plan for her future. She was free, free! She had paid back her sorry debt with labor, money and anguish. From now on she could do as she pleased. Almost she caught herself saying "something is going to happen." But she checked herself, she hated her old attitude.

But something was happening. Insensibly from the moment she knew of her deliverance, her thoughts turned back to a stifled hidden longing, which had lain, it seemed, to her, an eternity in her heart. Those days with Mrs. Boldin! At night,—on her way to New York,—in the work-rooms,—her mind was busy with little intimate pictures of that happy, wholesome, unpretentious life. She could see Mrs. Boldin, clean and portly, in a lilac chambray dress, upbraiding her for some trifling, yet exasperating fault. And Mr. Boldin, immaculate and slender, with his noticeably polished air—how kind he had always been, she remembered. And lastly, Cornelius: Cornelius in a thousand attitudes and engaged in a thousand occupations, brown and near-sighted and sweet-devoted to his pretty sister, as he used to call her—Cornelius, who used to come to her as a baby as willingly as to his mother; Cornelius spelling out colored letters on his blocks, pointing to them stickily with a brown, perfect finger; Cornelius singing like an angel in his breathy, sexless voice and later murdering everything possible on his terrible cornet. How had she ever been able to leave them all and the dear shabbiness of that home! Nothing, she realized, in all these years had touched her inmost being, had penetrated to the core of her cold heart like the memories of those early, misty scenes.

One day she wrote a letter to Mrs. Boldin. She, the writer, Madame A. Wynne, had come across a young woman, Amy Kildare, who said that as a girl she had run away from home and now she would like to come back. But she was ashamed to write. Madame Wynne had questioned the girl closely and she was quite sure that this Miss Kildare had in no way incurred shame or disgrace. It had been some time since Madame Wynne had seen the girl but if Mrs. Boldin wished, she would try to find her again—perhaps Mrs. Boldin would like to get in touch with her. The letter ended on a tentative note.

The answer came at once.

> My dear Madame Wynne:
>   My mother told me to write you this letter. She says even if Amy Kildare had done
> something terrible, she would want her to come home again. My father says so too. My

mother says, please find her as soon as you can and tell her to come back. She still misses her. We all miss her. I was a little boy when she left, but though I am in the High School now and play in the school orchestra, I would rather see her than do anything I know. If you see her, be sure to tell her to come right away. My mother says thank you.

Yours respectfully,
CORNELIUS BOLDIN

The letter came to the modiste's establishment in New York. Amy read it and went with it to Madame. "I must go away immediately. I can't come back—you may have these last two weeks for nothing." Madame, who had surmised long since the separation, looked curiously at the girl's flushed cheeks, and decided that "Monsieur Ween" had returned. She gave her fatalistic shrug. All Americans were crazy.

"But, yes, Madame,—if you must go—absolument."

When she reached the ferry, Amy looked about her searchingly. "I hope I'm seeing you for the last time—I'm going home, home!" Oh, the unbelievable kindness! She had left them without a word and they still wanted her back!

Eventually she got to Orange and to the little house. She sent a message to Peter's sister and set about her packing. But first she sat down in the little house and looked about her. She would go home, home—how she loved the word, she would stay there a while, but always there was life, still beckoning. It would beckon forever she realized to her adventurousness. Afterwards she would set up an establishment of her own,—she reviewed possibilities—in a rich suburb, where white women would pay for her expertness, caring nothing for realities, only for externals.

"As I myself used to care," she sighed. Her thoughts flashed on. "Then some day I'll work and help with colored people—the only ones who have really cared for and wanted me." Her eyes blurred.

She would never make any attempt to find out who or what she was. If she were white, there would always be people urging her to keep up the silliness of racial prestige. How she hated it all!

"Citizen of the world, that's what I'll be. And now I'll go home." Peter's sister's little girl came over to be with the pretty lady whom she adored.

"You sit here, Angel, and watch me pack," Amy said, placing her in a little armchair. And the baby sat there in silent observation, one tiny leg crossed over the other, surely the quaintest, gravest bit of bronze, Amy thought, that ever lived.

"Miss Amy cried," the child told her mother afterwards.

Perhaps Amy did cry, but if so she was unaware. Certainly she laughed more happily, more spontaneously than she had done for years. Once she got down on her knees in front of the little arm-chair and buried her face in the baby's tiny bosom.

"Oh Angel, Angel," she whispered, "do you suppose Cornelius still plays on that cornet?"

[*The Crisis* 20.4 (August 1920): 168–173; 20.5 (September 1920): 226–229; 20.6 (October 1920): 267–274]

THE FOOLISH AND THE WISE: SALLIE RUNNER IS INTRODUCED TO SOCRATES

by Leila Amos Pendleton

Mrs. Maxwell Thoro (born Audrey Lemere) tiptoed down the spacious hall toward the kitchen of her dwelling whence issued sounds, not exactly of revelry but—perhaps jubilation would be a better fit. For in a high soprano voice her colored maid-of-all-work, Sallie Runner, for the past half-hour had been informing to the accompaniment of energetic thumps of a flat-iron, whomsoever it might concern that she had a robe, a crown, a harp and wings.

Mrs. Thoro moved quietly for, enjoyable as was Sallie's repertoire, one could never tell when she would do some even more enjoyable improvising, and her employer knew from long experience that Sallie's flights were much freer and more artistic when she was unaware of an audience.

Just as Mrs. Thoro reached the kitchen door the soloist started off on the verse, "I gotta shoes," so she stood quietly listening until the verse ended:

> I gotta shoes, yo' gotta shoes,
> All a Gawd's chillun gotta shoes;
> Wen I getto hebben goin' to put on my shoes
> An'skip all over Gawd's hebben.
> Hebben, Hebben! Ever'buddy hollering"bout hebben
> Ain't goin'dere.
> Hebben, hebben, goin'to skip all over Gawd's hebben.

As the singer ceased she whirled around upon her employer with a loud laugh. "Ha, ha, Miss Oddry!" cried she. "I knowed yo'was dere. I sho is glad yo' done come, 'cause I'se mighty lonesome an' powerful tired. Jes' was thinkin' to myseff dat I'se goin' to try to swade Brother Runner to move away fum Starton. Nobuddy don't do nothin' here but git bornd, git married an' git daid, an' wurk, wurk, wurk! Miss Oddry, I'se goin' to tell yo' a secret."

"What is it, Sallie?" inquired Mrs. Thoro.

"I don't lak wurk. Nuvver did."

"Why, Sallie! That is a surprise," replied her employer. "I should never have guessed it, for there is not a more capable maid in town than you are."

"Yassum, I guess dat's right. I works wid my might an' I does whut my hands finds to do, but taint my nature doe. Muss be my Ma's trainin' an' mazin-grace-how-sweet-de-sound mixed togedder, I reckon. Miss Oddry, does yo' know whut I'd ruther do dan anything? I'd ruther know how to read an' write dan anything in de whole, wide world, an' den I'd nuvver do nothin' else but jes' dem two."

"Well, Sallie, I'm sure you would get very tired of reading and writing all the time; but you're not too old to learn."

"Nome, not too ole, mebbe, but too dumb an' too sot in de haid, I reckun. Miss Oddry, couldn't yo' read to me or talk to me on ironin' days 'bout sumpin' outside uv Starton? Cose I wouldn't want yo' round under my feet on wash-days but ironin'-days is fine fur lissening."

"Why yes, Sallie, I'd love to do that. Why didn't you ask me before? Mr. Thoro and I are re-reading an old school course, just for the fun of it, and I'll share it with you. I'm sure you would enjoy hearing about some of earth's greatest characters. How would you like to have me tell you about Socrates?"

"Sockertees? Huh! Funny name! Sockertees whut?"

"Well, in his time men seldom had more than one name, Sallie. He was the son of Sophroniscus and Phaenarete. He was a sculptor and a philosopher."

"Gosh!" cried Sallie. "A sculpture an' a lossipede! Wusser an' mo' uv it! But go on, Miss Oddry, tell me mo' 'bout him."

"Socrates was born about 469 years before our Lord, and died at the age of seventy. He is said to have had thick lips, a flat nose, protruding eyes, bald head, and squat figure, and a shambling gait."

"Why!" exclaimed Sallie. "He was a cullud gentmun, warn't he? Musta looked jes' lak Brudder Runner, 'cordin to dat."

"Oh, no, Sallie, he wasn't colored."

"Wal, ef he been daid all dat long time, Miss Oddry, how kin yo' tell his color?"

"Why he was an Athenian, Sallie. He lived in Greece."

"Dar now! Dat settles it! Ever'buddy knows dat my cullud folks sho do lak grease."

"Oh Sallie! 'Greece' was the name of his country, just as 'America' is the name of ours." Sallie grunted.

"Socrates," continued Mrs. Thoro, "was a very wise, just, and a good man, and he loved his country and his countrymen very much. He used to delight in wandering through the streets of Athens, conversing with those whom he met, giving them the benefit of the truths he had discovered and seeking to obtain from each more truth or new light. He spent the whole day in public, in the walks, the workshops, the gymnasiums, the porticoes, the schools and the market place at the hour it was most crowded, talking with everyone without distinction of age, sex, rank, or condition. It was said that 'as he talked the hearts of all who heard him leaped up and their tears gushed out.'"

"Hole on, Miss Oddry," interrupted Sallie, "Jes' wanta ax yo' one queshun. While ole Sockertees was runnin' round the streets, shootin' off his lip an' makin' peepul cry, who was takin' keer uv his fambly? Sounds mo' an' mo' lak Brudder Runner to me."

"Well, Sallie, he had a very capable wife who bore him three sons and whose name was Xanthippe. No doubt she managed the household. The only fault Socrates found with her was that she had a violent temper."

Sallie slammed the flatiron down and braced herself against the board, arms akimbo, eyes flashing with indignation.

"Vilent temper?" cried she. "Vilent temper? Whut 'oman wouldn't had a vilent temper in a fix lak dat? I sho do symperthize wid Zantipsy an' I doesn't blame her fur gittin' tipsy needer, pore thing. I betcha she was es sweet es a angel befor' she got mahred, 'cause whut it takes to change yo' dispotition, a man lak dat sho is got. It's jest' es much es a 'oman kin do to take keer uv her house right an' raise her chillun right wen her husbland is doin' all he kin to hepp her, less mo' wen he ain't doin' nothin' but goin' round runnin' he mouf. Dis ain't de fust time I'se met a gentmun whut loves he kentry mo' dan he do he home folks. Go on, Miss Oddry, dear, tell me some mo' 'bout Reveral Eyesire Runner's twin brudder."

"Of course, Sallie," said Mrs. Thoro laughing, "Socrates was human and had his faults, but all in all he was a noble character."

"I hopes so, Miss Oddry, but I'll have to hear mo' fo' I 'cide."

"Socrates," resumed Mrs. Thoro, "Believed in signs and omens and in following warnings received in his dreams; he also claimed that there was an inner voice which had guided him from childhood."

"Miss Oddry," expostulated Sallie, "yo' keep on tellin' me Sockertees warn't cullud, but yo' keep on tellin' me cullud things 'bout him. Wen we all b'lieve in signs an' dreams yo' all allus says, 'It's jes' darky superstishun an' ignunce.' How yo' splain dat?"

"Well, Sallie, in those days the most learned people were very superstitious. Of course we know better now."

"How yo' know yo' knows better, Miss Oddry? How yo know yo' don't know wusser? Dere's one thing I done found fur sho, an' dat is dat de mo' folks knows de less dey knows. I b'lieves in dreams an' wen I follers dem I goes right. Cose I ain't nuvver heerd do cujjus voice, but ef ole Sockertees say he heerd it I b'lieve he heerd it. Nobuddy can't prove he didn't."

"Very true, Sallie, but,—"

"Jes' one minute, Miss Oddry, please. Dere's sumpin' I been thinkin' a long time, an' now I knows it. An' dat is dat wen yo' come right down to de fack-trufe uv de side feelin's, peepul is all alak; black ones is lak white ones an' dem ole ancienty ones lak Sockertees is jes' lak dese here ones right now."

"I believe there is some truth in that, Sallie, but shall I go on about Socrates?"

"Oh, yassum, Miss Oddry, I do love to hear 'bout him."

"He tried most earnestly to make people think, to reason out what was right and what wrong in their treatment of each other. He constantly repeated, 'Virtue is knowledge; Vice is ignorance,' while to the young his advice was always, 'Know thyself.'"

"Humph! interrupted Sallie, "Mighty good advice, Miss Oddry, but it's some job, b'lieve me. I'se es, ole es Methusalum's billy goat now an' I ain't nuvver found myseff out yit. Dere's some new kind comin' out ev'ry day. How 'bout you, Miss Oddry?"

"I think you are right, Sallie. But don't you think we are better off if we study ourselves than if we just blunder along blindly?"

"Oh, yassum, I guess so. But how did ole Sockertees come out wid all his runnin' round an' talkin'?"

"Very sadly, I am sorry to say. Very sadly. Most of the Athenians entirely misunderstood him."

"Bound to," said Sallie.

"He made a great many unscrupulous enemies."

"Bound to," said Sallie.

"They accused him of being the very opposite of what he was."

"Bound to," said Sallie.

"And finally they tried him and condemned him to death."

Sallie set down the flatiron and folded her arms, while her eyes flew wide open in astonishment. "What?" she exclaimed. "Jes' fur talkin'? Wal I-will-be-swijjled!"

"Yes," continued Mrs. Thoro. "They imprisoned him and sent him a cup of hemlock, which is a deadly poison to drink."

"But he had mo' gumption dan to drink it, I hope?"

"It was the law of his country, Sallie, and Socrates was always a law-abiding citizen."

"Wal, fur gosh sake!" cried Sallie. "Whut in de world was de use uv him havin' all dat tongue ef he couldn't use it to show dem people wherein? He mouts well been es dumd es a doodlebug!"

"But," explained Mrs. Thoro, he had spent his whole life in trying to make the Athenians love and honor and obey their laws and he was willing to die for the same cause. He had many friends who loved him truly and they tried to persuade him to escape, but by answerable argument he proved to them how wrong they were."

"Humph!" grunted Sallie. "Tonguey to de last! An' in de wrong way to de wrong ones."

"Plato, who was a friend as well as a pupil," continued Mrs. Thoro, "tells how beautifully Socrates died. He took the cup of hemlock quite calmly and cheerfully and drained it to the dregs. When his friends could not restrain their sorrow for the loss they were about to sustain, he reproved them and urged them to remember that they were about to bury, not Socrates, but the shell which had contained him, for he, himself, was about to enter the joys of the blessed. He tried to the last to make them see that unless they honored and obeyed all laws, their country could not long survive, because lawlessness was the same as suicide."

"Miss Oddry," said Sallie, solemnly, "don't yo' wisht we had one million of dem Sockertees down here in ower sunny Soufland?"   [*The Crisis* 21.5 (March 1921): 210–212]

Two Americans

⸻≋⸻

by Florence Lewis Bentley

I

The little village of St. Gervais lay sleeping in the early dawn of a spring morning. St. Gervais was one of the first spots in France to feel the devastating fury of the Hun, and for many months it had lain deserted and desolate. After two years of exile, however, many of her people—tenacious homekeepers—had straggled back. Patiently they had repaired and rebuilt; and now St. Gervais, with the added help of Spring's healing touch, was looking a little like her old, picturesque self. The marks of the destroyer were still there. The broken church spire, the town-hall half destroyed, ruined fenced and shell-plowed farms still gave dreadful evidence, that Hate had passed that way. As a sleeping countenance sometimes shows marks of grief and passion not seen when the brave spirit of the sleeper is active and on guard, so the little village, asleep in the dawn, showed many scars often lost sight of when its people were bustling about, filling every corner with the spirit of their indomitable courage.

This morning the sleep of the villagers was early disturbed, for while the dawn was still gray, up the road came a well-known sound, the tramp, tramp, tramp of marching feet. From one window, then from another, nightcapped heads were thrust; out of doors tumbled the peasants, pulling on clothes as they ran—men, women and many children. The place was so near the actual fighting ground, that no man knew who that marching host might be, friend or foe. Huddled together in groups, the memory of old terrors holding strong, they anxiously gazed towards the approaching sound. Suddenly into their delighted vision, a khaki-colored host appeared. That uniform was already well known in this region and the relieved and delighted people with joyous accord cried, "*Les Américains, les Américains, vivent les Américains!*

A detachment of Pershing's men soon filled the road. Children ran to them and clasped their hands and tried to keep step with them. Their elders smiled and shouted and tried in every way to express from their French hearts a grateful love for the country that had sent these fine soldiers. The khaki line stretched out longer and longer and the clamor of greetings of an increasing number of peasants was at its height, when suddenly there seemed to be a curious change in the soldiers. The people stopped their shouting and stood bewildered and hesitant. These men now passing had not the accustomed face—these were not white faces, but black faces and brown. The French people of this countryside had never seen faces so colored and their astonishment was very real. The uniform to them, however, meant America, and one thinking more quickly and clearly than the others cried out, "*Ceux-ci sont aussi des Américains.*" ("These are Americans, too.")

The cry was taken up and repeated from group to group.

"*Ceux-ci sont aussi des Américains.*"

The little children ran to see these black men and smiled at them and clasping their hands, accompanied them far down the road, chatting and singing in their sweet childish voices.

For many days after this event there was excited talk in St. Gervais about the soldiers who passed through, especially concerning the black soldiers, who were also Americans.

Then shortly cannons were heard, the sounds becoming increasingly louder and nearer. War-ridden France had become so used to these sounds that they were scarcely allowed to disturb the routine of life. Women stopped oftener in the little church to say a prayer, children were kept closer to their homes—just little things like these indicated an apprehension which a long tried courage kept under control. One day a detachment of Red Cross doctors and nurses came, took over the largest barn in the place and made a temporary hospital. That same night ambulances slowly brought in their loads of wounded, and the little French village knew that once more it was in the fangs of awful war.

The cottage of Mère Pinchot stood at the west end of the village, nearest to the place of fighting. Late one evening, the good woman and her daughter, Zélie, were tidying up their little kitchen, preparing to go to bed when the quick ear of the girl heard a faint tapping at the door. Stray comers were not always safe visitors in these uncertain days and the two unprotected women drew together in terror, when Zélie told what she had heard. They listened for a moment and hearing no further sound, were about to mount the steep stairs, which led to their little bed room when once more the sound was heard—this time loud enough for the mother to hear. First sending her daughter upstairs for safety, the French woman cautiously approached the door. To her challenge twice repeated, there was no reply. Truly terrified by this time, she was about to run upstairs with her daughter when she heard a low moan, as if from one in extreme pain. Instantly she threw open the door when across the threshold tumbled two men—a black man and white man—both clad in the uniform of America.

The white man was on the shoulder of the black man, who evidently had been carrying him. Both seemed badly wounded and were covered with blood and mud, and to the frightened gaze of the French woman both seemed dead. She called her daughter and together they pulled the inert forms into the kitchen, cut the leather belt which strapped one to the other, and laid them gently side by side on the floor.

"Zélie, we must get help immediately. Will you stay with them and let me run to the hospital for the good nurse and doctor. Are you afraid?"

"No, mother," from the brave little French maid, "I can run more quickly than you, let me go. And I am not afraid, for with me always is the good God. I'll run as fast as I can." Throwing a shawl over her head, she sped away into the darkness, while the older woman did all in her power to resuscitate the two men.

In a short time the young girl returned with a doctor, a nurse, and stretcher bearers. While the stretcher bearers were carrying the men out, the doctor questioned the woman:

"You say one was strapped to the other's back?"

"Yes, monsieur, the black one had the white one strapped to his back. He must have carried him, you see."

"I see," agreed the doctor, examining the belts. "He must have strapped him on so that he would not fall off. And he full of wounds, himself. Some sand there, believe me."

The wounded men were taken to the barn-hospital where they were carefully washed and put to bed—both still unconscious. Their wrist tags showed that they were both from Huxton, Georgia.

"Same place," said the recording nurse. "Knew each other at home, very likely. Splendid courage in that black fellow."

Towards morning the Negro soldier regained consciousness and the first words he whispered were, "Did I save him?"

On being assured that his comrade was safe in an adjoining cot, a look of great relief passed over his face and he soon dropped off into a quiet sleep. On the next day the white soldier regained consciousness, but it was very evident that there was small hope of recovery in either case. The white man's wounds were so serious that the wonder was that he had lived at all; the Negro's, though not so serious at first, had been greatly aggravated and complicated by the superhuman exertion he had put forth in carrying his comrade from the battlefield, two miles away.

On the third morning the Negro soldier seemed a little stronger and the young doctor, who was more than ordinarily interested in this case of rescue, which indicated one man's sacrifice of life for another, said as he took his temperature:

"That was a brave thing you did, soldier boy." Over the large black eyes into which he gazed, passed an inscrutable look, but the Negro made no reply.

"You are both from the same place?" Still trying to make a friendly approach.

"Yes, from the same place," was the quiet reply.

"Knew each other pretty well, eh?"

"Yes, we knew each other."

"Well all I can say is that you did a mighty fine thing for him. If we pull him through he owes his life to you. Must care for him a great deal, don't you?"

"I hated him."

The words were said quietly, just stating a fact not to be added to by any inflection of voice or gesture. The doctor, now really mystified, asked, "Do you care to tell me about it?"

"Sometime I will, doctor. You seem very kind and I would like some one to know. Sometime—"

"Sometime," thought the doctor, "you haven't very much time, young fellow. "But he only said, "Maybe this evening, when I am off duty for a while."

The other tried to incline his head and for the first time smiled a smile that seemed to restore for a moment all the youth and brightness which much suffering and labor had banished from his countenance.

That evening a number of the wounded were transferred to the base hospital, and fewer patients gave the young doctor a few moments of needed relaxation. The huge doors of the barn were thrown wide to let in the soft warm air of the spring evening. Outside, the moon, almost at its full, bathed in its softening light the little village. A window in one of the barn lofts had been thrown open and through it a long bar of light penetrated the gloomy interior of the barn, throwing into deeper shadow, parts outside of its silvery beam.

Here and there a candle flickered at a soldier's bedside, doing its little best to lighten the gloom. One or two nurses moved softly about, their white clad forms making grotesque shadows when they crossed the track of light. The doctor stood resting in the doorway, looking out on the quiet night, when a movement in the cot of the Negro soldier attracted his attention and recalled to his mind the promise to talk to him that evening. He quickly approached the bed and taking a candle from a nearby table, anxiously examined the soldier, who was tossing restlessly on this narrow cot. To the experienced eye of the surgeon, there was a significant change in the patient and he knew that the young man's time was limited. He put down the candle and took the sufferer in his strong arms, turned him over in an easier position, smiling all the while into the upturned black face looking so wistfully up to him.

"Now, old man, that's easier. Take a sip of this," said the doctor, holding some water to his lips.

The Negro drank feverishly and said, "Doc, you must let me talk now, for I know I'm goin' soon an' I must tell some one before I go." The doctor pulled up a little camp stool and seating himself by the cot, assumed a listening attitude.

The Negro soldier told him this story:

"I was born and raised in Huxton, Georgia—me and my brother Joe. We lived with our mother and all three of us worked. We were happy enough until we boys began to grow up, and then it seemed that the white boys were pickin' on us all the time, and abusin' us. My mother told us to try not to mind, for when we all had saved enough money we could go North, where we could get a better show. But when you get little pay, it takes a long time to save any amount of money. And we boys were men when we at last got money enough to take all three of us away. All the time we were having trouble. Whenever the gang of white boys saw us or our friends, they would chase us and stone us. We always had to run, of course, 'cause we knew we would be killed if we hit back. One day the whole gang, about ten of 'em, met Joe walking alone and chased him for miles, until he rushed into our little cabin out of breath. He had been struck on the head with a huge stone. That night he said to me, 'That's the las' time I'll run. I'm goin' to act like a man. If I'm chased again before we leave this God-forsaken place, I'm goin' to show fight.'

"'What can you do?' sez I, 'You, one, against the crowd.'

"'I'll see to that,' sez he. And the next day he went to town and bought a revolver.

"Me and my mother saw that we must hurry to get away. All our little things were packed and we hoped to get away within the week. Me and my ma were both working one day at the same place, old Judge Canna's, whose house was on the Square. In Huxton the Co'te House, the store, the livery stable and one or two houses faced the Square, where all the meetings used to be. My ma was inside ironin' and I was working in the garden, when I saw Joe come out of the store with a bag of candy.

"Some of the white boys were standing before the livery stable and as Joe passed one cursed him. He seemed to say something back, because in a minute they were all after him. He started to run, but a white man tripped him up, and as he lay there they kicked and beat him. I saw him put his hand in his pocket and in a minute there was a flash, and one of the white boys fell. In the confusion (every one thought some one was killed) Joe got away. They found that only one boy was struck, and he only in the leg.

"I rushed into the house and told my mother, Old Judge Canna was in the house and he made my mother and me go up into his attic and stay there. Judge Canna was the one *white* white man we found in the South. We hid in the judge's attic for three days. The judge brought in word that the mob had burned our home, and that only he and the colored preacher knew where Joe was hiding and they hoped to get him out of town when the people had cooled down. On the third day my ma was sitting in the attic doing some mending for old Miss Canna, and I was peeping through the slats of the window on to the Square. Suddenly I heard a great shout and a noise like people running, and then I saw a crowd turn a corner and pour into the Square. They had Joe. He looked awful. One eye was out, the blood was trickling all around his face from a cut in the head, and one arm hung like it was broken."

II

"'O My God!' my mother cried. 'They got my boy!' and when she looked through the slats and seen him, she tumbled right down in a faint. Old Miss Canna and the Judge run in and took her in another room, where she couldn't hear or see if she come to. But I stuck to the window, and I saw them take my only brother—that crowd of white people—and lay him out on a table. They stretched out his arms like a cross and nailed down his hands and feet. Then they passed around the table and each one—men and women and children—struck him and stuck him and tore his flesh and spat upon him. I was almost crazy. I tried to rush out to my brother and die with him, but the old Judge, who had come back into the room, had locked the door.

"'Think of your mother, boy,' he said, 'you must be safe for her.' My poor mother!

"When I returned to the window they had stopped the torture and were preparing something else. I soon saw what it was, for a man stepped forward and poured kerosene on the body of my brother and the leader of the mob applied a lighted torch. I must have fainted then because everything grew black, but before I lost consciousness I plainly saw the face of the man who had been the ring leader and who applied the torch to my brother's helpless body—and it was the face of that man I brought in here."

The face of the Negro had become ashen and the sweat was thick on his forehead as he lay with closed eyes after speaking. The doctor wiped the wet face and moistened the purple lips. In a few minutes the dying man resumed:

"The next night the Judge drove me and my mother to the next town and we took train for the North. My mother didn't live long. Her heart was broken. And I was full of hate. I hated all white men, and I made up my mind if I ever met that man who led that mob to murder and to burn my brother, I'd make him suffer just what Joe suffered. I knew I would meet him. The world wasn't big enough to keep us apart. Then the war came and I was drafted. I was glad to get away from America, and I didn't care if I did get killed in the war. But I made up my mind that I would be such a good soldier that those white men back home would understand just what kind of real men we Negroes are. And I did fight well—did you save my cross, doctor?"

The doctor opened a bundle on the table and showed him the *croix de guerre* which they had found pinned to his torn and stained jacked. A pleased smile passed over the gray face.

"I got that in my first fight," he whispered. "Then one day we passed through this place and went to N—. There we certainly found hell. But I did my share before that shell got me. When I came to, all was so quiet that I thought I was in bed when I opened my eyes. But when I raised up, I saw the deserted field and dead bodies all around. It was then quite dark and I tried to rise and seek shelter somewhere. Then I heard a slight groan and saw that another soldier near me was still living. I went over to him and called but he was still unconscious, so I dragged him a little way under a hedge and lay down beside him to wait for daylight. That's the way the stretcher-bearer must have missed us—we were behind the hedge. I must have slept or become unconscious, because the first thing I knew I opened my eyes and saw sunlight. I was full of pain and my head hurt something fierce, but I knew I had to get myself and my comrade to a safer place. I looked over and saw him there, face downward. I turned him over to the light and I saw his face—the face of the man who had burned my brother! I remember I burst out laughing. I just laughed and laughed! I just couldn't stop. He must have heard me, for he stirred and opened his eyes and stared at me.

"'Who are you?' he whispered. 'Give me some water.' I just laughed and laughed! 'Water,' he says, kind of weak like. 'Some water, for pity's sake.'

"'Pity,' sez I, 'what you know about pity? Did you pity Joe when you burned him in Huxton? I'm Joe's brother!'

"He stared at me a minute, and then just begin to whimper like a little baby. 'Now you are going to suffer some what you made Joe suffer,' sez I. And I pulled him out from under the shade of the hedge into the sunlight. 'Now you'll burn and burn, and no water for you. And when you get to hell, remember Joe's brother sent you there.'

"And then I staggered up and left him. I heard him cry out once, but I just laughed and went on. I laughed all the way up the road, just staggering along from side to side and laughing fit to split, till I suddenly turned a bend in the road and come plumb face to face with—Joe. No, doctor, I'm not out of my head, my pulse is all right. *I was facing Joe.* There he stood as I last saw him. The blood all streaming down all around his head, like it crowned him, and his hands and feet showed where they had nailed him that day.

"'Joe!' I cried, and I stopped laughing. He looked at me so sad like, and he raised one of them scarred hands and pointed back down the road I had come.

"'Go back and save your brother,' he said.

"'He is not my brother,' I cried. 'You are my brother.' And I tried to laugh again but I couldn't.

"'All men are your brothers,' he said. 'Go back, go back.'

"I tried to answer, but the first thing I knew I fell flat on the ground and couldn't say a word. I lay flat on my face in that road in front of Joe. I knew he was still talking to me, though I could not make out the very words—the sense of it I felt. I'll try to tell you."

And with superhuman effort he raised himself on an arm and laid his black hand upon the doctor's white wrist.

Slowly, stammeringly, but most earnestly he continued:

"He made me know that this war—this war which I was fightin' in—has come to wipe away hate. That any one act of hate—like what I was doin'—only made the war longer. That all men *are* brothers, black and white, yellow and brown. That when hate was cleaned away, everybody would know this and act like brothers. That if I killed in hatred, I wasn't a true soldier, but a deserter—giving aid to the enemy and making things harder for all my comrades. And he said that if I did what I was doing, I was killing him again, just as the white mob did.

"Then I hollered out, 'O, no, Joe, not that—not that—I'll go back, I'll go back!' and I stretched out my arms to clasp him, but he was gone.

"Then I struggled to my feet and went back to the white man. He looked like he was a dead one there in the hot sun just where I had left him, but I felt his heart still beatin'. I had some water left in my canteen, so I moistened his lips and bathed his face before I took him on my back and started once more on the road. It was a long trip, Doc, and two or three times I thought I couldn't make it. When night came on again, I found some hay in a wagon in a deserted field. I made a bed for each of us, and when I lay him down I see that his eyes were open. When the moon came up I could see him still there, watching me all the time. Then he said:

"'I was in another place, wasn't I, and you came back for me?' When I nodded he sez, 'Why did you come back?'

"'Because I am a true soldier and want this war to end!' I sez.

"'What you mean by that?' sez he. Then I told him all about meetin' Joe, and all what Joe said to me. He lay quiet for a while and then he sez:

"'That sounds very queer, but many things over here seem queer and strange and different.'

"And then after a while he sez slowly, 'I'm thinkin' if those folks back home could see this Hell that hate has made over here—maybe they would get a light on some things. If I ever get back'—but he didn't finish that, he just turned over and soon I knew that he had fell asleep. I got a little sleep, too, and so in the morning we both felt some stronger. I strapped him on before we started, so that he wouldn't slip off if I grew too weak to hold him on.

"The day was a scorcher, though, and what with the heat and more loss of blood, it was real fierce. Two or three times I fell and we lay until I could go again; but I knew I just had to do that job, and when at last I saw the light of that farm-house I knew that God meant that I should do it. That's all, Doc."

The moonlight had long since faded away. The open loft window looked like a black patch against the barn wall. Outside, the darkness obliterated the village, and through the open door the chill air of approaching dawn penetrated the *quasi* hospital. The young doctor with gentle hands—hands that trembled in spite of himself—drew the covers close around the dying soldier and placed him in a more comfortable position. He closed the door, snuffed his candle and settled down again at the bedside of the patient. He felt that he should be taking the little rest which was now his due, but sleep was far from his thoughts, for he knew that the passing of a brave soul was very near.

Just before morning the Negro started from a seeming stupor. He sat straight up in bed and stretching out his arms as if to an invisible presence, he cried:

"Joe,—Joe—I did it—I overcame the enemy—I—I." Then the doctor caught in his arms a gallant soldier whose fight was now over.

The white soldier during the day was able to dictate a letter to his home folks, but before night, he too, had passed beyond.

These two men from Huxton, Georgia, were given a soldier's burial on the same day. Into the same wide grave were their rude coffins lowered and one American flag marks their place of rest. Flowers are planted there by the warm-hearted French people, and on fair days the little French children love to play softly around the grave of "Two Americans."

[*The Crisis* 22.5 (September 1921): 202–205; 22.6 (October 1921): 250–252]

BUYERS OF DREAMS: A STORY

by Ethel M. Caution

Spring and Summer had passed with their promise and visions of life. Now came Autumn—glorious fulfillment. She painted her pathway with reds, and golds, and browns.

Boughs that had once been showers of pink petals were now freighted with richly tinted fruits. Leaves to whom the wind had whispered shy little secrets covered the earth with their radiant hues, and as one trampled through them, the wonder and mystery crept up into one's very soul. If with Spring came restlessness and yearning, and with Summer thrills of experimenting, with Autumn came conviction and decision.

At this season of the year the Seller of Dreams was always very busy with folks wanting various and sundry dreams. So today he busied himself polishing his cases and placing his wares to the best advantage for inspection by Youth, Beauty, and Age who would surely visit him. His whole shop was radiant and inviting with cleanness.

And such dreams as he had!—marvelous things of costly price and others not so attractive and therefore to be bought for less. And because in the Autumn people usually paid highly for their purchases, the less expensive, ordinary little dreams were not given the place of honor.

It was early in the morning. The shop had scarcely been open when in came a dashing young lady needing a dream. She looked the wares over very carefully and asked prices. One that was all shining and dazzling appealed to her but the price was rather more than she had thought of paying.

"Here are some beautiful ones," said the shopkeeper.

"Oh, those!" answered the girl in disgust.

"Well, of course, they are not as gorgeous as the ones you like."

The girl pondered and pursed her mouth and made little mental calculations on her fingers. Finally:

"If you will agree, I will pay you what I have with me now and you can put the dream aside. I will come with the rest later. Will that be all right?"

"Yes, I shall be glad to oblige you if you are sure that is the dream you wish."

"Oh, but it is! Just see how it shines! Everyone will turn to look because it is so beautiful."

She went away with a satisfied smile on her face.

A few hours later another girl came in, dignified and impressive in air, and asked to see the dreams.

The shopkeeper showed her the shiny beautiful ones; but she wanted something out of the ordinary, something that everyone didn't have. So he showed her some that were very unique, even peculiar.

"That's what I am looking for. I want a dream that will make me stand out as one in a thousand. There can be lots of gorgeous dreams and many drab ones, but very few people would think of taking one like I want. That is why I want it."

She paid for her dream and took it away.

Then trade lagged until nearly closing time, when a very plain little girl came in and quietly closed the door.

"What kind of dream would you like?" asked the keeper.

"Oh, I'll look around and see."

"I have some very lovely ones, but," eyeing her plain clothes, "they are very expensive."

"It won't be a question of money. I have been saving and saving so that I would have enough for whatever dream I picked out."

"Do you like this one?" picking out the most gaudy one he had.

"No, no. That isn't a real dream. That is only a bubble. It costs a lot, but we can't always measure worth by cost. That dream is for the society butterfly. It means fine clothes, and expensive parties; late hours and breakfasts in bed; yachts and trips; perfume and paint; and in the end, emptiness and dissatisfaction."

"Then, maybe you would like this one. I sold one today."

"No, that is for the girl who wants a career. She wants a dream that means bringing the world to her feet for some wonderful bit of work she has cornered. She doesn't realize the emptiness of mere fame and of work done just for personal glory."

The shopkeeper noticed the wistful twist in her smile and discovered that when she looked him full in the face, there were golden lights in her deep brown eyes.

"I think I like that dream over there," she said, indicating a very inconspicuous one off in a corner.

"That looks like a real dream and I am glad it is not very expensive, because more girls can buy one. Let me show you how beautiful it is."

He handed it out to her and her eyes sparkled and there was a lilt in her voice as she held it up to the light and said:

"This dream means comradeship, and love, home and happiness. Can you not see the beautiful babies in it? See their laughing eyes, and the dimples in their hands and plump little knees. See them wriggle their toes and reach their little hands to love and caress your face! I wouldn't pay a penny for your flashy dreams. A pin prick, and they are no more. Neither do I want your dream of a career to end my life in loneliness and emptiness and bitterness. This is a dream I shall buy. Love, babies, life!"

And the shopkeeper decided that of the three, she had made the wisest choice.

[*The Crisis* 23.2 (December 1921): 59–60]

THE FOOLISH AND THE WISE: SANCTUM 777 N.S.D.C.O.U. MEETS CLEOPATRA

by Leila Amos Pendleton

The hour for opening had passed but, strange to say, Sister Sallie Runner, the All Highest Mogul of Sanctum 777, "Notable Sons and Daughters of Come On Up," had not yet arrived. The members stood around in groups and wondered what had happened, for Sis Runner was never late. True the Vice-All Highest, Sister Susan Haslam, was present and technically it was her duty to open the meeting; but the members of the Sanctum had a very poor opinion of her ability. Sally had once voiced the general feeling when she said to her:

"Sis Haslum, seems lak to me dat yo knowlidge box is allus onjinted an'de mentals of yo mind clean upsot. How yo spect to rule dis Sanctum wen yo time come I cain't tell. Pears lak to me de bes' thing we kin do will be to 'lect yo Grand Past All Highest an' give yo de grand claps now an' be done wid it. Den we won't have to worry wid yo settin' in dis cheer an' trying to zide."

The suggestion was not acted upon, but as the members waited tonight they wished very earnestly it had been; for then Sister Tulip Bawler would have been in line to preside (as she was Most Mightiest), and no one doubted her ability. When the thoughts of the members had reached this uncertain state, Notable Brother Brown spoke up:

"High Notables, Sons and Daughters, Brothers and Sisters, Officers and Members," he said, "I moves dat we close dis here Sanctum tonight befo' we opens it an' journey 'round to Sis Runner's house to see what all's de matter wid her."

"Sho! Sho! To be certingly," responded the Sanctum unanimously, but just as they were putting on their wraps, in bustled Sallie, breathless but smiling.

"I knowd it," said she, as soon as she could catch her breath, "I jes knowd you all would git tired a waitin'. I tole Reveral Runner so. But dat man is some sick an' whut part ain't sick is scared to death; an' no wonder, as much debilmunt as he's allus up to. Jes as I were puttin' on my hat to come here he dragged in de doe, lookin' lak a ghost. 'Brudder Runner,' says I, 'Is dat yo or yo apparatus?' He diden make no answer but jes pinted to his chist. Wal, yo orter seen me hop 'round. Yo know he already done had newmonny twict. I had some creso an' dats good for de longs'; den I chopped up some Turmooda onyuns an' bound him up in dat an' salt. When he mence to feel better I turned him over to Obellina. She's jes as gooda nuss as me an' she are wrapped up in her pa cause she ain't on to his curbs. Come on, chilluns, less open de lodge. We'll leave off, de gowns an' crowns an' mit de regular openin' cause it's so late, but I gotta fine ole anncienty story to tel yo an' dis time it's 'bout a cullud lady."

At this the Sanctum was all excitement and officers and members hurriedly took their stations. Sallie gave the altar in front of her five raps, then said she, "High Notibuls, yo kin pass to de secertary's desk one by one an' pay yo dues. Sis Dolum an' Sis Spots tend to passin' de cookies. Does yo all think you kin do all dem things an' lissen to me too?"

"Oh yes, All Highest," came a number of voices. "We's jes crazy to hear yo."

"Wal," proceeded Sallie, in her stateliest manner, "dis here lady I'se goin' to tell 'bout tonight were bornd right spang in Egupt an'dats in Afriky. She were a sho nuff queen too, wid lords an' ladies an' sojers an' servants. Her name were Clea Patrick."

"All Highest," cautiously inquired Sister Ann Tunkett, Vice-Most Mightiest, "is yo rale sho she were cullud?"

"I is," responded Sallie. "Cose, Mis Oddry beat me down she warnt, but I knows better 'cause I were lookin' right at her. She were one a dese here high browns wid wavy hair an' rosy cheeks, lookin' jes lak dat Donarine Elett what were rennin' arter Reveral Runner dat time. Least he 'cuse her of runnin' arter him wen dey got cot up wid, but I knows who were doin' de most runnin'."

"Is Mis Oddry got Clea Patrick's picter, All Highest?" inquired Sis Tunkett.

"Yas; an' de nex' time yo come 'round I'll show it to yo. Clea Patrick were one of dese here long-haided, long-nosed, long-eyed, slim gals dat jes nachel come into de world to make trubble. An' she sho made it. Fust off her King pa died wen she were only eighteen years ole an' lef his kentry fur her an' her lil brudder Tallmy to rule over togedder. But whut should Tallmy's gardeens do but grab de whole bisnuss an' leave Clea wid nuffin."

"Now ain't dat jes lak some men!" exclaimed Sis Bawler. "Seem lak de vurry idear of Wimmin rulin' anything but de cook kitching sets um wild."

"It's de fack—trufe," replied Sallie. "Yo all knows dat as long as I were settin' on dis floor Brudder Runner were a jim-dandy member of de 'Come On Ups.' Soon as I mence to move 'round de cheers, he mence to git restless. Den wen yo all 'lect me All Highest he jes nachel coulden stan' it. So he goes off an' jines dat 'Everlastin'Order of Hezzakites' an' he aint been back here sence."

"Dats right, All Highest. Dats jes whut he done, but I nuvver seen through it befo'," said Vice-Most Mightiest Tunkett.

"Wal I seen through him. He's jes de same as a winda-pane to me. But ef I'da knowd whut I knows now or ef I'da lissened to my ma he'd nuvver got me in his clinches. Longs as I diden do nuthin but work fur him an' be a skillyun he were as pleased as punch, but jes as soon as peepul act lak dey thot I could do sumpin else sides dat he got sore. An' dat was de vurry way dem men acted wid Clea Patrick. But dey diden know her yit! Ha ! Ha! Dey haden foamed her quaintence. She skipped 'round an' got herself a big army an' de way she fout um were sumpin pretty, 'cause evry one of dem sojers was in love wid her. Den right in de middle of all dat here come dat Julyus Siezer."

"Who were he, All Highest?" inquired Sis Haslum.

"Why he were dat great Roaming gineral sumpin lak Elleckzandry, only he were borned a long time afterward. Wal as soon as he got in gunshot of her, Clea Patrick mence rollin' dem long eyes at him. She done a right cute thing doe—she wind herself all up in a big bufull rug an' make her servants carry it to Siezer an' say, 'Here's a present Queen Clea Patrick sont you.' Den wen dey enroll it, out she jump an' dat ole jack went crazy over her. Now he were ole nuff to be her grandpa en' he had a wife at home, sides bein' bald-haided, an' dey warn't no scuse fur de way he carried on."

"Wal, All Highest," drawled Most Mightiest Bawler, "Yo know whut dey say bout a ole fool."

"Yas," returned Sallie, "an' I aint nuvver seen dat sayin' fail yit. Dis here Siezer were a good zample of it, too. Why he took Clea Patrick back to Roam wid him an' put her in a fine palace an' was gittin' ready to go fum extreemity to extremity. But dem Roamings say, 'Looka here, we's tired a dis foolishness. Nuff's good as a feast. We all caint die togedder— somebuddy is got to die fust an' it might's well be yo.' So dey jump on Siezer in de State House one day an' fill him fulla daggers."

"Oh! Oh! My! My!" cried the Sanctum.

"Yes indeedy," replied Sally nonchalantly. "Cose when I fust got quainted wid dem ale anncienties, dat murdarin' an' momockin'way dey had worried me a lot. But Ise usedta it now. Yo know you kin git usedta anybuddy dyin' but yosef. Wal wen dis here Siezer died, Clea Patrick lit out fur home an' took dey lil son Siezeron wid her. An' it's a good thing dey got away so slick 'cause dem Roamings woulda finished um bofe. But it do seem lak peepul nuvver knows whut day ralely wants. When Siezer were daid evrybuddy got sorry an' when his will were read an' dey found out dat he had left a whole lotta money to de vurry ones dat had kilt him, why dem Roamings rose up an' made dose killers fly an burnt up all dey homes an' done um up so bad dey wisht dey nuvver hada seen dat Siezer, less mo' kilt him."

"Wal," Most Mightiest Bawler interposed, "doesn't yo think dat were fair an' square, All Highest?"

Oh, I guess so," the All Highest replied, "but dem ole anncienties done so many quare things yo nuvver coud tell whedder dey was comin' or goin'. Wal, arter Siezer were daid his main frend name Mark an Tony took up de battle. Arter fightin' in evry derection he wint sailin' down to Egupt. When Clea Patrick heerd he were comin' she diden git into no carpet dis time. No indeed! She puts on her gladdes' rags an' jewls an' fumes an' gits in her fines' boat all kivvered wid gold an' silver, an' has her servunts all decked in dey grandes' clothes holdin' parasols over her an' wavin' fans at her an' way she sail to meet Mark an Tony. She already knowd him wen she were in Roam wid dat Siezer an'mebbe dey lak one another den, yo can't tell. Anyhow dey sho lak each udder arter at meetin'. Sho did!"

"Ef she look anything lak Donarina an' was all fixed up lak you says, I knows she were one uvvermo hartbreaker," put in Sis Haslum.

Sallie transfixed her with a look and went on. "Mark an Tony furgot all erbout Roam an' home an' wife an' everything but Clea Patrick. He warns no ole man lak Siezer so dey was mo' on a quality. Dey played games togedder an' went a huntin' an' a fishin' togedder lak lil boy an' gurl. Sides, Clea would sing to Mark an' play fur him an' talk to him in seben langwitches."

"It's a wunder Mark's wife haden got onto um," commented Sis Tunkett.

"She did. She were one of dem strong-arm wimmin an' she starts up a great war, hopin' dat Mark will come on home an' git into it; but he were too busy. He an' Clea useter dress up in masks an' servunt's clothes at nights an' run up an' down de streets an' play Holler Ween pranks on peepul when it warnt no Holler Ween. Den agin dey would put on dey grandes' robes an' crowns an' give de bigges' kinda ceptions to dey frends an' eat an' drink tel dey coulden see. An' den in the middle of dem doins Mark's wife upped an' died."

"Ah, de pore soul!" sighed Sis Haslum, "Dat Clea Patrick orta be shamed a hersef."

"Wal," resumed the All Highest, "Mark went on to meet the yuther great Roaming gineral name Tavius an' what should he do but make up a match 'tween his sister an' Mark."

Good gosh!" exclaimed Sis Bawler, "an' Clea Patrick yit livin'? Now don't you know dere's trubble comin' in lobs an' gobs ? Diden dat Tavius had gumption nuff to know dat a man whut won't be true to one wife, won't be true to two?"

"Wal," Sallie replied, "pears lak if he uvver knowd it he furgot it or else he were hopin' fur de bes.' Anyhow, fur a while Mark kep' rale straight. But arter while he hadta leave home to go to de wars agin an' when he got not so fur fum Clea Patrick—uh! uh!—he sent fur her an' give her not rings an' bracelits an' things lak dat, but rivers an' mountings an' cities an' countries."

"Jes whut I knowd!" triumphed Sis Bawler. "Dese here madeup matches alus scares me. Land knows deres times wen its harda nuff to stand a match yo done made yosef, less mo' one dats made fur yo."

Mark an Tony found dat out aright. He done a lil mo' fightin"round erbout den he hikes hissef spang down to Egupt an' dar he stays wid Clea Patrick."

"Ah ha!" Sis Bawler cried. "Tole yo so! Tole yo so!"

"But," Sallie went on, "dem Roamings feel dersef much more degraced by Mark an Tony's doins, an' dey is tired a Clea Patrick hoodoodlin' dey bes' ginerals so dey clar war agin her."

"Serve her jes right!" Sis Tunkett cried indignantly. "Don't care ef she were a cullud queen. I don't hole wid no sich capers. She orta lef dem wimmins' huasbunds lone."

"Dats right! Dats right!" chorused the Sanctum.

"Yas," Sallie agreed. "My ole mudder allus said dat 'Right wrongs no one.' Wal, Mark an Tony an' Clea Patrick gethered all dey sojera an' sailurs an' off dey go to fight de Roamings. Wen de battle got hot, Clea got scared an' back home she went ascootin. Stidda Mark an' Tony stayin' dere an' fightin' lak a rale sojer, whut muss he do but take a fast boat an' lite out arter Clea Patrick. Cose wen de leaders lef, the sojers stop fightin' an' de inimy captured dem all an' den hiked out arter Clea an' Mark."

"Wal warn's dat sumpin!" exclaimed Sis Haslum.

"Dem two," continued Sallie, "knowd evrything were over den, so dey et an' drunk an' carried on wusser den uvver, tel dem Roaming come clean into de city. Den Clea Patrick hide sersef wid her maids in a big monimint an' made her servunts tell Mark she were daid. I caint imagine why she done dat 'cause dat news on top small de res' of his trubbles jes nachel broke his heart an' he run his own swoad clean fru his body. Den when dey come back an' say Clea Patrick warnt daid he made dem carry him to her. I reckon dey love one another much as dem kinda peepul kin, 'cause when she saw him dyin' at her feet, she 'sides she diden wanta live widout him. So she put a pizenous wiper in her breast to sting her an' in a lil while she were dead."

"Poe thing," Sis Haslum sighed. "Poe thing. Mebbe ef her ma hada lived she woulda been a better gurl."

"Mebbe so," answered Sallie, "mebbe so. High Notabuls, de hour is late. We will close by singin' 'Dy soul be on dy gard.'"   [*The Crisis* 24.1 (May 1922): 17–20]

THE YELLOW TREE

―――∞∞∞―――

by DeReath Byrd Busey

Plum Street is a firm believer in "signs." It is not an ordinary street—not even physically, for it begins at Ludlow, stops on Clark where the trolley passes, picks itself up a half block south on Clark and rushes across the railroad straight uphill to the Fair Grounds. In the early nineties it was the thoroughfare for the "southend," but Jasper Hunley, who bought Lester Snyder's house at public auction, proved to be a "fair" Negro. Then the Exodus! In 1919 Negroes had been in undisputed possession for twenty years.

Like the colors of their faces, the houses vary. There is Jasper Hunley's big brown house with built-in china cabinet and bookcases, hardwood floors and overstuffed furniture. On either side of him in white houses live the Reverend Burns and Policeman Jenkins in a little less state, with portable furniture sparely upholstered, and carpets. Across the street lives Mother Stewart and Reverend Gordon in plain bare-faced houses with scarred pine furniture.

At the close of the January day, Mary Hunley sat watching at her window for Eva Lou's home-coming from the office. Again she recalled vividly the June day she had sat with bed-ridden Mother Stewart while Lucy went to market. She had been sitting at the second story window feasting her eyes upon her hard-won home across the street—a big house in a big yard with flowers and young trees in spring garb. The roses were beginning to open. She had smiled contentedly as her eyes lingered on each bush and shrub but a puzzled frown crossed her brow as she noticed her youngest maple had yellowed. She wondered if worms were at its root.

She turned her eyes to gaze down at the Reverend Mr. Gordon, who pulled his broad brimmed hat further over his eyes, squared himself on his bare board bench in the corner of the yard and sank into a reverie. Unpainted palings enclosed the tiny grassless yard about his unpainted weather-stained house, distinguished from its neighbors only by a bright blue screen door. The Reverend, tall, broad, his brown face growing darker with age, had lived on Plum street ever since he had been called from the janitorship of the Mecklin Building to the pastorate of the St. Luke's Baptist church. He had come to be the oracle of the street.

His dreams were respectfully broken by the greetings of returning marketers. Mary listened idly until Lucy stopped for a conversation. They spoke of the movies and the man there to whom the whole town was flocking for advance information on the future. Lucy thought his amazing replies all a trick. Mr. Gordon concurred.

"Yet," he said, "the Lawd do gives wahnin of things t' come t' them that believes, Miss Lucy. Ah'm not a-tall supstitious but when ah gits a sign ah knows it."

"Yassuh," Lucy nodded.

Las' yeah," he continued, "ah says to Mrs. Reveren' Burns that somebody in that house on the cornuh o' Clark would die 'fore spring come agin. She laffed. In Feb'uary the oldest boy died o' consumption. The new leaves on d' tree in d' front yahd turned yeller. When a tree does that, Miss Lucy, death comes in the fam'ly fore a yeah is gone."

He paused portentously. Mary Hunley leaned unsteadily closer to the window. He spoke solemnly as he pointed his long finger.

"That tree yonde' in Jasper Hunley's yahd turned yeller las' night. This is June, Miss Lucy. The Lawd do give wahnin's to them as believes."

Mary Hunley never knew how she got home. She only knew the Lord had sent her warning. She had always believed in signs—and the few times she had ignored them they had told truth with a vengeance.

When but a girl a circus fortune-teller had drawn a picture of her future husband who should bring money and influence. When Jasper Hunley, carpenter, came a-wooing, his likeness to the picture made the match. She never really loved him, but he was her Fate so they married.

The first year of her marriage she dreamed three nights that they had moved into a big brown house. When Lester Snyder went bankrupt—Jasper bought the house. They moved in and their neighbors moved out. Racial gregariousness was stronger than economy, so houses went for a song. Enough of them came to Jasper to make him potential potentate of Plum street. But Jasper was slow, not given to show, and contented to be hired.

Mary came to realize that he would only bring the money. She must make the influence. She had received diploma and inspiration from one of those southern Missionary Schools for colored youth and she had thoroughly imbibed "money and knowledge will solve the race problem." In ten years she had made Jasper a contractor. She read, she joined "culture clubs," she spoke to embroidery clubs on suffrage when it was a much ridiculed subject, she managed Jasper's business, drew up his contracts, and still found time to keep Eva Lou the best dressed child in Plum street school.

On Plum street as in some other Negro communities color of skin is a determining factor in social position. Mary had cared for that. Jasper was fair and she became fair. From the days of buttermilk and lemon juice to these of scientific "complexion beautifier" she kept watch on herself and Eva Lou. When Eva Lou came back from school in Washington she was whiter and more fashionable than ever; the street wondered, envied, resented.

Gradually Mary grew to feel that the glory of her ambition would come through her daughter. She centered all her love and energies upon Eva Lou—the promise and fulfillment of her life. Occasionally she thought Eva Lou indiscreet in bringing city fashions among small town people, yet she trusted her to have learned on her expensive trips what the great world does. Eva Lou and a few kindred spirits who had ventured far afield—to Chicago and Washington, Boston and New York—had established a clique of those who wore Harper's Bazaar clothes unadulterated, smoked cigarettes in semi-privacy, and played from house to house. Plum street's scandalized gossip joyfully reported by Lucy she ascribed to envy. Lucy, black and buxom, hated Eva Lou's lithe pallor. Mary smiled. Only those in high places are envied.

That June morning as she sat at Mother Stewart's window, she had breathed a sigh of relief. At last, she could relax. Jasper was a thirty-third degree Mason and Eva Lou was engaged to Sergeant Hawkins of Washington.

Then Gordon's prophecy smashed in upon her soul. For one panic stricken hour she was filled with terror. But the qualities that had fought for her family for twenty-five years came to her rescue. She knew the prophecy was of Eva Lou. And she who had believed implicitly and fearfully set out to give that yellow tree the lie. She shuddered with dread but she would not retract.

"If I tell Babe," she reasoned, "wor'y will make her sick. I'll just have to fight it out alone."

January was here now. Never a winter before had Eva Lou been so plagued with good advice and flannels. At first she had listened civilly but unheedingly. Finally she firmly refused both. She wore as many as she needed. As for spats and rubbers—

"Well, I'll say not. Pumps ah the thing this wintuh An' what if I do cough! Ev'rybodys got a cold this weathuh. You have yuhself."

Daily tears did not move her. Fear and a hacking cough were breaking the splendid courage of Mary. Plum street, informed by Lucy, waited the prophecy's fulfillment in sympathetic certainly.

Down the street Mary saw Dr. Dancey's car come slowly rolling. She had heard him say flu and pneumonia were rampant again. Suppose Eva should get either! She could not recover. That yellow tree would win and life come crashing to her feet.

"I'll just have to take care of myself and get rid o' this grip I have—"

Dr. Dancey was stopping at her door and helping Eva Lou alight.

"O Babe!" Mary cried as she dragged her unwilling body to the door and snatched it open. "Babe, are you sick? *Are* y' sick?"

Dr. Dancey tried to quiet her. Eva Lou had an attack of grip—nothing more. A hot bath, hot drink, and long night's sleep would set her right. Mary knew he lied. Grip did not make you look as Babe did. Mary knew for days that the aching limbs and throbbing head she had were signs of grip. When she asked Babe she said she just felt weak.

After Jasper and Eva Lou were asleep, Mary lay in bed and racked her fevered brain for means to thwart the threatening evil. Ah—the sure solution shone clear before her. Her tortured mind felt free and calm. A smile of cunning triumph crept over her face. She eased out of bed, slipped on her flannelette kimono and bedroom slippers. She crept in to look at Babe. She stared, then stooped and kissed the girl's hot lips. Sweet little Babe! Mother would save her. She raised her head and smiled in calm defiance across the sleeping girl at the shrouded figure of the waiting Death Angel near the window. Not yet would it get her!

She smiled with cunning triumph again at the silent figure. Why didn't it move? She knew. It was sorry. It had come in vain.

Down the back stairs and into Jasper's tool room she floated. All pain had left her. Her thinking was clear, and her body light as air. As she bent over the tool box she chuckled. She had never felt to certain of success since the day she married Jasper. Softly she drew out the bright, keen saw. In the kitchen she stopped for salt to sprinkle on the ice. She might slip. She floated around the house and to the youngest maple. Carefully she anointed its ice covered trunk and limbs with salt. Every crackle of the melting ice brought joy to her heart. When she felt a bare wet space on the tree she began sawing—haltingly, unrythmically. Over and over she whispered exultantly.

"The yellow tree lied! The yellow tree lied!"

Once she stopped to wonder why she was not cold, but she was so light and warm it seemed a waste of time. Not even her feet were cold.

The saw was almost through the tree. She raised herself to gloat over its fall.

But it was not a tree. It was that same Angel of Death. The laugh froze in her throat. His face was uncovered and he was smiling. He swayed toward her once—twice. Suppose he should rush over her and get Babe anyway! She laughed now—sweet, carefree. She still would win. She would hold him—if it were forever. The Angel swayed again and fell into her outstretched arms. They held each other.

Early in the morning slow moving Jasper found her there on the ice with the tree over her.

They buried her yesterday. Eva Lou wore white mourning. Lucy, voicing the query of Plum street, asked Reverend Gordon why the yellow tree took the wrong one.

[*The Crisis* 24.6 (October 1922): 253–256]

Aunt Dinah and Dilsey Discuss the Problem

by Mary Church Terrell

"Aunt Dinah, cullud folks is turrible bad, ain't they? An' they don' stop at bein' bad theirselves, but they learns white folks so much devulment, don' they?"

The shine on Dilsey's face made the kitchen range, which had just been polished, hang its head with shame and the expression thereon was a cross between a puzzle and a frown, as she asked Aunt Dinah the questions which she promptly answered herself.

"What make you so down on yo' own color, Dilsey? How come you don' neber see no good in nuthin' 'tall dey does an' says? Youse only twelve yeahs old, an' I 'low dey ain't no little white gal in dis town got more prejuder agin cullud folks den you is. Do you' teacher in de school larn you dat?"

Aunt Dinah's face was full of indignation and the glance she threw upon Dilsey might easily have withered her. But the child winced only for a second and then proceeded to give a reason for the faith that was in her with all the cocksurenes, characteristic of youth.

"'Deed my teacher don' learn me that. She is always tellin' us chilrun how many nice, grand things cullud folks have done and how many rich ones there are. But I tell you, Aunt Dinah, I don' put much 'pendence in what my teacher says, 'cause she's cullud herself. I heard some white folks, what eat at that resterrrant where I worked last summer, say that all cullud folks are ignant, even those that been to school and none of 'em can tell the truf neither. So I don' put much 'pendence in what cullud folks says—not even my teacher."

"But what makes you think dat all cullud folks is so turrible bad, Dilsey, an' how come you say dey larns white folks devulment?"

"Oh, pshaw, Aunt Dinah, you showly ain't askin' me fer serious earnes.' Don' you know that all cullud folks lie and steal and is mos' genully wicked, an' sets white folks a bad example all the time? An' that ain't the wust of it neither. Only yistiddy I heard Miss Nelson say that cullud folds had brought all kinds of turrible diseases from Africa an' give 'em to white folks.

"They brought a nasty, ugly worm here called the 'Hook Worm.' Ev'ry time it bites white folks, it makes 'em lazy an' they hates to work. But they ought to call it the 'Cook Worm,' 'cause when it bites white ladies, it makes 'em hate to cook. Ain't you never noticed, Aunt Dinah, how white ladies hate to cook? It's jes 'cause that old worm that black folks brought from Africa has gone an' bit 'em. An' jes ez that worm makes white ladies hate to cook, when it bites 'em, it makes nice, white gemmen hate to do any kind of work, lessen dey jest has to."

"Hesh, Dilsey, fer de Lawd's sake. Showly no white folks ain't layin' dere laziness on cullud folds. I ain't been to no school, chile, but I knows a heap mo' den dat. Dere wouldn't a been no cullud folks here 'tall, ef white folks hadn' always hated to work. White folks didn' go way over to Africky to steal cullud folks, case dey loved 'em, honey, but dey lef dere wives an' chillun fer weeks at a time an' dahed to brave de briney oshing wif all its sharks an' whales to get black folks an' bring 'em heah to make 'em work, so dey wouldn't have nuthin' to do deysef. Taint no worm black folks brung from Africky made white folds heah lazy, chile. De worm dat bit laziness into white folks, honey, stung em right arter Gawd made Adam and Eve."

When Aunt Dinah finished her speech, she was still shaking her finger at Dilsey, as though she were trying to press her words into the child's brain. Dilsey, a bit frightened at the old woman's intensity, stood at a respectful distance from her and listened to every word, but she was by no means convinced by the arguments she had heard.

"Anyhow, Aunt Dinah," she replied, "if cullud folks didn' raly make white folks lazy by bringin' a worm from Africa with 'em, they are spreadin' tuber-closis among white folks here, so the poor things are dyin' jest like sheep."

"What in de wurl is tuber-closis? Dat showly is some new kin' ub sickness. I aint nebber hearn tell ub tuber-closis befo.' It sounds lak it's a new-fashioned feber, aint it?"

"Fer goodness sake, Aunt Dinah, you showly has heard of tuber-closis. Miss Nelson said that ignant people call tuber-closis—consumption."

The slightest reflection upon her intelligence riled the old woman greatly, and she allowed Dilsey to go no further in her treatise on tuberculosis.

"I don' cyar nuthin' bout what Miss Nelson sed," she replied hotly. "Ole Marse John an' ole Miss, too, always called it cornsumption, and dere wan' nuthin' dey didn' know. Miss Nelson don' b'long to no fambly ub quality no how."

Dilsey could stand some things—indeed she knew better than to take audible exception to anything Aunt Dinah said, and she rarely dissented from any opinion the old woman expressed. But—Miss Nelson was the idol of her young heart and the apple of her big, black eyes. She would defend Miss Nelson to the very last ditch. Backing nearer to the door, she took up the cudgel of defense.

"Miss Nelson knows a heap mo' than some of the old quality folks, anyhow."

Alarmed at her own tone, she simmered down a bit and continued as meekly as her indignation would permit.

"Miss Nelson done graderated from college an' she knows mo' than some men, I tell you, Aunt Dinah. An' Miss Nelson said that cullud folks is spreadin' tuber-closis jes like a farmer sows seed, an' white folks is dyin' jes like sheep."

"Ain't you got no sense a 'tall, Dilsey? 'Pears to me lak de cullud chillun whut goes to school don' know ez much ez us whut didn'. I've hearn ole Marse an'ole Miss say dozens ub times dat all endurin' slav'ry, dere slaves didn' have no cornsumption a 'tall, and dat dere wan' no sich a thing ez cornsumption from one en' ub Afriky to anudder. An' I hearn ole Marse say dat cornsumption is called de 'Great White Plague,' case white folks wuz de fust to interduce it an' give it to cullud folks. An' now, bless de livin' Lawd, white folks is eben tryin' to lay de blame ub dat disease on po cullud folks. Dey don' stop at nuthin to clar dere awn skirts. Dey is jes so 'termined to lay de blame ub all dere sins an' sickness on cullud folks dat dey gone to 'cusin 'em ub interducin'a disease dat dey invented deyself. White folks show do beat de Dutch. Dey got de insurance to say anythin' 'bout cullud folks dey likes. An' arter dey says it nuff times, dey is so 'customed to hearin' it, dey raly b'lieves it is de truf.

"An' Dilsey, lots ub white folk hates cullud folks, case dey b'lieves things 'bout 'em dat aint so. Fer de Lawd sake, chile, don' you pattern arter dem low-lived darkies whut 'peats ebry thing dat white folks says agin dere own race, jes lak it was de truf spoke by de Holy Ghost. Tain't no race in de wurl back bites its own color like po' cullud folks. But—laws a mussey, chile, I mus' be goin' crazy. I ain't got no time to be argifyin' wid you, I got to do my wuk, an' you wash dem dishes jes ez quick ez you kin'."

[*The Crisis* 25.4 (February 1923): 159–160]

TO A WILD ROSE

by Ottie B. Graham

"Ol' man, ol' man, why you looking at me so?" Tha's what you sayin', son. Tha's what you sayin'. Then you start a-singin' that song agin, an' I reckon I'm starin' agin. I'm just a wonderin', son. I'm just a-wonderin'. How is it you can sing them words to a tune an' still be wantin' for material for a tale? "Georgia Rose." An' you jus' sing the words an' they don't say nothin' to you? Well listen to me, young un, an' write what you hear if you want to. Don't laugh none at all if I hum while I tell it, 'cause maybe I'll forget all about you; but write what you hear if you want to.

Thar's just me in my family, an' I never did know the rest. On one o' them slave plantations 'way down in the South I was a boy. Wan't no slave very long, but know all about it jus' a same. 'cause I was proud, they all pestered me with names. The white uns called me red nigger boy an' the black uns called me red pore white. I never 'membered no mother— just the mammies 'round the place, so I fought when I had to and kep' my head high without tryin' to explain what I didn't understan'.

Thar was a little girl 'round the house, a ladies' maid. Never was thar angel more heavenly. Flo they called her, en' they said she was a young demon. An' they called her witch, an' said she was too proud. Said she was lak her mother. They said her mother come down from Oroonoka an' Oroonoka was the prince captured out o' Africa. England took the prince in the early days o' slavery, but I reckon we got some o' his kin. That mean we got some o' his pride, young un, that mean we got some o' his pride. Beautiful as was that creature, Flo, she could ford bein' proud. She was lak a tree—lak a tall, young tree, an' her skin was lak bronze, an' her hair lak coal. If you look in her eyes they was dreamin', an' if you look another time they was spaklin' lak black diamonds. Just made it occur to you how wonderful it is when somethin' can be so wild an' still so fine lak. "My blood is royal! My blood is African!"

Tha's how she used to say. Tha's how her mother taught her. Oroonoka! African pride! Wild blood and fine.

Thar was a fight one day, one day when things was goin' peaceful. They sent down from the big house a great tray of bones from the chicken dinner. Bones for me! Bones for an extra treat! An' the men an' the women an' the girls an' the boys all come round in a ring to get the treat. The Butler stood in the center, grinnin' an' makin' pretty speeches about the dinner an' the guests up at the big house. An' I cried to myself, "Fool—black fool! Fool—black fool!" An' I started wigglin' through the legs in the crowd till I got up to the center. Then I stood up tall as I could and I hissed at the man, an' the words wouldn't stay down my throat, an' I hollered right out, "fool—black fool!" An' 'fore he could do anything atall, I kicked over his tray of gravy an' bones. Bones for me! Bones for an extra treat!

The old fellah caught me an' started awackin', but I was young an' tough an' strong, an' I give him the beatin' of his life. Pretty soon come Flo to me. "Come here, Red-boy," she say, an' she soun' like the mistress talkin', only her voice had more music an' was softer. "Come here, Red-boy," she say, "we have to run away. *I* would not carry the tray out to the quarters, an' *you* kicked it over. We're big enough for floggin' now, an' they been talkin' about it at the big house. They scared to whip me, 'cause they know I'll kill the one that orders it done first chance I get. But they mean to do somethin', an' they mean to get you good, first thing."

We made little bundles and stole off at supper time when everybody was busy, an' we hid way down in the woods. 'bout midnight they came almost on us. We knew they would come a-huntin'. The hounds gave 'em 'way with all their barkin', and the horses gave 'em 'way steppin' on shrubbery. The river was near an' we just stepped in; an' when we see we couldn't move much farther 'less they spot us, we walked waist deep to the falls. Thar we sat hidin' on the rocks, Flo an' me, with the little falls a-tumblin' all over us, an' the search party walkin' up an' down the bank, cussin' an' swearin' that Flo was a witch. Thar we sat under the falls lak two water babies, me a-shiverin', an' that girl a-laughin'. Yes, such laughin'! Right then the song rose in my heart tha's been thar ever since. It's a song I could never sing, but tha's been thar all a same. Son, you never seen nothin' lak that. A wild thing lak a flower—lak a spirit—sittin' in the night on a rock, laughin' through the falls, with a laugh that trickled lak the water. Laughin' through the falls at the hunters.

After while they went away an' the night was still. We got back to the bank to dry, but how we gonna dry when we couldn't make a fire? Then my heart start a-singin' that song again as the light o' the moon come down in splashes on Flo. She begin to dance. Yes suh, dance. An' son, you never seen nothin' lak that. A wild thing lak a flower the wind was a-chasin'—lak a spirit a-chasin' the wind. Dancin' in the woods in the light o' the moon.

"Come Red-boy, you gotta get dry." And we join hands an' whirled round together till we almost drop. Then we eat the food in our little wet bundles—wet bread an' wet meat an' fruit. An' we followed the river all night long, till we come to a little wharf about day break. A Negro overseer hid us away on a small boat. We sailed for two days, an' he kep' us fed in hidin'. When that boat stopped we got on a ferry, an' he give us to a man an' a woman. Free Negroes, he told us, an' left us right quick.

I ain't tellin' you, young un, where it all happen, cause that ain't so particular for your material. We didn't have to hide on the ferry-boat, an' everybody looked at us hard. The lady took Flo an' the man took me, an' we all sat on deck lak human bein's. When we left the ferry we rode in a carriage, an' finally we stopped travellin' for good. Paradise never could a' been sweeter than our new home was for me. They said it was in Pennsylvania. A pretty white house with wild flowers everywhere. An' they went out an' brought back Flo to set 'em off. An' when I'd see her movin' round among 'em, an' I'd ask her if she wasn't happy, she'd throw back that throat o' bronze, an' smile lak all o' Glory. "I knew I'd be free, Red-boy. Tha's what my mother said I'd have to be. My blood is African! My blood is royal!" Then the song come a-singin' itself again in my heart, an' I hush up tight. Wild thing waterin' wild things—wild thing in a garden.

Thar come many things with the years; the passin' o' slavery an' the growin' up o' Flo. Thar wasn't nothin' else much that made any difference. I went to the city to work, but I went to visit Flo an' the people most every fortnight. One time I told her about my love; told her I wanted her to be my wife. An' she threw back her curly head, but she didn't smile her bright smile. She closed her black eyes lak as though she was in pain, an' lak as though the pain come from pity. An' I hurried up an' said I knew I should a-gone to school when they tried to make me, but I could take care o' her all a same. But she said it wasn't that—wasn't that.

"Red-boy," she said, "I couldn't be your wife, 'cause you—you don't know what you are. It wouldn't matter, but *I* am *African* and my blood is *royal!*"

She fell on my shoulder a-weepin', an' I understood. Her mother stamped it in her. Oroonoka! Wild blood and fine.

I went away as far as I could get. I went back to the South, an' I went around the world two years, a-workin' on a ship, an' I saw fine ladies everywhere. I saw fine ladies, son, but I ain't seen none no finer than her. An' the same little song kep' a-singin' itself in my heart. I went to Africa, an' I saw a prince. Pride! Wild blood an' fine.

Thar was somethin' that made me go back where she was. Well, I went an' she was married, an' lived in the city. They told me her husband come from Morocco an' made translations for the gover'ment.

"Morocco," I thought to myself. "That's a man knows what he is. She's keepin' her faith with her mother."

I rented me a cottage. I wanted to wait till she come to visit. They said she'd come. I settled down to wait. Every night I listen to the March wind a-howlin' while I smoked my pipe by the fire. One night I caught sound o' somethin' that wasn't the wind. I went to my door an' I listen, an' I heard a voice 'way off, kind a-moanin' an' kind a-chantin'. I grabbed up my coat an' hat an' a lantern. Thar was a slow, drizzlin' rain, an' I couldn't see so well even with the lantern. I walked through the woods towards where I last heard the voice a-comin'. I walked for a good long time without hearin' anything a-tall. Then thar come all at once, straight ahead o' me, the catchin' o' breath an' sobs, an' I knew it was a woman. I raised my lantern high an' thar was Flo. Her head was back, an' she open an' shut her eyes, an' opened an' shut her eyes, an' sobbed an' caught her breath.

An', spite o' my wonderin' an' bein' almost scaired, that little song started up in me harder than ever. Son, you never seen nothin' lak that. A wild, helpless thing lak a thistle blowed to pieces—a wild, helpless thing lak a spirit chained to earth. Trampin' along in the woods in the night, with the March wind a-blowin' her along. Trampin' along, a-sobbin' out her grief to the night.

Thar wasn't no words for me to say; I just carried her in my arms to the fire in my house. I took off her coat an' her shoes an' put her by the fire, an' I wipe the rain out o' her hair. She was a-clutchin' somethin' in her hand, but I ain't said nothin' yet. I knew she'd tell me. After while she give the thing to me. It was a piece o' silk, very old an' crumpled. A piece of paper was tacked on it. Flo told me to read it. That time when we run away from the plantation she took a little jacket all braided with silk in her bundle. 'Twas the finest jacket her mother used to wear. This dreary night, when Flo come to visit, she start a-ransackin' her old trunk. She come across the jacket and ripped it up; an' she found the paper sewed to the linin'. An' when I read what was on the paper, I knew right off why I found her in the woods, a-running lak mad in the March night wind.

Her mother had a secret, an' she put it down on paper 'cause she couldn't tell it, an' she had to get it out—had to get it out. Thar was tears in every word an' they made tears in my eyes. The blood o' Oroonoka was tainted—tainted by the blood of his captor. The father o' her little girl was not Negro, an' the pride in her bein' was wounded. She was a slave woman, an' she was a beauty, an' she couldn't 'scape her fate. Thar was tears, tears, tears in every word.

I looked at Flo; her head was back. I never did see a time when her head wasn't back. It couldn't droop. She threw it back to laugh, an' she threw it back to sigh. Now she was a-starin' at the fire; an' the fire was a-flarin' at her. Wild thing lak a spirit—lak a scaired bird ready to fly. Oroonoka! Blood o' Oroonoka tainted.

"Red-boy," she said to me, an' she never look away from the fire. "Red-boy, I'm lookin' for a baby. I'm lookin' for a baby in the winter. How am I gonna welcome my baby? Anything else wouldn't matter so much—anything else but white. *That* blood in me—in my baby! Oh, Red-boy, I ain't royal no more!" I couldn't say much, but I took her hand an', I smoothed her hair, an' I led her back to the white house down the way.

Thar in the country she stayed on an' on, an' I stayed on too. Her husband come to see her every week, an' he look proud. He look proud an' happy, an' she look proud an' sad. She wandered in the woods an' she sang a low song. An' she stood at the gate an' she fed the birds. An' she sat on the grass an' she gazed at the sky. Wild thing, still an' proud—wild thing, still an' sad.

An' she stayed on an' on till the winter come. An' the baby come with the winter. She lie in the bed with the baby in her arm. Son, you never see nothin' lak that. A wild thing lak a flowerin' rose—lak a tired spirit. Flower goin', goin'; bud takin' its place. She said somethin' 'fore she died. She look at me an' said it.

"Red-boy, my blood is royal, but it's paled. Don't tell her—, yes tell her. Tell her about the usurpers o' Oroonoka's blood."

But I never did tell her, I went away again an' I stay twenty years. I just find out not long ago where her father went to live. I went to see 'em an' I make myself known. I didn't do so much talkin', so the miss entertain me. She played on the piano and forgot that she was a-playin'. Right then she was her mother. Yes suh, thar sat Flo. Wild thing! Royal blood! Paled, no doubt, but royal all a same.

Then she turned around, an' she wasn't Flo no longer. The brown skin was thar, an' the black, wild eyes, an' the curly dark hair. She spoke soft an' low, but she never did say, "*My* blood is royal! I am *African*." An' she never did say "Red-boy." Her father had never told her about Oroonoka—that was it. An' I come back too late to tell her.

Well it don't matter no how, I thought, so long as she can hold her head lak that, an' long as she can look so beautiful, an' long as she make her mark in the world with that music. But the little song started a singin' itself in my heart, an' I could see the flower agin.

Tha's your material boy. 'Member how I told it to you, a-fishin' on the river edge. 'Member how you was a-singin' "Georgia Rose." Thar's your material. Georgia Rose. Oroonoka. A wild, young thing, an' a little song in an old man's heart.

[*The Crisis* 26.2 (June 1923): 59–63]

DOUBLE TROUBLE

by Jessie Fauset

I

Angélique came walking delicately down Cedarwood Street. You could see by the way she advanced, a way which fell just short of dancing that she was feeling to the utmost the pleasant combination of her youth, the weather and the season. Angélique was seventeen, the day was perfect and the year was at the spring.

Just before Cedarwood crosses Tenth, she stopped, her nice face crinkling with amusement, and untied and retied the ribbon which fastened her trim oxford. Before she had finished this ritual Malory Fordham turned the corner and asked rather sternly if he might not perform the task. "Allow me to tie it for you," he had said with unrelieved formality.

"Sure I'll allow you." Angélique was never shy with those whom she liked. She replaced the subtler arts of the coquette with a forthrightness which might have proved her undoing with another boy. But not with Malory Fordham. Shy, pensive, and enveloped by the aura of malaise which so mysteriously and perpetually hung over his household he found Angélique's manner a source both of attraction and wonder. To him she was a radiant, generous storehouse of light and warmth which constantly renewed his chilled young soul.

"We're in luck this afternoon," said Angélique resuming her happy gait. "Sometimes I have to tie my shoes a dozen times. Once I took one shoe off and shook it and shook it, trying to get rid of make-believe dust; I was glad you didn't turn up just then for I happened to look across the street and there was cousin Laurentine walking, you know that stiff poker-like way she goes—" Angélique bubbling with merriment imitated it—"I know she was disgusted seeing me like 'my son John, one shoe off and one shoe on.'"

"It's a wonder she didn't take you home," said Malory, admiring her.

"Oh, no! Cousin Laurentine wouldn't be seen walking up the street with me! She doesn't like me. Funny isn't it? But you know what's funnier still Malory, not many folks around here do like me. Strange, don't you think, and me living all my life almost in this little place? I never knew what it was to be really liked before you came except for Aunt Sal. I say to myself lots of times: 'Well, anyway, Malory likes me', and then I'm completely happy."

"I'm glad of that," Malory told her, flushing. He was darker than Angélique for his father and mother had both been brown-skinned mulattoes, with a trace of Indian on his mother's side. Angélique's mother, whom she rarely saw, was a mulatto, too, but a very light one, quite yellow, and though she could not remember her father, she had in her mind's eye a concept of him which made him only the least shade darker than her mother. He had to be darker, for Angélique always associated masculinity with a dark complexion. She did not like to see men fairer than their wives.

Malory dwelt for several moments on Angélique's last remark. You could see him patently turning the idea over and over. His high, rather narrow, forehead contracted, his almond, liquid eyes narrowed. His was a type which in any country but America would have commanded immediate and admiring attention. As it was even in Edendale he received many a spontaneous, if surreptitious, glance of approval.

He evolved an answer. "I don't know but you're right, Angélique. I think I must have been home six months before I met you, though I knew your name. I seem to have known your name a long time," he said musing slowly over some evasive idea. "But I never saw you, I guess, until that night when Evie Thompson's mother introduced us at Evie's party. I remember old Mrs. Rossiter seemed so queer. She said—."

"Yes, I know," Angélique interrupted, mimicking, "Oh, Miz Thompson, you didn't ever introduce them! That," concluded the girl with her usual forthrightness, "was because she wanted you to meet her Rosie—such a name Rosie Rossiter!—and have you dance attendance on her all evening!"

Fordham blushed again. "I don't know about that. Anyhow, what I was going to say was if I were you I wouldn't bother if the folks around here didn't like me. They don't like me either."

"No, I don't think they do very much. And yet it's different," Angélique explained puzzling out something. "They may not like you—probably because you've lived away from home so long—but they're willing to go with you. Now I think it's the other way around with me. They sort of like me, lots of the girls at times have liked me a great deal, new girls especially. But they shy away after a time. When Evie Thompson first came to this town she liked me better than she did any one else. I know she did. But after her mother gave that big party she acted different. She has never had me at a real party since and you know she entertains a lot—you're always there. Yet she's forever asking me over to her house when she hasn't company and then she's just as nice and her mother is always too sweet."

They were nearing the corner where they always parted. Cousin Laurentine did not allow
Angélique to have beaux. "Perhaps they're jealous," Malory proposed as a last solution.

The girl's nice, round face clouded. She was not pretty but she bore about her an indefinable atmosphere of niceness, of freshness and innocence. "Jealous of the boys, you mean?" She bit her full red lip. "No it's not that; none of the boys ever treats me very nicely, none of them ever has except you and Asshur Judson."

"Asshur Judson!" Malory echoed in some surprise. "You mean that tall, rough, farmer fellow? I'd have thought he'd be the last fellow in the world to know how to treat a nice girl like you."

"Mmh. He does, he did. You know the boys—most of them"—for the first time Fordham saw her shy, wistful—"when I say they're not nice I mean they are usually too nice. They try to kiss me, put their arms around me. Sometimes when I used to go skating, I'd have horrid things happen. They'd tease the other girls, too, but with me they're different. They act as though it didn't matter how they treated me. Maybe it's because my father's dead."

"Perhaps," Malory acquiesced doubtfully, but he was completely bewildered. "And you say Asshur Judson was polite?"

"I'd forgotten Asshur. You didn't know him well, I think; he came while you were still in Philadelphia and he went away right after you came back. We'd been skating one day. I wasn't with anyone, just down there in the crowd, and I struck off all alone. Bye and bye who should come racing after me but Asshur. I looked back and saw him and went on harder than ever. Of course he caught up to me, and when he did he took me right in his arms and held me tight. I struggled and fought so that I know he understood I didn't like it, so he let me go. And then that hateful Harry Robbins came up and said: 'Don't you mind her, Jud, she's just pretending, she'll come around!'" Her voice shook with the shame of it.

"And then?" Malory prompted her fiercely.

"I heard Judson say just as mad, 'What the deuce you talking about, Robbins?'"

Malory failed to see any extraordinary exhibition of politeness in that.

"Oh, but afterwards! You know my Cousin Laurentine doesn't allow me to have company. Of course he didn't know that, and that night he came to the house. Cousin Laurentine let him in and I heard her say: 'Yes, Angélique is in but she doesn't have callers.' And he answered: 'But I must see her, Miss Fletcher, I must explain something.' His voice sounded all funny and different. So I came running down stairs and asked him what he wanted.

"It was all so queer, Malory. He came over to me past Cousin Laurentine standing at the door like a dragon and he took both my hands, sort of frightened me. He said: 'You kid, you decent little kid! Treat 'em all like you treated me this afternoon, and try to forgive me. If you see me a thousand times you'll never have to complain of me again.' And he went."

"Funny," was Malory's comment. "Didn't he say anything more?"

"No, just went and I've got to go. Got to memorize a lot of old Shakespeare for tomorrow. Silly stuff from Macbeth. 'Double, double, toil and trouble.' 'Bye Malory."

"Good-bye," he echoed, turning in the direction of his home where his mother and his three plain older sisters awaited him.

On his way he captured the idea which had earlier eluded him. He remembered speaking once, before he had met her, of Angélique Murray to his odd subdued household and of receiving a momentary impression of shock, of horror even, passing over his mother's face. He looked at his sisters and received the same impression. He looked at all four women again and saw—nothing—just nothing, utter blankness, out of which came the voice of Gracie, his hostile middle sister. "Good heavens, Malory! Don't tell me that you know that Angélique Murray. I won't have you meeting her. She is ordinary, her whole family is the last thing in ordinariness. Now mind if you meet her, you let her alone."

At the time he had acquiesced, deeming this one of the thousand queer phases of his household with which he was striving so hard to become reacquainted. He had been a very little boy when he had been taken so hurriedly to live in Philadelphia, but his memory had painted them all so different.

In spite of his sister's warning Angélique's brightness when he met her, her frankness, her merriment proved too much for him. She was like an unfamiliar but perfectly recognizable part of himself. Pretty soon he was fathoms deep in love. But because he was a boy of practically no ingenuities but mechanical ones he could hit on nothing better than walking home from school with her. She was the one picture in the daily book of his life and having seen her he retired home each day like Browning's lovers to think up a scheme which would enable him sometime to tear it out for himself.

Angélique, hastening on flying feet, hoped that Cousin Laurentine would be out when she reached home. She could manage Laurentine's mother, Aunt Sal, even when she was as late as she was today. But before she entered the house she realized that for tonight at least she would be free from her cousin's hateful and scornful espionage. For peeping through the window which gave from the front room on to the porch she was able to make out against the soft inner gloom the cameo-like features of the Misses Courtney, the two young white women who came so often to see Aunt Sal and Laurentine. They were ladies of indubitable breeding and refinement, but for all their culture and elegance they could not eclipse Laurentine whose eyes shone as serene, whose forehead rose as smooth and classical as did their own. The only difference lay in their coloring. The Misses Courtney's skin shone as white as alabaster; their eyes lay, blue cornflowers, in that lake of dazzling purity. But Laurentine was crimson and gold like the flesh of the mango, her eyes were dark emeralds. Her proud head glowed like an amber carving rising from the green perfection of her dress. She was a replica of the Courtney sisters startlingly vivified. Angélique, on her way to the kitchen poising on noiseless feet in the outside hall, experienced anew her thrill at the shocking resemblance between the two white women and the colored one; a resemblance which missed completely the contribution of white Mrs. Courtney and black Aunt Sal, and took into account only the remarkable beauty of Ralph Courtney, the father of all three of these women.

Aunt Sal in the background of the picture was studying with her customary unwavering glance the three striking figures. The Misses Courtney had travelled in Europe, they spoke French fluently. But Laurentine had travelled in the West Indies and spoke Spanish. When the time came for the Misses Courtney to go, they would kiss Laurentine lightly on both cheeks, they would murmur: "Good-bye, Sister," and would trail off leaving behind them the unmistakable aura of their loyal, persistent, melancholic determination to atone for their father's ancient wrong. And Laurentine, beautiful, saffron creature, would rise and gaze after them, enveloped in a somber evanescent triumph.

But afterwards!

Up in her room Angélique envisaged the reaction which inevitably befell her cousin after the departure of these visitors. For the next three weeks Laurentine would be more than ever hateful, proud, jealous, scornful, intractable. The older woman, the young girl shrewdly guessed, was jealous of her; jealous of her unblemished parentage, of her right to race pride, of her very youth, though her own age could not be more than twenty-eight. "Poor Cousin Laurentine," the child thought, "as though she could help her father's being white. Anything was liable to happen in those old slavery times. I must try to be nicer to her."

When later she opened the door to her cousin's tap her determination was put to a severe test, for Laurentine was in one of her nastiest moods. "Here is another one of those letters," she said bitingly, "from that young ruffian who pushed his way past me that night. If I had my way I'd burn up every one of them. I can't think how you manage to attract such associates. It will be the best thing in the world for all of us when your mother sends for you."

Angélique took Asshur's letter somewhat sullenly, though she knew the feeling which her cousin's outburst concealed. In that household of three women this young girl was the only one who could be said to receive mail. Even hers was, until very lately, almost negligible—a note or two from a proudly travelling schoolmate, some directions for making candy from Evie Thompson or from the girl who at that moment was espousing her inexplicable cause, a card or so from a boy and now this constant stream of letters from Asshur Judson. As she opened these last or sat down to answer them in the shaded green glow of the dining-room, she had seen Cousin Laurentine's face pale with envy under the saffron satin of her skin.

Laurentine received letters and cards from the Misses Courtney when they were abroad— a few bills—she made rather a practice of having charge accounts—and an occasional note from the white summer transient expressing the writer's pleasure with "that last dress you made me." Once the young divinity student who, while the pastor was on his vacation, took over the services of the African Methodist Episcopal Church, sent her a post card from Niagara Falls. Laurentine exhibited a strange negligence with regard to this card; it was always to be found in the litter of the sewing-table. "Oh," she would say casually to the customer whom she was fitting, "that's a card from Mr. Deaver who substituted here last summer. Yes, he does seem to be a fine young man."

Angélique did not at once open Asshur's letter. She had too many lessons to get. Besides she knew what it would contain, his constant and unvarying injunction "to be good, to be decent" coupled with an account of his latest success in some branch of scientific agriculture; he was an enthusiastic farmer. She liked to hear from him, but she wished his interests were broader. Laying the letter aside unregretfully she fell to memorizing the witches' speech in Macbeth and then in her little English Handbook under the chapter on "The Drama—Greek Tragedy," she made a brief but interested foray among the peculiarities of the ancient stage. Reading of Greek masks, buskins and "unities" she forgot all about Asshur's letter until as usual Aunt Sal put her fine dark head in the door and told her in mild but unanswerable tones that it was "most nigh bedtime."

She jumped up then and began to undress. But first she read the letter. Just as she thought it began like all his former letters and would probably end the same. No, here was something different. Asshur had written:

"My father says I'm making great headway, and so does Mr. Ellis, the man on whose farm I'm experimenting. Next year I'll be twenty-one and father's going to let me work a small farm he owns right up here in northern New Jersey. But first I'm coming for you. Only you must keep good and straight like you were when I first met you. You darn spunky little kid. Mind, you be good, you be decent. I'm sure coming for you."

It was a queer love-letter. "So you'll come for me," said Angélique to her image in the glass. She shook out her short, black, rather wiry hair till it misted like a cloud about her childishly round face. "How do you know I'll go with you? I may find someone I like ten times better." Dimpling and smiling she imitated Malory's formality: "May I tie your shoe for you?"

All night long she dreamed she was chasing Malory Fordham. Was it a game? If so why did he so doggedly elude her? Then when, laughing, she had overtaken him, why did he turn on her with round gaping mouth and horrid staring eyes that transformed him into a Greek tragic mask? Through open, livid lips came whistling strange words, terrible phrases whose import at first she could not grasp. When she did she threw her arm across her face with a fearful cry and fell back convulsed and shuddering into the arms of a dark, muffled figure whose features she fought vainly to discover.

II

Edendale, like many another Jersey town, as well as all Gaul, was divided into three parts. In one section, the prettiest from a natural point of view, lived Italians, Polacks and Hungarians who had drifted in as laborers. In another section, elegant and cultivated, dwelt a wealthy and leisure class of whites, men of affairs, commuters, having big business interests in Philadelphia, Trenton, Newark and even New York. Occupying the traditional middle ground were Jews, small tradesmen, country lawyers and a large group of colored people ranging in profession from Phil Baltimore, successful ash-contractor to the equally successful physician, Dr. Thompson. This last group was rather closely connected with the wealthy white group, having in far preceding generations, dwelt with them as slaves or more recently as houseservants. Sometimes as in the case of Aunt Sal Fletcher and the Courtneys, who following the Civil War, had drifted into Jersey from Delaware, they had served in both capacities.

Malory and Angélique came to know the foreign quarters well. Here on the old Hopewell Road beginning nowhere and going nowhither they were surest of escaping the eye of a too vigilant colored townsman as well as that of the occasional white customer for whom the girl's cousin sewed. Malory was in no danger from a possibility like this last for the Fordhams on the maternal side had been small but independent householders for nearly a century. Even now Mrs. Fordham lived on a small income which came partly from her father's legacy, partly from the sale of produce from a really good truck-farm. Her husband had showed a tendency to dissipate this income but he had died before he had crippled it too sorely. Malory was determined to have more money when he grew older, money which he would obtain by his own methods. He never meant to ask his family for anything. The thought of a possible controversy with the invincible Gracie turned him sick.

He would be an engineer, how or where he did not know. But there would be plenty of money for him and Angélique. Already all his dreams included Angélique. He had not told her but he loved her fervently with an ardor excelling ordinary passion, for his included gratitude, a rapt consciousness of the miracle which daily one wrought for him in the business of living. She was so vivid, so joyous, so generous, so much what he would wish to be that almost it was as though she were his very self. Every day he warmed his hands at that fire which she alone could create for him.

He it was who fought so keenly against the clandestine nature of their meetings. Not so Angélique. This child so soon, so tragically to be transformed into a woman, was still a romantic, dreaming girl. Half the joy of this new experience lay in its secrecy. This was fun, great fun, to run counter to imperious, unhappy Laurentine, to know that while her cousin endured the condescending visit of the son of the ash-contractor in the hope that some day, somehow she might receive the son of the colored physician, she herself was the eagerly and respectfully chosen of the son of the first colored family in the county. This was nectar and ambrosia, their taste enhanced by secrecy.

But Malory hated it. He had not told his family about the girl because clearly for some fool reason they were prejudiced against her, and as for Angélique's family—no males allowed. Hence this impasse. But he wanted like many another fond lover to acquaint others with his treasure, to show off not only this unparalleled gem, but himself too. For in her presence he himself shone, he became witty, his shyness vanished. The Methodist Sunday School picnic was to be held the first week in June. His sisters never went; proud Laurentine would not think of attending. He told Angélique that he would take her.

"Wonderful!" she breathed. She had a white dress with red ribbons.

They met on that memorable day, rather late. Laurentine could not keep Angélique from attending the picnic, but she could make her late; she could make her feel the exquisite torture which envelops a young girl who has to enter alone and unattended the presence of a crowd of watchful acquaintances. Angélique inwardly unperturbed,—she knew Malory would wait for her forever,—outwardly greatly chafing, enjoyed her cousin's barely concealed satisfaction at her pretended discomfiture. With a blithe indifference she went from task to task, from chore to chore. "Greek tragedy," she whispered gaily into the ear of Marcus, an adored black kitten.

Malory did not mind her lateness. Indeed he was glad of it. So much the more conspicuous their entrance to the grounds. As it chanced, practically the whole party was in or around the large pavilion grouped there to receive instructions from Mrs. Evie Thompson who had charge of the picnic. A great church-worker, Mrs. Evie. When the two arrived the place was in an uproar, Mrs. Evie, balanced perilously on a stool tried to out talk the noise. Presently she realized that her voice was unnecessarily loud, the sea of black, yellow, and of white faces had ebbed into quiet but not because of her. Malory just outside the wide entrance, in the act of helping Angélique up the rustic steps caught that same fleeting shadow of horror and dismay, that shadow which he had marked on the faces of his household, rippling like a wave over the faces of the crowd, touching for a second Mrs. Thompson's face and vanishing. Appalled, bewildered, he stood still.

Mrs. Thompson rushed to them. "You just happened to meet Angélique, Malory? You— you didn't bring her?" Her voice was low but anxious.

"Of course I brought her," he replied testily. What possessed these staring people? "Why shouldn't I bring her?"

"Why not indeed?" soothed Mrs. Thompson. She herself came from a "best family" in some nearby big city. "It's such luck that's all. I was wishing for Angélique. She's such a help at a time like this, so skilful. I want her to help me cut sandwiches."

Malory, rather sulkily accepting this, allowed his guest to be spirited away to exercise this skill. The crowd, drawing a vast, multi-throated breath dispersed. Mrs. Thompson was anything but skilful herself. In the course of the afternoon she cut her assistant's hand. "I don't anticipate any infection," she remarked, peering at the small wound with an oddly unrepentant air, "but you'd better come home with me and let Doctor dress it. Sorry I can't invite you too Malory, but there's hardly room the buggy for four. Evie and I are both fat."

Malory passed a night of angry sleeplessness. "I don't know what to think of these people," he told Angélique when they met the next day. "Do you know what I want you to do? You come home with me now and meet my mother and sisters. When they get to know you, they'll like you too and I know they can make these others step around." It was the first time he had betrayed any consciousness of the Fordham social standing.

Angélique, nothing loth, agreed with him. She too had thought Mrs. Thompson extraordinary the day before, but she had not seen as Malory had that strange shadowy expression of horror. And in any case would have had no former memory to emphasize it.

The two moved joyously up the tree-lined street, Malory experiencing his usual happy reaction to Angélique's buoyancy. Nothing would ever completely destroy her gay equanimity he thought, feeling his troubled young spirit relax. There was no one like her he knew. His people, even Gracie, must love her. He was living at this time in the last years of the nineties and so was given to much reading of Tennyson. Angélique made him think of the Miller's daughter, who had "grown so dear, so dear." What of life and youth and cheerfulness would she not introduce into his drab household, musty with old memories, inexplicably tainted with the dessication of some ancient imperishable grief!

At the corner of the street he took her arm. They would march into the house bravely and he would say, "Mother this is Angélique whom I love. I want you to love her too; you will when you know her." He perceived as he opened the gate that Angélique was nervous, frightened. Timidity was in her such an unusual thing that he felt a new wave of tenderness rising within him. On the porch just before he touched the knob of the screen door he laid his hand on hers.

"Don't be frightened," he murmured.

"Look," she returned faintly.

He spun about and saw pressed against the window-pane a face, the small, brown face of his sister Gracie. In the background above her shoulder hovered the head of the oldest girl Reba, her body so completely hidden behind Gracie's that for a second, it seemed to him fantastically, her head swung suspended in space. But only for a second did he think this, so immediately was his attention drawn, riveted to the look of horror, of hatred, of pity which was frozen, seared on the faces of his sisters.

"For God's sake, what is it?" he cried.

Gracie's hands made a slight outward movement toward Angélique, a warding off motion of faintness and disgust such as one might make involuntarily towards a snake.

"I'm going in; come Angélique," the boy said in exasperation. "Has the whole world gone crazy?"

Before he could open the door Reba appeared, that expression still on her face, like a fine veil blurring out her features. Would it remain there forever he wondered.

"You can't bring her in Malory, you mustn't."

"Why mustn't I? What are you talking about?" Strange oaths rose to his lips. "What's the matter with her?" He started to pull the door from his sister's grasp when Gracie came, pushed the door open and stepped out on the porch beside him.

"Oh Malory you must send her away! Come in and I'll tell you." She burst into tears.

Gracie his tyrant, his arch-enemy weeping! That startled him far more than that inexplicable look. The foundations of the world were tottering. He turned to his trembling companion. "Go home, Angel," he bade her tenderly. "Meet me tomorrow and we'll fix all this up." He watched her waver down the porch-steps then turned to his sisters:

"Now girls?"

Together they got him into the house and told him....

III

Angélique said to herself, "I'll ask Aunt Sal,—Cousin Laurentine,—but what could they know about it? No I'll wait for Malory. Can I have the leprosy I wonder?" She went home, stripped and peered a long time in the mirror at her delicate, yellow body.

Next afternoon near the corner of Cedarwood and Tenth she untied and retied her shoes twenty times. Malory did not come. She shook out bushels of imaginary dust. He had not come, was never coming.

At the end of an hour she went to the corner and peered down Tenth Street. Yes—no—yes it was he coming slowly, slowly down the steps of the Boys' High School. Perhaps he was sick; when he saw her, he would be better.... He did not look in her direction; without so much as turning his head he came down the steps and started due west. Cedarwood Street lay east.

Without a second's hesitation she followed him. He was turning now out of Tenth north on Wheaton Avenue. After all you could go this way to the old Hopewell Road. Perhaps he had meant for her to meet him there. A block behind him, she saw him turn from Wheaton into the narrow footpath that later broadened into Hopewell Road. Yes, that was what he meant. She began to run then feeling something vaguely familiar about the act. On Hopewell Road she gained on him, called his name, "Malory, oh Malory." He turned around an instant, shading his eyes from the golden June sunlight to make sure and spinning back began to run, almost to leap, away from her.

Bewildered, horrified, she plodded behind, leaving little clouds of white dust spiraling up after her footsteps. As she ran she realized that he was fleeing from her in earnest; this was no game, no lover's playfulness.

He tripped over a tree-root, fell, reeled to his feet and, breathless, found her upon him. She knew that this was her dream but even so she was unprepared for the face he turned upon her, a face with horrid, staring eyes, with awful gaping lips, the face of a Greek tragic mask!

She came close to him. "Malory," she besought pitifully. Her hand moved out to touch his arm.

"Don't come near me!" His breath came whistling from his ghastly lips. "Don't touch me!" He broke into terrible weeping. "You're my sister,—my sister!" He raised tragic arms to the careless sky. "Oh God how could you! I loved her, I wanted to marry her,—and she's my sister!"

* * *

To proud Laurentine sitting in haughty dejection in the littered sewing-room, fingering a dog-eared postcard from Niagara Falls came the not unwelcome vision of her stricken cousin swaying, stumbling toward her.

"Laurentine, tell me! I saw Malory, Malory Fordham; he says,—he says I'm his sister. How can that be? Oh Laurentine be kind to me, tell me it isn't true!" She would have thrown herself about the older woman's neck.

Inflexible arms held her off, pushed her down. "So you've found it out have you? You sailing about me with your pitying ways and your highty-tighty manner. Sorry for Cousin Laurentine,—weren't you?—because her father was white and her mother wasn't married to him. But my mother couldn't help it. She had been a slave until she became a woman and she carried a slave's traditions into freedom.

"But her sister, your mother," the low, hating voice went on, "whom my mother had shielded and guarded, to whom she held up herself and me—me—" she struck her proud breast—"as horrible examples,—your mother betrayed Mrs. Fordham, a woman of her own race who had been kind to her, and ran away with her husband." She spurned the grovelling girl with a disdainful foot. "Stop snivelling. Did you ever see me cry? No and you never will."

Angélique asked irrelevantly: "Why do you hate me so? I should think you'd pity me."

Her cousin fingered the postcard. "Look at me." She rose in her trailing red dress. "Young, beautiful, educated,—and nobody wants me, nobody who is anybody will have me. The ash-contractor's son offers,—not asks,—to marry me. Mr. Deaver," she looked long at the postcard, "liked me, wrote me,—once,—"

"Why did he stop?" Angélique asked in all innocence.

Laurentine flashed on her. "Because of you. You little fool, because of you! Must I say it again? Because my mother was the victim of slavery. People looked at me when I was a little girl; they used to say: 'Her mother couldn't help it, and she is beautiful.' They would have forgotten all about it. Oh why did your mother have to bring you home to us! Now they see you and they say: 'What! And her mother too! A colored man this time. Broke up a home. No excuse for that. Bad blood there. Best leave them alone.'"

She looked at Angélique with a furious, mounting hatred. "Well you'll know all about it too. Wait a few years longer. You'll never be as beautiful as I, but you'll be pretty. And you'll sit and watch the years go by, and dread to look in your mirror for fear of what you'll find there. And at night you'll curse God,—but pshaw you won't,—" she broke off scornfully, "you'll only cry—"

Angélique crept up to her room to contemplate a future like Laurentine's.

Hours later Aunt Sal come in, her inscrutable dark face showing a blurred patch against the grey of the room. In her hand something gleamed whitely.

"Thought you might want your letter," she said in her emotionless, husky voice.

Her letter, her letter from Asshur! Her letter that would reiterate: "Be a good kid and I'll come for you...."

She seized it and fell half-fainting in the old woman's arms. "Oh Asshur I'll be good, I'll be good! Oh Aunt Sal, help me, keep me...."

[*The Crisis* 26.4 (August 1923): 155–159; 26.5 (September 1923): 205–209]

BLUE ALOES: A STORY

—⚬∞⚬—

by Ottie B. Graham

Who can account for an impulse? Surely not a youth of twenty. Who would account on a day whose skies were blue and whose streams were clearest silver? Oh, not a youth of twenty.

Then Joseph was answering the call that only the young can know when he threw off shoes and top clothes and leaped into the silver of deep, smooth Little River. It flowed in front of Aloe House. Threw off shoes and stockings, and leaping, called to Melrose, living in Aloe House.

"Melrose!" he called, flashing through space and flipping into the water. Across to the opposite bank he swam, speeding like an islander. And climbing up to land by roots and hanging bushes, forth he stepped—youth on a sunny morning! Blessed son of the gods, singing impromptus to a maiden. "Melrose!" And the morning breeze carried the music over the water. Soon the boy followed. He had seen the slender form come out from the little house. But though he swam swiftly and straight, the girl was not there to greet him. He was disappointed but not surprised. Granna had interfered. He knew. Since she could not swim with him, at least they could walk together. So he threw himself flat upon the grass along the bank, stretching out full length to dry.

Little time passed before he heard a dragging footstep. For a moment he thought he was dreaming a dream that was bad. He was supposed to move away upon the approach of the dragging footstep, but he would not move today. He would remain and sing to Melrose if the old woman cursed him doubly. He would—ah, he could not move now if he wanted to. She stood over him.

"Lazy young dog!" she started, and there came such a torrent of maledictions as Joseph had never before heard. At first he had laughed at her. It amused him to hear an old hag going into fury because his young limbs, uncovered, breathed the sun; because he persisted in his love for the girl; because she loved him in return. At first it was funny but soon it ceased to amuse, and he joined in her tirade. Finally Granna dragged away, and she scowled and fussed. Fussed like something from the lower regions. Joseph hurried into his clothes and followed behind her, sullen and determined. Ach! she turned upon him.

"I tell yu, ef I puts a sho nuf curse on yu, yu won't forgit it soon. Runnin' aroun' heah half naked, an' callin' all ovah the place fo that gal, an' she ready an' fixin' to come out in the river with yu lak a young fool. Jus' come on an' take her out ef yu think yu kin. I'll fix yu!"

And the boy put in his part. "Oh, you think I'm afraid of your black magic, you old witch! But I'm not, and I'll teach Melrose not to be. And she'll stop making your aloes cures and the people will stop coming to bring you money for nothing. You old witch, you old witch! You old wi-hitch! Here's what I think of your aloes and your house full of aloes branches. *Now* conjure me!" And his laugh was so wild and shrill with anger it dulled the clanging of the falling tubs he had kicked over in his rage. They held the drippings of aloes.

With the dying away of the furor came a soft crying, then a young, tremulous voice. "Jo!" It wailed softly. "Jo! You don't know what you have done. Jo!" Around the corner of the little house crept the girl, Melrose, frightened and ready to flee. The old woman had disappeared into the house. Soon, however, she returned. Even before the girl could reach her boy.

"Come on, Melrose, come on," called Joseph. The girl had started back. "Come on, she won't hurt you." Granna stopped and glared upon them while the boy talked that she might hear.

"She hates you because you're more beautiful than she would have you; because you are younger than she would have you. She hates you because you love me and her aloes can't stop you," And he laughed long and lustily. Granna looked on.

Melrose had reached his side. "Hush, Jo, you've done enough. That was the last of the drippings from the blue leaves, and they came from far away. Someone brought them to her on a boat from an island. Listen!"

The woman, already bent from age, was bending farther over, and mumbling, mumbling, mumbling. The violet blue substance, part liquid, part resin, flowed past her in a slow stream. A slow stream from its tumbled tubs. And she, running with it, then running back, mumbled, mumbled, mumbled. The girl and her boy stood looking, the girl, frankly distressed, the boy alarmed in spite of himself.

"It's the curse!" Melrose trembled. Joseph held her hand. They were two children.

"How can it hurt? The stuff is no more than a medicine."

"Oh, but,—"

"It's her foolishness. I'll take you away from the South and its superstitions. Look at her now, the old witch." Granna was on her knees now, splashing handfuls of the substance.

Melrose turned where she stood. "I'll have to go away now, Jo. I can't go back. No! You can't go back either." Joseph had not turned where he stood. Instead, he moved toward the woman. The blue stuff flowed between them.

"Don't cross it, Jo. You can never get rid of the curse if you cross her stream!" And this served only to make him dare. He strode to the stream and jumped across.

"I'm going to take Melrose away!" he yelled. He was quite close upon Granna, but he hollered as though she had been deaf. Perhaps he did not know it. He trembled. "Melrose living under the roof with you. Lord, what a crime! I'll take her from you, old Ashface, out here in the woods. I'll take her from the South and superstition!"

Granna had been kneeling. Now she stood. But she did not measure to the height of the stripling before her. She squinted and blinked up at him, and her wrinkled black face *was* ashen with the heat of temper. She was wont to sing hymns as she brewed aloes, but she seldom talked. This late mad outburst had taken her strength, therefore, and she quivered as she stood. An aloe string hung about her neck. The Negroes of Africa's west coast wore such cords, but that gave no clue to Granna. None knew of her origin. They only knew of the pretty child she had raised. She looked up at Joseph, and he down at her. From a short distance came the soft crying of the young and tremulous voice.

"Takin' my gal, is yu? Well, tell uh don' come back when yu turn to anothuh. Ungrateful yaller devil!" A fresh thunder clap. They gyrated and all but spat in each other's faces. Youth is wild, and sometimes old age too.

"Oh, you say that again, old woman! You judge me by yourself, no doubt. I'll rid you of your hateful self!"

"Hi! You dar to tuch me." She was witch now, if ever. Her withered old hand touched the cord about her neck, and she snatched it off and dashed it in the face of Joseph. "Yu know what hit yu? Blue aloes!" And she screamed out a grating haw-haw.

Melrose ran to Joseph. For a moment he thought he was blinded. He went, by her hand, to the river, and together they bathed the bruised eyes. Then they started off to the future, empty handed, looking not behind them. Aloe House was still. And the silence deafened, so that neither heard the other catching little breaths at the outset of their journey.

Neither heard. The sun now was too hot, the day was now too dry. Melrose coughed. Joseph spoke.

"Her medicines don't cure your cough."

"I got the cough from her."

"Huh!"

"All medicines can't cure a cough." They turned from the road and sat under a tree. Town was still far off.

"What of magic, can it cure a cough?" They looked at each other.

"There isn't any magic, Jo. I'm not afraid of magic."

"You were afraid back there."

"But I've come away for good. Not afraid now." They resumed their walking—new pilgrims on the search for happiness.

"I'll take you away from the South," said the youth. Brave youth.

"Can't take me from the South, Jo. I have to stay in the South with this cough. It will go, but I'll have to stay here. Jo, where are we going?"

"Up on the hill to my father's house. It is all that I have, my father's house. When I came back last year I closed it. I paddled down Little River and found you. Now I shall open it again. We'll stay there until the cough goes."

"That will be a long time."

They neared the town. Silence had flown, but a town does not exist without its noises. This was called a pretty town, but the girl thought it drab and choky. The country behind was sweet. They entered the town. People stared or nodded, or smiled or shook their heads. In a very short time the whole town knew that Joseph was opening the old home for the girl from Aloe House. One street led up a hill overlooking its section of the town. Up the hill they went, Melrose and Joseph, looking back not once.

The house stood silent like the country along the road; the grounds were silent like the house. The girl felt thankful. They would be away from the town. The afternoon was waning. In its soft, drowsy heat Joseph went down the hill again. Melrose waited under a tree. The trees up here were gracious; their shade was cooling. How could men live in towns—narrow, stuffy places? Where had Jo lived down there? He had lived with the parson. The parson—the parson—oh! There was another thing about towns. They required parsons with love. Well, that would not matter, only it had not occurred to her before this. Love—parsons—what places were towns! Towns—country—country—Granna! But there was no magic. Aloes—just a medicine—no magic. "Till he turned to another—turned to another." But he was coming back already, and someone else was with him. The parson. She knew the parson. He had visited her when she first got the cough. Granna had been very rude. There were others coming too. Was the town moving up to kill the quiet of the hill? She sat still, rising not until Joseph spoke.

"You know who this is, Melrose. We let the others come. They can take back good news now. They'll take back one kind or another, you know." So they were married up on the hill. The crowd, curious, around them. The house, yet unopened. The "guests" carried their news back to the town.

At the parson's house they were feasted, Melrose and Joseph. The parson was kind; so was his wife. The house on the hill was opened and left to the night, that the stale air and the moths might drain out. At the parson's house they were feasted, and taught to look brightly on the future.

Youth must never fear the future. These were merely words of advice; there was no fear here. With morning came work for Joseph and gifts from neighbors for the girl. Southerners are good-hearted.

Time brought only happiness. Joseph taught his young wife all he had learned North in schools. He would take her there some day, to the North. Then the girl would cough and he knew she could not go. But it was happiness, this living on the hill where the town was out of sight, and the trees whispered, and the yellow-brown creature moved about singing with the low, tremulous voice. Children from the town came up. He taught her and she taught them. Children from the town—all kinds. Little pale things with scraggly locks, little pale things with heavy locks. Brown little things with silken curls, brown little things with kinky curls. They and Melrose. Melrose and they.

Time landed one day a strange cargo. Happiness a bit discolored, came with the bringing of a plant. With a plant. A gardener, an old man working about the town, brought it. A beautiful thing, and rare. Melrose thanked the man with slight strain in her voice. As soon as he had gone she dashed it on the ground, stamping it again and again, until it was bruised and broken. Bruised and broken beyond recovery. She knew most of the species of the aloe. This was akin to the blue. That Joseph might not know of it, she buried the fragments under a great flower jar. But fear and sadness descended upon her. She had brushed aside this silliness long, long ago, and now it had seized her again. Joseph said the mind could be better controlled. This she told herself many times, saying, "It is absurd to fear nothing. It is absurd!" But her cough grew worse and she trembled about her duties. She walked down the hill to meet Joseph.

"Jo, could you ever love anyone else?" They were coming to the house.

"Could anyone else be you, honey?" And he kissed her lightly as they passed the great flower jar. She shook just a little and coughed a lot. That night she sobbed aloud in her sleep.

Melrose grew paler. She felt that the cough was worse. On warm evenings Joseph paddled a canoe. Went drifting down Little River. Joseph was not afraid of things, yet he never took the left branch of the river. The left branch of Little River flowed past Aloe House. It had been several years now since he took Melrose away, and neither of them mentioned it. Whether it still was there he did not know, nor did he go to see. So the right branch of the river was his, and he nosed round the bend automatically. On warm evenings Melrose went with him. Now she stayed home on the hill. She felt that her cough was worse. Now Joseph paddled alone.

On the water he hummed little melodies. He wished Melrose could play the piano better. Then he wished she were here on the water. Here singing with him on the water. No voice sang like hers. In the morning he would send another doctor. She must not be pale. He splashed the water and drifted. The night. Melrose would love the night out here. They had never come this far.

There came on the still air music. When had he heard such music! Music from a piano. He paddled to come nearer to it. Looking around, he saw a huge mansion on a hill. From this mansion came the music. Came the tones of silver. Light streamed from a topmost window. To a landing he guided the tiny boat and listened. The music stopped and directly the light went out. Surprised, Joseph started back, paddling hard all the way. Melrose stood at the window when he reached the house. He told her of the night. Told her of the music. Told her how he had missed her.

Next night he went again. Went in the little boat down Little River. Down the right branch, drifting and paddling till he heard the silver melody. Music in the night from a mansion on a hill. Melrose would like it so. If she would come but once. Come but once to hear. He listened at the landing. The music ceased and the light went out. Immediately Joseph moved the canoe. At home on his hill Melrose waited. Patiently stood at the window. Again he told her of the night. Of the music.

Melrose next day was weary. She longed for the night to come. She would go this night in the canoe. Please Joseph and go on the river. But the day burned by. It was hot. When evening came she was tired. At the meal she smiled, but the smile was a dismal effort. Joseph set out earlier. Melrose was weary, the air was sultry. He must get out in the boat.

On the river it was cooler. He drifted all the way. And even at the mansion night had not yet come. No music sounded except the whirring of the wind through the trees. At the landing Joseph looked up. At the window, away up high, there stood a woman. The house below her was closed. Joseph started and stared. A paddle slipped from his hand into the river, and he uttered a short cry. "Melrose!" The house was near the river. He could see clearly, but he could not believe.

The woman stepped upon a little balcony outside her window and pitched something to him. It fell by chance into the boat—a beautifully grained paddle, its arm set with a gem of blue. She raised a finger to her lips and motioned him to go. The music came as he paddled away. As he pulled away in a daze. Night had fallen when he reached his hill. Melrose stood by the window. He told her of part of the trip. Of the music and of finding a paddle, but not of a woman who was her second self.

"Let me see the paddle, Jo," she asked. He brought it to her.

"The stone is lapis-lazuli." She was calm like mist on the bog. "The wood is aloe. It is very old; the fragrance is faint." She handed it back to Joseph. He looked at the paddle and then at his wife.

"Shall I throw it away?" She nodded. "I will." Late in the night Joseph awakened talking in his sleep. "I wish I could take her away," he was saying, "take her from the South."

Then he slept again and dreamed of her—of Melrose. But the dream became muddled, and he saw one time his Melrose—saw next time this woman. She came on the balcony and turned to his wife. Melrose came and turned to the woman. Then they came together and submerged into one. He was glad to awake. Glad to find Melrose whom he knew. At sundown he would go once more that he might see this person who was like her.

He went. At sundown he went that he might see. She stood at the window and waved to him. Again she was garbed in blue. Soft, sighing blue. She had worn blue on yesterday. Her window seemed a haze of blue. Joseph seemed rather to sense this than to see it. He gazed only at her face. "Melrose!" It was not her skin alone. There were hundreds in the South like that. Brown-yellow and yellow-brown. Nor was it alone her hair. Black—deep black like crows. Nor yet her gently pushed, red lips. But her sway when she stepped to the balcony. Her eyes like dark, melted pansies. Her waving—her languorous waving. Melrose was in her being.

Joseph returned the next evening, and the next, and the next. Many days he came at dusk, staring and bewildered. He spoke no more of his trips. Melrose asked naught about them. One time a rain came suddenly. All day the heat had stifled, but there had been little sun. Joseph was on the river. He would have turned and hurried back, but the music, more silver than the rain, came through the cooling air. He went to the landing and listened. Soon the woman, beautiful in her blue, appeared at the window. It rained too hard for her to step out, but she beckoned for him to come in. She dropped a big key, an old, rusty thing. A key seldom used, no doubt. Doing her gestured bidding, he opened a large side door. Steps, walled off from the rest of the place, wound straight up from the doorway to the top of the house. The lady, lovely person, met him. From a little anteroom she led him to where she had stood at the window. As he entered this larger room he was struck by the odor of aloes. Pleasant as the perfume was, it sickened him. For a second his head swam and he heard the low crying of Melrose's voice. He wanted to run away. Run like a little boy.

The rain on the roof was cheery but this scented, strange room was sad. It was blue. Blue from floor to ceiling, with rugs and low chairs of velvet and pillows and hangings of silk. A huge, blue opalescent dome hung low from the center ceiling. A piano, a handsome thing, stately in lacquered blue, stood beneath the dome. The walls were like a paneled, morning sky. Joseph gazed at the ceiling—at the floor—all about him. The woman stood at the window. "Like Melrose," Joseph whispered. She had forgotten him, no doubt. She was so still; he continued gazing. Now the dome. The woman turned, and while he gazed at pearl blue opalescence, she rested her eyes on him. He felt her looking and turned. And though he suspected the focusing of her eye, he flinched when their glances met. She came close to him and stood. At this range her face was older than his wife's. Even so, it was rather young, and almost as beautiful.

"The rain will cease," she said. Her voice was that of Melrose grown older.

She wore a string of aloes about her throat. Joseph noticed them and gulped.

"I thank you, Madame, for your kind favor. The rain has stopped already. You were good to take me in. Now I must leave." She held his arm lightly to detain him.

"It is almost dark," said she, "and the sky is clearing. The sky from my window is wonderful at night." She returned to her window without asking him to stay. Joseph went with her. Pale stars twinkled through sailing fleece. The sky darkened as it cleared.

"Why have you come in your little boat to watch up at my window every evening?"

"Your playing, Madame, and you." Then she played for him. Played on the blue piano and brought forth silver notes. He listened long to her playing before he arose to go. He thanked her once more and started but she held him again.

"You have not seen my treasures," she said, "I have treasures. Rare things from Sokotra." She turned to a curtained corner and opened a chest of deep drawers. Proudly she drew forth trinkets. Trinkets of many descriptions. Metal necklaces and anklets of aloes. Aloe bracelets and anklets of metal. Rings and head-dresses and luckstones and bangles. Powdered perfumes of aloes and myrrh. Wood of aloes set with jewels. Aloes and cassia for scenting garments. Joseph was in a stupor.

"Rare things from Sokotra—Rare things from Sokotra." The words hummed in his brain. His brain seemed tight and bursting.

"I must go now, Madame. I must go." He heard himself saying this.

"Yes, you must go now, hurry. Hurry or they'll find you here!" The surprise of this statement destroyed the stupor. Joseph fled from the room.

The woman came close behind him. At the top of the stairs they stopped. He would have taken her hand to say goodbye, but she clung to him until he kissed her. Kissed her many times. Half way down the stairs he heard her voice calling—calling to him, "Hurry!"

Outside the night was quiet. The stars, once pale, were glowing. This air was not laden with aloes. He paddled home in a listless fear. A fear that was dull and thumping. Melrose was sleeping—and the room was blue. Oh, this was delusion. He would sleep it away. Sleep it away forever. But the morning came and the room was blue. Melrose dressed in blue. She had draped their room in blue. This was pretty he told her. This change from rose to blue. But he wondered why she made it—why she made it.

Every evening he went on the river. Went before the darkness came. The woman stepped onto the balcony and threw her kisses to him. Each time he looked to see her beckon. But she did not call him, and he wondered who else was there with her. He dared not go unless she beckoned. Beckoned and dropped the key. He listened when she played, and watched her light go out. She made the room dark that the night might come in. The night with its flickering stars. He listened when she played, then paddled home.

At home one night he found aloes. Found his garden set with aloes. Straightway he sought Melrose. She waited at the window.

"Why do you have about you this thing which you fear?" he asked.

"But I do not fear it any longer. You taught me not to fear."

"They are beautiful. You did not find them here?"

"Imported. A species of the Blue from Sokotra."

"Where?"

"Sokotra."

Joseph hushed. Something rang in his mind. "Rare things from Sokotra. Rare things from Sokotra." He looked with unstill eyes at Melrose. She looked quite steadily at him.

"Did you ever have kin in Sokotra?" he queried.

"No one knows but Granna. I know nothing of myself."

"Where is Sokotra, Melrose?"

"Some place on an island." Melrose talked little recently; she moved about more, however. She felt that she was better. That the cough was growing faint.

On the night that Joseph brought the paddle Melrose had felt a quaking. Her heart had sunk within her. Within her something whispered, "When he turns to another. When he turns to another." Why she had felt this she did not know, but the quaking was there in her heart. Somehow she had known that the paddle had not been found. Someone had given it to him. The nights had passed slowly from that time. From that time the day had changed. There was something she must discover. Something was taking Joseph. She had followed him the next night. Down the river he had paddled his tiny craft and she had run behind along the bank. The trees and shrubbery had hidden her. She had followed to the mansion. Had seen the lovely creature; compared her with herself. She had returned the morning after while Joseph was away, but the house had been silent, and the woman's window closed. Again she had gone at evening, after Joseph rode ahead. With him she had seen the greetings and with him heard the music.

Once when rain showered he had entered the house. The woman had tossed him a key. Melrose had come out of hiding and run to go in behind him. The door had locked behind Joseph, and she had dropped to the ground. On her knees she had sobbed aloud. Had called out to her husband. She had not known that her voice reached him, riding on the night like a broken spirit. By the door she had remained until he passed her. Passed her without seeing, and in haste. The odor of aloes had passed with him and she had laughed in pity at herself. At home she had reached the bed just before he came. For some time their room had been blue (she had seen that the woman wore it). But Joseph had first noticed this this night.

Now Melrose felt sorrow in her heart. Sorrow mingled with disdain. Adorned in blue, she had moved about the hill, silent, but stronger and fearless. When the children came up from the town she laughed and told them stories. Stories of Granna, a shrivelled old woman who believed in witchery. Of an island where aloes grow—an island on the way to India. There people dwelt in rubble-built huts, and lived on dates and milk; and aloes kept them well and in health, and scented all their garments. Granna had lived there long ago, chasing goats and wild asses over the hills. Once Joseph listened to the tales, and he searched his wife's face for understanding. He did not know she ever talked of Granna. And Melrose felt sorrow in her heart. Sorrow and disdain. Her husband was bewitched, and she was losing fear. She seldom coughed.

At dusk she ran behind the canoe, trailing him down the river. The woman came on the balcony. She kissed him her hand and he stretched out his arms, pantomiming love. One night she dropped down an aloe leaf. Melrose found it later. At once she filled her home with aloes, rare specimens from the island. Joseph asked about them and found her unperturbed.

Soon one evening, Melrose went ahead of Joseph. Ran swiftly along the river to the mansion on the hill. At the window stood the woman. Waiting already for Joseph. She did not see the figure darting quickly behind trees, stooping under bushes, slipping to her stairway door. But soon she heard a knocking. A knocking, knocking, knocking, and she came very softly down the steps. Without asking from the inside what was wanted, she opened wide the door.

They stood like stone, these women. Stone images reflected in a mirror. Melrose had not seen her close before. She had not seen Melrose ever. But now a look of knowing flitted across her face, then a look of awful fear, and she backed to the steps and turned and ran. Leaped like a frightened deer. Midway she wheeled again. Melrose had not moved. Back down the stairs the woman came, the look of killing in her eyes. She muttered.

"They'll not know," came the words thick and bitten, and away she flew repeating, 'They'll not know!'

Melrose started after her, but she knew that Joseph would come. She expected the woman back also, and she must hold her ground. She ascended the stairs trembling. Trembling from what had passed, and what was yet to come. At the top was an antechamber. No one was within. In the large room she had a notion that she had walked into the sky. Into a sky perfumed with aloes. At the window she waited. Looked out on the river. Little River. She listened for the woman, but the woman did not return.

The canoe came gliding. Joseph's brown face was handsome. She would beckon as the woman had once done, Beckon and please him. He would come through the open door and she would kill him. Kill him in this room of blue. Yield to the curse. He looked up smiling and she tried to smile. Joseph frowned and looked harder. He would say goodbye to this woman; she was uncanny. No one should be like Melrose. He did not want this woman's smiles. He would say goodbye. Say goodbye and go. His boat nosed cross wise. He was turning.

"Jo!" came his name from the window. "Jo!" short and quick. "Jo!" the long wail. Melrose!

She did not call again. She leaned against the window, convulsed with tears and sobbing. Sobbing and shaking. Moaning. Joseph ran to the door and found it open. Found no one upstairs but Melrose. He gathered her up and took her, down like a baby in his arms. He could understand nothing, but he did not ask. It was not time to ask. Home he took her in the boat. Through the town they strolled, two lovers. Lovers reconciled.

Little groups of people stood about the streets. At the hill a crowd was jabbering. Eyes centered on Melrose and Joseph. Jabbering started afresh. Faces peered. Faces black and white and yellow, brown and tan and red and black. On the hill policemen guarded. Kept the crowd away. In a porch swing rested the body. The woman was dead. The woman from the mansion. She had tried to kill a white man on the street, and then she had run in the way of a horse. She had been insane. Now she was dead. They were awaiting the ambulance. Awaiting the coming of aid. The woman had been near the hill. People said she belonged there. Joseph chilled through. Melrose burned. They both said it was a mistake. The people had made an error. The ambulance came and took her away.

In the town the people whispered. Some said this woman was the mother of Melrose. Said Granna took Melrose when she was born. Was born of a father not black. Said the woman came from an island. Was brought by a southern family. In the town the secrets spread. The woman, frightened, had lost her mind. She would not leave the house. The family moved and provided for her there. They left someone to keep her. No one had ever seen the person." Joseph heard the whisperings. "Whoever came, she thought to be her lover. Whoever came, she wooed in careful secrecy. Melrose was her child. Melrose her child." The whispers came to Melrose.

Joseph and Melrose went to find Granna. Back in the country down Little River—down the left branch to Aloe House. After a southern secret. They knocked at the door. Granna was not there. Nothing was there.   [*The Crisis* 28.4 (August 1924): 156–162]

THE BEWITCHED SWORD

by Ola Calhoun Morehead

> "God's in his heaven
> All's right with the world."

That's exactly how Mary felt this morning as she repeated the last lines of Pippa's little song. As far as Browning was generally concerned, she did not care a great deal for his poems. They seemed trifle vague and obscure. Miss Hayes had analyzed "Rabbi Ben Ezra" and "The Last Duchess," her face aglow with the keen rapture of a poetry lover, but Mary, as the rest of the class, remained a lukewarm enthusiast. Miss Hayes, refusing to be discouraged, shook her head sagely as she remarked:

"It will come in time. Keep searching for the treasure."

But the treasure in Pippa's song was just beneath the surface and, to youth, it is so easy to find all right with the world. Mary repeated the last lines over and over again, but with an added fervor, because another circumstance had occurred to heighten her sense of the harmony of things—a very much more material circumstance than Browning's poem. She possessed five dollars and only five to buy a spring hat. The luck of it! Last night, all of the papers carried an advertisement that Bloch's entire stock of spring hats would be cleared at five dollars apiece.

She needed a hat badly. Her last summer's hat showed signs of its enforced duty. Twice she had tacked back the frayed straw. It was fading, too. Spring rains are not particularly kind to such delicate things as summer bonnets. Moreover, all of the girls in her set had new hats and she had begun to feel conscious of her old one. Now, displayed in the advertisement was the very hat she had seen in the window and admired. Ah, figuratively, she would laugh last and best!

Pippa's song fairly leaped from Mary's heart as she pulled her shabby hat over her newly shingled hair, throwing a hasty look at her dresser's mirror, in the meantime.

"Gee! I'd better hurry or they'll all be picked over. Think of it, values to twenty-five dollars!"

Bounding down the stairs to the street and to the "L" station she boarded a downtown car. As the train scurried, her dreams likewise scurried. She had bought the hat and its taffeta trimming was the same shade as that of her new flannel coat. Even now, she could hear the girls exclaiming over it. They always admired her taste. She had no cause for staying away from the lyceum now. She'd be there Sunday without fail. All of the young folks met there.

My! how she had missed being there the last couple of Sundays. Mary closed her eyes in delicious anticipation.

"State and Madison."

The girl started abruptly and left the car.

At Bloch's, she directed the elevator boy "Millinery." Ah! in the midst of dozens of women tables were heaped with the season's models—cunning taffeta turbans of every shade; chic, charming cloches; trim, tiny sailors; black, lacy, filmy things, ethereal as the air; and leghorns, velvet and taffeta-trimmed in dress sport styles. In the maze of all sorts of shapes and trims, she found at last the hat of her dreams and window gazing.

Searching out and finding an unoccupied dressing table, she tilted her hat to every angle and not at a single one was it unbecoming. Though, of course, she preferred to wear it slightly tilted to the left. She thought that angle gave a better shading to her eyes. Already, a saleswoman was coming toward her.

"I want this one," said Mary, fondling the leghorn and powder blue combination.

"Will you wear it? Then, I'll put the other one in a bag for you. And say, I want to tell you, you've got a bargain there, not only style, but lots of service and it's worth three times its price."

Wild with joy, Mary exchanged the five dollar bill for the hat. Tripping, all but, her heart a song, she left Bloch's to board the car at the next corner.

The car was filled, but even so, the girl's keen eye spied a seat at the front. She had scarcely sat down to weave more dreams when suddenly,

"*I won't sit by a nigger!*"

And Mary felt her knees rudely jostled as a tall blonde woman strode past her into the aisle.

Crash! fell Mary's dream towers and, instantly, she was swept back into the world of reality as eyes pinned themselves upon her—some pityingly, some quizzical, the most of them unkind.

With her lips tightly compressed, she felt the sharp point of the sword as it shot through her armor of happiness to sip, as it were, the blood of her heart.

A strange sword it was, too, possessing something of witchcraft, it could pierce iron; it could rend steel; it could break a heart of stone!

"Park Avenue!"

And, this time, a drooping little figure, limply holding a paper bag, left the car.

[*The Crisis* 29.4 (February 1925): 166–167]

"There Never Fell a Night So Dark"

by Mary Louise French

Dusk was falling, slowly hovering over earth, as a veil being gently dropped. Birds twittered. A soft wind stirred—night would soon be here with its millions of stars. Night—brooding and sweet.

He wondered how long she would sit there. He looked at his watch—three hours—and more, perhaps. But he had watched her for three hours and still she sat. She was well dressed. He could not see her face, but he knew that she was not very young or very old—there was an air of desolation around her—he dared not leave her alone. He was afraid. Years ago, he had waited—in this same park—motionless—waited for night. He felt responsible for this woman—sitting there—at the edge of things waiting for the night to help her on across. He knew; Life could treat one badly, make one long for the eternal darkness and yet, if one could smile, one could endure. Well, he would stay on a while longer, and if she continued sitting there so still, so very still, he would approach her—even if she misunderstood.

He had taken her in for three hours, at least her clothes. Dark clothes. Her dress was blue and soft and dark. He liked dark blue—always made him think of "sensible" and "independent." Well dressed but so still, so statue like. Dusk had turned into darkness, night had stolen upon them.

He would have to say something to her, to break that desolate spell around her. He approached her quickly, so tall and self-assured, so used to living to the edge of loneliness and misery.

When he stood before her he was unprepared for what he had thought would never happen. In the darkness the dim outline of her face was beautiful but her eyes were cold, lifeless and black like black marble.

She scanned his face—and met eyes that were eternally young. A smile—pleading and irresistible. There was something vaguely familiar about this man—and yet,—he drew a breath and seemed to steady himself. He sensed her torture. It was going to be harder than he had thought it would be. He was disconcerted to realize how unemotional she was. Surely, ah, surely she could not miss the beauty of the night. The night with its vast stillness and stars and somewhere a pale moon hanging low.

It was hard to meet the misery in her eyes. She spoke unemotionally, dully.

"Do you believe in God?" she asked slowly. And on hearing her voice his heart almost stifled him.

"How can you doubt? You can't look at that moon and the stars and doubt. Is it as bad as that, my friend?" He answered and took a place beside her.

After all nothing mattered to her. She was at the end. Let him sit, let him talk. It would make her last night shorter, make the hours pass more quickly.

"Tell me about it, won't you?" he asked patiently. He knew. He had watched the night come on—years ago—alone.

Strange—she felt no fear of this tall man beside her and there was something about him, something indescribable, something that made her want to sob and sob her heartbreak aloud. His smile perhaps reminded her so vividly of some one; his voice was an echo of some one's she had heard dimly, an echo of the past.

"Yes," she said bitterly, "Life is beautiful, beauty all around us; but I can't believe that there is a Just God. If there is, why does He make us suffer like this?" She was decidedly intense, and he felt that there was depth to her sorrow.

"Like this?" he asked, staring at the woman beside him. "Whatever it is, don't lose faith in yourself. Life without faith is indeed deplorable. One needs faith to live, you know." His voice went on: "When sorrow touches us the first thing that we are so willing to believe is that there is no God, or that He is angry and will not help—"

"But," she interrupted quickly, "suppose there were reasons that He should be angry, and suppose that His punishment was too severe, and suppose that one tried hard to make up for wickedness and finally found that it was useless—absolutely. What then?"

"You have lost your faith in yourself and life gets you on all sides. Unless," he paused for a second, "unless you smile, endure and go on and on. That's Life, you know. "

"But I can't go on, I can't!" she said emphatically, in a low voice. Her lips trembled and he wished that she would cry, instead of fighting the sobs back.

"You have lost some one, I know," he said quietly. He knew.

She nodded. "And I cannot bear it; you don't know, unless you have lost all your own too. This loneliness is unbearable and there is nothing—nothing—to go on for."

"I understand," he said soothingly. "I have seen and felt frightful things too."

"But your God took them! I know one has to pay. I deserved some punishment but not this—not this!"

He lighted a cigarette; somehow he wanted desperately to help her, perhaps because he had known loneliness; perhaps because her voice did not seem strange. "You are pent up; tell me about yourself; it will help you to talk."

She did, she told him of the years of struggle, of work everlasting—no end; of the man that deserted her with two children, a boy and a girl; of the eternal grind to give them a good education. And after all those years of work and sacrifice the war claimed her boy—so splendid.

"And when the war took my boy, although something went out of me, out of my life, I kept my courage. That sorrow was made beautiful because of the way he went. Brave! He went west smiling. My sorrow was made glorious! And then, and then there was my girl; young, wonderfully sweet to me, happy. How she could sing—so young, so unafraid; ready to meet life—and I lost her! How," she said, "can you tell me that God is somewhere?"

Silence, nothing but the wind softly blowing through the trees. Lights were dotting the darkness of the city.

"Just as you see me now I went to her. She was at school, nearly finished. They told me that she could not live and I left to go to her. All the way on that hot train I prayed, I pleaded with God to let me see her alive; I promised I would dedicate my life to Him if I could just see her alive. Torture! Endless hours of riding—ah!—Merciful God!—If you have to take her only let her know that I am with her; let her eyes look into mine and let me know! He didn't hear. I was too late; she had gone; only a little while—such a short time—before I arrived. I was alone, utterly alone. Why, can you tell me, did He do that? Why could she not live a few hours longer? Tell me that, if you can!" She sobbed. At last she sobbed.

She thanked him inwardly for his silence. But he was thinking. "Of course," he thought to himself, "she cannot understand why, since this girl of her heart had to be taken, why she could not have been spared a while longer. That is where the real hurt is; the one is deeper than the other. Funny we can never remember that time has not the slightest regard for one individual and Death not one favorite."

"After all," he said quietly, "there are so many things worse than death, so many sorrows deeper than yours, my friend." Silence. He did not expect a reply so he continued, looking far out into the darkness. "You have lost courage. Sure, Life has treated you badly and it'll get you if you don't buck up, smile and endure." She opened her lips and was going to speak, but his voice went on.

"I once knew a man. His name was Jim, steady, slow moving, decent. Married a girl, the only girl he ever loved. To him there never could be any one like Sue. They were happy for a while. She soon tired of the monotony. The town was small. The work was hard. Days of loneliness, drab days of drudgery, and the inevitable happened. There was a man that had always wanted Sue. Fool that Jim was, he gave her the divorce because he wanted her happiness. Providing that she would never interfere with the children; he thought that he would touch her motherhood, but—she failed him. She left him and the kids, and went her way. He was sure that he could not endure days alone. Days with his kids wanting their mother, But—he did; he had to—for them, you know. He suffered. But the years passed on, as they do. Jim worked hard. He was proud of the boy; real pals, he and that boy of his. And the girl, his heart. Friends all of them and that is something, to be friends with one's children. But Jim's boy is in prison; innocent—consider that—innocent!"

The woman trembled. But she was silent. "Jim's boy worked for a rich man that had a good-for-nothing son, always in some kind of a jam. He gambled and lost. Was heavily in debt. And his father refused to help him longer. So his son came home one night to take what he claimed would be his own some day. They quarreled; Jim's boy heard and came to see what it was all about. Just in time to see the old man fall—and foolishly in his horror over what had happened, he picked up the smoking revolver and paid—and pays—for a crime that he did not commit.

"Jim was like a man fallen in a puddle. He knew not what to do. He couldn't eat; he couldn't sleep; he could do nothing but curse an unjust God. His boy—innocent—in prison—not for a day—not for a month—but for life. God!"

The woman's low sobs had ceased; she drew her breath in shortly, but could say nothing. She was still, too still, like the night.

He went on in the same low voice. "Jim, of course, was unable to comprehend how such injustice could be meted out and he thought that he could not go on after that. But he did. Much worse that than the kindness of a death—a glorious death—is it not?" He turned to the silent figure beside him. "And the girl?" she asked, wiping her eyes.

"Ah! I am coming to her," he said. "The girl, as I told you, was sent to a good school and she came home, one day, unexpectedly. It was not long before he knew why. Insupportable calamity! Tragedy beyond realization! His boy, and now this—this." The man bowed his head in his hands for a fleeting second and it seemed to the woman, so very still beside him, that she could see a garden and a Man of Sorrows long ago. But his voice went on doggedly.

"When her time was upon her one night, it was Jim that went down into some place of pain, some horrible place of darkness with his little one. She was so young, so frail to suffer so much. And it was then that he bargained with God, as you did. He must have been heard—because when the dawn came Jim's girl went, smiling and unafraid, taking back to Him the cause of all her suffering. And," he turned to the woman quickly, "your girl went without pain, didn't she?" he asked, a bit savagely she thought.

"Yes," she answered softly, "she went like a flower in the evening time. But Jim, what happened to him?" Her eyes were tear-dimmed.

"Jim," he said, clearing his throat. "Jim of course knew that God was a Myth. Nothing mattered. Life was at its lowest ebb and dark as dark could be. He decided that the quickest way out of the darkness would be the happiest. So he sat, one day, and watched for the sunset, and after the night came he knew what he was to do. It was winter and it was cold and Jim was sick, body and soul, so he turned to his little room which was almost as cold as the night itself. Turned on the gas as he hovered between this world and some place of space, he was revealed to himself, he saw things he had never thought about. Darkness, one step on over, and he would be lost. And as he was wondering about the sweet coolness of that darkness, he seemed to hear some one say, 'How about that boy of yours that you are leaving, the years ahead of him with no one to care, no one to keep him smiling and help him through? Coward! Fight to get back!' And Jim tried as hard as he could to get back. He did not want to leave that boy of his alone, he wanted to help him live through the years that might be ahead, endless years of hopelessness. But try as he would, he was slowly being drawn on over—the blackness would soon envelop him. Only a miracle could save him. Oh, if God would only let him go back, and lo, when he raised his voice and cried aloud, 'Merciful God, let me go back, not for my wicked soul's sake but for the others that need me,' the miracle happened. Slowly he came back, with his landlady and a doctor over him. The cold night wind that reached him through the small window was sweet and he knew that he had been very close to the easiest way out; had been on a precipice with just a step between himself and the twilight. But he did not forget why he had been permitted to come back and he had been merciful too. A restlessness drives him at times and it is then that he finds peace, only by searching for someone that finds loneliness unbearable. And so," he said, turning quietly to the woman, "Jim learned."

"But the boy?" she interrupted huskily. He could feel her fingers gripping his arm.

"Has reason to hope for freedom soon. But Jim has been able to help him endure these horrible years unto the end."

She gave him her hands and in the darkness he could read the pleading in her eyes. "Could you forgive me, Jim dear, could you?"

Taking off her hat he searched her face. Her voice he had known, but so long ago, so many years. How could it be possible? And yet it was. In his heart, he had known, from the beginning.

"My dear, need you ask?" He answered folding her hands in his own.

She was no longer unemotional and dead; her eyes were no longer eyes of black marble. She was thrillingly alive.

"Jim," she said, "I have paid; teach me to smile and to endure. I have lost him and his children—yours and you; I know the thing that I did—to leave like that—is an injury irreparable; but my punishment for being wicked is more than I can bear. The days are so long and the nights—the nights—"

"'There never fell a night so dark that it could put out the stars,'" he quoted. "And Life is big; but Love is great, and greater."

There were tears in her eyes of black, but as they stood together and he looked deep into them, to him they were sweet and there was something deeper than understanding, something indescribable in his slow smile, as he said: "Life gets you on all sides—if you lose courage; so smile, dear; there is so much for us to do—together."

Triumphantly they passed into the night. [*The Crisis* 31.2 (December 1925): 73–76]

Three Dogs and a Rabbit

by Anita Scott Coleman

"This, that I'm about to relate," said Timothy Phipps, "isn't much of a story, though, you might upon hearing it weave it into a ripping good yarn. I'm not much of a talker or writer. Now maybe when I'm in my cups or in the last stages of a delirious fever—I might attempt to—write." He tilted his head, with its fringe of rough grey hair, a bit backwards and sidewise and laughed. His laughter seeming to echo—write, write, write.

Tinkling with fine spirits and good humor, he ceased laughing to inquire roguishly: "What, say, are the ingredients of a story? A plot? Ah, yes, a plot. Ho! ho! ho! The only plot in this rigmarole, my dear fellow, is running, hard to catch, a sure enough running plot. Characters. To be sure we must have characters: A pretty girl, a brave hero, a villain and love. A setting. Of course there must be a setting, an atmosphere, a coloring. We'll say moonlight and a rippling brook and a night bird singing nocturnal hymns in a forest and love. Love pirouetting in the silvery moonlight, love splashing and singing in a rippling brook. Love trilling and fluting in a bird's song—Love and a pretty girl—Love and a brave hero—Love and a villain made penitent and contrite; because of love. Bye the bye, there is no living person who could not fancy the beginning, imagine the entanglements, conceive the climax, unfold the developments, reveal the solution and picture the final, having such material at hand. But," laughed Timothy, "none such—none such in what I'm a-telling."

Shedding his joviality for a more serious mien, he queried—

"Have you ever thought how very few really lovely women one meets in a life time? Our pretty young debutantes are far too sophisticated; while our age-mellowed matrons affect *naiveté,* and our bustling house-wives are too preoccupied with directing the destinies of nations to be attractive in the least.

"Men? Bother the men. We are but animals at best. Alert and crafty, lazy and jovial; just as chance decrees, and monotonously alike in our dependence upon woman. All of us are made or marred by our contacts with women. Whenever chance draws her draperies aside to allow a lovely woman to cross our path, it leaves an ineffaceable mark upon our countenance and traces indelible patterns of refinement upon our character.

"Unfortunately, I am of a critical turn of mind together with a pernicious inclination to believe with the ancient Greeks that an ugly body houses an ugly soul and that loveliness dwells only in beautiful temples.

"Certainly, certainly this inclination has led me into more than one blind alley. Ah, if I could only wield the pen as skillfully as I can this—" He flourished a carving knife, for we were at table and he was occupied at the moment in carving the *pièce de résistance.* "I would tell the world how untrue my premise is. And what a cruel fallacy outer loveliness ofttimes proves itself to be.

"Despite this, my contrary nature clings like a leech to the belief that beautiful temples are invariably beautiful within.

"And it chanced, I say chanced, since there is the probability that someone not half so lovely might have done the same deed, and had such been the case my belief would have suffered a terrible set-back. It chanced that the loveliest woman I ever saw was the most beautiful.

"I saw her first under amazing circumstances. Circumstances so extraordinary they seem unreal to this day, but I won't linger upon them, because they make another story. My second sight of her was in a crowded court-room and it was then while she sat very primly upon the culprit's bench that I had my first opportunity really to see her.

"She was a little woman. Feel as you like towards all other types, but a little woman has her appeal. Especially, a little old woman with silvery hair, and an un-nameable air about her, that is like fingers forever playing upon the chords of sweetest memories. All this, and a prettiness beside, a trifle faded of course, but dainty and fragile and lovely—rare, you might say as a bit of old, old lace. And kindliness overlaying this, to lend a charm to her beauty that jewel or raiment could not render. Her silvery hair crinkled almost to the point of that natural curliness which Negro blood imparts. The kind of curl that no artificial aid so far invented can duplicate. Her eyes were extremely heavy-lidded, which is, as you know, a purely Negro attribute, and her mouth had a fullness, a ripeness, exceedingly—*African.*

"That she was anything other than a white American was improbable, improbable indeed. She, the widow of old Colonel Ritton, deceased, of Westview. As dauntless and intrepid a figure as ever lived to make history for his country. His career as an Indian fighter, pioneer and brave, open opposer of the lawlessness which held sway over the far West in the late sixties is a thing that is pointed to with pride and made much of, by Americans. Three notable sons, high standing in their respective vocations, paid her the homage due the mother of such stalwart, upright men as themselves. Two daughters, feted continuously because of their beauty, were married into families, whose family-tree flourished like the proverbial mustard-seed, unblighted before the world.

"There had to be some reason why a lady of her standing was forced to appear in court. The truth is, it was not because of the greatness of her offense; but because of the unusualness of her misconduct which had raised such a hue and cry; until drastic method had to be resorted to.

"The charge against her was one of several counts, the plaintiffs being three very stout gentlemen, florid-faced, heavy-jowled, wide-paunched to a man. Each of them diffused a pomposity; which while being imposing managed somehow to be amusing. Their very manner bespoke their grim determination to punish the defendant. Their portly bodies fairly bristled with the strength of this intention. The muscles in their heavy faces worked as though the currents of their thoughts were supplied by volts of wonderment, shocking and bewildering. They charged, first: That the defendant willfully hampered them in the fulfillment of their authorized duty. Second: That the defendant had knowingly aided a criminal to evade the hands of the law, by sheltering the said criminal in or about her premises. Third: That the defendant had spoken untruthfully with intent to deceive by denying all knowledge of said criminal's whereabouts. Fourth: That the concealment of said criminal constituted a tort; the criminal being of so dangerous a character, his being at liberty was a menace to the commonwealth."

Timothy Phipps paused, as he busied himself, serving generous slices of baked ham to his guests. In the act of laying a copious helping upon his own plate, he commenced again, to unreel his yarn.

"There is no joy in life so satisfying, so joyous, as that of having our belief strengthened—to watch iridescent bubbles—our castles in the air—settle, unbroken upon firm old earth. To hear our doubts go singing through the chimneys of oblivion. Ah, that's joy indeed. And it is what I experienced that never-to-be forgotten day in the dinkiest little court-room in the world.

"A rainy spell was holding sway and a penetrating drizzle oozed from the sky as though the clouds were one big jelly-bag hung to drip, drip, drip. I was sogged with depression, what with the weather and the fact that I was marooned in a very hostile section of my native land, it was little wonder that my nerves were jumpy and a soddenness saturated my spirits, even though I knew that the fugitive was free and making a rough guess at it, was to remain so. But an emotion, more impelling than curiosity forced me to linger to witness the outcome of old Mrs. Ritton's legal skirmish.

"From a maze of judicial meanderings, these facts were made known.

"The old Ritton house was a big rambling structure built at some period so long ago, the time was forgotten. It was not a place of quick escapes, for no such thing as fleeing fugitives had been thought of, in its planning. Unexpected steps up and steps down made hasty flight hazardous. Unlooked for corners and unaccountable turns called for leisurely progress and long halls with closed doors at their furtherest end, opening into other chambers, were hindrances no stranger could shun. All told, the house as it stood was a potent witness against the defendant, each of its numerous narrow-paned windows screeched the fact that none but the initiated could play at hide-and-seek within its walls.

"Many pros and cons were bandied about as to why the run-away Negro had entered Ritton's house. That he had done an unwonted thing went without saying—since hunted things flee to the outposts of Nature, shunning human habitation as one does a pestilence: to the long, long road girt by a clear horizon, where dipping sky meets lifting earth, on, on to the boundless space, away to the forest where wild things hover, or a dash to the mountains to seek out sheltering cave and cavern.

"At first, it was thought that entering the Ritton house was a 'dodge' but subsequent happenings had proven the supposition false. It was quite clear that he had gone in for protection and had found it.

"The claimants carefully explained to the court, how they had chased the Negro down Anthony, up Clements and into Marvin, the street which ran north and south beneath the Ritton-house windows. They were but a few lengths behind the fugitive—not close enough, you understand, to lay hold upon him; nor so near that they could swear that someone signaled from an open window in the Ritton house. How-be-it, they saw the Negro swerve from the street, dart through the Rittons' gate, dash down the walk, and enter the Ritton house. Less than five minutes afterwards they, themselves, pursued the Negro step by step into the building; to find upon entering it a room so spacious that the several pieces of fine old furniture arranged within it did not dispel an effect of emptiness, while the brilliant light of early afternoon showered upon everything, sparklingly, as if to say, 'No place to hide in here' and over beside an open window old lady Ritton sat very calmly, knitting. And upon being questioned she had strenuously denied that a black man had preceded them into her chamber.

"Finally the point was reached, when the defendant took the stand. And the Lord knows, so much depended, that is, as far as I was concerned, upon what she would or would not say—well, what she said, makes my story.

"'Gentlemen, the thing you desire me to tell you, I cannot. Though, I think if I could make you understand a little of my feelings, you will cease—all of you being gentlemen— endeavoring to force me to divulge my secret.

"'You, all of you, have been born so unfettered that you have responded to your every impulse; perhaps it will be hard to realize the gamut of my restraint, when I swear to you, gentlemen, that in all my life, I have experienced no great passion and responded to the urge of only two impulses—two—but two—and these, gentlemen, have become for me a sacred trust.

"'It was years ago when I felt the first impulse and answered it. It has no apparent connection with the present occurrence. Yet, possibly, for no other reason than an old lady's imagining, the memory of that first occasion has leaped across the years to interlace itself with this.

"'Wait, gentlemen. I will tell you all about it. This turbulence has awakened old dreams and old longings and opened the doors of yester-years in the midst of an old lady's musing; but it is worth all the worry. Yes, 'tis worth it.

"'It is strange what mighty chains are forged by impulses and none of us know the strength that is required to break them. My first impulse wrought me much of happiness— very much happiness, gentlemen. Bear with an old lady's rambling—your Honor, and I shall relate just how it happened.

"'I was ten years old, when my master—

"'Pardon? Yes? Yes, Sirs—My master.

"'I was ten years old; when my master gave up his small holdings in the South and came

West with his family, his wife,—my mistress—a daughter and two sons and myself. We traveled what was then the tortuous trail that began east of the Mississippi and ended in the rolling plains beside the Rio Grande. Our trip lasted a fortnight longer than we expected or had planned for. Once along the way, we were robbed. Again, we were forced to break camp and flee because a warring band of Indians was drawing near. Afterwards, we found to our dismay, that a box of provisions had been forgotten or had been lost. Misfortune kept very close to us throughout our journey, our food was all but gone. There was wild game for the killing, but ammunition was too precious to be squandered in such manner. Master had already given the command that we were to hold in our stomachs and draw in our belts until we reached some point where we could restock our fast dwindling supplies.

"'One day, an hour before sun-down, we struck camp in a very lovely spot—a sloping hill-side covered with dwarf cedars and scrub oaks, a hill-side that undulated and sloped until it merged into a sandy-golden bottomed ravine. We pitched our camp in a sheltered nook in this ravine. The golden sand still warm from the day's sunshine made a luxurious resting place for our weary bodies. Below us, a spring trickled up through the earth and spread like lengths of sheerest silk over the bed of sand.

"'In a little while our camp-fire was sending up curling smoke-wreaths, smoke-blue into the balmy air and a pot of boiling coffee—our very last—added its fragrance to the spice of cedars and the pungency of oaks. Sundown came on, and a great beauty settled over everything. Nature was flaunting that side of herself which she reveals to the wanderer in solitary places: the shy kisses she bestows upon the Mountain's brow and, passion-warmed, glows in flagrant colors of the sunset; the tender embrace with which she wraps the plains and the glistening peace shines again in sparkling stars. Beauty that is serene and beauty that brings peace and calm and happiness and is never found in towns or crowded cities.

"'Our three hounds—faithful brutes that had trailed beside us all the weary miles—sat on their haunches and lifted their heads to send up long and doleful cries into the stillness.

"Here—here—" cried Master. "Quit that!—Come, come, we'll take a walk and maybe scare up something to fill the pot tomorrow." He ended by whistling to the prancing dogs and they were off. Up the hillside they went, the dogs, noses to earth, skulking at Master's heels or plunging into the under-brush on a make-believe scent.

"'I sat in the warm sand, a lonely slave-child, watching Master and the dogs until they reached the hill-top. Almost on the instant, the dogs scared up a rabbit. What a din they made yelping, yip, yap, yap and Master halooing and urging them to the race. The frightened rabbit ran like the wind, a living atom with the speed of a flying arrow. Straight as a shooting star, it sped: until turning suddenly it began bounding back along the way it had come. The ruse worked. The dogs sped past, hot on his trail of the dodging rabbit, many paces forward before they were able to stop short and pick up the scent once more. And the rabbit ran, oh, how he ran tumbling, darting, swirling down the hillside, terror-mad, fright-blind, on he came, the dogs on his trail once more, bounding length over length behind him. One last frantic dash, one desperate leap and the rabbit plunged into my lap. I covered the tiny trembling creature with my hands, just in time, before the great hounds sprang towards me. With great effort I kept them off and managed to conceal my captive in the large old-fashioned pocket of my wide skirt.

"'Master, disgruntled at his dogs and quite ireful—it is no little thing for a hungry man to see a tempting morsel escape him—came up to question me. "That rabbit—that rabbit—which way did it go?"

"'When I replied "Don't know," he became quite angry and beat me. Gentlemen, the scars of that long ago flogging I shall carry to my grave. Our food was nearly gone and it was I, the slave-girl, who knew the lack most sorely. But I did not give the rabbit over to my master.

"She paused a little while and in all my life I never before knew such quiet; you could actually feel the silence.

"'It is strange, strange how far reaching the consequences of an impulse may be. Howard, my master's son, witnessed everything. He had always teased me. His favorite pastime had been to annoy the slave-girl with his pranks, but he changed from that day. That day, when he saw his father beat me. And it was he, Gentlemen, who taught me to forget the scars of serfdom and taught me the joys of freedom. In all truth, Sirs, I am the widow of Colonel Howard Monroe Ritton of Westview.'

"There is no use trying to tell you about that," declared Timothy. "It's an experience as indescribable as it is unforgettable. That little old white-haired woman standing alone in the midst of all those hostile people, tearing apart with such simple words the whole fabric of her life. I think it was her loveliness that held them spell-bound; the power of her beauty, that kept them straining their ears to catch every word she said. As if suddenly awakened to her surroundings, she cleared her throat nervously, and hurriedly concluded her story.

"'The necessity of my being here, Gentlemen, is the outcome of my second impulse, an impulse, Gentlemen, nothing more. Each afternoon I sit in my west chamber beside my sunny windows, there is a whole beautiful row of them, as one can see by passing along the street ... I like the sunshine which pours through them of an afternoon, and I like to knit. And I like to watch the passersby. And, I think, Gentlemen, whenever I sit there I can recall more easily the things that are passed, the old friends, the old places, the old loves and the old hurts, which, somehow, have no longer the power to bring pain.

"'So I was peering—my eyes are not so good—into the street and I saw a cloud of dust, all of a sudden. I thrust my head a little ways through the window, then, I saw a man running; on looking closer, I saw that he was black.

"'Then a queer thing happened, Gentlemen; the first time in years on years, I remembered the days of my bondage. And curiously, yes, curiously, I recalled. Wait. No, I did not recall it. I swear to you, Gentlemen, a picture formed before me; a hilly slope overgrown with trees of scrub oak and dwarf cedars—a golden sand-bottomed ravine and twilight falling upon miles on miles of wind-swept prairie, and peace, sweet and warm and kind, brushing my soul and turning my thoughts towards God. And I heard it, the strident yelps of three strong dogs. I saw it—a tiny furry rabbit running for its life. I tell you—it was real, Gentlemen. And while I looked, it faded—changed—glowed into another picture—the one that was being enacted out in the street. It glimmered back to fancy and flashed again to fact, so swiftly, I could not distinguish which. Then, Sirs, they merged and both were one.... The black man who was running so wildly was only a little terror-mad rabbit. The three stout gentlemen there, (she pointed, quite like a child toward the fat policemen, while a ripple of laughter floated across the room), and the crowd which followed after, very strangely, Gentlemen, every person in it had the visage of my master. I think, I cried out at that, Sirs. Yes. Certainly. I cried—at that.

"'Then the black man was in my presence, inside my sunny west-chamber, and I was forced to act—act quickly—.

"'The picture had to be finished, Gentlemen. The rabbit, no, the man—had to be protected. Thank you, Sirs. That is all.'

"Yes," said Timothy Phipps, pensively. "I was the running black gentleman in the story—

"He tilted his head a bit backwards and sideways and laughed. His laughter echoing—joy—joy—joy!   [*The Crisis* 31.3 (January 1926): 118–122]

THE PRISON-BOUND

by Marita Bonner

"God help the prison-bound this evenin'
Them within the four iron walls—."
From a prayer heard in a country church

It was supper time.

There was salt in Maggie's tea cup. She had not put it in there. She was choking on it.

—Did you ever try to swallow salt tears with food? It will choke you—.

Maggie did not know how the salt got in there. She had not put it in the tea and Charlie had not lifted his eyes from the plate since he had sat down. The salt was there, though.

Maggie held the cup to her lips and her eyes on a spot on the wall behind Charlie. The spot was greasy like all the rest of the wall.

It was greasy and dingy; yellow and cracked. It was smoked up to a sooty ceiling. It made even the window and the glimpse of house tops through the window greasy.

That's all the kitchen was anyhow. Greasy no matter how you scrubbed and dug.

Grease and soot and waterbugs always covered the kitchen. That's what everybody on the three floors above her and the three floors beneath her said. If you lived in a colored tenement you had to take grease and soot and waterbugs along with a constant "break-down" of things.

Yesterday the stove had smoked a little. Today it smoked a little more. Six months from now it would fill the whole room with smoke when you lit it.

The sink was stopping up. The zinc under the stove curled up and tore your skirts when you passed. Little crumblings of things that nobody fixed. Charlie would not. He was too tired when he came home. Always too tired. And the agent said the owner was abroad.

Abroad? Somewhere. Not there.

Everything was breaking down. Even Charlie himself looked broken down humped over his plate.

Why didn't he straighten up some time? His arm thrust out of a sweater with a flannel shirt showing beneath, plied back and forth, up and down, from plate to mouth.

His hands were even greasy and fat. His fingers almost overlapped. They used to be slender and strong. His very shoulders were like young hams. There was no sink, no slender hollow between his neck and shoulders. You could not lay your head there now. He was fat and greasy. Greasy like kitchen wall.

The fork beside his plate could not puncture the rolls of fat. Even Death himself would have to play with his ribs a half hour before he could find his way between them.

How long had Charlie looked like this? Six months? Six years? Must have been longer.

It must have been more than six years when he had begun to "call on her." She hadn't been so fat herself then. He came to call. That was all. There had been nothing compelling or acute about the calling. He had come dryly, placidly, consequentially.

He had squatted in the middle of a chair. Squatted in the middle of sentences that always began and always ended alike. Somehow or other they had married. Squatted in two rooms. Squatted in these. Now he worked in a mill.

She wished that they could get up. Move up. She looked out of the window. Even move up into one of the trees.

She wanted to be at the top of one of those trees. Maybe a leaf. She was a leaf. A leaf greening, drinking in the sun. Shaking on a thread of stem. Charlie—was squatting over his plate. Blind to everything. Blind like a mole.

She cried to him silently: "Mole! Mole! Can't you see the sun? Can't you see the rain? Gold and plenty around you?"

Blind to everything. Only after the rain and sun have become strength and sap—lost their freshness and become a something else—like warm love turned to tepid tolerance—does the mole answer. He sniffs and smells but never sees, and he answers, "Yes, leaf—I see it."

And he squats at the roots and thinks he is in the tree-tops with the leaf. He thinks his eyes are wide open and he is happy—.

Charlie ought to quit squatting. He ought to see.—She set the cup down.

—One iron wall—.

She wondered why he did not say anything. She could talk. He called her ignorant lots of times though. "You ain't never been higher than the fifth grade in Dexter County schools. You ought to learn up here. This ain't down home," he'd say.

She could talk about things though she never talked to people. All the women round about bore themselves with such assurance it shamed her. She hung out of the windows and watched them.

"You ain't nothin' but lazy," Charlie told her. "Stay in out them windows."

But she looked and held silent talks with the women who passed. Watched each one as she passed. Talked gayly to her if her eyes were gay. Talked soothingly and peacefully if their eyes stared through everything and saw nothing.

Told the women who passed below her things about herself too. How she would like a gas log in the parlor instead of that coal stove with the broken door. But Charlie grumbled like a whole hive of bees if she asked him to pay the gas bill. She wanted curtains and a new hat and carpet. The place could look nicer.—A long iron wall—.

This was a town where you could not go to the theatre if you were colored. Nobody wanted to sit next to you.

Pushed out, the colored people had one of their own. Charlie said no decent man took his wife there.

Still the woman across the hall—the one who could laugh until tears came to your eyes while you listened to her—that woman said her husband took her and he had even beaten a man once for looking at her too pleasantly.

She laughed all the time. She even made Charlie laugh. Maggie couldn't. Once the other had even laughed at Maggie herself. Laughed when she told her what Charlie had said about the theatre.

Laughed and called her green and countrified. Well, maybe that woman wasn't decent as Charlie said and she had better let her alone like he told her to. She'd never go over the hall into her house through she thought she had heard him laughing in there once. Still, he was a man and she, a woman.

Why didn't he look up? Or laugh, even? The kitchen walls were so greasy. She wanted to see some others. It was too cold to sit in the parlor. The fire was out all the time. It was silly to go to bed as soon as you have eaten. You might die of acute indigestion before morning.

She sat back and closed her eyes. Charlie looked up swiftly. Saw her face, swollen and shiny beneath the tears. Tears streaming down into her tea cup. The sight sickened him suddenly.

Why did she cry? Why didn't she say something? If he asked a question she acted like she had to get her mind together to answer. And then she only said, "Yeah—!"

Women were not supposed to be so soft. Supposed to be soft, but not so soft you could knock a rock through them without their saying a word.

She asked for things, too, as if she were afraid to ask. Why didn't she wheedle things from him? Put her arms around him?

Why couldn't he have a victrola and folks dropping in? Why didn't she dress and fix up the place? The kitchen walls were greasy. Maggie's face. Maggie's clothes—Maggie—.

Oh well! Things he couldn't walk out of. Could not walk around. Or walk beside. Iron walls.

He pushed his chair back.

Maggie raised her eyes slowly. Maybe he would talk to her now. Tell her something someone said. What they had said and what they had done. Where they had been. How he felt when they said it. Where they went to make people laugh like the woman across the hall.

He went into the bedroom. She heard them walking around. Walking heavily and slowly. Maybe he was tired. Tired enough to sit down and talk.

He called from the hall: "Guess I go 'long out. Least till you can stop cryin'."

The salt choked her. She'd been crying, then. She set her cup down. She wiped her eyes.

She'd wash the dishes and wipe up some of the grease. Might not be so bad tomorrow. Tomorrow—.

God help the prison-bound—
Them within the four iron walls this evening!   [*The Crisis* 32.5 (September 1926): 225–226]

NOTHING NEW

by Marita Bonner

There was, once high on a hillside, a muddy brook. A brook full of yellow muddy water that foamed and churned over a rocky bed.

Halfway down the hillside the water pooled in the clearest pool. All the people wondered how the muddy water cleared at that place. They did not know. They did not understand. They only went to the pool and drank. Sometimes they stooped over and looked into the water and saw themselves.

If they had looked deeper they might have seen God.

People seldom look that deep, though. They do not always understand how to do things. They are not God. He alone understands.

* * *

You have been down on Frye street. You know how it runs from Grand Avenue and the L to a river; from freckled faced-tow heads to yellow Orientals; from broad Italy to broad Georgia; from hooked nose to square black noses. How it lisps in French, how it babbles in Italian, how it gurgles in German, how it drawls and crawls through Black Belt dialects. Frye street flows nicely together. It is like muddy water. Like muddy water in a brook.

Reuben Jackson and his wife Bessie—late of Georgia—made a home of three rooms at number thirteen Frye street.

"Bad luck number," said the neighbors.

"Good luck number," said Reuben and Bessie.

Reuben did not know much. He knew only God, work, church, work and God. The only things Bessie knew were God, work, Denny, prayer, Reuben, prayer, Denny, work, work, work, God.

Denny was one thing they both knew beside God and work. Denny was their little son. He knew lots of things. He knew that when the sun shone across the room a cobwebby shaft appeared that you could not walk up. And when the water dripped on pans in the sink it sang a tune: "Hear the time! Feel the time! Beat with me! Tap-ty tap! T-ta-tap! Ta-ty-tap!" The water sang a tune that made your feet move.

"Stop that jigging, you Denny," Bessie always cried. "God! Don't let him be no dancing man." She would pray afterwards. "Don't let him be no toy-tin fool man!"

Reuben watched him once sitting in his sun shaft. Watched him drape his slender little body along the floor and lift his eyes toward the sunlight. Even then they were eyes that drew deep and told deeper. With his oval clear brown face and his crinkled shining hair, Denny looked too—well as Reuben thought no boy should look. He spoke:

"Why don't you run and wrestle and race with the other boys? You must be a girl. Boys play rough and fight!"

Denny rolled over and looked up at his father. "I ain't a girl!" he declared deliberately.

He stared around the room for something to fight to prove his assertion. The cat lay peacefully sleeping by the stove. Denny snatched hold of the cat's tail to awaken it. The cat came up with all claws combing Denny.

"My God, ain't he cruel," screamed his mother. She slapped Denny and the cat apart.

Denny lay down under the iron board and considered the odd red patterns that the claws had made on his arms.... A red house and a red hill. Red trees around it; a red path running up the hill.

"Make my child do what's right," prayed Bessie ironing above him.

People are not God. He alone understands.

* * *

Denny was running full tilt down a hillside. Whooping, yelling, shouting. Flying after nothing. Young Frye street, mixed as usual, raced with him.

There was no school out here. There were no street cars, no houses, no ash-cans and basement stairs to interfere with a run. Out here you could run straight, swift, in one direction with nothing to stop you but your own lack of foot power and breath. A picnic "out of town" pitched your spirits high and Young Frye Street could soar through all twelve heavens of enjoyment.

The racers reached the foot of the hill. Denny swerved to one side. A tiny colored girl was stooping over in the grass.

"Hey, Denny!" she called. Denny stopped to let the others sweep by.

"Hey, Margaret!" he answered, "What you doing?"

Margaret held up a handful of flowers. "I want that one." She pointed to a clump of dusky purple milkweeds bending behind a bush.

Denny hopped toward it.

He had almost reached it when the bush parted and a boy stepped out: "Don't come over here," he ordered. "This is the white kids' side!"

Denny looked at him. He was not of Frye street. Other strange children appeared behind him. "This is a white picnic over here! Stay away from our side."

Denny continued toward his flower. Margaret squatted contentedly in the grass. She was going to get her flower.

"I said not to come over here," yelled the boy behind the bush.

Denny hopped around the bush.

"What you want over here?" the other bristled.

"That flower!" Denny pointed.

The other curved his body out in exaggerated childish sarcasm. "Sissy! Picking flowers." He turned to the boys behind him. "Sissy nigger! Picking flowers!"

Denny punched at the boy and snatched at the flower. The other stuck out his foot and Denny dragged him down as he fell. Young Frye street rushed back up the hill at the primeval howl that set in.

Down on the ground, Denny and the white boy squirmed and kicked. They dug and pounded each other.

"You stay off the white kid's side, nigger!"

"I'm going to get that flower, I am!" Denny dragged his enemy along with him as he lunged toward the bush.

The flower beckoned and bent its stalk. On the white kid's side. Lovely, dusky, purple. Bending toward him. The milky perfume almost reached him. On the white kids' side. He wanted it. He would get it. Something ripped.

Denny left the collar of his blouse in the boy's hand and wrenched loose. He grabbed at the stem. On the white kids' side. Bending to him—slender, bending to him. On the white kids' side. He wanted it. He was going to have it—

The boy caught up to him as he had almost reached the flower. They fell again.—He was going to get that flower. He was going to. Tear the white kid off. Tear the white hands off his throat. Tear the white kid off his arms. Tear the white kid's weight off his chest. He'd move him—

Denny made a twist and slid low to the ground, the other boy beneath him, face downward. He pinned the boy's shoulders to the ground and clutching a handful of blonde hair in either hand, beat his head against the ground.

Young Frye Street sang the song of triumph. Sang it long and loud. Sang it loud enough for Mrs. Bessie Jackson—resting under a clump of trees with other mothers—to hear.

"I know them children is fighting!" she declared and started off in the direction of the yelling.

Halfway she met Margaret, a long milk-weed flower dragging in one hand: "Denny," she explained, holding it up.

"I knew it," cried his mother and ran the rest of the way. "Stop killing that child," she screamed as soon as she had neared the mob. She dragged Denny off the boy. Dragged him through the crowd under a tree. Then she began:

"Look at them clothes. Where is your collar at? All I do is try to fix you up and now look at you! Look at you! Even your shirt torn!"

"Just as well him tear that for what he said," Denny offered.

This approximated "sauce" or the last straw or the point of overflow. His mother was staggered. Was there nothing she could do? Unconsciously she looked up to Heaven, then down to earth. A convenient bush flaunted nearby. She pulled it up—by the roots.

On the white kids' side. The flower he wanted—

God understands, doesn't He?

* * *

It had been .a hard struggle. Reuben was still bitter and stubborn: "What reason Denny got to go to some art school? What he going to learn there?"

"Art! Painting!" Bessie defended. "The teachers at the high school he know how to paint special like. He'd ought to go, they said."

"Yes, they said, but they ain't going to pay for him. He ought to go somewhere and do some real man's work. Ain't nothin' but women paddin' up and down, worryin' about paintin'."

"He's going all the same. Them teachers said he was better!"

"Oh, all right. Let him go."

And Denny went to the Littler Art School. Carried his joyous six-foot, slender, brown self up on Grand Avenue, across, under, the elevated towers—up town. Up town to school.

"Bessie Jackson better put him on a truck like Annie Turner done her Jake," declared colored Frye Street. "Ain't no man got no business spendin' his life learnin' to paint."

"He should earn money! Money!" protested one portion of Frye street through its hooked noses.

"Let him marry a wife," chuckled the Italians.

"He's going to learn art," said Denny's mother.

Denny went. The Littler School was filled with students of both sexes and of all races and degrees of life. Most of them were sufficiently gifted to be there. Days there when they showed promise. Days there when they doubted their own reasons for coming.

Denny did as well and as badly as the rest. Sometimes he even did things that attracted attention.

He himself always drew attention, for he was tall, straight and had features that were meant to go with the blondest hair and the bluest eyes. He was not blond, though. He was clear shaven and curly haired and brown as any Polynesian. His eyes were still deep drawing—deep telling. Eyes like a sea-going liner that could drift far without getting lost; that could draw deep without sinking.

Some women scrambled to make an impression on him. If they had looked at his mouth they would have withheld their efforts.

Anne Forest was one of the scramblers. She did not know she was scrambling, though. If anyone had told her that she was, she would have exploded, "Why! He's a nigger!"

Anne, you see, was white. She was the kind of girl who made you feel that she thrived on thirty-nine cent chocolates, fifteen-dollar silk dress sales, twenty-five cent love stories and much guilty smootchy kissing. If that does not make you sense her water-waved bob, her too carefully rouged face, her too perfumed person, I cannot bring her any nearer to you.

Anne scrambled unconsciously. Denny was an attractive man. Denny knew she was scrambling—so he went further within himself.

Went so far within himself that he did not notice Pauline Hammond who sat next to him.

One day he was mixing paint in a little white dish. Somehow the dish capsized and the paint flowed over the desk and spattered.

"Oh, my heavens!" said a girl's voice.

Denny stood up: "I beg your pardon." He looked across the desk.

Purple paint was splashed along the girl's smock and was even on her shoes.

"Oh, that's all right! No harm done at all," she said pleasantly.

Nice voice. Not jagged or dangling. Denny looked at her again. He dipped his handkerchief into the water and wiped off the shoes.

That done, they sat back and talked to each other. Talked to each other that day and the next day. Several days they talked.

Denny began to notice Pauline carefully. She did not talk to people as if they were strange hard shells she had to crack open to get inside. She talked as if she were already in the shell. In their very shell.

—Not many people can talk that soul-satisfying way. Why? I do not know. I am not God. I do not always understand—

They talked about work; their life outside of school. Life. Life out in the world. With an artist's eye Denny noted her as she talked. Slender, more figure than heavy form, moulded. Poised. Head erect on neck, neck uplifted on shoulders, body held neither too stilt or too slack. Poised and slenderly moulded as an aristocrat.

They thought together and worked together. Saw things through each other's eyes. They loved each other.

One day they went to a Sergeant exhibit—and saw Anne Forest. She gushed and mumbled and declared war on Pauline. She did not know she had declared war, though.

"Pauline Hammond goes out with that nigger Denny Jackson!" she informed all the girls in class next day.

"With a nigger!" The news seeped through the school. Seeped from the President's office on the third floor to the janitor down below the stairs.

Anne Forest only told one man the news. He was Allen Carter. He had taken Pauline to three dances and Anne to one. Maybe Anne was trying to even the ratio when she told him: "Pauline Hammond is rushing a nigger now."

Allen truly reeled. "Pauline! A nigger?"

Anne nodded. "Denny Jackson—or whatever his name is," she hastened to correct herself.

Allen cursed aloud. "Pauline! She's got too much sense for that! It's that nigger rushing after her! Poor little kid! I'll kill him!"

He tore off his smock with a cursing accompaniment. He cursed before Anne. She did not matter. She should have known that before.

Allen tore off the smock and tore along the hall. Tore into a group gathered in a corner bent over a glass case. Denny and Pauline were in the crowd, side by side. Allen walked up to Denny.

"Here you," he pushed his way in between the two. "Let this white girl alone." He struck Denny full in the face.

Denny struck back. All the women—except Pauline—fled to the far end of the room.

The two men fought. Two jungle beasts would have been kinder to each other. These two tore at each other with more than themselves behind every blow.

"Let that white woman alone, nigger! Stay on your own side!" Allen shouted once.—On your own side. On the white kids' side. That old fight—the flower, bending toward him. He'd move the white kid! Move him and get the flower! Move him and get what was his! He seized a white throat in his hands and moved his hands close together!

* * *

He did move the white kid. Moved him so completely that doctors and doctors and running and wailing could not cause his body to stir again. Moved him so far that Denny was moved to the County Jail.

Everything moved then. The judge moved the jury with pleas to see justice done for a man who had sacrificed his life for the beautiful and the true. The jury moved that the old law held: one life taken, take another.

Denny—they took Denny.

Up at the school the trustees moved. "Be it enacted this day—no Negro student shall enter within these doors."

The newspapers moved their readers. Sent columns of description of the "hypnotized frail flower under the spell of Black Art." So completely under the spell she had to be taken from the stand for merely screaming in the judge's face: "I loved him! I loved him! I loved him!" until the court ran over with the cries.

Frye street agreed on one thing only. Bessie and Reuben had tried to raise Denny right. After that point, Frye street unmixed itself. Flowed apart.

Frye street—black—was loud in its utterances. "Served Denny right for loving a white woman! Many white niggers as there is! Either Bessie or Reuben must have loved white themselves and was 'shamed to go out open with them. Shame to have that all come out in that child! Now he rottenin' in a murderer's grave!"

White Frye street held it was the school that had ruined Denny. Had not Frye street—black and white—played together, worked together, shot crap together, fought together without killing? When a nigger got in school he got crazy.

* * *

Up on the hillside the clear water pooled. Up on the hillside people come to drink at the pool. If they looked over, they saw themselves. If they had looked deeper—deeper than themselves—they might have seen God.

But they did not.

People do not do that—do they?

They do not always understand. Do they?

God alone—He understands.   [*The Crisis* 33.1 (November 1926): 17–20]

IN HOUSES OF GLASS

by Ethel R. Clark

The soft, languid voice of Mrs. Langford, wife of a middle-class merchant in Xville, Georgia, interrupted the awkward, sorrowful silence.

"There, there, "Honey," don' take on so! Y'all must have some kin-folk back where you came from an' when they read of yo' mothah's death, they'll sure come for you. While you're waitin,' you just stay right heah with Willie Mae. We all 're right glad to have you."

"Honey" Davis, the girl addressed, made a forlorn-looking picture as she sat huddled on the top step of the Langford home, eyes swollen from weeping and bobbed curls in tousled disorder. There was something uncommonly attractive, wistfully appealing, about her. She wore a trig little sport dress of mystical mauve, set off by soft collar and cuffs of friendliest yellow. But it was the unlooked-for beauty of face in a child only fourteen years old that fastened one's attention. The summer's sun had poured a rich brown tint over the velvety olive skin, against which the appealing blue eyes and dark brown hair stood out in challenging contrast.

"But I feel so lonesome without Mothah! Y'all are powerful good to me (caressing the hand of Mrs. Langford), but you don' know how it feels to be all alone. You reckon folks will see that notice in the papah, sure 'nough? O, I wish I knew where Mothah's people are!"

"Didn't she ever tell you where y'all come from? Nor anything 'bout her folks? Y'all always looked like foreigners to me an' I set out several times to ask yo' mothah, but she was so sort o' tight-mouthed, a body didn't 'low to ask her many questions."

At the reference to her mother's much-discussed failure to talk about herself or her family, Honey's full lips disappeared into a stubborn, set line and her eyes flashed a warning not unheeded by the woman. In a conciliatory tone of voice she bade "Honey" make herself comfortable while she, Mrs. Langford, returned to the house to superintend the preparations for supper.

Left to herself, "Honey" resumed her mournful, tearful meditation, from which state, she was rudely roused by the sound of wild, hilarious laughter and rhythmical, racing feet. As she hastily peered over the railing, a ten or twelve-year-old boy rounded the corner near the Langford home, running at top speed and followed by a yelling, pelting trio of colored boys. No sooner did the runner catch sight of "Honey" than he dashed up the steps in search of refuge. "Honey" rushed the boy into the house. Returning immediately to the porch, she faced the chasing, barefoot trio who now stood defiantly bunched on the edge of the sidewalk.

"Go 'way from heah, you good-for-nothing niggers! How dare you chuck stones at a white boy? Y'all orter be skinned alive! Go on 'way from heah! Go on, I say! How come y'all don' move?"

"He beat up mah li'l brothah what wasn' both'rin' him a 'tall an we all gonna fix him," bravely spoke the oldest, aged eight.

"I don' believe it," shouted 'Honey.' "Leastways if he did, y'all ain't got no call to hit him. You're nothin' but niggers, nohow. Get away from heah!"

With which shrill command she reached for some nearby stones, but the dusky trio had already decided in favor of "safety first" and were retreating precipitately, with many a backward glance. When all was once more restored to tranquility, the white boy emerged in answer to "Honey's" call, curtly thanked her for her assistance and continued on his way. Scarcely was he out of sight when the unusually animated form of Willie Mae dashed up the steps.

"O, 'Honey,' look what I just got fo' you from the Post Office!"

"A letter? Sure 'nough! O, I do hope it's from some of Mothah's folks! Maybe they did see the notice in the papah after all. I'm so excited I can't open it and besides I've just had a time with these nasty, dirty nigger boys that live two streets back yonder in Sawdust Bottom. Mothah always scolded me for calling 'em 'niggers' but they are and I just can't help calling 'em that. I hate 'em all with their smelly black skins. Ugh! I nevah could see how she could take up fo' 'em so. I'm so nervous I can't read this letter. Read it fo' me, Willie Mae?"

"Sho.' Mighty pretty handwriting an' yes! it's signed 'Your loving Aunt, Etta Philips.' Goodness, 'Honey,' I reckon she's rich as anything! Now listen:

> —Hospital,
> Boston, Mass.
> August 12, 1921

My dear Niece:—

I can scarcely hold my pen for I am so excited, so anxious to see you. I have just read an overlooked copy of *The Blade*, the one in which your mother's death is announced and your search for relatives. I am your mother's sister, but we have neither seen nor heard from each other for more than fourteen years.

O! my little niece, how I long to go to you, but I am temporarily indisposed, the result of an automobile accident—nothing serious. So I have arranged for you to go to a board-ing school for girls at—N. C., until such time as I can make the trip and fetch you home with me. Miss Mabel Whitely, the principal, is a personal friend and knew your mother many years ago. I am enclosing a check to cover your expenses.

Meanwhile, be a good girl and bear up bravely.

> Your loving Aunt,
> ETTA PHILLIPS

"My, but you're a lucky girl, 'Honey'!"

During the reading of the letter "Honey's" eyes had grown positively luminous. As Willie Mae ceased speaking, the little motherless girl sprang to her feet, threw both arms around Willie Mae with boundless enthusiasm, then pulling Willie Mae by the hand, ran into the house calling to Mrs. Langford in high, exultant tones.

The train had deposited "Honey," three other passengers and some baggage at their mutual destination, a rural station in North Carolina. The three passengers and most of the baggage had disappeared. Only a small group of colored bystanders, men and a half-grown boy, remained within "Honey's" range of vision. As the girl remained standing there, the boy started toward her bearing a covered basket in one hand and a large pot of steaming coffee in the other.

When he was within hailing distance, he thus offered his wares:

> "Fried chicken, fried chicken,
> Right out'n de pan!
> Fresh coffee, hot coffee,
> Bes' in de lan.'"

"Honey" was too full of anticipation and anxiety even to think of eating, so shook her head impatiently and walked toward the section of the waiting room designated for the whites. Ere she reached the threshold, one of the blacks, an elderly man who had detached himself from the idle group, accosted her hesitantly, hat in hand.

"'Scuse me, Missy, but is yo' name Davis?!"

"Reckon 'tis. Did Miss Whitely send y'all fo me?" appraisingly.

"Yes, Miss, but I 'lowed 'twarnt you at fus.' Dis heah y'all's baggage? Jes' follah me. Heah's owah cyah."

"Owah cyah" proved to be a much-battered, mud-besmeared Ford and as the journey to the school progressed, the unsightly appearance of the car was amply justified by the terrible condition of the roads, most of which were deep, red mud. After what seemed to be the longest three miles in "Honey's" experience, the school was finally sighted.

As the Ford ground its familiar course up the driveway, the girl became a human whirlpool of conflicting emotions. Colored girls all over the campus! What was the driver taking her here for? Could he have mistaken her for some other person by the name of Davis?

Had her Aunt made a mistake in the name and location of the school? Surely not, for she had specifically said the principal and she were friends.

Feverishly she extracted her Aunt's letter from the handbag and re-read the instructions, comparing the name of the school given in the letter with the name written over the main doorway of the building they were approaching. The names there identical!

What could it mean? What was the trouble? Why was her Aunt sending her, "Honey," a white girl, to a colored school? There was some terrible, hideous mistake. She would see the principal!

"Welcome to our fold, dear! So this is the little niece of whom your Aunt wrote me? We are indeed glad to have you. Yes, I am I am Miss Whitely. Walker, please see that her baggage is taken to Room 8. Have you the trunk check?"

All this from a dark-skinned, portly woman. "Honey's" face had gradually been assuming the color of poppies. As Miss Whitely reached in the car to help the girl to alight, she could restrain herself no longer. Wild eyed, she wrenched herself free and literally screamed at the woman:

"Take yo' black hands off me! Take 'em off I say! Don't you dare touch me! Do y'all heah? Send those black devils away! Send them away, I tell you! I'll—I'll—Leave me alone! Let go! Don't you push me! Stop it, I say! Stop! Just wait till I—"

Only by sheer force, violent struggling, did Miss Whitely finally manage to get the biting, scratching, kicking girl into the office and close the door. She was as one insane. The scuffle had drawn a crowd of curious, eager onlookers, whose proximity served but to incense her the more.

At first the older woman had been frankly stunned by the outburst, but only for a moment. Intuitively she understood. Now taking from the wall a group photograph and looking intently at "Honey," the principal inquired whether the girl had ever seen her Aunt. Upon receiving a sullen shake of the head, Miss Whitely singled out a woman of pleasing appearance in the group and pointing to her said,

"There is your Aunt."

Amazement, incredulity, lastly fear, passed in swift succession over the face of "Honey." This woman with brown skin and curly black hair her Aunt! What a joke! What a silly, cheap, degrading lie! What was the matter with this woman, anyhow? How dare she! Her Aunt a nigger! Well I reckon not! Wasn't her Aunt her mother's own sister? And wasn't her mother white?

Wasn't her mother white? That phrase began to repeat itself automatically in her mind until with each successive repetition a hellish doubt began to take form. First one remembered trait of her late mother, then another doubtful characteristic suggested itself in embryo. Evidence of the growth and torture of these reflections was plainly visible on "Honey's" countenance. Mechanically she retreated step by step to the opposite side of the room, eyes riveted alternately on the photograph and Miss Whitely as if she would deduce from the one or the other the truth of this terrible accusation.

It was a lie! Of course! Of course! This Negro, this dark-skinned woman, her Aunt!

Now the hysterical laughter! Again the sudden contraction of the mouth and the dilating of the pupils as a seeming doubt once more entered the portals of thought. How Miss Whitely longed to go to her and clear away the vacillating look of terror! Now it was Miss Whitely's turn to question. Why had this girl been kept in deliberate ignorance of her racial identity? Yet even as she asked herself the question she knew only too well the answer. To enable "Honey" to receive the best in education and advantages, of course. But oh! the penalty of the awakening!

Now "Honey" was sitting down, still absorbed, verily hypnotized by the photograph. Suddenly she sprang to her feet, ran to a mirror in the corner of the room and gazed scrutinously at herself. What torture to watch her! Demented with fear. Hunted, hounded, by an invisible enemy which chased her in never-ending circles of doubt, broken only by fragmentary intervals of approaching hysteria.

At length, turning abruptly from the mirror, she advanced toward the principal and looked her full in the eye.

"Tell me honestly, truthfully, is she really mah Aunt ? And was my mothah colored, too? Am I—Am I—a—n—n—nigger ?"

O, the pathos, the quivering agony voiced in that query!

For reply, Miss Whitely inclined her head and extended two gracious hands. With a smothered shriek and a visible crumpling of the body as though a burden too heavy to be borne had suddenly been placed upon it, "Honey" sank to the floor, senseless.

For two long weeks, a motherless, raceless girl battled with delirium and soul-destroying humiliation. Eventually youth won. The period of convalescence over, she was permitted to leave her room the third week but remained a willfully solitary figure on porch or campus.

A month dragged slowly by, a month of unrealities, of searing pain and readjustments. The awful shame of it! She, "Honey" Davis, one of those things, a nigger! O dear God! Why hadn't someone told her before! What would her white friends say when they knew?

It was all so clear now. Mother's reticence! Their solitary existence! Mother, whom she had almost worshipped, only a nigger! O, well, maybe the dreadful sting of it would wear away after a while. Already she was beginning to like Miss Whitely.

What had happened to her, "Honey," anyhow? How had she changed? Wasn't she the same girl now that she had always been? Did her mind, her body, function any differently now than in former times? No and yes! To all outward appearance she was the same. But the inner self! Funny how just thinking a thing could change one so! Maybe that was all that really made things different anyway. Just thinking so.

Another change had been effected too. Whereas, heretofore, she had always thought of colored people as "niggers," the term now filled her with abhorrence and uncontrollable revulsion. Applied to herself it was intolerable!

How it must have hurt Mother to hear her, "Honey," use it! Mother! How she yearned for that presence now! Mother wouldn't have hurt her so! There! That was it! Mother had kept the knowledge from her to keep from wounding her.

"Honey" had wandered on during her silent soliloquy until now she found herself on the edge of the campus boundary with acres of ripening fields stretching before her. In the distance, Walker, general man-of-all-work, was busily working in the garden. As he worked he sang and the words of the song came floating brokenly to her:

> Although you see me goin' 'long so, O, yes, Lord!
> I has my trials heah below, Oh, yes, Lord!

With a brave little smile of resignation, she slowly recrossed the campus and, with determined mien, approached a group of girl-strollers and timidly asked to join them.

Here was the opportunity for which the girls had long been waiting! They would show the stuck-up thing that they were just as good as she! Forthwith, they proceeded to demonstrate the old Mosaic law by turning their backs upon her and walking away in high, sarcastic glee. The deliberate rebuff to her overt act of conciliation was the last straw. "Honey" took refuge behind the nearest tree trunk and burst into convulsive sobbing.

At this unexpected turn of affairs the girls stood stark still, looked at each other in unfeigned amazement, then, as if by common consent, made a simultaneous dive toward "Honey." Ere the girl could collect her scared and scattered wits, she was surrounded quite by an affectionate, chattering bunch of repentants who began at once to prove to her that the slate was wiped clean.

Later in the evening, Miss Whitely thought she heard a sound as of singing on the front porch. Going noiselessly to the door, she beheld "Honey" seated alone in the porch-swing, eyes gazing into space and singing with a conviction that could be felt:

> And He walks with me and He talks with me,
> And He tells me I am His own;
> And the joy we share as we tarry there,
> None other has ever known.

Hastily wiping away her tears, Miss Whitely stepped onto the porch.

"Come, dear, I think you have been long enough in the night air. Perhaps you would like to come into my office and read a nice, long, interesting letter I received today from your Aunt."

Smiling acquiescence, "Honey" graciously accepted the presence of Miss Whitely's arm about her waist and together they reentered the building.

"Honey" Davis "belonged," belonged to that great human race whose members form one brotherhood, acclaim one Father—God!   [*The Crisis* 34.4 (June 1927): 115–116, 133]

ONE BOY'S STORY

by Joseph M. Andrew [Marita Bonner]

I'm glad they got me shut up in here. Gee, I'm glad! I used to be afraid to walk in the dark and to stay by myself.

That was when I was ten years old. Now I am eleven.

My mother and I used to live up in the hills right outside of Somerset. Somerset, you know is way up State and there aren't many people there. Just a few rich people in big houses and that's all.

Our house had a nice big yard behind it, beside it and in front of it. I used to play it was my fortress and that the hills beside us were full of Indians. Some days I'd go on scouting parties up and down the hills and fight.

That was in the summer and fall. In the winter and when the spring was rainy, I used to stay in the house and read.

I love to read. I love to lie on the floor and put my elbows down and read and read myself right out of Somerset and of America—out of the world, if I want to.

There was just my mother and I. No brothers—no sisters—no father. My mother was awful pretty. She had a roundish plump, brown face and was all plump and round herself. She had black hair all curled up on the end like a nice autumn leaf.

She used to stay in the house all the time and sew a lot for different ladies who came up from the big houses in Somerset. She used to sew and I would pull the bastings out for her. I did not mind it much. I like to look at the dresses and talk about the people who were to wear them.

Most people, you see, wear the same kind of dress goods all the time. Mrs. Ragland always wore stiff silk that sounded like icicles on the window. Her husband kept the tea and coffee store in Somerset and everybody said he was a coming man.

I used to wonder where he was coming to.

Mrs. Gregg always had the kind of silk that you had to work carefully for it would ravel into threads. She kept the boarding house down on Forysthe Street. I used to like to go to that house. When you looked at it on the outside and saw all the windows and borders running up against it you thought you were going in a palace. But when you got inside you saw all the little holes in the carpet and the mended spots in the curtains and the faded streaks in the places where the draperies were folded.

The pale soft silk that always made me feel like burying my face in it belonged to Mrs. Swyburne. She was rich—awful rich. Her husband used to be some kind of doctor and he found out something that nobody else had found out, so people used to give him plenty of money just to let him tell them about it. They called him a specialist.

He was a great big man. Nice and tall and he looked like he must have lived on milk and beef-juice and oranges and tomato juice and all the stuff Ma makes me eat to grow. His teeth were white and strong so I guess he chewed his crusts to.

Anyhow, he was big but his wife was all skinny and pale. Even her eyes were almost skinny and pale. They were sad like and she never talked much. My mother used to say that those who did not have any children did not have to talk much anyhow.

She said that to Mrs. Swyburne one time. Mrs. Swyburne had been sitting quiet like she used to, looking at me. She always looked at me anyhow, but that day she looked harder than ever.

Every time I raised up my head and breathed the bastings out of my face, I would see her looking at me.

I always hated to have her look at me. Her eyes were so sad they made me feel as if she wanted something I had.

Not that I had anything to give her because when had all the money and cars and everything and I only had my mother and Cato my dog, and some toys and books.

But she always looked that way at me and that day she kept looking so long that pretty soon I sat up and looked at her hard.

She sort of smiled then and said, "Do you know, Donald. I was wishing I had a little boy just like you to pull out bastings for me, too."

"You couldn't have one just like me," I said right off quick. Then I quit talking because Ma commenced to frown even though she did not look up at me.

I quit because I was going to say, "Cause I'm colored and you aren't," when Ma frowned.

Mrs. Swyburne still sort of smiled; then she turned her lips away from her teeth the way I do when Ma gives me senna and manna tea.

"No," she said, "I couldn't have a little boy like you, I guess."

Ma spoke right up, "I guess you do not want one like him! You have to talk to him so much."

I knew she meant I talked so much and acted so bad sometimes.

Mrs. Swyburne looked at Ma then. She looked at her hair and face right down to her feet. Pretty soon she said: "You cannot mind that surely. You seem to have all the things I haven't anyway." Her lips were still held in that lifted, twisted way.

Ma turned around the machine then and turned the wheel and caught the thread and it broke and the scissors fell and stuck up on the floor. I heard her say "Jesus," to herself like she was praying.

I didn't say anything. I ripped out the bastings. Ma. Stitched. Mrs. Swyburne sat there. I sort of peeped up at her and I saw a big fat tear sliding down her cheek.

I kind of wiggled over near her and laid my hand on her arm. Then Ma yelled: "Donald, go and get a pound of rice! Go now, I said."

I got scared. She had not said it before and she had a lot of rice in a jar in the closet. But I didn't dare say so. I went out.

I couldn't help but think of Mrs. Swyburne. She ought not to cry so easy. She might not have had a little boy and Ma might have—but she should have been happy. She had a great big house on the swellest street in Somerset and a car all her own and some one to drive it for her. Ma only had me and our house which wasn't so swell, but it was all right.

Then Mrs. Swyburne had her husband and he had such a nice voice. You didn't mind leaning on his knee and talking to him as soon as you saw him. He had eyes that looked so smiling and happy and when you touched his hands they were soft and gentle as Ma's even if they were bigger.

I knew him real well. He and I were friends. He used to come to our house a lot of times and bring me books and talk to Ma while I read.

He knew us real well. He called Ma Louise and me Don. Sometimes he'd stay and eat supper with us and then sit down and talk. I never could see why he'd come way out there to talk to us when he had a whole lot of rich friends down in Somerset and a wife that looked like the only doll I ever had.

A lady gave me that doll once and I thought she was really pretty—all pale and blonde and rosy. I thought she was real pretty at first but by and by she seemed so dumb. She never did anything but look pink and pale and rosy and pretty. She never went out and ran with me like Cato did. So I just took a rock and gave her a rap up beside her head and threw her in the bushes.

Maybe Mrs. Swyburne was pale and pink and dumb like a doll and her husband couldn't rap her with a rock and throw her away.

I don't know.

Anyhow, he used to come and talk to us and he'd talk to Ma a long time after I was in bed. Sometimes I'd wake up and hear them talking. He used to bring me toys until he found out that I could make my own toys and that I liked books.

After that he brought me books. All kinds of books about fairies and Indians and folks in other countries.

Sometimes he and I would talk about the books—especially those I liked. The one I liked most was called "Ten Tales to Inspire Youth."

That sounds kind of funny but the book was great. It had stories in it all about men. All men. I read all of the stories but I liked the one about the fellow named Orestes who went home from the Trojan War and found his mother had married his father's brother so he killed them. I was always sorry for the women with the whips of flame like forked tongues who used to worry him afterwards. I don't see why the fairies pursued him. They knew he did it because he loved his father so much.

Another story I liked was about Oedipus—a Greek too—who put out his eyes to hurt himself because he killed his father and married his mother by mistake.

But after I read "David and Goliath," I just had to pretend that I was David.

I swiped a half a yard of elastic from Ma and hunted a long time until I found a good forked piece of wood. Then I made a swell slingshot.

The story said that David asked Jehovah (which was God) to let his slingshot shoot good. "Do thou lend thy strength to my arm, Jehovah," he prayed.

I used to say that too just to be like him.

I told Dr. Swyburne I liked these stories

"Why do you like them?" he asked me.

"Because they are about men," In said.

"Because they are about men! Is that the only reason?"

Then I told him no; that I liked them because the men in the stories were brave and had courage and stuck until they got what they wanted, even if they hurt themselves getting it.

And he laughed and said, to Ma: "Louise he has the blood, all right!"

And Ma said: "Yes! He is a true Gage. They're brave enough to put their eyes out too. That takes courage all right!"

Ma and I are named Gage, so I stuck out my chest and said: "Ma, which one of us Gages put his eyes out?"

"Me," she said—and she was standing there looking right at me!

I thought she was making fun. So I felt funny.

Dr. Swyburne turned red and said: "I meant the other blood, of course. All the Swyburnes are heroes."

I didn't know what he meant. My name is Gage and so is Ma's so he didn't mean me.

Ma threw her head up and looked at him and says: "Oh, are they heroes?" Then she says real quick: "Donald go to bed right now!"

I didn't want to go but I went. I took a long time to take off my clothes and I heard Ma and Dr. Swyburne talking fast like they were fussing.

I couldn't hear exactly what they said but I kept hearing Ma say: "I'm through!"

And I heard Dr. Swyburne say: "You can't be!"

I kind of dozed to sleep. By and by I heard Ma say again: "Well, I'm through!"

And Dr. Swyburne said: "I won't let you be!"

Then I rolled over to think a minute and then go downstairs maybe.

But when I rolled over again, the sun was shining and I had to get up.

Ma never said anything about what happened so I didn't either. She just walked around doing her work fast, holding her head up high like she always does when I make her mad.

So I never said thing that today.

One day I came home from school. I came in the back way and when I was in the kitchen I could hear a man in the front room talking to Ma. I stood still a minute to see if it was Dr. Swyburne though I knew he never comes in the afternoon.

The voice didn't sound like his so I walked in the hall and passed the door. The man had his back to me so I just looked at him a minute and didn't say anything. He had on leather leggings and a sort of uniform like soldiers wear. He was stooping over the machine talking to Ma and I couldn't see his face.

Just then I stumbled over the little rug in the hall and he stood up and looked at me.

He was a colored man. Colored just like Ma and me. You see, there aren't any other people in Somerset colored like we are, so I was sort of surprised to see him.

"This is my son, Mr. Frazier," Ma said.

I said pleased to meet you and stepped on Ma's feet. But not on purpose. You know I kind of thought he was going to be named Gage and be some relation to us and stay at our house awhile.

I never saw many colored people—no colored men—and I wanted to see some. When Ma called him Frazier it made my feet slippery so I stubbed my toe.

"Hello, son!" he said nice and quiet.

He didn't talk like Ma and me. He talked slower and softer. I liked him straight off so I grinned said: "Hello yourself."

"How's the books?" he said then.

I didn't know what he meant at first but I guessed he meant school. So I said: "Books aren't good as the fishin'."

He laughed out loud and said I was all right and said he and I were going to be friends and that while he was in Somerset he was going to come to our house often and see us.

Then he went out. Ma told me he was driving some lady's car. She was visiting Somerset from New York and he would be there a little while.

Gee, I was so glad! I made a fishing rod for him that very afternoon out of a piece of willow I had been saving for a long time.

And one day, he and I went down to the lake and fished. We sat still on top a log that went across a little bay like. I felt kind of excited and couldn't say a word. I just kept looking at him every once in a while and smiled. I did not grin. Ma said I grinned too much.

Pretty soon he said: "What are you going to be when you grow up, son?"

"A colored man," I said. I meant to say some more, but he hollered and laughed so loud that Cato had to run up and see what was doing.

"Sure you'll be a colored man! No way to get out of that! But I mean this: What kind of work are you going to do?"

I had to think a minute. I had to think of all the kinds of work men did. Some of the men in Somerset were farmers. Some kept stores. Some swept the streets. Some were rich and did not do anything at home but they went to the city and had their cars driven to the shop and to meet them at the train.

All the conductors and porters make a lot of scramble to get these men on and off the train, even if they looked as if they could take care of themselves.

So I said to Mr. Frazier: "I want to have an office."

"An office?"

"Yes. In the city so's I can go in to it and have my car meet me when I come to Somerset."

"Fat chance a colored man has!" he said.

"I can too have an office!" I said. He made me sore. "I can have one if I want to! I want to have an office and be a specialist like Dr. Swyburne."

Mr. Frazier dropped his pole and had to swear something awful when he reached for it though it wasn't very far from him.

"Why'd you pick him?" he said and looked at me kind of mad like and before I could think of what to say he said: "Say son, does that guy come up to see your mother?"

"Sure he comes to see us both!" I said.

Mr. Frazier laughed again but not out loud. It made me sore all over. I started to hit him with my pole but I thought about something I'd read once that said even a savage will treat you right in his house—so I didn't hit him. Of course, he wasn't in my house exactly but he was sitting on my own log over my fishing places and that's like being in your own house.

Mr. Frazier laughed to himself again and then all of a sudden he took the pole I had made him out of the piece of willow I had been saving for myself and laid it across his knees and broke it in two. Then he said out loud: "Nigger women," and then threw the pole in the water.

I grabbed my pole right out of the water and slammed it across his face. I never thought of the hook until I hit him, but it did not stick in him. It caught in a tree and I broke the string yanking it out.

He looked at me like he was going to knock me in the water and even though I was scared, I was thinking how I'd let myself fall if he didn't knock me off—so that I could swim out without getting tangled in the roots under the bank.

But he didn't do it. He looked at me a minute and said: "Sorry, son! Sorry! Not your fault."

Then he put his hand on my hair and brushed it back and sort of lifted it up and said: "Like the rest."

I got up and said I was going home and he came too. I was afraid he would come in but when he got to my gate he said: "So long," and walked right on.

I went on in. Ma was sewing. She jumped up when I came in.

"Where is Mr. Frazier?" she asked me. She didn't even say hello to me!

"I hit him," In said.

"You hit him!" she hollered. "You *hit* him! What did you do that for? Are you crazy?"

I told her no. "He said 'nigger women' when I told him that Dr. Swyburne was a friend of ours and came to see us."

Oh Ma looked terrible then. I can't tell you how she did look. Her face sort of slipped around and twisted like the geography says the earth does when the fire inside of it gets too hot.

She never said a word at first. She just sat there. Then she asked me to tell her all about every bit that happened.

I told her. She kept wriggling from side to side like the fire was getting hotter. When I finished, she said: "Poor baby! My baby boy! Not your fault! Not your fault!"

That made me think of Mr. Frazier so I pushed out of her arms and said: "Ma your breast pin hurts my face when you do that!"

She leaned over on the arms of her chair and cried and cried until I cried too.

All that week I'd think of the fire inside of the earth when I looked at Ma. She looked so funny and she kept talking to herself.

On Saturday night we were sitting at the table when I heard a car drive up the road.

"Here's Dr. Swyburne!" I said and I felt so glad I stopped eating.

"He isn't coming here!" Ma said and then she jumped up.

"Sure he's coming," I said. "I know his motor." And I started to get up too.

"You stay where you are!" Ma hollered and she went out and closed the door behind her.

I took another piece of cake and began eating the frosting. I heard Dr. Swyburne come up on the porch.

"Hello, Louise," he said. I could tell he was smiling by his voice.

I couldn't hear what Ma said at first but pretty soon I heard her say: "You can't come here anymore!"

That hurt my feelings. I liked Dr. Swyburne. I liked him better than anybody I knew beside Ma.

Ma stayed out a long time and by and by she came in alone and I heard Dr. Swyburne drive away.

She didn't look at me at all. She just leaned back against the door and said: "Dear Jesus! With your help I'll free myself."

I wanted to ask her from what did she want to free herself. It sounded like she was in jail or an animal in a trap in the woods.

I thought about it all during supper but I didn't dare say much. I thought about it and pretended that she was shut up in a prison and I was a crime fighter who beat all the keepers and got her out.

Then it came to me that I better get ready to fight to get her out of whatever she was in. I never said anything to her. I carried my air-rifle on my back and my slingshot in my pocket. I wanted to ask her where her enemy was, but she never talked to me about it; so I had to keep quiet too. You know Ma always got mad if I talked about things first. She likes to talk, then I can talk afterwards.

One Sunday she told me she was going for a walk.

"Can I go?" I asked her.

"No," she said. "You play around the yard."

Then she put her hat on and stood looking in the mirror at herself for a minute. All of a sudden I heard her say to herself: "All I need is strength to fight out of it."

"Ma'am?" I thought she was talking to me at first.

She stopped and hugged my head—like I wish she wouldn't sometimes and then went out.

I stayed still until she got out of the yard. Then I ran and got my rifle and slingshot and followed her.

I crept behind her in the bushes beside the road. I cut across the fields and came out behind the willow patch the way I always do when I am tracking Indians and wild animals.

By and by she came out in the clearing that is behind Dr. Somerset's. They call it Somerset's Grove and it's named for his folks who used to live there—just as the town was.

She sat down so I lay down in the bushes. A sharp rock was sticking in my knee but I was afraid to move for fear she'd hear me and send me home.

By and by I heard someone walking on the grass and I saw Dr. Swyburne coming up. He started talking before he got to her. "Louise," he said. "Louise! I am not going to give anything up to a nigger."

"Not even a nigger woman whom you took from a nigger?" She lifted her mouth in the senna and manna way.

"Don't say that!" he said. "Don't say that! I wanted a son. I couldn't have taken a woman in my own world—that would have ruined my practice. Elaine couldn't have a child!"

"Yes," Ma said. "It would have ruined you and your profession. What did it do for me? What did it do for Donald?"

"I have told you I will give him the best the world can offer. He is a Swyburne!"

"He is *my* child," Ma hollered. "It isn't his fault he is yours!"

"But I give him everything a father could give his son!"

"He has no name!" Ma said.

"I have too!" I hollered inside of me. "Donald Gage!"

"He has no name," Ma said again, "and neither have I!" And she began to cry.

"He has blood!" said Dr. Swyburne.

"But how did he get it? Oh, I'm through. Stay away from my house and I'll marry one of my own men so Donald can be somebody."

"A nigger's son?"

"Don't say that again," Ma hollered and jumped up.

"Do you think I'll give up a woman of mine to a nigger?"

Ma hollered again and hit him right in his face.

He grabbed her wrists and turned the right one, I guess because she fell away from him on that side.

I couldn't stand it any more. I snatched out my slingshot and pulled the stone up that was sticking in my knee.

I started to shoot. Then I remembered what David said first, so I shut my eyes and said it: "Do thou, Jehovah (which is God today), lend strength to my arm."

When I opened my eyes Ma had broken away and was running toward the road. Dr. Swyburne was standing still by the tree looking after her like he was going to catch her. His face was turned sideways to me. I looked at his head where his hair was brushed back from the side of his face.

I took aim and let the stone go. I heard him say: "Oh, my God!" I saw blood on his face and I saw him stagger and fall against the tree.

Then I ran too.

When I got home Ma was sitting in her chair with her hat thrown on the floor beside her and her head was lying back.

I walked up to her: "Ma," I said real loud.

She reached out and grabbed me and hugged my head down to her neck like she always does.

The big breast-pin scratched my mouth. I opened my mouth to speak and something hot and sharp ran into my tongue.

"Ma! Ma!" I tried to holler. "The pin is sticking in my tongue!"

I don't know what I said though. When I tried to talk again, Ma and Dr. Somerset were looking down at me and I was lying in bed. I tried to say something but I could not say anything. My mouth felt like it was full of hot bread and I could not talk around it.

Dr. Somerset poured something in my mouth and it felt like it was on fire.

"They found Shev Swyburne in my thistle grove this afternoon," he said to Ma.

Ma looked up quick. "*Found* him! What do you mean?"

"I mean he was lying on the ground—either fell or was struck and fell. He was dead from a blow on the temple."

I tried to holler but my tongue was too thick.

Ma took hold of each side of her face and held to it, then she just stared at Dr. Somerset. He put a lot of things back in his bag.

Then he sat up and looked at Ma. "Louise," he said, "why is all that thistle down on your skirt?"

Ma looked down. So did I. There was thistle down all over the hem of her dress.

"You don't think I killed him, do you?" she cried, "You don't think I did it?" Then she cried something awful.

I tried to get up but I was too dizzy. I crawled across the bed on my stomach and reached out to the chair that had my pants on it. It was hard to do—but I dragged my slingshot out of my pocket, crawled back across the bed and laid it in Dr. Somerset's knees. He looked at me for a minute.

"Are you trying to tell me that you did it, son?" he asked me.

I said yes with my head.

"My God! My God!! His own child!!!"

Dr. Somerset said to Ma: "God isn't dead yet."

Then he patted her on the arm and told her not to tell anybody nothing and they sat down and picked all the thistle down out of the skirt. He took the slingshot and broke it all up and put it all in a paper and carried it downstairs and put it in the stove.

I tried to talk. I wanted to tell him to leave it so I could show my grandchildren what I had used to free Ma like the men do in the books.

I couldn't talk though. My tongue was too thick from my mouth. The next day it burnt worse and things began to float around my eyes and head like pieces of wood in the water.

Sometimes I could see clearly though and once I saw Dr. Somerset talking to another man. Dr. Somerset was saying: "We'll have to operate so save his life. His tongue is poisoned. I am afraid it will take his speech from him."

Ma hollered then: "Thank God! He will not talk! Never! He can't talk! Thank God! Oh God! I thank Thee!" And then she cried like she always does and that time it sounded like she was laughing too.

The other man looked funny and said: "Some of them have no natural feeling of parent for child!"

Dr. Somerset looked at him and said: "You may be fine as a doctor but otherwise you are an awful fool."

Then he told the other man to go out and he began talking to Ma.

"I understand! I understand," he said. "I know all about it. He took you away from somebody and some of these days he might have taken Donald from you. He took Elaine from me once and I told him then God would strip him for it. Now it is all over. Never tell anyone and I will not. The boy knows how to read and write and will be able to live."

So I got a black stump in my mouth. It's shaped like a forked whip.

Some days I pretend I am Orestes with the Furies' whips in my mouth for killing a man.

Some days I pretend I am Oedipus and that I cut it out for killing my own father.

That's what makes me sick all over sometimes.

I killed my own father. But I didn't know it was my father. I was freeing Ma.

Still—I shall never write that on my paper to Ma and Dr. Somerset the way I have to talk to them and tell them when things hurt me.

My father said I was a Swyburne and that was why I liked people to be brave and courageous.

Ma says I am'a a Gage and that is why I am brave and courageous.

But I am both, so I am a whole lot brave, a whole lot courageous. And I am bearing my Furies and my clipped tongue like a Swyburne and Gage—'cause I am both of them.

[*The Crisis* 34.9 (November 1927): 297–299, 316–320]

DRAB RAMBLES

by Marita O. Bonner

I am hurt. There is blood on me. You do not care. You do not know me. You do not know me. You do not care. There is blood on me. Sometimes it gets on you. You do not care I am hurt. Sometimes it gets on your hands—on your soul even. You do not care. You do not know me.

You do not care to know me, you say, because we are different. We are different you say.

You are white, you say. And I am black.

You are white and I am black and so we are different, you say. If I am whiter than you, you say I am black.

You do not know me.

I am all men tinged in brown. I am all men with a touch of black. I am you and I am myself.

You do not know me. You do not care, you say.

I am an inflow of God, tossing about in the bodies of all men: all men tinged and touched with black.

I am not pure Africa of five thousand years ago. I am you—all men tinged and touched. Not old Africa into somnolence by a jungle that blots out all traces of its antiquity.

I am all men. I am tinged and touched. I am colored. All men tinged and touched; colored in a brown body.

Close all men in a small space, tinge and touch the Space with one blood—you get a check-mated Hell.

A check-mated Hell, seething in a brown body, I am.

I am colored. A check-mated Hell seething in a brown body. You do not know me.

You do not care—you say.

But still, I am you—and all men.

I am colored. A check-mated Hell seething in a brown body.

Sometimes I wander up and down and look. Look at the tinged-in-black, the touched-in-brown. I wander and see how it is with them and wonder how long—how long Hell can seethe before it boils over.

How long can Hell be check-mated?

Or if check-mated can solidify, if this is all it is?

If this is all it is.

THE FIRST PORTRAIT

He was sitting in the corridor of the Out-Patients Department. He was sitting in a far corner well out of the way. When the doors opened at nine o'clock, he had been the first one in. His heart was beating fast. His heart beat faster than it should. No heart should beat so fast that you choke at the throat when you try to breathe. You should not feel it knocking—knocking—knocking—now against your ribs, now against something deep within you. Knocking against something deep, so deep that you cannot fall asleep without feeling a cutting, pressing weight laid against your throat, over your chest. A cutting, pressing weight that makes you struggle to spring from the midst of your sleep. Spring up.

It had beat like that now for months. At first he had tried to work it off. Swung the pick in his daily ditch digging—faster—harder. But that had not helped it at all. It had beaten harder and faster for the swinging. He had tried castor-oil to run it off of his system. Someone told him he ate too much meat and smoked too much. So he had given up his beloved ham and beef and chicken and tried to swing the pick on lighter things.

It would be better soon.

His breath had began to get short then. He had to stop oftener to rest between swings. The foreman, Mike Leary, had cursed at first and then moved him back to the last line of diggers. It hurt him to think he was not so strong as he had been.—But it would be better soon.

He would not tell his wife how badly his heart knocked. It would be better soon. He could not afford to lay off from work. He had to dig. Nobody is able to lay off work when there is a woman and children to feed and cover.

The castor oil had not helped. The meat had been given up, even his little pleasure in smoking. Still the heart beat too fast. Still the heart beat so he felt it up in the chords on each side of his neck below his ears.—But it would be better soon.

It would be better. He had asked to be let off half a day so he could be at the hospital at ten o'clock. Mike had growled his usual curses when he asked to get off.

"What the hell is wrong wit' you? All you need is a good dose of whiskey!"

He had gone off. When the doors of the Out-Patient's Department opened, he was there. It took him a long time to get up the stairs. The knocking was in his throat so beads of perspiration stood grey on his black-brown forehead. He closed his eyes a moment and leaned his head back.

A sound of crying made him open them. On the seat beside a woman held a baby in her arms. The baby was screaming itself red in the face, wriggling and twisting to get out of its mother's arms on the side where the man sat. The mother shifted the child from one side to the other and told him with her eyes, "You ought not to be here!"

He had tried to smile over the knocking at the baby. Now he rolled his hat over in his hands and looked down.

When he looked up, he turned his eyes away from the baby and its mother. The knocking pounded. Why should a little thing like that make his heart pound. He must be badly off to breathe so fast over nothing. The thought made his heart skip and pound the harder.

But he would be better soon.

Other patients began to file in. Soon the nurse at the desk began to read names aloud. He had put his card in first but she did not call him first. As she called each name, a patient stood up and went through some swinging doors.

Green lights—men in white coats—nurses in white caps and dresses filled the room it would seem, from the glimpses caught through the door. It seemed quiet and still, too, as if everyone were listening to hear something.

Once the door swung open wildly and an Italian came dashing madly through—a doctor close behind him. The man threw himself on a bench: "Oh God! Oh God! I ain't that sick, I ain't so sick I gotta die! No! You don't really know. I ain't so sick!"

The doctor leaned over him and said something quietly. The nurse brought something cloudy in a glass. The man drank it. By and by he was led out—hiccupping but quieter.

Back in his corner, his heart beat smotheringly. Suppose that had been he? Sick enough to die! Was the dago crazy, trying to run away? Run as he would, the sickness would be always him. For himself, he would be better soon.

Peter Jackson! Peter Jackson. Peter Jackson. Five Sawyer Avenue!" The nurse had to say it twice before he heard through his thoughts.

Thump. The beat of his heart knocked him to his feet. He had to stand still before he could move.

"Here! This way." The nurse said it so loudly—so harshly—that the entire room turned around to look at him.

She need not be so hateful. He only felt a little dizzy. Slowly he felt along the floor with his feet. Around the corner of the bench. Across the space beside the desk. The nurse pushed open the door and pressed it back. "Dr. Sibley?" she called.

The door swung shut behind him. Along each side of the room were desks. Behind each, sat a doctor. When the nurse called "Dr. Sibley," no one answered, so Jackson stood at the door. His heart rubbed his ribs unnecessarily.

"Say! Over here!"

The words and the voice made his heart race again.—But he would be better now. He turned toward the direction of the voice, met a cool pair of blue eyes boring through tortoise—rimmed glasses. He sat down.

The doctor took a sheet of paper. "What's your name?"

His heart had been going so that when he said "Peter Jackson," he could make no sound the first time.

"What's your name, I said."

"Peter Jackson."

"How old are you?"

"Fifty-four."

"Occupation? Where do you work?"

"Day laborer for the city."

"Can you afford to pay a doctor?"

Surprise took the rest of his breath away for a second. The question had to be repeated.

"I guess so. I never been sick."

"Well, if you can afford to pay a doctor, you ought not to come here. This clinic is for foreigners and people who cannot pay a doctor. Your people have some of your own doctors in this city."

The doctor wrote for such a long time on the paper then that he thought he was through with him and he started to get up.

"Sit down." The words caught him before he was on his feet. "I haven't told you to go anywhere."

"I thought—," Jackson hung on his words uncertain.

"You needn't! Don't think! Open your shirt." And the doctor fitted a pair of tubes in his ears and shut out his thoughts.

He fitted the tubes in his ears and laid a sieve-like piece of rubber against his patient's chest. Laid it up. Laid it down. Finally he said: "What have you been doing to this heart of yours? All to pieces. All gone"

Gone. His heart was all gone. He tried to say something but the doctor snatched the tube away and turned around to the desk and wrote again.

Again he turned around: "Push up your sleeve," he said this time.

The sleeve went up. A piece of rubber went around his arm above the elbow. Something began to squeeze—knot—drag on his arm.

"Pressure almost two hundred," the doctor shot at him this time. "You can't stand this much longer."

He turned around. He wrote again. He wrote and pushed the paper away. "Well," said the doctor, "you will have to stop working and lie down. You must keep your feet on a level with your body."

Jackson wanted to yell with laughter. Lie down. If he had had breath enough, he would have blown all the papers off the desk, he would have laughed so. He looked into the blue eyes. "I can't stop work," he said.

The doctor shrugged: "Then," he said, and said no more.

Then! Then what?

Neither one of them spoke.

Then what?

Jackson wet his lips: "You mean—you mean I got to stop work to get well?"

"I mean you have to stop if you want to stay here."

"You mean even if I stop you may not cure me?"

The blue eyes did go down toward the desk then. The answer was a question.

"You don't think I can make a new heart, do you? You only get one heart. You are born with that. You ought not to live so hard."

Live hard? Did this man think he had been a sport? Live hard. Liquor, wild sleepless nights—sleep-drugged, rag-worn, half-shoddy days? That instead of what it had been. Ditches and picks. Births and funerals. Stretching a dollar the length of ten. A job, no job; three children and a wife to feed; bread thirteen cents a loaf. For pleasure, church—where he was too tired to go sometimes. Tobacco that he had to consider twice before he bought.

"I ain't lived hard! I ain't lived hard!" he said suddenly. "I have worked harder than I should, that's all."

"Why didn't you get another job?" the doctor snapped. "Didn't need to dig ditches all your life."

Jackson drew himself up; "I had to dig ditches because I am an ignorant black man. If I was an ignorant white man, I could get easier jobs. I could even have worked in this hospital."

Color flooded the doctor's face. Whistles blew and shrieked suddenly outside.

Twelve o'clock. Mike would be looking for him.

He started for the door. Carefully. He must not waste his strength. Rent, food, clothes. He could not afford to lay off.

He had almost reached the door when a hand shook him suddenly. It was the doctor close behind him. He held out a white sheet of paper: "Your prescription," he explained, and seemed to hesitate. "Digitalis. It will help some. I am sorry."

Sorry for what? Jackson found the sidewalk and lit his pipe to steady himself. He had almost reached the ditches when he remembered the paper. He could not find it. He went on.

The Second Portrait

By twelve o'clock, noon, the washroom of Kale's Fine Family Laundry held enough steam to take the shell off of a turtle's back. Fill tubs with steaming water at six o'clock, set thirty colored women to rubbing and shouting and singing at the tubs and by twelve o'clock noon the room is over full of steam. The steam is thick—warm—and it settles on your flesh like a damp fur rug. Every pore sits agape in your body; agape—dripping.

Kale's Fine Family Laundry did a good business. Mr. Kale believed in this running on oiled cogs. Cogs that slip easily—oiled from the lowest to the highest.

Now the cogs lowest in his smooth machinery were these thirty tubs and the thirty women at the tubs. I put the tubs first, because they were always there. The women came and went. Sometimes they merely went. Most all of them were dark brown and were that soft bulgy fat that no amount of hard work can rub off of some colored women. All day long they rubbed and scrubbed and sang or shouted and cursed or were silent according to their thirty natures.

Madie Frye never sang or shouted or cursed aloud. Madie was silent. She sang and shouted and cursed within. She sang the first day she came there to work. Sang songs of thanksgiving within her. She had needed that job. She had not worked for ten months until she came there. She had washed dishes in a boarding house before that. That was when she first came from Georgia. She had liked things then. Liked the job, liked the church she joined, liked Tom Nolan, the man for whom she washed dishes.

One day his wife asked Madie if she had a husband. She told her no. She was paid off. Madie, the second, was born soon after. Madie named her unquestioningly Madie Frye. It never occurred to her to name her Nolan, which would have been proper.

Madie bore her pain in silence, bore her baby in a charity ward, thanked God for the kindness of a North and thanked God that she was not back in Culvert when Madie was born, for she would have been turned out of church.

Madie stopped singing aloud then. She tried to get jobs—dishwashing—cleaning— washing clothes—but you cannot keep a job washing someone's clothes or cleaning their house and nurse a baby and keep it from yelling the lady of the house into yelling tantrums.

Madie, second, lost for her mother exactly two dozen jobs between her advent and her tenth month in her mother's arms.

Madie had not had time to feel sorry for herself at first. She was too busy wondering how long she could hold each job. Could she keep Madie quiet until she paid her room rent? Could she keep Mrs. Jones from knowing that Madie was down under the cellar stairs in a basket every day while she was upstairs cleaning until she got a pair of shoes?

By the time she went to work in Kales's Hand Laundry, she had found the baby a too great handicap to take to work. She began to leave Madie with her next door neighbor, Mrs. Sundell, who went to church three times every Sunday and once in the week. She must be good enough to keep Madie while her mother worked. She was. She kept Madie for two dollars a week and Madie kept quiet for her and slept all night long when she reached home with her mother. Her mother marveled and asked Mrs. Sundell how she did it.

"Every time she cries, I give her paregoric. Good for her stomach."

So the baby grew calmer and calmer each day. Calmer and quieter. Her mother worked and steamed silently down in Kale's tub-room. Worked, shouting songs of thanksgiving within her for steady money and peaceful nights.

June set in, and with it, scorching days. Days that made the thick steam full of lye and washing-powder eat the lining out of your lungs. There was a set of rules tacked up inside the big door that led into the checking-room that plainly said: "This door is never to be opened between the hours of six in the morning and twelve noon. Nor between the hours of one and six p.m."

That was to keep the steam from the checkers. They were all white and could read and write so they were checkers.

One day Madie put too much lye in some boiling water. It choked her. When she drew her next breath, she was holding her head in the clean cool air of the checking-room. She drew in a deep breath and coughed. A man spun across the floor and a white hand shot to the door. "Why the hell don't you obey rules?" He slammed the door and Madie stumbled back down the stairs.

A girl at the end tub looked around. "Was that Mr. Payne?" she asked.

Madie was still dazed; "Mr. Payne?" she asked.

"Yah. The man what closed the door."

"I don't know who he was."

The other laughed and drew closer to her. "Better know who he is," she said.

Madie blinked up at her. "Why?"

The girl cocked an eye: "Good to know him. You can stay off sometimes—if he likes you." That was all that day.

Another day Madie was going home. Her blank brown face was freshly powdered and she went quietly across the checking-room. The room was empty it seemed at first. All the girls were gone. When Madie was half across the room she saw a man sitting in the corner behind a desk. He looked at her as soon as she looked at him. It was the man who had yanked the door out of her hand, she thought. Fear took hold of her. She began to rush.

Someone called. It was the man at the desk. "Hey, what's your rush?" The voice was not loud and bloody this time. It was soft—soft—soft—like a cat's foot. Madie stood still afraid to go forward—afraid to turn around.

"What, are you afraid of me?" Soft like a cat's foot. "Come here."

—Good to know him—

Madie made the space to the outer door in one stride. The door opened in. She pushed against it.

"Aw, what's the matter with you?" Foot-steps brought the voice nearer. A white hand fitted over the doorknob as she slid hers quickly away.

Madie could not breathe. Neither could she lift her eyes. The door opened slowly. She had to move backwards to give it space. Another white hand brushed the softness of her body.

She stumbled out into the alley. Cold so sweat stood out on her.

Madie second had cost her jobs and jobs. She came by Madie keeping that first job.

Madie was black brown. The baby was yellow. Was she now going to go job hunting or have a sister or brother to keep with Madie second?

Cold perspiration sent her shivering in the alley.

And Madie cursed aloud.

* * *

Not in my day or your tomorrow—perhaps—but somewhere in God's day of meting— somewhere in God's day of measuring full measures overflowing—the blood will flow back to you—and you will care.   [*The Crisis* 34.10 (December 1927): 335–336, 354]

BATHESDA OF SINNERS RUN

———∞∞∞———

by Maude Irwin Owens

It was like reading the Books of Chronicles, to read in the Thornton family history of the attending succession of slave women that formed the single line of Bathesda's ancestry. The Thorntons had always boasted of their seven generations of slave housekeepers who had directly descended from the housekeeper of the first American Thornton. They would proudly point out the precious, faded entries, so faithfully recorded in the old genealogy. The paternal side of the issue was always politely ignored in strict accordance with the manners and customs of the South.

The scapegrace younger son of an English baron, Richard Thornton, was founder of the family. When gambling debts and foul dueling forced him to flee his native land, he decided upon the colony of George II under Governor Oglethorpe. His first slave purchase was written in two sentences, which seemed to wink and laugh up at the reader with its tan ink and old fashioned lettering. It read: "On this day did I barter my gold hilted sword, some lace and several shillings to that villain from the Virginia colony whom I do sorely despise—for a black wench to cook my porridge, brew my tea and wash my linen. She is comely withal and methinks, the temper of a noble blooded colt: so I have named the vixen, Jezebel."

From this Jezebel on the issue became mulatto and less mulatto: for it was written that Jezebel foaled a likely mustard-colored filly whose father and master, with malicious humor, named for his King and the colony.

So Jezebel became the mother of Georgie; who begat Abigail; whose brat was Callie; whose offspring was Ruth; whose child was Viney; whose daughter was Anne; and twenty years after slavery, came Bathesda.

To the utter amazement and chagrin of her erstwhile master and mistress, when the bell of freedom tolled for those in bondage, Anne betook herself from under the Thornton roof, in spite of all the inducements and cajoleries the Thorntons offered.

She married Enoch Creek, a fusion of Creek Indian, Negro and white and who chose to select his surname from the Indian blood which dominated his being. He was a bitter man, having no faith or belief in mankind or the institutions and principles of mankind; a religion of hatred that banned all but Anne and much later little Bathesda.

They founded a tiny home at Sinners Run, the Negro suburb of Thorntonville, Georgia, that had been called after a famous camp-meeting revival sermon preached there, years back. Their cabin was a little apart and elevated from the other huts and shacks of the Sinners Run people, so that they could look down upon the road which was alternatingly red clay or yellow mud and note the comings and goings of those who lived upon it.

Anne attended the Sinners Run Baptist Church regularly and prayed that her husband find salvation. Enoch traded at the store because it was necessary—but after that, all socializing with their neighbors ceased; unless in the case of illness, when Anne was administering angel and healer of the small community. Within her lean yellow hands was the strange, soothing power to allay pain, and from her husband, she learned much of the Indian mysteries of roots and herbs for medicinal use.

They were thrifty and got along. For twenty years they worked, saved, improved their little two room home, and the acre upon which it stood. Anne was an expert needle-woman as Viney, Ruth and Callie had been before her; and she was in great demand in all the big houses down in Thorntonville. Enoch hired himself out as a plantation farmer, and in spite of his scowling silence, was known as a good hand.

Then, at the age of forty—when all hope of bearing the traditional one girl-child had flown from the heart of Anne, it happened; and Bathesda made her advent into the life of Sinners Run.

Enoch smiled for the first time—his squinting Indian eyes snapping with delight at the yellow gypsy-like Anne in the role of Madonna, with the robust little papoose that was his. Of course the Thorntons got wind of it, investigated and greedily annexed one more generation to old Jezebel's descendants, although the essence of reflected glory had lost its flavor since the inconvenient Emancipation. The distinction of being the first of her line born out of slavery, was the most disgraceful thing that could have been written about Bathesda, into the sacred Annals, according to Thornton opinion.

Two weeks later, Enoch stepped on a rusty spike. Blood-poisoning set in and, in spite of their combined knowledge of medicine and healing—his time had come to leave Anne and Bathesda, before Anne had convinced him there was a God.

Anne turned from the unmarked grave, and faced the world alone with her baby, unflinchingly, with that calm independence that asked no pity. She went about her sewing at the houses of her patrons, for a while, carrying her infant with her.

But as Bathesda began to toddle about, Anne realized her child should have home life, and be allowed to play in the vegetable patch and flower garden which Enoch had so painstakingly planted. So Anne took only work such as she could do at home, and her little daughter grew to be the marvel of the country side—a healthy, lovely child.

She attended the broken down school-house to be taught by a wizened old maid from Connecticut a few months a year, and she sat at her mother's knee, during the school period ... both struggling eagerly to master a clear fluent English. Anne, being, ardently religious, insisted that the little girl read her Bible and attend church regularly, in which she was reluctantly obeyed.

Thus Bathesda grew up to womanhood. Beautiful—of deep-rooted intelligence handicapped by inadequate schooling, a pagan love for the gorgeous wonders of Nature and a passion for all things artistic. She became adept at the fine French seams and hemming; learned to feather-stitch the picturesque quilts on the huge frame, to weave highly imaginative Indian designs out of the bright silken rags into rugs and mats, to make the difficult Yankee hook jug, the knowledge of which had been introduced South by a Yankee Thornton bride; and best of all, she became an expert copier of the old ante-bellum samplers. Anne's sampler embroidering frame looked worm-eaten—it was so old; and Bathesda considered it with great reverence.

They made a picture to be remembered, sitting together at their artistic labors—the older woman and her daughter. Anne invariably talked religion to Bathesda having sensed a silent indifference which bespoke much of Enoch's atheism. When at the stuffy little church, the sermon had become highly exhortive, and the worshiper's down-trodden souls burst forth in howling primitive devotion to a God they desperately believed in—even when great tears spilled down her quiet mother's cheeks, Bathesda's sole reaction was a disdainfully cold squinting of her pretty black eyes.

"It's Enoch! It's Enoch!" mourned old Anne, as she watched the child of her old age flower into radiant womanhood with no change of heart.

"But Mother," Bathesda would say, "you take on so 'bout nothin'. Ain't we happy? We have always been different from them in our way of livin' and doin' things and so how can you expect me to be like them in their church doin's? You are not like them when you feel the spirit, Mother. You cry a little bit, but I have never seen you rear and tear and stomp and scream 'halleluliah' like someone crazy.... I hate it! My church is the purple mist stealin' ahead of the red dawn—the chirpin' woodchucks; wild wood blossoms! If I ever 'get religion' Mother 'twill be in that kind of church, and not among the sweaty, hysterical hypocrites of your church. Why! I believe to my soul, Mother, you are the only real Christian among them, and do the least testifyin'!"

"Child—you don't understand. It is as real with them as life itself! It is given to each to work out his own destiny in the Lord, in his own way. It is the feelin' that they are weak and sinful that overpowers them so—in their strivin' to follow the Good Book."

"I don't care 'bout them anyways, Mother. We are better colored folks ... that's all. It just ain't in them to be better. Look at their homes! Bare plank doors that all their scrubbin' and scourin' don't improve; walls plastered with newspapers full of pictures that they think are pretty; gunny-sacks tacked up to the windows ... ugh! Give them their winter supply of potatoes, rice and hog meat ... let them go to church and give chitterlin' suppers ... plenty of shoutin' and back-bitin' and they are happy all winter long, Mother. But look—at our home!"

She waved her pale brown hand proudly around the room in which they sat. The walls were whitewashed. The floor was covered with a huge rag rug rich with colorful stripes and the single square window was draped with deep rose curtains that fluttered happily in the breeze. They had been made from flour bags soaked in kerosene to remove the printing, and dyed with berry juice. There were two fine old pieces of colonial mahogany in this outer room—a gigantic highboy and a marble-topped medicine chest The other articles of furniture were three rush-bottomed chairs and a table that Enoch had made, and carved all over with the weirdly grotesque totem-pole gargoyles. Upon the mantel over the fireplace revere a brilliant basket and two odd potteries also relics of the Creek strain in the father of Bathesda. Small, painted tubs and cans were in interesting groups about the room, filled with plants of various sorts.

"I don't suppose I should say I hate them, Mother dear," Bathesda continued, "but I can get along without them. I shall do as you have always done ... when they're sick, I'll make them well if they call upon me—but I don't ... I can't be one of them in religion or otherwise."

"Ah, my child," sadly smiled Anne, "you may have inherited the sense of medicine from Enoch, your father, but the Divine gift of healing can never descend upon a disbeliever ... and you are the first of us women who has not been born with the gift since Mother Jezebel. She, even in her early day, was a Christian convert."

At this, Bathesda would shake her head impatiently as if flinging aside the admonitions of her mother, and the two long black braids would flare about her arms and shoulders. Then, bowing earnestly over her work, she would concentrate upon the exact copying of probably old Viney's intricately designed sampler with the words,—"Little flakes make the biggest snow," ordered by an antique dealer from Savannah.

Bathesda's mother died in her sixtieth year, and never had there been such a funeral in the history of Sinners Run. Unlike her husband who had only a faithful wife and new born babe to follow him to his grave—the entire countryside turned out to do honor to Anne Creek. All of the present generation of Thorntons came from their town house in Savannah, in full force, much to the awe of the Sinners Run folk. They even hinted about how appropriate and fitting it would be if Anne were buried beside Viney, in Thorntonville; but Bathesda was obdurate.

"Thank you, Mr. and Mrs. Thornton, but my mother's place is beside her husband. My father has been alone out there, long enough."

So the Thorntons had a second lesson in Negro independence.

"Promise me, my daughter, that you will seek Jesus!" gasped Anne in her last consciousness. "Go to the church—seek Him until you find Him ... and He will give you your birthright like he has given it to all the rest of us. Promise your poor old Mammy, Bathesda ... baby!"

And so she had promised to seek religion and the power to heal the sick.

Bathesda lived on, as the years rolled by, much as when Anne lived. She made beautiful things with her graceful slender hands, and more money than she needed in her simple mode of living. She lived alone with the spirit presences of her parents, except for the loyal protection of a watch dog. She cared for the gay little flower garden tenderly and kept her graves freshly decorated in flower season. She grew her vegetables, also the roots and herbs with which she concocted her famous medicinal recipes. She attended the Sinners Run Baptist Church and contributed to its support; but the Indian in her worshipped only the wonders of Nature and she put no other gods before the beauty of the earth.

The colored people of Sinners Run envied and hated her, yet maintained a deceitful courtesy that permitted them to call upon her when in need of intervention with white people, money or in sickness. Her ability to always smooth the way for them, in any form of distress, was known with a certainty that was uncanny to their superstitious minds. She could do all except smooth out actual pain like her mother had done. However, she did her all, in the name of Anne ... she herself caring little for these crude mean-hearted and petty people, who grinned in her face for favors, and hissed "half white bastard" behind her back. This last amused her, however, since her intelligence allowed her to see no difference between the black and yellow progeny of the illicit unions of slavery.

"What queer religion these folks have," laughed the woman, "it breaks forth in a certain place, and at a certain fixed time, then they lose it 'til the next time."

The women were especially incensed against her, because—if they married at all, they invariably married men who Bathesda had rejected. She allowed each suitor in his time, to visit her, sit as long as he pleased admiring her at the embroidering rack, while she, with serene indifference hoped he would make his departure in time for her to take her dog and to go the crest for the sunset, or some such solitary jaunt. She could say "no" with a cool pleasantness that retained their goodwill; but the wives to whom she gave the men up, hated her venomously for so doing. Hated her for wrapping her long glossy braids around and around her head in a coronet which made her a queen among them. Hated her for appearing so youthful despite her forty-seven years. Hated her for not shouting at church, and for failing to testify or profess. Hated her for having the prettiest house and garden in the community—for making the medicine that cured them. Hated her for weaving and embroidering while they took in washing, or labored beside their men in the cotton and corn fields. Hated her for her chaste aloofness of man, while they bore large families in the morass of poverty and misery. Hated her for showing contempt for the edicts of fashions and mail order houses up North or the cheap stores in Thorntonville and Savannah and for wearing the simply made, richly embroidered garments which none could duplicate. For all these reasons, the women of Sinners Run despised Bathesda.

Among them, she had one sincere friend in the person of young Becky Johnson. The dark-skinned girl had sought Bathesda in a frenzy one stormy midnight. Bathesda had donned her cape and accompanied the wild young mother to the bedside of her baby who was strangling with dyptheria. It was a simple deed; the swabbing of the little throat with boiled vinegar and salt, with a few directions, but the brown girl had hugged Bathesda's knees and kissed her comfortably shod feet in feverish adoration. The father, too, had looked dumb gratitude with brimming eyes. After this incident, Becky took Li'l Jim up to see Bathesda regularly, and Bathesda became greatly attached to the small family such devotion from Becky having awakened within her cold nature, something akin to affection.

Becky's sister, mother and grandmother, strongly disapproved of this friendship. The sister, whose name was Cisseretta, was somewhat of a belle, and when rigged up in the cast-off clothes of the white people for whom she worked, was, for Sinners Run, quite elegant. She was light brown, with hazel eyes that were sly and coquettish. Her hair was of that yellowish cotton-barren sort, known as riney. She meant to marry better than had her older sister, and scorned the field hands as prospective husbands, although she was not averse to keeping them from dancing attendance on the less discriminating girls of her set.

The mother, Eliza Lambert, was about Bathesda's age and a malicious "yes" woman to gossip and trouble making, although too stupid herself to even investigate a healthy lie.

The grandmother, Granny Lou, was an ancient crone, black as pitch, who had lost trace of her age, but knew everything pertaining to a scandalous nature concerning the families of both races for miles around. She sat in one corner year in and year out, wrapped in filthy shawls and hoods summer and winter, smoking her foul clay pipe, and spitting snuff into the maw of the tumble-down stove, or gumming her vicious old tales. She was reputed to be the oldest woman in that section of Georgia, and to have borne more children than she herself knew; Eliza, being her youngest, to whom she had hitched herself. Just as most of the trouble making and under-current of evilness in the neighborhood could usually be traced to the chair of Granny Lou and Lambert household, so was she guilty of inciting most of the fierce antipathy among the women, against Bathesda.

One particular early autumn morning, she pursed and screwed her shrunken lips around to settle the snub and saliva making a "Mpwhumn-mpwhumn" noise, and began lisping to Eliza who was washing:

"Heh, heh!" Ah sees whar dat-ar new ministah done gine sottin up to Thesdy's already—heh, heh! 'Pears lak to me dat you 'omans ain't slaves no moah an' oughten't go fer to put up wid sich cayyin' on. Lise ... Yo' Cissy tryin' to sot huh cap foah him, but 'pears lak to me, effen she gits him, won't be twell dat Thesday's chawed 'im up an' spat him back at huh! Heh, heh!" and as if to suit the word with the action, she spat into the pink wood ashes which were falling out of the stove pit.

"Taint nothin' to them Jezebel 'omans, noways. De white folks make me sick cayin' on so high 'bout dem. Day all sold dere souls to de debbil. Don't dey fool 'round wid roots 'n things? ... mind how dey nebber show dere natchul age lak we'uns does?"

The silence that followed was broken by the sudsy slapping of wet clothes with home made lye soap. Eliza was too busy to bother about her old mother's chatter this morning, but Granny Lou was nothing loath to amusing herself.

"Becky, lak a li'l fool ... she run up dere case day yaller 'omen do foah dat brat ahern, jis what any of ussen coulda did. Ah knows, chal! Yo Granny Lou knowed dem f'om way back to Callie!"

"Kyah, kyah, kyah! Granny Lou hush yo mouf," laughingly yelled Eliza above the suds, steam and slop, with perspiration dripping from her corn-rowed head into the tub.

Cisseretta, who had entered the room unnoticed, flared up angrily at the old hag's challenge—

"I wants Brother Parson Brown, and I's shore goin' to git him. 'Taint goin' to be after Thesday done chawed him, either, Granny!" So saying, she jammed her hands down upon her hips with her legs astride and frowned belligerently from her mother to her grinning grandmother.

The pine door swung open admitting Becky, resplendent in a soft white dress carrying Li'l Jim who was sportive in a blue smock and cap. The three women were aghast at the sudden picture. Poor Becky who was content to drudge in a one room cabin with her baby, for a husband who scarcely could pay for his fat back and meal down at the store,—what right had she to look nicer than Cisseretta, the acknowledged social leader of Sinners Run!

"Whar'd je git dem cloes?" darkly inquired Eliza of her daughter.

"Oh Mammy! Ain't dey jist swell? Miss Thesdy done made dis up special for me out o' brand new goods case ah told huh 'twas my second year married, today! See Li l Jim? Ain't he grand? I had a big suppah foh Big Jim when he gits home and thought I would run in an let you folks see us."

"Humph! 'Miss' Thesdy! Since whin did we start 'Missin' yaller niggers? Was Parson Brown anywhere bouts up there?" this from Cisseretta.

"Seems to me dat dose clo'es would scorch yo' skin, chal. Dat Thesdy is a woman wid no religion whatsomever," exasperatingly sighed Eliza.

"Jes' gib yo all dose cloes fuh to git yo' wrapped up in huh, fudder—den she gine conjuh yo ... heah me, now heah me!" snapped old Granny Lou with a portentious shaking of her beshawled head.

Poor Becky! All her joyous happiness so quickly transformed to bitter antagonism.

"How come yo' all hates that pore woman so? What she done done aginst you? All I seed she done was good! She's up dere in huh own pretty li'l house, amindin' huh business, and you folks down heah hatin' huh! Cisseretta? You won't make no hit wid Parson Brown... hatin' Miss Thesdy, 'case he thinks she is jest grand! As for me and Big Jim, she saved our boy's life which is moah den you what's his own kin-folks done, and we loves huh, even if she ain't done professed 'ligion. From what I seed of huh and knowed of younes, she's a heap sight nigh to God den you folks who eat out yo hearts wid hatin' huh!"

She gathered the bewildered Li'l Jim up and left the scene of unsympathetic relatives, muttering to herself—"Gawd! Effen I stayed widdem any longer I would lose my own 'ligion. They's my own folks, but dey simply breed evilness, and I doesn't blame sweet Miss Thesdy from not minglin' wid 'em, 'ceptin' when she has to."

In the Lambert cabin, Granny Lou was grunting—"See dat? She done got dat chal tu'ned agin huh own folks already ... an de preachuh eatin' out ob huh hand,"—with a cunning glance at Cisseretta.

"For two cents, Granny—" whined Cisseretta, petulantly, "I'd git the women together and go up to her ol' house and beat her up!"

"Kyah kyah! Lawsy me! Hush yo' motif, chal!" elaborately guffawed her mother.

"Go hade, den ... go hade! Do moah—an' talk less, honey!" huskily whimpered the old woman to her infuriated grandchild.

The day had been a busy one for Bathesda. She had contracted to make reproductions of the old samplers for an important Jewish antique dealer of Atlanta. Little Alice Thornton, quite grown up, and home from college, had motored out to see her, bringing with her her fiancé from Boston, an artist. He had begged for the privilege of painting Bathesda in all the glory of her little cottage and embroidering frames. To please Alice, she consented, on condition that it wouldn't interfere with her work.

"Like one of Millet's peasant women," he had said—"and that interior! Worthy of the old Dutch masters."

The young minister had sat awhile, explaining his well meant plan of progress for his congregation, which she knew would never be accepted by the deluded Sinners Run folks, the present pastor being their first seminary man. They understood only the old fashioned untrained "called-but-not-sent" type of ministering.

Becky and Li'l Jim dropped in with the new things she had made for them, and the sight of the mother and child transformed by her handiwork, thrilled her deeply.

She bent her queenly head over the crimson, green and purple threads she was inter-weaving so intricately into the words—"Heart within, God without" on the square of yellow, and smiled the smile of the middle-aged who had all they wanted in life—peace, pleasant labor, and contentment. Why should she be sad because of a God who withheld Himself, or the doubtful power of healing a people who despised her?

She decided to pick a fresh cabbage for her supper, and going to the door, was surprised to see Cisseretta Lambert approaching. With shifting eyes, and lowered brow, she informed Bathesda they had come to fetch her for a friend. At the little picket gate stood an old rickety home-made cart with ill matched wheels, drawn by a sorry nag whose hips punctured his skin in miss-meal significance. Eliza was driving and perched beside her for all the world like a bundled up mummy, sat Granny Lou.

"We kin fotch you there and back in no time, Thesdy. New folks jest come to Sinners Run, and powerful sick."

Bathesda hurriedly threw a light shawl around her shoulders with a strong sense of foreboding which she forcibly thrust out of her mind, and joined the trio at the cart.

She and Cisseretta rode backwards with their feet swinging, and nothing was said by the four women as the half dead animal faltered along the lonely road pulling the unbalanced, lurching, wabbling vehicle behind him.

Then Eliza ...

"Kyah kyah! Heah we all is, folksies! Kyah Kyah! Lawdy, Lawd!"

Bathesda turned from the back end of the wagon and saw glaring malevolently at her, the dark faces of ten or twelve women. They were as a pack of hungry hounds eager to be off on the chase. Cisseretta leaped from her seat on the wagon and rudely grabbed Bathesda, causing her to stumble to the ground on her knees. As if waiting for the initiative action from their leader, they pounced upon her, dragging her by the arms up the sloping hill side. The decrepit conveyance with the beswaddled old woman, was left standing on the road.

The maddened women yelled violent invectives—brandished whips, twigs and sticks aloft, dragging her roughly uphill, not allowing her to regain her foothold or the freedom of her arms.

"Thought you'd git yo claws on Revern Bro Brown, didn't you? We see 'bout dat, won't we? Cain't feed him none o' yo hoodoo vittles ... nu-huh!"

"Yes indeedy. We is gwine to see 'bout all dis heah monkey business yo been cayin' on all dese yeahs wid de men folks ...."

"Think you better don ussens, doesn't you? Humph! Old half white riggers make me sick ... caint be white an' caint be black!"

"Naw! We niggers don't want you and de white folks won't hab you!"

"Lawdy, Lawdy, Lawd today! Yeowh!"

"Pull huh ol' plaits down! Make me tiahd wid huh ol' dawg har! Wouldn't have straight har, mahself—Revelations say as plain as day—'har lak lambs wool' like ussen got...."

"Sis Grenn? Dis is shoah a holy deed Cisseretta done called on us to do ... to pertect ouah poah pastor from de wiles ob dis sinner woman..."

"Kyah hyah! Lawd today!"

They reached the summit of the hill which was capped with a small patch of woods. A few of the trees had recently been chopped down, judging by the fresh stumps. The several women in whose clutches Bathesda had fallen, suddenly released their hold on her and jumped back out of her reach. But Bathesda merely stomped the caked dirt from her shoes and torn skirt, thru a quiet searching glance around the semi-circle of women, and made to swing her loosened braids around her head.

This action galled Cisseretta, who saw in it a self assurance, a composure that was shaking the courage of her vigilance committee. She sprang at Bathesda heavily with an angry snarl, pushing her back into a tree which instantaneously crashed to the earth, sideways, sending Cisseretta and all the women scrambling and yelping down the hill.

"Conjuh woman! conjuh... Lawd ah's feared!"

"Hoodoo stuff! Told yo'all we oughten to bother wid huh!"

"Lewd! Jist 'low me to git home oncet moah ... please!"

"Cisseretta done got ussen into dis mess...!"

From the opposite direction came two white men, hurrying toward Bathesda who stood arranging her hair beside the fallen tree.

"Anybody hurt, Auntie? We are clearing these here woods for Ben Lovett who has bought the strip, and my buddy here—he sprained his joint while chopping dozen that 'un a few minutes ago. We went up to my shack, after some liniment and we didn't 'reckon anyone would come along before we got back. The tree was nearly cut thru and I 'spec a slight jostle knocked her over."

"No one was hurt. It fell to the side," murmured the yellow woman absently—eyes searching into the distance.

A delicate tenderness played over her face, and kindly wrinkles appeared about her mouth and forehead. Like Haggard's "She," Bathesda unexpectedly looked her age, all at once. She had dropped the cloak of a hardened, held-over youth, and taken on the ethereal robe of an inner beauty—a soul transformation had taken place.

She, for the first time, turned directly to the lumberjacks, and asked of the one with the bandaged arm—

"Is it bad?"

"Hurts mightily and swellin' every second."

She unwrapped the crude bandage, wiped away the stench of liniment, cupped her two hands about the swollen arm and gazed upward—her thin lips moving almost imperceptibly while the men stood transfixed.

She finally withdrew her hands, clenched them into tight fists and then shook them open and away from her, as if throwing off the contamination of alien flesh.

"Now ... it is well!"

"Bill! Honest to John! She's right! The dadburned misery has gone completely and look! The swellin' is goin' down right before my very eyes!"

"Good God! 'tis a miracle we've just witnessed! The woman's a saint." And he hastily crossed himself, while the other man tested his healed arm by swinging an ax.

Bathesda went down the hill with wide masculine strides—the light winds causing her snagged skirt and white apron to billow and flurry. Her eyes were two muddy pools of tears. She was testifying.

"Up Calvary's rugged brow did I go, this day with Thee, dear Lord ... to the very foot of the Cross ... and I saw the bloody nails in Thy precious feet ... the cruel thorns ... and the bitter cup was spared me ... me, a worthless worm ... but Thou didst drink it to the dregs!"

And she went home with a new power—with understanding, tolerance and forgiveness; to be one of her people; to take care of Becky with her Li'l Jim and Big Jim; and the fragrant drops of rain pelted her in gentle benediction.

[*The Crisis* 35.3 (March 1928): 77–79; 35.4 (April 1928): 121–122, 141–142]

DAYS

by Brenda Ray Moryck

There was the day that Mrs. Randolph went to see about the apartment.—A silver day.—A silver day in a silver month. Silver sunshine,—silver sky,—silver trees,—silver sidewalks,—and silver promises everywhere in the air.

The Greek real estate agent shrewdly eyed his client and rubbed his hands appreciatively over the dingy radiator in his grubby little office.—Not in appreciation of its faint heat however,—no,—only in happy anticipation of securing at last a desirable tenant for his tiny, third-rate flat.

Mrs. Randolph was desirable,—eminently so. In the first place she had money. Diamonds on her fingers,—not too many,—just enough to announce wealth and good taste,—furs around her neck,—elegant fur,—fine gloves which fitted hands that had never known work,—dainty shoes,—a soft, dark, silk dress occasionally disclosed between the flaps of the handsome, heavy coat, and a small beautiful hat, very attractively tilted to the left side of the head.—And serene eyes and quiet hands.

The rent would never be late.—Money.

And culture. Mrs. Randolph was a lady. The low, mellow voice accompanied by the swift, direct look out of kindly, yet experienced, dark eyes,—the rare, flashing smile,—the well-chosen words of her language, the deliberate manner, at once charming and practical, so easy and yet so elegant,—the whole general air about her bespoke the gentlewoman. Such a fine-looking woman too. Tall, handsome, statuesque, with curling raven's-wing hair most unexpectedly streaked with gray, framing a face mature with worldly wisdom but still young in sympathy and outlook. Such magnificent bearing and carriage. Of course she was dark— very dark,—almost black enough to be a nigger. French perhaps—or Spanish. Yes, that was it,—Spanish. That accounted for the slightly oriental expression in the eyes, and the high-bridged nose and the protruding white teeth gleaming between the small pretty mouth. Of course. Spanish.

A tenant like that would raise the value of property all around,—lift the whole tone of the neighborhood. He sighed and rubbed his hands again, this time with appreciation and regret. What a pity he had placed the rent at such a low figure since she particularly wanted to locate in that vicinity.

"Your husband is lawyer, Mrs. Randolph?" he inquired ingratiatingly.

"Yes, he is a lawyer. His offices aren't far from here,—in the Lawyer's Building. That is why this is such a convenient location. We haven't been married very long," (this simply, and without any self-conscious smirking), "and I am a stranger here. I'd like to be near enough to his business so that he can come home to lunch. Then, too, this is near the Tubes."

Oh! Of course. Five minutes' walk—twenty-five cents taxi fare to the rapid transit line to New York. She would spend much time in New York. All fine ladies did. It would be some time before she discovered that the neighborhood was déclassé. By that dark time, the lease would be in operation and she would be used to the convenient nearness of all things desirable.

Yes, she could have the flat—have it at once.

"But I'd like to bring my husband first," Mrs. Randolph demurred as the agent prepared to bind the bargain immediately. "Perhaps you wish to talk with him."

"No need—no need." He waved his hands and laughed facetiously. "I know who is the boss in any family when I see the lady, I don't need to see the husband. If you're satisfied,— well,—the same here."

So Mrs. Randolph rented the apartment.—And went forth into the silver day, in the silver month, key in hand, to measure the windows for the dainty voile curtains she meant to put up, and to estimate the amount of old ivory enamel and floor stain and wax, and the number of rolls of imported paper she would need to make the little place over into her home,—her first home with her husband.

A silver day in a silver month,—and silver promises everywhere in the air.

* * *

There was the day that the neighbors went to demand satisfaction from the landlord who had rented to niggers.—A black day. A black day in a treacherous month. Treacherous skies, and black clouds,—black clouds too sullen to rain,—leaden mood, menacing, threatening, and hate everywhere in the air,—black looks and hate.

Outrageous, insulting, unendurable. The very idea! Niggers living on the street. Right next door and across the street, and down the street and around the corner! Niggers! They'd see about this thing. Those niggers would either move or they'd know the reason why. What did Rocci think they were anyway, a bunch of wops or sheenies that they'd live in the same row with niggers? Besides, they had their business interests to look out for. No paying roomers would take lodgings on a block with niggers,—not even the most undesirable. And Mrs. Keenan had lost trade recently. The fellows and girls didn't come in any more in the day like they used to,—only at night. And Mrs. O'Hennessy's beaus sort of quit showing up before dark, and went out so quietly you couldn't hear them, which was a bad sign. They were always quiet when they didn't get what they wanted or quite *all* they wanted. Now it was niggers that had scared them. As for Mr. Schlitski and the still in his cellar—! *Still* was right since that damned nigger lawyer had moved into the block. Gosh! What was the country coming to? It must be darned hard up when it had to get a nigger for assistant district attorney.

They'd see.

"Rocci thought he was puttin' one over on us,—the damned skunk!" Mrs. Heery announced angrily to Mrs. O'Kelley as she jabbed a gaudy, brass hat-pin into a loud, cheap hat, and jammed it down rakishly over a somewhat bleery blue eye. "I smelt a rat the minute I put my peepers on the woman. I sez to Mick that night when he come home, 'Gosh, there's a swell-lookin' dame took Rocci's empty flat at 68' 'Yea' he answers, kind o' disinterested like. You know Mick. 'Any kids?' Mick's death on kids. 'Not so's you'd notice 'em,' sez I. 'I ain't seen nobody but *her yit*. But b'lieve me, Kid, somepun's wrong when a dame what kin wear them cloes an' has got them manners moves into a little flat like that in this here neighborhood.'"

"H'mph!" sniffed Mrs. O'Kelley. "This neighborhood ain't so bad. I've seen lots worse,—over in Jew town an' out in little Italy. When you look up an' down this here street an' don't know nuthin' about it, it looks swell as it ever was. That's why I like it. It looks classy."

"Yea, *looks!*" Mrs. Heery gave a shrill guffaw and poked her companion familiarly. "But me an' you knows diffrunt. We lives here. But we ain't a-goner have the tone spoiled by niggers, I'll tell the world. Gosh! When I seen that nigger husband o' hers, I near died. An' Mick wanted to right down an' knock Rocci's block off, only I wouldn't let him"

"Yea, this is much better. Do it dignified. All of us together,—a delegation like,—protestin' against insult. Jim was fer callin' out the Ku Klux right away. He's Grand Goblin of the branch you know, but I sez we don't want to give this thing too much air. It'll hurt the roomers an' then,—well, we don't want the p'lice snoopin' around here. Sometimes they take up fer these niggers. Sure! An' since the coon's got a official position too. Jim sez he stands in down at the City Hall."

Mrs. Heery snapped shut the clasp on her yellow fur neck-piece and jerked aside the tawdry lace curtains screening her wide second-story window. "That's neither here nor there," she tossed over her sharp little shoulder. "I ain't half so mad at the niggers as I am at Rocci fer puttin' 'em in. My Gawd! Was it midnight when he looked at the man? I kin see where he got took in on the woman, especially with them cloes and that air. Even Dutchy says he can't believe she's a nigger. He says she talks an' acts just like them swells down on Clinton Avenue when he used to keep a shop down there before it went sheeney and she buys the same kind o' meat. But my Gawd! Her husband—! Come on,—Mrs. Keenan and Mrs. Stebbins and Mrs. Schmidt is all ready, an' the rest'll be there. All except that damn dago. Said he wouldn't join in. Said he saw them all the time and their company an' they was nice people,—kind and like fine ladies in the country. His country! Gosh, that's what comes o' lettin' scum o' the earth run all over the United States."

"He always did look simple to me. Always bowin' an' grinnin'. He did good work though, an' he's cheap.

"Yea, but nary a shoe o' mine will he ever remember fixin' fer me again.—Look they're going.' Gosh! Wait 'till we git through with Rocci, the rotten bum."

"What can you expect?" asked Mrs. O'Kelley with rhetorical airiness, as she flipped a dirty powder-puff against a thin turn-up oblong-tipped nose and gave a final squirt of cheap perfume to some frizzled ash-blonde hair. "Rocci's nothin' but a dirty foreigner hisself. Maybe he did it a purpose."

"Well, we'll see."

So the notice to move was angrily served.—And Mr. Randolph went blackly forth to court to battle about his lease while Mrs. Randolph remained at home and cried.—Her cozy little apartment which love and taste and money had made so beautiful,—her first home with her husband!

A black day. A black day in a treacherous month and hate and evil everywhere—black looks and hate.

Then there was the day that lovely Mrs. Leighton came to call,—a golden day—and the neighbors decided that those colored people needn't move. A golden day in a glorious month. Golden sunshine,—pink-blue sky,—yellow-green buds, and glowing mood. Precious mood and radiant sky—and golden promises in the air.

And lovely Mrs. Leighton driving up to call. An exquisite woman altogether,—patrician from the smart, little, black silk hat, covering the masses of glorious gold-brown hair with copper glints, to the daintily shod, high-arched feet,—fair-skinned, wistful-eyed, sweet-mouthed,—sweet.

Mrs. O'Kelley, sweeping off the front, spied her first and rang Mrs. Heery's bell. And Mrs. Heery called up Mrs. Stebbins and left it to her to tip off the rest of the neighborhood as to the worthwhileness of suspending all regular afternoon operations in order to keep a sharp look-out front, before she accepted the box seat next to Mrs. O'Kelley in the latter's parlor bay window.

Those colored people couldn't be just ordinary niggers after all. Not when they had elegant white people like that coming to see them. Of course, Mrs. Leighton was white. Certainly. She had a nigger chauffeur and niggers didn't work for other niggers.

Then too, there was that time before when she came in the taxi and that grand looking man and another fine lady had come with her. The dago across the way had told them Mrs. Randolph had gone away,—he was always mixing himself up in other people's business, trying to please,—bowing and grinning from his shop window like a silly ape. They had written a note and then walked leisurely away. Mrs. Keenan had followed them and they had gone to the Robert Treat and had dinner. Niggers weren't allowed to put their peepers inside the door there,—not even as bell-hops. Mrs. Keenan had engaged the table next to theirs so she could hear them talk and gee! they were some swell. Of course, she was white. Cadillac car, nigger chauffer, astrakhan coat, kolinsky trimming! Some rich!

"They must be terrible intimate," Mrs. O'Kelley smacked out as she wallowed the huge gaub of gum under her upper lip to the left jaw teeth and rocked to and fro complacently. "She comes here quite often. Noo Yawk license too."

"Yea," responded Mrs. Heery reflectively. "It's a swell car, sure. An' that fur coat! I priced 'em. Fifteen and eighteen hundred dollars. Salisbury-Jacobson's the only place that carries 'em in the burg."

"I mean the whole she-bang looks good, car standin' in the street,—coon sittin' on the front an' that swell dame on the stoop. 'Course, all her company's been good-lookin' an' some of 'em mighty near white, too, an' never nothin' dirty or suspicious-like about their actions either."

"Yea. It makes the street look good. Anyone comin' along an' seein' this here friend o' hers goin' in an' out so often would think all the swells that used to live here didn't move away after all.—Listen, Celia,—*look*, here they both come! Now ain't they a grand sight!— Umph! Look at the coon hold open that door! My Gawd! See him touch his cap to *her* too! Gosh!—I wonder where they're goin'."

"Noo Yawk, you bet cher life!"

"Yea—mos' likely."

Silence for some time afterwards. A slackening of the violent gum-chewing and softening of the raucous squeaking of the rocker. Silence and much thinking.

Then:

"Say Celia,—listen," slowly from Mrs. O'Kelley. "I been thinkin' maybe Rocci wasn't such a dumb fool after all for puttin' 'em in. Maybe he was lyin' when he said he never seen the husband 'till afterwards, an' thought the woman was Spanish."

"Yea," in a squelched tone from Mrs. Heery. "I bin thinkin' the same thing. So's Mick."

"Maybe we was kind o' hasty-like when we made Rocci serve 'em notice," timidly ventured again by Mrs. O'Kelley. "Jim sez her husband knows O'Hara an' O'Toole an' Teeling down at the City Hall an' they all say he's a good fellow.—What d'ye say we tell Rocci—."

"Yea, let's."

So the Randolphs were told that they needn't go,—a golden day. A golden day in a glorious month. They needn't move because the neighbors had decided that high class colored people wouldn't ruin the block. Of course, they hadn't known what they would be like. Down where they came from niggers did nothing but wield razors and drink booze. The Randolphs were different. So clean and quiet and so refined.—Yes,—they might stay.

A golden day. A golden day in a lovely month, and radiance everywhere in the air,— radiance everywhere in the air,—radiance and tolerant feeling.

Then followed the days that the Randolphs remained,—more golden days.—The days when Mr. Randolph came to have the time-o'day speaking acquaintance with his neighbors in the evening, and Mrs. Randolph came to give the children of the neighborhood piano lessons and receive their adoration and their little bunches of flowers in return. Days when the women learned to enjoy her music and admire her beautiful home and to marvel at her fine standards;— days when they tried to fix up their own places and copy her taste—days when the men came to respect Mr. Randolph, the man, as well as his name and power;—days when all was well.

All golden days—golden days in warm, golden months—and fulfilled promises everywhere—radiance and kindly feeling.

* * *

And then, finally, there was the day that the Randolphs moved,—a gray day. A gray day in the sultry month,—rain clouds,—misty air, drab sidewalks and gray mood. Gray mood and sorrow everywhere,—sorrow and regret.

Those nice colored people were moving away. What a shame! They wanted their own home, of course, but if Rocci hadn't been such a fool when he served the notice, they might have stayed,—one year anyway. Why, the rotter actually swore at Mrs. Randolph when she told him that she couldn't possibly know that he wouldn't recognize her race. She had come from parts where one's face made no difference in one's status, so it was honest and clean. She had wanted him to talk with her husband in the first place. The dirty rotten foreigner! Her husband couldn't forget that. You couldn't blame him.

Such lovely people,—so clean and nice. And such high class company. Just like white people. And that little, fat friend with the round, brown face and the big, black eyes, who was always there, actually had her own car! And so many changes of clothes,—hats too, and never any men hanging about her, either. Gee! They made Mrs. O'Hennessy feel cheap. It was a shame they were leaving. Gee!

With the avid and pitying interest the neighbors watched,—watched the men sling the pretty new furniture into the vans and struggle under the beautiful baby grand piano,—watched until the rag man had scraped up the last choice debris,—watched until the last load left—watched until Mrs. Randolph gave a final gingerly pat on the many, many dainty dresses laid for safe-carrying on the rear seat of Bunny's coupe,—watched as she settled herself wearily against the little, fat brown friend as the latter shifted into gear.

Then:

Over came the Italian shoemaker,—the handsome, gentle, diffident shoemaker, with the big, beseeching, tragic, child-eyes and the soft, alluring voice and manners. Out came the neighbors.

"I sorry you go," ventured Tony shyly. "I so sorry. You fine lady. Your husband—he fine man. I sorry." (It is impossible to describe the inflection of his tone). "No more nice music."

His voice choked on the last phrase and water welled up in the gentle eyes. He shook his head dumbly and moved away.

"Aw, cheer up, Tony," Mrs. Heery attempted jocosely. "Come over an' git them tan shoes o' Mick's tonight an' you'll feel better. Mrs. Randolph ain't goin' so far away she can't come back sometimes, huh?" But her own hard Irish eyes filled with moisture just the same. "It's a darn shame you're movin' away, Mrs. Randolph. We'll miss you."

"Yea, we will that," vouchsafed Mrs. O'Kelley honestly. "Seems like it's kind o' hard to part, we got so used to you."

"May-be when you're down this way sometimes,—shoppin' or on your way to the Tubes or somethin' you'll stop in sometimes, huh?"

"Yea, an' play fer us a little, huh" I guess I could scare up a cup o' tea an' a little grub,—some o' them sausages an' a little o' that pickle you liked so much, yea?"

"Well, good-bye and good-luck to you!"

And all along the block, they waved and called good-bye as Mrs. Randolph kissed her hand to the charming nest which love had made so dear, and took a last look at her beautiful, little home,—her first home with her husband.

A gray day.—A gray day in a rainy month, mist and sadness everywhere,—sadness and regret.

* * *

Just days.   [*The Crisis* 35.6 (June 1928): 187–188, 206–207]

House of Hark Back: A Tale for Young Folk

by Effie Lee Newsome

You'll doubtless say that Phyllis dreamed it all. And it might have been a dream. It began this way. Phyllis was watching a clear stream. The water kept playing over vermilion and white and purplish pebbles and made them look very clean and cool. Phyllis thought of the poem about the water nymph and the boy and how the nymph had drawn the child into the pool. Dreadful!

She hurried her thoughts on to something else. "I've known rivers," she recalled lines from a poem by Langston Hughes that her elders had repeated, "ancient dusky rivers." She knew what "ancient" meant, but "dusky," what did that mean? Dusky?

The little summer winds in the water willows blew softly and a bee, gold barred like a royal bee from Italy, kept humming near her. After that—*What did "dusky" mean?*

Phyllis found herself at a great entrance. At first it seemed to be the hollow of a huge tree. Indeed I think it was a tree toad that met her at the threshold with a tart demand, "are you looking for data?"

"Data?" Phyllis gasped.

"Never mind, I see you don't know anything about it. Come in."

Phyllis obeyed and seemed as she went through the opening to see walls hung with bats upside down as these creatures fix themselves for winter in tree hollows. Then the bats became dull bronze sconces. And the one or two owls on the walls were doubtless stuffed birds, Phyllis thought. "What is this place?" she asked.

"House of Hark Back," came a voice from no living thing that she could see unless it could have been one of the owls. "And the entrance fee," went on the voice, "is a thought. Only people who think can come in here. Of what were you thinking?"

"Rivers and runlets? Yes, rivers and runlets."

"'Rivers and runlets'?" Sure enough, it was one of the large owls speaking. "Oh, then it's data you want. The tree toad at the door—he's grouchy enough—may have mumbled something against data. Data and warts furnish him something to grumble about. But reason ought to tell him that a House of Hark Back is the very place to which to come for data. Let me call Mary's Lamb."

"Mary's?" Phyllis gasped, wondering if she was about to see that well known creature.

The owl gave a piercing cry. "Yes," beginning again to talk to Phyllis, "after the way it's worked all these ages, seems only reasonable that it should have a little rest in the House of Hark Back, when they will allow it to rest! Some one is always calling it out. Mary's Lamb"—the lamb entered—"that holds the honorary post of keeper of parchments in this the House of Hark Back." Evidently the owl was presenting Mary's Lamb.

It was white to Phyllis's amazement and not stone gray like most of the lambs that she had seen.

"Now you want data, you say, on rivers?" the owl went on while Mary's Lamb waited as it had waited on Mary.

"I don't know now," Phyllis replied growing weary of the persistent owl. "I'd just been thinking something from a piece called 'The Negro Speaks of Rivers,' I believe. I forget."

"Oh, 'The *Negro* Speaks of Rivers'? That would come under the record of darker peoples. Suppose I call Aben Hamet. Chateaubriand the great French writer created him. He is a Moor of long ago. The Spaniards, you know, drove the Moors from magnificent Granada. But Aben Hamet continued to go back over the water again and again to Granada."

"But why did Aben Hamet go back?"

"For two reasons," the owl said. "One of these was because everywhere in Granada he could find marvelous monuments in fret work and tower that his people the Moors had placed there. He loved to see them. Aben Hamet is a prominent figure here in the House of Hark Back. Here he is."

In walked Aben Hamet, a slender graceful man with rich tinted skin and dark hair and eyes.

"Was it an Italian painter, da Vinci, Aben Hamet, who studied and loved the course of waters? Tell this child, please," suggested the owl.

"Leonardo da Vinci was ever interested in hydraulics. But this little girl"—he turned to Phyllis who had never seen any one more graceful—"might want to know that there was once in old Egypt a man with a strange name, C-T-E-S-I-B-I-U-S. He it was who centuries ago invented that branch of engineering science that is known as hydraulics."

"That's another terrible word," Phyllis cried. "And what does it mean?"

"Hydraulics?" asked Aben Hamet with a pleasant smile. "The regulation of liquid motion to laws and the application of these laws to marine engineering."

"But I would rather talk with Mary's Lamb. I think Mary's Lamb didn't go inside the school. And perhaps it will not be too wise for me to understand."

Aben Hamet smiled again. "Yet I have told you something that it would be well for you to pin to your mind. A man of dark skin invented that science which deeps the fair skinned man's world rushing forward. Call Mary's Lamb. But hereafter whenever you happen to hear the gurgle of waters remember what Aben Hamet has told you: A man heard waters gurgle in old Egypt and made them force."

Aben Hamet swept softly away. And Phyllis began calling, "Mary's Lamb! Mary's Lamb!" The words seemed strangely hard to say. She was trying with all her might. But was she not only gurgling after all?

Then something happened. Phyllis opened her eyes. You're right if you guessed that she had been asleep. She was sitting against a great oak that had a hollow on the other side. And not far beneath Phyllis's toes that dangled over the ledge on which the oak grew, ran the stream.

"I wonder," was her first thought on waking, "if it is true that an Egyptian was first to discover how water could be used in engineering. I shall ask mother."

And Phyllis did ask when she got home and learned that Ctesibius of Egypt truly had invented hydraulics, the science of fluids in motion.

[*The Crisis* 35.10 (December 1928): 331, 350]

ANNA

by Iva L. Cotton

"White people are mean and I hate 'em." Anna told Judge Maket Wright, in the juvenile court, "I don't care if Dr. Robinson does say I'm white. I'm black and shall always be black. I hate you, too."

The question of whether Anna is colored or white, came up after the little girl of ten years, who had always lived with a colored family and believed herself colored in spite of her fair skin and light hair, had followed a carnival company from Eighth and State Streets to Cudahy, where police found her and sent her to the detention house.

"Why *I* like *you*."

"Yes, that's cause you don't know me, I reckon. Wait till you know I'm a nigger, then you'll hate me, just like all the kids at school hate me. I know. They liked me at first, too, used to give me apples, put their arms around me, choose me for a partner till—till," she choked a little, but soon regained her fighting control, "—till some of 'em saw me with my ma and pa."

"Now, now—let's quiet down and not frighten all these people out of the room. Even Mr. Copper here is almost ready to drop his billy and run," the judge said teasingly. "But what about your ma and pa the kids don't like? If they are like you I'd like them."

"That's just it, they are 'zackly like me, only the kids don't think so. They only see ma and pa's skin. They call us 'nigger' and now 'stead of giving me apples they throw stones at me, 'stead of puttin' their arms around me they push me off the side walk, and 'stead of wantin' me for a partner, they don't want me in the ring. I know what it means to be colored—even if my skin is white and I'd d'rather be a 'nigger' than be one of you cruel white people. You are all mean and I despise you."

This was quite a long speech for Anna to make in public. She had said the same things many, many times to herself, as she lingered after school, waiting for the rest to 'get gone.'

Judge Maket Wright, a young man of thirty-six, rather enjoyed talking to this little spit-fire; and the more she said she hated him the more he knew he liked her.

"Tell me where you live I will take you there," he said.

"I know where I live and I can go there myself, if you'll let me," she answered.

The judge wanted to know for reasons of his own. He insisted. "Tell me, won't you, as nearly as you can, about yourself, Anna?"

Anna straightened up, trying not to be afraid, set her eyes on the strange man, and began:

"I don't know where I was born. The first thing I remember was a whippin' they gave me at the orphanage for tyin' a handkerchief around a clothes-pin to make a doll. I wanted somethin' that would love me and that I could love and tell my secrets to at night when I went to bed. They said I had been snooping; that's how I got the clothes pin, they said. They wouldn't believe me when I said I found it under the clothes line where one of the big girls had dropped it while hangin' up the clothes. They took it away from me and whipped me for stealin'."

Anna's fingers twitched and jerked as if fumbling a rag doll.

"Well, after that I did steal a clothes-pin and I made me another doll. I called her 'God' 'cause I used to pray to her. God and I slept together every night after that as long I stayed there. I used to tell God all the good things I did and all the naughty things too. She never once told on me. I used to hug and kiss her every night and we used to imagine we weren't orphans, but were real ladies and gentlemens ... We don't want to be ladies and gentlemens now,—'cause we know too much about 'em.... But we did then.

"Then one day about a year after that, I was about seven years old, I 'spose, among the many people that came to the Memphis Orphanage, came Ma and Pa Olds. They seemed to look at me more than any one of the other girls. Pretty soon old Miss Whip, that's what God and I called her—I've forgot her real name—came to me and said these people were going to adopt me.

"Then I took my first ride. It was in a buggy behind an old horse, black like Pa Olds. I always liked old Jim that was the horse's name. Pa Olds afterwards gave Jim to me for mine.

"We had only got started away from the orphanage when they spied something in my hand and ast what it was."

Her eyes grew a little brighter. A faint smile came on her face.

"At first I was scared. I was afraid if they found out they would take her away from me. But Ma Olds laughed a little, then pulled out of her pocket a real sure enough doll and handed it to me. It had a black and white checked skirt on it with a turkey-red shawl around its shoulders. She said Rachel would be a good name for it, so I called it Rachel. But I never trusted Rachel like I did God. I only told Rachel of the good things I did.

"Ma and Pa Olds used to build campfires in the evenings on the banks of the Mississip. Other nigger kids used to gather 'round and Pa would play nigger music and tell us stories. Then "—she stopped, her face grew sad again,—"then Ma Olds, after the other kids had gone home, used to tell me about her own little girl that she once had and didn't have any more. And she would hug and kiss me. Pa Olds would pull a big red handkerchief out of his pocket, and wipe away tears. Then with his big, rough black hands he would stroke my hair and I would grab his hand and kiss it ... Then we wouldn't talk at all for a long time."

"Two years ago we moved up North." She slid to the edge of her chair and again regained her granite-like character. "Here we are in Madison and I don't like it and that's all there is to it." She drew a long breath and quit talking.

The judge looked at the officer. The officer looked out of the window.

After a long silence, the judge asked, "And where is—God?"

Anna thought for a minute as if forming her words, then she said, "You know, God never liked it up here either. The air and sunshine ain't the same as in the South. Even Pa Olds says that babies and melons don't do down there. We, God and me, talked it all over many, many times. Many times we played we were down South again. We always wanted to go back. I couldn't go, I couldn't leave Ma and Pa Olds, 'cause I knew they couldn't get along without me. So I started to figure and plan how I could get God back to the country she liked.

"One day in school I was studyin' g'ography, I noticed that the Yahara River flowed south and south and south. So I ast our teacher, 'Does that water go into the Mississip?' He said it did. Then I ast him if it went passed Memphis and he said 'Yes.'

"That night, when I went home, I went to the bed-room, and got God. Ma and Pa told me I'd better give her a different name and I did—for them—but when we was alone I always called her just 'God.' Well, we talked it all over. She was tickled and wanted to start right away. I could hardly give her up. But I loved her so I couldn't make her stay any longer. I did it for her sake ... The last I saw of her she was floating south, toward the Mississip and Memphis."

Anna looked up as if to ask if there were any more questions.

Again the judge looked at the officer. Again the officer looked out the window....

After a long silence, during which Judge Maket Wright's meditative stare seemed to take him far away, he said:

"I guess she's black, ain't she, Murphy?"

"I think she is," the officer gulped.   [*The Crisis* 36.4 (April 1929): 117, 134–135]

THE PAPALOI

by Annice Calland

The topaz fire of full sun was upon the royal palms and red flowered poinciana trees, waiting, waiting in the silence of the summer moon of the year 1912 in Haiti.

Leconte, the President was uneasy among his palace guards for a revolution was brewing. And though the President was uneasy among his guards, a white woman traveled alone through the Black Republic. Traveled with but one purpose in mind, to save her son from a shameful death, or to die with him for he was all that was left to her in this world.

She had heard of an old and wise Papaloi, a native of Haiti. She had been told that if any one on the Island could help her, it would be Soulouque, the Papaloi.

Arriving at the dark jalousied store building in the Rue de Dessalines, she entered without hesitation and inquired of the silent footed attendant who came to meet her for Soulouque. Beckoning her to follow, he conducted her through the dark cluttered curio store room, through another room richly furnished and softly lighted through half closed jalousies, and pulling aside heavy curtains of rich tapestry, he bowed her into a room hung with priceless silks and furnished in costly woods. Before her, seated at a massive mahogany desk was a scholarly looking gentleman in rich robes. Soulouque was not black. According to the painstaking classifications of Moreau de St. Méry, he was a marabout, that is to say he was eighty parts black and forty-eight parts white.

Soulouque looked up; before him stood a lady more delicately beautiful than a La France rose tree in full bloom.

Soulouque desired all beautiful women, all women sleek and beautiful; above all women Soulouque desired this beautiful white woman.

"Your wish, Madame?" he inquired in French, bowing courteously to her.

Her eyes glowed with subdued fire as she answered him:

"My son is a prisoner. He is accused of having plotted against the Haitian Government. He is to be executed in the morning for a crime of which he is as innocent as you or I. Since there is no escape for him, we would die together. I endeavored to smuggle a dagger to him, but the guards searched me and found it. He is being subjected to such indignities of which you may know much more than I. But he can tell nothing of the revolution because he knows nothing.

I have heard that you have a knowledge of many native drugs and of poisons; and have come to you for a poison that can be carried past those who will search me."

"That would be a pity, a very great pity," said Soulouque; and fell to musing.

No one knew Port au Prince as Soulouque knew it. He had seen *les blancs* come and he had seen *les blancs* go, driven away by petty persecutions. He had seen them absorbed by the Blacks. He had seen many of those destroyed who would not be driven away and who would not be absorbed. Soulouque pondered. He knew the lady and her son were exiles who had fled from Russia in the year 1906. They had gone first to Paris; from Paris the son had come to Port au Prince, and promoted a company for buying and selling the coffee which grew with so little cultivation on this sun-washed Island. He had succeeded; better, perhaps for him had he failed. Now he was a prisoner, and a beautiful white woman had come to Soulouque.

Soulouque sighed.

"That would be a pity, a very great pity," again said he, then continued:

"I will give you a poison; it will be in a small silver tube that you can carry under your tongue without inconvenience; but," Soulouque hesitated and fell to musing again, "after you have given the poison to your son, you must return here. You will tell him that you, too, will partake of the poison at a certain hour, but you must return here."

As Soulouque spoke he drew back a heavy tapestry that concealed a door which he opened and motioned the lady to enter. No one passing on the mean and dirty streets in front of Soulouque's curio shop could possibly guess the beauty of the room disclosed. Rugs of beauteous Oriental pile in delicate and harmonious colors covered the door. Pottery and porcelains of quaint and curious designs were about. Tapestries covered the walls, tapestries of Chinese textiles of gold and silk woven in elaborate patterns, gorgeous pieces of textile art of the richest decorative effect. And books, books, old and strange, that at a happier time she would have enjoyed to read and handle.

Soulouque offered her a chair and she sat down, looking at him expectantly. It was plain that she had not comprehended and was waiting for him to explain more fully. A servant brought tea and curious little confections, serving her daintily.

Soulouque left the room for a few minutes and returned with two tiny silver tubes, which he explained, contained the deadly poison. One tube was for her son, the other for herself; both could be carried easily in her mouth at the same time, and were so sealed there was no possible danger to the person who carried them.

"This afternoon you will go to your son at the prison; as you kiss him good-by for the last time you will pass him one of these tubes. You may tell him that you will swallow the contents of the other tube at the same hour. Then you will return to this room—and to me."

Slowly, slowly, Soulouque's meaning came to her. Her dark eyes widened in horror and she shuddered. Her face could be no paler after death. Her lips trembled when she tried to speak; her mouth opened and closed but no words came; it seemed that she had lost the power of speech. One thought only came to her over and over:

For her son's sake; to end his unendurable sufferings; for his dear sake; to save him from torture and shame; that he might die in peace. Steadily she looked at Soulouque for a moment.

"I will return," she said, and held out her hand for the poison. Soulouque gave it to her and silently held open the door for her, bowing gravely as she left the room.

Down the sun-filled, sleepy street she passed. Beggars showed her their sores, some smiling ingratiatingly, others threatening her if she did not give them a *sinq cob*; but she did not see them. Two long lines of market women passed continuously, baskets poised upon their heads, driving patient *bouriques*, their paniers piled so high with market produce that the tiny animals were scarcely visible, chattering and gesticulating like mad the women passed, but she neither heard nor saw them. Over the high stone walls, Bougainville, jasmine and *bois lette* showered her with perfume but she was not conscious of it. Nude street urchins hurled vile epithets at her, calling her "chein Russiane," but she did not hear them. A "high yellow" passed in his automobile, his driver honking loudly, but she was not aware of it; and he was obliged to drive around her. Up, up, up the steep, dusty street she climbed; a greater horror in her heart than she had ever known. Her one thought, that she must convey the poison to her son and return.

That gypsy king, the trade wind breathed softly through the white city by the dark blue Caribbean Sea, glittering and smooth under the afternoon sun. White-sailed fishing craft were wafted slowly over the silvery blue Gulf of Gonaives, to be seen in the distance. A steamboat's whistle sounded its hour of departure. Up, up, through the hot street she hurried, blind and deaf to it all. To the gods of the sea and the land and the sweeping winds that were talking to her, from far away they were talking to her of a veil in the meeting of winds; of leaf shadows through jungle dusk; of cobweb threads of sound, subtly enchanting; of tree bells' silvery tinkle, lovely, elusive. As a flash through the dark she saw only her son.

She submitted mechanically to the search of the guards, scarcely conscious of it. At sight of her son, her courage almost failed her, but his relief when she whispered to him of the poison restored her confidence, and strengthened her will. Her weary eyes devoured his loved face.

"It is better this way," she told him, "we will cheat death of its greatest sting. We will be spared the greater shame and the terrible torture, for this death will be quick and painless."

"God bless you, little mother," he whispered as she kissed goodbye and passed him the tiny tube. She was fiercely tempted to tell him all and both so allow the poison immediately, but—she followed Soulouque's instructions.

A servant showed her into the beautiful room upon her return and served her a delicious dinner while she sat and waited. She did not taste of the food, but sat as if turned into a lovely marble statue. Hour after hour passed. At times thoughts raced through her mind. Again time passed without registering on her numbed brain. Doubts of this mysterious Papaloi assailed her. What if he should betray her to the Government officials, who would take delight in shaming her, torturing both her and her son. But the hideous night finally passed. Soon the east began to glow softly pink. A sound came from an opening door but she did not glance up as foot-steps moved toward her. Someone stood before her; she raised her eyes, then suddenly sprang to her feet.

"Mother, mother, dearest mother," her son exclaimed and caught her wavering form and held her to him.

"Mother, mother, mother," he crooned, half sung to her, "you are the most wonderful little mother in all the world."

"Yes," said Soulouque, who now entered smiling, "and the most wonderful woman in all the world. Had you been tempted to take the other tube of poison after your promise to return, you both would have been buried alive and I would have left your son to die, but you I would have resuscitated.   [*The Crisis* 36.9 (September 1929): 297, 316]

WHITE LILACS

—∞∞∞—

by Edith L. Yancy

You needn't look so skeered, honey. I was ju' a-movin' dis here chair close to de winder, so's I could look at dem white lilocks a-growin' down dere in yo' yard. Dey's real pretty, honey—real petty wid de sun a-shinin' on 'em.

You is de sheriffs' wife, aint you? I done seed you goin' by on dat ole road what leads pass Mister Rankins' house. I done watched you many a time out o' de kitchen winder. I'se real sorry, honey, I done disturbed you f'om yo' work. 'cause whilse I'se here, I ain't a-meanin' to be no trouble—you done fetched yo' tattin' wid you, aint you, honey? Dat's 'cause you is gwi' sit a piece wid me, aint you? I'se glad, honey. De good Lawd knows I was gittin' kinder lonesome lak.

It be real comf'table up here, though,—dis nice mattin' on de flow,' an' de cot so's I kin lay down on an' rest, an' dis here easy-chair. I reck'n now, you thought to cheer a body up a bit, hangin' dese nice yaller curtains, wid de blue-birds on 'em. Dey's real pretty, honey. Dey hides, too dem iron bars de sheriff's done put 'cross de winders. Dey sho' do make it pleasant in here, wid de sun a-shinin' thoo 'em.

An' dem white li-locks—now. I was jus' lookin' at 'em, honey. I was jus' lookin' at 'em... She was plumb took 'way wid 'em, honey—my Eugenie—plumb took 'way wid 'em. Dat was my baby—Eugenie—honey. She be eighteen her las' birthday, which was in March, pass... An' when he seed how wild she was 'bout 'em, he up an' set out a whole lot uv 'em in de garden what he done make fur her.

'Twas lak a bit o' dem woods, what's out back o' his place, honey,—dat garden,—wild lak wid honeysuckle vines mos' nigh hidin' dem stone walls roun' it, an' wid birch trees an' yaller dogwood trees an' flowers a-growin' evah which-aways, an' dem white li-locks. It was kinder nice, honey,—dat garden.

I ain't nevah set foot in it though. An' he guessed I was skeered on 'count o' dey mought be snakes in it. An' he laugh, an' he say, dey wasn't none out dere, 'cause he done took a stick an' prodded all roun' an' he aint nevah foun' non...'Pears lak, at fust, he nevah thought nothing 'bout it,—howcome I done shun de place, an' done kept to my room, 'cept when I was in de kitchen... It wasn't on 'count o' no snakes, nuther, honey...

I done spoke to Eugenie 'bout it, dat she ought'n to do it, dat we ought to go 'way. She wasn't seein' it her ole mother's way, though. An' seemed lak, I couldn' bring mys'f to go 'way wid out her, honey....

Dey wasn't no place fur me to go no ways. My pore Ellick done been dead three months, an' me an' Eugenie was stayin' wid frien's—dey done bu'nt up ev'vy thing on de li'l plateau what we own, honey, whiles dey was huntin' Ellick—when Mr. Rankin ax me to come an' keep house fur him, lak I done fur his mother, befo' him, an' bring Eugenie wid me....

I done spoke 'bout it to Eugenie, honey. But she wasn't a-s-eein' it her ole mother's way,—dat dey was sin in it. I dunno—I reck'n, I wasn't strict enough wid her. Seems lak I nevah could say much to my Eugenie, no how....

Dey ain't no-body evah knowed she was dere in dat ole house, honey. Aint no-body evah seed my Eugenie. He done fetched me an' her here in one uv dem automobiles. We nevah knowed none uv de culled folks here in his town, honey. We be strangers here, me an' my Eugenie. We nevah went no where—jus' stayed on de place.... 'Peared lak he done talked to Eugenie befo' he ax me to come an' wuk fur him.

Dey ain't no-body knowed she was dere. Dat's howcome, honey, dey's a'cusin' me fur what done happen to him. Dat's howcome dey to fetch me here...

I done spoke to Eugenie, lak I say, honey. She was'nt thinkin' 'bout nothin' 'cept livin' fur him, an' bein' happy, though.

She was happy, honey—my Eugenie. She was happy, an'—him. I use to watch 'em in de evenin' when dey'd be together in de garden. I use to watch 'em—him, always quiet lak, an' her a'stoppin to smell de flowers, an' put her arms, wid de gold bracelets, he done give her, on 'em roun' dem white li-locks—An' wid de blossoms brushin' 'gin her face, an' fallin' off an' gittin' caught in her hair—I watched her 'cause she was so happy, honey... so happy, an' pretty, an' wild lak—jus' lak de garden he done make fur her.

Den some how—way after de li-locks done gone an' 'twas de fall o' de year—'peared lak sometin' done come betwixt 'em. He was real uneasy lak, den. An' he was'nt inclined to talk much, neither. An' days when he done come home early, he stayed out dere in de garden,—all unhappy an' desperate lak,—'twel 'twas dark, diggin' 'mongst de flowers.

An' Eugenie, she was all de time in her room. Only was'nt she staying dere, a-crying? I done seed she was'nt aimin' to let on lak dey was sump'n wrong be-twixt 'em. An' I open her do' soft lak. She was'nt a-cryin' though... only sittin' in dat big chair in front uv de fire place, wid de light a-flickenin' on her an' her head layin' back lak she was restin'... all de time restin' hers'f—an' him in de garden, unhappy an' desperate lak.

Den one day, when de snow done come, an' de garden was white wid it, he come up dem stairs to her room, a-fetchin' her a lil' birch twig wid one o' dem moth c'coons on it. I was in my room wid de do' open, honey, an' I heerd her when she speak—her voice a-tremblin' kinder sad an' kinder happy, too. An' she speak 'bout how when it done come spring a gin, when de flowers'd be bloomin', an' dem white li-locks 'd be out, de pretty moth a-layin' close an' warm inside o' de c'coon, would free itse'f an' come out.... Den she fell a-cryin'. An' I heerd him a talkin'—trying to comfort her. An' I knowed Eugenie was a-needin' me. I knowed I could nevah go 'way an' leave her dere by hers'f....

I couldn't make it out cl'ar, honey, 'bout de way she speak an' all. An' I was a-tremblin' an' afeared. 'Twas lak de good Lawd done put a nudder cross on my shoulder's fur me to bear an' done put de trufe in my way wid it. Den I thought 'bout her pappy—I thought 'bout my pore Ellick. Den—I couldn' listen, no mo; cause dey was somethin' done commenced leapin' up inside o' me,—a tearin' me to pieces.

An' when she done come to me wid it, honey, I couldn' hold in no mo.' She nevah say nothin' at fust, though, 'cause she knowed I was thinkin' 'bout her pappy,—jus' stood wid her head hangin' down... Den—all o' a sudden, she commenced cryin' out fur me to stop, 'cause she couldn't stand me a-thinkin' such things, an' 'cause she wasn't a-meanin' to heap no mo' trouble an' werry on my head, an' dat I couldn't understand how it be wid her,—dat she couldn't hold what'd been done to her pappy, 'gin Mr. Rankin jus' 'cause it was his culla what done it....

An' den when Spring done come, an' I seed her an' him in de garden together agin, an' wid her so happy, I prayed de good Lawd to let her go on bein' happy to let dat part o' dey sin what was hers, be on my head. 'cause I done suffered a lot a-ready anyways an' I could bear it....

But He nevah seed fit to let my baby's happiness go on, honey. When de flowers was all bloomin' an' de white li-locks done come—I was settin' in her room a knittin'—dese ole han's ain't so quick lak dey once was—I was knittin', an' my Eugenie an' him was at de winder a-lookin' down at de garden. She was so happy, my Eugenie.... She was holdin' out her han' so's de moth—it'd done come out o' de c'coon, honey, an' she was a holdin' out her han'd wid it clingin' to her fingers, so's it could fly into de garden. An' when it done got its strength, an' gone off into de garden, she turned roun' to him, an' I seed she was'nt smilin' no mo.'.. only looking sad lak, lak all her happiness done clean gone wid de moth into de garden.... An' den she fell a-weepin', wid him wid his arms roun' her, a-trying to comfort her....

My Eugenie nevah smiled no mo,' honey. De good Lawd nevah seed fit to let her take up her happiness, agin.... An' de li'l one,—it went away lak de moth... My baby nevah got to hold it long in her arms.... An' den—she went—too....

When I seed she was gittin' low—when I done done all I could fur her, she ax fur him to come, dat dey was sum'n she wanted to say to him, by hisse'f.

I didn' go way, honey. I stood out side my baby's do,' 'cause I knowed she mought be goin' any minute.... an' when he come an' fetched me, agin, I seed her propped up wid pillars, an' wid her bes' dress—it was made out o' yaller silk, honey, an' trimmed wid beads—an' her slippers, wid de gold 'broidery wuk on 'em—layin' on de foot uv her bed. She made me put 'em on her, honey, wid him he'pin', 'cause my ole han's was a-shakin' so....

Den layin' dere, she make us burn up in de fire-place, ev'rything dat was hers.... Dey was a shawl she done wore out in de garden, when him an' her was a-walkin' dere an' 'twas kinder cool. He pleaded wid her fur her to let him keep it, but she only looked him sorrowful lak, an' shook her head.... An' he stood dere befo' de fire-place wid his han's behin' him, an' his head hangin' down, watchin' it burn, 'twel she commenced pleadin' wid de Lawd dat day was nothin' left o' her sin but hers'f, an' she was ready to go....

She looked lak a pretty bride—my Eugenie—honey. Dat was why she wanted de silk dress on, an' de slippers, so's she mought look lak one, 'cause she'd nevah been none on earth. An' wid de big basket uv white li-locks, he done cut an' brung up out o' de garden fur her to look at, standin' at de head uv her bed, an' de li'l one a-layin' in de holler uv her arm— my baby looked lak a pretty bride, honey.

An' den all de afternoon wid me a-standin' by her bed a lookin' down at her an' de li'l one, an' a-listenin' to de soun' o' his hammerin' an' sawin' down dere in de cellar—

I seed den honey, he was'nt aimin' fur nobody to know 'bout my Eugenie an' de li'l one. But I couldn't go down dem stairs to him to hinder him... I couldn' do nothin'. I couldn' do nothin' but stand dere at de foot o' my baby's bed, an' look down at her an' de li'l one....

When he done come up agin to my Eugenie's room, an' done took her up off'n her bed, an' in his arms—her an' de li'l one—she look lak he mought be jus' carryin' her, wid her li'l one down to de garden to set dere in de sunshine an' look at de flowers, an' dem white li-locks. Only—I knowed honey, she'd nevah open her eyes no mo', an' it done got dark in de garden....

It peared lak, honey he seed den how 'twas wid me. I 'spec' it come to him den, too, how it had been wid me all along. 'cause he drapped his head down, an' he say dat she done make him promise to do it, when she done speak wid him, by hisse'f.... An' den I couldn' stand no mo', honey, de things dat was leapin' up in me fur me to say to him. But I couldn' say nothin', nuther, fur I couldn' make 'em out, dey done all turned black in my head. I couldn' make out nothin' only, dat I done fell down on my knees 'cause my strength done left me, an' dat my ears was full o' de soun' uv him a-walkin' down dem stairs, wid my baby an' her li'l one in his arms....

'Peared lak honey, he'd nevah git to de bottom uv dem stairs... nevah git thoo carryin' my baby an' de li'l one, down... an' down... an' down....

An' den, I heerd him a-hammerin' agin....

An den I couldn' heer nothin' but de soun' uv de wind a-blowin' thoo de trees out dere in de garden....

It done commenced gittin' day outside, honey, an' a drizzlin' rain done set in, when he come back up dem stairs to my Eugenie's room. An' he walked lak he was a fetchin' her an' de li'l one back, agin. But when he stood in de do,' I seed he was by hisse'f. An' he act lak he nevah seed me. He stood dere a-clutchin' de do' wid both han's lak he was afeared o' sump'n. Den bracin' his han's 'gin de wall, he walked roun' to de big chair in front o' de fireplace. An' when he done come to it, he shrunk down in it an' bowed his head in his han's.

I got up off o' my knees den, honey. An' when he heered me git up, he reared his head up wild lak, an' commenced shakin' all ovah an' mumblin' sump'n—I couldn' make it out— an' twistin' his han's together.... Den he riz up out o' de chair, only he drap down on his knees befo' it, lak his strength done gone from him. An' den, all de time a-mumblin' sump'n, only now it 'peared lak he was a moanin', too, 'cause sump'n inside o' him done start hurtin' him, he drug hisse'f long side my Eugenie's bed. An' he took hold on de basket uv li-locks wid both his han's, an' turned to her bed, wid her an' de li'l one gone, an' commenced cryin' out fur her to open her eyes, fur her to look at de white li-locks—lak she was still a-layin' dere. 'Twasn't long, though, fur he fell to mumblin' agin—mumblin' an' cryin', wid his head bowed down 'mongst dem li-locks, 'twel it done come ovah himn dat my baby couldn' evah answer him no mo', couldn' evah look at dem white li-locks, no mor.' An' den, honey, he fell to tearin' 'em to pieces an' to cursin' de good Lawd 'cause He done took Eugenie an' de li'l one away....

I seed den how 'twas wid him. An' I got afeared. I knowed I couldn' do nothin' wid him by myse'f, so I run to fetch him he'p....

Honey, I wasn't a-runnin' 'way when dey found me on dat ole road. I was jus' a-goin' to fetch him he'p. Only—I done got turned roun' lak I'd nevah been on dat ole road befo.' I wasn't a runnin' away lak dem what foun' me 'lows I was 'cause I done done sum'n to him. I ain't nevah knowed nothin' 'bout conjurin' folks, honey. No mo'n dem what 'lows I done it. But 'cause dey found me a wanderin' long dat ole road in de rain, an' wid only my ole shawl an' dis ole flannel wrapper on—'cause dey foun' me dat a-way, an' dey foun' him a kneelin' side her bed wid dem li-locks all torn up, an' a-callin' her name, an' pleadin' wid her, an' dey ain't nevah foun' nothin' what'd sho' my Eugenie been a-living dere, too—dey 'lows I done put all dat on him, an' dat dey could'n a-been no-body in dat ole house 'cept me an' him.... But I nevah done nothin' to him, honey.... I done suffered a lot, but it ain't nevah make me want to harm no body....

An' I been a-thinkin', too, honey,—he must a-loved my Eugenie lak he'd love one o' his own women kind, fur dem li-locks to turn him dat away....

Dem growin' down dere in yo' yard—now. Dey's real pretty, honey, wid de sun a-shinin' on 'em.... real pretty—an' cheerin' lak.   [*The Crisis* 37.1 (January 1930): 9–10]

DEEPENING DUSK

by Edith Manuel Durham

If you were very bright, with silky hair instead of wool, pomaded and hot-combed dead straight, you had to be careful. You must never dare to laugh at the amusing fancies, bobbing so deliciously into your brain, else the grinning, frisking black girls, who found so much to giggle over, would freeze you out of the fun. They would get mad and accuse "Stuck on your color. Trying to be white." They would say you were laughing because they were black; they might even call you "White folk's nigger." Vivvie Benson had learned to be careful. She knew all this and thought it silly. White was nothing to be stuck on. Black wasn't funny.

Ma was black and wooly headed but didn't Vivvie love her? Love her? Why Ma was all the world! No one would dare to laugh at Ma. Out of nothing Ma made the prettiest clothes for Vivvie and twisted her hair into perfect curls; Ma kept the neatest house, had the earliest garden, hung out the whitest wash. Vivvie was proud of Ma, the strongest, smartest, best woman in the world. Vivvie loved her black.

There was Tim, so slick they called him "Shine." Vivvie never used that name though she loved it. "Shine" fitted Tim, fitted pat to his satin polished skin. Everything gleamed about Tim; his hair was not plastered like the rest of the boys,' it was crisp live crinkles of blackness; his straight teeth flashed with glistening whiteness; he had eyes that sparkled, that danced when they looked at Vivvie, and changed to rolling fiery balls in a sea of white when other eyes danced at Vivvie.

No other girl so fair as Vivvie, no other boy so dark as Tim, yet Vivvie loved him, next to Ma. Girls younger than she had steady fellows but Ma said seventeen was much too early. Tim could not be her beau. He might only come now and again to sit and look at Vivvie while she chattered. Always Ma was close at hand. Kate Benson's eyes were keen for this only child. Tim often felt them, cutting under his skin.

This summer afternoon, in the spotless dining-room, Tim looked across the checkered cloth of the table, at the fragile blossom that was Vivvie, a creamy, tender bud in her cool green frock, tissue thin, still dainty and fresh after many launderings; Vivvie looked back at Tim, wholesome and strong, not minding his faded overalls and the tear in his chambray sleeves. She knew he would leave her for the heat of the foundry where he would sweat all night. For six years he had done the labor of a man. Vivvie was proud of the brawn of Tim.

Vivvie was retelling stories, the kind she delighted to read (the boy delighted in any tale that had her voice for the telling) of beautiful damsels, lovely princesses in distress and of gallant knights to the rescue. "Oh, Tim," she sighed, but happily, "if I might have lived back then and been a lovely damsel."

The boy answered the wish in a voice that had grown deep early and rumbled:

"If any fellow ever bothers you I'll knock the guts—" Tim bit the offending tongue into confusion for daring to spit out rough talk before Vivvie, "I mean the stuffin' out of him!" How else could he tell his princess he would die to be her knight? He had no words to speak his heart.

The girl flushed, in no other way would she let him know her ears had caught the ugly lapse, that she wanted him to knock the stuffings out of anyone who came between them. Vivvie loved the sparkles in his eyes, the glossed slain of his muscular arm, showing through the torn chambray sleeve, satin casing steel. It looked touchable, only girls did not touch boys nor let boys touch them. Ma said so. That has what made dancing wicked, touching. A girl might get bad, and there would be a baby, the most wicked thing that could happen, unless you were married. Tim's mother was not married. Vivvie could not believe it wicked for Tim to be born. Not Tim. The soft cheeks grew warm and dark with color.

Fascinated by the unusual play of color in the girl's face, the boy watched, breathless, till the questioning dark fire of his eyes drew the dreaming gray of Vivvie's; one growing second Tim held her gaze, then long lashes curled downward, veiling the glory in. Once only, in a lifetime has man a right to such a vision.

Her hand lay on the table against the red ground of the checked cloth, tiny, blossom like. Tim stretched his calloused, great, dark hand beside it, marveled at the contrast. Vivvie forgot what Ma had taught. Her hand crept over the little space between them. "Tim," she whispered, shy, sweet,

"Tim."

Slowly his palm closed over her fingers, tightened.

"Vivvie, oh Vivvie!" Shoulders inclined forward, chins tilted, over the table their lips met.

"Vivvie!" Another voice was calling. Like guilty sinners they started, grew rigid in their chairs. "Time this boy was leaving if he means to hold his job." Ma followed the voice into the room. She glanced from one to the other casually, then keenly as she saw something new in the two faces. Tim had grown ashy, Vivvie deeply pink.

Slowly Vivvie recovered her voice, "Yes, Ma," she answered, and rose to get his cap. She did not look up as she placed it in his hand, but Vivvie felt Tim looking at her, caressing her with his smile. She was glad he was going, she wanted to tell Ma all about it, that she loved him. Next to Ma!

Kate Benson stood, watching, waiting. "I want to talk to Tim a bit. You go in the kitchen, Vivvie, and see if the kettle's boiling." An excuse to be rid of her, the door closed between them by Ma's firm hand. Vivvie pushed her curls far back behind her ears. She had to hear. When she heard she could not see. Impatiently she alternated eager eye and ear at the keyhole. This was her affair, not even Ma could shut her out of it.

Tim was twisting from toe to toe, awkward beneath Kate Benson's determined gaze.

"I couldn't speak before the child," Ma was saying, "but you are near grown and will understand. You like my baby, Tim?" The voice was soft and kind, but some undertone left Vivvie afraid. Her heart stopped for the boy's reply.

"Awf'ly," proud and ashamed was Tim, "worse than likin'," he added boldly.

"I thought as much, and I'm sorry, but you will get over it before you die, boy. I'm asking you now, don't come here any more." What ailed Ma, was she crazy? Why Tim had to come there, how else were they to see each other. "I want you and Vivvie not to see each other."

The applied eye saw Tim, writhing in wordless confusion. Vivvie longed to help him talk up to Ma, Ma who was spoiling every thing. "Why, Mis' Benson, why, I been comin'." No use looking, she had to hear.

"When Vivvie was a little girl; but things seem to be changing. I've been watching you cast sheepeyes at my little girl lately. I ain't going to have you fooling with her."

Tim stuttered miserably, "What you mean, Mis' Benson?"

"You are old enough, twenty ain't you? You understand me well enough. There's to be no fooling with my Vivvie!"

Tim was not stuttering now. Vivvie's heart leaped, he was angry, had found his voice at this sacrilege. He understood Ma now. "That's awful, Mis' Benson. Why Vivvie is good. She's good, I tell you. I wouldn't try! I want her always good. It's not fair, what you're thinkin'. Not Vivvie." Tim was talking up.

"And you don't get a chance. I ought to know my girl is good without your telling. I mean her to stay that way till she finds some man fitting to marry her. You never could."

"Why?" he dared. No answer, so he found his own. "You mean on account of Ma."

Vivvie saw the ashy agony in Tim's young face. Her heart was wrenched for him, and strangely for his mother. Terrible to have her son ashamed of her. Never, never, vowed the peeking Vivvie, shall child of mine be shamed for me. But listen, Tim had something to say for her.

"Ma ain't really bad, folks are just down on her because she got the worst of it. Do you s'pose I could treat Vivvie like that—, I can't call him the right name before you, Mis' Benson, like that thing treated Ma?" That was it, it was his father he was ashamed of. Vivvie was glad; it was unthinkable having to be ashamed of one's mother.

"I guess Vivvie is safer with me, on account of that, than some fellows with fathers. I wouldn't treat the worst girl like that, I couldn't fool Vivvie. She's good. She's—, she's a queen to me." Oh, never could Vivvie have resisted that pleading voice, "Please, Mis' Benson, let me come see her like always. I won't talk no love to her. I won't make up to her, till you say she's old enough. I—I won't even touch her hand. I gotta come, Mis' Benson, I gotta."

Ma could deny him. "No, Tim."

"But, Mis' Benson, you gotta be fair. How could I help my father? I ain't blamin' my mother none, not for nobody. I ain't bad."

Ma's voice was kindlier, though still there was rock behind it. "I am sorry, Tim. I'm not thinking you worse than the others. You may be better. Only I got higher plans for Vivvie. None of them are going to hang around her. There's lots think she is easy falling, but I mean to show all these folks how to raise a lady, even though her daddy was a white man."

Vivvie saw and heard no more. That last sentence had left her sick and sore with a great disgust. She did not hear when Tim was eased onto the porch and the door shut firmly behind him, alone in the dusk, but not in his misery. Vivvie was suffering a pain she had never known before,—shame! Shame. Her father a white man! She knew now why the black girls had shut her out, they thought she was trying to be white. Only the trashiest white men and the trashiest colored women—she tried to stop the trembling of her hands, they were hot, her face was burning with shame. Ma couldn't be wrong. She never had been. She stood there, burning and shaking, waiting for Ma, for Ma who must set things right.

Kate Benson started in surprise at the stern eyed Vivvie waiting in the little kitchen for her, pouncing on her accusingly:

"I heard you, Ma, I heard you. I must know why you did it. I must."

The mother stared, never before had the child been rude. A good thing she had dismissed that boy, her baby was getting serious about him. They ripen so early, these children of the sun. Kate Benson hoped she had not waited overlong. Her attempt at amused laughter was shaky, "Why? Because you are only a baby, honey, just Ma's baby yet, sweethearting is for women, Vivvie. Ma has to guard you from the beaus yet awhile."

"Oh that!" Vivvie waved Kate's words aside. "I am not talking about Tim. It's you I am asking about, about you and my father. You have to tell, Ma."

What under heaven ailed the child? "Tell you what, girl?" What was she bawling about? "What is there to tell about your Pa? What is wrong? Answer Vivvie." But Vivvie was crying, crying. The mother's heart was shot with fear, the big fear that dims all others for the mothers of girls. If she had not watched close enough? If she had not been in time? Nothing like that could happen to her baby! "Tell me what ails you, girl," she bade, her voice made sharp with pain. "Answer, you hear me, mind your Ma."

"You never told me my father was a—a," (whisper,) "a white man."

Relief, perplexity, it was not the great fear any longer. "What need? You ought to remember your Pa, and there hangs his picture in the room," her eyes rested on Vivvie, unbelievingly, "you mean you thought all this time your Pa was colored?"

"I thought he was light complected like I am."

The dark woman gazed at the creamy, crimson flushed face before her, and her own eyes filled with determined light, "He was, like you; but he was a white man, and you are white, too, if your Ma is black."

"I am not! I won't have him for a father; I won't have you for—" the child stopped, frightened by her own vehemence. Almost she had disowned Ma. She still loved Ma. Tim loved his mother, bad as she was.

"Now listen, girl. You are not old enough yet awhile to call your Ma to account, and it strikes me you're a bit behind hand choosing your Pa and Ma. Everybody always knew who your Pa was, and as much as folks enjoy minding my business for me, with all the gabblers in the world, ain't you never heard remarks?"

So that was why the girls stopped talking, the kind ones, and the mean ones said things about "white trash" when she came on them suddenly. Only now, did she know, why those things concerned her. All her life they had taunted her, about her shameful parents, and she had been too dumb to see. She spoke slowly, her tears dry.

"They say about colored with white—, they say all the colored ones must know her too well is why she had to mix with trash. They say it's an accident when that kind gets married. They said it to me and I never knew they meant you. I never knew what they meant."

"I should think you wouldn't understand them, the hussies."

Timidly, Vivvie put her question, "Were you married?"

"I was married, tight enough, and I'll have pay of anyone, white, black, grizzly or gray that says I wasn't. I should think you'd be ashamed, asking your Ma such a thing?"

"I am not, I'm only ashamed of that."

"Well, you can stop having tantrums, if you are, my miss. Many a girl would be proud she had a white Pa to give her a bright skin and good hair."

"I am not. I am ashamed that I had to be born. I had rather be black, like Tim."

"Hush up, girl. You are as glad of your good looks as the next one." This was a hardness she had never dreamed to face. Who would have thought the child could take on so? "You know, baby, white and colored have always mixed, since slave days. You mustn't carry on so."

"Slavery times were different. They couldn't help themselves. You don't have to do such things now. No one made you."

Kate's sharp angry voice cut her off. "Vivvie! Stop that talk this minute! You hear me! A child of mine to be so bold. That comes of letting you talk with that Tim, putting the devil in your mind."

"He never, he never," Vivvie defended. "Tim wouldn't say a word to me that an angel couldn't hear." Oh, it was terrible for them both, standing hard eyed and angry, they who loved each other so.

It was time to end the scene. The child would be falling out next thing. "Be that as it may," Ma's voice rang with the old firmness, "You march yourself up the stairs, and wash your face in some good cold water, see if that will calm you down. Having tantrums all over the place like a five year old. March! before I turn you across my apron like you was one."

Left alone, the woman dropped on a kitchen chair, rocking her gaunt shoulders backward and forward, moaning, weeping. "My one little baby, my baby, I lost her now, I lost her, Lordy, Lordy, my baby. Oh mercy, mercy." Presently she rose, they must eat. Setting the kettle on the stove, she poked the fire viciously beneath it. "Did I know who said such things to her I could twist their neck with a grin."

* * *

In the trim little chamber above, a girl writhed on the bed, twisting her face in hard, dry, sobbing, a fit of shame, and rage and utter wretchedness. Having tantrums. Her slim body, wearied with its angry twitchings grew still, out of the welter of unaccustomed emotions two thoughts stood out clearly; Ma, who had forced "trash" on her for a father, had dared to despise Tim, Tim who loved her. The other thought? She was going to get up and walk straight out to Tim, he was black enough for both of them.

Sliding from the bed, she stood looking down at the crumpled pillow, at the bright counterpane, wrinkled and soiled where her heels had dug in. Automatically she patted and smoothed them. Vivvie had her mother's taste for tidiness. Something of softness crept into her eyes, as her fingers touched one bright square, and then another, scraps from gay blossom colored frocks made for Vivvie, only here and there a sober blue or gray bit from Ma's work dresses. Ma had given Vivvie the best, always. Too bad she must be hurt. Turning from the bed Vivvie's sober gaze was caught by the fluttering whiteness of the frilled curtains. Ma preferred stiffly starched Nottingham, but it was Vivvie's choice that framed the window. It was Kate Benson's hand that kept them snowy and fresh. Vivvie need never touch a washboard. She held her hands idly before her, soft, creamy, flawless, and thought of Ma's, roughened and black, of Tim's big strong wrists, beside her own on the redchecked table. Too bad they both loved her. She could love only Tim.

At the washstand she lifted the pitcher and poured cool water into the big bowl. The baby Vivvie had been bathed in that bowl. Often had Ma told her so. Too bad, she supposed Ma would be hurt. Vivvie patted her face dry, rehung the towel neatly on its rack.

Beside the bed was Ma's deep chair, a towel pinned to its back protected the new cretonne covering; the covering had changed many times but the chair and its mission had been the same since first Vivvie could remember. It was there every night that Vivvie would snuggle into Ma's arms and tell her all the story of her day; every night she would kneel before it, with Ma's hand upon her head, "Bless Ma, make me a good girl," she would pray, then "Bless my baby, keep her a good girl," that was Ma. This night there would be no story and no prayer.

Afterward there would be goodnight. Vivvie could sleep so calmly knowing Ma was there beside her, to cuddle and warm next when nights were cool, to waken for comfort when Vivvie dreamed of scary things. It had all been so sweet, not to last.

Vivvie gulped, but couldn't cry, there was work to do. In a corner was Vivvie's desk. Ma had placed it where she need not be disturbed in her study by the noise of sudsy smells from the kitchen. From its nooks the girl drew paper and pen. The note took but a minute,

"Ma, I have gone to Tim."

It was bald. What else was there to say? Nothing. The note slipped finder the inkwell. Ma would find it when she dusted in the morning. After Vivvie had gone to Tim tonight, Ma wouldn't dare to stop her in the morning.

Down the narrow stairs, calling "Ma, oh, Ma!" She must act like nothing had happened. She would tell her that she must see Rosie Kauffman next door about her algebra. That would give her an hour to locate Tim, before Ma got uneasy. She called again, funny Ma did not answer. As she stepped down into the kitchen, Vivvie crinkled her nose. Not like Ma to let her kettle burn, she must be upset. Vivvie lifted the smelly thing from the fire. If Ma was in the back yard Vivvie would walk out the front; save questions.

Halfway across the dining-room, she stopped short, hands fluttering to her breast. Something was wrong. Why was Ma lying on the door, her head under the table?

"Ma," shrilled Vivvie, "Ma!" Never had Kate Benson failed that cry. Vivvie dropped on the faded carpet beside her, shaking the huddled form, calling without answer. Ma must be deaf, or dead. Her shrieks pierced the air,

"Dead! I killed her! Ma! Ma! Ma!"

Pushing through the narrow door they came, plump Mrs. Jacobs, slim Mrs. Harris, anxious to aid. The Jewish woman's white hands were stained pink from the berries she had been hulling, the dark woman's brown hands were dusty, straight from the biscuit pan; busy women, both of them, dropping everything for a child's cry of terror.

Vivvie did not look up, intent only on making Ma answer. Jane Harris pulled her away, straightened the crumpled figure. Vivvie screamed again.

"Quit that noise, girl," the woman gave sharp command, "Screechin' can't help your Ma. Go to my house and 'phone the doctor."

The girl stood there, silenced by this briskness, but with no power of motion.

"The child is useless," Mrs. Harris complained, chafing Ma's wrists. Mrs. Jacobs was bringing water. Behind her mother's broad shoulders, Rosie Jacobs appeared.

"Rosie, you go," Jane Harris directed, "tell Doctor Talbert to come right off. Vivvie here is nothing but a stick."

With only time for a pitying glance at Vivvie, Rosie sped on her errand. Vivvie was seeing only Ma. She was trying to ask these women a question. Funny how loud she was screaming till Mis' Harris hushed her, now her throat wouldn't work at all. Still she had to know. Had she murdered Ma with the terrible things she had said, and the worse things she had thought and had not dared to say? There was a question she must have answered. Haltingly the syllables came,

"Is she—is Ma—dead?" Vivvie had spoken so low she was surprised when Mrs. Jacobs answered,

"The poor maidala," plump hands patted the girl's rigid shoulders, comfortingly, "the mama you have still by you."

Then she was not dead. Tears came. A soothing voice, "So, so, you should not cry."

Through the unchecked tears Vivvie questioned further, "Will she die?"

The crisp Harris voice answered, "If she looks to you for help she will." The brisk cruelty of the sentence as the brown woman meant it to, dried the tears and checked the hysteria she had seen rising.

"Go you up and get your Ma's gown ready, and turn down the bed."

Climbing the stairs like a freshly wound mechanical toy, the words followed her, "A thin woman, but long and heavy, can we manage her Mis' Jacobs? Here's Rosie back, better let her. Here, you Rosie, you're young and strong, we can carry Mis' Benson up."

Vivvie had a gown unbuttoned and spread on the chair-back, a best one Ma had laid away for sickness, she who had not needed a doctor since Vivvie was born in this bed whose covers were turned so neatly back. Vivvie stood watching while they laid Ma on the sheet, but put her hand out for a bar when they reached for the gown.

"No, I will do that, I can fix her," she told them. Mrs. Harris eyed her keenly. "Well," she agreed. Understandingly they left her alone with Ma. It was the first personal service the daughter had ever rendered. Somehow she undressed Kate, she could see plainly now that Ma still breathed. Like someone asleep, somehow Vivvie got the nightgown smooth under her, and pulled the sheet up under her chin. Some of Vivvie's terror was gone though she was still afraid.

"Overwork, the heart weakened evidently she has had a shock," that was the doctor's verdict. Perfect rest, quiet, to be guarded from unpleasantness, was all Kate Benson needed, he did not wish to be alarming, but another shock might prove fatal. He and his little black bag were gone. Jane Harris had followed him down the stairs, Vivvie was alone with Ma who was breathing easily, and sleeping. Vivvie sat there, her hands light on the pillow, her eyes waiting, intent on Ma's face. Oh, she had so very nearly killed her! If only Ma would get well, Vivvie would never, never hurt her again; she would learn to work so Ma might rest; she would even give up Tim; everything Ma wanted of her Vivvie would do, if only she would get well.

Ma opened her eyes, smiling into Vivvie's anxious face. Oh, it was heaven to see Ma smile again! Nothing should ever come between them! Not a dozen white fathers should separate them!

"Well, Vivvie, have you forgiven your Ma for not making you black?" surprising how natural Ma sounded, "for letting you be born?"

"Oh, Ma! Nothing matters if you will get right again. I love you, Ma, if I am a wicked little fool."

"Don't say such words, Vivvie, they ain't lady like. You're not ashamed to be my baby?" Kate caught both the child's hands.

"Oh, Ma!"

"Well, then, that's good because I have to talk to you about these things, I thought you always knew." Kate tightened her clasp on Vivvie's fingers. "Hard on you finding out like that. Ma's going to tell you all about it."

Something warned Vivvie, she did not want to hear, "Not now, dear, the doctor says you must be still."

"What's that doctor know about my business," it was the old Ma speaking, "you listen to me. More room out than in and I want to tell you all about it now. About me, and your Pa."

Vivvie didn't wish to listen, but she must.

"Your Pa's people were quality, well off. He was a youngun' still when he came here and stopped at the Brittney House, on his first job just a kid, though he was twenty-five or some; I was young too, not twenty yet, but I felt lots older, because I had made my livin' so many years then. I was doin' chamber work at the Brittney House. You can't know about such things, baby, so, I'll slur it over much as I can. I was makin' his room one day when he came in. Well, he wanted me, bad."

Vivvie turned her head away, it wasn't fitting to hear these things about Ma. It didn't sound like Ma, and she wasn't speaking right. Ma who was so proud of her schooling.

"You needn't flinch away, baby, Ma isn't going to shame you." Kate had sensed Vivvie's uneasiness. "I pulled away from him and gave him some sass, but I didn't report him.

The manager expected us girls to take care of ourselves. He would only have blamed me and maybe I'd lose my job. Well, to make a long story short, he wouldn't let me rest. I was a good girl, raised decent, so I made him see he couldn't have me, not the way he wanted me. Well, he hadn't ever been denied anything in reach of his hand, and he thought he had to have me. So we got married. You see it pays a girl to be good, Vivvie!"

It paid, yes, and here was Vivvie paying, because Ma had been "good"!

"Well, it raised a stink. Colored folks like to talk their heads off. I quit the Brittney House and your Pa's boss fired him soon as he heard what he'd done. That wasn't good for him. He never had done any laboring work and that was all there was for him after he married colored in a small place like this, where everybody minds your business. He never got hardened, it killed him earlier than he was due to die.

"Well, if either of us was ever sorry we never let on. He wrote his folks he had married a servant, without saying I has colored. The servant part was bitter enough to them. They forgave him after a while, but never came near him. He used to visit them when we could scrape up enough to dress him fitting. He was proud and scared when you came, Vivvie. Tiny and red, but we could see then you were to be bright, and I was tickled."

Vivvie interrupted, choking over the words, "You loved me because I was fair?" Kate Benson drew her child's averted head down to her breast and held her close, so the girl could not see the tears rising, holding back.

"As if I couldn't love my baby just the same, white as milk or black as coal, ma like or pa like. It was only we felt it would make things easier for you. Your Pa said then, 'If the dusk doesn't deepen, Kate me can send her home and make a lady of her.' He loved you, Vivvie. He took you with him once, but you were too little to remember. Your Grandma was crazy after you. He said it again when he was passin', and I promised him. And almost I waited too long. Your Grandma wrote me for you. Time I sent you away. You can pass."

This was shameful, abasing; Vivvie's cheeks burned. She wasn't going to try any such thing. It was foolish, wicked, mean. It would divide her from Tim. She nipped the hot protest on her tongue. Opposition would excite Ma. She asked, calmly as she could, "Is it right, Ma?"

"Think your Ma would tell you wrong?" Ma demanded. "Go look in that glass." Obediently Vivvie crossed to the tall old dresser, looked long and despairingly into the mirror. She had no need to look. Vivvie knew what it reflected, and now that Ma had spoken she knew what she had not thought of before: it was the face, the hair and the eyes of a white girl looking back at her, and Vivvie did not want to see it, now.

"Come back now, babe." Ma's eyes were on her, ruling her, beseeching her. "Now tell me what's wrong with our plan? Don't that glass say you are more white than black?"

The mirror said it, though Vivvie knew it lied. Lied, because it could not reflect her heart, her heart full of love for the black mother she used to have (this was not really Ma, saving such terrible things, only some one she had to be careful not to shock), full of Tim, Tim, Tim! Yes, her face was the dawn, but in her heart! What had Ma said? Deepening dusk? Too bad the mirror could not reveal the soft, brown dusk in her heart. She could never pass, if that should show.

Ma was speaking again, waiting for an answer. "Well, Vivvie?" The answer wouldn't come. Ma's eyes crew keen. "You aren't bothered over Tim, a baby like you. Wasn't anything serious?" she queried. Vivvie could not trust her voice, words might come with a violence that would shock Ma and kill her. Vivvie had promised obedience if Ma lived, and Ma was living, demanding, "You don't think you're in love with that black boy?"

Slowly Vivvie shook her head. Ma pulled Vivvie down to her again, "Well I'm glad. Nothing stands in our way. Not for nothing have I slaved to keep you a lady, babe, your hands white and soft. You never will have to come the hard way your Ma did. You needn't marry a poor man that can give you only a livin'. You can choose from the finest."

The finest? Tim. "I will never marry, Ma." Vivvie broke her silence to say. Never marry Tim, never to have chubby brown babies with dancing eyes!

"Glad that is settled, Vivvie, I will rise from here in the morning, Doctor or no. You go down now and tell Sis' Harris she can go home to her men folks. You and me will be all right. I mean to nap a bit. Kiss me, babe."

Vivvie put her lips to Kate's and went from the room on her errand. Ma did not sleep, she lay there with eyes closed, wondering, fighting, aching. She shouldn't have asked the child to kiss her, the caress had said too much, had near shattered the plans of a lifetime. Vivvie's lips had been hard and cold, the kiss of one already slain for sacrifice; it lay heavy on her lips, too lifeless to strike in. She had never counted on the child turning from her like that.

After all it was babe's happiness they had planned for, Pa and she. Ma would have to decide alone, her pale skin or the dusky. How could she tell? Babe must be happy.

Down in the kitchen, Vivvie delivered her message. Mis' Harris was re-inforced by three other neighbor women, all crooning songs; they hushed when Vivvie came in. Jane Harris was the first to speak, as one with authority.

"You can tell Kate Benson I stay right here. Who she thinks is going to see after her? Not you. It's a disgrace, sisters, and I say it right to Vivvie, here, that a woman with a grown daughter falls out from overwork. You ought to be ashamed, child, and mend your ways, the way your Ma has slaved for you."

Vivvie said nothing, what they said mattered little. "Sis Harris," one of the other women remonstrated, "you oughtn't be so hard on the girl. It's her Ma's fault for not teachin' her, lettin' her loll around fine lady like with her Ma in the tub. I never had any too fine to put their hands in suds, but I started them early. It's a shame how this child's been raised."

Vivvie turned on them all, furious, drowning their chorused approval.

"You stop blaming her. Ma knew what she was doing. She was minding her own business like you busybodies better do."

"Well, sassy, too."

"Youngun's don't have respect."

"Mine better have."

"A girl of mine talk like that—"

"I'll talk worse than that if you blame Ma anymore," Vivvie shamed and hurt, struck back, she wanted someone else to suffer, as she did, and Ma, as Tim would suffer when she turned away from him. She had to hurt them. Slowly she said:

"Ma was shocked, you heard the doctor say it, Mrs. Harris. You wish to know how? I told her the talk that your fine daughters have been doing, because my father was white; their nasty hints and slurs. Of course the daughters repeated what they had heard their mothers say. It hurt and angered her. That is why Ma is ill up there alone."

Before the women recovered breath, the girl had turned her back upon them. Their comment followed her up the stairs.

"If it was one of my girls I'll whale the sin out of her, talking about Mis' Benson where the girl could hear."

Jane Harris spoke soberly, "It wasn't just the girls, that talked. The Lord forgive us all for a bunch of gabbing fools. Making the child's way still harder with our scoldings, and her heart sick about her Ma."

Vivvie closed the bedroom door behind her. Ma's eyes mere tight shut, she crossed the floor and stared out the window into the growing twilight, gazing across the field behind the house as darkness gathered over it. She could not see, but beyond that marshy field was the river. Tim had taken her there, to teach her to swim, oh long ago, before she knew that Tim was a boy and she was a girl, that Tim was black and she was white; when she was only Vivvie and Tim was only Tim. They had whipped Tim for leading her off to drown, as if Tim would ever let her be hurt!

But she was hurt, now, and Tim could not help her. She was hurting, hurting all over, with the ice that lay on her heart. No one could help her. She had even lost Ma. Thinking, thinking, of the hard bare road before her, Vivvie, threw out her hands in a vague appeal to the dark, the warm, kind dark, in a wordless prayer for the laugh and song of her own kind, for Ma to come back like Ma again, for Tim, Tim, Tim, and the round brown babies she would never see. Only lies, and fear, and more lies, with the ice growing around her heart. Oh the warm sunshine of her own kind, that could be felt even in the darkness, and she had to leave. She couldn't kill Ma. Her hands fell in helpless surrender, her head bowed with the weight of it.

"Vivvie," the voice, faint so low she scarcely heard it, "come here to Ma, babe."

It was difficult crossing the floor, Vivvie did not want to talk, she wanted only to stay by the window, staring into the growing dark, mourning. She stood by the bedside looking down at this stranger, an alien demanding obedience.

"I thought you were sleeping."

"No child, I've been waking up. Kneel by the bed so I can see you better. Your face is all over shadow."

"It is nearly dark."

"Kiss me again, Vivvie." Wondering, the girl bent her clouded face to Kate. It was not like Ma to sue for caresses. Another frozen kiss lay on Ma's lips. With both hands Ma pushed the girl's head up again.

"Look at me, Vivvie, straight at me! You've been lying!"

"Ma!" rather feeble, the protest.

"Lying," Ma repeated, accusing, "you are grieving your heart out."

"No," Vivvie denied dully, "no."

Kate Benson's voice rose in an exalted chant, "Yes, oh, yes, glory be! You've been lying to your Ma."

"No."

"The truth, Vivvie," Ma charged her sternly, "I was primin' you to lie, but not to me, babe, not to me. You're lovin' Tim."

Vivvie pulled away from Kate and drew herself erect, tall with a new dignity as she stood above her mother, "Yes, I always will. He is worth loving. I will not be ashamed."

"You had rather wash and scrub and sweat? rather be poor and fretted with a swarm of black and brown and yellow little darkies than do what I tell you? rather than be white and rich with your path easy? Answer, Vivvie."

Her path easy? Vivvie saw nothing but thorns. Must she cling to her lie? She had promised, Ma was not to be hurt again, whatever happened. "No," she said steadily, "no."

"Vivvie, I'm askin' once more. The truth, child, if it kills us both."

Moments passed in silence, then, "Vivvie, mind your Ma."

The sobs came, dry and hard, "Yes, Ma. I lied, I tried to lie! The more I think white the better I love black. Oh Ma, I had rather a thousand times! How can I leave my own? How stop being what I know I am?" Dropping to the floor she buried her face in the quilts. "Oh Ma, Ma, let me stay, those others aren't my kind, not my people, they don't want me, I don't want them. I only want, Tim, and you, and my own, only want to stay where I belong. Let me stay, let me stay!"

Ma's long arms tightened round the trembling shoulders. "Sure, honey, you're stayin' right here."

Tears came, warm tears. Ma mingled hers with Vivvie's. They washed away the glacier that had risen in Vivvie's heart, that divided her from Ma. "Guess," Ma said slowly, "I haven't broke that promise to your Pa. That dusk seems deepenin' down where it can't be seen."

Vivvie was pressing kisses, soft and fragrant against Ma's cheeks. Forgotten doctor's orders, the growing darkness. She could no longer see Ma. It was enough to know Ma, the real Ma, was there. That she could tell her everything, how she loved Tim and the sparkle of his eye.

The door opened noiselessly. Behind Mrs. Harris and the lighted lamp she carried came the sound of singing, hymning voices from downstairs. Kate Benson greeted her neighbor with a broad grin. "Thought I ordered you all home." Vivvie gained her feet, stood dewy faced in the soft lamplight.

"We decided we could stay with you a spell. You sure are getting well in a hurry. Declare you don't look sick a bit."

"Who said I was? That Doctor? What's he know about black folks insides? Just soldierin' on you Mis' Harris. Pull that shade, and set a chair for Mis' Harris;" Kate commanded, complaining fondly. "This girl don't know the first thing about a house, Mis' Harris. Soon as I rise from here she's going through a course of sprouts. She thinks she wants to marry Tim when she's out of school. Babe is goin' back home."

Jane Harris looked puzzled, "Back home?" She echoed.

"I chose outside the lines, but Vivvie here, wants to bring the color back."

Mrs. Harris fidgeted in her chair, then blurted, "See here, Kate, that youngun' of yours let out something, said you was upset by gossip over that chosin' of yours."

"Go long, Harris. Ain't I been colored too long to let colored talk worry me? Vivvie, go down, tell those sisters they needn't be selfish with their tunes; bring that meetin' sound up here."

Jane Harris wondered why Ma whispered, "Glory, glory. My babe's come home to stay."

[*The Crisis* 38.1 (January 1931): 12–14; 39.2 (February 1931): 49–52]

HONOR

⌒⌒⌒

by Lillian Beverton Mason

There is Venice, Italy, with gondolas and singing gondoliers, with tall spired churches and red clad priests, with palaces of old and yellowed marble and enclosed gardens with fountains of dewy, misty waters and pouting pigeons sipping on their ledges, varied colored market stands with old market women like old masterpieces; houses lichen covered with headless ghosts inside. There are skies, crystal blue and olive groves and dark eyed maidens with old ivory skins. Night—when there is singing and shapes of things in the past, Caesar and stamping soldiers and the Medici and then—there is Venice, Mississippi.

Venice, Mississippi with its mud-rucked Mississippi and patched canoes and Negro fishermen with sun-curled hair and red bandannas, singing haunting blues and moaning Baptist hymns, and shacky houses on stilts looking like boney-legged gals in short skirts; houses with tin can weather boarding and rag stuffed windows. These houses reek of the smell of fish and too many humans in one place.

Of evenings there is song, not the chant of monks, but the remnant of song of a lost race and fiddles squeak and black women, fat and unshapen, sit in doorways and look at the men who pass. Some of them have youngsters pulling at their breasts like young animals, some are smoking and some sitting silent. The stars come out and a breeze from the river stirs up the smell of fish and encircles it about and its scent reaches Magnolia as she comes wending her way down the hill, the hill that divides Upper Venice or white folks' Venice from Lower Venice or colored folks' Venice.

* * *

Magnolia coming down when Venice is singing and loving, for that is all that is left to a lost race, singing and loving, and the women who feel the men's strong arms, wish for something better and holier, but you know there is a saying in Venice among the women, "If a nigger don't get you, a white man will."

The colored men curse themselves and feel ashamed and determine to do better by their ole woman and the kids. They look up the hill and see afar the gold crosses on the churches, the houses and the schools and they think of the praying and singing and loving of white folks in clean white places and little children in clean white beds, colored nurses singing them to sleep; their own houses like pig pens and their children—a hard slap from a fat hand and "Go to sleep, devil," that was colored "chilluns'" lullaby.

But even in such humble places as Venice are bred white souls and in the muck of Venice there was a white soul, Magnolia. They do not bother with the Jones or Smith part of your name in Venice, anyway. Magnolia had no Jones or Smith part. Her mother had given her to Granny Morris. Her mother had not been glad of her coming and had given her unwelcome offspring away more gladly than she would have parted with a pocket handkerchief.

Magnolia was a flower, a honey yellow flower, honey colored skin, with dark brown eyes, black curly hair, soft and silky, and a little pink mouth with lips the pink of luscious melons, and a slim little body that carried castoff white folks' clothes like a princess. The way she held her head and the determination in her eyes, Magnolia had honor. She wasn't going to belong to any man.

Magnolia was second girl at Rippleys. Every evening when the big cook folded her hands and said, "Guess we's through," then Magnolia slipped away for a while with Gran.

Every evening at singing and loving time she came down. Past Caroline's place, where there were awful women and where Big Bill Harris banged away at rags and whose look filled her with fear. Past them all to Gran's house.

Gran's house where every evening she swept out the dirt that daily accumulated and nightly repeated her commandments of cleanliness to Gran. Gran was wizened, shriveled and asthmatic. She was old and had colds in her head, therefore it was a necessity for her to wear at least seven head rags like the proverbial seven veils. Her feet were bare; bare, black and ashy. Yet to Magnolia she was Gran. Gran who so obdurately made her all this work every evening.

* * *

"Gran don't hang the slop jar on the door jamb. It's terrible."

"Nothin' terrible about thet. Everybody knows you gotta have one."

"What's this pile of dirty little rags?"

"Empty baccy sacks. Savin' em for quilt pieces."

"Oh, Gran don't. I'll buy you some nice clean pieces for your quilts. Gran what did you take those nice curtains down for?"

"Them's too good to be usin' everyday."

Patiently she put the shack in order only to have to do the same thing the next night but Gran had been faithful to her and she wasn't going to scorn her or make fun of her.

She stayed in the hot little shack all evening, even when it was very warm, it kept the men from annoying her. They were always after her, luscious Magnolia who wasn't to be touched by men.

Granny sipped something out of a yellow cup, something draughty and black. When she was through with the draught she drew on her pipe and asked questions about Magnolia's work folks.

"You mean to say Nola, they bought forty chickens and only used the breasts! I'll tell you white folks has all the hevin they's gonna git. Has they got anything new?"

"They bought a tapestry that cost one thousand dollars to hang over the buffet."

"A thousand dolla picture to look at while you eats! Why they's chilluns here in Venice ain't had a square meal all their lives."

"I know it Gran and I can't explain it; but theirs is a beautiful life."

Magnolia stood still, thinking and wishing things—of a school where you could go and work and where colored boys were learning about the higher things of life and learning to look at girls with honor and cleanliness. As soon as Granny was gone—but never would she leave her.

* * *

A man came to the door, breaking up the dream. "How do, Missus Morris, how you?"

He talked to Gran, but his eyes peered at Magnolia.

"I'm all right. How are you, young man?"

"Fine. Hello Nola."

The girl stiffened, did not answer.

"Stuck up ole gal ain't you? Neva mind, someday you gonna be glad to talk to a nigger."

He turned and went away. Magnolia covered Gran and started back to Rippleys.

Big Bill, tall, powerful, yellow, saw her passing and whispered a whisky scented request in her ears. She pushed him away.

"All right, all right," he answered in a surly tone, "Big Bill will get you some day."

Magnolia went on. She wanted to cry. Six long years of fending them off. Wolves! Why couldn't they learn about the school and go away and learn to honor women. She always took the street car as soon as she reached Upper Venice. There were white wolves up there.

But as spring came on, came other worries: rumors of the river rising and people having to leave, people being drowned and diseases on rampages. Gran sick and weak, refusing to budge and the water like a hungry demon, rising higher and higher. Magnolia stayed with Gran all the time now. The people in Venice were fleeing, a few every day. Gran pleaded to stay there. Pap had died there and there she was going to die. Magnolia stayed; closed the windows and doors to make the rescuers think there was no one there.

* * *

All alone in deserted Venice. Gran didn't know her now. All her talk was of Pap. Like a little child she looked, only a little child that is shriveled and old. Magnolia lifted her about like a child. Gran didn't eat anything. Magnolia wouldn't eat in another day.

The murky water rising higher, higher like a sleek and slimy monster, hundreds of feet long, it moved. Then late one afternoon Magnolia saw it with terror, the water moving under the door had formed a wide puddle on the floor. She wrapped Gran in her patch-work, a quilt of washed baccy sacks and hoarded calico pieces. There was no way of getting to the roof. She reached the window with her burden and sat there. The water under the door had trickled every place. The legs of the bed were covered. Her feet dangling from the window-ledge almost touched the flowing water below.

There was only miles and miles of water with partly submerged houses.

Magnolia looked down in terror at the water and in greater terror at the bundle in her arms. She couldn't pull back the quilt and see how Gran was, she would over-balance and they would both fall. The bundle grew heavy in her arms, so heavy that Magnolia thought the bones in her slim arms would crack. Gran was dead.

* * *

The yellow moon like a laughing Chinaman lit up the water and showed terrible things; things with stiff long ears—dead rabbits; things that were alive—snakes; boards, pans, a floating potted geranium and something that looked like a little child.

Magnolia screamed, but terror only made of her voice a hoarse whisper. She was sleepy. God!—but she couldn't go to sleep, but her eyes, they closed. For a minute she couldn't see the laughing moon. She shook her head. "Help! Help! Help!" and the echo was Help! Help! Help!

In spite of will she fell asleep. Numb legs, numb arms. It couldn't have been five minutes, yet it had been time enough to relax her arms and when she opened her eyes, the tiny, thin thing in the big quilt had slipped away. Magnolia swayed with sickness. She had let the body of Gran slip out of her arms into the witch's caldron of thick gray waters.

She went crazy. One scream after another she emitted, each weird and distressful. She listened for an answer. She heard a piano playing. She was crazy. There was a tinkle of a piano and a man singing:

> Today, tomorrow, all the time
>   She's my baby, yes sir.
> Brown skin gal, yellow skin gal
>   Slim black moma, thets my gal!
> A—you—a—me—a—you—a—me
>   Sittin' neath the moon all alone
> A—you—a—me—a—you—a—me
>   Ole owl askin' who is you!

That was Big Bill Harris playing and singing. She was crazy. There was no one in Venice but she and this monstrous river. She shrieked again.

A wooden window three houses down swung open. Big Bill poked his head out. There was a girl screaming out there somewhere. He had thought he was the only one in this "No Mans' Land." He had been drunk when the exodus took place and they had left him. He had expected to die. Sing a little and die. What was life about anyhow?

The girl was in the third house. Old Gran Morris's house. Must be Magnolia. He believed he could swim it. He shed his shoes and coat and jumped into the muddy waters. He put his immense arms up and caught the window ledge and pulled himself up beside her. He put his arms around the shrieking girl.

"Magnolia be still. What's the matter? Hush!"

The girl finally quieted. Big Bill Harris crooked up in the window, humming, quieting her and it was he who saw a boat passing, like a shadowy ghost, and hailed it.

Magnolia clung to him all the way to the refugee camp, crying and telling him about letting Gran go, and she didn't mind his arms at all,—Big Bill Harris, who played at Caroline's and never worked.

* * *

Fall, and Lower Venice almost like itself. At least Caroline's place, where Big Bill played, was open. It was Saturday night and Magnolia was leaving for school next day. She had come down to tell all she knew, goodbye. Magnolia was the first one that had ever left Venice to go away to school. She came at last to Caroline's place, the place that represented everything she hated, women without honor and Bill in there playing ragtime.

She went in. Went in Caroline's place Bill sat at the piano. The girls looked at her. She went over and touched Bill.

"Bill, come outside. I want to tell you goodbye."

He got up, his head almost bumping the ceiling as he arose. Magnolia stood constrained.

"Bill, I am going to school but I kept thinking about you saving me and how you never tried to be friendly since, and I felt I owed you something."

Puzzled, "Owe me something,—what, little girl?"

"I thought if you wanted me to, I'd stay here with you and—be your girl."

Big Bill stood motionless. Magnolia offering to give up everything; school, honor and end up at Caroline's place! That's where she'd end up at, 'cause he knew he would never work. Magnolia blossom!

"Why—No—'Nola," he actually stuttered, "You go on to school. If I ever has a gal, I want a college gal. You go on. You don't owe Big Bill a thing."

And the only credit Big Bill takes for himself is when they hear of some new honor that has come to Magnolia. He turns to Caroline and says, "I know a time thet girl would a went right down to the dogs, if it hadn't been for me, right down to the dogs!"

[*The Crisis* 40.7 (July 1931): 229–230]

THE PRODIGAL

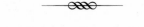

by Laura D. Nichols

A sudden hush fell on the congregation, and the faces of the listeners assumed the leaden stillness of masks. Only the startled black eyes that stared out from the vari-colored wall of faces told the earnest, young preacher that his people were listening as never before. A child cried, and its mother dropped a full, golden breast into its mouth, not once moving her eyes from the preacher's face.

Perturbed by this unwonted stillness that held a people usually so ready to respond with "Amen" and "Tell the truth, brother," the minister went on in his cool, even voice, "And God holds us to this commandment as it is written. 'Thou shalt not commit adultery.' Inquire into your own lives, my brothers, my sisters. Too many of you are living in a way to shame your church and your profession as Christians."

"Do that young fool know what he's sayin'? Don't he know he's hittin' some of the best givers in the church? Who he hittin' at anyhow?" Deacon Jones shook his head and sighed. He knew what this sermon would mean to the collection. And the responsibility of raising the preacher's salary rested heavily upon the shoulders of Deacon Jones.

"Thank God it don't hit me." Mama Jane shifted her snuff to the other side of her mouth, and managed a mulled "Amen." Mama Jane did not know her age, but she was "a good-sized gal in time of Abraham Lincoln's war." She had come north with her children and grandchildren during the industrial boom that had followed the World War, and had aided in establishing this little church. The migrant Negro did not often find the established churches of the North to his liking, and so began his own. Mama Jane continued to mutter to herself, "Old as I is, do,' and many preachers as I'se heard in my time, I ain't never hear one ain't got no mo' sense dan to badaciously insult de people wa' he got to git his bread and butter f'om."

Her mumbling did not stop the preacher. Indeed, he must have taken it for sanction, for sharper, more trenchant words fell from his lips, and hung like small, glittering blades in the air. His voice rang out once more, "The wages of sin is death, but the gift of God is eternal life."

The service was over, and the people swarmed out to the lawn surrounding the pretty little church, to give vent to feeling that this morning had not found the usual emotional outlet. An odd picture they made, these transplanted human beings, pulled up from their rural homes in the Southland and dropped in the heart of an eastern industrial city. The problems of adjustment were often disconcerting, but they had kept their religious life entirely apart from the changes. There was to be a lodge funeral this afternoon, and many of these people must "turn out." While they waited, they fell into groups on the ill-kept green to discuss the sermon.

"Ef I had only known that was wha' he was goin' to talk about, I'd a' sho stayed home and baked my rolls dis mornin'. Spec dey riz all out de pan by now." Sister Mary was plainly peeved. She had on a good-as-new black straw hat her "Tuesday Lady" had given her, and not the least excuse to shout. Sister Mary was an expert shouter. She always circled the church before the 'spirit' departed from her. She sometimes embraced happy fellow Christians, but she never committed the blunder of hugging comely Anna Brown. Not since Big Lige Pierce had taken up with Anna over a year ago.

Partly hidden by the fragrant, feathery beauty of a lilac in full bloom, a group of men, strong, black and young, passed a bottle from hand to hand, and shakily condemned the sermon and the preacher. "Better learn to tend to his own business if he wants to stay here." "How come you so touchy, big boy? Eve'y body know Anna Brown' husband aint's dead. Wouldn' I love to see him walk up someday when you' busin some o' his childen! Preacher sho have one mo' sermon to preach. Fesser Brown plumb crazy 'bout his lil yaller children." Big Lige made no answer to this.

On the steps a group of deacons and other officers of the church smoked and spat and studied. Deacon Jones grumbled, "Collection was powerful small this mornin'. That man go' ruin hisslf yet. Better be studyin' bout them hongry children o' his'n, stead o' insultin' some o' his best payin' members." The old man spat viciously into space.

Apart from these various groups, Anna Brown and her three attractive children laughed and talked happily together. The sermon was not mentioned. Anna was by far the best-looking woman in the congregation, and by the same token, one of the least popular. Though rather given to plumpness, she was both neatly and becomingly dressed. Her small bright eyes twinkled in a yellowish brown face, like stars peeping thru a sunset sky and laughing because they shouldn't be there. She was the sort of woman who says little soft, kind things to people when she might just as well say nothing at all. Mama Jane, who took care of the children while Anna went out to sew by the day, often said of her, "Poor chile, she don' do nobody no harm, only wha' she do to herself." Though for the life of her, Mama Jane couldn't see what Anna wanted of that big, rough Lige Pierce hanging around, and her husband a school teacher in the South, and as nice a boy as ever drew breath. She could never understand why Anna and Hal had separated, for Anna was a closemouthed woman, for all her gentle, smiling ways. Her lips could close in a hard, straight line, and the warm twinkle in her eyes change to the cold gleam of burnished steel.

The people began to move quietly toward the church door, as the funeral cars approached. From hidden recesses in bags and purses, quaint little black and purple bonnets appeared, along with big, bright badges. Hands slipped awkwardly into white gloves, and the order formed in solemn procession behind the bier and followed it into the church.

Lige Pierce sauntered over toward the little group that remained outside, for Anna did not belong to the order, and had only tarried because the children wanted to see the order turn out. Lige's hungry eyes rested, not on the familiar form of the woman, but on the slim, brown girl at her side. Esther, still unconscious of the charm of youth's first rounding out, felt his look, and flinched. Anna saw it with her smiling eyes, and the glint of steel veiled the smile. The words of the preacher fell again on her heart and cut like small, sharp blades. "The wages of sin is death." Death, yes; but that caressing look at her girl meant hell itself.

All the sorry memories of these past three years came to her as she walked slowly to the car line with her children. Lige was a few paces behind, and her heavy heart told her where his eyes rested now and again. Hal's voice rose in her ears as on the day he left to go back South to his schoolroom: "I cannot do the rough railroad yard work which is all our men find to do here now that the boom is over. We can make it at home on my salary, and send the children away to school later on." And her own voice, "Never. I'd rather wash and iron and be free than to have my children grow up in the South." Hal had gone, and Lige had drifted into her life. Hal's letters always begged her to return, but without avail. She could think of no reason why she should. Until today.

When the little party stopped in town to transfer, Anna slipped around the corner and sent Hal the following terse message: "Home next Sunday." She would need a few days to get the children ready.

And on the next Sunday, all the pent-up emotion of the worshippers burst forth when the earnest young minister thanked God that his words had borne fruit in one heart. Sister Mary gave two or three quick, frog-like jumps, and let the 'spirit' have full sway. She circled the church three times and fell exhausted in her seat. Mama Jane, too old for active shouting, fanned her vigorously and murmured, "God do move in a mysterious way. Bless his name."

In a little southern city, Hal Brown welcomed his loved family home, and thanked God piously that his prayers had at last been answered.

And Anna held her peace and smiled her quiet smile.

[*The Crisis* 40.9 (September 1931): 302–303]

THE GREATER GIFT: A CHRISTMAS STORY

by Marie Louise French

All around Elizabeth Ann was pandemonium: Five and ten cent stores. Things that squawk for a nickel. Bawl and shimmer from Christmas trees. The glitter of silver paper. Salvation Army kettles—the bells tinkling.

Christmas time—Snow time—the tilting of little, clanging cars around the curves.
You felt all tight at the pit of you, with the thrill and glitter of expectancy.

There were rows and rows of electric lights, red and green and blue.

Elizabeth Ann—hugging herself in her shabby coat, with a shabbier collar, hurried along, and always—there was a face, a misty face. Very clearly and closely it bobbed alongside with myriads of others, except that it was more clear. And there was a man dressed up as a Santa swinging a great razzle-dazzle. And Elizabeth Ann, who had a sob in her throat, thought of Betty—Betty who just could not get well—Betty, who might not see another Christmas! For an instant, Elizabeth Ann thought her throat would burst; but she hurried on—glimpsing the windows,—seeing nothing. There was Jen, the eldest, poor, dear Jen, always needing something. So much you had to do for her and her family. And you wanted to do, so very much more always. Jen, who tried to be so independent, you loved her so, because she was so utterly dependent. And of course there was Paula—the baby Paula was always laughing, her large brown eyes danced and her dimples were forever playing, flashing over her face.

It was good to work. But you wanted to. And anyway, Elizabeth Ann was a real person to the people for whom she worked. Twenty years of her life for one family—

Why, only this morning she had received from "The Boss," as she called him, her annual Christmas present—three hundred dollars!! He had smiled that wistful smile of his, bid her good bye and wished her a merry Christmas. With all his money, he was unhappy. Christmas meant nothing to him. There was nothing that he wanted, there was no one who loved him,—for himself—except, perhaps—Elizabeth Ann—!

There, there was that face again!—The black face—it looked sometimes as though there were a hint of a beard; but the wind, blowing flurries of snow in your face—you were never sure. Oh, the lovely din of everything! And,—glory be!—you would buy what you wanted with your own Christmas gift. You could give Betty—oh—what wouldn't you give Betty! your lovely Betty waiting for you—her great dark eyes looking at you—beyond you. If she would only get well—if some miracle would heal Betty; she would never want or ask another thing in the world. Always that face—a haunting face—above the poor frayed collar—or was it frayed? You could never tell for the snow.

Elizabeth Ann—her eyes sparkling, felt for her pocketbook. Her Christmas money—her girls' Christmas—and it wasn't there.

Where—? What—? When—? There were no words to answer. Her heart beat piteously. Of course, she would find it. Oh, it could not be lost—It must not be!

Up the street—one block—she walked. Tears—snow. The tears seemed to freeze with anguish on her cheeks. It was not true. It couldn't be—on she walked—blindly.

The sob in her throat would not be swallowed. And you glanced back—only for an instant to see that face again. And the man dressed as a Santa—you asked him, and you knew it was a waste of words. You knew it was useless—to wander around in a circle—longer. You met a neighbor and borrowed carfare home. And somehow you reached home. Might as well tell them, even Betty. Might as well get that over—poor dears. Elizabeth Ann knew she would feel the loss more than they would. They would try to comfort her. Paula, the youngest, would kiss the frozen tears away Jen, the eldest, would smile the disappointment down. Jen was a widow with three children—and took care of Betty. Paula worked too. But still—she was her baby. Betty would kiss her eyes—and say, "It doesn't matter, dearest. We have each other!"

Elizabeth Ann came near the house and desperately tried to square her shoulders. She tried to wipe her tears away from always sparkling eyes. But the minute she opened the door, they knew. Each one, almost in one breath asked her—

"What has happened, Mother? What is it?"

Betty was sitting up in the big chair today. She had made herself very beautiful for Mumsie, that she might think she was better. She stretched her arms to her now, and Elizabeth Ann ran to her. Jen, calm outwardly, but—wondering, waited. And Paula—the youngest—was waiting too, breathlessly.

Elizabeth Ann finally told them. She did not cry real tears, not those kind that hurt so—inside.

And Paula said, "Oh, my dear, is that what it is? I thought the Boss had kicked in or something—!" And Betty kissed her eyes tenderly, as she knew she would, and Jen logically wanted to know when and where she had missed her pocketbook? And perhaps you couldn't tell,—perhaps a nice person found it—

"Or an honest one"—said Betty.

"And anyway—we have you—Mother dearest, and we are all together—And that is everything—!" Paula said, laughing.

"But it meant so much to me—to all of us. Why, I was going to buy everything—the whole world with that Christmas present."

What peaches they were, Elizabeth Ann thought. She knew that they were disappointed; but no reproaches, only words of tenderness and eyes of love for her. She was overwhelmed.

And then the bell rang. Jen was nearest the door. She opened it, and there stood the stranger. He of the dark, dim face and frayed collar, the face that had followed Elizabeth Ann through flurries of snow.

Her smile could be like the flash of a wing. She smiled now. There was serenity in that face, that caused an enormous quiet. And he stood just within the door.

"Who are you?" asked Elizabeth Ann. "What is it?"

"I am a man—a working man; and I have come to return this."

And there in his hands, which were so beautiful was Elizabeth Ann's bag. And somehow, she could not open it. She knew—that everything was in it that had ever been there. She couldn't, just couldn't, offer him money. But the desire to do something, the desire to keep him standing there,—the need of his serenity and quietness,—the ache of everything in the world, inside her own heart.

"What can I do—!" she asked falteringly, "What—shall I do"

"Tell us—too!" the three girls said.

"You have power to be and to give—without that," he said in his quiet voice. And he pointed to the bag in her hands.

He took them in with his eyes,—and they rested longer on Betty. And she smiled, as though they held a secret together, a knowing smile—in her eyes—on her lips.

And he said, as he turned to go, "You have *love*, the greatest gift of all. Good-night!" "God bless you!" And as they followed him—beyond the door, "Good-night!"

The snow was so thick suddenly. Only with their hearts did they know that he was gone.

Outside it was snowing so—but it did not matter now—there was the Greater Gift— within. [*The Crisis* 40.12 (December 1931): 415–416]

THE THREE MOSQUITOES:
A STORY OF MARRIAGE AND BIRTH

—— ⚬⚬⚬ ——

by Anne Du Bignon

1910

Three girls were walking down Seventh Avenue talking excitedly. You would have seen at first a tall white girl, a chunky, pretty mulatto and a small lithe black. In fact, all three were colored and coming from a high school basketball game where they played right forward, guard and center.

"Oh boy," said tall, white Mary, "but didn't we put it over that snooty bunch of Mayflower descendants from Hempstead High!"

Of course, only Jewish and Italian girls would play on the team when the coach let in the three colored girls. "The Three Musketeers," they called themselves proudly, having just discovered Dumas and his Negro blood. But the boys nicknamed them "The Three Mosquitoes." They accepted.

"And watch your witchhazel," retorted golden Pinkie pertly.

They sauntered on, until Pinkie noticed a boy on the opposite sidewalk. She nudged Mary. Mary glanced at the unconscious dark girl, Sal, and said:

"Yes, I'm going to get married and I'm going to marry a white man. Why not? Of course I know they'll try to take advantage of me first, but I can take care of myself, if they get fresh. I know just what to do. He's going to be good-looking and rich. Children? I think not. You see they might show my other blood. Oh, they'd be pretty, of course. But they would raise difficulties. Well,—perhaps one. No, I'm not going to live abroad. I'm going to live up in Westchester. I have already picked out the house."

Pinkie interrupted. "Have you picked out the man?"

"Perhaps," said Mary, tossing her head.

"I'm not going to get married," said Pinkie—pretty, yellow and perhaps fifteen. "I'm going to write. You know my themes made a big hit this term. Say, I m going to write up this game for next week! No, I'm not going to write about Negroes or about 'races' at all. I don't care what that professor advises. I'm just going to write about people."

The youngest girl, dark-brown and a bit shy, said:

"But what people do you know, except colored people? And the whole point of this game was us!"

"Oh, well, after all, people are alike. And Mary, you can count on it no brats for me. There were seven in my family. That will do for two or three generations." Sal was not listening. She had just seen the boy across the street and was greeting him diffidently.

"Of course, Sal," said Mary, impishly, "You're going to get married."

The little girl assented gravely. "Yes, I think so."

"Love him?" asked Pinkie.

"Who?"

"Him!" Pointing across the street.

Sal's smooth face grew warm. "I—I don't know. Perhaps. You see Jack and I have been friends all our lives, and our families are friends and we seem sort of lost without each other. Of course, I suppose I shall marry him—he says so."

"But he's awfully black," said Pinkie. Mary nudged her and Sally tossed her head.

"I really hadn't thought of that. And what of it? So am I and I like his color. He's handsome."

"He is good-looking," said Mary. "But the children will be pretty dark."

Sal considered, "I suppose we'll have children if they come, and I wouldn't want white ones."

"They don't come uninvited," asserted Pinkie.

"Well, I may invite two or three. Goodbye. "

"Goodbye, Sally," added Mary, "that was a mean crack but I'll forgive you. Here he comes."

Jack started across the street, while Pinkie and Mary, turning up 135th Street, nodded toward him indifferently.

"He doesn't like us," said Mary. "I rather like him, but really, it's awkward to meet him on the street. People think I'm white and they surely couldn't mistake him."

1920

Pinkie was wading through mud out in Jamaica, Long Island.

"My God, this mud!" she said, and then as the door opened, "Sal, you dear old thing."

"Where did you ever come from, Pinkie! I haven't seen you in years. I'm so proud of you. I read both your books. They're ripping."

"Thanks; they aren't ripping off much coin for me. White folks don't like them and colored folk don't buy books; they borrow them, sometimes."

"Oh, I'm sorry. Baby, don't put your hand on the lady's dress."

"Never mind! What a dear! What is it? How old is it, and how many have you?"

"This is Thomas. He's just a year old. I have a boy of six and a girl of three."

"How splendid. So strong, healthy and beautiful."

"They are dears, even if their hair is difficult."

"Pish! Didn't we use to be fools, Mary and I. What's lovelier than color? And I never saw any hair that didn't have its difficulties."

"I was just joking. The real difficulties are much more important. Pinkie, it's a solemn thing to bring human beings into a white world when they're black. My children are fine, strong and bright. The boy is a favorite and leader in kindergarten with one of the highest I. Q.'s—but Lord, we had to fight to get him in and one teacher is still too mean for words."

"I just couldn't stand it, Sally."

"O yes you could and you'd thrill with the fight—if you could just keep it up.

"Why can't you?"

"Money. Jack's doing well—for a young man—for a colored man. You know he was crazy about electricity and he's got a job with the Universal Electric. He's even had one promotion after a fight and gets $1,200 a year. But what's that going to be as the family grows up? Will he ever get more? Will he even keep that?"

"Why worry? Times are changing. He may make it and you can move from this mud hole to Forest Hills."

"Yes? His boss lives there. He'd be fired for seeking social equality! Mind you, I'm not complaining, Pinkie; I wouldn't have missed the glory of this motherhood for worlds—but now I want to see daylight for them. But enough of selfish me. Now about you. Talk about yourself while I get dinner. Jack's due in an hour. Did you ever marry?"

"No, but I'm going to."

"Splendid—love at last!"

"No, not love. You beat me there, Sally. You loved and married. I waited. No, not love. Meal ticket. Literature don't pay unless it's 'Nigger Heaven' stuff. I'm going to write what I want to write. Remember what you said once about knowing our own people best? Well, it's more than true. I tried to write about 'people' but they all turned out colored only not the kind publishers pictured. Well, hereafter I'm writing about the only kind I know—real flesh and blood. I don't care if nobody reads my work. I must write. Also, and incidentally, I must eat. So I'm marrying Dr. Brown."

"Oh, the rich widower."

"Yes; he's a dumbbell but he's a good sort. And no babies. He never had any."

"Babies are a bother."

"Liar, they are dears and how I envy you. But my job's different. Only I don't fancy Brownie as an ancestor. But what's the racket I hear?"

"It's the other two kiddies. They always meet Jack up the road and ride home in the new flivver."

Jack came in alone and greeted the guest.

"Welcome home, Pinkie. But isn't this fine. Sally has been missing you all these years. 'The Three Mosquitoes' again,—but where's Mary?"

"You know you never liked Mary."

"Well, I liked her well enough, only—well, the girl is named after her. Sally insisted—Margaret Mary."

"But really," asked Sally, setting the table. "What has become of Mary? I've had no word in seven or eight years."

Pinkie sauntered over to the window and looked out on the trim little porch, the well-kept yard, and the contrasting mud of the street.

"Married white money—tried Westchester two years; had a baby and went abroad. Baby too golden to be quite white, I gather. I heard from her occasionally until the last two years. Parsons, her husband is dead, you know. He never was strong, and marrying Mary sort of cut him off from his old-time friends. He was a brick about it, for he understood. Junior is in boarding school in England. He's gorgeously beautiful. Mary sent me a picture and added whimsically that it is 'intimated' that he has Spanish blood! Poor kid."

"Dear, dear, what a funny world," said Sal. "I'll have dinner ready in a jiffy. I suppose I must apologize to you for doing my own housework."

"What on earth is coming?" suddenly said Pinkie. "An earthquake."

"No," answered Jack. "It's the kiddies. And Jack, Jr., off with your hat. Meet another Mosquito."

But Pinkie ran and kneeled before the girl.

"And this is Margaret! Sally, she's mine forever. It's a case of love at first sight."

1930

The "Bremen" was swinging slowly into Pier 42. A tall, thin and tired lady looked listlessly on. She did not scan the crowd for friends. She expected no friends. She did not recognize loved and familiar sights. She hated America. Yet she had come back. She was almost the last one on the dock and paid $500 duty with scarce a murmur and only a brief glance.

"The jewels?" They were in her small handbag. She tried to open it. It stuck. That patent Swiss lock always stuck. The obliging and deeply impressed inspector started to offer aid but she pried the case open impatiently, breaking the delicate mechanism. This diamond bracelet and that string of pearls and emeralds were new and had been declared. The others were old—quite old, as old as they were gorgeous.

The inspector was all apology and helpfulness. He warned against the half-locked case, now stamped and tucked carelessly under her arm. Thieves and gangsters were so prevalent. But the lady paid slight notice. There was a sort of defiant suffering in her face. She corralled a porter and followed him carelessly out and down, threw bills for tips and climbed into a cab.

"The Gotham," she directed and sank back listlessly, dropping the jewel case on the seat. One little tear crept down her face and she wiped it angrily away. Suddenly she leaned forward—

"Not the Gotham—the Grand Central Terminal," she ordered, and for the first time noticed the cabman—a boyish figure, chunky, almost too young for a license and with a good-looking but sullen face. His skin was deep brown and his hair closely curled. A Red Cap took her bags but the jewel case remained on the seat. She hurried to the ticket office. The cab drove off.

"Scarsdale."

"Round trip?"

"One way."

She came slowly back to the porter, looking at her watch. The porter lifted her bags, and then she remembered her jewel case. Quickly she reported the matter to the police and gave her address at the Gotham.

She stood in the middle of her sitting-room, perplexed. Somehow, she remembered the cabman's face vividly. He reminded her vaguely of someone. She hoped desperately he would return the case. It was not the jewels, it was about the boy she was inexplicably worried.

Early next day came a knock at the door. A bell boy ushered in a policeman and a colored boy. She recognized him as the cab man and stared at him.

"This fellow brought in your jewels this morning of his own accord. If they are all there we're booking no case against him, although we've taken his license away. It belonged to his father who he says is sick. The boy is way under age and had no business driving a cab at all. Then again he was a long time returning this property which looks suspicious. Please check up on the jewels carefully."

"They are quite all right, Officer and here is your reward."

"You don't want to make a case against him?"

"Oh no, but I'd like to talk to him—alone."

The policeman glanced at the check and went out cheerfully. She pointed to a chair but the boy continued standing as she sat down. He squared his shoulders and looked straight at her.

"I lied," he said briefly. "I meant to steal the jewels. I saw the case immediately [after] you left the car. I picked it up and started to call you, but it flew open and the jewels fell out. I drove away quickly. I meant to keep them."

"Why?"

"I just graduated from DeWitt Clinton High. I led my class in marks. I was on the baseball and football teams. I knew I was first in line for the college scholarship offered each year. But I didn't get it. That Southerner who was Assistant Principal canned me. The catch was that the one who got it must not only excel in marks, but he must be the boy "of greatest promise"—what promise was before a colored boy? He was right. I lost my only chance to go to college."

"And your parents?"

"Father has been out of work for three months; tried this cab and fell sick and there are two younger children. It is no use. I meant to steal your jewels."

"And why didn't you?"

"I couldn't think out a safe way. I studied plans all night. I enquired cautiously in Harlem and on the east side. Then I saw in the morning papers the notice of the loss. It was useless to try to keep them without letting mother and father know and risking jail. I didn't care for myself but I couldn't drag in the family. So I brought the case back. There now, you know the truth. I don't want any reward because I didn't earn it."

He turned to the door.

"Wait," she said—"I want to talk. Won't you sit down?"

"No," he said abruptly, but he faced her standing squarely on his two feet.

"I knew a boy like you once," she began slowly—"only he lacked your courage. I started to educate him but he knew—too much already. Now I've found you and I like you. There are few people on earth whom I do like. But I like you, because you are honest, blunt and human. I'm going to send you to college."

The boy stood very still holding desperately the hard lines of his dark face; but a tear rolled down and splashed on his hand. She reached over and took the hand and drew him to her. He crumpled to his knees and sobbed.

They talked a long time and then as he started to go, she said, "Tomorrow, Jackie, you'll bring mother here to dinner. I want to know her."

* * *

Seven came next night. Her guest was late. The 'phone whirred.

"Madame, they won't let mother come up on the passenger elevator."

Angrily, she dropped the 'phone and swept down in lace and silver and velvet. The manager hurried forward, but she ignored him and hurried toward a neatly dressed brown woman. She stopped and stared.

"Sal," she gasped and had the woman in her arms.

"Sal—good heavens, my own little Sal. It was your dear eyes I saw in Jackie's. And I never dreamed of his being your son. I didn't even recall Jack's name. I had forgotten you these twenty long and awful years. I had forgotten everything. Oh Sal, but it's—it's great to see you again. Come let's go eat—I'm starved. I don't know when I ate last. But I'm alive again and hungry."

"But Mary dear—not the dining room—there's sure to be unpleasantness."

"Fiddle-sticks, follow me!"

"But Mary dear, even if—if nothing happens I couldn't stand the stares and I'd hear all they said and all they didn't say."

"All right, Mouse,—sweet old mouse. Come up to my room. "I'll order a feast with roses and champagne."

* * *

Next day they foregathered in Pinkie's rooms in the Dunbar Apartments overlooking Seventh Avenue.

"'The Three Mosquitoes' again," laughed Pinkie.

"Who's that?" asked a pert little dark fairy of thirteen who was sketching the group industriously.

"Never mind—off to school. This is Friday and tomorrow the week end home. You see Pinkie and Dr. Brown have let Margaret stay here and go to the art course in Ethical Culture High."

"Let her! Begged for her you mean—we're both crazy about her but we had a hard time getting Jack's consent."

Mary looked at them both, her hard, tired eyes breaking in a mournful smile.

"And now I come begging," she said, "to my only friend." She paused and they all sat silent. Margaret sketched industriously.

"Aunt Mary," she said, "Smile more. That's ever so much better."

Mary continued, "You see I'm childless now and I think you will have to help me with Jackie."

"Childless," cried Pinkie and Sally.

"Yes," said Mary. "The boy's twenty and really is a gorgeous looking kid educated like an English gentleman. The family wanted him and didn't want me. I put it up to him. I just told him exactly who I was and what the difficulty in the marriage had been. I suppose I sort of thought that he was going to fall on mother's neck and say, 'Hurray for colored America!' But he didn't. He fell the other way. Damn it, he almost shrunk from me. Well, they wanted to annex him entirely as their breed was running out. I was silly, of course; what did he have in common with us but a tiny drop of blood? And he hates us. Can you imagine? He despises 'Niggers.' He raged at me. He declared it must be a horrible mistake.

"'Why, you're white,' he screamed. 'You're white as—'

'Hell.' I said calmly—'Never mind, Junior, go on and be white. You are already, body, soul and tailor. We're through forever. I'm handing you back your Spanish Grandee for ancestor. I'm going back to Harlem.'" She paused and closed her eyes a space—"And here I am."

"I'm glad," said Sally, "and sorry. I don't know what I'd do to lose a child. And you have just saved my first born. He told me all. How can I ever make it up to you."

"By giving him to me," said Mary. "He's the sort of human being I love—full of good and evil and with the grit to fight. I lacked the grit. I tried to run away."

"I can't give him to you, dear, not exactly. Remember, Jack. He's so shy and sensitive and tries to be so bluff and hardboiled. He couldn't stand the thought of not being able to do for Jackie. Losing his job upset his world. He'll never make a taxi driver—he's not strong enough and much too honest."

"That's all right. I've got a block of Universal Electric. He'll have his job back this week or I'll dump it on a falling market. Don't worry. Merit wins, backed by bonds."

"Impossible!—but don't say anything. Let him think merit did win. It'll bring back all his pride and manhood. And don't speak of taking Jackie away. Just say you'll help—see?"

"Saw!" said Mary with more of her old whimsical smile.

* * *

It was a week later. Jack, Sr., walked into his home with what was for him an almost jaunty air. He had on a new suit and his clean-shaven face showed returning health. Pinkie was there with little Margaret in a lovely fur coat. They were just about leaving for Manhattan.

"I've got my job back," announced Jack.

"Good," chimed Pinkie and Sally with excellently simulated surprise.

"Yes—President sent for me and said he just couldn't get on without me. I knew they couldn't. These young white dubs they were pushing in didn't know much. Yes, and I get a raise to $1,500. That nearly bowled me over. Nobody's getting raises these days. Reckon they were afraid I might refuse. Gee, they didn't know."

He walked over and put his arm around Sally and then noted Margaret's new coat. He glanced at the car outside. "Fine—fine, but you don't have to go back now. Reckon we'd better not sponge on Pinkie any longer."

A hush fell and Pinkie's golden face went sallow. The little wrinkles near her eyes worked through the light film of powder.

"Jack," she said. "You won't take her from me now."

Jack frowned uneasily and sat down.

Sally looked at him sorrowfully and Margaret wanted to cry.

Pinkie sat down beside Jack and spoke slowly.

"You see, Jack, you couldn't do this to me. You just couldn't. Brownie and I'd just die. You see little Margaret is Me. She's what I meant to be. She's my great Work of Art that I was too lazy and selfish ever to do myself. She has rare talent in her pretty hands and a dream of color in her eyes. Herr Schlesinger says so. She's not too strong and must not overdo. She needs money, lessons and attention and she'll get it. And," she laid a hand on Jack's tenderly, with a hint of tears in her eyes. "We're not really taking her. You're loaning her to us. She'll be home every week end—yes—twice a week. Oh, Jack, you won't—."

"Of course I didn't mean to hurt you," said Jack awkwardly. "You've been darned nice to us in our trouble, but you know how I hate charity—"

"Charity!" snapped Pinkie. "My God! I'm the one that's begging!"

"And Mary's got Jackie tied to her golden chariot," grumbled Jack. He looked up at Tommy who was tearing through the house from the back yard.

"I presume I may keep Tommy." But Tommy had darted to the door to greet the big Lincoln which was rolling up and carefully avoiding the deep mud holes. Mary and Jackie, Jr. came in.

"I've matriculated at Columbia," cried Jackie beaming, "and got a room in the dormitory. You ought to see Aunt Mary put that over."

Mary who looked almost happy out of her somber eyes and dead white face took Sally in her arms and looked past her to Jack and Pinkie.

"They're quarreling over the ownership of my children," sobbed Sally happily. Mary's old superior smile crept back.

"Dumbbells," she said. "Don't you know that these three children belong to us three women?—each for all and all for each—The Three Mosquitoes!"

THE DOCTOR'S DILEMMA: A STORY OF TUBERCULOSIS

by Anne Du Bignon

Dr. Brown smiled a bit impatiently.

"Suppose she did have a little fever," he said. "It's gone now and it's the natural result of a cold."

"But," insisted Pinkie, "sometimes she has fever and sometimes her temperature is way down. I'm a little anxious."

"You are always anxious about Margaret. You coddle her too much. Of course she is working a bit hard and she doesn't take enough outdoor exercise. Why don't you make her go to some of the parties or play cards, dance a bit?"

"You know how little Margaret goes in for that sort of thing, and then, too, I tell you she hasn't the strength. She's tired all the time."

"Oh, nonsense," said Dr. Brown, as he hurried out. "I'll examine her again, of course, but you're too anxious about her."

He was late for the meeting of the Manhattan Colored Doctor's Association but found that others were still later. The President, young Doctor Taylor, was there fuming and swearing.

"Darkies are always late," he growled.

Dr. Taylor was a dynamo, swift, always at work, accurate, up-to-the-minute in his knowledge.

"See here, Brown," he said. "That damned Van Vranken Sanitorium is still refusing to admit Negroes. It gets a hundred thousand a year from state and city taxes, from you and from me, but because it has got a big endowment and a stuck-up Board of Directors, they do as they please, but we've got to force them, I tell you. We've got to force Negroes into that sanitorium."

"Sure," said Dr. Brown, and then suddenly he looked up. "By the way, my wife is continually bothering me about Margaret."

"Margaret? Who's Margaret?"

"Our daughter."

"I didn't know you had a daughter. Oh, yes, you mean that adopted daughter of yours."

"Well, she isn't exactly adopted. Her parents live in Jamaica but she's more than a daughter to us. She's been a little peaked recently, and, of course the wife is afraid of T.B."

Dr. Taylor almost said: "Good—we'll force her into the sanitorium." But he caught himself.

"Well, well, want me to help you look her over?"

"Yes, I would like it. Of course, I have examined her several times and had her sputum examined. No traces. Ray is negative except for an old bronchial node infection. What young adult does not have this?"

"Was she not well cared for when little?"

"Ye-es, I rather think so."

"Well," mused Dr. Taylor, "all young adults do not have bronchial node infection. You never can tell. The only sure way is to have her carefully watched and her temperature taken and more specimens examined. Is she tired?"

"Well, yes, she is rather tired these days. She's working like the dickens for a competition at Art School."

"Well, then, she ought to rest. I'll tell you what we'll do. We'll put her to bed for two weeks and have a nurse go twice a day and take her temperature. Then we'll take sputum and see what we can find." And Dr. Taylor almost rubbed his hands.

Ten days later, Dr. Taylor called Dr. Brown over the telephone.

"Come over here" he said. But Dr. Brown had a number of calls and didn't get there until hours later. When he came in, Taylor took him over to a microscope:

"There it is," he said. "It's a tubercle bacillus and while there are only two or three in the whole specimen, we are finding this when there is no fever nor acute cold. Your 3 analyses and 5 of my own reported no results. The 9th got this clear glimpse of a tubercle. Now, I'll tell you, Brown, what we've got to do. I have already made application to the Van Vranken Sanitorium for a private room, and we must put your daughter there. A few months up there and she'll be fit as a fiddle."

But Dr. Brown was standing stock still, looking sallow and grayish under his dark skin.

"My God!" he said. "Couldn't those two things be artifacts?"

"Not on your life—not these—but snap out of it. It's nothing. Any number of people are walking about good and well with more tuberculosis than Margaret's got. And say, what a chance it will be! Here you are, able to pay for a room, and independent of white charity, with no political debts! Why we can make a fight that will revolutionize things."

"Yes," said Dr. Brown, slowly. "But you don't understand, Taylor. Margaret is not a thing to fight with. She's a lovely, delicate thing. She winces and cringes under the mere thought of discrimination and dislike. She's about the last person in the world to put forward as a battering ram to break down prejudice. She's too sensitive. Good Lord! It will kill me to think of her having to stand what she'll have to in that sanitorium."

"I tell you, Brown, it's your duty. It isn't a matter of sensibilities or persons. Here's the great principle to be fought out. Think how many valuable lives we are going to save if we can keep these damned thieves and upstarts from using the public money to boost their own private prejudices! And besides, if she doesn't go there, where can she go? What can you do to cure her?"

Brown said slowly. "Well, you know, Abyssinian Church is trying to establish a small sanitorium—."

"Hell!" blurted Taylor. "It will be 'try' and 'small.' You know what a proper sanitorium costs and where are they going to get the skill to treat their patients. We can talk of what we've done in medicine but how many colored specialists in tuberculosis have we developed or had a chance to develop? What right has the state or city to confine the skill which it helped pay for to one group or one race. And beside, the whole principle of segregation in medicine and hospitals is wrong and we've got to fight it out if we lose a hundred patients."

Brown look at him and Taylor caught himself.

"Sorry, old man, I know how you feel about Margaret. Of course, quite natural."

"Have you ever seen her?" said Dr. Brown.

"No, not to know her; meant to call last week, but sent my best nurse. O, I've heard of her and I know what fine work she's doing."

"Well, we'll see how this thing turns out."

It was a month later and Doctor Taylor descended from the train at the little station in

Northern New York, near the Van Vranken Sanitorium. One could see it on the side of the hill, high, airy and roomy, in the white snow. Wide verandas stretched out with white beds. Trained nurses, carefully buttoned up, were hurrying about. Dr. Taylor walked in. The officials in charge glanced at each other. He was not aggressively colored, and yet a second glance showed his Negro blood. Beside, they knew he name. They were silent and a bit stern and he was gruff. Abruptly, he walked out on the veranda and looked about. Then he sought another veranda. There was no dark face.

Huddled in a dark corner, surrounded by very sick patients, he found her; a tray of untouched food stood on a table at an inconvenient distance away. He knew at a glance how little care or thought she had had. He took her pulse and temperature. She had not improved. In fact, if the truth were known, she was worse off, than when she came. She had been very silent as he worked, with a frightened look in her dark eyes that Dr. Taylor persistently ignored. Fierce red anger swelled him, and at last he looked her square in the face. There was something tremendously appealing about this girl of 22. She was not beautiful but her skin was velvet; her hair, close-curling and her eyes, appealing eyes almost ethereal. Impulsively, he took her up in his arms and wound the bedclothes around her. She put her arms around his neck and nestled with a sigh as though recue were near.

"Please take me home," she whispered. "It will be much nicer to die there."

"No dying yet," he grumbled as he held her tenderly and close.

He took her out to the office and deposited her gently in an easy chair, and then did just the thing that he had not intended to do. Instead of arguing with the superintendent and the head nurse and showing them how this girl had been willfully neglected, he damned out the whole outfit with every oath he could think of, and again taking the girl in his arms, stepped outdoors and hailed a taxi which had just depositing a newcomer.

"Where to," said the man. Taylor was about to say: "To the train." Then he was a little scared, as he glanced down at the girl's face. Beneath the warm brown was a certain dead pallor that he was afraid of. The taxi man was helpful.

"There's a little colored sanitorium up beyond the hill," he said.

"Drive there," said Taylor.

He found a small cottage of four rooms but perched on a hill with plenty of sunshine. There were three patients and one nurse. But she was the kind of woman who is a born nurse. In a little while they had Margaret out in the sun on the one veranda. They had warm food for her, and before Taylor was ready to leave, she had dropped asleep. Then Taylor gave orders and emptied his pocketbook.

"By the way, to whom does this place belong?" he said.

"The Abyssinian Church," said the nurse smiling, and added: "Dr. Taylor."

Taylor hadn't blushed in several years, but he did this time and made no further comment. When he got back to New York, he reported that Margaret was improving, and in order to make this true, he neglected his practice shamelessly for the next month and twice a week. Sure enough Margaret did improve. Also, Taylor improved until finally, he knew that if by chance Margaret did not get well, he, personally, would be perfectly willing to die.

After the second month, he brought Margaret himself back to New York and had her installed in a roof apartment with an open garden which Dr. Brown had rigged up on top of their house in 138th Street.

There was a meeting of the Manhattan Society that night. Taylor was gay and Brown happy. But Dr. Williams said, scowling:

"I understand, Taylor, that you are now on the staff of that 'Jim Crow' sanitorium which the Abyssinian Church has up in Northern New York." Taylor looked uncomfortable.

"I reckon, I am," he said, and then he added, "You see, it was either 'Jim Crow' or death for the girl that I am going to marry."

Williams interrupted bitterly. "And so you traded a wife for one of your great principles."

"I am afraid I did," said Taylor.

"And those white skunks are still getting away with stealing public money to use for their private prejudices?"

"Yes," said Taylor.

"You're a hell of race leader," said Williams.   [*The Crisis* 40.2 (February 1933): 36–37]

THE FARM ON THE EASTERN SHORE: A STORY OF WORK

by Anne Du Bignon

1927

"There's no two ways about it, Jim. You are a damned fool."

The speaker was tall and thin, nervous and yellow; a handsome young fellow, Frank Farley by name. He was, as he insisted on being called, a Realtor. It was in New York, in 1927, in a beautifully furnished house on the north side of 139th Street, just west of Seventh Avenue. On the first floor, a polished, brass plate announced the office of Dr. Harry Forbes. On the second floor was a long parlor and in the rear a table set and shining for a small but elaborate dinner. Farley was talking to Jim Holmes, and his wife, Anne Edwards Farley, was with them. Anne looked at Jim and her eyes softened. She remembered him vividly when they had all finished Howard together. The three boys had roomed at the home of Anne's aunt and being classmates this had enabled them to discuss life and to disagree with great enthusiasm. These three boys had been her almost constant escorts. She had liked Jim; in fact, of all the young men who had danced attendance upon her beauty, wit and beautiful clothes, Jim was by far the most loveable, with his shyness and deep feeling. But she had married Frank. She looked over at him, and insisted that she had done well. Yes, he was the kind of man one marries, and yet she was afraid.

"Jim, you are too soft," she had said. "You just can't make it in this world with all your sympathies and loyalties and sensibilities. This is a hard world and it takes a hard man to get through it." And so she married Frank, who has a dynamo.

Of course, Frank must become a lawyer. Anne liked that, but even when she had accepted him, she resolutely refused to marry him immediately.

"Nonsense," she said. "You finish your law course first. I'm going to teach." Frank blustered. He didn't believe in women working. Women were made for the home, etc. But Anne just smiled at him. She took a year for her Master's, and then went into the Dunbar High.

Harry Forbes was going to study medicine. He didn't like it particularly, in fact, he didn't know anything about it. But it seemed a good way to make money. And Harry said that he had been without money long enough. But Jim was the despair of all of them.

They liked him. He was easily the most popular boy in the class of nearly a hundred. But instead of going on to study business, which he seemed cut out for, he was going home to run a farm! Could you imagine? Frank had called him a fool in those days.

"You know that your father could mortgage that farm and get enough, with what you could make, for you to study commerce or medicine, or whatever you will. It's idiotic for you to stick yourself down on the eastern shore of Maryland. It's a God-forgotten country. It's the last place on earth, except Mississippi."

"I know," said Jim, "and I hate to go back. But you see it's this way: my father is getting old and he's done a lot for me. He's awfully keen on having me back to run the old place. And then again, he's deathly afraid of mortgages. He never had a mortgage on his place or any part of it. He's got now two hundred acres down there, some of it pretty fine land. Runs from the Choptank back up into Talbot County."

"Where they lynched a nigger last year," said Frank, grimly; but Jim continued:

"He says we will always have something to eat, but that if he mortgages the farm, white folks will get it."

"Let 'em have it," said Forbes. "That wouldn't be so bad."

"No," said Jim. "It isn't really my fear of losing it. It's fear of hurting Old Aaron. He's been good to me and he and Mother and sister are alone now. I'm going back. I may be able to make the thing go." The others hooted.

* * *

Now they were all in New York on one of the few reunions that they had been able to keep. They had met once in Washington, and always when they met, the four of them went off and chummed together. This time they had left the class reunion in Washington because Forbes couldn't be present and had gone up to see him. They were in the parlor of his lovely bachelor home waiting to have dinner with him.

Frank was already rich,—at least on paper. He had gotten through law school; held a civil service appointment; then gone into real estate, and was talking in five figures now. He had driven them up in his new Packard car; he had a substantial equity in a beautiful home on "R" Street, and plans for a summer cottage on his lot at Arundel.

Anne looked at the two of them. Softly at Holmes, and anxiously at her husband. Frank was successful, terribly successful, but Anne just couldn't follow his figures. He was all the time buying and selling, making big mortgages, negotiating loans, signing bonds, and spending, spending money; they entertained at bridge; they took trips to New York theatres because Washington theatres would not admit them and they had a happy, swift life full of fun and work. And yet she felt breathless, as though they were floating on something very unsubstantial. She just couldn't grasp it. Dr. Forbes interrupted her train of thought, as he rushed up from his office,—velvet-brown, debonair and jovial, and yet with a tired face. His Lincoln, with a chauffeur was parked outside. Brooks Brothers made his clothes and shirts.

"Through at last," he said, peeling off his white coat, and rushing up to the third floor.

Soon he returned, immaculate in white shirt and tuxedo. Two girls appeared in the dining room door; one was evidently his head nurse. She had relieved a bit the severeness of her uniform, but stood dark, slim and silent, and yet with a certain air of efficiency. He introduced her offhand.

"My nurse, Miss Benson, who thinks she's keeping me from going right to hell!"

Miss Benson bowed without a smile, and said simply: "My friend, Miss Harriet Fisher."

Harriet was a large, well-built, cream-colored young woman with humorous eyes, evidently in perfect health, and quite unhurried. She took competent charge of the situation and soon they were seated and beginning what was evidently going to be an excellent dinner, served by a man servant. They had hardly finished the soup, however, before there was a faint sound of a bell, and the nurse, excusing herself, arose. Dr. Forbes tried to stop her, but she went out. In ten minutes, she had returned and quietly bent over him.

"Tell her to go to hell," he said briefly. The nurse was evidently remonstrating, almost insisting, but Forbes was obdurate. He ordered the fish.

"I don't care, I don't care. Let her get Smith. I'm tired. This damned nurse of mine is a regular gad-fly. Here I was up until four."

Harriet looked across humorously.

"Well, yes, some medicine and more cabaret. Fellows from Chicago, insurance gang. Poker, and oh well,—Jim, old thing, you're a sight for sore eyes. Still the old stick-in-the-mud. How's the farm?"

But the nurse talked long and earnestly with Harriet Fisher, and then again went silently out.

Dr. Forbes laughed and sampled his sherry.

"Frank," he said, "you ought to be interested in Harriet here. She's a business woman."

Frank glanced at her with evident doubt in his eyes.

"Yes, and what's your line?"

"I own a beauty parlor," said Miss Fisher.

"Oh," said Frank, briefly.

1929

Anne looked old and tired as she sat in her bare Washington parlor talking to Jim Holmes. Workmen were tramping through the house and removing the furniture. Frank, who had just rushed out, rushed back in.

"Jim," he said. "I tell you they're robbing me." And he threw up his hands dramatically. "And taking everything. Can you imagine, everything! Just squeezing me dry of my real estate, even this home and my new car. Jim, I tell you, my real estate alone was worth at least $200,000, not to mention my stocks and bonds. But when they get through, they'll have me with nothing and buried under debt. There's the Barth National Bank. I was down there yesterday and the day before. I've just been there this morning. I've been doing $100,000 worth of business with them a year. And do you know, they won't loan me a cent. Not a single cent."

"Oh, well," said Jim, uncomfortably, "after all, you've got yourself and Anne."

But Frank stormed out again.

"I haven't got a damned thing," he said. Jim arose and walked slowly back and forward.

"Now Anne," he said, "buck up. What we've got to do is, first, to get this bankruptcy over; then get Frank out into the country and let him sleep and eat until he finds himself."

But Anne felt tragic. "It isn't myself," she said. "It isn't even what has happened to Frank. Somehow, dimly, I always knew this was coming. But it's what people will say about us. I can hear our friends chortling."

Jim grinned. "Well, you know, that's a nice thing about trouble. It isn't so much what happens to us; it's what people say about it. That makes it so easy. All we have got to do is to give up caring and suddenly it's all right!"

Anne sniffed and Frank rushed back. Jim took him by the arm.

"Say," he said, addressing Anne again. "This bozo's got to go to the country and take a nap."

"Do you think I'm going to bury myself in the country," snarled Frank.

Anne looked at him. "Well, if you don't," she said, "You'll bury yourself here and that soon. You go down with Jim and I'll follow later. I must begin to lay plans to get back into the schools. He needs air and quiet and rest. He is a nervous wreck and Harry Forbes has warned him of tuberculosis."

But Jim interposed. "No, now wait. Let me tell you something. Really, you know, in spite of all you say, there's a chance down on the eastern shore to do something. Father and Mother are dead, as you know. They had a quiet and happy old age. There's only myself and the young sister. Now one thing that we have got down there is plenty to eat and warmth and shelter in the big, old farmhouse. We have got communication by water and rail and good roads to the markets of the nation. And it's even possible that we can sometimes use Chesapeake Bay for boats to Haiti and South America, because our land runs right down to it. Now why not all go down and start something? And you can't think who's going to join us. You remember Harriet Fisher, the friend of Harry's nurse?"

"That business woman!" sneered Frank.

"Well," said Jim, "it seems that the bottom has fallen out of her business, and when I wrote Forbes to come down and start a hospital and bring along a teacher, she answered and offered to come. It seems she has a pretty good education, an A.M. from Columbia in commerce."

"And running a beauty parlor!" said Frank.

"Well," sighed Anne, "The bottom seems to have fallen out of both the real estate and beauty parlor business. But what did Forbes say?"

"He didn't answer, but that little nurse, who evidently attends very carefully to his correspondence, said that he ought to come. He's wasted not only his money but his health, and she's going to do what she can."

Frank started to the telephone. He had to keep doing something. "I'm going to get Harry over long distance," he said. "And see if he really will come. Perhaps we might start something down there."

But Harry was not attracted by the prospect of the eastern shore.

"Not by a damned sight," said his crisp voice over the telephone.

They were in the back, living room of the farm house on the Maryland eastern shore. Blazing logs were burning and the radio was turned low. Beyond the grey waters of Choptank were tossing toward the bay. Anne was in one armchair with a baby in her arms. Harriet was in another, and Jim on the floor beside her. Frank was walking up and down waving his hands.

"I'll tell you," he said: "Our fortune's made. Listen, with $5,000 we can transform this place. We've got plenty of good food and some which we could sell in the markets of Wilmington, Washington and Baltimore, if we only had a big, fast truck! Then we could get in some laborers and put in a big crop of melons, plant some peach trees and try some other stuff. Drive it right up to Dover, Wilmington, Baltimore and Washington. I tell you, I can see some big things."

Harriet Fisher looked at him quietly and said: "The school is really getting on splendidly. Awfully interesting children, but we need a new modern schoolhouse and more money from the county. Then we ought to have a hospital. I'm still hoping that Billy Benson is going to fetch Forbes down here. That would be a big thing. Then we have got to start some industries for furnishing some of our own needs. We can make our own furniture, simple, mission sort. I believe that we can do something in spinning and weaving with small machines, once we get electric current wires in here from Delaware. Then, with some tailors and dressmakers, we'd settle the matter of clothes."

"But," said Anne, "How about money. How about something to sell?"

"Just what I was saying," said Frank.

But Harriet interrupted. "We have got to have a surplus, of course, to sell outside. But first we must be self-supporting. Then, we must get buyers. In fact"—continuing to interrupt Frank,—"we must get buyers before we sell. We must organize groups of colored people in the cities North and find out just what they want to buy, the colored teachers and clerks as well as the laborers. We could engineer a big, organized co-operative effort to furnish them with vegetables and chickens and perhaps even meat and eggs and milk."

"Where are we going to get the money?" said Frank. "You have got to have capital. All we have to do is mortgage this farm for, say, $5,000."

But Anne interrupted. "I never want to hear the word mortgage again."

Jim looked at Harriet and then at Frank. Harriet looked into the fire.

"No," said she, "no mortgages."

But Jim got up and stretched. Then he frowned a bit.

"Frank and I were down to the banker in town this morning," he said, "and after Frank left for home, I went back there."

Frank looked at him eagerly, and Jim looked a bit uncomfortable.

"Well," he said, "Perhaps I'm a fool, but I mortgaged the farm today and here's the $5,000."

Harriet started up with something like fear in her eyes. All her secretly cherished plans seemed in danger. But she held herself well in hand and reached out for the check.

"It's for $4,750," said she, "I notice."

"Yes," said Jim. "You see, I had to pay $250 bonus."

"And 6 percent?"

"Yes."

"Let's see," said Harriet with her pencil. "That would be really 11 percent in all; and for three years?"

Jim looked more uncomfortable. "Yes, of course," he said, "that is, as a matter of fact, we made it out for a year, but I have the banker's word that it will be renewed."

"And if he breaks his word?" said Harriet, slowly.

"Oh, but he won't," said Frank.

"No, no, of course he won't," added Jim. "He's a gentleman."

"Oh, I see, a gentleman! Well, Jim, just endorse this check," she said.

He looked at her curiously, but before Frank could interrupt, he endorsed it with a smile.

She folded the check slowly. "Now," continued Harriet, "You boys listen to me. You did the borrowing, but we, Anne and sister and I, will do the spending. I somehow just don't trust you spending money any more than I would have trusted you borrowing, if I had known it."

"I don't like that," grumbled Frank. "Anne don't know anything about money, and Harriet keeps her cash in her stocking."

"And where do you keep yours, dear?" asked Anne.

1933

The sheriff was sharp, not to say truculent.

"Mortgage is foreclosed," he snapped, spitting on the white porch, "and due notice has been given. I'm here to take possession."

The blood surged up in Jim's neck and Frank went white with anger. The five or six deputy sheriffs, with their badges hastily pinned on and their pistols quite evident, moved a little nearer. Outside the gate there was a crowd of white neighbors, which began to have the appearance of a mob, growling and throwing out epithets. Only Harriet seemed cool.

"All right, sheriff," she said. "Sit down. He started to enter the door but she pulled the chair out on the porch. "First, let me talk with the banker on the telephone?"

The sheriff hesitated and then sat down. Jim and Frank started to enter with Harriet but Harriet intimated that they ought to watch the porch. Then she telephoned. There was a brief colloquy.

"Sheriff," she said, at last, "The banker would like to speak to you."

He turned toward the door but she handed the telephone out the window.

"What!" he said. "Well, I thought,—oh, all right! But how long? Tomorrow at noon? Very well."

He almost threw down the telephone, and then he turned to the group on the piazza.

"I'm coming tomorrow at noon to take possession and I'm going to do it if I have to kill every nigger on the place. And listen, I'm going to leave a deputy here and nothing is to be moved. Nothing. Neither crops nor that auto truck. The mortgage and mortgage bond cover everything."

He strode out; the mob milled about the gate, and one armed deputy sat all night on the steps. Within the men were desperate. Frank drew the curtains and Jim got out the shot-guns, oiled and loaded them grimly.

"I don't understand," Frank kept saying. "The banker promised us. He said it was only a form, that one year mortgage, and that, of course, he'd renew. How much of the money have we got left, Harriet? We haven't spent very much. Perhaps he'll take partial payment?"

"No, he won't. He said he must have it all," growled Jim. "The liar!"

Harriet got out her books. "There was the $250 for the bonus; $1,000 for the truck; $1,000 for lumber; $500 for seed and fodder and fertilizer; $500 in wages. We have got about $1,750 left; but you know most of that is due on the contract which Frank arranged for machinery."

Frank groaned. "We ought to have gotten a cheaper truck and bought less seed and stock; and we didn't need that machine until next year."

"I said something like that," said Harriet.

"Oh, I'm to blame," said Frank. "I'm always wrong; but I tell you what I'm going to do." And he got up and seized his coat. Anne stepped quickly to his side.

"What do you mean?" she said.

"I've got a truck of melons," he said, "all loaded and ready for the market. I'm going to run it through to Wilmington tonight. I'm going to talk to Forbes in New York and call up all my Washington business connections. I'm either going to bring back that money or else I won't come back myself."

Harriet's voice was cool. "Don't be a fool, Frank," she said. "You can't fight the law."

"Damn the law," he blustered.

"Telephone Forbes, that's all right, and telephone him right from here. But don't run out and get murdered in the dark." Frank rushed to the telephone and after a long delay got Forbes in New York. At least, not Forbes, but Miss Benson. He came back radiant.

"Forbes is coming and starting tonight. She says he's sick and got to get away or he'll be in the psychopathic ward in Bellevue. Seems he hasn't got much money, but she says she'll bring what she can. She was a bit perky, that nurse of his, but she seemed to know what she was talking about."

All night the men figured and worried, but Harriet and Anne went quietly to bed and what's more, went to sleep.

"That's what women are good for in a jam," whispered Frank.

"Hush," said Jim.

Anne and Harriet got an early breakfast and sang at the task. Jim and Frank could not eat but the armed deputy sheriff on the front porch received a plate of hot cakes and sausage and a cup of aromatic coffee with almost affable condescension. Inquisitive and scowling neighbors began to gather again.

At nine, Harriet called the bank again and shut the parlor door on the conversation. About eleven o'clock a big Lincoln car drove up. Harriet rushed out to greet Miss Benson. A pale, thin Forbes shook hands listlessly with Frank and Jim, and then out of the back of the car stepped a white man.

"We called at the bank," explained Miss Benson. "This gentleman said he had business out here and we offered to bring him along."

The banker looked about doubtfully.

"Where is—" he hesitated. He did not want to say "Miss," for he feared the woman he was seeking might be colored. She was, for Harriet said sweetly, "I am Miss Fisher. Won't you sit down?"

They sat down on a bench in the yard. They read papers and signed and exchanged papers. They argued. The banker seemed both embarrassed and angry. He kept his hat on and talked brusquely, but when at noon the sheriff appeared, he met him at the gate. They called the deputy from the front porch and without a word rode back to town. At the front gate, the crowd faded away. Jim and Frank stood on the porch and stared, while Harriet sauntered back toward the house, fingering a large paper, with a red seal. Jim's sister disappeared into the kitchen and began washing dishes. Frank could stand it no longer.

"Well, when you have time," he said at last, elaborately, "and can spare the words, Miss Fisher, would you mind telling us just what the hell this is all about?"

"Why, certainly," said Harriet. "Come girls and let the dishes rest."

They sat down around the fire.

"Now, boys," said she, "I hope you won't get angry. The girls know what I'm going to say. First of all, the mortgage has been foreclosed and the house has been sold."

Jim stood up taut and gray and stared at her. She continued without looking at him.

"I've bought it," she continued.

"You," blurted Frank.

"Well, at least I was the agent. The real buyer is the Aaron Holmes Cooperative. Now don't interrupt. You see, it was this way. When Jim and Frank borrowed that money, I was in despair. I took the check, cashed it, and put it in the safe deposit vault in town. Then I looked around to see what funds we could get hold of. I had saved $2,500 but had already lost $1,000 in a nice little bank which failed in New York. That left $1,500. Anne had $1,000 tucked away." Frank growled but kept still. "Oh, it was hers,—"

"Cash for a fur coat or a diamond, I forget which," from Anne.

"That made $2,500. And dear, little Miss Benson, here, found us $2,500 more money belonging to Forbes which she had tucked away and kept him from wasting."

Forbes sat with dull eyes but smiled.

"That made $5,000, and out of that we have been spending money and not out of the mortgage money. I knew the banker was going to foreclose. He had to. He was in a jam and needed cash. I offered him anonymously through the Dover bank $3,000 cash for the place and to my great surprise, he took it. I would have given him $5,000. So I formed a corporation and the Directors are us. The women will out-number you men four to three, which is," said Harriet, reflectively, "about as it should be."

"And what are you going to do?" said Frank.

"I'll tell you," said Harriet. "I'm not going to use this farm to make money. I'm going to use it to make people happy, with plenty to eat and wear. Then, I'm going to spread the happiness by selling its products to people that need them."

"Charity?" asked Frank.

"No, business. But co-operative business and not to make money. Benson says that Dr. Forbes' car there cost $7,000. We plan to sell it for a little hospital. I'm going to use our lumber to put up homes for the best of the colored families around here instead of building warehouses.

"Frank and Jim are going to take trips to Washington and Baltimore and Wilmington and organize some food buying units. And thus, we're all going to be well-fed, well-clothed, healthy and happy."

"And poor and idiotic," said Frank, as he flung out of the house and walked angrily down toward the bay. Anne took the baby and followed him. Miss Benson took Forbes and finally persuaded him to lie down. Jim walked out and wandered aimlessly up toward the little graveyard where his father lay buried. He stood a long time looking at the fresh flowers upon it. Then he turned suddenly.

Quick footsteps were approaching and Frank came running.

"Jim," he said excitedly. "I see it all now—look, here's the afternoon paper. Melons are up in the New York market. I'll bet fruit and produce are in for a big rise after the slump. The crackers knew this and tried to steal our farm. They want us to dump our fruit and vegetables in town so they can sell it and clean up. I tell you Jim, we can beat them and I'm going to begin right now. I'm going to run those melons to Dover and ship them to New York."

"But it's late, Frank—after four. It will be dark long before we get to town. Let's make an early start tomorrow after we talk to the girls."

"I'm tired of apron strings. Cooperation! It's all poppy-cock. I'm rushing these melons to market. With the cash; I'm going to get new seed and tools and hire more laborers. Let the women think we're drumming up customers if they want to, but I tell you, business is selling not buying. Let the buyers go hang. The woods are full of them."

"I don't know about that," said Jim, doubtfully. "I sort of reckon that after this crisis, the Buyer is going to begin to assert himself—going to organize and think and plan and stop being kicked about like a dumb pawn. Harriet—"

"Harriet be damned. She's pulling the wool all over you and you're too goofy to see it. The way you turned over that mortgage money made me sick."

"But Frank you shouldn't go alone and I can't leave the women. The white neighbors are sore and ripe for trouble. If you swagger through town alone on that new truck and they are sore at missing truck and farm, some of them will be just drunk enough to pick a row. Wait until morning or at least until after midnight."

"I'm gone," yelled Frank.

Soon the truck tore out of the shed, scattering melons. Harriet rushed to the door and Anne, toiling up from the sea, called sharply, "Frank!"

But Frank was gone. They waited—just why they could not say, or would not. He might 'phone. Someone might 'phone. If not, they'd call Dover.

"I ought to have gone with him," complained Jim.

But Anne hugged her child close and stared into the night. Already she knew—she knew.

Then it came—at midnight; the slow, halting puff and roll of a crippled truck; the yellow radiance of pine torches, hushed voices. Silently they hurried to the door. Some colored men were bringing the truck home. On a bed of green and crimson melons lay Frank, shot through the head.

* * *

Jim stood at sunrise alone by his father's grave where Harriet suddenly joined him. He looked up in surprise and down in shame for tears were in his eyes.

"Well," he said slowly. "It's over—and I've failed. I'm beaten, just as years ago they said I'd be. The Eastern Shore's too much for me. Oh, I've got to stay—but I'm going to pay back all the money—"

"I'm staying right here, too," said Harriet quietly.

"What?"

"The time to fight is when you're licked. The time to win is after you're beaten. I came down here to help make this farm go on a new plan and we're going to do it. They've only killed one of us so far and as I figure it there are three more to kill, not counting Forbes, who's half dead with liquor.

"Why Harriet, you—darling." And then suddenly he became apologetic. "I didn't quite mean to say that. I don't know why I said it."

"I do," said Harriet, "and the answer is Yes. And now, Jim, sit down here and put your arm around me and let's dope this thing out. There's no use of our trying to win this bread and butter game by bucking the white competitive market. They control credit, markets, prices and all the tricks of trade. They've got us beaten before we start. Our only hope is, first, a colored group of buyers held together not by law and police but by a new religion of race salvation. We'll buy black because we must or starve. We'll regiment and stabilize and systematize our wants along simple, primary lines which we can supply with our own hands, our own brains, our own unmortgaged land. We'll make a community not of exploited serfs but of friends and neighbors and educate, keep them healthy and make them work like the devil or get out.

"First, we'll feed and wash and serve ourselves; and then build our own homes, and after that work toward gradually making our own sheets, shoes, hats and clothes. We'll organize town and city groups and solemnly bind them to buy such things as we can furnish and which they must have, whether these are the best and latest and cheapest, or poorest and dearest and last year's style. They'll buy because black lands made the goods and black wants support black work. Year by year we'll do better work and turn out better goods and extend wider and wider this perfect, unbreakable circle, punishing economic traitors with pitiless ostracism and social death. We'll let the closed colored economy grow to a thousand and a hundred thousand, a million, ten millions; with factories, power, wholesale and retail depots— money, credit and insurance.

"We don't need to fear. If we stand firm they can't stop us. We'll be impervious to retaliation or boycott. Once on our feet, we can draw white labor into our circles so far as they follow our rules and yield to our leadership. And then when the new Social Commonwealth appears, as it must, we can bargain as trained and independent leaders and not sue as ignorant and blind beggars."

They arose together, facing the glory of the rising sun. Jim Holmes held her hand tightly in his.

"That is the Promised Land," he said. "And we must reach it over this morass of white ignorance, poverty, envy and murder. Old Aaron there, lying cold and still, points the way. He was silent and worked hard. He did not boast nor crawl. He did good for evil but he never called evil good. He forgave his enemies, but he neither loved nor forgot them and wasted no precious time in hate. He knew no color in pain and turned no beggar, white or black, away. He was long-suffering but he had two shot guns always in his home. They were loaded and his neighbors knew it. He died poor but rich in friends. Dear, we'll work and build and organize. We'll send our fruit and food to market, but we'll go by daylight and ride with a rifle in our hand."

"And I," said Anne, coming on them quietly and dry-eyed, her suitcase in one hand, her baby in the other, "am leaving today. You see, I could not stay here—now. Poor Frank, fighting white folk he was enmeshed in their own crazy net. He thought he must be rich and reach wealth by cheating the poor, any poor—all poor, white and black. I am going back to Washington to teach my child and all little children that Happiness not Wealth is Life. I'm going to organize black Washington to buy your fruit and food and all you learn to make, and to them who will not work with us I will be an avenging angel driven on by my husband's blood."   [*The Crisis* 40.3 (March 1933): 61–62 70; 40.4 (April 1933): 85–87]

TWO OLD WOMEN A-SHOPPING GO!: A STORY OF MAN, MARRIAGE AND POVERTY

———— ❧ ————

by Anita Scott Coleman

Without a doubt, Nell had Horace on her mind. There was no forgetting the way he had pleaded with her, the night before. She had fallen to sleep thinking of him, not as on other nights when imagery made vivid by love, brought his dear presence near in her last wakeful moments to drift pleasantly through her dreams. No, not that way, but an unhappy picture of him, nervous and moody, penetrated her sleep and leaped to aliveness with her first wakefulness.

She remembered every word he had said, unfair, cruel words; now they formed crookedly and apart like bits of a jig-saw puzzle as she dressed. His arguments repeated themselves:

"Each day, we are growing older—"

Nell leaned nearer the mirror, and scanned her piquant face. Could it be, that she really was aging and losing her charm, as surely as yesterday's flowers that drooped beside her in their squat, brown jar. A tiny line brought Nell's brows, silky, high-arched, brows like the sweep of bird wings, together. She brushed her hair with brisk strokes, while thinking dejectedly:

"You will be old and gray."

Sudden panic seized her; she would not look for gray strands; no, not yet. She was not old, and she would not allow Horace to hurry her, frighten her into marrying him.

She put on her hat, a little round crocheted affair that she had made herself. She put on her coat and drew on her gloves, picked up her bag, and went out, an altogether lovely colored girl.

Nell thought how many mornings had she gone out, thus. Five years and every morning except Sundays, she had taken this same way: three steps down the cobble-stoned walk to the green latticed gate; half a block to the corner, turn North; four blocks to the car-line; a wait five or more minutes for the car; an hour's ride to work.

Last night, Horace had said, pleadingly....

"You'll be worn out, all fagged-to-death and, I—I—don't want the girl I marry worked to death before I get her."

Nell tried to brush her troublesome thoughts aside and quickened her steps, then as quickly found herself agreeing with Horace. She was tired, so tired. Unconsciously, the line that drew her lovely brows together, deepened.

She heard voices, and looking up, she saw two old women come trundling towards her.

One was a very black and very stout old lady buttoned to the throat in a long black coat that fitted tightly about the waist and bulged loosely about the hips. She carried a basket on her arm.

One was a very stout and white old lady with near-white-folk's hair straggling from beneath a brown bonnet. She was buttoned into a red knitted sweater. She wore a heavy worsted skirt, and over that, a white, starched apron that tied around her waist. She carried a black shopping-bag in her hand.

Thought Nell; two old ladies out to do their shopping. Making a lark of it, too, she decided as their high cackling old voices came to her. Said one:

"No suh, they'll never come through what we done come through."

The other old woman tuned in quaveringly:

"Lord, chile, they couldn't begin to do't."

"Not wantin' 'im 'cause he ain't rich." Chimed the first.

"Ain't none of us that, neither." Vouchsafed the other.

"The ideas and the whimsies of these 'ere young'uns do beat me." They broke into high cackling laughter. The black old woman changed the basket to her other arm. The old white woman shortened the strings of her bag.

Then they were abreast of Nell. They smiled broadly upon her. The old mulatto nodded her head until the brown feather atop her brown bonnet danced like a live thing. The black old, woman called out: "Howdy!"

"None of 'em will ever stand what we done stood," floated to Nell, like the refrain of a song, as she waited for the car.

Somehow the passing of those two old women changed Nell's day. For the first time, she noticed that the morning was very bright, the sky was blue and tiny knobs of green were putting out on a tree near by.

"They were so cheery, the dears!" She said of the two old women, and sought to dismiss them. She wanted to think of her own perplexities, but the old ladies insisted upon rising up before her... Their cackling words: "None of 'em will ever stand what we done stood," caused Nell to toss her head defiantly. How could they know, those two.... Old issues that they were! Why, she herself had had her share of trouble, and she was but one of a legion of "Young'uns" as they termed them.

Had she not toiled every day except Sundays for five years, denying herself everything save sheer necessities for a chance to enjoy at some future time the heritage of every human creature, love and home and children. Undoubtedly, she had saved a little, her dowry, she called it, but its amount was written in her brain and on her heart. Tolling off their joint income, dollar by dollar, penny by penny, she and Horace together, was a part of their Sunday's routine.

Sundays Nell often said were Horace-days. Horace had Sundays off also, and they spent their one free day together. For the most part they spent the day, planning, making schemes to make their dreams come true. While she had merely worked, Horace had slaved; he had scraped together a sum that matched her own savings and there was a little place up-state where he wished to make their home.

He wanted to marry at once, now that the little place was paid for, but then, Nell countered, when during the long years since they had known they belonged to each other, had he not wanted to do so?

As though some of the glow from the steady flame of his adoration reached out to her, Nell felt her cheeks grow hot.

Suddenly, she knew that it was hard on Horace, harder than upon herself. Black men really had tougher sledding than black women, she thought, tenderly. She loved him so, she communed in her heart. That's why she wanted things; demanded them, those things that later, would insure their peace and contentment in their nest of a home. That's why ... She checked herself, smiling whimsically at finding herself beginning to use all the arguments that she was wont to use upon Horace over and over to convince him that they must work on and wait a little longer.

Then for no reason at all, two old figures lumbered through her consciousness, glimmeringly like moving shadows on a wall.

One very black and stout old lady, one very stout and white old lady said: "No suh, they'll never come through what we done come through."

"Lord, chile, they couldn't begin to do 't."

Nell tossed back her head and laughed... The darling funny old dears!

Aroused from her day-dreams, her slender brown fingers played for a time, on the keys of her typewriter, but thoughts of Horace would not down. As the moments sped, her thoughts became laden with foreboding; she decided to call him. It was against the rules, but just this once.

—Employees must not use telephone during working-hours,
except emergencies.—

A placard advised her as she dialed. It was emergency she concluded grimly. Never before had such warning intuition driven her. Never before had a desire to call to Horace through space tormented her as it did now; never before had longing, intense as pain made her want to stretch out her arms and encircle him close, close to her heart...

"Horace Canning has quit the company!" an ironic voice informed her over the wire.

"Horace—quit—his—job?" Nell I gasped the words foolishly and was restored to sanity only by the sound of a faint click striking into her ear.

She alighted from the car four blocks from home. She had not found Horace though she had verified the information received by telephone. Horace had given up his job, though, that no longer mattered; she had lost hers too. She had given it up to look for Horace.

She could not avoid seeing the knot of people gathered on the corner. A cursory glance revealed it to be several boys in their teens and younger mingling with the usual motley street-crowd that is attracted willy-nilly to anything that happens. Intent with her own concern she was hastening on when some horrid cataclysm rushed out to meet her, paralyzing her until sight and sound and feeling swirled and clashed into one agonizing tempest of emotion that sent her running, screaming headlong into the crowd. Horace was in the midst of it, a disheveled funny-looking Horace, but her Horace!

Magically, they made way for her to pass ... Save for a few taunts—a prolonged "Boo," "Sic 'em, sic 'em," "Atta Girl, Geese—nothing was done to hinder her. Presently, she was beside Horace, placing trembling hands upon his shoulder. At her touch, he turned, looked at her a moment, unknowingly, and announced thickly:—

"I need-sh my girl, hic, but she-sh won't-sh have me!"

Nell's grasp on his shoulder tightened; she shook: him furiously... "Horace, oh Horace, how could you? How could you?"

The crowd dwindled away. As for that, Nell had forgotten that there ever was a crowd. She looked for a taxi. Horace lurched heavily against her, and asked in ludicrous bewilderment:

"Is-sh you, hic, Nellie by-sh any chanc-sh."

"Tut, tut..." said someone close beside her, with a voice whose high old cackle dropped through Nell's dismay like a ray of sunlight into a dark crevice.

"He be your'n, honey, your man?" queried the voice. Nell knew it belonged to the old black woman of the morning.

"Take 'im, chile don't you dast to leave 'im when he needs yo'" chimed in another quavering old voice.

"Just you take 'im home. A cup of right hot coffee'll fix 'im or a speck of tomatoes 'will be better."

Without more ado, they were walking together. The trundling gait of the two old women matching nicely with Horace's unsteady steps.

"'Tis a trouble men folks be," offered one.

"But a sweet trouble 'tis," proffered the other.

"Trouble ain't never harmed nary one of us. What's more, us wimens can make men folks what us choose to."

"'Deed so! Us 'tis what makes 'em or breaks 'ems."

Then they performed a tempered replica of their high cackling laughter of the morning. Soon afterwards, they left her, turning off down their street.

The next day, while Nell sat waiting proudly high-heading looking straight ahead, she was not certain that these two old ladies had really joined her. Yet without effort, she could vision the black old woman in her queer black coat and the old white woman in her brown bonnet and red-knitted sweater. Oddly enough, their high cackling old voices still rang in her ears:

"Trouble ain't never harmed nary one of us," made a tune like a Spiritual...

"The idees and the whimsies of these 'ere young 'uns do beat me," was an epitome of the wisdom of old age.

"No suh, they'll never come through what we done come through ..."

"Lord, chile, they couldn't begin to do 't," was like a skit of Negro comedy, and Nell tossed back her head and laughed.

The intangibleness of those two old women enthralled her. Life, too, was like that, Nell mused, made up of intangible veils that became real only as you lifted them one by one, always, to find others and yet others, on and on. Love was one of the veils, so gossamer and fine, so fragile and easily broken. Love was one of life's veils that could never be brushed aside to grasp another. If you dared, once having it, to let it go, it was lost forever. You had to take it when you came to it, but once you caught and held it, it became for all time, a magic carpet.

Horace was coming towards her; tickets were in his hand. The porter was calling their train. Above all the ensuing bustle of departure, she caught the sound of a high, old cackle:

"Deed so! ... 'tis us what makes 'em or breaks 'em."

All Aboard!

At last, Horace and she were settled in their seats, on their way to the little place up-state, still short thousands of dollars of what they intended having. But she was glad, oh so glad.

"Happy?" asked Horace suddenly, his arm going around her.

"Happy!" breathed Nell with a great content.   [*The Crisis* 40.5 (May 1933): 109–110]

THE THOUGHTS OF A COLORED GIRL: A STORY OF REALIZATION

by Margaret K. Cunningham

AS FLAPPER

It is the funniest idea that most folks have about us youngsters.

Now there is Mim or Mother, who is not old, but her ideas concerning me are hopeless; talking to me about reserve—why she doesn't seem to know that our day calls the very same word, "old timey."

I get a lecture every time I turn around; about this and that: knots are forming on the back of my neck from having it shaved: she says I should never have a razor put on it; as if I could go around and sterilize all the barbers' razors.

What are we going to do anyway? For nearly three hundred years, the women of my race have been the burden-bearers and the frumps of creation: and Lordee! we are expected to go on with this heart-breaking, soul-searing grind; bearing children, digging, scrubbing far into the night; never asking any questions, until the final night.

For what, I should like to know! The selfishness of our men, and the boys are following their footsteps; my daddy, his daddy, to the fourth generation, of the twelve tribes of Adam.

Why can't I feel free to wear what I want to, so long as I honestly labor for it? To go with my men without being humiliated by them and others? What is the matter with the world?

I have no patience. Why? Because Mim was too patient. The hours she spent "letting patience do its perfect work," prenatally have left me bereft. If she could have known clean joyous hours, need I be restless for them?

Need I go forever hunting, longing for that which lies just beyond the grasp, ever near, ever fleeting, ever elusive.

The other night, I saw a "bully" knock down a girl. Two years ago she was a high school junior. He put the "skids" under her feet and started her downward trend: and now he continues his brutalizing, I wanted to scream, to tear him. I did scream, I did start at him; but Ted put me in his car and carried me from this scene of degradation, home to Mim's arms.

Ted laughed and said, I had better be glad it wasn't I. I could have died. I tell you if our mothers had been more emotional as human beings, we would be more divine. I know we should.

The bitterness locked in their hearts, as they worked and waited for, the Lord only knows, what, has encased us. Better they had drunk of Solomon's "stolen waters" and caught remorse than this thirst.

I am told, that as a race we are too young to follow the white race of women; that if they average one child each, we must average eight times as many. King of Italy! Where will they get food, clothes and learning?

Ted is not strong, so he says; and we have so many Teds too. I suppose the race is almost full of Teds. If I should resign myself to such a fate, I would have to mother Ted as often as I would the infant. It's what the mothers and wives do. Guess I'll play I don't hear.

Adam surely was a black man, for his grumbling at Eve, telling her she was the cause of his having to work, is certainly handed down. I hear it on every side. I see all these things and I tell you my heart is wormwood.

To see the rank and file of my men going along in the same old rut, hiding behind that helpmate gag, when it's all-mate—is too much for me. Just the other day, a woman who works close to me, returned home to find it bare, her husband (who swore at the altar, "I will" and "I do" in tones like a bomb) had showed his clayhoofs.

Oh! I am beyond faith, until our men take the heavy load from our backs. Until they do, they may look, and look in vain for the tot at the door.

Ted cries: "Go fifty-fifty with me, and we will buy a home, before the knot is tied." If I help to increase the population—which I shan't do—there is no way earthly for him to make it fifty-fifty if he buys fifty homes, eh?

"Pray, child," Mim says, as if I can pray when my heart is barren.

Pretense! O Columbus! I am sick almost to death of pretense.

Mim, and a great many of Mims, can smile a glad smile when their hearts are ashes. Can I? Yes, I can, but I won't.

Have I been disappointed—crossed in love? Yes, from my mother's womb, and will be until I find what she looked for and failed to find, unselfishness, trust, protection—these three—but the greatest of these is the first. The other two are embodied therein. I repeat until I find these in the future fathers of the race, I shall be restless, without patience, without faith, encased in bitterness, layers of bitterness.

AS WIFE

I have played the fool to confound the wise, I hope. Ted and I are one. It seems but a short while, yet in truth, it is two years. The bitterness is still there in my heart, but not the boiling, seething kind. It is submerged in—no, not patience—I will not have it so, but in peace.

Ted has sold his car; had to to meet the first payment on our nest. I don't mind much, only we can't take long joy-rides as before—but we can hold hands at home,—our home.

Ted says my hands grow more lovely each day, fancy the truth of it, but Ted says it, and it sounds like new wine feels, all joyous, full of beauty.

I cannot bear the word "patience," yet Ted tells me, I have an abundance of it; and because he avows it, I am exalted.

When—but never mind that now. Do you know I have not had to mother Ted once? I am his friend, his bosom friend.

Thank God; of all the abominable atrocities the vine supporting the oak, that one stands head and shoulders, like Saul of Israel, over all others; nothing to it.

As Mother

My mother was right, was right, when she so kindly told me: "You will see clearly some day, dear." Ages have seemed to pass away. Dear God, forgive; I have not meant one word I have stormed. I have fought the Dragon; I have bruised the Serpent's head.

My son, my first born son! Would—What was I going to say—surely it was not bitter grief like David's—I know now. I was going to say: "Would you could know that all my bitterness has turned into a sweet smelling savor, all my restlessness into peace."

[*The Crisis* 40.8 (August 1933): 182]

BLACK MESTIZA

by Madelen C. Lane

Mariana Greene glanced casually about the room. She hoped her eyes held just the right touch of disinterestedness. She wanted to give her companion the impression that she was accustomed to eating ice cream and angel food cake in a white sweet shop.

But she was interested and thrilled—tremendously so. She cast her eyes at the people in the other booths. There were several white couples within view, the painted faces of the girls a striking contrast to the black and silver modernistic background. And on the end she saw a couple with olive skin and black hair—Mexicans.

Once again Mariana felt a sudden rush of helpless anger and something akin to bitterness surge through her being. She always felt that way whenever she saw dirty, greasy Mexicans or Indians eating in places where decent, well-groomed colored people could not enter. But even as she raged inwardly another self took it all calmly. She was not a colored girl that night; she was a Filipino. She batted her eye-lids to remove any trace of her injured feelings and turned toward Juan.

"Nifty place for a town like Phoenix, don't you think?"

Mariana spoke with feigned nonchalance. Juan must not know that this was the first time she had set foot within the place, that her heart had been gripped with cold dread when he had first mentioned coming here. But it was so. Born eighteen years before in the Philippine Islands of a native mother and a Negro father (that is, he was called a Negro although his skin was of a creamy yellow color), Mariana had lived for five years in this little Arizona town associating with the colored people and assimilating their views regarding the world in general.

Unconsciously she had absorbed their hatred and prejudice against, and also their feeling of inferiority before, the white race. She attended the colored high school and most of her friends were Negroes. Whenever they wanted to eat out they always tacitly avoided those places where there was any possibility of being refused service or insulted. Hence it was that Mariana had never entered this sweet shop.

But now she was here with Juan, a Filipino, Mariana glanced at her reflection in the mirror that lined the wall and smiled with satisfaction. Why had she ever been afraid to enter white shops? She had her mother's round face, her transparent, light-brown skin showing creamy underneath. Her hair, coal black like her mother's had deep natural waves. In these days of beauty salons who could tell that they were not artificial? She should take advantage of her looks. And after all, wasn't she as much a Filipino as she was a Negress?

Suddenly, Mariana felt that the cage in which she had lived for five years had been opened. She felt free and, somehow, exhilaratingly happy. Her early childhood days, like a dream forgotten and suddenly remembered, flashed through her mind. She recalled that she used to play with other Filipino children under her *nipa* house in the Philippines. She also remembered the years she had spent in San Francisco and Chicago where her friends were of different races and nationalities. Mentally she stretched herself and prepared to test her new freedom.

The light of admiration in Juan's eyes added confidence to Mariana's newer self. She must have kept up her end of the chatter while her mind had been occupied for he did not act as if anything was amiss.

"Shall we take in a dance after this? The night is still young." Juan was speaking.

Mariana caught her breath. Here was a test indeed! To mingle with other people, to dance with them could she carry it off?

"I'd love to," she replied, "but where?"

"There's a dance hall ten miles from here where the Mexicans dance on Sundays."

"All right. Let's go."

In Juan's auto later, Mariana talked rapidly. She tried not to think of the ordeal to come. That would only make her more nervous. So she rambled on, talking in Tagalog the native language which she found she had not forgotten.

Finally they arrived. Cars surrounded the barn-like hall. The exotic strains of a Mexican orchestra came out to them as they parked their car in the wide enclosure. Mariana's heart was in a panic. All the fear she had tried to repress on their way over came surging to the surface. She paused a moment with a pretence of powdering her nose to quiet the nervous quivering of her knees. She looked at her reflection in the mirror of her compact to reassure herself that she looked all right. Then with a defiant tilt to her chin and a laugh on her lips, she tripped gaily inside.

Nothing happened. Nobody shouted insults at her. The girl at the cashier's window barely glanced at her as Juan paid the admission. The men about her and leaning against the railing looked eagerly at her as any bunch of stags would in the hope of obtaining a dance.

"*Ay, que linda!*" she heard some one whisper. She had picked up enough Spanish to understand what that meant. The man had said she was pretty. Some of the tightness about Mariana's heart relaxed. The orchestra started off and Juan guided her onto the floor. He danced divinely and Mariana followed him naturally, answering to the pressure of his arm with light grace.

All too soon the dance ended. Juan found a seat for her between two girls on the long bench against the wall. He stood near by and they conversed in Tagalog. Two Mexicans stood in front of her but Mariana paid no attention to them. They must be friends of some of the other girls, she thought.

Just then the music started. Both boys held their right arms, elbows bent, toward her at the same time murmuring something that sounded like "*por favor, Senorita*" Mariana gasped and turned to Juan.

"What are they saying?"

"They are asking for a dance."

That would be fun, she thought, but—"should I?" she asked.

"Well—if you like."

Mariana placed her fingers on the arm of the taller one who led her triumphantly away. He was, if anything, a better dancer than Juan. His steps were long and graceful.

"You are a Filipino girl?" he asked in stilted English

"How do you know?"

"Your friend, he's Filipino. I know. You look like him, too, and you talk different language."

"Yes." It was exhilarating, this wine of victory. Mariana drank deeply of it. She had won! Now she could go anywhere like other people and not feel inferior—.

Several hours passed, hours brimful of joy and fun. She danced with other Mexicans after that and with Juan quite often. He hovered protectingly near her and she was glad for his presence.

On their way home Mariana looked at Juan with new eyes. There was something glamorous and thrilling about him. He had come to Phoenix three weeks before—a contractor with boys to harvest cantaloupes. She had seen and talked with him as she did with other Filipino boys. But she had never paid much attention to them. Her gang, her circle of friends, were Negroes. Filipinos had no place in her scheme of things. Several times before some Filipinos had asked to take her out but she had always refused. That night she had gone with Juan in a spirit of fun and now she was glad.

New worlds had opened before her. She was grateful to Juan for it. He was no longer just a farm worker. He became embodied in her eyes with all that was romantic and thrilling. So when he took her in his arms on the front steps of her home and kissed her, she did not resist.

The next night Earl called to take her to the movies. Earl was her "steady," a Negro. Not that there was any definite agreement between them, but he was the one who took her to dances and shows and treated her to dinner once in a while. And he it was on whose lap she sat in the overcrowded car when the gang went for a joy ride.

Mariana had always been rather fond and proud of Earl. He was nice looking in a brown skin way, tall, slender, with a thin face offset by merry eyes and a most engaging smile. To top it all he was attending the Junior College and was to become a lawyer some day.

Yes, Mariana was proud of Earl. But that night, when the flippant white usherette shooed them to the balcony, to that part at the top known as "Nigger Heaven," Mariana had a change of feeling. Earl was all right; he couldn't help it that people of other races treated him as if he were dirt. But she was not going to stand for such things any more. She expected better things of life than that.

Mariana did not mention her thoughts to Earl. But she feigned a headache when he suggested an after-theatre supper and made him take her home.

Thus began a new existence for Mariana. She went out quite often with Juan, reveling in the freedom she had found. Each night with him was certain to bring new thrills, new adventures in a world from which she had been shut off so long.

Earl called up quite often. He did not understand Mariana at all. He did not know, or pretended not to know, the double life she led. Once in a while Mariana consented to go out with him for old time's sake but her thoughts were for Juan.

Mariana's father noticed her interest in Juan and was afraid. Juan had little or no education or money. He worked in the fields for his livelihood. Mariana would lose quite a lot if she married him. Her father realized the seriousness of the situation. He knew that Mariana was attracted to Juan by the lure of new and stolen adventures. Yet, being, wise, he said not a word of his fears.

But he began inviting Juan to dinner with the family, bringing up questions and discussions on history, literature, politics. Earl could always be depended upon to say something worthwhile on any of these topics but Juan only looked blank. The father suppressed a smile of satisfaction.

However, his work seemed all in vain. Mariana was blind to everything except how romantic Juan was. Did he not play the banjo and guitar, captivating her afresh? Her father suffered, but could only sit helplessly by and look on. This could not go on forever. Something was bound to happen soon.

And it did. At the end of the cantaloupe season, Juan proposed to Mariana.

"Oh, no." She was startled.

"Why not? I love you and I thought you loved me, too. Don't you?"

"Y-yes."

"Then there's nothing to prevent us. We could get married now and go to California for the cantaloupe season."

"But I don't want to get married yet, I want to finish school."

"Then you care more for school than you do for me."

"No—Wait, let me think! I'll let you know tomorrow night at the party."

All that night Mariana turned and tossed sleeplessly. She could not think clearly. Her thoughts went around and around in a dizzy whirl out of which came flashes: Juan playing a guitar and smiling at her in that charming way of his—sitting at the counter in the drug store with Juan eating pineapple sundae—finishing school and becoming a teacher—sitting in "Nigger Heaven" at the movies with Earl—to be the wife of a Filipino farm laborer or of a Negro lawyer—.

When at last she fell into an exhausted sleep toward morning, she had not yet made up her mind although the balances of the scales weighed heavier in Juan's favor.

The next day Earl called up. "Hello, Mariana. Are you coming to the moonlight picnic with the gang, tonight?"

She wondered why she had never noticed before that Earl could not pronounce her name correctly. He spoke it so awkwardly.

"I can't Earl. I have a date."

"What's the matter, Baby? You don't run around with our gang like you used to."

"Now listen here, Earl, I do too."

"No you don't."

"I do too."

"Well, come tonight. I'll drop by and get you."

"How many times must I tell you that I have a date?"

"Oh, Mariana! Don't you know how I feel about you? Don't you know that I—well, listen here: If you change your mind call me up, won't you?"

"All right, Earl."

Mariana felt sorry for Earl. He was so devoted to her. He thought that there was no one else in the world so wonderful as she. But she had made up her mind to marry Juan so she cast the feeling aside. There was no one so wonderful, so much the Prince Charming, as Juan.

When Juan came that evening, Mariana was not quite ready. She had only to put on her dress and a few finishing touches of rouge. Every one else was gone so she opened the door herself. Two other boys were with him. After the introductions were over and they were seated, Mariana started to excuse herself to finish dressing. But one of them spoke up.

"I haven't seen a Filipino girl in a long time. Gee, it's good to see one; makes me think of home."

"Yes?" Mariana smiled.

"By the way, what part of the Islands were you from?"

"Batangas."

"Then you're a Tagala."

"No-o."

"You see she's not a full-blooded Filipino," Juan explained, "she's a *mestiza ng etim*," (black mestiza). Her father is a Negro."

"Oh." The other's voice was suddenly cool.

"But, of course, Negroes are a nice people," Juan was saying, "I like them better than some other races. Many people do not like Negroes but I—"

Mariana's brain grew numb. There was something about Juan's tone, something about the quickness with which he defended colored people that hurt her to the quick. It was as if he was apologizing for her, as if he was trying to convince himself as well as these other boys, that she was all right despite her Negro blood. Was he ashamed of her, she whom Earl considered the height of perfection?

Suddenly Mariana laughed aloud. The men looked at her in surprise but she laughed on—a brain-clearing, dream-routing laugh. Then she excused herself and, going to the phone in the dining room, dialed Earl's number.

"Earl, this is Mariana. Are you still willing to take me to the picnic?"

"Of course, Mariana!" (Gee, it was good to hear his pleasant voice again, to feel the eagerness that throbbed as he called her name.)

"Then call for me in half an hour. Juan is still here but I'll pretend to have a headache and get rid of him."

"Great!"

"And listen, Earl. You can have all my dates from now on—always."

[*The Crisis* 41.3 (March 1934): 63–64]

BLACK VELVET

by Juanita DeShield

Boy, that's pretty good, even if I do say so myself. What a break if I could win that prize. Well I've got two weeks to practice."

Humming her song, she looked over the handbill again.

"Amateur Nite! Local Talent!! Cash Prizes!!!"

Straightway she fell into a reverie dreaming of her conquest, picturing every small detail of her performance: how she would stand, how she would throw back her head as she sang, how swell she would look up there on the stage.

The happy smile died on that last thought. She pursed her full lips tight together and ran to the closet. A brown silk street-dress was the best thing her skimpy wardrobe offered. She took it down, scrutinized it with narrowed eyes, tried it on. It was short, had pleats, and long sleeves. Not so hot. She certainly wouldn't make a very commanding personage in that. She just looked clean and scrubbed—she wanted to look glamorous and intriguing she wanted to exhibit some *savoir faire*. Now black velvet, long and clinging....

The striking of the clock called her back to reality with a start. Six o'clock and no supper ready. Sis would be home in a few minutes, tired, hungry, and irritable. She put away the dress and the dream, and began to prepare the evening meal for Sis and herself. Sis was working in a factory; she was not working, and had not for some time. She had been studying music while she worked. To meet her fees, she had to deny herself the frivolities and personal gadgets most girls admire.

There was a goodly wind blowing as she walked along Seventh Avenue. She folded her coat more tightly around her and pressed her underarm purse more tightly against her. The monetary contents of that purse totaled five dollars for the weekly budget. She turned into One hundred twenty-fifth Street. The bright windows with their attractive merchandise occupied not a little of her attention. She pressed her broad brown nose against the window, her lips parted in admiration, her eyes half-closed with envy.

"Come in dearie, come in," called the proprietor, a fair daughter of Israel.

"Oh, I'm not buying anything," she replied quickly.

That's nothing," said the other with a characteristic shrug. "Just look around."

A young salesgirl sidled toward her. "What can I do for you?" she inquired sweetly—too sweetly.

Up to this time she was quite sure of herself; but the salesgirl showed her a black velvet; then she was not so sure of herself. She hesitated a moment. That was all the salesgirl wanted. And now she was in a dressing-room clad in black velvet, long and clinging. She regarded the reflected person in the big mirror and found her glamorous and intriguing. She felt herself growing pale beneath her dusky skin. All her sense of reason was deserting her; she could feel her brain shrinking and weakening; the primal instinct "take what you want" filled the vacancy. Her long-suppressed desire overwhelmed her and, like long-imprisoned musty air, stifled her.

The salesgirl kept cooing, "just a little down and a few cents a week."

* * *

She left the shop feeling a little bewildered and with only three of the five dollars left in her purse. As she walked her bewilderment changed to chagrin, and the grim realization of what she had done broke upon her.

"Good Lord what have I done? I couldn't pay ten cents a week much less fifty. Yet I must have that dress for that Friday night. I've just got to do something between now and then."

* * *

She never fooled with "the numbers." She knew quite well that almost every one else did, but she had never bothered herself with them. Now she ran over to the shoe-shine stall where Sis's boyfriend worked. "Listen," she whispered sheepishly, "put these few cents on our house number. But please don't tell Sis. I'm in a mighty tight corner. I can trust you can't I?"

The number did not come out.

Poor child. She had figured that two "hits" would net her the eleven for the dress. There was no one who could lend her the money, especially now that she wasn't working. She had forgotten all about the song and how she was going to sing it. The dress loomed above all.

A flashily dressed man eyed her lewdly. "This must be the point where girls go wrong," she thought to herself as she noted his crude appraisal. "I could go mighty wrong right now for that eleven dollars." The full import of her unexpressed thought surprised more than shamed her. She turned her mind into other channels.

Idling around in the waiting rooms of employment agencies irked her, yet she was there the next morning bright and early with the best of them. Oh, she'd take anything.

A "sleep-in" (a room on the job) for a week at seven-fifty? Yes, anything.

Sis was glad to hear of the job; but she had brought home some piece-work from the factory.

"I'll take it with me." Sis wondered at this newly developed energy.

The next morning found her up early. All day long till evening she was washing: washing dishes, washing clothes, washing floors, washing tiles, washing paints. The last of the chores completed, she gulped an aspirin and started on the hand-work for the factory. Midnight found her a pretty tired girl. And so on for a week. Then she went off Thursday for the afternoon she spent her leisure cleaning paints in an apartment down the block. But first she had to go down to the factory with the garments. When she got in that night, her head felt as big as a pumpkin.

The next afternoon was Friday and she quit the job. Her eyes were burning, her head ached, her feet were sore, her muscles were stiff and she wondered how long it would take to manicure her hands back into shape. When she walked into the shop and paid the balance down in one cash payment, my! what a good customer! She must come back again. She felt like choking the salesgirl and tearing up the dress. She dragged herself home, chucked the dress in a corner, and got into bed. It seemed to her only a minute later that Sis awakened her. She was finally dressed, and so tired and disgusted with herself she didn't know whether her black velvet was long or short, loose or clinging; and she didn't care.

* * *

At the theatre she certainly looked better than anyone else, but she scarcely noticed that. All the torture of the past two weeks, physical and mental, rose before her. As she took her cue and walked onto the stage, she wasn't thinking of how she looked, nor how her dress hung. She just had to confide in someone. She had to tell somebody what a little fool she had been, so she opened her mouth and sang. She didn't sing as she had in the apartment, wondering about the effect; she sang for her own comfort and solace. Her eyes were wide and misty, and her voice was deep and sweet.

* * *

As she was presented with the prize, a woman in the wings remarked, "A crow could sing in a dress like that. Some folks get all the breaks." Little that woman knew.

[*The Crisis* 14.5 (May 1934): 130]

EMERGENCY EXIT

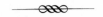

by Carol Cotton

Helen dropped her pen when the queer staccato rhythm sounded again from beyond the open windows, and jagged little splatters of ink flew across her letter. With a detached interest, she watched her hand and arm tremble. It was vaguely annoying that they did not quiver in time to the sharply marked tempo outside. Keep tempo. That was the thing. "I got rhythm ..." but she hadn't. The faint familiarity of the noise was annoying, too. Carefully she watched her mind step around the edges of fear. Where was it she had heard that sound before? ...The telephone ripped across her taut nerves like a buzz-saw across a cello. She watched her hand pull the instrument toward her as if it belonged to someone else. Then her voice, as detached as the hand....

"Hello."

The voice at the other end was startlingly close, and very clear. There was fear in it ... or merely concern? Who could tell?

"Marshall, from Durham, speaking. Is Professor Wallace in?"

"No, he's out of town. He'll be back Monday."

"Mrs. Wallace?"

"No, this is Helen. Mother's in New York."

"Who is there with you?"

"Nobody. I'm alone on the campus ... why?"

There was a brief moment of hesitancy. She could feel the second dragging out like a rubber band. Then the band snapped.

"The Durham militia was just called out to go over there to help quell a race riot. We were worried about you people ... is everything all right? Is there any danger?"

Her voice, she discovered, was still steady. "I haven't seen or heard anything."

"If you need any help, we'll send someone over."

"Thank you. It won't be necessary, I think.... Goodnight."

Marshall was a big man. Banks, insurance companies, business ventures ... when Marshall said there was a militia call, he wasn't joking. So it had come, then, this thing they had always feared.... Suddenly her thoughts dropped into place, and she knew where she had heard that pattern of sounds before. Tack-a-tack-a-tack-a-tack-a ... it was in *Wings*. Submachine gun. She leaned over; looked past the desk toward the window. Dark out there ... pitch dark. Nothing to be seen. For a moment longer she sat there, watching her hand. It was getting the rhythm, now ... keep tempo ... then she laughed. Durham was over forty miles away. Send someone ... what good would that do? What could the militia do?

The room was full of air which seemed to solidify into jelly. Crickets had stopped chirping an hour before; now the deep boom of the frogs down in the bottoms was stilled. No moon, of course. Nothing but darkness ... even the wind had dropped, and the leaves were silent. The silence was heavy, clammy. Absently she touched her forehead ... then she knew that she was covered with sweat. So this was fear. She drew deep, deliberate breaths to keep down hysteria. *"Fear is an instinctive reaction to an unfamiliar situation. It is an emergency measure. Fear does not exist when the individual is capable of managing the situation..."* the lines, in her own handwriting, took shape on the desk. Beside them, in the margin, she could see tiny figures ... a lop-sided elephant, a man with long, curling mustachios, two girls jumping rope. Her psychology note-book. She could hear the low, dry voice of her psych professor ... accented heavily by the rasping snare-drum effect of the guns.... "IT is highly PRObable that eMOtions do not exIST for unimaginative PEOple..."

Suddenly she wanted to run. The room was stifling. She looked wildly around ... rose jerkily and pulled the windows down, locked them. Then she ran through the house to the kitchen. There were no light on except the one desk lamp in the library. She stumbled against a chair, skinning a knee. Heedless, she ran on. The kitchen was warm, with a smell of soap and wax. She had cleaned it thoroughly that day, scouring all the pantry shelves, waxing the linoleum. Waste of time, that ... to clean a place which might be ashes so soon ... Rough, hoarse breathing startled her until she realized that it was her own. She latched the screen, pulled the kitchen door to, locked it savagely. Then the windows. One of the faucets was leaking, and mechanically she went across to the sink to shut it off. She could leave ... the hospital was less than a block away. They would take her in ... surely even a mob would not bother a hospital. If the close dark outside did not hide men, many men, she could get that far. She thought of Joe Ridley. He and Ethel had tried all day to persuade her not to stay at home at night.

"*You're crazy, Helen, to even consider it ...*"

"*I'm not afraid. What could hurt me on the campus?*"

"*There are a dozen places in town you could stay those three nights ...*"

"*Yes, but I like my own bed best ...*" They had called her stubborn.

She thought of her mother's cherished hundred-year-old quilt, and the jewels, turquoise and gold, which her grandfather had mined and made with his own hands. There was something else she should remember....

Starting back through the house toward the front, she caught a stealthy sound on the porch ... could they be here? A minute passed, two, three. Standing there in the dark, she could twist her head around and see the faint glow from the lamp in the library. Mistake, that. She should have turned it off. Then, maybe, they would have thought there was no one at home; would have left her alone. She stole, cat-like, to the door. Nothing there. She started to slam the door shut, but at that moment the lights from a car were reflected in the windows of the building opposite, and she hesitated. The car was two blocks away ... on many summer evenings they had all sat on the porch and watched the lights of far-off automobiles reflected in just that way. That was the dormitory ... "*representing an expenditure of one hundred thousand dollars, money scraped from low funds by the God-fearing men and women of our great church for the benefit of these unprivileged Negroes of the south: a testimony of the love of humanity for humanity ...*" The rolling sonority of the white Treasurer of the church board echoed back to her over the years. It had been the first building of any size she had ever seen erected. It was all mixed up with her first lover ... if Tom could be called a lover. She and Tom were up on the third floor one Sunday afternoon, inspecting the progress of the week just passed, before they put the roof on. She had stepped too close to the edge of the scaffold, and Tom had pulled her back, roughly, and kissed her. It was an awkward kiss, but it had been so quick ... she could feel the hot sun beating down on her head; feel the slight dizziness the height and the kiss ... her first ... had together aroused in her.

Listening carefully, she opened the screen and stepped out on the porch. Down to the left was the boys' dormitory. Like the other, it was a replacement following a disastrous fire. Nearly new, too. Memories went swirling through her head in confusion. It was put up the summer Dad went abroad, and she had charge of the payrolls. She had a major operation that summer, and bit her tongue to keep from talking while the anesthetic wore off, because Joe Ridley had told her he was going to bribe the nurses to repeat whatever she said. She and Joe had gone fishing in the long afternoons, played tennis, argued, all summer. Once she had bet Joe a dollar he couldn't eat a half-gallon of ice cream by himself ... and lost.... There was a break in the rapid-firing. A new rhythm ... iambic ... no, dactylic. That was it; dactylic hexameter....THIS is the FORest PriMEval ... a queer pain in her fingers pulled her attention away. She was clutching the door-frame, so tightly that her fingers had cramped. Carefully, she opened them, closed and opened them again several times with painstaking attention. The starlight showed a pale blur where the white paint made the janitor's cottage stand out. When Dad found out he had gone away with his family for the week-end, leaving her alone on the campus, he'd catch hell. When Dad found out ... maybe they would hall have caught hell first. She was trembling again and, deliberately, she swung around to face the administration building. Huge in the dim starlight, it somehow filled her with a degree of comfort. It had always been there ... it was inconceivable that it should cease to be. All her school life until after high school had been spent there, all her friendships and hatreds formed there, every party, movie, lecture, basket-ball game of her first sixteen years had been experienced within those walls. (NOTHing could be FINer than to BE in Carolina in the MORNing ... another metre now. It was definitely closer, too. She looked east, to the cotton mills, almost a half-mile away across the open fields. There were tiny figures running about a building which held the half-lurid light of the covered wagon scenes in the circus. They had used red flares in the circus ... this wasn't red flares. It must be fire. Then ... they would be here soon.)

If she was going, she'd better go. The shouting was coming closer, too. Then, as if a stubborn lock had tumbled, somewhere, she got the combination to the thing which had been hovering just on the edge of her consciousness. She couldn't go. She was in charge. Dad had always been half-afraid of a race riot some day ... Negro schools are not regarded with a uniform kindness ... and Dad had prepared.

Swiftly she moved back in to the house, not stopping to close the door behind her. The library was stuffy ... the closed windows were a mistake on such a hot night. After a moment of indecision, she opened them. A window or so wouldn't make much difference for very long, anyway. Then she opened the closet door, found what she searched. Her hands were steady enough now, but she wasted no thought on them. Two rifles ... here they were. Shot gun ... no, she couldn't' pull the trigger without using both hands ... risky, when you must aim straight. She left it. Revolvers ... three. There was an automatic somewhere, that Rob had used in France ... breathless with hurry, she ran upstairs, felt under her father's pillow. Here was one she wouldn't have to load ... but she remembered that he always kept one chamber empty, the one directly under the trigger. Mechanically she turned the magazine. Now for the automatic. She had to hunt for it ... finally found it, in the bottom of Rob's long-unused bureau drawer. Last, her own pet ... the tiny 22 her grandfather's father had fashioned; mother-of-pearl handle, silvered barrel. A toy. Her father had told her once that he would stand in the road all day and let her shoot at him with that thing. She had cut her teeth on it because her mother thought a "Kentucky baby" should grow up true to form. Take that, too ... if there were bullets for it. Yes, here they were ... a box nearly full. Then, arms full, she sped back into the library. Steadily, methodically, she loaded them all. Rifle ... 38 ... 16-repeater. Rifle, 32 (The Winchester ... darling of Dad's heart) ... 14 repeater. Two revolvers ... 32. One revolver, 38. Army automatic, of German make. There were cancelled German words along the barrel ... careful about the safety catch ... there. Her own tiny toy ... seven chambers. Dad's big Smith & Wesson, already loaded. Fifty-nine bullets. Well, that ought to give her a chance to take a few "pecks" to glory with her. She laid them out in a semi-circle; stared at them. Her jaw felt tired, and, after a moment, she unclenched her teeth. One person to defend a sixteen acre campus ... it was folly. But it was her father's life, this campus, and she was her father's daughter ... the daughter of the Kentucky mountains. She could shoot. Suddenly she wondered about the trembling, and looked again at her hand. Steady. She took a paper-knife from the desk, balanced a bottle of ink on its edge, held it out at arm's length. Steady. That was that, then. "*Fear does not exist when the individual is capable of meeting the situation....*"

She had a moment of panic when she realized how open the house was. There was absolutely no way to barricade it. Perhaps the top of the stairway was the best place to wait....

She made two trips, getting the guns up. Then she went back down to turn off the light. Wild shouts from the cotton mill were clearly audible now. Suddenly, the telephone, again. In the darkness, she answered.

"Hello ... Professor Marshall?"

"No, it's Helen. Dad's out of town until Monday."

"Oh. This is Donaldson, in Raleigh. The Raleigh militia is on its way over there to stop a race riot ... anything to it?"

"They haven't bothered us yet. I can hear some shooting."

"Are you all right?"

"Yes."

"You aren't alone, are you?"

"Yes, but I'm all right."

"Listen. Get a car ... there must be one on the campus ... and take the old Raleigh road. We'll send someone out to meet you ... "

"No. I'll stay here. It will be all right. Thanks."

Raleigh, too, was forty miles away. Houses could be ashes by the time a car could get to Raleigh ...

Carefully, she went back up the stairs, past the open front door. It was better open; bodies pressed against the framework would be a fair target.

It was hot upstairs, and close. Breathing was not easy, either, crouched on the floor as she was. Minutes dragged by, while she slowly, regularly, opened and closed her fingers to keep them awake. Once she picked up a rifle ... the 38 ... then noiselessly put it down. The town clock struck ... eleven. Or was it twelve? The wind was rising ... she could hear it over the pine grove back of the barns. Suddenly something new startled her nearly upright. For a full minute she couldn't place it. Her rifle was ready, pressing hard against the hollow of her shoulder. Then, abruptly, she knew. The shooting had stopped. The night was absolutely still. She waited; motionless, ready, but the stillness lengthened, pulling at her finger tips. Carefully, she set the rifle on the floor, stepped across it, and crept down the stairs. The reddish lights from the cotton mill section were slowly dying down. Once more the telephone rang. It was a sacrilege, this noise in the midst of the breathless silence. She covered the distance into the library with what seemed like one leap; removed the receiver.

"Hello ... Helen? This is Joe. Ethel thought we ought to call to tell you not to worry about that shooting you've been hearing. Strikers at the cotton mill got hold of a machine gun and ripped up the place. Sheriff sent for the militia ... colored folks over in Raleigh and Durham got all excited ... it had to be a race riot, of course ... say, are you listening to me?"

She was ... but, suddenly, she wasn't. Huddled on the desk, her head buried in her arms, she was crying ... great, heavy sobs that tore her lungs. Then she was desperately, terribly sick.

"Fear is one of the emergency emotions; necessary under primitive conditions, perhaps, but having no real meaning in modern civilized life...."   [*The Crisis* 41.6 (June 1934): 159–160]

THE FARMER

by Violet G. Haywood

"So you don't want to sell, huh, Jim? I'll give you good money enough for you to go up Nawth and be with yo' boy. You can do the same thing that us white folks kin do up Nawth!"

He spat viciously. "Reckon you'd rather do that than stay down here and work a little old farm like this?" Mr. Hilton laughed heartily, condescendingly. This was the way! Talk about that boy of his. He would make him sell.

"Well?" he queried when Jim remained silent.

"I—reckon I don't want to sell, Mr. Hilton." Haltingly, yet firmly Jim replied.

(God-damn you!! God-damn nigger—)

"But why? Why?" Mr. Hilton's voice rose shrilly. He looked cuttingly at Jim out of the corner of his eye. Did he, could he know? But that was impossible. This stupid black fool, he could *not* know!

"Remember I allus deal fair with good niggers, Jim, and you're one of the best. Reckon you are more like a white man than any nigger I heard tell of." He slapped Jim on the back and wondered vaguely at that queer fire that flashed in his eyes for an instant.

"Yes sir, Mister Hilton, yes sir—"

"You'll sell?" Jim heard the exultant note in the white man's voice.

Jim looked over his little farm. The cotton crop had been sparse; the land was so poor! Three bales of cotton the land had given him; not much, but enough to buy food and clothes for Mandy and him. Maybe next year—. Three bales home from the gin-mill, seeded and all ready to be sold. His very own! Not much, compared with other farms but—his own bales! Under the shed of his barn. His farm! his cotton, his! Yet, how could he say all this, how could he tell anyone?

"No sir"—A dream come true all his life he had worked, *slaved*, prayed. This was his prayer. A little farm of his own. Mandy had worked by his side (faithful, oh! faithful). His dream, her dream, their dream. Go North and live with his son? Cooped up in the city away from the sun and the wind and the sod? But this was his. He and Mandy belonged here.

"You mean you ain't gonna sell?" Mr. Hilton broke in upon his thoughts. Jim looked into his cold, blue eyes and suddenly was afraid. Why should this man want to take his farm from him?

"No-sir."

Without another word the white man turned on his heel.

"You'll get out," he thought. I'll run you out. What would a nigger do with oil! Black—"

Jim was sorry about Mr. Hilton. He didn't like to cross any white folks, and seldom did. But he would not sell his farm. He looked over his little farm; standing with his face to the sun. "This," he thought, "is mine. Why should I sell it?" He picked up his bucket and went to milk the cows.

At supper that night he told Mandy about it.

"You was right, Jim," she said, as he had known she would say. "Reckon this is ours and we don't want to sell."

"But it's little and po', Mandy. Maybe we could do better up No'th—" Mandy stopped short, the spoon ladened with black-eyed peas halted in mid-air.

"What ails you, Jim, honey?" she looked anxiously at him, but Jim avoided her eyes. He himself could not have said what the trouble was.

"You know yo' self, Jim, that we wouldn't like no city. This here is ours, and we ain't never going to leave it! Come on now, it's gettin' late and tomorrow is Sunday."

Jim sat a while and smoked his old corn-cob pipe while Mandy did the dishes. Then, tired out by the day's work, Mandy went to bed, leaving Jim alone with his pipe.

Sleep refused to come to Jim immediately. He turned and tossed until Mandy began to stir sleepily. Then he forced himself to lie still and close his eyes tightly. Finally sleep did come and with it bad dreams. He dreamed that he was trying to hide from Mr. Hilton, but always the cold blue eyes would find him. Only the eyes were no longer cold. They were hot and searing and a peculiar smoke came from them.

Jim and Mandy went to church the next day. Their buggy was old and somewhat inclined to rattle; the horse, tired and slow. The ride from their little farm "in town" to church was long, but they didn't mind.

Mandy sang in the choir and Jim was proud of her deep, sweet voice. He patted his foot in time with her song, his shoes making little squeaky noises. He kept himself awake during the long service by crying "Amen" now and then.

After the service he noticed the "sisters" speaking to Mandy with much respect. "It's because of our farm!" he thought proudly.

They saw it before they got there. Almost at the same instant their eyes spied it and together they pointed and exclaimed, "Look!"

Great clouds of smoke rose from their shed and curled gracefully toward the heavens, eventually losing themselves in thin, blue lines. Flame, great licking, hungry tongues reared themselves, growing larger and more cruel. Jim jumped from the wagon and broke into a run across his field of cotton stalks. When Mandy finally arrived after having urged the horse to his poor fastest, Jim was fighting the fire madly, bravely and hopelessly. How can a man fight fire without water? Mandy hurried to his aid, but realizing the utter hopelessness of the situation they stood helplessly by, watching with sad eyes and bleeding hearts, the rapid disappearance of their three bales of cotton. Food for the winter, clothes, freedom from debt—Ah! Jesus!

"I heard tell of yo' misfortune, Jim and sho' am sorry about it." This was Mr. King. Jim had come to him to borrow money. Mr. King was sitting with his feet on the banister of his porch. He was a nice white man. He let colored folks sit down on his porch with him. He was silent a long time then—"But I can't lend you no money," he said.

"I kin pay it all back to you next fall after cotton time, Mr. King"—

"Well I can't do it, Jim. Sorry!"

Jim rose to go. He twisted his hat nervously.

"Well," he said, a smile on his lips but a groan in his heart, "thank you, jess the same, Mr. King—Good-night, sir—." As he began to walk away Mr. King called after him as if on second thought:

"I'd buy yo' farm from you, Jim."

"No, no, Mr. King, I reckon I'll get along!"

The next day Jim went to borrow money from the government agent. He was a farmer sorely in need of a little help. He would pay it all back come cotton time another year. But the agent glared at him.

"Lend you money?"

"I—I can pay it back—"

"Hump!"—All niggers want to borrow. Why don' you try working for a change? No, we can't lend you any money!" He stuffed his hands into his pockets and walked away.

Vaguely Jim noticed Mr. Hilton there. Smiling. He put out his hand and said something, but blindly Jim pushed him aside. Like a sleep-walker or one of those rare beings who are dead yet continue to function as though alive, Jim climbed into his buggy. His hands were folded idly in his lap. Death was in his eyes. From long habit the horse without being guided, found his way through the little town and finally on the long road home.

As Jim sat there, silent and motionless many things became clear to him. The dog missing, the strange, blue flame with which the cotton burnt; that cold look of hate in Mr. Hilton's eyes: Mr. King's refusal of a loan; the government agent's answer; that triumphant smile on Mr. Hilton's face.

In the moments required for the trip from town to the farm, Jim was transformed from a strong man, in the prime of his life, to an old man with empty eyes and a heavy heart. Lines seemed to have creased the brown of his face like tiny streams breaking the smoothness of firm, brown soil. The proud flash had gone from his eyes and his shoulders were stooped and old and tired.

"All my life, all my life, and this is what I've got. I have worked, and prayed and lived clean and upright. I have never crossed white people. Yet they take my farm from me. They want everything. They want the world. We do not matter to them—"

Perhaps this is what was passing through his mind, could he have straightened it out.

The horse turned in the gate. Jim dumbly looked at the little farm that meant so much to him. He and Mandy must leave it. Tomorrow he would see Mr. Hilton. They would go North. The tears that his eyes would not shed gathered in his heart and swelled it until he was afraid to speak lest his heart burst and spatter blood from his parched lips. Dimly he saw Mandy come out to meet him. He wanted to comfort her, she looked so scared. He moved to get out of the wagon and pitched face forward at her feet. Just an old man, lying still in the dirt. Drunk maybe—What right have niggers with oil? With anything?

[*The Crisis* 42.2 (February 1935): 40, 50]

MASQUERADE

by Isabel M. Thompson

"... they learned the white man with whom they had to deal. They learned him through and through, and without ever completely revealing themselves."
From *Along This Way* by James Weldon Johnson

* * *

I was hunchin' maw an' pointin'. "Maw! Look, Maw. It's a-movin'!"

An' sure 'nough, when maw look up, the magnoly tree in front o' the cabin was tremblin' like it done got chills an' fevah—but they warn't no air stirrin'.

Maw reach ovah to where I was settin' on the do'-step (I warn't but twelve then); she tech my shouldah, an' says low an' kinda shaky, "Hattie, honey, they's somep'n in the air."

Then I sho did feel funny. Wondah if maw was readin' my min'. 'cause I jus' been sayin' to myself, "I cain't figgah what makes maw ac' so sot all time, like she's tickled to death with what we gettin' down heah in Miss'sippi. How come she don' jus' up an' tell the white folks that we's tired o' slavin' away fo' nothin'? Else why don' we pick up an' run away up no'th, like Birdie an' her maw done? ... Co'se Marse Robert's good 'nough, but I wants to be free!" I didn' aim to say nothin' out loud, yet 'n still maw done tech me.

Right then a man drap down out o' the tree an' run up to us. He grabbed maw by her shouldah an' I was gonna hit 'im—but he whispahed so hoarse-like, "Maw Haney!"

An' maw, she say, "Jake! How come you ac' like this?"

"Maw, I'se gonna run away, but they's aftah me! Hide me 'way quick!"

We could hear folks a-talkin', an' they was three dogs a-barkin'. Me, I jus' stood there shakin'. But maw! You shoulda saw her. So calm an' peaceful, like we was jus' talkin'.

"Hattie," she say, "What you shakin' 'bout! ... No, Jake, I ain't gonna hide you. Let's set down on the do-stop fo' a spell."

Jake didn' move from that spot. "Maw, is you crazy? Cain't you see they'll git me? I'd jus' soon be daid as to get cotched. You know what Green-Eye done to Slim t'othah day. Please, Maw!"

"Son' you trus' me, Jake? Don' I allus tell folks right—white folks an' ouah folks too?"

"Sho you does, Maw Haney, sho. Evvabody come to you with they troub—" Jake put his han' ovah his mouth. "Maw, I see the to'ch-light. They is a amos' here. Help me!"

We could see one light, an' soon they was lots of 'em shinin' right on maw an' Jake. But when I looked at maw, seem like her eyes was givin' off mo' shine than the to'ches. I couldn' take my eyes offn' her. Neithah could Jake.

Then up come the crowd with Green-Eye Jackson in the lead. (He was right young, but they had him fo' haid-man ovah to Ralston's.) "Wa-al, Maw," he say sorta slow an' nasty, "I didn' expect this of you."

Maw got up an' planted herself in front o' Jake. Fo' quite a spell, she didn' say nothin'—jus' fold her arms an' look straight at Green-Eye. Now, Maw warn't so big, but when she look at you that way, you was boun' to melt down to nothin', an' tha's what Green-Eye done. He look so shame' an' kinda stepped back. Maw took a deep breath an' smiled! She say real sof'-like, "Jake, he's a good boy, Mistah Jackson. Somebody jus' been puttin' queer notions in 'im. S'pos'n you-all lets him stay ovah heah on Marse Robert's plantation fo' a spell. I bet it'll be all right. An' I'll git Jake all straight on things."

Green-Eye, he look at the rest of 'em an' say, "That suits me fine, Maw. We can always count on you.... Come on, boys, let's get some sleep."

The lights was all gone an' the dogs was barkin' a long ways off, befo' maw said anothah word. "Son, ain't you jus' a trifle hongry? We's got some hawg-jowl an' wil' greens lef' from suppah...."

At las' we was all three out on the do'-step once mo'. Maw puff away on her ol' cob-pipe an' say, "Jake, you is got a heap to learn in this ol' worl'. You is the kin' o' li'l fellah what would fight barehan' 'gainst the hefties' man on earth, ef he had somep'n what you want. Now that soun' good, but hit ain't good sense."

When maw stop to puff away once mo', she could heah Jake breathin' heavy an' even. She got up. "Come 'long, Hattie' we is gotta fix a place fo' this boy. I'll jus' hang two o' my undah-shirts on a line 'cross the room.... Hit's been a long time, since they was men-folks in this heah shack." ...

Nex' day, through the grape-vine, we heerd tell how ol' Green-Eye done scairt the guts out o' Maw an' make her take keer o' Jake. An' they was othah things nasty too.

Jake, he got so mad, an' at dinnah time when they was lots o' folks come ovah to see us, he jus' blowed up. I reckon ol' Green-Eye nevah tol' 'bout how Maw scairt him to death." He look 'roun' at maw, but she didn' pay no min' to his talk. She was too busy bouncin' Sistah Dolly's li'l baby on her lap. Lots mo' chillun was hangin' 'roun', pullin' on her skirt with the pretty red figgahs on it.

So Jake kep' on. "Yas, suh, you shoulda saw the way me an' maw stan' right up to that po' white trash, an' says, 'Go min' yo' own business!'"

The chillun was beggin' maw, "Please, cain't you tell us jus' one li'l story, Maw Haney? Jus' one."

"Wa-al, ef them big folks would shet they mouths onct in a while, maybe I could." Maw was talkin' loud fo' her; so they all got real quiet. They wasn' a soun'.

An' this is what she tol':

"They was onct a li'l rabbit what had a good-luck chahm. Hit was strongah than them asafittidy bags you-all weahs roun' yo' necks. Hit was pow'ful strong. An' all the time, this rabbit was so happy a-jumpin' roun', 'cause couldn' nothin' hahm him, long as he had the chahm could they?"

"No, ma'am," says the chillun.

"So, one day he come home, pull out his chain, an' set down to look at the chahm so as to say some magic words. But lo an' beholst the good-luck chahm was gone! The li'l rabbit, he was almos' crazy a-runnin' heah an' a-runnin' theah to find it. An' he didn' have no luck. He sho felt bad.

"'bout fo' five days aftah, when he was hoppin' 'roun' behin' a grea' big rock, he heerd somep'n growl. An' what does yo' think he seen, when he peep out? They was a big ol' brown beah holdin' the li'l rabbit's good-luck chahm an' playin' with it!

"Now the rabbit, he was mad an' staht to run up an' grab his chahm. Then he figgahed he might git et up; so he hopped on home an' scratched his haid fo' a long time.

"An' so evvaday, unbeknownst to the beah, the li'l rabbit followed behin' him evvawhere he go. Then one day, the rabbit hops up to the beah an' say so sweet an' nice, 'Mistah Beah, I brung you a big pot o' honey!'

"The beah jus' growl at firs', but when he taste o' that honey, he say, 'This the bes' honey I evva had! Weah yo-all git it?'

"'Ef you like it, Mistah Beah, I'll bring you some evvaday.'

"'Why yo-all is jus' fine,' say Mistah Beah. 'Won' yo-all come in my house an' set down fo' a spell?'

"So the rabbit walk in an' visit. When he was a-gittin' ready to go, he say, 'What's this, Mistah Beah? Hit sho is sweet-smellin'.'

"'Oh, that ol' bag ain' nothin' much. I found it on the road one day. Reckon it's one o' them silly chahms. Yo-all can have it, ef yo' wants.'

"'Oh, thank you, Mistah Beah. Hit sho do smell sweet. An' tomorrow, I bring you some mo' honey.'

"'Tha's fine, li'l rabbit, 'cause I sho do love honey!'"

Maw stop an' grin, showin' all them white teeth o' hers. She say, "Yas, *suh*, big brown beah sho do love honey."

The chillun all clapped they han's an' kep' shoutin', "Big Brown Beah sho *do* love honey!" Then all the grown folks staht to have fun; so they make up this verse:

> Big Brown Beah sho do love hon-ey,
> Big Brown Beah sho do love hon-ey,
> Big Brown Beah, he ac' so funny
> But Big Brown Beah sho do love honey.

They all joined hands an' skip roun' an' roun'. "I be the Beah," say Long-Tall Joe, the bes' cotton-pickah in them pahts. "Leave me be the li'l rabbit," say Merry, the littles' one in the ring. An' whilst they went through the whole thing, evvabody was happy. They fo'got they was slaves; they fo-got they was boun' to work whethah they want to or not leas'ways, evvabody but Jake.

Jake, he look like a tree wha's been chopped down. He didn' say nothin', wouidn' look at nobody—jus' set theah an' then sneak off behin' the cabin.

Two Sundays pass by, an' Jake git worse an' worse. One day, whilst maw was up to the big house a-washin' clothes, Jake come runnin' in the cabin an' staht to roll up a bundle o' things. "I ain' gonna stay heah no longah. Don' nevah keer, ef I do git cotched or die. Tha's bettah than to stay heah an' listen to Maw Haney sweet-talk the white folks, whilst they drives us clean to the grave. That ol' woman ain' got no sense ain' nevah gonna git none. I wants to be free!" When he say this las', he pick up his roll but he drap it right quick.

Jake was lookin' at the do.' "Maw! Maw Haney, don' look at me lak that!"

Maw walk in so easy, an' say, 'Jake, I got somep'n to say to you, but don' nevah tell nobody else.... I jus' come from talkin' to a white lady an' a gen'-mun from up in Ill'nois. They is nice folks. I knows that, 'cause I got 'em to git Birdie an' her maw 'way from down heah, an' take 'em up no'th."

Jake an' me was almos' chokin'.

Maw kep' on, "Now they is gonna see to you, come sun-down. They is gonna wait fo' you, right behin' the magnoly tree."

Jake, he stumble ovah the bench. Whilst he was down on his knees, he grab maw's skirt with the red figgahs on it, an' whispah so hoarse-like, "Maw! Maw Haney!"

[*The Crisis* 42.7 (July 1935): 201, 217]

SERENA SINGS

———— ✕ ————

by Octavia B. Wynbush

"All service ranks the same with God."
—Browning

The moon, a pendant lamp in the cloudless sky, radiated soft light over the bit of garden in front of Serena Sayer's little cottage. Serena, leaning back in the old hickory rocker under a huge magnolia tree in full bloom, was drunk with the wine of the Louisiana night.

"Lawdy, I sho' could sing this night! I could just throw back my head and hollah! If 'twasn't so late, I *would* sing, but I'm feared I'll wake some o' these early sleepin' plantation hands."

She drew in a deep breath, and with it the fragrance of tea-roses, cape jasmine, magnolias, and wild honey suckle.

"An' them flowers! They don't smell half so sweet by day."

Out of the shadows rose the song of a mocking bird.

"Listen to that bird. He's praisin' his God for this beautiful night, an' why can't I, even if 'tis nigh twelve o'clock? 'Tain't my fault if folks want to close they eyes early this lovely night."

Her eyes once more caressed the night scene. The grass, blue in the moonlight, lay a rich carpet under her feet, and stretched along the yellow river-road winding past her white-washed picket fence. At the bend of the road, and completely hidden by a thick grove of beeches, lay the grounds surrounding the "big house," where lived the Marshalls, owners of the plantation on which Serena's little cottage was situated.

Tomorrow morning Serena would walk into the old-fashioned high-raftered kitchen as usual, and send the smell of rich coffee, waffles, eggs, and bacon floating upstairs to the bedrooms of the Marshall family.

Thinking of the family tonight brought a sign from Serena. Something was wrong. She had sensed it that evening, with Mr. Ned's return from "up No'th." She had felt an unaccustomed restraint in his greeting when he had come into the kitchen before dinner.

Then, after dinner, there had been that quick withdrawal of the family to the library. Mr. Tom had not come into the kitchen for his nightly round of teasing; Miss Jean had not spoken her appreciation of the chocolate cake and vanilla ice cream, especially prepared for her; nor had Miss Alice spoken her usual word of praise concerning the meal.

"Something's wrong!" Serena's muttered comment had its confirmation in the sight which she had surreptitiously witnessed. On departing that night, instead of leaving by the back gate as she always did, she had stolen to the front of the house and under the protection of Miss Alice's prize rose bushes, had seen the four members of the family in the library.

Mr. Ned his face wrinkled and drawn like a mummy's, was standing with his back to the old-fashioned fireplace. He looked as if he had added ten years to his fifty. Mr. Tom was sitting in one of the high-backed chairs that had belonged to his great-great-grandfather, looking at Mr. Ned as if he were a ghost, instead of Tom's father. Miss Alice sat on the sofa, her lovely gray hair blending with Miss Jean's brown, they were so close together. The sudden rising of Mr. Tom, and his movement toward the long window, as if he were going to step through it to the porch, brought Serena's spying to an end.

"Something's wrong. Something's mighty wrong." Serena's head wagged solemnly.

Once more the mocking bird's clear notes filled the stillness. Well, morning would tell the tale. Just now it was night, and the night was calling for song.

"Lawdy, I jus' mu' sing!"

Throwing back her head and folding her plump brown hands across her broad stomach, Serena began to sing. One song after another swelled from her deep throat, and floated off down the river-road, to be lost on the river rolling at the foot of the bluff on which the "big house" stood.

In his bedroom Ned Marshall paced slowly to and fro. His white hair, in greatest disorder, added to the ghastly appearance of his face. His hands were thrust deep into his pockets. His voice was a broken mutter.

"Broke! Ruined! Not a damn cent left. My fault, too. Should've listened to Alice. She's a damned good business man, even if she is my wife."

He walked to the long window opening out on the balcony which ran around the upper story of the house. Stepping out of the window, he looked around. As far as his eyes could see, lay the Marshall holding. Like a wayfarer who is returning home after years of exile, his eyes dwelt upon each well-known landmark. There was the hibiscus set out by his grandmother's gardener, while the kindly, silvery-haired lady stood watch; the smooth, shrub-and-tree-dotted lawn immediately surrounding the house, and enclosed by a wrought-iron fence forged by slaves in days gone-by; the hitching-post, wrought in the form of a grinning Negro boy holding an iron ring in the hand that protruded from a tattered shirt-sleeve. Outside the fence spread the plantation; sugar cane, cotton, and other green stuff; some of the land, newly ploughed, lay black in the moonlight. And too far away to be seen, lay the cabins and the cottages housing his hands.

It had all been gained and held by thrift and good management. Now, at one stroke it was gone. At least it was as good as gone, for it would take all his land would bring to pay for his gambling on the stock market.

Ned winced. His family—he couldn't blame them, he reckoned, for the stand they were taking. Alice hadn't said a word. That was what had made it so hard. It would have been a damn sight easier if she had even said "I told you so." She had always remonstrated with him for playing the market.

And tonight, after he had broken the news, she had offered him the use of her private fortune. Ned shuddered in the warm night air as he felt again the prickles of shame which had run over him when he had confessed that he had spent her money, too. He couldn't blame Tom for looking him full in the face and then withdrawing to the verandah. And Jean, his favorite of the two, had thrown her arms around her mother, and held her close. Ned had felt horribly alone when at a word from Tom when he re-entered the room, all three had gone upstairs to Alice's sitting room, leaving him without a word. After he had heard her door shut, Ned had gone to his own room to face himself, and fight it out alone.

Now he stood on the balcony, alone and wretched. He felt a sudden irritation creeping over his deeper emotion. Then he became aware of the cause. A voice—the voice of a Negro woman singing in the distance was disturbing him.

"Damn! Who in hell can sing at a time like this? Why couldn't she choose some other time to howl?"

He forgot the nights on which he and his family had sat in the moonlight and listened appreciatively to the mellow, untamed voices of the plantation workers. But tonight this lone singer angered him. He could choke those notes back into her throat.

Slowly he walked to the railing of the balcony and looked down. Falling from the balcony, a man might break a leg, or possibly paralyze himself, but the distance was not great enough to insure instant death. True, there was always a revolver, but insurance companies had been known to balk at paying widows of suicides. And his insurance would go a long way. His eyes roved absently across the lawn to the yellow river-road.

The river! How easy! To go for a row in Tom's row-boat, anchored in the cove where the river bent away from the road. To overturn accidentally. No one could refuse paying the widow of a man who drowned when a boat upset.

Briskly he stepped back into his room, passed quickly and quietly through the door and down the wide staircase to the hall below. Opening the outside door with great care, he stepped upon the verandah, moved down the stone steps, and started across the lawn. Once more, across the river-road, came the rich voice of the colored singer. Involuntarily, Ned Marshall listened. He recognized the voice, now. It was Serena's:

> Look down, look down, this lonesome road,
>   Before you travel on.
> Look up, look up, and see your Maker,
>   'fo' Gabriel blows his horn.
> True Love, True Love,
> What have I done,
> That you should treat me so?
> You caused me to walk and talk
> Like I never done before.
> Weary totin' such a load,
> Travelin' down that lonesome road.
> Look down, look down, that lonesome road,
> Before you travel on.

As the golden notes gave place once more to silence, Ned Marshall walked slowly to the edge of the circle of beech trees and stood silently with bowed head in the shadow of their arms.

"It's a pretty shabby trick, I call it."

Tom, standing with legs far apart, and hands, thrust deep into his trousers pockets, faced his sister and his mother as they sat by the long window opening on the balcony outside his mother's room.

Alice Marshall was thinking how like his father Tom was, standing almost exactly as the former had stood downstairs those few tragic moments just passed. Instead of shame, however, anger throbbed in every movement and tone of the speaker.

"To take Mother's money, above all things!"

"Don't talk about your father, Tom."

Alice said the conventional thing, but her bearing gave the lie to her words. Yes, she was bitter against her husband. The unnecessary humiliation which he had brought upon his family was enough to make one bitter. Numb as she still was from the shock, she yet had sense enough to realize what was ahead for them—for her two children, especially.

The humiliations of poverty; the loss of social standing, and the withdrawal of their friends would be hard enough for her and Ned, but for Tom and Jean, it meant stark tragedy.

"If he had only listed to you, Mother. But he never does. Grandmother used to say it runs in the Marshall family. Marshall men never listen to their wives. They're all like that."

Tom whirled on his sister. "Not all! I'm one, but I don't hold with the old man's action at all! But gee, that's not the main thing now. The mischief's done. The question is, where do we go from here? How shall we stand in the sight of our friends, if any?"

Jean staring at the floor, sat up and turned eyes full of sudden fright upon her brother.

"Were—do—we—go? Friends—if—any?" she spoke in a dazed fashion. "Why—I hadn't thought of that. You don't suppose our friends will go back on us?"

"But I have thought of it." Alice rose and stood looking at first one and then the other of her children. "The thing that's happened to us is as hard to get adjusted to at once as a sudden death in the family. As long as the body is in the house, we feel it can't be so. Then, suddenly we realize it *is* so, and the whole thing comes down on us, at once."

"But what do you mean?" Jean's eyes were those of a person fighting hard to disbelieve something which he feels he must believe.

"Sis, can't you understand?" Tom was nearly shouting in his exasperation. "We'll have to leave all this—go away—move! Everything's gone—money, plantation—everything. We—we're just beggars, not even as well off as the darkies who work for us." He gave a short laugh. "It'll soon be 'worked,' instead of 'work,' I reckon."

Walking to the window, he stared out at the night scene. Beyond the clump of beech trees, and across the river-road, lay the unseen quarters of their plantation workers.

"At least they're carefree," continued Tom. They don't have any fortune to lose. Their friends won't turn their backs on them because they don't have a dime in the world."

"How could Father bring this on us?" Jean's voice was a moan.

Alice and Tom looked across her bowed head at each other. Tom's fist clenched. He didn't give a hoot for himself. He could give up the university, his fraternity, and everything and do a man's work. But Jean—just when things were about to be clinched between her and Beauregard LeClerc. They couldn't expect him to propose to a penniless girl, and anyway, Jean wouldn't want his proposal now—would seem too much like charity. And then LeClerc's were snobs, to boot.

"We may as well face facts, children." Alice's voice was decisive. "Your father has lost every thing we called our own. From what he said tonight, our remaining at Marshall Hall is only a matter of days. Jean, it is just as well to realize at once that we cannot and do not expect our friends to be our friends any longer. We do not want them, for all they can do for us is to give their sympathy. The Marshalls and the Whittakers accept no man's sympathy. We fight and win our own battles."

Tom applauded. "Spoken like a man! We'll stick to you, Alice Marshall."

"It was so unfair of Dad. I don't care if I never see him again." Jean's eyes flashed as she spoke.

"It was rotten. But we're not concerned with him, any more. It's we three. He got himself into this mess, and he can get himself out." Tom's voice was like a metal rasp.

Saying nothing, Alice slipped to the balcony. Her children were saying the bitter things which were in her own heart. But she could not sanction them. She looked out over all the dear, dear things which had twined themselves into her life for the twenty-five years she had been Ned Marshall's wife. The sharp pictures in the moonlight became blurred by tears. Dimly, she could see the form of a man standing in the wide sweep of the beech trees. His head was bowed upon his hands. Turning, she called to her children.

"Tom, Jean, come here."

Before the two had taken their places beside her, there broke upon the stillness the voice of Serena Sayer's—Alice recognized it at once—singing triumphantly. When Tom and Jean appeared, they thought that Alice had called them, as she often did, to listen to the singing. So they listened this time, and Alice, laying aside her original purpose for calling them, was silent. On the stillness of the night, came the song:

> Do you think I'll make a soldier,
> Do you think I'll make a soldier,
> Do you think I'll make a soldier,
>   Soldier of the King?
> Rise, shine, give God the glory,
> Rise, shine, give God the glory,
> Rise, shine, give God the glory,
>   Soldier of the King?
> Yes I think you'll make a soldier,
> Yes I think you'll make a soldier,
> Yes I think you'll make a soldier,
>   Soldier of the King?

As the last note finished, Alice turned to her children.

"Your father is down yonder under the beeches, alone. A good soldier never deserts a comrade in distress. Come, let us go to him."

Every time I look up to the House of God,
The angels cry out, "Glory!"
Glory be to my God who lives on high!
To save a soul from danger!

With the last notes of this song, Serena arose from the hickory chair. Once more she caressed the night scene with her gaze, smiling a loving, troubled smile as her eyes came to rest on the beech grove which concealed effectively any glimpse of the Marshall grounds.

"Well," she murmured, as she turned her footsteps toward her own little cottage, "I don't know if I disturbed nobody or not. But anyhow, I sho' feel powerful good myself."

[*The Crisis* 42.10 (October 1935): 296–297, 313]

ECHO OF THE DISTANT DRUM

————— ∞∞∞ —————

by Carol B. Cotton

It was the day before Christmas. Becky tucked her feet up in the hem of her flannel nightie and bounced up and down in bed. She slid one warm hand up from under the blankets and touched the tip of her nose. Grandma said Becky's nose was cold, like a puppy's, every morning. It must be time for Grandma to come and call "Double up, little sister!" That was the way Grandma had called Mother when she was six-going-on-seven. Grandma was always talking to Becky about when Mother was six-going-on-seven, and everything that Mother did then, Becky must do now. Some of the things were fun; coloring the dresses of the ladies in the *Godey* books, and making little paper boats for Grandma to put honey-caramels in, and popping corn in the wire popper. But Mother never had any roller skates, nor any paper dolls, nor ... oh joy ... any Sunday School s'tif'cate. Becky wasn't exactly sure what a s'tif'cate was, but Marjorie and Priscilla and Walter and a little fat girl named Mary Sue ... and Becky ... were going to get one today. And Becky was going to send hers to Mother for a Christmas-birthday present. Mother never had a Christmas-birthday present like that before, she'd reck... think. (Think, Becky, try hard. *Don't* say "reckon." If you can't speak correctly and say I suppose or I think for pity's sake don't say Ah reckon. She could hear Grandma saying that now).

Even Grandma never had a Sunday School s'tif'cate, nor Grandpa. He said they would frame Becky's and hang it up beside Mother's college diploma in the little red room upstairs where Becky lived in summer, that used to be Mother's room. But Becky knew he was only teasing. That was to be Mother's very own Christmas-birthday present.

Grandpa was in the sitting room now whistling while he made the fire in the big fireplace. There were only heavy curtains between the sitting room and the room where Becky slept in the winter, down near the fire so she wouldn't get too cold. She could hear Grandpa's chair creak as it was moved around to the wood-box. "Sweet dreams, Grandpa!" she called. "Please whistle Humpty-Dumpty!"

"Sweet dreams, Sunny," Grandpa said just like always. That was funny. Grandpa called Mother Sunshine because she was always laughing and singing, and he said Becky was Little Sunny, like the little girl in the red book over in the tall bookcases across from Becky's bed. Next to it was the Mother Goose that had Merry Christmas and Happy Birthday to Rebekah written in it. That had puzzled Becky until they told her Mother's name ... *Mother's* ... was Rebekah too! Daddy always called her Bee ... But Grandpa was whistling HumptyDumpty ... a tune he had helped Becky pick out on the square piano in the parlor before it got too cold to go in there. Becky bounced in time to Grandpa's whistle ... Humpty-Dumpty *sat* on a wall; Humpty-Dumpty *had* a great fall; all the King's horses and *all* the King's men never could put him *together* again ... there was a picture of poor Humpty, fat and smooth, sitting on his wall with his legs crossed, and then another of him, with a big crack in his face, and his legs all twisted, on the ground ... Never could put him together again ...

She was walking in time to the same whistle on her way to Sunday School. Grandma had made her put on lots of clothes, because it was so very cold. She had Grandma's stockings on over her shoes, which she must take off as soon as she got to Sunday School, so her feet wouldn't get wet. She walked as fast as she could, but the snow was thick and slippery, and she wasn't used to snow yet. Once two boys ran past her, on the bridge over Plum Creek, and pushed her down, right across from where all the King's horses stayed. In the summer you could see them standing in their stalls, or waiting in the little yard next door to get some new shoes, but today the big doors were shut tight. Becky wondered if the horses would kneel and pray to the Little Lord Jesus tonight, like the animals in one of Mother's books. All the animals must kneel on the night before Christmas. That was the night that Santa-Claus came, too. Becky stopped to look in the windows of Haylor's Furniture Co., at the doll bed with a real mattress and two real pillows. She had begged Grandma to let her hem some sheets and pillow cases for the bed *if* SantaClaus should happen to bring it, and Grandma had told her she could, if she would hem Daddy's Christmas handkerchief very carefully. Becky rubbed her nose up and down on the cold window pane. Daddy's handkerchief had been hemmed and mailed to him. But Mother was to get the s'tif'cate, and Grandpa had bought a special-delivery stamp so Becky could send it that very day. Walter said it would have her name on it, a big blue seal, and maybe a tassel, like the cradle-roll s'tif'cate. Walter knew everything because his papa owned a store, and Walter could have all the candy he wanted free. She began running, slipping over the snow, at the thought of the blue seal and the tassel, maybe. That was all they had talked about in Sunday School ... the birthday of the Little Lord Jesus and the s'tif'cates. Mother had the same birthday the Little Lord Jesus had, so she must have the s'tif'cate too.... The children were to be promoted from the Primaries into the Children's. The Primaries was very nice, with a soft carpet and little red chairs, but Walter and Marjorie and Priscilla wanted to go into the Children's, so Becky did too. She never saw them except in Sunday School, except when Walter came to his papa's store, next door to Becky. But she thought Marjorie's long brown curls were the prettiest things in the world, and Priscilla had a fur muff that was soft as soft. Last Sunday the teacher had taken them up into the church and made them stand up nice and tall on the platform to sing, Away in a Manger and Silent Night, Holy Night. Becky and Walter stood in the very back because they were so tall. Then the teacher said "When you come down come past this little table and get your certificates, and then next year, in the nice new year, you will go in the Children's Room for your lessons."

The church was warm all over not just near the fire, like at Grandma's. Becky hurried past the big doors that led into where the man preached, and where she waited for Grandma every Sunday after Sunday School. She went downstairs quickly. She had a new dress to get her s'tif'cate in. It was blue, with what Grandma said were red pipings, and it had red and silver buttons. And Grandma had tied a red ribbon at the top of her head, and another at the end of her braid. Becky hung her coat and other wraps up carefully, put her mittens in her sleeve, and sat down to take off Grandma's stockings. Marjorie had blue ribbons on her curls. Priscilla had a big white bow on her yellow bob. Walter had his red hair slicked down tight. Mary Sue hadn't come in yet. The teacher said they must all sit quietly until it was time to go upstairs. Becky could hardly breathe. Then she thought of something terrible. Suppose they spelled her name wrong! Then Mother wouldn't know it was truly her own s'tif'cate, because Becky's name was spelled a particular way. She went up to the teacher and waited. The teacher smelled like Mother's garden, back home, where it was never cold enough to snow. She smiled at Becky. "What is it, dear," she said.

"Did they spell my name right on my s'tif'cate " Becky asked, very low. The children laughed at the way Becky said things, sometimes.

"Why, Rebekah! Did you think... come here dear." The teacher took Becky's hand, and led her over to the windows. Jack Frost had drawn ferns and trees all over them so that you couldn't see outside. Inside there was a real fern, green, but just like the white ones that Jack Frost had drawn. Becky felt trembly inside like she did the day they told her Mother must go away to the hospital for a year, or maybe two years, and Becky must live with Grandma for a while. She looked hard at the ferns.... white ones, green one. Green one, white ones.

"You see, Rebekah, you haven't been here but a few months. Marjorie and Priscilla and Walter and Mary Sue have been in this church since they were babies on the Cradle Roll. And you don't really live here, do you? You're just visiting your grandmother, aren't you?"

Becky nodded. The trembly feeling wouldn't let her talk.

"Well, we can't give you a certificate. You can go on in the other class with the rest, because you're quite a big girl, but since you're not really a member.... "

Becky turned away. It had been bad enough to go to school to Grandma, with a little green table and a little chair instead of to the big brick school house on Prospect Street. And now.... the new blue dress was scratchy. The red ribbon was tied too tight it hurt. That was why she was crying. Daddy said no Brooks would ever cry. But she wasn't really crying. The ribbon was tied too tight, and forced the tears out of her eyes....

"Aren't they goin' to give you a s'tif'cate?" That was Walter, whispering so the teacher wouldn't hear him. "No." "Well, it's because you're a nigger," he said. Becky looked at him, in wonder. "What's a rigger?" But Walter just laughed. Becky could hear the tump-tump-tumpety of the organ upstairs. Down here it sounded just like a drum. "You're a nigger too," she told Walter. "No, I'm not. I'm not, and Marjorie's not and Priscilla, and nobody is but you... y-o-u, that's who!" Then Walter ran to get in line. Upstairs the organ was beginning to play Away in a Manger. Becky went over to the hooks and got her things. The cattle are lowing ... the baby awakes ... but Little Lord Jesus no crying he makes... She put on her sweater then her muffler, then her coat. She buttoned it high and tight, and pulled her hat down over the red ribbon. Grandma had put it on carefully so the ribbon wouldn't wrinkle. She pulled on her mittens before she thought of Grandma's stockings. She'd better not leave them. She rolled them up in a tight ball and held them in her hand. Upstairs, as she crept past the big doors, she could hear the children singing Silent Night, Holy Night. Soon they would come down to get their s'tif'cates. She wouldn't get one. Walter said, because she was a nigger. The teacher said, because she was living with Grandma. Did it make you a nigger to live with Grandma? Then Grandpa must be one, too. Maybe that was why mother never got a s'tif'cate, or Grandpa. Now Mother wouldn't get any Christmas-birthday present from Becky. Maybe she, Becky, wouldn't get anything ... did Santa Claus come to niggers? She thought he had come last year, at home, but then when she was at home, she wasn't a nigger. Nobody had ever called her one, anyway. She stopped at Haylor's Furniture Co. to look at the bed just once more. Then she cried, hard. She couldn't help it. The bed looked so lonesome. And Mother ... what could she give Mother? Mother didn't want books, she had plenty. She might ... oh, she could send Mother her skates. They were in a box in the little red room that used to be Mother's, and where Mother was it was warm. There wasn't any snow. So Mother could skate, maybe. Becky dug her heel in the hard top of the snow until it broke. Then she dug out some of the soft snow underneath and washed her face. She dried it on Grandma's stockings and went on.

At home, Grandma scolded because Becky had left Sunday School. She asked Becky questions. Why did she come back? Why didn't she have her certificate? Nonsense, she said, when Becky told her what Walter said. Then she said, "What did you say, Rebekah?" Becky told her again what Walter said. Grandma's face got mad. "Never say that word again as long as you live, Rebekah Brooks. Do you understand me?"

Grandma went out walking angrily. Becky crawled up on the arm of Grandpa's chair. It was nice and wide, for Grandpa kept all his small tools in the arms of his chair. "Grandpa ... what's a ... you know, what Walter called me?"

Grandpa wasn't like Grandma. He never asked questions, and he always answered them. But this time he was still so long Becky thought he hadn't heard. She must say it ... just once more.

"What's a ... nigger ... grandpa?"

Grandpa's face was sad. "Nothing, Sunny, dear, ... just something that is a part of some people's imaginations...." Then he looked down at Becky, and put his arm around her, tight. "Just a sort of Humpty-Dumpty idea that got pushed off its wall and is pretty badly smashed."

Becky thought she understood. Humpty-Dumpty was fat. So was she. So was Santa Claus. So Humpty-Dumpty was one too! Was...

It was warm in the sitting room. Becky put her head on Grandpa's shoulder and snuggled close. "Grandpa, is Santa Claus one, too, maybe?"

"Maybe, Sunny."

"And Little Lord Jesus ... maybe?"

"A good many people treated him like one, Sunny."

"Are you one, Grandpa ... are you, too?"

"So I've been told. Sunny ... and your Daddy, and your Mother."

"Why, then, I don't mind, not a bit!"

She slid her arm around Grandpa's neck, under his collar. She could feel herself going all limp, close against Grandpa. "In fact, I b'lieve I'm a little bit glad."

And, contented, Becky went to sleep.   [*The Crisis* 42.12 (December 1935): 362–363]

THE CONVERSION OF HARVEY

------ ⨯⨯⨯ ------

by Octavia B. Wynbush

Harvey halted suddenly in his wandering among the tangled vines, the close-grown trees and the mossy stumps of Devil's Swamp. He had penetrated to its center. He knew that by the soft, blanket-like stillness which lay over everything, as well as by the fact that he was standing under the moss-draped arms of his favorite live-oak tree.

The gay song of a late autumn bird trilled from some bough far above his head. The scarlet, yellow and brown leaves of the trees and bushes which shed their leaves in spite of the fact that they were growing in the southern part of Louisiana, floated in silent gracefulness to the rich dark mould beneath Harvey's feet.

But neither the leaves nor the song of the bird thrilled the boy as they usually did. He was all melancholy. A heavy weight lay on his spirit—the weight of sin and wretchedness. He had been attending the fall revival services at Jerusalem Church two miles down the river road, and he had been convicted of sin on the first night of the meeting.

Harvey remembered that night in the crude little church with its rough benches crowded and creaking under the bodies swaying in time to the spirituals. After the praying, the singing and the preaching, the minister had extended the invitation for all sinners to come forward. No one responding, he had asked all present to stand up. Then he had requested all who were saved to sit down, leaving the sinners exposed standing.

Under the spell of the preacher's pleas, or the cries and urgings of friends and parents, or perhaps because of embarrassment, or emotion, Thad Smith, the leader of Harvey's gang, had stepped forward and knelt at the mourner's bench. A distinct electric thrill had shot through the "Roughnecks," as this gang of boys ranging from fourteen through sixteen had styled themselves, to see the toughest member of this company surrender to prayer and entreaty.

Amid shouts of "Praise God!," "Glory hallelujah!" and "Thank you Jesus!" one by one the other Roughnecks had stepped from the crowded benches and gone to the mourner's bench in the front of the crude pulpit stand. Never 'till his dying day would Harvey forget the pandemonium that reigned as he and the rest of his companions knelt for prayer. Jumping bodies—waving arms—hysterical shouts—broken snatches of hymns—cries of women— hoarse shouts of men—and above all the booming voice of the preacher "Praise God! Praise de Lawd for his goodness! Children, let us pray!"

Under the spell of the preacher's prayer, Oliver Gray, one of the weaker and less tough- ened member of the Roughnecks had cried out and staggered to his feet. Instantly Miss Susan Helm, one of the sisters of the church had grabbed Oliver around the neck, shouting, "Honey, you is got it, you's come through. Praise His holy name!"

Then, at the close of the meeting, Oliver had been taken inside the deacons' little room of the pulpit stand for questioning. The next night he had made a brilliant and moving tes- timony of his conversion, after which statement he had been received as a candidate for membership.

One by one during the following week the other "Roughnecks" had come through, each bearing a wonderful testimony which, to quote Deacon Eldem, had "set the meeting on fire."

Now, after seven days, there remained of the original group of mourners, only Harvey. For some reason he couldn't explain he had yet failed to see the light. And tonight marked the close of the revival.

Although he could not explain his failure to "come through" with the others, Harvey's family found no difficulty in discovering a number of reasons for his dilemma.

"You ain't in earnest, boy, you cain't be," his Uncle Butler said.

"You must go to sleep when you kneel at the mourner's bench, Harvey. You know you're too lazy to stay awake 'cept only when you're moving or eating," his sister, Harriet, giggled.

"You mus' be holdin' on to the world, son," his mother had told him, "but jus' keep prayin' an' cut aloose from everything."

Boy, you is harborin' some secret sin," Granma Brown quavered, on the occasion of his weekly visit to carry her some of his mother's Saturday baking.

"You mus' be, fo' it ain't natchel fo' a young one lak' you to be so hard to come ovah. How old is you, anyhow?"

"Fourteen, going on fifteen, Big Mama," came the gloomy response.

"Fohteen, an' still fritterin' away time asettin' in school eight months outen twelve! Jean sho' be's de beatinest woman fo' havin' queah ways. She didn't git no sech schoolin' but she sho' is workin' herse'f to death for all you big strappin' young uns. Hit's a shame befo' de Lawd to have a big strappin' six-foot man fritterin' away time in school."

Harvey looked down at this long, lean length, feeling more awkward and miserable than ever. Big Mama, usually so sympathetic, had evidently got up on the wrong side of the bed today.

"I don' know if eddication an' religion mixes, nohow. I ain't never seed nothin come of eddication but stuck-upness an' high falutin' ways us folks cain't reach wid with a six-foot pole. I serously doubts whethah sich a pusson can be saved."

A cold shiver ran up and down Harvey's entire length and across his back. Not be saved! That meant eternal fire—hotter than the fiery furnace—flames mountain high—the never dying worm—devils skewering souls over the hottest part of searing flames, just as he and his friends skewered weiners on a weiner roast.

"You go 'long home now, an' pray. Put up dem books fo' a while and devote yo' time to God. Dey is what's standin' between you an' de light. Book learnin' and true religion don' set together, some how. Ain't you goin' kiss you' Big Mama goodbye?"

Harvey, already retreating from the door, came slowly back and dutifully but unenthusiastically kissed Grandma Brown goodbye. He could not for the life of him put into that kiss the tenderness and enthusiasm with which he usually bestowed it. Then he swung his ungainly length down the garden path, through the little gate and into the dusty road.

He went past the swimming place to have a swim with the other fellows who were sure to be found there. On his arrival he had found their favorite meeting place deserted. It was only then that he had remembered Thad's telling him that a good Christian didn't go swimming. With that recollection, Harvey felt more acutely, if possible, his own lost and undone condition. To want to go swimming when his very soul was hanging over Hell's dark door!

So he had straggled back from the pool to the road—knowing not whither he wanted to go. His feet, responding to some subconscious guidance, had carried him along the dusty road, past Deacon Eldem's prosperous well-cared acres, around the bend in the road and over the bridge whose rotting planks afforded precarious protection from the narrow, sluggish stream below, and led him deep into Devil's Swamp under his favorite oak.

Slumping down in an untidy heap of long legs and dangling arms, Harvey leaned his head against the trunk of the tree and pursued his disheartening thought. He recalled conversations of his parents and testimonies of others of his elders, concerning the miraculous visions and signs and omens that had attended their conversions. He remembered old Mother Henshaw's tale, told on every occasion possible since it happened nearly fifty years before,—Old Mother Henshaw, who on week days and between revivals kept the whole village agog from end to end by her gossipping and tale bearing—yet, she had seen a miraculous sight.

"As I was on my knees, down in the deeps of the woods, askin' fo' mercy on my lost an' undone soul, I heard a voice cry, 'Look an' live!'"

"I looked up, an' I saw the heavens open, an' a blindin' flash of light come down. An' the voice from some unseen angel cried once mo', 'Rise, Martha, go in peace an' sin no mo.' Brethren and Sisters, I rose to my feet. I looked at my han's an' my han's looked new! I looked at worl' aroun' me, and all de worl' was bathed in the grace an' glory of God Almighty, new streamin' from de heavens."

Harvey could hear her cracked voice taking one melody as she intoned the words to the accompanying chorus of amen's and hallelujah's, and the undertone of melodic humming of the congregation. He could see the rapt look on Mother Henshaw's withered brown face as she rocked and swayed to the rhythm of her own words.

A wicked thought flashed through Harvey's mind. How could a woman who caused so much disturbance be admitted to such a beautiful experience? He curbed the sinful thought and bowed his head in his hands. Again there beat upon his brain and through his consciousness the utter wretchedness of his own sinful mind. His thinking became less and less connected. Surely the end of all things was in sight for him, if he failed to have a vision. Hadn't all the others had visions? Hadn't Thad even seen a miraculous handwriting in the darkness? But Thad's vision was mighty like the one Farmer Stodgers had told year in and year out as long as Harvey could remember. Yet that didn't keep Thad's story from being true. With so many people in the world, maybe there weren't enough visions to go around. He, Harvey, would try his best to have one before he left the swamp.

And so he sat there in the drowsy atmosphere of the swamp, listening with unwilling ears to its thousand little noises. Surely such a place of quiet was the right place. Slowly the opiate stillness had its effect. The seeker after religious grew less rigid, and finally stretched full length at the foot of the oak.

The early dusk was creeping up from the earth, and the river mist was rising when Harvey slipped out of the swamp, thoroughly disgusted with himself, and thoroughly convinced of his doom to eternal damnation.

When he entered the kitchen of his home, his nostrils were greeted by the savory smells of the evening meal already spread on the clean blue and white-checked tablecloth. His two brothers and three sisters greeted him from their seats at the table.

"Hi, Harve' where you been all day?"

"Ain't you the lazy loafer, sneakin' off and leavin' us to do your share of the work!"

"Shet up!" His mother's voice brought sudden silence. "Cain't you all see yo' brother's still seekin' peace? Set down, Son, and eat."

"I don't want much, Ma," Harvey answered, lounging into his seat, terribly conscious of the battery of eyes trained on him. He felt that his sisters and brothers regarded him with contempt, amusement or awe, according to their several natures. His father, tall, stalwart of body and sparing of speech, seemed not to notice his son's arrival. But Harvey knew that behind that seeming indifference the "old man" was doing his own thinking.

Despite his avowal that he didn't want much, Harvey ate ravenously. A fellow still got hungry even if he was seeking religion. Twice Bennie, opposite him, kicked him on the shins under the table.

On looking up, Harvey had beheld his brother's eyes opened wide in mock horror, while his mouth pantomimed the words, "Oh, no, you didn't want much." An unholy temptation to return the kicks with compound interest surged over Harvey. But even such an act might mean the withdrawal of whatever mercy the Lord might have in mind to extend to one so sinful.

The time after supper passed at last, and Harvey was again swinging down the road under the first cool stars. The family was going as a body to the last service. Harvey walked along rapidly, head sunk on his chest, hands deep in his pockets, oblivious of the rest of the family who kept up a constant chatter in all keys. Harvey's one aim was to reach the church as quickly as possible. He wanted to take his place at the mourner's bench before there were so many spectators.

On reaching the church grounds, fairly covered with church-goers moving about in the dusk and the cool of the evening, Harvey slipped through the throng, as inconspicuously as possible. He dreaded being stopped and questioned as to the progress he was making in being converted. He was glad to find only five or six people in the long, narrow, low-roofed room which would soon be stifling with the heat and the smells of closely-packed bodies.

By the glow of the oil lamps suspended from the rafters in the ceiling, and hanging from wall-brackets on the sides of the room, Harvey strode past the rough-hewn planks set on trestles that served as benches, and sat down on the very front bench dedicated to mourners. He must pray tonight as never before. If this revival closed on him as still a sinner, he would be disgraced forever, an outcast from Thad and his other pals, a laughing stock in the community.

His thoughts turned to Thomas Leppard. Thomas had come through four revivals unsaved. At first the community had regarded him as an object of pity, then of despair, and finally as an object of contempt and humor. Thomas was now the standing joke of the community. Harvey winced. He could never stand to be in Thomas' shoes, but Thomas did not seem to mind.

But this wasn't praying! He must pray. And he began to whisper over and over, "Lord have mercy on me, a sinner."

So rapt did he become in the prayer, that the first indication he had of the fact that the church had filled, was in the first notes of a spiritual.

> Lord I want to be a Christian,
> In-a my heart, in-a my heart.

Voice after voice took up the strain until the raftered ceiling rang with the refrain,

> In-a my heart, in-a my heart
> Lord, I want to be a Christian,
> In-a my heart.

Through the stanza voicing the wish

> to be like Jesus,
> I-na my heart, in-a my heart,

and the one,

> I don't want to be like Judas
> In-a my heart, in-a my heart....

went the song, and when the last strains had quivered to rest in the furthermost corners of the church, Harvey heard the voice of his Uncle Billy's wife, Rose, raised in prayer. Through his bemused brain floated snatches of her phrases, time-worn, but sweet to Harvey every time he heard them.

"Lord, we thy servants come to thee, like empty pitchers before a full fountain, waiting to be filled."

Later on, her familiar petition for the preacher: "Bless this thy servant that shall break the Bread of Life to us.—Crown his head with wisdom from on high.—Rough-shoe him with the preparation of the Gospel—Put the silver trumpet of salvation in his mouth that he may call dying sinners to repentance."

Her words for the sinners sank deep in Harvey's heart.

"Have mercy, Master, have mercy, on those po' sinners hangin' over hell's dark door,—who are on the road to destruction and seem to love their distance well. An' specially, dear Jesus, come down and touch the hearts of those po' mourners aroun' the mercy seat tonight. Put the live coals of the grace into their hearts that they may use and give Thee the glory for evermore."

She closed with the request for a general blessing for "all I'm duty bound to pray fo',", and the hope for her own final rest, half-spoken, half-sung in rhythmic strains:

"Now, Father, when I'm done comin' an' done goin', in that great gettin' up mornin', when the big bell tones in Zion to raise the quick an' the dead, give me a resting place to rest my weary head forevermo.'"

The whole lyric utterance, intoned as it was in a voice beautifully mellow, and accompanied by a subdued undercurrent of humming in rising and falling cadences by the congregation, and interspersed with the shouts of some of the members, helped increase Harvey's trance-like state between despair and ecstasy.

Two or three more spirituals were raised at the same time, the victory going to the most persistent and most powerful-lunged of the contestants, and the building reverberated once more with the strains of "Let my people go."

Through the mazy spell the singing and the prayers and the continuous undercurrent of rhythmic humming had woven around him, Harvey finally heard the words of the preacher, echoing like peals of thunder and crashing through the building like sharp flashes of swift lightning. His picture of God's mercy to the three sinners on the mourner's bench was the first knowledge Harvey had that two other lost souls were keeping him company. Peeping through the fingers of the hand supporting his bowed head, he saw a girl and a boy at the far end of the bench.

"And, God, friends, is settin' without a doubt, on his great white throne tonight, along side the battlements of glory. An' on one side, stands de angel wid de great trumpet in his han's—de trumpet that's to wake de quick and de daid on dat las' day. An' de angel wid de trumpet says, 'Lewd, mus' I blow dis trumpet?' an de good God say, 'Not yet. Not yet! Wait twell dese po' los' sinful souls at de mourners bench in Jerusalem Church come home!'

"An' on de other side of God's white throne stans de angel wid Death, Hell an' Destruction in his han's, de Angel wid de vials of God's wrath. An' de angel says, 'Lewd, mus' I let loose destruction on dis wicked worl' below?' An' God Almighty says, 'Not yet! Not yet! Wait till my po' los' lambs come home!'

"But brothers an' sisters, he ain't always goin' to keep on extendin' mercy. He's goin to get tired of havin' sinnahs turn der backs on him an' still crucifyin' his only begotten Son. An' some of dese days dis ol' worl's going to reel an' rock from the very foundations of hell, to de battlements of glory. An' sinful men and women is goin' call on de rocks an' de mountings to fall on dem an' hide dem f'um de wrath o' God, but God ain't goin' pay 'em no mind. An' 'Too late! too late!' will be de cry of souls hurled into everlasting fire, fire where the worm never dies, an' life is never quenched."

Sinking deeper and deeper under the spell of the magnificent, full cadences of the preacher's voice and the ejaculations and rhythmic "moaning" of the congregation which had swelled from a soft monotone to an antiphonal accompaniment, Harvey became aware after a while that the sermon had reached its conclusion. The preacher had called for members of the congregation to come forward and labor individually with the mourners.

Aunt Rose stepped to Harvey's side and knelt with him on the hard, bare planks. Deacon Mayberry raised his voice in prayer. The congregation began its antiphonal chorus. A sudden cry from the girl who knelt beside Harvey. She sprang to her feet clapping her hands and shrieking in ecstasy. The chanting accompaniment to the Deacon's prayer grew louder and more melodic. The boy at the other end of the bench staggered to his feet and was surrounded by a group of people who had surged forward from the congregation.

Harvey's heart beat wilder and wilder. His brain whirled faster and faster. "Lord have mercy! Lord have mercy on me, a poor sinner!"

Aunt Rose prayed louder and louder. The group that had surrounded the two converts joined their prayers with hers and pressed in a suffocating semi-circle as close to them as possible. The old building rocked and swayed with the incessant patting of many feet keeping time to the rhythm of their own ejaculations and responses.

Suddenly the preacher strode through the semi-circle raising his voice in the melody:

> Ride on King Jesus!
> Ride on King Jesus!
> Ride on conquering king
> I want to go to heaven in the morning.

Bending over Harvey, he laid his broad, strong, black hand on the boy's head.

The experience of the preacher had taught him that, in most "stubborn" cases, the touch of his hand on the head of the mourner provided as a last resort, the necessary stimulus for conversion. But to Harvey, the heavier the moist fat hand pressed his head, the farther and farther within himself shrank that elusive something for which he wished to find expression.

Finally, after the strain had become unbearable, he rose to his feet, hot and cold by turns with the daring of a sudden resolution. The shouts and cries of the congregation became redoubled in intensity.

"Glory, hallelujah!"

"One mo' soul snatched f'um de jaws of hell!"

"Thank you, Jesus!"

The whole church surged forward to shake the convert's hands, but Harvey held them off in desperation, shaking his head and trying to make himself heard above the general clamor. The preacher raised his hand for silence.

"Brothers and sisters, dis young man got somethin' to tell you. He wants to tell you of his crossin' ovah—"

"No! No I don't!" Harvey's voice had the boldness of despair, and the shrillness of courage screwed to the sticking point. Sharp ejaculations and cries of wonder greeted his words. The preacher thrust to him sharply.

"What's dat you say?"

"I—I don't want to tell them I've crossed over cause I ain't. I can't do it. Don't pray for me any more—least not tonight. I can't stand it." Then Harvey bolted down the aisle and out of the door.

Straight home he fled, and had been there an eternity, locked in his room, when his sister called through the keyhole,

"Harve! Gramma and Dad and Mother want you. They're in the kitchen."

In a moment Harvey found himself standing in the kitchen staring toward the table where sat his parents and his grandmother gazing up him with conflicting expressions on their faces.

Harvey faced them sullenly. He wasn't afraid—no, he wasn't afraid. Let them do what they darn please. He hadn't felt what the other mourners said they had, and he wasn't going to lie about it. Not that his friends had lied. Oh, no, he didn't mean that, but to say he had felt the spirit when he hadn't—well, that would be lying against God, and that meant damnation, sure and certain.

It was Grandma Brown who, as usual, took charge of the family council. From her seat at the head of the table she began to speak, pointing her finger at the culprit.

"Boy, you is a disgrace to yo' ma an' yo' pa an' me. Don' you stan' starin' at me lak dat, sah! Wheh is you manners? Look a dat boy, Jean! He ain't got de grace to bow his head in shame. He look at me jes' as brazen as if he was my equal in age an' Christian experiences. How dare you, sah? If I was in yo' place, I'd keep my eyes on de groun' and crawl in de presence o' God's children, I would.

"But you cain't do nothin' wid dis present generation. Dey haids ain't dry fo' dey begin actin' high an' mighty, an' flyin' in de face of Providence. Dat's what comes o' all dis yeah book-learnin'. I done tole you all along, Jean, to stop sendin' dat boy to school. Nothin' good nevah come o' no sech truck. Look at him now! Hardenin' his heart and stifferin' his neck against de true religion an' de voice o' God! Settin' all through dis revival, an' lettin' all de good sermons Rebben Smith been preachin' run offen his mind like water offen a duck's back.

"He's disgracin' de family name, he lets all dat trash gitin' converted while he jes' sets down. Ef he was my son, I'd teah up ev'y book in ten miles o' him, put him to plowin' wid his pa, an' set his feet in de path o' righteousness, dat's what I' do."

Having exhausted her breath, her vocabulary and her wrath, Grandma Brown sat back, queenlike, in the old split hickory chair, folded her arms and gazed through and beyond Harvey into space.

Unable to make up her mind, Jean looked distractedly from her mother to her husband. In every controversy she sided with the most persistent and most vociferous speaker. Reuben, her husband, until now calmly silent, turned to Harvey and beckoned him to the chair at the other end of the table, facing Grandma Brown.

"Set down, Son," he said in a kindly voice.

Grandma Brown shrieked in fury, and rose to her feet, all a-tremble.

"Set down, an' in front of me? That impudent young rascal what don't know enough to look humble when he's bein' chastised? Set down wid me, a true believer, when his own heart's too hard to be touched? Well, of all de mistakes! No wondah dis young generation goin' to de debbil! I'll trouble you fo' my hat and walking stick, Jean."

"Don't go, Ma! Harvey needn't set down. Wait, an' Reuben'll go home with you, soon!" Jean put her hand on her mother's arm.

Reuben's fist rang on the table, making both women jump.

"Ashes to ashes an' dust to dust ain't been said over me yet, so I guess I'm still head of dis house! When time comes one of my children cain't set at the table wid one of my guests— well—I guess it's time fo' that guest to—depart!"

"Reuben!" Jean s eyes were wide with fear and astonishment.

Grandma Brown stood frozen with surprise. In all her eighteen years acquaintance with her son-in-law she had never heard him speak as long or so forcibly. He had always been "easy" to get along with. Realizing that to stay would be to sacrifice her dignity, the old woman gestured feebly to her daughter for her stick and hat. Receiving them, she hastily jammed the hat on her white head, grasped her stick, and, with as much hauteur as she could muster, strode out slamming the door behind her.

"Now, don' you worry," Reuben said, seeing tears in Jean's eyes. "She'll git over it an' come around tomorrow out o' curiosity to see if I done whaled the life out o' Harvey, or jes' pitch him in the Mississippi, instead. Now, you go to bed, an' me an' Harvey'll talk this thing over."

Bewildered completely, Jean turned to go, patting Harvey on the shoulder as she passed him, and turning an imploring look on her husband, over the boy's shoulder, as she passed into the adjoining room.

"Well, Son, since we got rid o' them women-folks, I guess we can talk this thing over man to man."

The kindness in his father's voice put Harvey at ease. He had been as astonished as the others at the sudden outbreak from his taciturn parent. As he approached the table to sit down, a passing breeze blew through the curtains of the kitchen, parting them and revealing the white light of the moon.

"Gee, Dad. I wish we could talk outside!" The words spilled out before Harvey had time to wonder what his father would think of a boy who was carried away by the sight of the moonlight.

"Jes' thinkin' the same myself. Let's go out."

Opening the door, Harvey allowed his father to pass out first, and then followed him. They stood a moment on the porch, looking out on the night scene. Before them, across the road, was the black line of trees and bushes marking the river's edge; to their right, the black trees and denseness of the swamp; to their left the fields under cultivation.

Together they passed down the steps of the porch, and walked slowly to the fence in front of the house.

"Well, Harvey, Grandma Brown thinks you've disgraced us, but I'd rather you acted as you did, than lied about it. At least you're honest."

"Thanks, Dad. I—I tried awfully hard, but something just stuck inside me. I couldn't see any vision; I couldn't hear any voices, an' I couldn't feel like the others said they did, even when Preacher Smith put his hands on my head. I give up, Dad. Guess I'm goin' to be another Thomas Leppard."

"No, I don't think that. Thomas never was in earnest, accordin' to my way of thinkin'. He liked bein' made over—havin' people notice him, an' he took that way to get it. But I been noticin' you. You is in earnest, I see that. No, you ain't goin' be another Leppard. You ain't got the no 'count blood in you that's in him."

"Well, somehow I feel pretty much ashamed. I tried hard, and I can't help wondering why I couldn't feel religious like the rest. I went into the swamp today to—to see. Dad, does everybody have to go through the same experience?"

"I been wonderin' about that same thing for years, Harvey, an' I been studyin' these folks that gets religion every revival, for the past thirty years, an' this has been my observations. Some of those that has the long-windedest tales to tell about what they's felt and what they's seen, stay pretty straight for five or six months—an' some not that long. Then, the next things anybody knows, they's back to all the tricks they knew before they confessed religion, with a few fancy ones added.

"Then, I've seen some who jes' had a talk with their Maker earnest and quiet like, an' who didn't have no long, fancy tale to tell, join the church and go about in they quiet way doin' more good fo' the kingdom an' God with one finger than the whole passel of loud speakers put together."

"Then we all don't have to come the same way?"

"It's like this, to me, Son. Jes' as God don' use the same way to make a summer day pretty, He don' use the same way wid us. Sometimes He sends lightnin', thunder, and rain to make the grass greener and the flowers prettier—sometimes he sends jes' a soft, gentle shower, an' again he jes' sends a tiny breeze to ripple the grass an' pass over the petal of a flower, givin' it color an' beauty you'd never guess was ther. That's jes' the way He comes to different ones of us, to my way of thinkin'."

"'Taint jes' a ticklin' good feelin' makes religion, nohow. When you get so you understan' God ain't settin' off somewhere manufacturin' visions an' feelin's an' experiences to order for us, but that He's filled the worl' with visions of Hisse'f in everything that's in the earth, an' sent us His message in the water, the breeze, the sky, why I reckon you're on the right track."

Harvey drew in his breath—the first light-hearted breath he had drawn in days. Turning to his father, he cried:

"After all, Dad, getting converted is a matter between God and me, ain't it? Whatever way it comes, I can't make a mistake when it does come. Look at that moon! Don't it seem like it's just hanging low tonight to tell me God understands my heart?"

[*The Crisis* 43.3 (March 1936): 76–78, 93–94]

MOB MADNESS

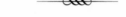

by Marion Cuthbert

Lizzie watched Jim stir his coffee. Her eyes were wide with fever and horror. Around and around he stirred, and the thin stuff slopped over and filled the saucer. But he did not notice because he was talking to their son.

"Shore, we got 'im at the very spot I showed you and Jeff. Lem would o' slit his throat right then, but the fellers back on the pike was waitin' an' wanted to be in on it, too, so we drug 'im out o' the brush. The boys wanted ter git at 'im to once, but some o' the more experienced on 'em cooled us down. You was there last night, so you know as much o' that end o' it as anybody."

He turned to the neglected coffee now and downed it in great gulps. The thirteen year old boy watched, his face set in a foolish grin of admiration and wonder.

"Jeff said he heard a man down to the square say you all got the wrong nigger. Said this one didn't do it."

"Guess he did it all right. An' if he didn't, one of the black—stretched out Ole Man Dan'l, an' the smell o' this one roastin' will teach the rest o' 'em they can't lay hands on a white man, b'Gawd!"

"Les see the toe again."

The man took a filthy handkerchief out of his overalls pocket, and unwrapped carefully a black object.

Lizzie swayed, and fearing to fall against the hot woodstove, sank into a chair.

Then Jim and the boy finished breakfast and went out.

For a long time Lizzie sat in the chair. After a while she got up shakily and went in the other room. Little Bessie was still sleeping heavily. She was ailing and her mother had been up with her most of the night.

But she would have been up all of that night, that terrible night, anyway. Neighbors had run in on their way to the square to ask her if she was not going, too.

She was not going.

Jim had come in long past midnight, little Jim with him. His eyes were bloodshot. She would have believed him drunk, but there was no smell of liquor on him. The boy was babbling incoherently.

"Maw, you should a seed it!"

Big Jim shut him up. The two fell into bed and slept at once.

After a time it was day, and Lizzie moved like a sick woman to get breakfast.

She stood looking down now on little Bessie. The child's yellow hair had fallen across her face. This she brushed back and looked for a long time on the thin little oval of a face. The purple veined eyelids were closed upon deep blue-gray eyes. Lizzie's own mother had said she was the living image of little Bessie when she was a child. Delicate and finicky. But when she was sixteen she had married six foot, red-faced Jim. He was always rough, but men seemed all like that. She did not know then that he would....

After a little the child awoke. She gave her some breakfast, but would not let her get up. Allie Sneed from next door ran in.

"Everything's as quiet as kin be this morning. Not a nigger on the street Lizzie, you missed it last night!"

Jim drove the truck for the store. He had gone to Terryville and did not come for lunch. Little Jim came in swallowed his food and was off. It was cold, so Lizzie kept the woodstove going smartly. She held little Bessie in her arms and rocked back and forth. All day she had not eaten, but she was not hungry. She rocked back and forth...

... they got It down in the brush on the other side of the branch ... they took It into the woods ... at dark they tied It to a car and dragged It back to the town ... at the square they piled up a huge bonfire ...

... Jim had helped by bringing crates from the store...

... they had cut parts of It away...

... Jim had something black in a handkerchief...

... then they put what was left of It on the fire ... their house was quite a way from the square, but she had heard the shouting. Every house around was emptied...

... once her brother had had an argument with another man. They fought, and pulled knives on each other. Both were cut pretty badly and they feared the other man would die. But she never shrank from her brother after that. All hot words and anger. He did not shout, crazy. Afterwards he did not brag...

... they did not fight It ... they caught It like an animal in the brush ... if It had been an animal they would have killed It at once... but This they took in the woods...before they killed It outright they cut off Its fingers and toes...

... Jim had something black in a handkerchief .

She put the child back in bed and went out in the yard to pump some water. She leaned her hot face against the porch post. In the dark by the fence something moved. It came nearer.

"Mis' Lizzie? O my Gawd, Mis' Lizzie! Dey burned me out las' night. Ah bin hidin' in de shacks by de railroad. Waitin' fo 'de dahk. You allays good to us po' cullud people. Hope yo' Jim put me in de truck an' take me to Terryville tonight. Tell 'im he'p me, Mis' Lizzie, tell 'im he'p me!"

She could only stare at her. The voice of the black woman seemed far away, lost in the shouting in her head.

Their home was quite a way from the square, but she had heard the shouting.

The voice of the black woman seemed to go away altogether. So Lizzie went inside and began supper.

Soon after Jim came home and ate his supper. He was weary and dour. As soon as he was through he went to bed, and the boy, too.

Lizzie sat by the fire. Little Bessie was better and sleeping soundly.

... if Jim had not been so tired he would have come to her...

... he did not yet know she was going to have another child. This child, and little Bessie, and little Jim, had a father who helped catch a Thing in the brush... and cut off the quivering flesh. It seemed that all the men in the town had thought this a good thing to do. The women, too. They had all gone down to the square...

... little Jim was like his father. The other day he had spoken sharp to her. As big Jim so often did. He said she was too soft and finicky for her own good. Most boys were like Jim. When little Bessie grew up she would marry a boy like this...

... when little Bessie grew up...

... some boy who could touch her soft, fair flesh at night, and go forth into the day to hunt a thing in the brush, and hack at its flesh alive...

Lizzie looked and looked at the child. She remembered things which she had thought were true when she was a child. She was a woman now, and she knew that these things were not true. But she had thought they were true when she was a child.

The fire in the stove went down, then out. She made no effort to replenish it. Toward morning she went to the table drawer and took something out. She went in the other room and looked down on the uncouth figures of the sprawling man and boy. It was over the boy that she finally bent, but she straightened at once, remembering that the man and the boy were one. So she turned to the little girl, and the lifted blade of steel did not gleam any more.

Jim had had a good rest and awakened early. He found the bodies, already cold.

When the shock of the first terror let him find his voice he declared he would kill with his own hands every black man, woman and child within a hundred miles of the town. But the sheriff made him see that it was not murder. All this she had done with her own hand.

"She didn't touch me, ner the boy. When they go mad like this, sometimes they wipes out all."

Out in the yard Allie Sneed said to an awestruck group, "I knew it was somethin' wrong with her when she held back from seein' the burnin'. A rare, uncommon sight, that, and she hid in her house missin' it!"   [*The Crisis* 43.4 (April 1936): 108, 114]

LADY BLANCHE AND THE CHRIST: AFTER THE MANNER OF THE MEDIAEVAL TALE

by Octavia Beatrice Wynbush

The minstrel's song had ceased, and the last harpstring had trembled into silence. Sir Rupert, the Lady Blanche, and their laughter Hildegarde, and all the household roused and shook themselves as people waking from a dream, and gazed into the great hearth-fire in silence.

And Sir Rupert said, "'Tis a strange tale ye tell, and a strange song ye sing, Minstrel. Your lodging from the bitter cold, and your Christmas feast at our board tomorrow shall be your reward."

Then, he turned to his serfs and thralls who sat apart around the roaring fire, to hear the teller of tales and the singer of songs, and bade them go and take with them the singer.

When they had gone, Sir Rupert said lo Lady Blanche, "Why art thou so quiet? Likest thou not the minstrel's song?"

And Lady Blanche answered, "Aye, I liked it over much. Many a song have I heard, but never one like this."

"But it is not so much the song," spoke the little Hildegarde, "as it is the minstrel. Sawest thou ever a minstrel like him?"

"Yes, that is it," quoth the Lady Blanche. "The minstrel! A man as uncommon as the song he sang."

"He sang of the great oak, and said that any one might see the Christ under its branches tonight, the eve of Christmas," whispered the little maid.

"And at what a price," said Sir Rupert.

"To give him the thing one holds most precious," mused the Lady Blanche.

"Nay, not that," quoth Sir Rupert, "not that. He said the thing hardest to give."

"Is it not the same?" asked the little maid.

"Methinks not," said Sir Rupert. "In my mind there is a difference. But it is time to go to bed, ere Christmas Day dawn and find us here."

And as they left the hall, Sir Rupert and the little Hildegarde talked and laughed, but the Lady Blanche said naught, for she was wrapped in deepest thought.

The rush lights had long ago ceased to glow. Only the Yule-log burned brightly on the hearth when the Lady Blanche came back into the now-dark hall. And she was clad in warmest garments from head to foot, for she would go to the great fire-oak, to see the Christ of whom the minstrel told. And ready was she to give the hardest gift the Christ might ask, if he would bless her soul.

She drew the well-wrought bolts and walked into the night. The wild wind blew, the white snow swirled, and the frost gleamed on the frozen earth. The moon shone full and bright, and by its light the lady wended her way to the great oak. Straight and strong it stood, where four roads met—a broad road which men said led northward to an unknown land, and southward even into Rome;—a narrow, winding road on which the knights went venturing east and west.

The Lady Blanche smiled when she stood beneath the bare and black branches of the oak. Right glad she was for shelter from the wind and the snow. And glad again she was, for she would see the Christ, and receive his blessing.

So by the oak's strong stem the lady waited, saying her prayers the while.

And lo, when the midnight came, the whirling wind died down, and swirling snow lay suddenly at rest. And across the snow, to eastward, came the tinkle of a far-off bell. The Lady Blanche looked up from her prayers, and a strange sight did she behold.

Across the snow there came a man, the likes whereof the fair lady had never seen. Tall he was, and straight. Broad of chest and strong and shapely of limb. But the lady marveled at his dress and at his features, for he was clad in flowing robes of white, and around his head was wound a turban of white cloth, pinned with a crescent moon. His face was swarthy, even unto brownness, and his lips uttered strange words.

When he had come to Lady Blanche, he did obeisance, bowing himself low, yet there was nothing servile in the gesture, nor was it one of fulsome flattery. And though he spoke in a strange tongue, yet could the lady understand his greeting, that it was full of friendliness.

Now a great loathing filled the lady fair, so that she turned her from the brown-faced man, and said, "Begone! I wait the coming of the Christ."

And even as she spoke, the white-robed man moved on across the snow.

Then clasped the lady her great cloak closer about her, and waited wondering. Nor had she waited long, when down the self-same road the man had trod, a woman came. Small she was, and curiously dressed. Her long black hair was piled high upon her head, and pierced with many a jeweled pin. Her shapely hands were crossed upon her breast, upon a flowing, widesleeved silken robe embroidered in golden threads, and a wondrous yellow cast was her face.

When she came near the Lady Blanche, she stopped and smiled; and though her tongue was strange, the lady understood her words a greeting full of cheer and goodliness.

But though the woman's rich embroidered robes and softlyuttered words did tell her high born state, yet did the Lady Blanche withhold her speech for very scorn, and turn away her high-held head.

"I wish," cried she, "the Christ would come!"

With slow step the woman in the flowing robe passed on and went the way the turbaned man had gone.

Then stood the Lady Blanche, pressed close against the huge oak's sturdy stem, and held her fur cloak close. Down the four roads she looked, north, south, east, west.

Then as she gazed down the northern road, a cry arose behind the tree. Then stepped the lady toward the sound, and there behold a sight! A child, all black, with close-curled hair, stood with bare feet and ragged garments. And he did cry and piteously beg for food and warmth. When he saw the lady come around the tree, he started toward her.

"Away! Go to your own," cried Lady Blanche. "I wait the Christ. Away!"

With a deep cry the black child turned and walked into the night.

Then, sudden on the lady's ear, a burst of music fell. It was the self-same song the minstrel sang, a wondrous melody, sweet yet so very sad. And sadder now it seemed to Lady Blanche, than when she heard at her hearth-stone.

"Perhaps the minstrel too, would see the Christ," she mused, as the sound came nearer.

Then the minstrel came in view, harping his strange, sad melody. And by the lady's side he stopped.

"What seek ye Lady Blanche," he asked.

"The Christ, of whom ye told, good minstrel," spoke the lady.

"And have ye not seen him, Lady fair?" asked the minstrel.

"Nay, though I have waited long, and am cold, even in my warmest cloak," answered Lady Blanche.

"Did no one pass this live-long night?" asked the minstrel.

"Aye. Three people passed, but they did not count," answered the lady.

"Who were these people who did not count?" The minstrel's voice was stern.

"The first to pass was a man. All brown of skin he was, and dressed in flowing robes, and wearing on his head a turban pinned with a crescent moon," made answer the lady.

"Spake ye to the man, fair lady?" asked the minstrel.

"Nay. He was not of my kith and kind," quoth the lady, upraising her hands.

"And who passed next?" and the minstrel drew a deep, sad note from his harp.

"A woman passed," answered Lady Blanche, "a woman yellow of skin, and wearing robes richly-wrought with threads of gold."

"Gave ye the woman a sister's kiss?" asked the minstrel, and his voice was low and kind.

"Oh, nay! My kiss was for the Christ!" cried the lady, "and the woman—she was not my kind."

"And then who passed?" the minstrel asked, and he drew a note from his harp that was deep and sad, so that it brought tears to the lady's eyes.

"A child, all black, stood just behind this tree," answered the lady, "and he was hungry and cold."

"Fed ye this child, and gave ye him a cloak" asked the minstrel.

"Nay! He belonged not to my kind," answered Lady Blanche.

Then did a wondrous thing come to pass. The minstrel threw his harp on the ground, and where it fell sprang up a bush with deep green leaves and berries like two drops of deep red blood. And the minstrel grew terrible to behold. His stature was greater than the stature of any one on earth. Around him floated robes whiter than the sitting snow, and seamless from top to hem. And a great light shone around him, and he spoke in a voice soft and sad, yet terrible, like the sounds he had drawn from his harpstrings.

And Lady Blanche fell on her knees, and hearkened to the words he spoke:

"Know ye, proud lady, that the Christ ye seek has passed ye thrice this night?

Each time he asked for the thing that is hardest for you to give, and that is love to all mankind. Know ye not, fair lady, that your Christ saves all manner of men? Then henceforth see ye me in all men. As long as ye live, remember what the minstrel sang at your hearthstone; Christ blesses those who give what is hardest to give."

Then the sad voice ceased; there was a rustle as of a wind of spring, and then the silence once more. When Lady Blanche unveiled her eyes, she was alone. Then with slow steps she went back to her proud castle. But ever since that night, the gates swing wide to all men, whatsoever their kind.   [*The Crisis* 44.1 (January 1937): 11, 21]

THE RETURN OF A MODERN PRODIGAL

—∞∞∞—

by Octavia B. Wynbush

The Illinois Central Flyer spun along the gleaming steel rails, farther and farther from the chill, blustery shores of Lake Michigan, deeper and deeper into the balmy warmth of the southland. Past Memphis, past rich fields of cotton, sugar cane and rice, deep, threatening swamp, and romantic vistas of old plantation mansions dating 'way before the days of the Civil War, rushed the train, while the wheels hummed and sang to the steel rails.

To Slim Sawyer, reared back in the Jim Crow smoker, his hat on the side of his head, a huge cigar in his mouth, and his feet planted comfortably on the cushion of the seat in front of him, the wheels spinning on the steel rails were singing, "Going home, Going home!"

There was a pleasurable exhilaration in listening to their steely song, an exhilaration mixed at the same time with a heaviness and an apprehension that was growing momentarily with the shortening of the miles between him and his destination. Slim was wondering. Would his folks know him after twenty-five years? He would know them, without a doubt.

His hand strayed to the side of his head uncovered by his hat, and felt the close-curled hair that covered it. He smiled as he had smiled a hundred times after performing the same act. A crop of hair felt good after a man had been forced to keep his head clean-shaven for nineteen years. Slim jerked himself out of his reverie and looked around with the air of one who fears he has whispered a secret too loudly. No one was paying him any attention. Evidently nobody had heard his thoughts.

Staring out the window at the fields, trees, mules and cabins that went spinning by, Slim saw back and beyond them all, the panorama of his own life unrolling. It had been boyish restlessness and dissatisfaction that had shaped his life into what it now was.

He saw himself as he must have looked at fifteen—like that youngster out there, leaning against the fence, watching the train rush by. He must have been like that—a tall, slim, youngster out of whose face blackened by the intimate acquaintance with the Louisiana sun, shone two eyes eager and alive with the dreams and longings of youth. Many a time when unobserved by his father, he had let the mules stand idle in the field at plowing time while he leaned against the fence and stared down the road that wound away into the distance. It always fascinated him, that road, yellow with powdery dust in the dry season, churned into black, sticky mud in the wet.

There, somewhere at the end of that road has a railway station where trains came puffing in three times a day and once at night. And these trains carried people away from the never-ending toil of the plantation. Somewhere in the great unknown these trains stopped at New Orleans, Memphis, Chicago and God only knew where else in that heaven called the North.

One day in plowing time the lure of the road had proved too strong for his boyish imagination. As he came opposite the fence on this particular day, he had dropped the reins of the mules, bolted over the fence, and taken to the road. His action was entirely unpremeditated, and was simply the result of dreams, and the day which had beckoned him with teasing finger ever since he had risen at dawn.

Once in the road there was no turning back. Too many things lured him on. Every curve in the road, hidden by trees and clumps of bushes, hinted of something more alluring around the bend. That night he had slept in the station where he hid behind a pile of old boxes. At day-break he had started on his trek to New Orleans. Slim smiled as he pictured the dirty ragged black boy who had ventured from house to house begging food, and who had slept in field corners at night, and had stolen from those fields under the shadow of night what he needed to eat.

The man's smile was sadly reminiscent as his mind flew back over the many vicissitudes through which he had passed during the following years spent in New Orleans, in Memphis, in Chicago and Detroit. His mouth twisted wryly as he thought of Detroit. That city had been the scene of his undoing. A cloud of sadness and of shame descended upon him. Drink— a fight—fumes of poisonous whisky clearing away from his brain to reveal to him the still, dead form of a man they said he had killed—the trial—the cold pronouncement of the sentence by the judge—nineteen wasted years in the penitentiary, his time had been shortened to nineteen years because of his good behavior. He had spent the year following his release trying to lose the prison traces. His hand involuntarily went back to the hair on his head.

He wondered how the old folks would take his return. He did not wonder whether they were still alive. His first concern after leaving prison was to find that out by devious secret means. They were just as poor now as they were the day he had walked off. Certainly they were feebler. The years and the hard, back-breaking, spirit-grinding toil had taken care of that.

Slim smiled broadly. In an inside belt he was carrying enough money to put his parents on Easy Street the rest of their lives. Bootlegging had been the easiest and the most profitable business he had found open to him after his release. He had saved nearly every penny of his profits for the old folks.

The shadows cast by the coaches were gradually lengthening; the sky was growing less and less light. Evening was coming, quickly to be followed by the night. One more night in the uncomfortable coach, with his long body doubled "S" fashion on two seats in lieu of a berth, and he would be in New Orleans. From that point a local would carry him by slow, perspiring stages to the station in which he had slept the night he had run away.

The lights in the coach flared up. Night had fallen. Slim's preparations for retiring were simple. He removed his hat and placed it in the rack above him. Then he threw the remaining part of his cigar out of the window, removed his shoes and accommodating his long body to the two seats drew over him a lightweight overcoat to keep out the chill of the night.

It was six o'clock the next morning when the train pulled into the station in New Orleans. As he stepped from his coach Slim saw the local on the next track, getting up steam to pull out. Quickly he was aboard and settled in a seat. This train did not move with the speed of the flyer he had just quitted. The wheels, however, sang, "Going home," but with a difference. It was like a funeral dirge now. "I feel more like a corpse than a livin' man," Slim muttered, wiping his face with a large fancy silk handkerchief.

The day was exceedingly warm and as the local crept from station to station, stopping often for a longer period than it was in motion, the oppressive heat weighed on Slim to such an extent that it gave him an oppressed feeling. Somehow, the nearer he was borne to his home, the farther away he felt from all that home represented. His mother, a saintly well-meaning woman; his father, a practical, hard-headed man who worshipped his God and measured mankind by the Ten Commandments.

The utter simplicity of their faith, the purity of their lives, the shining whiteness of them served only to make his misspent years stand out boldly black and ugly. His hand surreptitiously patted the money belt. How would these dollars be received? He had concocted a tale that to his ears had seemed plausible enough when he boarded the train in Chicago.

But now at the thought of looking into his mother's calm, trusting eyes and telling the carefully planned lie, a feeling of nausea swept over him. Under the keen, shrewd, soul-scrutinizing eyes of his father, the best planned tale would seem weak and futile.

The tortuous hours crawled on. Noon had enveloped and smothered the passengers with its heat, and the slight breeze that had sprung up drove clouds of smoke and showers of cinders into the windows of the Jim Crow car. Slim noted with increasing irritation that his cuffs, collars and shirt front were growing momentarily dingier. Every now and then he removed his hat and carefully flicked the soot and cinders from its surface. He sighed with relief when the conductor shouted the name of the station.

Gathering his luggage, Slim made his way to the platform and sprang to the ground as soon as the train stopped. He looked around him. The dingy unpainted shed of a station that had once sheltered him was gone. In its place arose a trim bright yellow building bearing on one side the legend, "Laurelville." There were two waiting rooms, also, one bearing the sign "White Waiting Room," the other, "Colored Waiting Room."

The next question was how to get to the plantation on which his father lived. Slim did not relish the long walk through the yellow dust. Surely there must be someone with a wagon and mule, who wouldn't mind earning a dollar by carrying him up that road.

He walked around the corner of the station, and there came upon a crowd of young men lolling and sprawling in all degrees of idleness and inertia. Looking at their dull, stagnant, yellow, brown and black faces. Slim reflected that here, but by the grace of chance, was Slim Sawyer. Singling out one of the group he walked up to him and spoke.

"Buddy, do you know where I can get a wagon to carry me out to Logan's plantation?"

The fellow questioned spat carefully into the dust beyond Slim, wiped his mouth on his ragged shirt cuff and answered, "Sho.' I'll take y' in my ole flivver. It's jes' around' the cornah behin' de station. Come, git in."

Slim followed his guide to the rear of the station, where stood the great, great grandfather of all flivvers. Battered, dented, with great gaping wounds in the top, and every shred of upholstery vanished from the interior, it looked entirely incapable of motion. Gingerly Slim deposited himself on the front seat through which a broken spring protruded. He made an effort to keep the spring between the owner and himself.

After much cranking, kicking, and coughing, the ancient chariot started off with the noise of a cannon shot. Its bounds and leaps at the starting made Slim think of a passage his father had once spelled out in the family Bible—something about horses pawing in the valley.

The light yellow dust rose in clouds from the dry road, sprinkling the vehicle and its occupants with a fine yellow film. It seeped between Slim's lips, making his mouth feel rough and gritty. He was thankful for the dust, though, for it kept his companion from asking the very personal questions that every native felt privileged to ask every newcomer.

The heat and the dust played havoc with Slim's freshly washed face and clean clothes. He cursed inwardly for not having kept on the clothes he had worn during his journey on the train. The handkerchief with which he swabbed his face came away streaked with dirt and perspiration. His silk shirt grew stickier and stickier. A longing to exchange his summer weight woolen suit for the airy tatters of his companion overcame him. The car engine seemed to add twenty degrees to the temperature of his feet.

At last the car turned a bend in the hot unshaded road and entered a narrow lane lined on either side with magnolias, live-oaks and a sprinkling of pecan trees. Slim sighed with relief for their shade. He knew that in a few minutes his ride would be over. The thought brought a flood of conflicting feelings.

"Well, hyah you is," drawled the owner of the car, bringing it to a standstill in front of a gate in a barbed wire fence.

Slim climbed out and took the luggage which the man handed him from the car.

"How much do I owe you?" he asked.

"O, 'bout two bits, I reckon."

Reaching into his pocket, Slim drew out a dollar and handed it to the fellow, saving with a smile, "Keep the change for lagniappe."

Ignoring the voluble thanks that followed his generosity, Slim turned and opened the gate. He stood just within it until the car had hiccoughed out of sight. He suddenly felt bewildered, frightened and very small-boyish. Strangely enough his mind flew back to a day in his childhood—a day when often, having disobeyed his father's injunction to stay out of the creek because the water wasn't warm enough yet, he had stood at that same gate, making up his mind to go to the house. He remembered wondering whether all signs of his disobedience were destroyed, and feeling then exactly as he felt now.

Slowly closing the gate behind him, he advanced up the path, merely a ribbon of trodden grass threading through a grove of trees similar to those lining the lane. A few moments of slow walking brought him to the end of the path and into an open grassy space. There, under the wide-flung branches of a live-oak whose Spanish moss dipped and touched the much-patched roof, stood the little cabin. It was black, now, with the wind and the sun and the rains. The same flower beds were flung out in front of it. The little path led to the cabin sips. The railing around the porch supported wooden flower boxes similar to those Slim had seen there in his boyhood.

He halted again. Sudden panic overcame him. He wanted nothing so much as to run away. But any such intention was quickly put to an end by the appearance in the doorway of an old woman. The short, thin gray hair, the spectacles, the deep furrows on her brow and thin cheeks and the stoop that comes of old age and labor could not disguise her. It was his mother. His heart quaked into stillness. Would she know him. Did he want her to know him?

The old woman looked at him questioningly yet with a smile of unmistakable hospitality.

"Good evenin', sah," she said in a somewhat thin tremulous voice.

"Good evening, ma'am." Slim accompanied the words with a sweeping bow. His mind was made up as to the course he would pursue until she recognized him, or until he decided to drop his disguise.

At the beginning of his journey he had hoped for instant recognition. Now, somehow, he was glad it had not come. In a few words he established his assumed identity. His name was Adams, Lee Adams, and he was on a long journey from Chicago to a point still farther away. He wanted to break the trip by stopping somewhere tonight. On the train from New Orleans someone lead told him of Mr. and Mrs. Sawyer as nice people to stop with, and here he was. Would she put him up overnight? He would pay her well for her trouble.

With true Louisiana hospitality Sarah Sawyer invited him into the house.

"Sho' you kin stay. We ain't much of a place, but ef you kin put up with it, why we'll be glad to have you. 'Tain't often strangers draps aroun' heah."

Slim followed her into the cabin. How familiar everything was! The oven of the big cook-stove in the center of the wall opposite the outside door, was sending forth fragrant whiffs of something baking. On the stove were a sauce pan, a kettle and a big black iron pot. In a corner of the room, near an open window was the table spread with a neatly patched blue checked table cloth, and laid for two people. Slim thrilled to think that soon another place would be there for him. The willow rocker that he had helped his father make sat turned toward the door, as if Sarah had been sitting in it looking out when the stranger came up the path.

She led him across the kitchen to a door on one side of the stove. Opening this door she stood aside with fine courtesy to let Slim enter.

"I'm sho' it ain't what you is used to, sah," she apologized, "but sech as it is, you is welcome to it. Jes' mak yo' se'f comfatible. I'll bring you some hot watah so you kin wash de dus' off yo'se'f. Dis Looziana dus' sho' sticks. My husban'll be in f'm de fiel' soon, and we kin have suppah."

She walked out, closing the door behind her, and leaving Slim to look around him. He was in his own room once more. The rafters were darker now than they were when he used to lie in the white covered bed and look up at them at night. Vivid colored pictures from magazines, posters and newspapers were pasted on the walls. He fingered some of the prints tenderly, realizing the fact that he had often helped his mother paste such on the walls when he was a boy. White barred dimity curtains hung at the two windows. A rag carpet covered most of the floor. Near the door through which he had just come stood an old-fashioned wash stand with a large tin bowl and pitcher.

"Heah's yo' watah."

Stepping to the door Slim opened it and received a bucket of cold water and a kettle of hot water from Sarah.

When he reappeared in the kitchen, he was rewarded with a smile and an appreciative glance from Sarah.

"Son, yo' sho' looks a heap bettah sence gettin' shet of some of dat dus.' Dey ain't no dus' nowheres else in de whole worl' lak dis Looziana dus.' It sticks lak leeches. Set down an res' yo' se'f. My husball' be comin' any time now. Set in de willow rocker."

"But won't I be robbing you?" Slim's whole being was throbbing with a strong ache at sound of that word "son." But he realized that it was only a term of kindness and friendliness, nothing more.

"Shucks! A woman don' have time to set down near meal-time," he heard Sarah say, as she stooped to open the oven door.

Slim sat in the rocker, his eyes on his mother. She was so much thinner than he had ever known her. Already the trembling, uncertain movements of old age were creeping upon her. The spryness, while not altogether gone, was somehow less dynamic, less vital. A step on the porch—Slim looked up into the eyes of his father. Involuntarily he rose to his feet.

Sarah had heard the step, for she came forward.

"Andrew, dis is Mr. Lee Adams. He come f'rum Chicago an' is on his way to Baker, an' he ast to stop heah ovah night. Mr. Adams, dis is my husban', Mr. Andrew Sawyer."

Feeling the shrewd, close scrutiny of the tall, straight old man's eyes, Slim felt a chill as he stretched out his hand to meet the other's. As their hands clasped, Slim's thumb doubled under his finger in a movement he had not made since leaving home. He felt a sudden fear. This little trick was one his father had taught him. It was their sign of sticking together in any plot conceived and carried out against the wishes of Sarah. Slim looked searchingly into Andrew's eyes, but they were the unfathomable, scrutinizing eyes of one meeting and appraising a stranger.

After a few words of formal greeting, Andrew withdrew to another room opening out of the kitchen. Slim remembered again. No matter how hungry or tired her men-folks, Sarah always made them "fresh up" before eating their evening, meal.

By the time Andrew appeared once more the supper was sending out tantalizing odors from the table. The three sat down and began to eat. Little was said, except by Sarah, full of womanly curiosity as to the ways of city folks. Andrew ate in silence, but Slim knew that the old man was mercilessly scrutinizing, analyzing and classifying him.

When the meal was over the two men repaired to the porch, Andrew to smoke, and Slim to watch the advancing night as it slowly conquered the west and spread up the heavens. Finally Sarah joined them and began to speak.

"I put Mr. Adams into the little room, Andrew."

"Uh huh," grunted Andrew between puffs at his pipe.

Sarah leaned toward Slim.

"You know, Mr. Adams, it's our boy's room. He lef' us twenty-five years ago."

"Dead, you mean?"

"No. He runned off. Jes' lef' one day 'thout rhyme or reason."

Slim expressed his sympathy. Encouraged by his words Sarah poured out the whole story of her fears, her sorrow and her sleepless nights.

"Hadn't a night passed sence then what I don' pray for him. I ast God to let me see my baby boy once mo.' We ain' nevah knowed why he runned away. Lawd knows we was as kin' to him as we knowed how to be."

"Perhaps he'll come back some day, rich an able to help you," suggested Slim.

"Dat's what I tells Andrew all time," answered Sarah, looking in the direction of the glowing pipe embers, "but he say de boy is daid, or good as daid."

"Good as dead?"

"Yes, he say ef his tuhned out to be a worthless no-count rascal, his good as daid to him."

"An' I'm right!" exclaimed Andrew, and the glowing embers in his pipe came to rest with a slight thud on the railing. "A man what don' say nothin' in twenty-five years to his parents what done all they could fo' find him, is daid or a no-'count rascal."

"He may have been hindered in getting in touch with you. Maybe he couldn't send you anything. That is—something may have—"

"Ef he's lived de right kin' o' life, he'd write to his folks even ef he ain't got nothin' to send em."

"Andrew, go in an light de lamp." Sarah's tone was peevish. She didn't want Andrew giving this stranger the wrong impression of her boy.

Slim leaped up. "Let me!" he exclaimed, "I know where it is."

In the darkness he walked across the porch into the kitchen. Unconsciously as he crossed the porch, there was a slight dragging sound as if one of his feet had gone suddenly lame, or was moved with difficulty because of a heavy weight.

As he placed the chimney on the lighted lamp, a cold sweat broke out on him. He realized what he had done. After a year of practicing and being on his guard, he had gone back to the habit burned into his blood by nineteen years of wearing the ball and chain. Cautiously, every nerve on guard, he walked back to his seat in the far corner of the porch. In passing, he cast a glance at Andrew's face, dimly visible in the faint reflection of the lamp in the kitchen. The old man was looking off into the darkness, smoking away. Slim fancied that the muscles of his mouth quivered an instant, and then set in a granite line.

Sarah took up the conversation. "My boy wouldn't do nothin' whut wuzn't right," she declared stoutly, "ez hard ez we tried to raise him right."

"But it might be easy for a young lad to get into trouble. Maybe he did go wrong, but if he was sorry an' wanted to come back—"

"He could come, bless God," cried Sarah. "But my baby wouldn't do no wrong. He's alive, too, somewhere an' he'll come back yet. I don' believe he's daid—"

"It would be too bad," murmured Slim.

Removing his pipe once more, Andrew remarked in low, tense tones. "I'd rather believe he's daid than come to some things I can think of. Some things is worse than death."

A slow tightening around Slim's throat and chest. "What, for instance?" he asked, after a thick silence.

"Servin' time in the pen," returned the old man.

"No mattah whah he is, or what he done, he's my own little baby whut I borned into dis worl.' He kin come to his mammy f'um any place he's at," sobbed Sarah.

With an effort Slim spoke again. "Suppose he had—served time—an' had got out—an' made money an' come back to take care o' you—"

Andrew bit in savagely, "Ef he done made his peace with God an' made his money clean, he be welcome. Ef he ain't, he could take hisse'f an' his money an' hit de highway. We kep' de family name clean an' clear fo' lo dese many yeahs, an' we don' what was right in de sight of de Lawd. We ain't gwine be disgraced an' made ashame in ouah ol' age. Honest want is bettah den dishonest' plenty."

The yellow moon was now shining directly upon their faces. To hide whatever his countenance might betray, Slim leaned back in the shadow of the vines covering one side of the porch. He knew too well that old man. Arguing with him was about as effective as using one's fists to beat a way out of a tomb of solid granite. His mother, rocking softly, had covered her face with her apron and was sobbing softly.

At last Slim arose, said goodnight and went to his room. Locking the door he sat on the side of the bed. Dejectedly his head sank into his hands. For a long time he sat there. Finally he arose, walked to the chair upon which his bag rested, opened the bag and took there-from a writing case. After taking out an envelope and a piece of paper he closed the bag and seated himself beside the lamp stand. Slowly he began writing:

> Dear Mrs. Sawyer,
>   I have decided to take the three o'clock morning train. So when you get up I'll be gone. I'm leaving a little gift in the letter. Think of me sometime.
>   Thank you,
>   Lee Adams

From his money belt he counted out some of the currency—fifty ten dollar bills, twenty fives and twenty twenties—$1,000 in all—placed it in the envelope with the letter, and stood the sealed letter against the bowl on the washstand.

* * *

The stars dimming in the early morning sky looked down upon a man trudging through the dusty road leading back to the railroad station. His well-tailored clothes and expensive luggage were covered with a film of yellow, clinging dust.

[*The Crisis* 44.10 (October 1937): 300–301, 306, 311]

THE CHRISTMAS CANDLE

by Octavia B. Wynbush

The tall red candle flickered thinly a moment, and, simultaneously with the unsteady match, died out. Linda Cavell lighted the third match and sighed.

How like her life, her hopes, her dreams! Everything which she had lighted for her happiness had flared, flickered an instant, and died out. Steadying her shaking fingers, she held the light once more to the candle. Once more a flicker, a flare, and then a steady glow. The third time was the charm.

Stepping back from the window which formed a fitting frame for the light, Linda smiled bitterly, ironically. Lighting the candle—that was her last gesture before leaving this. She turned and surveyed the room in which she stood. Long, low-raftered and tastefully furnished and softly lighted, it was an ideal setting for the old-fashioned fire-place occupying nearly the entire side of the wall to her left. They had built the room for this fire-place, and the fire-place for the Christmas trees which were to be Ted's for a long, long time.

The flames from the log in the fire-place grew suddenly dim and distorted. Tears have a way of playing such tricks. This year there would be no Christmas tree.

"He was with us such a little while," whispered Linda, "just six tiny years. He was such a good child, too." She leaned against the fire-place weeping.

"Linda, why are you here?" The voice, slightly harsh in its concern and insistence, broke in upon her sorrow.

Turning her back to the hearth, she faced Theodore, standing there, in his overcoat, with his hat in his hand.

"Lighting the Christmas candle. Can't you see it? You know, it's supposed to bring us happiness."

Her own voice had a certain edge on it, now. Lately their voices had taken on that rasp when they addressed each other, an occurrence which was becoming noticeably less frequent.

Theodore came forward, and stood in front of his wife, looking down into her eyes. People were always attracted to Linda by her lovely eyes, but they had never seen them filled with the dislike and smothered anger which clouded them now.

Bracing himself for whatever might follow, Theodore spoke. "Linda, Darling, stop torturing yourself so needlessly, by remembering with such bitterness. Get your wraps and come with me to the Christmas Eve service. Afterwards we'll go to Mother's. It will be better."

The smoldering fires in Linda's eyes flashed into flame. Fury twisted her beautiful face into ugliness.

"Go, on this night of all nights—the anniversary of our last Christmas tree for—him? If you had a heart, if you loved him as you say you do, you wouldn't go yourself—you couldn't You'd stay here with me, and—remember. You'd let your assistant take charge of the service tonight."

"Linda, must we go over all that again?" Cavell's voice was weary and broken.

"No! we needn't go over it again, or ever." Turning her back, Linda walked over to the window and gazed down on the candle.

"I lighted the candle tonight," she continued, "just as I did last year. I wanted to remember how pleased he was when he saw the light as he came back with you from the service. He said it made him happy."

As soon as she had spoken, she was penitent. Although her back was to Theodore, she could picture the grayness of his face, and the wince of pain. It was on that last Christmas Eve trip with his father to church that Ted had contracted the cold which had developed into pneumonia. She had spoken, however, so she might as well continue, thought Linda.

"Tonight you will stand there in the pulpit, talking about the Shepherds and the Wise Men and the Christ child just as calmly as if nothing had happened in your own life. How you can do it, I don't know, unless it is as I said: You never loved him. If you did, you couldn't be so calm and self-contained all the time."

She heard him stoop slowly to pick up his hat which had dropped with a thud on the rug.

"You never loved him," she sobbed, and her tears caused the candle flame to waver unsteadily.

"Good night, my dear."

Linda made no answer to his farewell. She stood bowed above the candle, listening to him moving slowly to the door where he stood a moment fumbling with the knob, as if he were not quite certain as to where it was. Then the door swung quietly open, to be closed gently in an instant.

From her position at the window, Linda saw Theodore silhouetted in the oblong of light from the open front entrance as he stepped upon the porch. Then, as he closed the door, he became one with the blackness of the wintry evening.

Continuing to stare out into the darkness, Linda pictured the scene she knew so well.

Up here on the hill, the whistling wind sifted the snow from icy branches, piled it here and there, only to return and shift the piles to some other place. Up here were the homes of the few hundred prosperous residents of Castleton. On the hill, in every home but hers Christmas trees were being dressed and loaded with presents for starry-eyed youngsters and happy grown-ups.

Down below, in the valley now blotted out by the darkness, the snow lay more quietly, for the hill on one side, and the freight houses, sheds and various buildings of the train yards cut off the boisterous wind. Down there, were the huts and the shanties housing the poverty-stricken of Castleton. In the valley, the Christmas trees, if there were any, would be wretched little affairs form the "five-and-ten."

"Money, or no money, Christmas trees, or no Christmas trees, every one down there is happier tonight than I." Her words were bitter with envy.

"Excuse me, Mrs. Cavell, but I've packed everything you asked me to."

Linda turned to smile at the soft-spoken maid who stood in the door.

"Thank you, Jean, thank you." Linda moved through the door held respectfully open by the girl.

"Did you mean to leave the candle burning, Mrs. Cavell?" Jean made a movement as if to cross the room to the window. She stopped, jerked up by the sardonic laughter which gloated back to her as Linda paused, already at the top of the stairs.

"Yes, let it burn. It will be a light for Mr. Cavell when he returns from his service. It may bring him happiness. By the way, Jean, be sure to look on the dining room table for your package before you leave. Merry Christmas, and many of them."

"Thank you, Mrs. Cavell, same to you," called Jean, in a voice dutifully grateful.

Her hand on the door knob she looked around the cozy, soft-lighted room. Tears came to her eyes as she, too, remembered the Christmas Eve of a year ago. Then, a wrathful fire in her eyes, she began muttering to herself.

"It's not fair, the way she's treating him, and his heart about to break. She thinks she's heartbroken for Ted, but it's just for herself she's sorry." Jean shook the door knob as if it had contradicted her.

"He blames himself somehow for Teddy's taking cold that night. And now he's about to die from the way she's acting."

Walking over to the window, she stared out into the night, down toward the valley, where people had a right be heartbroken and sorrowful.

"Funny how some folks think servants don't have sense," mused Jean. "She's leaving him flat, never to come back, or my name's not what it is. She's not fooling me about any surprise visit he's planned for her to her folks. She don't any more intend to come back here after Christmas than I intend jumping down this hill into the valley. I'm sure glad I won't be here tomorrow to see Mr. Cavell's face. Christmas Eve, of all times!"

Moving from the window, she crossed the room, and pausing on the threshold, to switch off the electric light, passed out, closing the door behind her. The candle flame, fanned by the slight breeze from the closing door, wavered, flickered, and then burned steadily into the darkness.

Upstairs in her bedroom, Linda's nervous fingers retarded her change into street clothes.

"I can't help it," she gasped. "I can't stand another day of this. And tomorrow, I'd die here. We've had enough of each other, for a while, anyway. That Jean," she continued, unbuttoning her fur coat in order to put the second button into the second button hole, "I know she's seen through me. But what of it? She's just a servant."

She shivered as she wondered what Theodore would do when he found her note tucked under his pillow. How would he look? What would he say? Would he think her cowardly, especially at Christmas time? Well—The rest of her thoughts went into a contemptuous shrug. She looked at her watch. Time the taxi was here. Then the doorbell rang.

Down in the valley, in a two-room shack at the bottom of a crazily twisting lane close to the railroad tracks, Jonathan crouched shivering by a cracked, black, icy stove. Biting his thin drawn lips and blinking his eyes to keep back the "sissy" tears, he wrapped himself tighter in the rag rug which he had drawn over his thin shoulders. Despite the rug, however, the wind, nosing in through the jagged pane in the window opposite the stove, sank its sharp fangs into Jonathan's quivering flesh.

If Mumsy would only wake up! Jonathan cast his eyes toward the doorway into the other room. There, in the rags and tatters of what had once been somebody's bed-clothes, his mother lay, so very still since yesterday afternoon. Jonathan shivered. He was cold, but, when he had crept in to see Mumsy, she was even colder.

Of course he was glad she didn't moan and groan any more, but the stillness of her made him feel so queer. All day he had waited for her to wake; all day he had hoped some one might knock on the door of his house, although it was a long way from the few houses in the lane. As long as the coal and the sticks of wood had held out, he had kept the fire going, hoping the warmth would make Mumsy's hands less cold.

A small pile of coal and a few sticks of wood did not last very long in the cold December weather. Since noon there had been so spark in the stove. With the coming of evening, the cold had grown worse, until now, as the grayness blended slowly with the black of night, every inch of the two rooms was filled with the cold.

Suddenly Jonathan stood up. He must go and ask some one to come and help Mumsy get warm. All day he had waited, hoping, but now, he must act. Dropping the rug, he rose from his crouching position beside the cold stove, shook loose the few threads adhering to his coat from the rug, and crossed the creaking bare floor to a peg beside the outer door.

There, within easy reach of his six-year old hands, hung his overcoat and worn cap with the mufflers.

With cold-stiffened fingers he pulled on the cap and buttoned the overcoat. There were no overshoes or mittens. Mumsy had promised them to him for Christmas, so he could go back to school after the holidays.

The sharp blast of air which met him as he opened the outer door, almost drove him off his balance. Slowly he slipped outside, straining with all his might to pull the door shut behind him. Succeeding at last, he crept down the icy steps, and slipped and slid along the snowy track that led through the tiny yard to the lane.

He would stop at Mrs. Farr's house. She had been in to see Mumsy yesterday morning. The Farr home was so distant from Jonathan's yard that, by the time he had fought through the snow drifts, he was quite breathless. Successive knocks on the door brought no response except from the echoes within. Had Jonathan but known it, Mrs. Farr and her "young uns" had gone that morning to spend the Christmas with her aunt in a neighboring town.

Frightened by the darkness and silence surrounding him, Jonathan scrambled from the porch and fled through the gate to the lane black now from the shadow of the hill, which rose almost perpendicularly above it. At the gate he paused. Unable to see the darkness, he turned his eyes in the direction of his own home where, closed in by shadows, Mumsy lay.

For a while he clung to the gate, faltering between a desire to run back to his home, and a desire to go farther up the lane, to where the street intersected it. There, at the intersection, was a light, sending a yellow murkiness into the gloom.

Hugging himself closer in his overcoat, he turned toward the street light. Under the lamp, he paused once more. Now where should he look for help? Then he remembered. The lady with the kind eyes—he would go to her. He had been to her home twice with Mumsy, when she went to wash there, and last Christmas Eve, he had gone there with Mumsy after dusk. They had known the house because it was the only one on that street that had a real candle burning in the window. The others had electric wreaths and candles. That lady would help Mumsy. Her eyes were too kind to say no.

Head bent against the wind which grew sharper and stronger as he climbed the long, steep street, Jonathan felt strangely happy. He knew he would find help, now. The snow feathered inside his shoes, and seeped through their thin soles. Many times he stopped, back to the wind, in the shelter of a lamp post, to get his breath. Reaching the top of the sharp ascent at last, he turned to look down over the way he had come.

Then he turned, triumphantly, to search out, in the night, the house where the candle had burned in the window. Clinging to ice-coated iron railings which shut in each lawn with its bushes and trees rising like sheeted ghosts in the glow of electrically lighted fir trees and window wreaths, he searched eagerly, as he moved up the street.

Another fear seized him. Suppose the lady had put up an electric wreath, herself. Then, how would he know the house? It was too dark, and the house was too far back from the street to know it in any other way. Again he fought back the tears. He'd keep on, any way.

There is was! He was standing even now before the gate, and there in the window glowed the tall candle, its steady soft light seeming brighter because the room behind it was dark. The sobs could come now. The lady with the eyes would understand. Rushing through the half-open gate, Jonathan ran up the path, and stumbled up the steps to the door. With vigor that flowed from somewhere into his stiff fingers, he pushed on the bell as hard as possible.

It was only a short while before the door opened, and the lady with the kind eyes, stood before him. Jonathan did not understand, for she was dressed in hat and fur coat, and was carrying a traveling bag.

"Why, what is it?" Linda's voice expressed her extreme surprise. "I thought it was the taxi driver. Come in child. Who are you? What do you want?"

Setting her bag in a corner of the hall, Linda seized the weeping six-year-old by his hands, and dragging him into the warmth, shut the door behind him.

"You poor darling," she cried, "you are almost frozen. Are you alone? Come in here."

Opening the door, she stepped into the room lighted by the candle. Jonathan, encircled by her arm, stumbled after her, dazed by the sudden warmth.

"Please Ma'am, I came for Mumsy." He gasped as Linda, having set him on a stool in front of the fire, and taken off his wet shoes and stockings, threw her own hat, gloves and coat on the divan near the fire-place.

"For Mumsy?" How kind her voice was, just as kind as her eyes.

"Where is your Mumsy, and what does she want, sending you out like this?"

Jonathan, unable to bear that accusing tone in Linda's voice, began at once to tell his story. It was easy to tell, as she bent over him, chafing his feet with her soft, tender hands. Of course the words got tumbled together and mixed up a bit, but the lady listened until he got to the part about Mumsy lying so still since she stopped groaning yesterday. Then, Linda sprang up abruptly, and, without a word, rushed into the hall, leaving a very wide-eyed boy staring after her.

In the hall, Linda closed the door to the room which she had just left, stood for a moment, to gain her self-control, and then sat down at the telephone stand in the niche under the stairway. Hastily she dialed a number—the number of the telephone at the home of Theodore's parents. He would still be there, as it was yet too early for him to go to the church.

"Hello?" Thank the gods! It was Theodore himself calling. In a voice as steady as she could make it, Linda told Jonathan's story. When she came to the part about Mumsy sleeping so long, she found it impossible to go on.

"All right, sweetheart. I'll get some one out there as quickly as possible. Meanwhile, look after the little tyke. Maybe—maybe—"

Linda had one of her rare flashes of understanding.

"Yes, dear," she answered, "he'll share our Christmas with us tomorrow, and from then on. You see, darling, the Christmas candle brought him."

[*The Crisis* 44.12 (December 1937): 358–359, 378]

MARCH WIND

by Edna Quinn

The night winds spoke of death. The cold March wind that howled round the little cottage, and tapped at doors and wept at windows in a futile effort to communicate to any who would listen, the secret of the death that had befallen Bessie Craven.

Bess Craven was dead. Dead after a marriage of eleven months to Eric Finley.

To begin with, it was remarkable that Bess Craven and Eric Finley had ever married. It was like the grotesque mating of a jack-daw and a sparrow. Eric Finley would remind you of the jack-daw. Tall and large and black was Eric, with an overwhelming and unscrupulous love for the glittering things of life, and possessing an enormous gift of gab. A gift, by the way, that served to make Eric distasteful to most people who knew him, for invariably, Eric's chief topic of conversation was himself. But it was this very gift which had endeared Eric to the heart of Bessie. Bessie was the sparrow: little, drab, and homely, loved by none, execrated by many, maintaining her existence by sheer pluck and effrontery.

Bessie was a cook. And so was Eric. But Bessie had cooked fourteen years straight for the wealthiest white family in town, while Eric was occasional cook for a gang of construction laborers. It is a far cry from sweetbreads and apricot mousse prepared by an expert like Bessie and served to the cream of the quality by a dapper, brown-skinned butler, to mulligan stew and thick corn cakes dispensed by a perspiring, grinning Eric to a band of husky compatriots.

But one night at a picnic as Bessie sat solitary on a bench and watched the dancers inside of the pavilion swing easily through the bone-twisting gyrations of the Haile-Selassie, Eric and a boon companion had dropped down on the other end of the bench and begun to talk. That is, Eric talked. And as he held forth upon his skill in preparing hash and slum and other plebeian dishes, Bessie's dull eyes brightened and her heavy lips parted with rapt and eager interest. Noting this, Eric talked on apparently un-noting. Six weeks later Bessie Craven and Eric Finley were married.

Folks had always called Bass Craven queer. An orphan at the age of twenty, she had worked on and converted the rambling old shack left to her by her parents into a neat five-room cottage, furnished from front to back in irreproachable taste. This was all very well, but when Bess persisted in living there all alone, steadfastly refusing the companionship of her sister or her sister's children, folks called her queer. But then, the older settlers said, her mother had been queer before her. Born and reared in the town of Sundale, at the time of her death Bessie had not one real friend. As a maiden, she had kept to herself; as a wife, she had been amply satisfied with Eric's company.

The way she shunned her sister and her sister's children was queer enough, declared Sundale, but her marrying Eric Finley was the queerest yet. Eric Finley, who hadn't a dollar he could call his own, who lived a semi-vagrant life; Eric, part-time construction gang cook, part-time plain bum.

In the face of all that, however, Bessie Craven married Eric. What is more, she was happy with him, happy up to the very day of her death. Now, after eleven short months of wedded life, she lay dead at the age of thirty-five. She lay in her pretty little parlor, stretched stiffly inside the beautiful lavender half-couch casket, while outside the cold March winds sobbed and shuddered, whistled and sighed as they attempted to tell the facts about her demise.

It was the night before the funeral. The watchers at the wake, just two in number, sat beside the glowing stove in the dining room and listened to the prattle of the wind. In Sundale two beside the family was an unheard of small number to be present at a wake, but Bess had kept to herself in life, said Sundale, so she was left to herself in death. Only these two, who were the maid and the laundress at the house where Bess had been cook, chose to sacrifice a night's rest and watch beside her bier. Eric sat in the kitchen conversing in low tones with his aged mother and Bess Craven's sister who, even now, although the night had just begun, was preparing to depart.

"I must go home and see about my old man and the kids," Bess's Sister was saying, "tomorrow will be a hard day, with the funeral an' all. An' I need the rest."

The two watchers by the stove in the next room exchanged sly smiles. It was known that Bess's sister and her kids had been cut off without a cent. Bess had left her house, lot, all personal property, money on hand and in bank to her beloved husband, Eric Finley.

"Tomorrow will be a hard day, all right," whispered one watcher to the other, "tomorrow an' a great many other tomorrows. She's so disappointed she's almost dead, too. She thought maybe Bess would leave her or her kids something. An' now, not to even get a old dress. An' this nice house! I saw Bess's bank book, by accident, just before she took sick. One round thousand dollars in the bank! That Eric Finley is a lucky scoundrel, sure."

Lucky Eric may have been, and scoundrel he surely was, but at that moment his conduct was above reproach. With his eyes tear-reddened to just the proper degree he was lamenting his wife's death to his sister-in-law.

"We was made for each other, me an' Bess," he quavered, his sleek, black face twitching with emotion, "an' to think that we only got to spend such a short time together. We'd loved each other all our lives, me an' Bess, but we was kept apart by fate, an' when we did meet her time was almost up. But I'd 'a' never dreamt it then." The winds joined their lamentations with Eric as Bess Craven's sister went out into the night. Still gently weeping Eric stoked the fire in the dining room, nodded and smiled meekly and apologetically at the two watchers, then subsided quietly into a large easy chair.

"Well, it really don't seem possible that Bess's gone," observed the house maid, tentatively, after a brief silence, "we'll sure miss her at the house, won't we, Mag?"

Mag, the laundress, nodded emphatically, "Fourteen years she worked there an' the white folks thought their eyes of her. Fourteen years. Long before you or me ever thought of starting there. An' longer by a long sight than I'll ever stay if Mis' Fabin don't stop puttin' in so many white clothes for the children." And the laundress shifted her gum with a determined air.

Eric spoke now. "Yes, fourteen years," said he, with a trumpet-like blow of his nose, "That's a long time to stay by one family. But Bess was faithful. That was Bess faithful as the sun. If we'd 'a' lived together eleven hundred years instead of eleven months Bess would of still been faithful to the last. Oh I know it's all for the best, but I can't stand it—I can't."

Slumping down into the depths of his chair he buried his face in his hands. His old mother hobbled in and, with much ado, proceeded to comfort her grieving son. "Well," said Eric at length, as he pocketed his handkerchief with a long sigh, "you're right, ma. I must brace up an' be a man—I will." Suiting action to word he went into the kitchen and bestirred himself manfully with the result that within a short space of time the maid and the laundress, his mother and himself were seated cosily around the dining room table, enjoying a lunch that had no parallel in all the previous wakes observed in Sundale. Hot hamburger patties, with onion and pickle, french-fried potatoes, coffee with real cream, tea for the laundress (who by reason of a weak heart eschewed coffee) home made chocolate covered drop cakes, thick slices of home made bread and butter.

"No," repeated Eric after an interval, his utterance slightly thickened by food, "it seems like I really can't realize it. Bess dead! An' we loved each other so.

"She was sick a month, just about, wasn't she, Mr. Finley?" queried Mag the laundress.

"In bed just a month to the day," answered Eric, solemnly and heavily, "she had ulcers of the stomach, that's what caused her death."

The laundress and the housemaid exchanged covert glances. So the thing was out at last. They'd often wondered just what had ailed Bess. Some had said one thing, some another. But you could be pretty sure that blab-mouthed Eric would tell the thing just like it was.

"Ulcers of the stomach," the housemaid was thrilled, "but whatever causes such things, Mr. Finley?" Eric bit into another drop cake. "It's hard to tell just what does cause things like that," he said, "I just don't know—she was complaining before she quit work. I made her go see the doctor, but Bess got bedfast an' first thing I knew she was gone. Yes, ulcers of the stomach that's what's on the death certificate."

The lunch was ended. Eric's mother cleared away the dishes and the others drew their chairs closer to the fire. "Yes, she's gone," the bereft husband repeated thoughtfully, "an' she's left every thing to me. Made a will in black an' white, two weeks before she died." He went to the sideboard drawer, returned with a folded document which he handed to the housemaid. "Read for yourself," he said, and with staring eyes the housemaid read. It was true. Bess had bequeathed him everything. Lucky Eric Finley!

Now Eric proceeded to divert and entertain the watchers. He showed them silverware, beautiful hand-worked covers and bed-sets, handsome quilts, towels and comforters, all left to him by his loving, thrifty wife. And when these things had been admired and exclaimed over and returned to their proper places, he sat him down to talk. The clock struck two, and Eric still talked on. Struck three, the watchers stirred and nodded, nodded and roused, then to themselves cried plague on Eric's never-ceasing voice. He talked of many things: of how and when he first had met his wife, told tales of the construction camps, tales that were more thrilling than true.

Outside the wind screamed, moaned, then sobbed, then died. Beside the porch the house dog and a friend bellowed and bayed in the frenzy of their efforts to tell the wind that they, at least, understood. Finally, abandoning all hopes of sleep, the watchers settled themselves doggedly to listen.

"You see," came Eric's mellow voice, "Bess loved me because I was so good to her. An' I've been good to women all my life. Bess was my only love, the only woman I ever thought enough to marry. Of course, I took up with other women. Remember, Alice, ma, before we come to this part of the country?" His aged mother nodded affirmatively and sucked upon her pipe. "Alice was a woman I took up with. She was older than me 'cause I was just a kid. She was a pretty yellow woman, too. An' I made good money, six bucks a day, workin' on the concrete. Alice had a husband, but she put him out an' took me in. That's what made— Ma, don't this make you think somehow, of the night that I killed Charlie? Remember?" The mellow tone had left his voice, his eyes were wide and bright, his dark face twitched, so did his hands. The watchers noted these things sleepily, uncomprehending.

His mother cried out sharply, "Now Eric, don't start that! Remember? I've prayed to God every night since that night to please help me fergit!" Eric was standing up. "I didn't really know the man was dead," he said in a low voice, eyes fixed in space as though his listeners were forgotten, "Alice was in bed. I was in the kitchen readin' the paper. Somebody knocked on the door. Boom! Boom! Just like that. It was Charlie. Alice screamed: "Eric! Don't you go to that door!" But I had forgot to lock it. Charlie had been threaten' me—he was sore—He come in with a big, springback dirk knife—My gun was in the washstand drawer in the room where Alice was. He drawed back his knife—there was a shoe-hammer layin' on the floor—Alice used it to hold open the middle door. I reached down an' picked it up an' busted Charlie. An' his head split right half in two. But I didn't really know the man was dead."

As he sank to his seat his mother, somehow infected with this strange delirium, took up the fearful saga. "Eric gived hisself up," she proclaimed shrilly, "he run away that night, but after a while he gived hisself up. Then he killed a guard in the pen." "He knocked me down an' cussed me," defended Eric sullenly, "I knocked him in the head with a pick."

The housemaid, aroused at last, burst out, "Why, it's a wonder they didn't give you life for that! But I guess they never caught you." This interruption staunched the flow of reminiscence. Eric grinned sheepishly and poked the fire, his mother settled back into her chair.

"Just listen to that wind! It's gettin' colder," said the laundress after some deadly quiet moments had passed, "That wind is surely screechin'." Then later on. "It's five o'clock. We better go. We want to git an early start with our work so's we can git off for the funeral. Mr. an' mis' Fabin's goin' to the funeral, too." And Eric sighed and nodded, showing just the correct amount of resigned, yet heartfelt grief. "I thank you for comin', ladies," he said "to set the last night with me. The last night that Bess will ever spend in her home—our home. We loved each other so."

The two watchers delicately averted their faces that they might not look upon his tears. The door shut behind them.

Eric glanced around and saw his aged mother sleeping in her chair her mouth wide open. For a moment he stood there, then tiptoeing cautiously into the bedroom—his bedroom and the late Bess Finley's—he fumbled about in the dim glow that came from the dining room lights. From deep down in his trunk he drew forth a vial.

For a long moment he gazed at it, then stealing silently into the kitchen he proceeded, with a minimum amount of noise, to crush the vial to atoms beneath his heavy heel. Then carefully he swept the crumbs of glass upon the dustpan, made certain that his mother till slept, and tossed the contents of the pan into the fiery maw of the dining room stove. This done, he settled himself in a chair beside his mother for a brief nap until it should be time to prepare for the funeral. Outside the wind was crying, crying with rage and disappointment. As the housemaid and the laundress struggled down the street the cold March wind seized them roughly, snarled in their ears in a last vain attempt to tell them, buffeted them, flung them hatefully aside.

"That wind!" exclaimed the laundress, testily.

"It sure has been some night," gasped the housemaid, as the wind strangled her yawn, "Just us two sittin' up with poor Bess. An' Eric with all that talk. But about him killin' them men—that sure was news to me. We sure have heard revelation on revelation this night."

"Lie on lie, you mean," contributed the laundress, made irritable by lack of sleep and the torment of the wind, "If Eric Finley had done all that killin' they'd have strung him up as sure as he's born to die. He wouldn't have nerve enough to kill anybody—a boaster's always a coward. Eric Finley's just a big windbag, full of noise an' bluster, just like this March wind."

And the cold March wind, insulted and affronted by such incredible stupidity, stuffed back the words into the laundress's throat, and screamed: "Fools! Fools!"

[*The Crisis* 45.1 (January 1938): 16, 18, 27]

CONJURE MAN

———— ✸ ————

by Octavia B. Wynbush

Her beady old eyes glittering through narrow slits of lids as she peered through an opening in the leafy screen, Maum Samba sat behind the matted honeysuckle vines framing her front porch. Across the dusty strip of road in front of her rickety fence, a group of men was assembled in the semi-circular clearing in front of Devil's Swamp. The eldest of the group, a tall, muscular fellow, weathered by the Louisiana sun to a blackish hue, appeared to be giving orders.

What worried Samba was the fact that the men were carrying implements suggestive of digging. What could it mean? Was the gossip which had come to her ears of late about to become a truth?

"Mornin' Maum Samba."

Startled, Samba looked up. By her rocker stood the grinning twelve-year-old son of a neighbor.

"Lawd boy! Don' never come on me like dat agin. What you want, anyhow?"

"Ma done sent me for your risin' sun quilt patte'n. She say len' it to her, please."

Rising stiffly, Samba stepped into the house, from which she returned soon, bearing the pattern tied in a neat package. Before giving it to the boy, she queried; "What's goin' on 'cross the road, Luther?"

"Mistah Wesson's goin' build his new home 'cross from you, Maum Samba," grinned the boy, watching the old woman with a queer gleam in his eye.

The mottled yellow hand plucking the string around the package stopped suddenly, as if stricken with paralysis.

"Yes?" The tone was as unconcerned as Samba could make it.

"Yas'm. He bought dat strip of clearin' from Big Jim Handy, an' is goin' to live there with his fambly an' Miz Amanda."

"I reckon yo' ma's waitin' fo' dis patte'n, boy. Run 'long home."

When the boy had gone, Samba resumed her seat behind the vines. So it had come to this! Mark Wesson was going to bring his wife and Amanda to flaunt themselves and their prosperity in her face the rest of her life. Their new home would be across the road from her own dilapidated cabin with its run-to-weeds garden in which she had lost interest since the death of her husband two years ago.

What a reversal of the picture she had painted it in her youth! Samba's mind flew back to that happy time, so hazy now that she often wondered whether it had happened to her, or to some one she had once known. She moaned softly to herself. Surely what she had done did not demand life-long punishment.

She was beginning to believe what Nana Marshall had hinted to her once.—"God hain't punishing you, Samba. Hit's yo' bitter enemy what's put a spell on you, an' dey's only one human in dis parish what kin tek hit often you—dat's ol' Elias, what lives close to de cypress swamp. He kin tek hit off, or put a worser one on yo' enemy. An' you know who dis enemy is."

Samba sighed. How could she help it, if Bob had turned from Amanda Hartwell to her, forty-odd years ago, even after his word had been given to Amanda? He hadn't been able to help himself when the sprightly, beautiful girl from St. Martinville had danced into his life on the occasion of her visit to her aunt and uncle at Eglanville.

Maum Samba,—Seremba they called her then—had been beautiful in her youth, with her olive complexion, flashing, black eyes, blue-black hair sweeping below her waist, slender ankles and dainty feet that outdanced the best of the belles of Eglanville. She hadn't meant to take big Bob Moore completely away from his "promised" bride, at first. It had just been fun to see the big fellow fall so desperately for her. But Amanda's furious jealousy and bitter words had spurred the visitor to do her utmost.

Never would she forget the thrill of that evening on the outskirts of the swamp, just where the clearing was now. It was all thicket and trees, then. Bob and she had stopped under the live-oak, since felled by lightning, and there Bob had proposed. Samba recalled her own demurring because of Amanda. Even now she heard again his vehement declaration that Amanda had long since ceased to interest him. Even in her present state of mind, she could not forbear a tender, reminiscent smile.

Then, acres and acres of the rich soil had been Bob's, even the land upon which they had become engaged. And now, Amanda's son-in-law was building his home upon that spot— a home to which he could bring his children, his mother-in-law, Amanda, and his wife, Rose Ellen. Thought of Rose Ellen stirred the fire in Samba's soul to fiercer heat. With what vengeance had Amanda retaliated!

Of all their six children, Bob and Samba had held their daughter, Lucille, most dear, partly because she was the only girl, and partly because she was such a delicate creature. When Mark Wesson, superior in every way to the young fellows of Eglanville, had come from up the river to settle and open a combined store and "refreshment parlor," he had taken immediately to Lucille.

In a short time they became engaged. Samba had been wild with joy. Every girl in the village, Rose Ellen especially, had made desperate efforts to get this man whose energy and ability marked him as distinctly different from the indolent, shiftless fellows of their acquaintance. Even now nausea and weakness swept over Samba as she remembered—Lucille, slim, brown, lovely in her wedding finery, standing before the mirror, taking the last look at herself before starting for the church—Hannah Washington, frowsy, dusty, excited and perspiring, rushing in and blurting out the brutal fact that Rose Ellen and Mark Wesson had slipped off to the next town that morning, and had married. Samba had never been able to forgive Hannah for her tactlessness in blurting out the truth before Lucille. The scorching humiliation which had finally burned up Lucille's vitality and killed her, had shriveled Samba into a mummified version of her former self.

Behind the honeysuckle vines Samba stirred and sighed as she wiped her eyes with one corner of her blue-checked apron. Then she rose resolutely and stood a moment, her fists balled tightly at her temples. Resolve shone in her eyes, as she straightened at last.

"Tonight, at fust dark, I'll do it," she muttered.

The last rays of the sun had been conquered by the night rising from the earth, and the peculiarly velvety darkness that precedes the rising of the moon in Louisiana lay thick on Devil's Swamp. Samba, standing with her hand on the latch of her sagging gate, looked sharply up and down the road, listening for any sound of approaching footsteps. Assured that no one was coming, she swung open the gate and stepped into the road. After carefully closing and latching the rickety barrier between her weedy yard and the open highway, she began walking along in the dust, as fast as her wizened legs could carry her thin body. She must get off the main road before the moon rose. It was a long way to the big oak where she could take the snake-trail.

"I'm goin' to do it! I'm goin' to do it!" she muttered continually, savagely, as she strode along.

"I'm goin' to do it! I'm goin' to do it!" her footsteps seemed to echo back as she moved forward through the powdery dust. The close heat of the night, unfavorable for her pace, soon sent streams of perspiration coursing over her body.

For once fortune favored her. When the moon rose she was deep in the woods through which wound the crooked little snake-path that began at the base of the big oak by the main road. The big, yellow, eye-like moon made the trees stand in sharp, black, outline. Deeper and deeper into their midst went Samba, following the narrow path which led finally to a natural lane of pine trees, ending abruptly before a long, low shanty in a small clearing.

In the light of the moon, the cabin was oddly fantastic. Its roof appeared to be made of bits of tin, tar-paper, and slate. The sides were pieced together from scraps of timber, boxes, and boards from box-cars, the latter still bearing their legends of weight and capacity.

From one window of the shanty came a feeble ray of light. Creeping up to the window, Samba looked in. She could see a crudely made table covered with a dirty, much-marred oil cloth on which stood a flickering smoky lamp. At one end of the table, his face buried in his hands, sat an old man deeply absorbed in thought. Standing tip-toe, Samba craned her neck from side to side. She could discover no one else in the room. Elias was evidently alone. Samba was satisfied.

Mounting the two rickety steps leading to a little stoop before the door, she knocked cautiously and softly. The door was cracked. A rasping old voice inquired,

"Who dat?"

Samba's reply, though soft was somewhat scornful.

"You oughta know. It's part of yo' trade."

The door was opened still wider. Old Elias peered out, the beams of the moon falling over his fuzzled white head, his black, wrinkled face with its two sharp, ferrety, red eyes, and his ragged, open-at-the-neck shirt and tattered, dirty overalls.

"Maum Samba! Well, I *is* surprised! Come in."

The room in which Samba found herself was as grotesque as the outside of the shack. From the rafters, over which the shadows of herself and Elias sprawled in gargantuan proportions, hung all sorts of curious and startling things. Bunches of dried herbs, curiously-tied packages dangling from long strings, animal skins, gourds, and three dried snake skins, were distinguishable in the dim light.

The walls, bare and unplastered, with nothing to obliterate entirely the fact that they were simply the outside boards seen from the inside, were hung here and there with more of the things which dangled from the ceiling. Over the bunk with its grimy bedclothes hung a horseshoe and a wool-card. On a small table in one corner stood a collection of bottles and jars filled with weird-looking roots. Besides them lay a rabbit's foot, a crystal for gazing, and a luck stone.

Samba looked directly at the man in front of her.

"Elias, you knows I don' hol' much wid yo' trade. I bases my life on de Bible an' prayer, but I needs yo' help now fo' a quick act."

"Set down."

Samba took the stool Elias drew from under the oilcloth-covered table, and plunged immediately into her recital.

"Elias I wants you to help me get shet of a enemy."

"A enemy?"

"Yes. I name no name, an' I bear no blame."

"You bring anything belongs to yo' enemy?"

Samba's face fell.

"I didn' know I had to."

"How kin I wuk 'thout sumpin' to wuk on?"

"But you is done it, ain't you?"

"Not on no one ez pow'ful ez yo' enemy bes. Hit ain't so s'cessful. But I'll give you a luck ball twell you brings me sumpin'."

Elias went to the corner table where reposed his magic potions.

"What mus' I bring?" Samba's voice was guarded and low. Even the rafters might hear.

"Some of yo' enemy's haih, a piece of yo' enemy's clo'es, an' sumpin' yo' enemy's done wrote."

Samba's rigid back did not reveal her dismay. Getting these things from an enemy she had not spoken to in over forty years! Getting them from Amanda Pierre! Well, this was her problem. She would solve it. Impatiently she awaited Elias' return from his table.

When he finally returned to Samba, Elias laid before her a round, evil-smelling black ball, and a coarse brown bag containing something hard and pungent.

"Now," he began, "put dis yere black ball somewheah on yo' enemy's grounds, somewheah he'll have to walk over it. Put dis bag away somewheah in yo' own house, an' when you gits back home, sprinkle a cupful o' mustahd seed on youah walk an' do' step to keep off de evil sperrits yo' enemy might send agains' you at night. Dis will gib you a little pertection, but it ain't gwine be complete twell you brings me de haih, de piece o' clo'es, an' de writin'."

Samba stood up and fumbled in her apron pocket, a question in her eyes.

"One dollah only, bein' as it's you," Elias replied to the unspoken query, "an' to complete the work it'll cos' you twenty-five dollahs."

"Twenty-five dollars!" Samba's voice rose in a screech. "Wheah you think I kin get twenty-five dollars?"

"O, you kin git it, all right. You kin go dis minute an' lay yo' hen's on fo' times dat much. Don' look at me lak you's s'prised. I knows dat. Haint it paht of my trade?"

Elias laughed heartily at the opportunity to fling Samba's words back at her.

"And 'sides," he added after a moment, "de chahms you already has is 'versible. Dey kin wu'k against you ef de one what gave 'em to you wills, as well as fo' you, you knows. W'en will I be favored wid you' comp'ny agin, ma'am? Thanks fo' de dollah."

"Some time ve'y soon."

Gathering up the ball and the bag, and thrusting them into her pockets, Samba moved toward the door. Gallantly Elias stepped forward to open it. Samba breathed a long sigh of relief as she stepped outside and descended the rickety steps. Pausing for a moment on the ground in front of the shack, she expelled the rancid air of the hut from her lungs, and filled them with the sharp fragrance of the pine grove.

Before Samba's problem of obtaining the hair, the piece of clothing and the writing of her enemy had reached its solution, the finishing touches were being put on the Wesson house. The hot days of summer were giving way to slightly cooler autumn weather when a garden party given by Samba's friend, Teresa Claudin, furnished the occasion.

It was a beautiful night when Samba joined the crowd flocking over the broad expanse of unfenced, grassy ground Teresa pleased to call her "lawn." Elbowing her way through the crowd, Samba, a little black silk bag dangling from her left wrist, a short thin shawl over her shoulders, went straight to a group of which Teresa was one. Greetings over, Samba refused the hostess' offer to escort her to the room where the women had left their wraps.

"Thank you, thank you, Teresa, but you knows I knows ev'y inch of yo' house. I'll go by myself."

Up the path to the house went Samba, greeting friends right and left. It was just a step across the long front porch of the house into the room where lay all the light wraps brought by the women in anticipation of the cool breezes that often sprang up after sundown in the autumn.

Approaching the bed on which the garments lay an assortment of scarfs, jackets and coats Samba stood quietly searching with her eyes for one particular wrap. There it was! Amanda's black silk shawl with the red embroidered roses, and the deep, heavy black fringe. Mark had brought it to her from Baton Rouge.

Opening the bag on her wrist, Samba drew out a pair of tiny scissors. Making sure that she was unobserved, she began dipping a bit of fringe from each of several bunches of the knotted silk. Snip, snip, hurriedly yet carefully, the work was done. The clipped fringe and the tiny scissors reposed in the black bag.

Removing her own shawl, Samba placed it on the bed with the other wraps, and moved leisurely to join the group on the lawn. Once there, she moved around slowly, until she found herself next to Amanda who was receiving congratulation from a number of friends, who were loud in their praises of the new home. All of Samba's hot hatred boiled in her breast, but she was outwardly beaming as she joined the group. Uncomfortable silence fell as she sidled up to Amanda.

"I des wants to add my compliments to de res', Miz Pierre," she began. "It's a mighty fine house, an' I'm glad you's buildin' it in front of me. It gits awful lonesome sometimes fo' me now, 'specially at night. I kin hardly wait fo' you all to move in. Seems to me we mought as well be frien's, sence we's goin' to be neighbors. An' it ain't any better time to staht than right now."

An approving chorus arose from the listeners as Samba finished speaking and laid her hand beseechingly on Amanda's arm. For a moment Amanda stood stiff and frozen. Then, with as good grace as possible, she thanked her erstwhile enemy for her good wishes, and expressed her willingness to be friends.

Samba stood awhile, laughing and chatting with the others, and receiving congratulations along with Amanda. Then, excusing herself, she withdrew to a darker part of the yard, shaded by a huge magnolia tree. With the tree trunk between her and the people she had just left, she opened the bag. Something, clutched tightly between her thumb and forefinger, was dropped lightly within. It was a long, coarse gray hair she had found lying on Amanda's shoulder.

The night moved on. The guests grew merrier and merrier. Refreshments were served— all sorts of meats, preserves, chicken, cakes and cream. Samba ate sparingly, complaining of "not havin' felt well in my stummick sence day fo' yestiddy."

Suddenly a commotion arose in the group where she was sitting. Samba had fainted. One big husky young fellow picked her up and carried her into the house. No one noticed that even in her faint Samba clutched the little black bag tightly in her hands. The crowd, gathered on the outside of the house, and pressing up to the screen door, whispered, prayed, or giggled, according to their various natures.

"Lawd, I hope she ain't done got her las' sickness!"

"Mebbe dat's why she mek up wid Miz Pierre. Mebbe she done had a warning."

Presently Teresa came to the door, and called, "Miz Pierre, come dis way, please ma'am."

Ejaculations and comments followed Amanda's progress to the door. In a few minutes every one knew just why she had been called. Samba had expressed a belief that this was truly her last sickness. She wanted Amanda to do her one favor to show that all was well between them. Amanda must write a letter to her son, Andrew, bearing his mother's last words.

When the letter was completed, Samba suddenly took a turn for the better. She was soon able to rise from the bed where she lay and to set out for home in the rattling Ford belonging to one of the guests. The letter to Andrew lay in the black bag alone with the fringe and the hair.

For three days Samba was in bed to all visitors, but the fourth day found her up and about. She spent the morning behind her vines watching the men who had come to unload the furniture for the new house. Mark Wesson had gone his limit in building this new house. "Spot cash" had been paid for everything, even for the new furnishings, almost to the complete depletion of his bank account. He had not yet insured the house. That would be taken care of in a few days, after the family had moved in.

On the night of the fourth day, Samba set out on her second journey to the hut of Elias. The sky was covered with scudding clouds that intermittently cut off the light of the moon. They promised rain, but rain that would not come before morning. The darkness necessitated Samba's carrying a lantern to light her way. Arrived at the cabin, she knocked softly. The door opened, and Elias' woolly head appeared.

"Who dat?"

"Me, Samba," in a breathless whisper.

"Come on in."

"Anybody else inside?"

"No."

Quietly Samba stepped over the threshold into the miserable, foul-smelling room. After locking the door behind her, Elias stepped to the table, rubbing his hands and chuckling as if at some joke known only to himself. He peered at Samba, his red eyes glowing with malicious pleasure.

"You got dem t'ings?"

"Heah dey is." Samba placed in his outstretched hands a brown paper parcel. Placing the parcel on the table, Elias bent over it to untie its careful wrappings. The strand of gray hair, the knot of fringe and the letter lay before him.

"You played pretty slick to git dese, Samba." Elias' ragged, yellow teeth gleamed in a crooked smile.

"O, it didn't take no oncommon amount of brains," disclaimed the woman, bridling nevertheless at the compliment. "Now, what's de nex' step?"

Elias' rheumatically-knotted, dirt-encrusted hands, that had been playing idly with the contents of the package, came to a sudden stop. He folded them across his chest and stared long and searchingly at Samba, who began to grow uneasy under his gaze.

"Dat is right," he began musingly, stroking his chin with one dirty hand, "dat is de nex' 'sideration. Set down."

The rickety chair creaked as Samba adjusted her meager body to it. Elias took the stool at the end of the table opposite the woman. He gazed and gazed at her with a steady, unfathomable look. To Samba, whose nerves were already a-tingle, the look took on a quality of deepest penetration. Elias was seeing through her, beyond her, into her present—and past. He was seeing everything that she had ever thought, said, or done.

Finally Elias arose, walked over to the table where were spread his roots, charms, and other mysteries. Picking up the crystal, he turned to his seat. Placing it on the table in front of him, he stared intently at it. In the silence Samba could hear the rustling of the trees outside, as tiny breaths of air passed over them. The ticking of the Ingersoll watch in Elias' pocket was like the beating of a drum to her. At last the old conjurer began to speak in his slowest, deepest, most mysterious tones.

"Samba, I sees a heap in dis yeah crystal. Hit's tekin' me 'way back to de pas.' His' tekin' me back twenty yeahs, an' some ovah. I sees a low, shackly buildin'—low an' long. De front is lak a sto.'—Yes, I sees de wo'ds, Gin'ral Sto' on a long, uster-be-white boa'd cross de front.—Don' move, you clouds my vision.

"Hit's fo' noon on a hot day. I sees a man—hit looks lak Bob, yo' husban', comin' in de do.' He got up to de countah; he speakin' to do white man behin' de countah. De man is cloudy. Now he's comin' cleah. Hit' Mistah Thornton. Don' jump like dat, Samba! You 'sturbs me. Mistah Joe Thornton, what owned de gin'ral sto' heah long time ago. De two men talks. Dey is gittin' angry, somehow. Bob seems to be speakin' mighty imperdent to Mistah Joe. Mistah Joe jump ovah de countah—an' lams Bob in de face. Bob, he sprawls in de flo.' Now he's pickin' hisse'f up. He goes out. He done learn hits dang'ous speakin' back to a white man in Louisiana."

"'Tain't so, Elias, 'tain't so! I'm goin' out fum heah! Let me out!" Samba had arisen swiftly and was even then on her way to the door.

"Set down!' Elias' bellow filled the little shack and rolled back from every rafter and corner. Samba shrank back to her seat. Elias resumed his steady gazing at the crystal.

"Hit's mighty cloudy, now, 'cause you done broke in. Now, now hit's clearin' once mo.' Hit's black night—no moon, no stains, I sees two figgahs, a man an' a woman—"

Samba moaned.

"—creepin' up to de side of de gin'ral sto.' Dey looks in de back winder, what's pahtly open. I sees Mistah Joe sprau led ovah a table—he drunk, as usual. He done fogot hisse'f, too, fo' de big safe whut stan's in dis room be open. De two at de winder waits an' watches. Now de man be climbin' in. What's dat he got in his hen'? I b'lieve my soul hit's—a—club. Dat's what hit is!"

"You're makin' that up, Elias!"

Ignoring the woman's wildly shrieked words, the old man went on: "He bring hit down on Mistah Joe's haid. Mistah Joe falls ovah—daid. De man grabs de big sack o' money outen de safe, an' passes hit thoo de winder to de 'ooman. Now he's settin' fiah to de room, now he's climbin' outen de winder. Him an' de 'ooman goes back o' de sto', an' down to de woods, but not fo' I done seen dey faces in de crystal. Dey is—"

"No! No!" Samba fled shrieking to the door. She rattled it, shook it, but the lock held fast.

Unperturbed, Elias continued. "Dey is Bob an' you, Samba. Lucky fo' you two, de fiah done swep' de shack clean as a whistle, an burn de dead man to ashes, 'fo hit was put out. Ev'ybody thinks to dis day dat Mistah Joe done upsot his lamp an' burn hisse'f to death. Dey thinks de little box o' coin an' bills dey foun' in de safe was all he had, 'cause he was always close-mouthed 'bout hisse'f.

"But two folks knows bettah, doesn't dey? An' dey's 'fraid to make no display wid de money dey's stole, so dey meks 'way wid hit. I can't see whah, jes' now, 'cause no noise done clouded dis ball. Come here an' set down agin."

Whimpering, Samba sat down once more. Elias eyes her sternly.

"Samba, yo' whole life's done been cursed by dat evil deed. Now listen to me. Dey is one way fo' you to end yo' days in peace, an' git de bes' o' yo' enemies. Does you want to know dat way?"

Samba's "Yes" was smothered in sobs.

Elias nodded his head slowly, sagely.

"Now, dis ve'y night, aftah you leaves heah, walk back de way you come twell you reaches de end of dis lane of trees right befo' my do.' Den take de path dat leads to yo' right. Follow hit twell you gits to de aidge of de bayou in de cypress swamp by de big cypress what was struck by lightnin' las' summah. Now, when you git there, follow dese directions close. Is you listenin'?"

Samba nodded mutely.

"Fust, call on de sperrits of de air three times. Name de place whah dat money's hid, an' lif' de curse f'um hit. Jest say, 'Go to—name de place—an' bless what's there. Den, name aloud three times whatever hit is you wants done dis night by de spell I puts on dese token you done brung. Aftah de third time, drop dem in de bayou. Wait right whah you is at on de bayou aidge fo' forty-five minutes. Den go home, an' when you gits da, what-so-ever you want did will be did. You got a watch?

"No."

"Well, heah's my turnip. Dat lantern you got will he'p you see de watch face. You kin return my timepiece in de mornin'."

Samba slipped the watch into her apron pocket. Her hands trembled so that she almost dropped it. At a sign from Elias she arose from the table.

"Remembah, Samba, ef you does one little thing wrong, de curse what you brings on yo' enemy will bounce back on you. Onnerstan'?"

Again Samba nodded. She was past the power of speech. "You's sho'? Well, den, you may go, as soon as—"

Elias paused with a cough intended to be delicately suggestive of what he expected the next step to be.

Turning her back to him, Samba drew from her bosom a bulging, tightly-tied handkerchief. Loosening the knots with teeth and fingers, she finally untied it. Holding it carefully by the four corners, she placed the handkerchief on the table, and revealed its contents, a pile of quarters, fifty-cent pieces, silver dollars, and an occasional dollar in currency. Together they counted the pile—twenty-five dollars, exactly.

Smiling grimly, Elias said, "T'anks. Now do as I said, an' repo't to me in de mornin', or some time tomorrow night, ef hit suits yo' modesty bettah."

Mumbling that she would, Samba passed out of the door into the cloudy night. As she moved down the obscured path, the numbing sensation which had enveloped her body seemed now to invade her very brain. She could not think—she dared not. Her mind was a jungle of bewilderment, fear, hate, and wonderment. How had Elias found out all this? Was it really through the crystal, or had he known it all these years—that terrible secret Samba had thought buried with Bob?

Why had Elias directed her to take this path, when the one leading from the west side of his shanty was the shortest and the most direct route? He had made her take the longest and most indirect way through dense bushes and tall, darkly towering trees. For a moment she was tempted to try the shorter path, but fear of what might be the consequence of such disobedience held her feet in the path Elias had said she must follow.

It was a journey of torture. There was no light save that of her lantern, which served only to make the darkness more dark. The clouds in the sky were now like a heavy black curtain, a canopy drawn close around the earth, shutting out moonlight, starlight and air. Not daring to look back, hardly daring to go on, fearing almost to put her feet on the ground because of the possibility of stepping on some unseen, fearful night creature that might be in the way, she moved forward. Once, in a pine thicket, some drifting needles sifted against her cheek. She choked back a terrified scream. Again, a dark figure very much like a black cat, scudded across her path into the underbrush.

At last, sheer in her path, like one leg of a black giant whose body reared above the clouds, and whose other leg might be forty leagues away, there rose the trunk of a mighty cypress tree, which had been excoriated by lightning. To Samba, the marks left by the lightning danced and wriggled in the lantern light like so many snakes. On either side of her there spread a dense mass of bushes, tangled grasses, dipping willows whose feathery leaves caressed the black bayou waters, indistinguishable now in the blackness.

At the foot of the tree Samba stood still. The deathly silence filled her ears and her heart. The trees and the bushes, save for those that had lately been stirred by her passing, stood like immovable shadows, merging into indissoluble blackness. The yellow flame of the lantern lighted up the ripples in the stygian waters at her feet. A few paces away a bull-frog croaked and plopped suddenly into the inky depth.

Samba tried to stand bravely erect, but the horror and fear of the place bore down her shoulders. A cold, unseen hand was pressing her down, down, upon her knees. She opened her mouth to speak the charm. Once—twice—thrice—before the words finally came:

"Speerits of the air, go to my bedroom, lit' up de hearth-stones, an' lit' de curse, an' bless what's hid beneath it."

Half expecting a ghostly reply, she stopped. A bird roused by the unaccustomed noise chirped sleepily from the trees.

After the third cry, Samba sank down breathless. Would she have the courage to call on the spirits of the air to put the curse upon her enemy? For five minutes she sat at the foot of the cypress tree, panting, gasping, striving to command her voice. At last, she cried:

"Sperrits of the air, set fire to Mark Wesson's new house tonight an' burn it to ashes!"

Utterance of the wish gave strength to her vindictive nature, so that the second and the third times her voice was strong and confident.

When the preying, crouching silence had sprung upon and overpowered the last echo of her voice, Samba rose to her feet. Bracing herself against the tree trunk, she dropped the three tokens into the water. The hair slid from her grasp like something alive, twining and clutching at her fingers. The pebble-weighted fringe met the water with a soft splash. A thin, swishing sound told of the meeting of the water and the letter.

As the last token fell, Samba was startled by the sudden snapping of a twig behind her. For a second she forgot her perilous position on the edge of the bayou. Then, cautiously, she stepped out of danger and looked around. Nothing was visible beyond the circle of light cast by the lantern. Picking up the lantern, she turned to go, only to remember that she must remain where she was for forty-five minutes more of fear and terror.

She sank down at the foot of the giant tree, took the watch out of her pocket, and waited—waited—waited. Thrice she screamed aloud; once an owl in a nearby tree hooted, another time when something long and black with shiny eyes slithered by her in the bayou waters, and a third time when a sudden breeze shook the willow tree close beside her.

But all things come to an end. When forty-five minutes finally crept away, Samba discovered by the watch that it was exactly midnight. Trembling and quivering she made her way back, muttering, laughing, crying, babbling. When she reached the familiar open road, her legs doubled under her body, and she sank weak and helpless in the dust. Great sobs shook her, and tears rained down to mingle with the powdery yellow dust.

Suddenly, her sobbing ceased. A distant angry glow in the skies attracted her attention. The fiery red was in the direction of home. Chuckling, Samba scrambled to her feet. It was a fire, that's what it was. It must be Mark Wesson's place. The charm was undoubtedly working.

A sudden ecstasy made her forgetful of the experience through which she had passed. Wild, mad exultation lent speed to her feet. However, when she arrived at the scene of the fire, the crowd was already scattering. Nothing remained of Wesson's house but a few charred rafters, glowing tin and red hot nails.

Samba mingled with the crowd so naturally that each group thought she had been with some other group during the entire excitement. She was one of the most sympathetic who spoke to Mark and his family, and she even wrung Amanda's hand in commiseration.

Day was breaking when Samba, the last of the spectators, turned her back on the smoking ashes and smoldering rafters, to enter her own house. As she stepped into her bedroom, her first impulse was to turn up the irregular stones forming the hearth, in order to ascertain whether her treasure still rested in its hiding place. Exhaustion lay so heavily upon her, however, that after a glance to satisfy herself that the stones were in their usual position, she made ready for bed.

It was noon when a sudden loud sound, repeated at irregular intervals, aroused Samba out of a heavy sleep. Drowsily, stupid with fatigue, she raised herself on her elbow to listen. The door was slamming in the kitchen. Climbing out of the high bed, she padded barefoot into the next room. A high wind had risen, and was playing havoc with the things in the kitchen, as the rear door swung noisily to and fro. Pulling the door shut, Samba attempted to lock it. A sudden look of surprise swept over her countenance. Then dismay and fear struggled for mastery of her senses.

"Fo' God, dis lock's been broke!"

What did it mean? She knew that she had locked the door before leaving. Never in all the years of her life had she failed to do so. Had some one broken in, under cover of the fire? She had nothing anyone would want. A sudden constriction of her throat made her gasp for breath. Suppose—

Losing her hold on the door, Samba flew back to her bed-room, knelt by the hearth and began wildly pawing the stones out of place. Finally they were all thrown back, all over the small room. To Samba's eyes was revealed what had once been a hole, filled with fresh dirt. Screaming she sprang to her feet and seized a small fire-shovel leaning in one corner of the chimney. As she picked it up, she became aware of bits of fresh, damp dirt clinging to it. Sobbing wildly, talking brokenly, she stuck the shovel into the soil, which, piled loosely, allowed it to sink down, down, down. Desperately she shoveled out pile after pile of loose earth until there was left only a yawning, oblong cavity.

Weak and sick she sank weeping to the floor. No spirits had done this trick to her. The broken lock, the earth-smeared shovel, and the dirt-filled hole told her better. She had done everything Elias had said. Elias—She checked her sobbing. She sat open-mouthed. Elias— Elias—

With sudden resolution she rose to her feet and began to dress. Now and then she went to the window to look out. Yes, it would rain soon, but she would go. She had to.

A few seconds later, having made the back door fast with a piece of rope, she was on her way to Elias' shack. The first drops of rain were falling as she knocked at his door.

Surprise and great interest shone in Elias's eyes as he opened the door and saw Samba standing on the step. He took her umbrella and assisted her out of the old raincoat she wore.

"Set down! Set down, Samba, I didn't 'spect you 'fo' night. Set down!"

"No, Elias, dis ain't setting down time. I done come to ask you where my treasure be."

"Yo' treasure? Hain't hit whah—"

"No, it aint, an' somehow I believes you know dat it ain't."

"Now, Samba, I hain't looked in de crystal, an' I hain't t'ought of you sense I put your affair in de hain's of de sperrits. Ef yo' treasure's gone, de speerits seed fit to tek hit. You bettah thank yo' God dey let you off so easy!"

"Dat's a lie! No sperrits got my money."

"Keerful, keerful! Don't you talk to no conjure man lak dat. Is you lost yo' min'?"

"Los' my min'? Los' my min'?" Samba's voice rose to a shriek. "Los' my min' w'en I ain t got nary a cent in dis worl' an' nary a one to gib me a penny? Los' my min'?"

"Huh! Dat ain't so, an' you knows hit. Whah's dat strappin' boy you still got? Let 'im do somethin' for you."

Samba's voice took on a pleading strain. "Elias, set down an' look in dat crystal an' tell me where my money is."

"Woman, does you want to git found out? How could you count for having so much money, even if you knowed who had it now? What kind of a tale would you tell, an' 'mek any reasonin' person believe it? Ansuh me dat."

Samba sat in silence, head bowed in her hands. Suddenly, a gasp of astonishment tore from between her lips. With a scream she dropped on her knees, and grabbed from the grimy floor an object which had drawn her attention.

"Look! look. Elias!" She waved a long, clumsy, old-fashioned copper key, on whose dull surface glowed three long scratches.

At sight of the key, Elias, who had stepped to Samba's side, recoiled and seized the edge of the table to steady himself. His jaws worked, but he made no sound.

"Dis is de key to dat box, Elias! I knows it by dese scratches what I made de las' time I opened de box. Bob took de key an' de lock from his mother's old armoire."

Samba rose to her feet and faced the conjure man, who was drawing all his wits together for the final cursing of the old woman.

"You got my money yo'self," Samba babbled. "I unnerstan' evahthing. You wanted me to take de long way to de cypress tree las' night, so's you could go de shortest way and hide behind the bushes en' hear all I was sayin', and then you lit out fo' my house—Gib me back my money!" Her words ended in a wild screech. Elias turned his back on her, and walked to the blackened, littered fireplace.

"An' you set fire to Mark Wesson's place, to fool me into thinkin' sperrits did it," Samba wailed, twisting her hands. "You was probably hidin' somewhere about Mistah Joe's house that night they burned it down. You an' he was moughty thick at dat time. You just been waitin' a chance all dese years to git even 'thout hurtin' yo'self. You was too scared of Bob to do anything, while he lived. You ain't seed nothin' in de crystal, atall."

Composed once more, Elias turned toward Samba.

"Well what ef all you say *is* true?" he demanded about it? "What kin you do about it?"

"Do?" screamed Samba. "Do? I'll have de law on you, an' have yo' 'rested fo' de thievin', house-burnin' scoundrel you is! Dat's what I'll do!"

"An ef you does dat to *me*, jes' what does you 'spec' I'll do to you?" Elias drawled, insolently.

"You—you—wouldn't tell on me, Elias." quavered the woman.

Clapping his hands to his head, Elias teetered back and forth, roaring with laughter.

"Lissen to dis woman talk. She gwine turn me over to de p'leece, an' yit I mustn't say nothin' 'bout her, under no circumstances. Ain't dat rich!" His voice choked in another outburst of loud laughter.

Samba sank down on the chair. The room with all its grotesque furnishings whirled round and round her. As through a fog, and at an immeasurable distance, she heard Elias' voice.

"Now, I got de upper han', Samba, but I gwine be generous. O yes, I gwine be generous. I'll keep de money, an' your secret, too. Youse an' ole woman, now, an' ain't got much longer to live. Dat boy o' yourn kin keep yo' the three, four years yo' got to live. But membah dis," as he shook his dirty finger in her face, "Efn you, or anyone meks one move agin me, I'll tell everything, from A to izzard."

He moved to one side, still keeping his beady eyes on Samba's terrified face.

"Furthermore, I got it all wrote out, an' done put it where it kin be got in case anything happens to me, 'fore anything happens to you. Co'se, I won't use it, onless push comes to shove, you onnerstan'."

Moaning into her apron which she had thrown over her face, Samba rocked slowly back and forth.

Crossing the floor, Elias threw open the door, admitting the pelting rain.

"Heah, put on yo' coat, ole woman. Time to be on your way. Come on! Git out! Take your umbrella!"

Samba, her coat hung crookedly about her shoulders, stumbled over the rotted door-sill. The door slammed behind her. Dazedly, mechanically, she raised her umbrella against the slashing rain drops, and crept off through the wet grass.

[*The Crisis* 45.3 (March 1938): 71–73, 82, 89–90]

BRIDE OF GOD

by Octavia B. Wynbush

Leah stood in the flower garden situated on the west side of the little red cottage in which she lived with her aunt Sabriny. It was a rare day in May. The sky was blue as only the Louisiana sky can be blue, with two white clouds chasing each other across it, passing now and then over the sun in their play. A breeze that had wondered up from the Gulf and had lost its way, rustled the stiff leaves of the magnolia tree, sending a few petals of the white-cupped flowers floating to the ground at Leah's feet, and sending the mingled scents of jasmine, honeysuckle and roses to her nostrils. From the thorn bush growing in one corner of the garden, a hidden bird trilled as if his heart were bursting with the beauty and the odors of the morning.

And Leah listened, smiling. She was as happy as the singer, and therefore able to understand his feelings. They were closely akin. Neither had the power of words to express the ecstasy, but each could sing it.

"Yo sho' is happy, little bird. You mus' know how I feels dis mawnin'. Is you in love, too? Is you goin' be ma'ied tonight you'se'f?"

She laughed at her own foolish conceit, but felt at the same time that she and the bird were kin. He must be in love, he must be, for only love and its near fulfillment could make even a bird so happy.

She moved lightly, gayly among the flowers, caressing the leaves with her long, slender brown fingers, stooping to press her nostrils close to the velvety red, white and delicately pink and yellow roses, bending over the white jasmine throned in their dark green leaves. She leaned over just enough to catch their cloyingly sweet scent without letting her warm breath brown their sensitive petals. Moving to the screen-in side of the porch which formed the side of the garden enclosure, she buried her face in the cool fragrance of the clambering honeysuckled vines.

"Lawdy, Lawdy! What a beautiful day! God mus' know dis is de crowningest day of my life, He done made it so beautiful! Deah Lawd, I'm so happy I jes' can't beah it, I'm 'bout to die o' happiness. God sho' is good to let a fine man like Aleck love me 'nough to want to ma'y me."

Crossing to the north side of the paling fence that enclosed three sides of the garden, she climbed upon the stile which formed the entrance, and sat down. Turning sideways to the west, she gazed over the bluff on which her home stood, into the river flowing placidly below. Her thoughts were not of the river, however, but of her own romance. She was reviewing the incidents of her courtship.

Through her reverie she was pleasantly aware, now and then, of the stir and bustle going on in the house. Quick feet passing to and fro, laughter, much clanking of spoons in pots, the odors of delicious things in process of baking for the feast that would follow the wedding—whose heart would fail to be joyous under these conditions? Aunt Sabriny, a host of female relatives and friends were bustling and turning in the kitchen from which they had forcibly barred Leah a few minutes before.

Feet beating a quick crinch, crinch on the cinder path leading to the house roused Leah. She looked up quickly. Helen, a dear friend of hers from the village a mile distant, was coming up the path as fast as she could. Her round dark face was covered with perspiration, her plump bosom was rising and falling sharply as if she were at the point of exhaustion. Her shoes and the lower part of her stockings were covered with the yellow, powdery dust of the village roads.

"Hello, Helen, what's yo' hurry? What's de mattah?"

Leah waved her hand in accompaniment with her call. Helen gave her one glance and rushed by, into the house. It was only a glance, but it made something inside Leah stand still. What did it mean, that strangely compassionate, commiserating look in Helen's eyes?

Through the open windows of the house came the cheerful greetings of the busy women.

"How you, Helen?"

"Bless my soul, gal, what you doin' in sech a sweat?"

"What's de mattah? Why you cryin'?"

Then, suddenly, a lowering of voices, a buzzing, a sharp silence, then exclamations.

"What's dat?"

"What you say, Helen?"

"I don't believe it!"

"No, he couldn't do—"

Several loud "sh! sh's," silenced the last speaker, but Leah felt certain that the news concerned her. Quickly, with fast-beating heart she climbed down from the stile and ran to the porch.

"O God, don' let it be that somethin's happenened to Aleck. Don' let him be hurt or killed! I couldn't bear to live if somethin' happened to him!"

With almost strengthless fingers she opened the door to the screened porch, entered the house and walked unsteadily through the narrow hall to the kitchen door. There she saw the group of women huddled together, looking at each other in helpless anger, dismay, consternation. From the way in which they started at sight of her, Leah's suspicions and fears were confirmed. Straight, slim and tall, she stood in the doorway, one hand resting on either side of the entrance.

"What's wrong, you all? I know its somethin' bout Aleck. I kin feel it. Tell me! Is he hurt—or—daid?"

"Daid? I wish he was daid, the dirty scoundrel. Death's too good for him!" It was Helen who spoke so wrathfully, striking her fist on a table near which she stood.

"What you mean, Helen? Tell me, somebody, what's de mattah?"

It was Aunt Sabriny who moved out of the group and came over to stand before Leah. Tall, broad-shouldered, stout, she towered over the girl for a few moments, looking at her silently and keenly. Then, taking her gently by the hand, Aunt Sabriny led Leah into the little parlor, where the shades had been drawn to keep it cool and free from dust. There, she placed both hands on the girl's shoulders and said, looking her steadily in the eyes.

"Leah, you's a Sommers, ain't you?"

"Yes, Aunt Sabriny, but why—"

"Us folks, all us folks, yo' gran'ma an' yo' ma, an' yo' pa, an' all o' us, has a name fer bein' able to stan' up straight undah de hahdest kin' o' blows. Us ain't nevah hung we haids in front o' no kin' o' folks. If ouah hahts is breakin', us smiles befo' folks, even if us has to cry ouah eyes out when we's alone. No Sommers ain't nevah let de worl' know how he haht is bleedin'. Honey, you got to beah a hahd blow now, but you got to 'member you's a Sommers, an' no mattah how killin' it is, you ain't got to let on, even to dem women in de kitchen. Honey dat no 'count rascal Aleck done ma'ied Lisette Harris in de village ea'ly dis mawnin', an' done gone 'way wid her."

In the cool of the night, while the last breeze from the Gulf of Mexico still wandered among the flowers and the trees in the garden coaxing down adventurous petals, Leah walked to and fro, her paradise of the morning now her Gethsemane. The shock of a few hours ago had left her first of all dazed, bewildered. Then had come hot anger at both her utter impotence and her debasing humiliation. Like streaks of scorching flame and scalding water had the keen sense of her humiliation seared her spirit. Yet she was trying to follow Aunt Sabriny's advice and take it "standin' up."

"God, deah God," she moaned helplessly, weakly, leaning against the trunk of the magnolia tree and gazing at the placid river.

How could she stand it? To go on day after day, year after year, living under the shadow of such a cruel thing. Aunt Sabriny could talk about "standin' up." She hadn't gone through anything like this. She had never experienced the scorching humiliation, the shock of shattered faith, of love turned to mockery. She did not have to face living with this dumb misery in her breast. It would be easier just to climb the stile clamber down the bank, step into the river and float down, maybe to the Gulf from whence the breeze came.

Following her thoughts, she climbed over the stile and walked to the edge of the bluff. A narrow path obscured by the branches of some close-growing thorn bushes led to the river shore below. Carefully putting aside the branches, Leah began her descent. The moon shining over the middle of the river gave her aid in finding the path. Sliding and slipping, she finally stood on the sand of the shore. The waves flowing past, endlessly rippling, endlessly murmuring, dizzied her eyes and lulled her ears.

"Leah, honey!" Aunt Sabriny's arm slid suddenly around Leah's waist. How she had come there, the girl could not fathom.

"Honey, don' do it! De,' ain't no man God evah created worth a woman's killin' herself about. Life's got bettah things ahaid fo' you, honey. Bettah you foun' him out befo' den aftah ma'yin'. Mebbe it's God's way of tellin' you you'll be bettah off an' have a beautiful, happier life not tied to no wuthless man nohow. I been thinkin', Chile, mebbe you's to be a bride o' God."

"Bride o' God?"

"Yes. Mebbe you ain't to marry. Mebbe you's to spen' yo' life doin' good fo' peoples, like he'pin' de po' an' de sick, and comfortin' de widow an' de fatherless. O, I don' mean you got to go into a convent, or nothin' like dat, but I means you kin do de same good outside, right aroun' heah. Why, you kin be de light o' dis yere parish. Come honey."

They climbed slowly back up the narrow path to the cottage. After kissing her aunt good-night, Leah went to her own room. The odors of the cooked foods still lingered in the house. She knew that there after the very scent of cooking food would make her ill.

Arriving in her own room, she lit the lamp on the dresser and turned to lower the shade of the window opposite her bed. On crossing the floor, her feet caught in something soft and filmy, and ripped it. Stooping, she picked it up. It was her wedding dress. She had thrown it there in the first violence of her frantic grief. Crushed and torn, it was an emblem of herself, she thought, turning it over in her hands. Then suddenly, with a rush of tears she pressed her face into the soiled whiteness, saying with a whisper that was half sob and half hysterical laughter, "Bride o' God! Bride o' God!"

Time, that will not stay for joy or sorrow, passed on its way to Eternity, bringing with it inevitable changes. Leaning on Aunt Sabriny's firm, proud personality, Leah learned to walk calmly among her fellows, to hold her head up, and to smile, in time, as if nothing untoward had ever happened in her life. There grew to envelope her an air which, while not exactly aloof, warded off the too inquisitive and the too sympathetic. Her friends and neighbors had very soon discovered that "Leah ain't askin' nobody fo' sympathy."

As the years passed, her already kindly spirit grew more and more kindly, more gentle, more understanding. She set up for herself the ideal Aunt Sabriny had pictured that night on the river bank—"Bride o' God"—and, with little, unpretentious acts here and there she wove herself into the pattern of the community life so delicately, so subtly, that people soon found it a matter of course to refer all knotty problems to Leah Sommers. Mothers sent for her when children became suddenly ill. Wives came to weep out their vexations over wayward husbands; husbands consulted her about careless, wanton wives. Lovers sought her aid in patching up quarrels. Even the pastor of the little church came to look upon "Sis' Leah" as his unfailing source of inspiration and aid. Yet, it all came about so quietly, so unassumingly that no one, and Leah least of all, was really aware of how great a place she held.

By the time Aunt Sabriny died—an event taking place fifteen years later—Leah had established her place in the village completely. She continued to live alone in the cottage, spending most of her time in the garden. Here, on beautiful days and soft nights she met and talked with many of the people who came with their various troubles.

It was on one of these calm nights in early May that she sat quietly on a rustic bench that had been placed in the garden after people had begun coming to visit her there. Her arms were folded across her bosom, somewhat ampler than in her girl-hood; her eyes were fixed on the river flowing majestically by, at the foot of the bluff. She was thinking of the past.

Twenty years ago that very night she had suffered death without being able to die. Twenty years! The pain she had thought undying had worn first to a dull ache, and then scarcely to the echo of that ache. She was wondering tonight, as she had often wondered what had become of Aleck and his bride. No one had heard of them since. Lisette's family had been very closemouthed about the whole affair. Nobody had ever been able to pry the details out of them.

Leah sighed softly. After that unhappy incident, she had rejected every suitor, partly from pride, which made her feel that people would say she was snatching at any man to cover her humiliation, and partly from lack of faith in anything her suitors said.

But tonight she wondered. Had she done right? What would her life have been had she married? A kind husband, obedient children, happiness perhaps? Or a shiftless man, wayward children and a heavy heart? Had she really chosen the better part?

After all, she wasn't too old to marry. Only last week a woman of forty-five had been married in the village. And she, Leah, was only thirty-eight, and plenty of people said she didn't look a day over thirty. It was all right living alone now, but when old age came, and she grew too feeble to do for herself—.

A step on the cinder path roused her. Her mind flew back to Helen's flight over that path twenty years before. Leah sat still and waited. The person who was coming moved slowly, hesitatingly.

"It's a man's step, but it don't sound like no step I know. He don' know whether to come or go, 'cause they's no light in the house, I guess," she murmured to herself.

Rising, she climbed over the stile and walked across to the steps. The man was so far down the path and coming so slowly that she had ample time to enter the house and light the lamp. She was standing in the door when he opened the screen and crossed the porch.

"Good evenin', ma'am," he saluted in a deep voice.

"Good evenin', sir," responded Leah. It was a stranger. She hesitated about asking him in. He did not wait for an invitation, however, but began talking at once.

"I'm lookin' for Miss Sommers,—Miss Leah Sommers—if you please."

"I'm her. What kin I do fo' you?" A kindly tone took away any brusqueness from Leah's answer.

The man stood twisting his hat, looking at her trying to say something, evidently.

To relieve his distress, Leah repeated kindly, "I'm Leah Sommers. What kin I help you do?"

From his lips as from a dry, husky cavern, came the words, "Leah, don't you know me? I'm Aleck."

Leah's form stiffened. She drew back into the room, her hands on the door. A surge of anger, hatred, bitterness she had not dreamed of rose suddenly prompting her to shut the door in the face of the man who had so cruelly humiliated her.

"Leah! Fo' God's sake don' shet de do' on me! I know I deserves it, I know it, but I'm in trouble, an' I come to you fo' help. Please! Please! I won't come in—I ain't fit—but I needs yo' he'p." He was clinging to the outer door knob with all his might, frantic and piteous as a frightened child.

"What do you want o' me, Aleck Kingston, after twenty years?"

"Leah, I ain't had nothin' but bad luck sence I did de way I did. Things is gone f'um bad to wuss, an' now, now, I'm in de wuss trouble I evah did see."

"What's de mattah? What yo' done?" There was something sinister in the way Aleck had spoken the last words.

"Leah, 'bout a yeah ago, Lisette 'n' me, we got tiahed bummin' f'um place to place in de city, up north, an' we came back to de plantation 'cross de rivah. Two nights ago I got drunk an' los' mah haid, an' when de boss spoke to me de nex' mawnin' in a lonely path o' de fiel—" his voice choked; he stopped.

Leah knew what was coming. Her quick mind flew back to a rumor she had heard the day before. The overseer on the plantation across the river had been found with his skull crushed in. A posse had been searching for the murderer ever since.

"You mean you's de man what killed—"

"Yes, Leah, fo' God's sake help me. Hide me somewhere tonight an' tomorrow, an' de nex' night I'll leave."

Leah looked at the poor, shivering creature before her.

"But why'n't you travel tonight? Why'n't you try to get on? Why did you come here, anyway, Aleck? You mek me buck de law? Why fo' Gowd's sake—"

A sound in the distance broke up her speech.

"O Lawd, dey's aftah me! Leah, please, please!"

Before she could answer him, he had bolted into the house and crouched in the corner farthest from the light. Leah turned to him. Pity for an object so weak, so cowardly abject, flooded through her.

"Go up into the loft above my room," she whispered commandingly. "Nobody's in sight yet, an' mebbe dey won' come dis way, who knows? Go on, I tell you!"

As Aleck crept off, she turned to the door and stood framed in it awhile. Way in the distance came the sound of voices shouting, yelling, angry, frenzied voices, mixed with the deep voiced baying of blood hounds.

"Dey's found his trail, I know it," she thought, "Deah Lawd, help me do de right thing."

The yelling and the baying came nearer and nearer. Lights from torches, from flashlights could be seen. A great mob was swarming up the path and over the yard, a yelling, screaming mob.

Leah surveyed them calmly. One of them, a tall, commanding man, walked up to her and spoke.

"Leah Sommers, we want you to hand over Aleck Kingston, for murder."

Leah looked at him and smiled. "Lawd sakes, Mistah Johnny, ef yo' daid mothah knowed you was traipsin' 'round heah at de haid ob a crowd a no 'counts lak dat, she'd tuhn ovah in her grave. Whah's yo' raisin' any how? Don' you know de law kin handle a man lak Aleck Kingston, ef he's to be found? You don' fo'got how often I've trotted you 'roun while yo' mammy lived, ain't you?"

The man flushed deeply. He was evidently embarrassed, but did not intend to be put down so easily. So he repeated his command, but in a more mollified tone. Evidently the crowd was subject to his will, for as he talked to Leah, they contented themselves with trampling over the ground, keeping up a great hubbub, but made no attempt to enter the house.

Suddenly, behind the crowd another noise could be distinguished. Soon a troop of mounted police came riding through the mob, hurling them to left and right before the swift pace of the horses. With shouts and oaths the erstwhile clamorous, blood thirsty group melted into the night.

One of the officers, evidently in command, dismounted. The others followed suit, and spread out around the house. The first officer mounted the steps to the porch and entered it. Brusquely he demanded the business of the men in conversation with Leah.

"He's jes' a frien' o' mine, sir, came to see me on some personal mattahs," she answered quietly.

The officer then demanded the surrender of the hunted man, if he was in the house. Knowing the peril she was running into by concealing Aleck, and feeling at the same time profound pity for him in his mortal terror and abjectness, Leah prayed inwardly for help. It came, even as she prayed. Out of the shadows behind her came Aleck, straight and composed, his face alone working spasmodically. He stretched out his hands for the handcuffs.

"Officer, here I is. I've been a wicked man all my life, I guess, I gotta pay now fo' killin' dis man, an' fo' spoilin' yo' life, Leah," he said, turning to her as the officer snapped the handcuffs shut.

Leah looked at him pityingly. She knew he did not understand when she said quietly, "You ain't spoiled my life nohow, Aleck. No man kin spoil the life of a Bride o' God."

[*The Crisis* 45.10 (October 1938): 325–326, 340–342]

HATE IS NOTHING

by Joyce N. Reed [Marita Bonner]

The door would not open.

Lee's key hung in the lock. She pushed against the door with the fur coat that was slung over her left arm.

It would not yield.

She rattled the knob. And with the sudden perversity of old doors in old houses, the door swung wide.

Roger—Lee's husband—was coming down the stairs with the measured leisureliness that always marked his every move.

"Hey, ole Injun!" she started to greet him, but a door creaked open somewhere toward the back of the house.

That meant her mother-in-law was standing somewhere between the kitchen and inner hall

In the shadow.

Listening.

Why didn't she walk out where they both could see her? Why did she have to stay out of sight—keep silent—and listen?

"Where were you all morning, Lee?" Roger asked and walked toward her.

Lee left the door and met him.

"I've been in jail! Lee said distinctly so her voice would carry back in the shadow between the kitchen and the inner hall.

Roger moaned. "Anything left of the car?"

"The car? I wasn't in an accident. The car is all right. I was in a morals case—morals court or whatever you call it when you are taken out of a raided house!"

That banged the door shut.

That made the door bang shut in the shadow between the kitchen and the inner hall.

Roger said nothing. He took the coat gently from Lee's arm and stood aside so she could go upstairs. When he had laid the coat on the arm of the chair by the table, he came upstairs too. His steps were unhurried.

Lee was in her room, tossing off her hat, tearing off her gloves. She breathed in deeply and let her eyes rest on the color and loveliness that made the room.

"This is one place where Hell isn't. It has not brimstone in here yet!" Lee thought.

She touched a chair, a shade, fussed with her hair, then dropped back on the couch.

Roger closed the door carefully.

Lee turned her eyes up to the ceiling so that she would not see Roger.

There were times when she loved him for his calm immobility.

But when there was a tale to tell that carried her in quick rushes before everything—a speck of dust in the winds of Life—she never looked at him. He always made her impulses seem bad taste with his patience and aloofness.

Right now he sat silent.

There were no rays of disapproval pricking against her, but she could sense that he had gone deeper within himself. He was not reaching out to her.

"I aint approved!" Lee commented racily to herself.

Then she began to talk.

"I couldn't sleep last night," she began then waited.

Her husband did not say anything.

She started again, "My mind was hurling and racing and hurdling and hopping and skipping—so I got up at half past four—"

She stopped once more. He had told her where the keys to the car were before she went—so he knew all that.

He knew everything, too, that had kept her awake.

They had been reading—Lee had gone so far into what she was reading that she sensed rather than saw that Roger had dug a pencil out of a vest pocket and was scribbling—

He had spoken all at once. "Lee! Don't you think you spend too much money on the house?"

He had had to say it twice before she really heard him.

But she finally asked, "Why? I am spending no more than usual!"

Roger had tapped the pencil on the paper for a moment. "Well—," he seemed to be searching for words. "My mother said that she thought that we spent altogether too much!"

A geyser of angry words had roared inside of Lee's mind. "Tell your mother to end her visit that started six months ago and go home! Tell her that I did not spend nearly so much money until she decided to cook the meals alternate weeks!—And since she serves her Roger the fatted calf in every form from roast through salad and stew in her cooking weeks—my own menus have to be anemic assemblings of what I can afford! She blasts the hole in my household money—and I sweep up the dust! Tell her to go home!"

The geyser only roared inside. Lee only answered aloud soberly, "I'll look into it."

Then she had to grip her toes down in her slippers to keep from rushing out of the room at once to search out his mother—and tell her all the things that six months of pricking and prying had festered in her soul.

Lee did not go.

At thirty-three Lee was still struggling with impulse—for impulse had tangled her once in the barbed wires of an unhappiness that still—nine years after—was hard to heal.

With her eyes still on her book, Lee could see all of that unhappiness—her first marriage—spread out before her.

That first husband had drunk all of the time, yet Lee had never seen him reeling.

In the morning he would grab a cigarette in one hand, his bathrobe in the other and he would go and mix a drink.

That lit the devilish quirk in his eyes that some people called personality.

Lee had once thought that it was charm. Later she learned it was a tip of a flame from the hell-fire of the fastest living.

He drank in the morning, then he would go to see his patients and attend clinics.

Drunk—but not staggering. Only too gay, too cocky, too glib to be entirely sober.

Lee hated it. She had been afraid not for him, but for the people he treated. A drunken doctor with needles and knives in his hands!

But nothing had ever happened. His touch was too devilishly sure. Still the fear had shadowed all her life with him.

That whole marriage had been uneasy from the start—stable as the shadow of a leaf.

He had already lived three years for every year of his chronological age. But the keen edge of his excitement of living had cut new paths for her away from the conservative reserve of life as she had known it for twenty-two years—away from her Self—away from the sorrow that had given her no rest after both her parents had been swept away from her.

For awhile her impulses outstripped his insatiable hunger for good times, until finally, so sawed by the teeth of his sensuality that her soul retched when she heard him leaping upstairs (for he could never seem to walk) Lee loosed herself suddenly from him.

"I am good to you, Lee! Why can't you stay?" he had pleaded at first.

(Good to you, Lee! Good because I never knocked you down! Never bruised or hurt you with my fists! But I say nothing of the blows I have hammered on YOU!)

"Why can't you stay Lee?" (Stay and blot out more of your real SELF every time we quarrel and curse each other! Stay and blot out your Self! See if I can't make you and God lose each other!)

"I love you, Lee. There is something different about you! You are not stale—surfaced like most of these sisters! Stay with me!"

He had called Lee all the refreshing things like wild rose and sea breezes—and then he had gone off to stay with the stale-smooth-surfaces.

—Perhaps to test the surface tension of stale surfaces.

It was too much for Lee. You cannot live twenty odd years with the Ten Commandments then drown your Self in liquor and mad kissing in one year of unreal living.

Anyhow—who has ever been able to soak a wild rose in whisky, flail it to straw on the threshing floors of fleshly lust, and then care for the rose—the straw—tenderly.

Lee cut herself away.

He fought to get her back. But by knowing the right persons here and there the marriage was annulled.

People called Lee odd.

Odd. The flavor of something foreign to You grafted on to your life.

You cannot lose both your parents at twenty-two—be married and divorced at twenty-four—anneal the surface of a second marriage so that your background, your pride, your prejudices, your likes and dislikes are fused to those of another so there will be no seams nor cracks that are loose enough to separate into chasms between you—and be a "placid pool of sweet content."

The tense aching spots left by the two edged sword of sorrow—the fearful doubt and shattering devastation of a disgusting love—stoke fires of unrest in you that will not cool to ashes no matter how many tears you pour over it all.

"It won't break me to lose you!" he had sneered at the last.

God did that breaking.

One night, following a lonely country road home from a gay carouse, his car turned over and pinned him underneath. Only ashes and charred metal were left next morning.

Some people say another man's wife was with him, but it was never known. It was all hushed up, erased by the sleight-of-hand coups of a society that whitewashes the crimson of Babylon with the blandest perfumes of deceitful sophistry.

It did not matter.

Lee had never loved him truly and intensely as she did Roger. But what woman who has been close enough to a man to have been his wife could hear that his funeral pyre had been lit one drunken midnight on a lonely road without a shudder? Who could have him in the arms of a weak fool and not burned with remorse because she had left him as had found him—a weak fool?

Lee shuddered and wondered what the Great One had said to a man who had lived for and by all the things He had told men to leave alone?

What had God said to a man who—drunk with all the excesses of living—had met Death on the run?

Just because a jumble of creeds have created a mist that blurs the simple boundaries of the Way, men who live as he had lived, think Truth lies smothered under the dust of centuries of men's willfulness—blotted out so that a God cannot even know the Way.

Cannot know the Way—or still see every man.

There could be, then, no mild ordinary wonder about painful things in a mind that had suffered as Lee's had.

If Roger's mother told him when Lee was not present that his wife spent too much of his money—and said nothing to Lee—she meant to cause trouble.

Trouble.

The first shadow of Hell once more across Lee's path of living.

Lee had thrown her book from her and left the room where she and Roger had been reading.

"Is she trying to turn him from me? It's a slow process—this turning a person away from someone else! A paw here! A claw there! A knife thrust there! Some wicked tonguing everywhere!"

Lee had run a warm bath to sooth herself. All the unspoken bitterness fretted her still, though.

—Was the snake curled up in the center of Eden from the very start—or did she just happen to come and visit one day? And when she had observed the love, the loveliness, the peace and plentitude, did she decide that all this was too good for a poor fool like Lee—and straightway begin her snakiness?

By three o'clock in the morning Lee had worked over a dozen-dozen unpleasant situations that had been set up during the past six months. They all chained together and led to what?

Now it happened that Lee's mother-in-law hated her. Mrs. Sands belonged to that generation of older Negroes most heavily cursed by the old inferiority hangover left from slave days.

She was one of those who believed that when an exceptional Negro is needed for an exceptional position—or when a colored man in an exceptional position marries—only the nearest approach to a pure Caucasian type is fit or suitable.

Mrs. Sands had never forgiven Roger, her only son.

He had raised her hopes to great heights when she saw him, an exceptional colored man in an exceptional position—and then he had dashed her sensibilities by bringing home a brown-skinned wife whose only claim to distinction was good breeding.

Not that Mrs. Sands conceded good breeding to Lee. To her the most necessary ingredient for anything that set a person apart was the earlier or later earmarks of bastardy.

Mrs. Sands hated Lee.

As long as the contacts between the two women had been limited to casual visits, there had been enough frosty smiles and felt-covered nippy remarks on the one hand and smothered annoyance on the other to pass for polite courtesy.

But when the frost and nippiness became a daily portion, the world inverted itself and what had been harmony and peace began to crack, and hell peeped through.

It was deep down. Only women know about claws sunk so deeply in an enemy's flesh that they are out of sight.

The surface skin—the civilized covering—is unbroken.

So small a thing as "my mother says we spend too much"—was like a fuse that might lead to one stick of dynamite—or it might lead to a whole mountain range of high explosives.

By four o'clock in the morning, hot-eyed and restless, Lee crawled out of bed. She lifted herself carefully so she would not waken Roger.

His breathing was even, steady and placid.

The very calmness of his sleep fretted her. She hurried into her slippers and crossed the hall to her own room.

Even here ugliness had stalked her.

"Why do you need satin chairs in a room that you use every day?" Mrs. Sands had asked her once.

"Because I love lovely things around me every day," Lee had retorted.

Had she been trying to make Roger think her extravagant even then?

What was she trying to do? Why was she always picking, twisting, prying, distorting the most ordinary things of their life together?

"I am going out! I can't stay in this place. I'll drive out on the river road," Lee decided suddenly.

She pulled on a black corduroy suit—yellow sweater—a yellow felt hat—caught up her fur coat.

She felt in her bag. Roger must have the keys to the garage. She opened the bedroom door again and went in.

Roger spoke suddenly through the darkness. "Lee?"

"Yes."

"The keys are in the gray tweed vest in the closet."

She turned on a small light, opened the closet door, inserted swift fingers and found the keys.

"Be careful!" Roger said and held out one arm.

That meant that he expected to be kissed.

Lee did not want to kiss anybody. She began a struggled to enter her coat drawing nearer to the door all the while.

"I am just going to take an early drive! Can't sleep!" she offered from the doorway.

Roger shifted his position in the bed.

"You live too intensely, Lee!" he replied and yawned.

"Some more of Mama's talk!" Lee's mind clicked. "We can't all take life in cow-like rhythmics!" she shot at him.

Then she raced down the stairs, crossed the kitchen and went out to the garage.

The city slid away behind her and the twists and turns of the broad road beside the water made her forget herself for awhile.

It was not until she had run as far out as the little colored settlement—Tootsville—that she stopped. And then she had only stopped because the paved road ended where Tootsville began.

Deep yellow streaks were showing to the east where the sun was coming up out of the river mists. The tar-paper and tin houses of Tootsville looked so inadequate and barren of any beauty that Lee began to wish that she had driven in another direction.

But what was the need of trying to leave ugliness? It had to be seen through—and lived through—or fought through—like her own troubles.

Tears gathered swiftly in her eyes and she laid her head on her arms, crossed on the wheel and cried for a long time.

Lee had raised her head to wipe her eyes when she saw running toward her, a colored woman so stout that she might have been running off of a comic strip.

Though the fog of a wintry morning was just beginning to rise from the water, the woman was dressed only in a cotton housedress, a ragged sweater and a huge pair of felt bedroom slippers.

Stumbling and slipping grotesquely in the muddy road, she came abreast of Lee's car.

"It must be pretty terrible, whatever it is to drive you out in those clothes on a morning like this," Lee thought to herself. She ran the glass down swiftly in the door beside her and called to the woman, "Need any help?"

For an answer the other woman wrenched at the back door of the car. Lee pivoted and unlocked the door.

She sat silent and waiting while the woman lay back against the cushions and puffed.

"Jesus sure sent you to help me!" the woman managed finally. "I got to go to the lockup! Annie Mae is in there!"

Lee turned her ignition key and put her gloves on. "I am sorry I don't know where the lock up is. Can you tell me?"

"O, shure, honey! You just go back down that away apiece and turn at Sis Joneses house and cross the railroad track and its right nigh to the preacher's!"

"May God forgive us," Lee prayed to herself. "Suppose you tell me as I drive along. Get up front with me."

The woman began to outshout the motor. "Willie Shack, he come busting up to my door talking about my Annie Mae! She and Lee Andrew Miller both been put in the lockup! I keep telling that gal to let Lee Andrew alone! She aint but eighteen and here now they gits into one of them raids last night and now she in jail this Sunday morning! I gonna stop at the preachers if God helps me and see if he can't go up to the lockup with me!"

"Will he bail your daughter out?"

"Naw! I can do that myself!" She patted her bosom with the palm of her hand. "Got my rent money here! Landlord, he have to wait! The reverend he gonna marry them two right in the lockup so when some of these nosey niggers says to me long about next week— 'Seems like I heard somebody say your Annie Mae was in the lockup lass week!'—Then I can bust right back and say, 'You liable to hear 'bout anything child! Meet Annie Mae's husband!' Then they'll heish! See?"

"I see," Lee told her.

"Here's de preacher's! Let me git out!" And she was out on the pavement and up the stairs before Lee had warped the car into where a curb should have been.

The Reverend must have been accustomed to being roused at dawn to minister to his flock. He came out surprisingly soon neatly dressed in a frock tail coat.

No one asked Lee her name, so she did not offer it. She merely drove off and pulled up before a two story tin shack that sat directly on the ground.

"Here's where that fool gal is!" the mother burst forth. "Git out Reverend! Gawd have mercy! Much as I tried to do to raise that gal decent! That Lee Andrew Miller! Dirty dawg!" She muttered to herself and she waddled up the stairs.

Lee locked the car and walked in behind her.

A dirty slouch of a white man was sitting half asleep in a chair tilted against the wall. The chair crashed down as the woman and her minister walked in.

"What you want?" the man in the chair growled.

The reverend was the spokesman. "We want to see about the lady's daughter, Annie Mae Smith."

"When did she git in?"

"Last night, mister!"

"Hey Jim," roared the man from his chair. "Second back!"

There was a sound of doors opening, of feet stumbling and an undersized black girl, shivering in a cheap velvet crumpled dress, came walking out.

"This must be Lee Andrew," Lee thought as the swaggerish black man followed the girl.

Annie Mae was blinking dazedly. "Morning Reverend," she offered sheepishly. "Lo' ma!"

Ma sniffed and spoke not a word.

The man who had been asleep in the chair yawned to his feet and moved over to an old desk. "Couldn't you find no better place to take your girl, Willie?" he growled at the black man.

"Naw, sir." Lee Andrew accepted the "Willie" and all the rest of it with an apologetic grin.

"All right! That little visit will cost you fifteen bucks!"

Lee Andrew dug deep in a pocket and dragged forth a crumpled mass of dirty bills. He flung a ten and a five down on the desk with a more-where-that-came-from swagger.

"Why the hell didn't you make your boy friend take you somewhere else?" was the next demand—this time of Annie Mae.

She could only grin dazedly. She seemed to be wincing in fright, more from her mother than the officer.

"Fifteen bucks, too, sister!"

Lee Andrew dug deep again, swaggered a little more, but could only produce ten dollars in singles. Mama bustled forward and laid three dollars more on the desk. But there were still two dollars missing.

A panicky hiatus followed. No one seemed to know what to do.

"There are five dollars remaining for my table next week in my bag!" Lee calculated to herself. "If I risk two of them on this girl, I'll have to serve Roger tinted broths for dinner! And his mother—!"

Lee drew out the five dollar bill.

As he made the change, the man at the desk swept Lee with his eyes.

"Who are you? The dame that was running the joint?"

Before Lee could select the worst of the retorts that avalanched through her, the Reverend spoke. "She is just a lady what helps the community at times!" he supplied smoothly.

The other man made no reply. He made a great show of writing with a scratching pen.

From the place where she was still fastened with rage, Lee could see what he wrote.

"Willie Lee Miller—five dollars. Annie Mae Smith five dollars." He wrote beside the two names.

"Dirty thief!" Lee had to choke the words deep in herself.

But already the mother and the minister, with much whispering and bustling were pushing Lee Andrew and Annie Mae to the back of the room.

And standing right there in the ugliness and the dirt, the minister began; "Dearly beloved! We are gathered to unite this man and woman in the bonds of holy wedlock!"

Holy wedlock—

Tears crowded into Lee's throat. She looked at the mother. She was grinning joyfully. Lee Andrew smirked. Annie Mae was still dazed and frightened.

Lee could feel that old tangle of barbed wire eating into her flesh. Her first marriage— a runaway affair. A justice of the peace. Liquor on *his* breath.

Drunken fingers gripping tight—eating down into the flesh of her arms the way barbed wire does when it is settling for a grip.

Settling for a grip that always digs a scar too deep for eternity to ever fill again.

Lee told Roger all this.

Even as she talked there was a knocking at the door. A soft knocking, but a sharp insistent rupture of the peace in the room.

"It is time for dinner! Roger? Roger!! Your dinner will be cold!"

It was his mother, calling Roger for dinner. Calling Roger for dinner from his wife's room as if she were not there. All the prongs of ugly thoughts pricked Lee at once. "In my own home—she means to omit me!"

Roger stood up hastily. "Glad you could bail Annie Mae, Lee, but we'll talk about it all after dinner. It is time to go down, so we had better hurry." He left the room.

Lee did not follow him at once. She stood up and took off the jacket of her suit.

"I'd rather go out again. I can't sit to the table with her!" Lee stood alone with herself again.

But she had gone out hours before. She had driven fast and far and come back with still no peace in her.

"Oh there's no need to run and to think and talk to myself! Wrong things can't whip you around in Arabian cartwheels forever! There is a place where they have to stop! Things have to stop! Gouging into you! Something will turn it all aside and there'll be peace and no more whipping and gouging! I'll go down!"

She freshened her face.

She would have to step aside—let go of her own thoughts—push them aside and rest the case with herself and God.

It was the point where no human mind could unravel or untangle the snarls of her life. Only a greater mind could untangle—unravel—could go before her and straighten the crooked places.

Lee went down stairs.

Roger's mother was preening herself excitedly in the chair opposite her son. Lee sat at the side of the table.

As a guest should have sat—Lee sat at her own table.

The mother began to talk. "Lauretta Jones is having a little tea—a sort of wedding reception—for her son Henry and his bride this afternoon!"

"Oh did they finally work up to launching the bride?" Lee asked. "There was some talk the last time I heard as to whether she would be accepted."

An angry red crept over the older woman's face. "Any connection of the Jones family is most certainly the best this city can offer! Why Lauretta's husband, Atty. Henry Lyon Jones, represents the third generation of lawyers in that family! And Lauretta was a *Brewster* before she married! The Brewsters can trace their name back to the old aristocrat who owned their grandmother! The Jones family is certainly one colored family that can claim aristocracy, I can tell you! Acceptable? Any Jones is accepted!"

("The man who owned their grandmother." Lee's mind echoed. "Aristocratic!")

"Must is!" declared Roger. "If Miss Lauretta's darling Henry never went to jail for petty larceny—then they really must be exceptional! Why Lee, when we were all living in the frat house back at college, that guy would swipe anything hockable from anybody's room! Overcoat—watch—fountain pen—typewriter—anything! He even took my cuff links! Some that had belonged to mother's grand-father!"

Mrs. Sands red glow deepened. "Roger, you must never tell that! It might get to poor Lauretta's ears and it would hurt her so! I just believe that you lost them yourself."

"I couldn't have lost them myself! I never wore them. I always kept them in my case!"

"Maybe the women who cleaned up stole them. Those ordinary Negroes are such petty thieves! I'll never believe Henry took them."

("The *man* who owned their grandmother!) The Brewsters trace their *aristocratic* name to him. Now—! Those *ordinary* Negroes"! Lee repeated this all to herself.

"I wouldn't believe it either if Atty. Jones hadn't had to come up to school every year and pay off different guys for the stuff old Henry had swiped during the semester! I mean things they saw afterward in the pawn shop themselves! Everybody knew about Henry!"

Lee spoke suddenly. "Well, I don't understand why they are laying the red rug and elevating the canopy for Henry's Pearl—isn't that her name? They surely shut the door in Ann's face when she married six years ago! Mrs. Jones's daughter Ann certainly deserves as much as her son Henry!"

Mrs. Sands voice took a higher note: "But look at what Ann married! Some *janitor's* son! And they say his mother was a perfect Aunt Jemima. Why poor Lauretta nearly died! She was so afraid Ann would have a child that she didn't know what to do! Why there has never been anybody as colored as Ann's husband in any of the Jones's family for generations!"

"Yet when Ann's husband bought up half the Negro district a little later, poor Lauretta began to ride everywhere everyday in one of her son-in-law's cars," finished Lee drily. "I won't be at the tea this afternoon! All of Ann's friends—her real friends—those who went to see her all the years when Miss Lauretta wouldn't—swore we'd never go to anything that the Jones's tribe might give for Henry's wife. She and Henry lived together for two years before they finally decided to get married! Ann has really never forgiven her mother."

"Oh, you say the worse things, Lisa! (Mrs. Sands never called Lee by her short name.) Why shouldn't a girl forgive her mother—the one who gave her life?"

"And what a life! They tell that she always nagged Ann to death! Anyhow—why should a mother shut the doors of her home in the face of her daughter because she chose to marry a man blacker than her mother would have chosen for her son-by-marriage?"

Mrs. Sands drew her lips in with a I won't-push-this-fool-argument sneer. "I shall want you to drive me to Lauretta's after dinner, Roger," she told him after a slight pause. "Lauretta expects you! She and I were girls together!"

"Roger," Lee asked. "Do you care to meet a bride who spent two years as a wife before she was finally married?" Mrs. Sands red paled to a gray. Roger laughed.

"Don't be so shocked, mother! That was town talk all the years Henry was supposed to be off on that tour for an intense study of business. Of course everybody who spent those years hashing over the situation is going to fall into Miss Lauretta's this afternoon! They'd be afraid to stay away for fear someone might think they didn't belong!"

"And they want to add a deceitful simper to the hee-haw chorus they'll all be pouring out to draw attention to the loveliness of their cliques—to see if they can perfume away the stench around the bride's past!" Lee laughed.

Mrs. Sands laid her fork down. "Really, Lisa, if you are going to carry on this objectionable talk at the table, I'll have to excuse myself. Lauretta Jones is my best friend"—with a cross between a snort and a sniffle—"and anyone dear to her is dear to me."

Roger's voice curved gently across to his mother: "But mother!" he laughed apologetically. "Lee is only stating plainly what every durn one of them there will *know* this afternoon! Lee is just separating the marrow from the bones for us."

(So! I am at the point that he needs to explain me to her! Upstairs will be better for me after all. At least there won't be any prejudiced ignorance in my own room! She can have the chair—the room—Roger—and everything!) Lee thought to herself. "Sorry," she said aloud coolly to the mother, "the truth always will be the light, but light really blisters certain types of skin! I'll take a cup of tea upstairs in my own room."

Her chair went back in one swift push....—"If you'll excuse me!"

—So the cartwheels were still there.

—So this was not the time to straighten the crooked path.

Lee went out of the dining room to the small inner hall, where there was a cabinet of glass and dishes.

"I'll take my tea-pot and use my best small cloth upstairs. Maybe the touch of elegance will take my mind off of things."

She opened the drawer where the linens were and reached into a special corner where the cream damask lunch-cloth stayed.

It was not there.

Only two large table-cloths were left in the drawer.

"I know it isn't in the laundry! What on earth has happened to it!" Lee spoke aloud to herself.

She drew out an old stool and stood up to open the cabinet door.

Lee owned a tea set of cut glass with black inlay, a lovely Victorian ornate thing that had been her great grandmother's. That grandmother had been a seamstress for a wealthy group that had brought her gifts from every country they had visited.

Lee kept the tea set on a top shelf where nothing could possibly hurt its old fashioned loveliness.

She climbed up on the stool.

The top shelf was bare.

Lee stared at the empty space.

Roger's voice reached her; "Lee! Telephone! It's Mrs. Jones! She's having some sort of hysteria on the wire! She says Henry's new wife just dropped two of your cups—Say! You ought not to jump off of that chair like that! You will break your neck in those heels!"

Lee pushed Roger out of the way and threw the dining room door wide open.

Mrs. Sands was still in her seat. Something in Lee's face made her half rise.

"You gave Mrs. Jones my tea set!" Lee did not speak loudly at first. "You took my grandmother's tea set—without asking me!"

The older woman dropped back. Her ready sneer rode her features. "Surely anything in my son's house is mine too!"

"There are some things in your son's house—(which happens to be my house too)—that do not belong to your son! That tea set was mine! You had no right to touch *one thing* in here without asking me!"

"Asking *you*? I am his *mother*!"

"And I am his *wife*!"

This was one of the spots where life left no words to fight with.

But *eyes* can carry a battle forward.

Roger spoke, "Answer the phone, Lee!"

"Throw the phone and everything else out the window!" Lee told him. ("Any fool could have said something wiser!") Lee told herself.

And she ran all the way up stairs to the couch in her room.

She heard Roger come up the stairs soon after.

He walked into his rom. There was a sound of his closet door opening. He came out into the hall again and walked along the hall.

"Don't let him come in here!" Lee prayed to herself.

But the door opened. She kept her face buried on the couch. She could hear him cross two of the small spaces between the rugs. Then he stood still.

"I am going after your tea set, Lee," he said after a moment of silence.

There wasn't anything to say now. There was nothing to say unless you meant to use your words as a hatchet to hack out the roots of bitterness.

And Lee was too tired to hack. She'd spent too much strength trying to keep from blasting roots at the wrong time.

She kept her face turned to the pillow and waited.

Lee waited to hear Roger walk across the two small spaces between the rugs again. That would have meant that he was going out of the room.

But the sound did not come.

She twisted over suddenly.

Roger stood looking out of the window, his face in profile to her. Tense lines furrowed deep with a bitterness within, were drawn around his mouth. He stared far before him with the glaze of sadness you see in a person who has had to look a long time—alone—at some deep wound life has gashed in him.

"Why—*he* has seen how hatefully highhanded his mother can be—before this!" Shot swiftly through Lee's mind. "He has seen her do things this way before! *Her own* way! And to hell with you—your sense—your sensibilities—your property—or even your own soul! He has seen this all his life."

She started to rush over to him and throw her arms around him. But if she did that, the glazed sadness and the tense bitterness might run together. Then things might be said that could never be unsaid.

She would have to put her mind ... and not herself—between him and the thing that was hurting him.

That thought made her able to drop her feet to the floor.

"I'll go with you Roger," she suggested. "There's a detour on the river road that I saw this morning. You might miss it in the dark. Better wear a heavy coat. It's damp over there near the water."

She began to talk lightly while she powdered her nose, touched her lips and her cheeks, put on her hat and coat.

Then she ran downstairs ahead of him.

Passed the dining room door.

Talking—talking—lightly—lightly—lightly—spinning a gossamer of light talk so that there would be no chance for even one weighted word.

There are some cancerous spots in people's lives that no one ever wants to touch.

She did not wait for Roger to answer. She did not want him to answer, until the lines in his face were softer.

There are some cancerous spots in people's lives that no one ever wants to touch. Never.

She shook the door of the car a dozen times before she realized it was locked and Roger was digging in his pockets for the keys.

They were ten miles out on the River road before Roger spoke: "You take much better care of me than I do of you. I am afraid, Lee!" was all he said.

It was enough, though.

His face was not bitter drawn, hard and old now. He was himself once more.

It was enough.

She had blurred, then, some of the saw-toothed edges of hatefulness that must have eaten into him before this.

"Why *she* meant to go! *She* wanted to go to the tea! And we forgot her!" Lee remembered suddenly.

"We forgot her!"

And the fear of the hate that had seemed so strong—so full of power?

"I even forgot to be afraid while I was trying to help Roger get back into himself!"

And if you can forget the fear of a hate—walk out even for one second from under the shadow of the fear—that means it is nothing.

Nothing.

No hate has ever unlocked the myriad interlacings—the *front* of love.

Hate is nothing.   [*The Crisis* 45.12 (December 1938): 388–390, 394, 403–404]

Ticket Home: A Christmas Story

by Octavia B. Wynbush

"There, I reckon that'll do."

With a last part of her gray-streaked hair showing beneath the dilapidated felt hat whose draggled feather still made a gallant fight to stand erect, the woman turned from the cracked mirror above the scarred washstand perched crazily on its three good legs in the corner by the one window of the small, dark, musty room she called home.

Home! The very thought called up a vision of what she would soon see. No more of the smelly, stuffy hole for her—at least for a few days, maybe forever, if things broke for her this time.

The word "if" drew her thin, pasty-colored lips into a grim, sardonic smile. That little word was such a mighty one. All her life had been conditioned by it.

If, at the death of both her parents, she had not been reared by an older sister whose tender heart forbade her chastising "the poor little orphan," she would not have grown into a willful, head-strong girl. If she had not been so willful, she would not have married Andrew against her sister's wishes. If Andrew had not been the cruelest, meanest man on God's earth, she would be with him now, and with their baby—only the baby wouldn't be a baby any more, for by now she must be—. The woman ticked the years off on her fingers. Fourteen, fifteen, sixteen. Yes, the girl was now sixteen.

"I hope to God she isn't headstrong like me. Hope she doesn't spoil her life like I did mine at her age."

Well, spilt milk can never be collected. The grim mouth softened slightly, as the woman walked to the window, streaked and grimy with successive layers of soot, dried rain drops, and melted snow crystals. She looked down into the street below.

For a while, any way, the clattering vine street cars, the dashing taxis, the unkempt men and women drifting in and out of the Piccolo club, the dirt and trash in Eighteenth Street, would be something she used to know in Kansas City.

Turning from the window, she leaned over the low foot of the once-white iron bedstead, and picked up the old black pocketbook resting on the torn spread. She viewed the pocket-book with pride. Bought for five cents at the rummage sale, it showed class, just the same. It had been a mighty nifty bag in its day. Folks would think she had owned it a long time.

Once more she opened the bag; once more she removed a newspaper clipping so worn that the print was scarcely legible. Not that she needed to read it, for she knew the contents by heart. After carrying one clipping for six months and a few days, one should know its message. Mechanically she read it.

"PROMINENT CITIZEN FOUND DEAD

LAOTA, LOUISIANA, June 16—Louis Tourquee, one of Laota's oldest and most prominent citizens was found dead in his home yesterday, the victim of a heart attack.

At one time Mr. Torquee was rated among the wealthiest Negroes of this section of the state, but suffered severe financial losses in 1929.

He is survived by one niece, Mrs. Nanette Waller, of New York City, and a grand niece, Evelina Harden, aged 16, of Laota. Another niece, Mrs. Margaret Harden, disappeared about fourteen years ago, and has not been heard of since."

The tears blurred the picture which accompanied the clipping, but she knew every feature of that kindly face by heart. After six months, she was assailed once more by the desperate ache and grief which had borne down upon her that first day when she realized that her poverty forbade her returning to look just once again upon the face of him whose gentleness and love she had flouted. Never would she forget the longing to smooth down those two wild tufts of hair which had always stuck out from his temples.

"Well," she muttered, snapping the clasp on her pocketbook, "I didn't get to see him, but anyway I'll get a wreath for his grave. I'll maybe get a peak at the baby. Only she isn't a baby any more."

Again she wondered, as she often had during those fourteen years, how "the baby" had fared with her father.

"He'd be kind to her. He'd love her. She was such a sweet baby."

It was the same thought with which she had sought to soothe her conscience through all the years.

Even after Andrew's second marriage, two years after her disappearance, she had soothed herself with this idea. Now she remembered the pictures of that wedding—pictures in every Negro newspaper in the United States. It had all been carried out in grand style, that wedding, true to Louisiana traditions. It had taken place on Christmas Day, on the lawn of the Thiaux home, under a natural arbor of roses.

Margaret sighed. Roses at Christmas time. They were never more beautiful. She would see them again, and maybe, pluck a few growing through the fence pickets in Uncle Louis's garden. No one would grudge her a rose or two.

She moved to the faded green cretonne curtain hanging across the corner behind her door, drew it back, and took down the black coat hanging there. Every time she put it on she breathed a prayer for being lucky that week before Thanksgiving when the Hurst Loan company was giving coats away. She patted the inner pocket to be sure the cloth bag with her forty dollars was still there. Her round-trip ticket would cost about thirty-five dollars and a few cents.

Besides taking care of a few incidentals such as car and taxi fare, the balance would get her lodging and food in one of the humble homes where she would go. She would not go to the home of any one of her girlhood friends for shelter, not from any fear that they might recognize the slender, almost beautiful girl of sixteen in the thin, hard-featured, cynical-mouthed woman who looked at least twenty years older than she actually was, but because she knew that not one of them would open a door to the type she now represented.

But knowledge had ceased to worry her, the only thing that mattered was that she had been able to scrape together enough money to buy her ticket home.

Ticket home! Her eyes sparked as she buttoned her coat around her.

Ticket home! Her face lighted with a smile that found for an instant traces of her girlhood's beauty as she picked up her pocketbook and lifted the cardboard suitcase from its place on the floor.

Ticket home! Her hands trembled with eagerness as she stood in the dim hall and turned the key in the lock of her door.

Ticket home! Her feet recaptured the lost buoyancy of youth as she flew down the dirty, dark stairway to the street.

The chill of the day, the grimy slush of trodden snow in the street, were unnoticed as she lifted herself aboard a street car; nor did she feel her usual annoyance at pushing through the crowded aisle to find a strap to cling to.

Ticket home! Her heart sang as she lurched and swayed with the other passengers, on their way downtown, no doubt, to do last minute Christmas shopping. December 22! In the twenty-four hours from the time her train left, she would be in Louisiana, where the roses were, and her baby.

Forgotten were the sacrifices and the expediencies by which the forty dollars had been obtained. The sacrifices had lifted her soul; the expediencies—well. Only one thing mattered now—How would she manage to get sight of Evelina?

"I want to see her. I gotta, even if it's just a tiny glimpse. I gotta see my baby."

The frank, questioning stare of the woman above whom she was standing made Margaret realize that she must have spoken aloud. Her confusion vanished before the kindly, understanding smile which came into the other woman's eyes.

"I have to be careful," Margaret told herself, "or someone'll think I'm crazy."

The walk from the transfer point at Eighteenth and Walnut streets to Main street, and the wait there for the Union Station car, did not fret her as it usually did. Nor did she mind the honking, rushing taxis which interrupted her progress from the car through station plaza.

Not until she had passed through the revolving doors into the foyer and felt the warmth within, did she realize that she was shivering from cold and excitement.

"Gotta warm a minute, if I have time."

She glanced at the clock. Yes, plenty of time—forty-five minutes, in fact.

"I'll warm first, then get my ticket."

Crossing the foyer and entering the women's waiting room, she was making her way to a radiator, when her attention was drawn to a group of white women in a corner by the washbasins. Curiosity made her pause to stare at the group, but instinct reminded her:

"They're white. I got no right to stick my nose in their business. Better tend to my own."

Sound of sobs mingling with the distressed, coaxing voices of the women, each of whom seemed trying to give some one advice, roused Margaret's curiosity further.

"None of my business," she shrugged, turning her back just as one of the women glanced up at her. Evidently the woman who had looked up said something to the rest of the group, for the talking ceased.

"They needn't stop chattering. I'm not listening to what they're talking about." Margaret felt a hand on her shoulder. Turning, she faced the woman who had noticed her entrance.

"Excuse me," began the stranger, but perhaps you can help us."

"Help you?"

"Yes. You see, there's a little colored girl over here in distress. She's crying her heart out. She won't tell us what the matter is. When one of us suggested having the Traveler's Aid look after her, she nearly had a fit. Maybe you can get her to talk to you."

Margaret's eyes widened. Through her mind flitted the thought that no discerning woman of her own race would approach her to help a girl in distress.

She said, however, "Sure, I'll find out. I understand my girls. Just leave her to me."

With the expression of washing their hands of an extremely disagreeable piece of business, the white women picked up their luggage and left the room.

For a second Margaret and the girl stared at each other. What Margaret saw was a slender, graceful, dark, brown-skinned girl of sixteen, wearing a chic dubonnet velour tam aslant gleaming black curls, which framed her delicately-featured, tear-stained face. Her navy-blue coat, of good warm woolen, stopped at the stylish length from the floor above shapely, silk-clad legs and small, well-shod feet.

"Class, all right. Belongs to the upper crust. Probably'll give me the high and mighty." But the smile Margaret gave the girl was returned readily.

"Come over here and sit down, and tell me all about it, little miss."

"Thank you." The southern accent was unmistakable. It had the flavor of Louisiana.

"Well?" They were seated side by side in two low rockers.

The girl began to talk.

"I know you'll think I'm an awful nuisance, carrying on as you saw me, but I'm in awful trouble."

"What happened?"

"I—I've lost my ticket money, and all I had, besides."

"How'd that happen?" Margaret asked quickly, to check another flood of tears she saw rising.

"Some one cut the handles of my bag while I was coming from the train up here. There was such a crowd—"

"Had it dangling from your arm, I bet? You should know better than to do that trick in Kansas City, or in any city, for that matter."

"Well, you see, I—I've never been in any big city, before—except New Orleans."

"New Orleans?"

"Yes, and then I was with my—my—father."

"Why didn't you let those women take you the Traveler's aid? They'd at least see that you could telegraph your father."

"Well—"The girl hesitated. She looked at Margaret questioningly, suspiciously.

"Go ahead, tell me. I won't make you any trouble. Only, make it snappy. I've gotta buy a ticket and grab a train myself."

"You see. I'm running away—to my aunt in New York—I can't let anybody like the Traveler's Aid know, because they might send me back home."

"Now, sister, you're a nice girl, from a nice home. I can see it in your manners and your clothes."

"Nice home!" There was anger and hate in the young voice. "If you mean a modern home and money and people to wait on you, like most people do when they say 'nice home,' then it was a nice home. But if you mean a place where there's love and kindness and understanding, it—it—was hell to me."

"That's not the language for a girl like you to be using. Suppose you start in front and tell me everything, so's I can understand. I'll have to know, if you want me to help you."

"I'm not going to tell you where I'm from."

"You don't have to."

"Nor my name."

"You don't have to do that, either. But you're wasting my time."

"My father is the meanest man in the whole world."

"He couldn't be."

"Yes he is. He's so mean that my mother left him and me, when I was only two years old. She stole away one night, after putting me to bed."

The girl was too absorbed in herself to notice how Margaret's fingers suddenly tightened around the arm of her chair. Nor did she see the frozen, set look which stole over her face.

"My uncle took me to live with him, after mother ran away."

"I—thought you said you were living with your father."

"I have been, since June. My uncle—he really was my great-uncle—died last June."

"And your father was mean to you, after you went to live with him?"

"Yes, and his wife—my step-mother—was jealous of me. Between the two of them, I was almost crazy."

"How did you get money to run away?"

"My uncle had put some money in a Christmas saving for me. It was enough to buy my ticket to—where I want to go."

"Where's that?"

"New York."

"Why New York?"

"My aunt lives there. She wrote me to come if I could get my fare. She didn't have money to send for that, but she said she could take care of me until I could find something to do, or until things worked out for me. She feels that father will be glad even to pay her to keep me, although he was too mean to give me money to go to her."

"But why did you come through Kansas City? It's way out of your path."

"You won't laugh at me, if I tell you?"

"Of course not." "Well, when I went to buy my ticket, I had a hunch that if I came through Kansas City, I might see my mother, although none of us has had a word from her since she left us."

"What makes you think she is in Kansas City?"

"I don't know why I think she's here, but I think so, just the same. I thought maybe I'd find her, somehow, and we'd live together. That's one thing I've missed—a mother."

"You'd never find her here. If she's alive, and has stayed away this long without saying anything to you, she wouldn't want you to find her. I'd like to believe she's dead."

"Why?"

"She couldn't possibly stay away from a child as sweet as you for fourteen years, otherwise."

"Why, how do you know it's been that long?"

"You said you were two when she left you. You look to be about sixteen. I can do a little arithmetic, myself."

"Excuse me."

"You know what I think?"

"No. What do you think?"

"You'd better grab an armful of the next train going to New York, and go to that aunt of yours. I reckon she's a mighty fine woman."

"Uncle always said so. He—said she was made of sterner stuff than my mother."

"I'm sure he was right."

"But how can I go on, with no money?"

"How much is the fare?"

"Thirty-one dollars and ninety-eight cents from here."

Margaret's rocker came to a quick stop. "How long before your train leaves?"

The girl rolled back the cuff of her fur-lined kid gloves and looked at the infinitesimal gold watch on her wrist.

"Just fifteen minutes," she answered.

"Wait here." Margaret rose. "I have a friend who will lend me the money."

"But how can I pay it back?"

"I'll give you my address. When you get to New York, and get to work, you can send it to me."

"But—"

Margaret was already out of the door. It was only a few minutes, but it seemed hours to the girl, before the door opened again, to re-admit this woman who was taking such an interest in her. She bore in her hand two envelopes.

"Here," she said thrusting the narrow one into the girl's hand, "is your ticket to New York. And for God's sake don't lose it. It'll get you there in time for Christmas, I hope."

"But what—"

"No time for question and answer period now. This one," thrusting the square envelope into the pocket of the girl's coat, "has some extra change my friend loaned me, so's you could have something for eats and taxi fare. Pick up your bag, honey, and move!"

One hand grasping her own suitcase, the other firmly holding the girl's free hand, Margaret raced through the door to the gate through which the crowd bound for the New York train was passing.

"Goodbye, and always be a good, sweet girl, and always do what your aunt says. She is a real woman."

For a moment the two looked into each other's face. A bewildered expression, a puzzled questioning look, which reminded Margaret of the sun trying to break through a fog, clouded the girl's face.

"Merry Christmas," breathed Margaret, turning quickly to join the people crowding toward the exit.

Just outside, she reached into her inner coat pocket, drew out the bag in which her ticket money and the five dollars extra had been pinned. Opening her fingers, she let the bag, now limp and empty, float away with the gust of wind which swirled stinging snowflakes in her face.

She smiled. It was just as well. There was no point in going back to Laota just to put a cheap wreath on Uncle Louis' grave, and just to see roses bloom at Christmas time.

[*The Crisis* 46.1 (January 1939): 7–8, 29–30]

OUR HOUSE

by Elisabeth Thomas

"Yes, built by Edward. Of course I planned it. A good many years ago ... been with us a long time...."

"I don't know; Negroes live forever."

As Dorcas went in and came out, the door let the diners' voices through to Edward who stood beside the pantry table. Mr. and Mrs. Burden were going away this evening for their usual autumn holiday and he had been told to be at hand for any last instructions. Waiting, he listened absently as they answered their guest's remarks about the panels, the fireplace and the moldings of the dining room.

"In all Cumberland county you won't find a better house, if I do say so. My plan of course."

Edward had his brother to help him, you must remember, dear," Mrs. Burden's voice said. "They were all young fellows then, quick and obliging. Cephas married first, didn't he? Or did Amser? They took other places with their wives. Ungrateful after we'd given them work. But we'd have had to let them go later, so it was just as well. Then Edward married and his wife came to cook for us. She was an excellent cook, for years ... but she died."

Yes, Lulie had died; first she had lived though, that gentle smiling brown girl Edward had found and brought here long ago. In the cabin beyond the orchard she had raised their brown smiling babies; here in the big house she had worked for the white folks and pleased them. In that cabin and this kitchen she had lived all of her gentle life; as he stood and watched his granddaughter in her trim apron and skimpy black dress pass through the pantry carrying the dishes of succotash, tomatoes, hot rolls which his cousin Tilly had cooked, the memory of Lulie was a pleasant scent to him.

Jelly?" Mrs. Burden's voice urged, "a little with your meat? I put up more than a hundred glasses of jellies this summer ... to my friends at Christmas ... of course I don't do the preserving myself."

Edward heard without giving much thought to what was being said. Mr. and Mrs. Burden had been talking for a good many years: to their son grown and gone now, to their guests, to each other, to him and his kin. Sometimes they spoke crossly, sometimes they complained or called in a hurry, but mostly they just talked. The sound was as much a part of Edward's working life as was the sound of the animals breathing in their stalls, the whispering of the brush harrow he dragged over the garden, the creaking of winter boughs in the orchard. Like the other creatures and objects they, too, said their own words over and over.

Yet this evening they were saying something he had not heard before or hearing had not heeded. 'Edward growing old'—yes he supposed he was, with his occasional miseries, though he had no exact record of his age. After this house was built Mr. Burden had given him charge of the land. Cornfields, calves, peach trees and apple trees, he had raised up the land as carefully as he had raised up the house. For awhile his children had helped him— white teeth shining, bare toes shoving the dust—but they had grown up and gone out to their own work, and he was still in charge, still worked the land. When the Burdens gave up the horses he had learned to drive a car. And only this afternoon he had carried out on his shoulders the trunk packed for a month's visit; a heavy trunk, but he had black man's shoulders—

His proud reflections were broken into by the tinkle of the bell.

"Well, Edward, trunk off?"

"Yes, sir." He handed the check to Mr. Burden.

"Edward, this is Mr. Doby who is going with us tonight. He has been admiring the house. I told him I never could have built it without you."

The guest set down his wine glass and looked up at Edward.

"Did you make these fireplace columns, too? And that corner cupboard?"

Edward glanced at the two flat pillars which held up the mantel protecting the drowsing red fire; he glanced toward the corner where china was ranged on carved shelves; he smiled down at the guest.

"Yes, sir," he said.

"Wonderful. And that great door and those windows?"

"Yes, sir, Mr. Burden he chose the wood, I worked it for him."

"You did some fine work in this room. Such dignity, so tranquil—that's one of the handsomest doors I've ever seen."

Edward's brothers stepped into his heart.... Those days when all of them worked together, big strong fellows, prising the ox-huge foundation stones, stringing the long boards over their shoulders, black boys' shoulders.... Sometimes they sang or shouted for pleasure in the feel of their strength as they worked.

"Thank you, sir," Edward said. "It's a long time ago."

"It is indeed," said Mr. Burden. "I couldn't build a house like this today, Doby. Eh, Edward?"

"No sir, not like this."

"Well, come now, we must get that 7:45. Bring the car around. We'll leave it at Romer's to be overhauled while we're away. But no you can't get back then."

"I'll get back, Mr. Burden."

"Any last orders to Edward, my dear?"

"No. I don't think so. I've talked over everything with Tilly. She and Dorcas will get the canning finished and clean the house. You're going to help them with the windows and rugs, Edward. Take good care of the house. It will be a vacation for all of you."

"Yes'm, thank you."

Edward helped Mr. Burden up from his chair, the guest helped Mrs. Burden up from hers and they went out of the dining room by the big door. Edward went out by the pantry door, through the back entry, and brought the car around.

It was late when he got back from the station. Tasting crisp autumn air, he hoped Tilly was saving him some supper. But though the kitchen waited in warmth with a spicy smell from the stove, no one was there. The table was crowded with glass jars and with the baskets of beans, onions, cucumbers and corn he had carried in that afternoon. "Two-three days' work for Tilly to find the top of that table," he said to himself, going on through the entry into the large square hall.

From the library came the glow of the lamp and the sound of swing on the radio. Edward looked in. Dorcas in a blue silk frock stood at the telephone snapping the fingers of her free hand and swaying her thin little body to the music while she giggled and chatted with a friend.

"Who's gonna fetch you to the hindy? Stan an' the others is comin' for me. Uh, huh...."

"Who told you, come into Mr. Burdens's library without a dustcloth in your hand?" he began. "Who told you, call on his telephone? For all the world like this house belongs to you"—

"Edward," came Tilly's voice, "supper; come eat now."

He went back across the hall. The radio stopped and Dorcas scurried past him to the dining room. There his cousin Tilly stood by the table, a tall black woman in a cotton dress, her hair braided in three tight little braids close her head. She held a pot of coffee in her hand.

"In here," she said.

The doilies, the wine and water glasses still marked the family places. They sat down and helped themselves from the warm dishes Tilly put back on the table.

Presently from the kitchen came a soft low whistle. When Dorcas answered, it came again. Then there was the sound of footsteps and murmured words. The pantry door was pushed open and one by one they edged slowly in, the colored boys and girls on their way to the shindy. Edward knew them all. Here came Stan, here came Amser's grandchildren who worked in white folks' houses too, here came Cephas' two youngest boys, mechanics in a garage, and a cousin driver for a truck gardener. Tonight they had rubbed off their work and wore their finery. Their sleek brown faces were listening with pleasure. "Evenin' Uncle, evenin' Tilly. 'Scuse us," they said respectfully, "we've come by for Dorcas." They stood around the table or backed themselves shuffling against the wall. The younger ones rolled their eyes.

But when Dorcas invited them to draw up they became easier and soon drew chairs to the table. "You got any for us, Tilly?" they asked, and sat down and ate. Seeing a little wine left in the decanter, "Let's taste that," they cried and poured it into a glass and passed it around. They talked and laughed; they made a warm gay circle around the table. Slowly, wonder filled Edward looking at them. It wasn't only the supper and so many eating. There had always been plenty on Lulie's stove and she could make it seem like more than it was and serve it round to everybody who came. No, it was ... my folks, he thought, my folks sitting here around this table; and wondered if he had spoken out loud, or if it seemed as strange to them as to him.

Here was the same room he had stood in a few hours ago. He had been praised for it; his moldings, his windows, his mantel shelf—see those old red woodcoals blinking to sleep in the ashes—his house. "My plan of course," Mr. Burden had said. Edward and his brothers had built long and foursquare with large square rooms, and their kin had taken care of the house ever since: kept it warm, kept it clean, fed it, dressed it and the white folks inside it. White folks ... he hadn't built it for himself, none of his kin had worked in it for themselves, yet now they were sitting here like it belonged to them.

Edward's working day had been long, he was tired. He pushed aside his plate of uneaten supper, went to the kitchen and, putting his hand into the back of the oven, brought out some sweet potatoes which he put on a plate. Taking his bowl from the kitchen dresser he went back to the dining room. Here he sat down again, filled his bowl with milk and coffee, and ate his sweet potatoes, breaking them with his hands. He pushed his chair a little sideways from the table toward the fire. The young people were making ready to leave. Dimly he heard them telling their thanks to Tilly and Goodnight, Uncle; but he made no reply, though what he was studying about as he looked at the coals and ate slowly in silence, he could not have told.

He was engrossed in watching a crowd of colored folks who appeared to be coming and going around a house. They walked in groups, in friendly twos and threes. The men wore overalls the women aprons and they carried things in their hands: a broom or a saw, a hoe, a mop or a hammer or shovel. Some carried heavy boards and stones, some guided animals.

Edward grew dreamy watching the vision of them. Who were they and what house was it? He couldn't rightly make it out. Looks like it's this house, looks like it's their house....

The telephone rang and Tilly being busy with the dishes Edward answered the call.

"No sir, Mr. Burden he's not here.

"This his house, you ask?"

The question seemed part of his dream by the fire and out of his dream he answered.

"Somehow I don't rightly know, his house or mine. Looks like it must be our house...."

[*The Crisis* 46.2 (February 1939): 47, 59]

THE COON HUNT

by Thelma Rea Thurston

Joel didn't know how long he had been aware of the baying of the hounds, but suddenly it seemed that they were just outside the yard of his Uncle Tate Mosby's house, and his cousin, Lil Tate, was wide awake, shaking him and shouting, "C'mon, c'mon, Joel! Thar's a-goin' to be a coon hunt, and Pa sed I could bring you 'long."

"A coon hunt?" Thirteen-year-old Joel Smith rubbed his eyes sleepily. Since coming to Mena to spend the summer, he had observed a lot of queer Arkansas customs, but this was the first time he had been aroused from a pleasant slumber to go on a coon hunt. He looked at the radium face of his wrist watch. It was a quarter past three.

"A coon hunt?" he repeated. "What's a coon hunt?"

"Git yore clothes on, 'n' c'mon an' you'll see." Lil Tate grinned in anticipation. "You ain't never seen nothin' like it, I'll bet."

He hurried into his shirt, putting it on wrong-side-out. "Hurry Joel," he cried. "All the fun'll be over by the time we git thar."

Outside the house, Lil Tate cut across the Crosby garden patch, leading Joel eastward in the direction from whence came the deep baying tones of the hounds.

"Gawd, listen at them haounds," Lil Tate breathed, "they mus' be almos' on him. C'mon, this is goin' to be good." With his long, freckled face thrust forward and his unkempt, red hair blowing back, his cousin reminded Joel of one of the hounds. Momentarily, it seemed to him that Lil Tate must stop short and bay long and mournfully.

Soon Joel began to wonder wearily if all coon hunts were so long and led over so many rocky hills and so many almost impassable stretches of marsh land and thickly wooded gullies. After what was only an hour and twenty minutes, but seemed an eternity, they were still far behind the baying hounds, and Lil Tate was still urging Joel on.

"You don't wanta miss this'n. It war ol' Shiner Brooks' gal, Nannie, who tol' 'bout it; an' Shiner's up thar in front with the haoun's. I wouldn't miss this'n for anything. Hurry up! You don't wanta miss this'n!"

Still the hunt for the elusive coon seemed to Joel without any reason. It night have been fun to traverse the same route in the daytime and at a more moderate pace. But he was getting tired.

Despite the fact that they had hounds, the hunters apparently did not know where to look for their quarry. Once they stopped to pound on the door of an isolated Negro cabin. Then an old, colored man came to the door, one of the men in the hunting crowd knocked him down with the butt of his gun.

Lil Tate laughed as if it were a part of the sport. Joel was not near enough to hear the men's conversation with the old man, but the act appeared cruel and unnecessary. Trying to keep up with Lil Tate in the boulder-and-stump-filled darkness, Joel reflected on the way he saw his uncle and other men in the vicinity of Mena treat the colored people. In the hilly, back-country areas, he had seen them treated as if they were without human feelings. He wondered if it had been a part of the coon hunt to awaken the old, colored man and knock him down when he opened his cabin door He asked Lil Tate, but that young man just redoubled his panting speed.

Joel was aware that the baying of hounds was become more frenzied, and the shouts of the men more excited. Somewhere ahead of him, several shots were fired in quick succession.

The breath of Lil Tate, climbing a hill ahead of Joel, was coming in panting gasps. "They mus' have him almos' treed by now. My Gawd, ef you don't hurry, we'll miss everythin'!"

Joel thought of the poor, pursued animal somewhere ahead of them, out there in the East, where darkness was beginning to give way to dawn. It must be terrible to be a fugitive for so long, he thought—half the night and into the morning. Somehow—he kept thinking—that hunted creature ought to welcome the end. Surely, anything would be better than the awful suspense of being always just inches ahead of the hounds. Joel felt that he could not have endured it.

Then, without realizing how he knew it, the young northerner sensed that the hunt was over, that the hounds had closed in and that the object of the bloodthirsty host of men was at their mercy. Perhaps it was the excited yell that burst from Lil Tate's throat just as all the hounds lifted their voices together in a high, doleful cry. Or perhaps it was another sound— a shrill, suffering, human scream that rose above Lil Tate's excited outburst, above the hounds' cries, above the vicious voices of the men. A sound that rose higher and higher until it seemed to go on past the twinkling morning star and to pierce the celestial blue beyond.

As he heard that sound, Joel felt that he could not go on and witness the end of the coon hunt. There was something human in that shrill, piercing cry, something that made him wish that he had never come on the hunt, or, indeed, that he had never left the hustling sanity of his northern home town for the dull confusion of the Arkansas backwoods.

Just beyond a hill several feet ahead of the two boys, the underbrush gave way to a small copse, from the center of which came sounds that unmistakably indicated the end of the hunt. The coppice was slightly thicker at the edge by which the boys approached it than at its center. In the middle of the thicket a group of men and hounds milled around a bonfire which threw weird shadows on the ground behind them. Nearing the fire-lit clearing, Joel seemed to see the men for the first time. He was aware of things he had not noticed before: their drunken laughter, their slinking, furtive movements, their coarse talk and swearing. Several of the men had bottles in their hip pockets. Occasionally there was a flash of amber as a bottle was raised to blasphemous lips. Some of the men held rifles, and many were armed only with heavy sticks and clubs.

Joel was almost at the center of the thicket when he looked past the smoking end of the rifle held by his uncle. A lone hound crouched on the ground nose pointed upward, baying mournfully at something in the branches above him. For a sickening instant, Joel looked up into the branches. When he turned away to look into Lil Tate's grinning face, he was sick to his stomach.

"Aw, shucks," Lil Tate lamented, "we missed the best part of it. They've done it already."

As if urged by some magnetic force, Joel turned again to look at the object in the branches above the lone hound. For an unforgettable moment, he stared, fascinated at what he saw there. He could not see quite all of it, but he saw enough: above the mournful, crouching hound, above the leaping flames of the bonfire, two black feet dangled grotesquely from the legs of a pair of blue denim overalls. One of the bruised feet had a wound where there should have been a big toe, and there were no nails on any of the remaining toes. High up on the blue denim overall legs a dark splotch grew larger and larger. Once, Joel thought he saw one of the toes twitch slightly.

Then through the crowd he saw a big red-faced man push his way roughly, a long, hunting knife in his hand. "Lemme at the black nigger," the man demanded. "I'll teach him to bother a white woman! I'll cut his livin' guts out!" Joel recognized the speaker as the man Lil Tate called Shiner Brooks. He was apparently the leader of the mob, and as he finished speaking, half a dozen smaller knife blades flashed in the light of the fire, and the men took up the cry in a swelling refrain: "Cut his livin' guts out!"

Through the copse, far, far to the East, dawn was breaking. But Joel saw silhouetted against the roseate splendor which was the promise of dawn, only a hound baying up at two black feet that dangled from a pair of blue overall pants legs. "Cut his livin' guts out!" The cry rang in his ears—the battle cry of the coon hunt. And for the first time in his thirteen years, Joel Smith went back on all his pre-arranged patterns of one hundred per cent American boyhood and fainted.

A few hours later the same morning, heavy-eyed and nervous, Joel was vainly trying to eat breakfast in the Mosby kitchen, when a neighbor woman came in. Joel did not know her, but he had seen her about the neighborhood many times—always talking or looking for something to talk about. Her sharp eyes fell on him as she entered.

"What's the matter with him?" she asked Joel's aunt.

'Lina Mosby poured a spoonful of batter on the sizzling griddle, before she answered, "Oh, he went with Lil Tate to the lynchin' las' night. An' it war his first un."

"Humph! That warn't nuthin' to git all pale and sick-lookin' 'bout." The neighbor woman shrugged her shoulders in a gesture of disappointment. "I thought there war somethin' wrong with him."

Then she perked up again. "But what do you reckon?" she asked. And before 'Lina Mosby could say a word, she went on to answer her question: "That Nannie Brooks jes' fibbed! She never seen that nigger before. There warn't a man near her, 'ceptin' Hank Jarbors. An' do you know why her clothes was all tore off her like that? 'cause Lettie Jarbors caught her an' Hank together. Lettie was a-tellin' everybody in taown 'bout it early this mornin' after the lynchin'. She said she tried to beat the life outa Nannie. An' Nannie knew her pa'd finish her if he foun' out, so she said it was a nigger, an' run off to Fort Smith. They say Shiner is going after her, and get her to make her pay him for all the moonshine that he give the men who helped him hunt for that nigger. He's mighty riled, too 'cause he had to pay 'Lige Jarbors five dollars for usin' them haoun's." The neighborhood narrator paused for breath.

"My ol' man," she continued after a moment, "brought home a toenail for a souvenir, an' I hear that Sam Jokum got a big toe. Ef I'd a-been thar, though, I'd a-got a piece o' his pants. It would-a made a right nice quilt patch, don't you think?"

While the griddle cakes burned on one side, 'Lina Mosby solemnly declared that she "should say so!" Lil Tate snickered over his breakfast of side meat and hot cakes.

But Joel, choking on a sorghum-soaked piece of fried batter, did not hear them. He heard again the frenzied baying of a pack of hounds, and the excited yells and curses of a mob of lynch-crazed men. He heard again the bloodthirsty cry: "Cut his livin' guts out!" And still he saw silhouetted against the roseate splendor of the dawn, a crouching hound with head upturned to bay at two black feet dangled grotesquely from the legs of a pair of blue denim overalls.   [*The Crisis* 46.4 (April 1939): 109, 120]

CALL IT SOCIAL SECURITY

by Edwina Streeter Dixon

Elaine suddenly left the room. The entire situation, the setting, the guests, their conversation, clipped speech, the very atmosphere, were all so incredible! She felt she had to leave that swarm of eating, drinking, talkative people all smelling horsey, all speaking a horsey language and seek some spot or some face, that would bring back to her bewildered brain sights and sounds more familiar.

With her hand on the dark oak of the balustrade she halted abruptly. She had heard Clyde's voice above the din drifting from the library door at the end of the vast hallway, and knew he was inquiring her whereabouts. It recalled her to responsibility. It reminded her that this, her first social venture on a large scale since coming to her husband's family home, was to make or break her socially; and would mean much more to her husband's career than she understood.

She smiled grimly as she retraced her steps. Little had she thought when she used to ride with Lester, Jim and the girls in Washington Park that such experience would be a stepping stone to friendly footing with these horse-and-hunt minded English folk in Windringham-on-the-Thames. From Washington Park in Chicago—good old U. S. A.!—to England. From park riding on a rented animal to an English hunt—pink coat, fox, suet pudding, and ale! Not to mention the excellent mounts that were her husband's personal property.... Funny!

Two steps from the library door she sobered, and with palpitating heart, entered.

Most of her guests were standing about the fireplace, heavy plates in hand, their ale mugs on the mantle above the blue-tipped flames, while they lured steam from the damp riding breeches grouped about.

Clyde's eyes called her to his side, and apparently without losing a word garrulous Lord Bigham growled to him, consigning Chamberlain, Hitler and Mussolini to unhappy ends. Elaine knew he was, body and mind, aware of her. Her heart and face glowed with a warmth of love for him that seemed never to lessen—that must never!

While she sipped from the glass of sherry Clyde handed her, she looked about her and tried to realize that this was her home, these utterly foreign people were ones she hoped desperately to make her friends; and this long, lounging aristocratic Englishman, Sir Clyde Montague Inniss. M.P., D.S.C., V.C., her husband. Could she ever believe it? The score or more books she had read of English people of the upper classes came to life bit by bit as she looked about, as her small pink ears seemed to twitch like a puppy's, reaching for sounds familiar to her eyes, new to her ears. To be a part of this setting.... To be married into a family as old, and distinguished as this (forget how you deceived to get into it!).... To be accepted by this difficult-to-please set of people only because she rode well, or because she was Clyde's wife or—oh, some reason, she wasn't particular *why*. Enough to be accepted....

Tonight would be the hunt ball. The Hunt Ball! First panic had subsided to dull, gnawing unease under Clyde's insistence that his brother and sister-in-law would handle all details with her standing by to learn what she could, naturally and reminding her, too, that a round half dozen old family servants were long accustomed to such festivity. Woman-like, the memory of the gown she would wear that night, of the exquisite pearls Clyde had given her—creamy as her baby skin, he had told her shyly—lifted her spirits somewhat.

At the far end of the room, where a group of guests were bemoaning the change of weather while looking out the door-length windows into the drenched garden, cries of delight and curiosity attracted Elaine's attention. Clyde squeezed her arm and murmured:

Johnson s making a bid for popularity, old thing. He will get it with those drinks of his!"

He chuckled delightedly, and they watched the scene with mixed emotions.

Clyde felt he was as fond of their old colored servant as his wife. When he had gone to Washington to serve as Embassy secretary, he had his first contact with American people of color. He had been drawn to them inexplicably. His contact had been limited to the few he had met at a tea at one of the large Negro universities. He was so levelheaded an individual he was not too surprised that they were men and women no different than fairer skinned Americans with whom he was in daily contact. They were simply Americans of different ancestral background; but having the same hopes for a brighter future; the same interests in politics, economics, entertainment. At the places of amusement he secretly felt them far more entertaining and naturally vivacious than other folk.

When he met Elaine at the home of blonde and lovely Aleeka Karenov, a student in the States from Soviet Russia, and subsequently learned of the devotion she had for the old Negro, Johnson, who travelled, he understood, wherever she went, caring for her with a devotion typical of the old family retainers of his own homeland, he felt doubly attracted. Since the time he discovered that family, caste, money meant nothing to him if they meant preventing making Elaine his wife, he had grown increasingly fond of the old man. He had, in fact, insisted that he come to make his home with them, continuing his work or not as it suited him and Elaine. He felt satisfied that all was well.

To Elaine alone came thoughts, chilly with doubt, quivering with fear. Apprehensively she watched the scenes across the room, while slicing another cut of cold beef for Clyde from the large round of pink and brown meat on the cutting board of the buffet.

Johnson was dressed as was the butler, Hallet, his gray trousers neatly brushed and pressed, his coat equally so, his tie perfection, his scant gray hair as smooth as much brushing would make it. But the expression he wore upon his face was far more attractive than his sartorial perfection. Expression of delight. Expression that said, "Say, this is *something* and I like it!" It was that shining smile that lured a "reasonable facsimile" onto the cold faces turned toward his great tray of long, cool drinks. Elaine observed. Johnson stood, as Hallet would have never dared, while heads thrown back drained the glasses, his eager face telling any observer he was waiting for compliments on his concoction. Elaine had no idea that his delight at the rain of excited comments was mirrored in her own face.

Lord Bingham, Clyde and the few remaining about the fireplace clamored for their share and were served immediately by the brownskin Johnson. When the drinks were completely gone, Clyde urged his guests into the game room, across the vast hall, where the larger group dissolved into several, some to excitement over ping-pong; others to a more subdued interest in cribbage or bridge. Without fully understanding her own restlessness, and the growing feeling of sadness and regret of which she grew more conscious, Elaine strolled from group to group, her smile as vivid as her hair, coiled her creamy neck, her witticisms always evoking laughter, never resentment—secret of her charm and social success.

She had traversed the length of the room. Her cigarette was almost burned but, her restlessness at a new high. Without conscious reason or aim she was out in the hall again; and as though drawn by some unknown magnet, she continued slowly, more slowly, toward the library again. Pausing on the threshold, she stood, one slim hand clutching the door, her cigarette held near her mouth, her eyes drifting about the dimness of the room. Fire almost out ... scent of food, drink, smoke, scarcely noticeable with all the windows open now ... chairs pushed about, neglected.... The sound of deep humming and the clatter of dishes, out of sight at the other end of the room, made her aware of her reason for coming here; and she ran between chairs and footstools to Johnson's side.

"Oh Daddy! Daddy! What have I gotten us into!" she cried, ignoring his horrified expression, as she flung tweed-clad arms about his neck.

Firmly grasping her arms and forcing them to her sides, he looked sternly at her while he reminded:

"It's nothing to what you *will* have us into if you don't stop this foolishness." Tears in her eyes melted him completely, but just "in case," he fussed with assembling plates, silver and mugs on the tray, and continued:

"Honey, I wish to God I could make you stop worrying about me. Can't you see I'm happy?" His eyes ashine testified, his eager voice verified. "Why, working with those folks in Washington didn't hold a candle to what I'm doing here."

His voice ceased, but his thoughts raced about crossed and recrossed the Atlantic, laughed with his lips and eyes when he thought of their background, looked about their present, speculated on their future. Elaine stood mutely caressing the sleeve of his coat, and silently agreed there was no turning back, no regrets for either. She had been born for this, white Negro that she was. He had been born for it—keen sense of humor, adventurous mind, connoisseur of bizarre situations. Try to tell him this wasn't better than old age pension, or social security!

"Honey, I've got some prayin' to do, I know. I *am* sorry about all these lies I've been telling; and all this fooling I've been doing of people who believe in us. But I know it hasn't hurt anyone. You got the man you love. You have security and a future that depends wholly on the way you handle this situation. If you lose, you lose what you want most—the man you love. Now get on back in there and behave yourself!"

When she hesitated, Johnson, who knew her so well, murmured, "Your ole Dad knows you love him. And I'm not a bit lonesome, honey; as long as I know you're happy, I'm happy too."

Back in the smoke-filled game room, swallowing repeatedly the lump that rose in her throat, Elaine strolled as nonchalantly as possible across to her husband's side.

"Darling, I do like these cigarettes," she drawled and leaned toward his lighter with the cool composure of an English gentlewoman to the manor born. She puckered smooth, full lips to release the fragrant smoke, and as she watched its spiral climb ceilingward, then to nothingness, she prayed silently that all her fears had just reason to go with it.

[*The Crisis* 46.5 (May 1939): 141, 157]

THE WHIPPING

by Marita Bonner

The matron picked up her coat. It was a good coat made of heavy men's wear wool and lined with fur. She always liked to let her hands trail fondly over it whenever she was going to put it on (the way women do who are used to nothing).

She shook it out and shrugged her shoulders into it.

"I'll be back home again in time for dinner!" She smiled at the warden as she talked. "Helga will have 'peasant-girl.' for dessert, too!"

The hard lines that creased around the man's eyes softened a little. "Peasant-girl-with-a-veil! Ah, my mother could make that! Real home-made jam, yellow cream!—good! Nothing here ever tastes as good as it did back in the old country, I tell you!"

The woman balanced her weight on the balls of her feet and drew on one of her leather driving gloves. Through the window she saw her car, nicely trimmed and compactly modern, awaiting her. Beyond the car was a November sky, dismal, darkening and melancholy as the walls that bounded the surrounding acres of land which belonged to the Women's Reformatory.

At the end of her drive of thirty-five miles back to the city again, she would go to her apartment that—through warmth of color and all the right uses of the best comforts—seemed to be full of sunshine on the darkest days. She looked down, now, as she stood near the warden and saw her right hand freshly manicured.

Her mother's hands back in the stone kitchen with the open hearth found in every peasant home in Denmark, had always been grey and chapped with blackened nails this time of year. No woman who has to carry wood and coal from a frozen yard can have soft clean hands.

The thought made the matron shrug again. "I like things as they are here—but it would be good to go home some day to visit!"

She hurried a little toward the door now. Nobody lingers in the impersonal greyness of an institution whose very air is heavy the fierce anger and anguish and sorrow, buried and dulled under an angry restraint just as fierce and sorrowful.

She had nearly reached the door before she remembered the colored woman sitting alone on the edge of the bench beside the window. The matron had just driven up from the city to bring the woman on the bench to stay at the Reformatory as long as she should live.

She had killed her little boy.

The judge and the social worker said she had killed him.

But she had told the matron over and over again that she did not do it.

You could never tell, though. It is best to leave these things alone.

"Good bye. 'Lizabeth!" the matron called in a loud voice. She meant to leave a cheerful note but she only spoke overloud. "Be a good girl!"

"Yes'm!" Lizabeth answered softly. "Yas'm!"

And the women separated. One went out to the light. The other looked at the grey walls—dark—and growing darker in the winter sunset.

Everything had been grey around Lizabeth most all of her life. The two-room hut with a ragged lean-to down on Mr. Davey's place in Mississippi where she had lived before she came North—had been grey.

She and Pa and Ma and Bella and John used to get up when the morning was still grey and work the cotton until the greyness of evening stopped them.

"God knows I'm sick of this!" Pa had cursed suddenly one day.

Ma did not say anything. She was glad that they had sugar once in a while from the commissary and not just molasses like they said you got over at McLaren's place.

Pa cursed a lot that day and kept muttering to himself. One morning when they got up to go to work the cotton, Pa was not there.

"He say he goin' North to work!" Ma explained when she could stop her crying.

Mr. Davey said Pa had left a big bill at the commissary and that Ma and the children, would have to work twice as hard to pay it up.

There were not any more hours in any one day than those from sun-up to sundown, no way you could figure it.

The Christmas after Pa left, Mr. Davey said Ma owed three times as much and that she could not have any flannel for John's chest to cover the place where the misery stayed each winter.

That was the day Ma decided to go North and see if she could find Pa.

They had to plan it all carefully. There was no money to go from Mississippi northward on the train.

John had to get an awful attack of the misery first. Then Bella had to stay home to take care of him.

The day Mr. Davey's man came to find out why Bella and Jim were not in the field, Bella had her hand tied up in a blood soaked rag and she was crying.

The axe had slipped and cut her hand, she told them.

That meant Ma would have to wait on Bella and John.

Lizabeth worked the cotton by herself and the Saturday after Ma laid off, Mr. Davey would not let them have any fat back.

"Y'all can make it on meal and molasses until you work off your debts!" he told Lizabeth.

Ma had said nothing when Lizabeth had told her about the fat back. She had sat still a long time. Then she got up and mixed up some meal.

"What you makin' so much bread to oncet?" Bella asked Ma.

"Gainst our gittin' hungry!"

"Can't eat all that bread one time!" John blared forth. "Better save some 'cause you might not git no meal next time! We owe so much!"

"Heish, boy!!" Ma screamed so you could hear her half across the field. "I aint owe nobody nuthin!"

Lizabeth's jaw dropped. "Mr. Davey, he say—!"

"Heish, gal!" Ma screamed again. "I sent owe nuthin, I say! Been right here workin' nigh on forty years!"

She turned the last scrap of meal into a pan. Then she stood up and looked around the table at three pairs of wide-stretched eyes.

"I'm fixin' this 'gainst we git hungry! We goin' North to find Pa tonight!"

You would not believe that three women and a half-grown boy could get to Federal street, Chicago from Mississippi without a cent of money to start with.

They walked—they begged rides—they stopped in towns, worked a little and they rode as far as they could on the train for what they had earned. It took months, but they found Federal street.

But they never found Pa.

They found colored people who had worked the cotton just like they themselves had done, but these others were from Alabama and Georgia and parts of Mississippi that they had never seen.

They found the houses on Federal street were just as grey, just as bare of color and comfort as the hut they had left in Mississippi.

But you could get jobs and earn real money and buy all sorts of things for a little down and a little a week! You could eat what you could afford to buy—and if you could not pay cash, the grocer would put you on the book.

Ma was dazed.

John forgot the misery.

Bella and Lizabeth were looping wider and wider in new circles of joy.

Ma could forget Pa, who was lost, and the hard trip up from the South when she screamed and shouted and got happy in robust leather-lunged style in her store-front church run in the "down-home" tempo.

John spent every cent that he could lay a hand on on a swell outfit, thirty dollars from skin out and from shoes to hat!

Bella's circles of joy spread wider and wider until she took to hanging out with girls who lived "out South" in kitchenettes.

She straightened her hair at first.

Then she curled her hair. After that she "sassed" Ma. Said she was going to get a job in a tavern and stay "out South" too!

They heard she was married.

They heard she was not.

Anyway, she did not come back to 31st and Federal.

John's swell outfit wasn't thick enough to keep the lake winds from his misery. He began to have chills and night sweats. The Sunday he coughed blood, Lizabeth got a doctor from State street.

The doctor made Ma send John to the hospital.

"He be all right soon?" Ma asked after the ambulance had gone.

The doctor looked grim. "I doubt if they can arrest it!"

"Arrest it! Arrest what? John's a good boy! He sent done nothing to git arrested!"

The doctor looked grimmer. "I mean that maybe they can't stop this blood from coming!"

Ma looked a little afraid. "Well, if they jes' gives him a tablespoon of salt that will stop any bleeding! My mother always—"

The doctor put his hat on and went out. He did not listen to hear any more.

The second fall that they were on Federal street, Lizabeth met Benny, a soft-voiced boy from Georgia.

Benny said he was lonely for a girl who did not want him to spend all his money on liquor and things for her every time he took her out. That is what these city girls all seemed to want.

They wanted men to buy things for them that no decent girl down home would accept from men.

Lizabeth was glad for just a ten-cent movie and a bottle of pop or a nickel bag of peanuts.

They were married at Christmas. The next year, in October, baby Benny came.

In November John died.

In February of the second year Benny—who had begun to go "out South" in the evening with the boys—suddenly stayed away all night.

Ma had hysterics in the police station and told the police to find him.

"He may be dead and run over somewhere!" she kept crying.

The policemen took their time. Ma went every day to find out if there were any news. Lizabeth went too!

She stopped going after she saw the policeman at the desk wink at another when he told her; "Sure! Sure! We are looking for him every day!"

Mrs. Rhone who kept the corner store asked Lizabeth one morning, "Where's your man? Left you?"

Lizabeth bridled: "He was none of these men! He was my husband!"

The other woman probed deeper: "Who married you? That feller 'round to the store front church? Say! Heehee! They tell me he ain't no reglar preacher! Any feller what'll slip him a couple of dollars can get 'married'—even if he's got a wife and ten kids "out South," they tell me!"

Lizabeth shrank back. Benny had been truly married to her!!

This woman just did not have any shame!

But after that Lizabeth grew sensitive if she went on the street and saw the women standing together in gossiping groups.

"They talkin' about me! They saying I weren't married!" she would tell herself.

She and ma moved away.

The place where they moved was worse than Federal street. Folks fought and cursed and cut and killed down in the Twenties in those days.

But rent was cheap.

Lizabeth only got twelve dollars a week scrubbing all night in a theatre.

Ma kept little Benny and took care of the house.

There was not much money, but Lizabeth would go without enough to eat and to wear so that little Benny could have good clothes and toys that she really could not afford.

"Every time you pass the store you 'bout buy this boy somethin'!" the grandmother complained once.

"Aw I'd a liked pretty clothes and all that stuff when I was a kid!" Lizabeth answered.

"How she buy so much stuff and just *she* workin'!" the neighbors argued among themselves.

"She must be livin' wrong!" declared those who could understand all the fruits of wrong living in all its multiple forms.

Little Benny grew to expect all the best of things for himself. He learned to whine and cry for things and Lizabeth would manage them somehow.

He was six years old in 1929.

That was the year when Lizabeth could find no more theaters to scrub in and there were no more day's work jobs nor factory jobs. Folks said the rich people had tied up all the money so all the poor people had to go to the relief station.

Lizabeth walked fifteen blocks one winter day to a relief station. She told the worker that there was no coal, no food, the water was frozen and the pipes had bursted.

"We'll send an investigator," the worker promised.

"When'll that come?" Lizabeth demanded vaguely.

"*She* will come shortly! In a few days, I hope!"

"I got nothin' for Ma and Benny to eat today!" Lizabeth began to explain all over again.

"I'm sorry! That is all we can do now!" the woman behind the desk began to get red as she spoke this time.

"But Benny ain't had no dinner and—"

"Next!" The woman was crimson as she called the next client.

The client—a stout colored woman—elbowed Lizabeth out of the way.

Already dazed with hunger and bone-weary from her freezing walk, Lizabeth stumbled.

"She's drunk!" the client muttered apologetically to the woman behold the desk.

Lizabeth had had enough. She brought her left hand up in a good old-fashioned back-hand wallop.

Everybody screamed, "They're fighting!"

"Look out for a knife!" yelled the woman behind the desk.

Her books had all told her that colored women carried knives.

A policeman came and took Lizabeth away.

They kept Lizabeth all night that night. The next day they said she could go home but it was the third day that they finally set her on the sidewalk; and told her to go home.

Home was thirty blocks away this time.

"Where you been, gal!" Ma screamed as soon as the door opened. "You the las' chile I got and now you start actin' like that Bella! Ain't no food in this house! Aint a God's bit of fire 'cept one box I busted up—!"

"She busted up my boat! She busted up the box what I play boat in!" Benny added his scream to the confusion. "She make me stay in bed all the time! My stomach hurts me!"

Lizabeth was dizzy. "Aint nobody been here?" She wanted to wait a little before she told ma that she had been in the lock-up.

"Nobody been here? For what?"

"Get us some somepin' to eat! That's what the woman said!"

"No, ain't nobody been here!"

Lizabeth put on her hat again.

"Where you goin' now?" Ma shouted.

"I got to go back."

"You got to go back where?"

"See 'bout some somethin' to eat, Ma!"

Benny began to scream and jumped out of the bed. "You stay with me!" he cried as he ran to his mother. "I want my dinner! I—"

"Heish!" Lizabeth out-screamed everyone else in the room.

Frightened, Benny cowed away a little. Then he began again. "I want to eat! The lady downstairs, she say my mother ought to get me somethin' 'stead of stayin' out all night with men!"

Lizabeth stared wildly at her mother.

Hostile accusation bristled in her eyes, too.

"That's what the lady say. She say—" Benny repeated.

And Lizabeth who had never struck Benny in her life, stood up and slapped him to the floor.

As he fell, the child's head struck the iron bedstead.

His grandmother picked him up, still whimpering.

Lizabeth went out without looking back.

Fifteen blocks put a stitch in her left side. Anger made her eyes red.

The woman behind the desk at the relief station paled when she saw Elizabeth this time. "You will have to wait!" she chattered nervously before Lizabeth had even spoken.

"Wait for what? Been waitin! Nobody been there!"

"We are over-crowded now! It will take ten days to two weeks before our relief workers can get there!"

"What's Ma and little Benny going to do all that time? They gotta eat!"

The other woman grew eloquent. "There are hundreds and hundreds of people just like you waiting—!"

"Well I stop waitin'! Bennie got to eat!"

Fifteen blocks had put a stitch in her side. Worry and hunger made her head swim. Lizabeth put one hand to her side and wavered against the desk.

This time the woman behind the desk *knew* that Lizabeth had a knife—for her alone! Her chair turned over as she shot up from the desk. Her cries brought the policeman from the next corner.

"We better keep you for thirty days," the police court told Lizabeth when they saw her again.

"But little Benny—!" Lizabeth began crying aloud.

There was a bustle and commotion. A thin pale woman pushed her way up to the desk. Lizabeth had to draw back. She stood panting, glaring at the judge.

He had been looking at her at first in tolerant amusement. But while this pale woman talked to him across his desk, cold, dreadful anger surged into his eyes.

"What's that you're saying about little Benny?" he demanded suddenly of Lizabeth. "He's dead!"

Lizabeth could not speak nor move at first. Then she cried out. "What happen to him? What happen to my baby?"

"You killed him." The judge was harsh.

A bailiff had to pick Lizabeth up off of the floor and stand her up again so the judge could finish. "You whipped him to death!"

"I ain't never whip him! I aint never whip little Benny!" Lizabeth cried over and over.

They took her away and kept her.

They kept her all the time that they were burying Benny, even. Said she was not fit to see him again.

Later—in court—Ma said that Lizabeth had "whipped Benny's head" the last time she was at home.

"I aint hit him but once!" Lizabeth tried to cry it to the judge's ears. "He didn't have nuthin to eat for a long time! That was the trouble."

"There was a deep gash on his head," testified the relief worker. "She was brutal!"

"She brought knives to the relief station and tried to start a fight every time she came there!"

"She's been arrested twice!"

"Bad character! Keep her!" the court decided.

That was why the matron had had to drive Lizabeth to the Woman's Reformatory.

She had gone out now to her car. Lizabeth watched her climb into it and whirl around once before she drove away.

"Won't see her no more! She's kinder nice, too," Lizabeth thought.

"It is time for supper! Come this way!" the warden spoke suddenly.

Lizabeth stumbled to her feet and followed him down a long narrow hall lit with one small light.

That relief worker had said she would see that Ma got something to eat.

That seemed to settle itself as soon as they had decided they would send her to this place.

"You will work from dawn to sundown," the matron had said as they were driving up from the city.

She had always done that in Mississippi.

It did not matter here. But she asked one question "They got a commissary there?"

"A commissary!" The matron was struck breathless when Lizabeth asked this. She had decided that Lizabeth was not normal. She had seemed too stupid to defend herself in court. "She must be interested in food!" the matron had decided to herself.

A slight sneer was on her face when she answered, "Of course they have a commissary! You get your food there!"

Lizabeth had drawn back into her corner and said nothing more.

A commissary. She understood a commissary. The same grey hopeless drudge—the same long unending row to hoe—lay before her.

The same debt, year in, year out.

How long had they said she had to stay?

As long as she lived. And she was only thirty now.

But she understood a commissary and a debt that grew and grew while you worked to pay it off. And she would never be able to pay for little Benny.

[*The Crisis* 46.6 (June 1939): 172–174]

HONGRY FIRE

by Marita Bonner

God—it was good to be lying in the bed at eleven o'clock on Monday morning and hear somebody else on the washboard!

Only thing, Margaret never did wash real clean!

—"I've tried ever since that gal was old enough to work to git her to do things up real finished! Jes' listen to her! Missin' those rubs! Be leavin' the dirt in and everybody'll be laughing at my wash!! First time in my life anybody ever laughed at it, too! Jes listen—!!—Aw Margaret? You Margaret!" Ma yelled aloud and pounded on the bedroom floor so that Margaret, in the kitchen below, could hear.

Heavy footsteps thudded along the lower hall.

That gal even walked fat!

Steaming and puffing, fatter and blacker for the greasy perspiration that glistened on her broad face, Margaret thrust herself into the room.

—"What you say Ma?"

—"You wash them clothes clean, you hear?"

—"Oh, course I will Ma? You jes lay there quiet and I'll tend to every thing! I gotta get back down stairs 'cause the baby'll be gettin' at that lye water!"

"You puttin' lye water on them clothes!! Don't put none on Pa's Sunday shirts or none on Vernice's fancy underclothes!"

"Aw corse not, Ma! Jes lay still! You want some of your medicine?"

"No!!"

"Well,—I'll git back down! The baby'll be in the lye water!

Ma listened until she could hear Margaret and the baby. She began talking to herself again:

"Just 'cause the doctor said something about 'cardy—something and said to lay quiet they think I'm sick! What I need with that dark green stuff! Twenty drops of that, and take the yellow stuff to sleep! What ever heard tell of a woman what raised six children and worked all her life all day every day needin' somethin' to make her sleep? I'm jes' going to lay here peaceful and let them take things as they find 'em themselves!"

Ma stared around here. Funny how the furniture looked sort of marked up and dirty!

Somebody ought to wash the marble tops on that bureau and table in soap water. Somebody ought to shut the drawers tight and ... her feet were on the floor before she remembered.

"I'm jes 'sposed to lay here quiet like! Too bad I had to lay right down there in church yestiddy mornin' when the reverend was preachin'! But Lawd! Did seem like I'd never draw a clean breath again! Hope nobody'd be evil enough to think I was drunk! A deaconness twenty years! People so mean in their hearts they think anything 'bout anybody!"

The pillows became too hard, too hot, too lumpy and smothering.

The front door struck to downstairs.

That would be Pa, getting back from the foundry. Why did he have to shut the door so noisy? Seemed like the noise was right under her bed.

Ma hung her body half off the mattress and looked at the faded rug under the bed. One spot seemed to sag a little. She pushed it. The end turned up.

"Here's the old hole where Pa took out the hot air heater! Always gonna fix it. Hole still here. I can even see down in the kitchen."

Pa's voice eddied up through the hole.

"Hey, Margaret. Gal. Put the little pot in the big pot. I could eat the half side of a ram I'm so hungry! How's Ma? What the doctor say?"

"Aw. She's all right. Able to eat and tell me what to do. The doctor he say she got to lay still a piece."

They both laughed loudly.

"That's ma, all right. Guess I better get on up and see her."

Heavy crunching footsteps along the hall.

(Here's that Margaret comin' up behind Pa. Anything to leave that wash tub. Them clothes ought to been out by nine o'clock.")

"Hello Pa. Yeah I'm all, right. Be up tomorrow I reckon."

You better stay there 'till the doctor say git up."

"Aw my Lawd. You all make me sick. I ain't dying. I ought to know how I feel."

"Luly and Sam be here this afternoon, Ma."

"What they coming for?"

"See how you feel and stay 'till you are better."

Aw you make me sick. Who's that slamming that front door again?"

It's me, Ma!"

"What you coin' home from work Jim?"

Though he was twenty-six and though he had the dirty overalls of a mechanic, Jim dropped on the side of Ma's bed like a child.

Everybody eyed him.

"You lost your job?"

"Aw no, Margaret! I jes run home a minute to see Ma! Was takin' Mr. Drake's car to be greased."

"Well git them greasy clothes off my clean sheets! What the name of God ails you, boy?"

"Ma!—Artie's married."

Jim said it as if he were dropping a load.

"Artie!!"

Ma snapped up right in the bed. Pa jack-knifed down on the trunk. Margaret's mouth dropped open wide and she let it stay wide.

In spite of that pumping and jumping that started in her left side, Ma spoke first.

"Who says Artie's married? My boy ain't going to take no wife 'thout telling me and Pa! You always talk too much Jim!"

"I ain't jes talkin! He is so married! Fellers was tellin me down the oilin' station."

"Who he marry?"

"Mrs. Fannie's Jule!"

"You mean that gal what kept a sportin' flat over the drug store? My God!"

"Aw hol' on Pa! How you know where she keep her flat?"

"Aw, Ma! Everybody in town knows about Jule!"

"Ma!"

It was Margaret who saw the tears on Ma's face. "You all stop telling Ma all this stuff!"

"Aw heish! Ef Artie's married I'm the mother what borned him and I'm gonna know about it," Ma panted as she said it.

Margaret stabbed a mean look at Jim. "You always talk too much!"

"Y'all stop that fussin!"

Ma had to breathe strong to keep going but she talked to Pa. "You say this Jule belongs to Miss Fanny? She bound to be bad then, cause Fanny ain't never been a God's bit of good! Maybe, though, if Artie's married her and he brings her home we can git her to join church!"

"Aw Ma. You don't know that gal!"

"Heish, Margaret! Don't speak light of the church!"

Pa snorted: "That gal's been all over town all her life!"

"Pa! No deacon ought to talk that away! Jim! You tell Artie come home and bring his wife!"

"That means I got to git out of his room! Where'll I sleep—in the attic?"

The front door shook the house. John the youngest boy, raced into Ma's room.

"Hey, ma! Ole Artie's married. The kids out at school tole me!"

"That ain't no reason you got to come splittin' in here like any Indian! Don't you learn no manners at the high school?"

"I am an Indian, Old Margaret! Ain't I, ma? You said your great, great grand-pap lived in a tent and had fifteen wives!"

"I sent never said no such a lie! I said he married one Indian woman. I said he saw these Indians burn up some town and he run off from slavery with 'em and married one!"

"At's the time ma! At's the time! That ole guy is the one you say said them arrows them Injuns was shootin' had fire on them! Jes ate up everything in town."

"Hongry fire!" chanted Jim like a child finishing a well-known story. "Hongry fire! Et up everything it hit!"

Ma laid down suddenly. "You all go on out of here! Go on out!"

"Aw Ma!! Better take some of that medicine what the doctor left."

"No!"

"Aw Ma!"

"Well—Pa you fix it! Only don't give me much! 'bout ten drops'll do! You Jim? Tell Artie come on home!"

And up in the flat over the drugstore, Artie was with his Jule.

"You come on home and stay! Leave your ma have the flat to herself! She won't be lonesome!"

Jule had a butter-colored skin and hair that was bleached red. She did a lot of things to her eyes and lips and kept putting on layers of rouge.

Artie was still breathing as if the ceremony in the city hall and the taxi ride back to Jule's flat had been a marathon.

"Gee I never thought you'd marry me Jule! All the guys you could get!" Artie kept saying it in a dazed murmur.

Jule let her lips curve a little. "You're a good guy Artie! But why can't you stay here with Ma and me! Plenty of room!"

"I'm going to take you home! You're my wife and I'll look out for you! See? Honey—!"

Finally Jule said—"Aw—! All right!" But she said it slowly and began to pick up things and pack her bag slowly too, as if she did not want to put them in it.

Funny Artie could not see she was glued in her own home!

It was a Monday again. Ma Jones was still in bed.

—"'Pears like to me that doctor don't know what he doing! I been taking that green stuff nigh on four months now and I ain't been outside this room yet! Do look like to me—"

A double chorused shout of laughter cut across her thoughts. Jule was down in the kitchen with Margaret.

"Gal, you sure are dumb! Dumb! Ain't six enough! You don't need no more! Gawd knows you don't, Margaret!"

The hole under the carpet still linked Ma with the family life down stairs. She leaned out of bed swiftly and listened.

"But Jule! I'm scared! Suppose this stuff kills me too."

"Aw take it!! I always use the same thing!"

There was a little silence. Then Margaret began to cough and choke. "Sure tastes bad enough!"

Was that Jule teaching her Margaret to drink? Her Margaret what never had a foot on a dance hall floor and was a married woman with six children at twenty-four? Ma called aloud.

"You, Margaret?"

"Ma'am?"

"You, Margaret? Come up here!!"

"Yas'm."

Two sets of footsteps came along the hall and Margaret stood only a little inside of the door. Jule's eyes peeped sleepily over Margaret's shoulder. She had a green silk kimona around her, but her body was bare. She never did wear any clothes in the house.

"You, Margaret." Ma sat up in the bed. "You been drinkin'?"

"Drinkin'!! No Ma!"

"What was you all doing downstairs?"

Jule eeled in. "Aw Ma! I'se jes fixing up a little something for Margaret's cold,"

"Cold! What you doin' lettin' yourself ketch cold, Margaret! You know you told me you thought—!"

"The doctor says he gotta wait another month to make sure!"

"He aint sure yet? I thought he said you was about four months along!"

"Aw no—Ma!—I—!"

"No Ma, he told Margaret he didn't think nuthin' tall was the matter with her! That's what he tol' her las' time she's there!"

"How you know Jule?"

"'Cause I went with her! Went with her one night you was sleeping."

Ma laid back again in her pillows. Jule went along the hall to her room. Margaret scrabbled heavily down stairs.

She couldn't remember any time that Jule had gone to the doctor's with Margaret.

There went that front door again. Why couldn't Johnny ever come in decent—like—?

John's steps pounded up the hall.

Jule opened her door. "Aw Johnnie? Johnnie? Come here, dear! I want you to reach down this window shade for me!"

And John streaked on past Ma's door without stopping to glance in, though he did yell, "Hey, ma!"

Ma waited for him to come back. It only took a few steps to cross the room. It only took a minute to stand on a chair and reach the shade—then come out and into her room.

Ma waited.

She heard the chair scrape, she heard the shade roll down—then she heard Jule laughing and laughing and talking as if she was telling some joke that was real funny.

("Wasn't that gal stark naked when she stood in this here door five minutes ago?")

"You, Johnny? Johnny!" Ma sat up in bed to shout it.

"Ma'am!"

John stood outside on Ma's door sill and said again, "Ma'am"'

"You stay out of Artie's room—heah me? Stay on out of there!"

Johnny turned and went down the hall toward the steps. "Yes'm!" he called back from the head of the stairs.

Ma heard him walking down stairs. Ma heard the front door click softly.

Johnnie had gone out. Johnnie had shut the door. Quietly.

Ma panted back in her pillows. She'd better pray. Her breath came so hard!

("I better get up from heah!")

She took hold of the table by her bed so she could support herself. The bottles of medicine in it clinked and rattled.

"Believe I'll try some of the yaller stuff this time. Get some sleep and stop worrying about these children's foolishness! How many drops the doctor say take? Ten! Don't want too many! He say this stuff kill anyone that takes more'n ten—!"

The street lights were slicing the darkness of her room when Ma opened her eyes again. Someone was talking downstairs. It was Luly and Sam having their supper.

"I wish them children'd all eat together at the same time like I always had them! Still I s'pose all them brats of Margarets are too much with Luly and Sam and Johnny and Pa and Vernice! Don't seem like no family—all eating at different times."

Luly was talking. "I wish we'd go on back home, Sam! Don't seem right to stay here on Pa and Ma all the time!"

Sam must have been chewing. There was a silence before he spoke. "I tol' you I put the stuff in storage! Might as well stay here! Save money!"

"You put my furniture in storage! You ain't never tol' me!"

"I did so! You ain't been listenin' to me!"

A sharp wail cut in all at once.

"Can't you never keep that baby quiet, Luly?"

His stummick bother him, Sam! All I do is keep looking out after him all the time!"

"Wish to God you'd keep him still! Look like a man could have some peace when he gets home after a day's work!"

"Aw shet up!"

This was Sam and Luly!!

"And another thing, Luly! Why didn't you make me no light bread like I ast you this mawnin ? A man had ought to be able to eat what he wants at his own home? You don't have nuthin t'all to do all day but 'tend the baby!"

"I tol' you that baby had a stummick ache! I couldn't find no time!"

"Why couldn't your mother keep him? She ain't doin' nuthin but layin' in the bed!"

"Ma's sick! You know the doctor said she'd ought to be quiet!"

"Aw—my mother had the same thing she's got! And she never missed a day at the tobacco factory down home neither! These women get too soft and lazy in these big cities!"

—Her own home!—

Her own daughter!

And her own food—Pa said Sam gave next to nothing toward the food bill.

Making a table of discord out of her food!

And Sam suppose to be such a Christian! Superintendent of the Sunday School. Always rolling his eyes and actin' so sanctified! Like some old nanny goat baa-in"! ("Whyn't Luly sass him back and really shet him up. I'll call her right up stairs, and tell her something— tell her something—")

That sleeping medicine must not have let go of Ma entirely. She dozed again and when she woke up it was to struggle with thumping and bumping that tore loose in her left side every once in a while.

The thumping and the struggling kept up all next day. When Ma saw Luly she forgot whether she had heard her quarrelling with Sam. She wasn't even sure whether it was Luly or Margaret or Vernice.

On Thursday she did ask Margaret what the doctor had said about her.

"Did he say you gonna have another baby, Margaret?"

"Heh—heh! No. Ma! Everything's all right. I come all right again!"

"You come all right again! I thought you tol me you was 'bout the fourth month."

"I guess it was cold! I guess I caught cold or somethin!"

Jule had been sitting on the trunk listening. Now she began to laugh and laid back against the wall. She got up all of a sudden and walked out and went into her own room.

"That gal sure laughs like the devil Margaret!"

"Yes'm! You want anything else, Ma? I gotta go down stairs—see 'bout somethin' I left on the stove!"

Margaret went down the stairs bumping the railing, then the wall. Something surely must be burning! Margaret never walked down-stairs fast.

Ma went back to struggling for a clear breath over the thumping in her side in her throat—all over her.

By Saturday morning she seemed to have won the race, but Ma lay more tired than ever in her bed.

"Lawd this house seems quiet! Ain't that Luly's baby hollering somewhere?"

Ma listened and rapped on the floor for Margaret.

"What ails little Sam, Margaret?"

"His stummick Ma! Don't seem to git no better!"

"Whyn't Luly give him some castor oil?"

Margaret took hold of the spread on Ma's bed and began shaking it to fluff it up. "I did, Ma," she answered after a minute.

"I ain't asked you why didn't you try castor oil! I said—why don't Luly use it on little Sam?"

"She ain't here no more!"

"She ain't here!! Ain't Sam and the baby here? Where's she at?"

Margaret lifted an arm toward the window. "She gone! Lef a letter! Tole Sam—tole him she ain't never loved him or the baby neither 'cause the boy was his'n!"

The pain in Ma's side knocked her to her feet this time.

"Where's my child, Margaret!

"Where's Luly? Aw—Jesus!"

"Jule say she went on with Dick!"

"Dick? You mean that no 'count trash I stopped her from runnin' with 'fore she married Sam! God help me—".

Jule came running when Margaret screamed. She helped Margaret put Ma back in bed and then she went out to the corner drugstore and called the doctor.

"She can't have any more excitement," the doctor told Pa. "You'll have to see that she's kept quiet! She can't stand another attack like this one!"

"Yas sir!" Pa promised. "You Johnny and you Vernice!" he threatened his two youngest. "You'll act like you got some sense and keep quiet in this house! Heah me?"

"Yas sir!"

Johnny took to hanging around Pete's Pleasure Pool Parlor. Vernice began walking out with Jule. Sometimes she would go down to Miss Fannie's,—Jule's mother's—with her.

Vernice was sixteen and had velvet black brown skin. You could tell by her walk that her suppleness would make any dance graceful. Ma had made Bernice join church when she was twelve. She had never danced—a Christian could not dance—and she could only see a movie when she slid off without telling anyone at home.

But she wanted movies and dancing, and all the other things anybody sixteen anywhere ever wanted.

She began walking with Jule every evening. She would talk to Jule, too.

"Jule—don't it feel swell to have somebody takin' you places and everything like old Artie does for you?"

"Yeah—I dunno!—sure!"

"Lord! I'd know it was swell!"

"Any girl can get something for herself! Just gotta know how! Now take you—you're too slow! You gotta act hot—get out—get a string of guys crazy about you—then pick the one that's the biggest fool over you for your husband! That's all!"

"Yeah!"

"Say! I know a swell feller! Come down to my mother's with me next Friday—"

"Gal's got to know everything in all the books when she starts percolatin' with a guy like Eddie!" a man told this to Artie one night in the barber shop.

"You ain't tellin' me nuthin!" Artie agreed. "Who's Eddie bustin' around with now."

The other man looked surprised—then he masked his expression with a bland wariness. "Better ask Vernice," he laughed.

Margaret was asleep when Artie jerked her door open.

"Where's Vernice?"

"She went out with Jule!"

"What you let her go out with her for?"

"What you talkin' 'bout, boy? Ain't Jule your wife?"

"Yas, Jule's my wife—! You ought not to let Vernice stay out after eleven!"

"What time is it now? Aw she's all right long as she's with your wife! They say they goin' to Miss Fannie's!"

"Miss Fannie's!! You let Vernice go to Miss Fannie's?"

"How I going to stop her from going to your wife's mother's house?"

"Aw go to hell!"

"Heah! Don't you curse me!"

Sam, already awake with the baby and on fire with a longing to fight the world—came into the room, too.

"What ails y'all? Quit yellin'!"

Pa came out of the kitchen. "What the name of God is the matter with y'all? Heish!!"

"Jule's taken Vernice down to Miss Fannie's!!"

Pa cursed so long and loud that Ma rapped on the floor. "Pa!! Pa!!" Her voice sounded as if she were ten stories away from them. "You a deacon! Pa, what's the trouble! I'm gonna come down."

Pa yelled back. "Heish, y'all!! Stay up there, Ma! I'll be up there!"

Everyone trailed Pa up into Ma's room.

"I'm gonna beat Jule for takin Vernice to Miss Fannies!" Artie shouted at the door.

"Is Vernice down there? Lawd!" Ma had to pant a while, but she fought to keep on talking. "Ain't no sense to beatin' no wire, Artie! Jes' you go down and git the child!"

"I'm gettin ready to throw that Jule out on the sidewalk and set her trunk on top of her!"

"Aw, Pa, heish! You ain't gonna do nuthin of the sort! She could go room somewhere else and get 'round the child better then!"

"Well, I feels like blowin' her brains out 'cause she's the one what sent Luly on to her destruction! Luly never'd of thought 'bout leavin ef Jule hadn't put her up to it!"

"Aw Sam! Don't talk no foolishness! You helped send Luly away your own self!"

"What!!"

"Yas!" Ma's voice rallied to a shout.

"I ain't never sent my lawful wife to no bed of sin!"

"Tain't whilst to argue with Ma, Sam! I'm the head of this house!"

Pa's thunder silenced the room.

"Well—I'm going to tell Jule what I thinks of her!" Margaret offered after a while.

"That'll just be bustin a hornet's nest." It was odd how Ma could silence the flood of pain long enough to silence each one of them. .

"Y'all come on out of here!" Pa shouted at them all. "Ma got to be quiet. Come out!!!"

They herded out still yapping and snapping at each other the way people will do when they are wrought up, bewildered, set on—and cannot see a door or a window or even a crack to get out of their tight spot.

The thumping made Ma get out of bed this time. She was feeling for her slippers when the front door opened.

"Here's Jule! Here's Vernice!" Ma wanted to run downstairs in the instant between the sound of the door opening and its closing to hold Pa and the rest of them back in the kitchen.

The door closed.

Jule laughed and called out, "Artie," Oh! honey! Artie?"

"Heigh, honey!" Artie's answer was slow.

"Artie! I left my little bag you gave me down to Ma's. You run on down there and get it for me! Some of Ma's friends'll be pickin' it up and I don't want to lose it—'cause you gave it to me!"

There followed a long quietness. Then Ma heard the door close again. Artie was going for his Jule's bag.

"What'cha sayin', Pa ?" Jule's voice swaggered. She was in the kitchen now. "Gosh that ham sandwich looks good to me, old dad! Gimme a bite! Say, Sammy? Ma says to give your kid some arrowroot in milk."

Ma sat down heavily on the side of her bed.

All of them—every one of them—was scared of that gal!

They didn't dare say anything to Jule! And Jule—just like a fire—was burning holes into the lives of each one of them.

That Margaret would never make heaven. That Margaret had had more than a "cold" that time when she and Jule were drinking something in the kitchen.

Luly had turned to be a bad woman—and Jule had led her, had told her how to get out and to be one!

That gal was a fire—a hongry fire—burning up the house just like them Indian's arrows—burning that town.

And nobody had been able to jump on the house tops and stamp out the fire. It had taken a sudden rain from heaven to do that.

"God! What'll I do? I could only see the reverend—I'd ask him! Vernice ain't never even come up stairs to see me yet!"

The thing that plunged and tore loose in Ma s left side pressed her back against the head of the bed. She wanted to scream out but she was too spent when she could get up again.

She kept talking to herself. "Ain't one of 'em left to be saved for the kingdom after this gal gets through! Not a one of 'em but Vernice and Johnny—and she been after them! God! I wisht there's some ways to stop her! Wisht there's some ways to stamp out her fire!"

Jule was laughing on the stairs. Pa was laughing with her. Margaret joined in and Sam said something. They all laughed louder.

"Well—night y'all! Guess I'll be ready to turn in time my Artie gets back," Jule announced.

"Yeah!" (That stupid Margaret!)

"Night, Jule!"—(Pa was *so foolish* sometime!)

"Night!" (Dirty thing! answering so sure of herself)

Jule was walking up the steps. Jule was going by Ma's door.

"Aw Jule? Jule!"

"'Scuse me, Ma! You wake? What you want?"

"Ah—you get me a little water—will you? Got—got to take some medicine."

"Aw sure, Ma! where's the glass! This here? Whyn't you have a light in here?"

"I kin see all I want with the street lights!"

Ma fumbled under the table. "You get it, Jule? Thanks. Say Jule I got a little peach brandy here Miss Johnson brought me las' week. Don't you want a taste?"

"Aw thanks, Ma! I'll take the bottle in the room so's Artie can have some too. Thanks!"

"Oh, now Jule! I—I—I got some all poured out in here for you! You drink it right here! Then you take the bottle in the room for Artie, too! Wait'll I drop my sleep medicine!"

"Here! You ain't sposed to take but ten drops of that, ain't you, Ma? You putting in too much, ain't you!"

"No!! Thirty drops! Thirty-five!"

"Aw no! Wait'll I call Margaret—"

"Aw leave that gal downstairs! Leave them all down there—!! I ain't puttin' in too much—!! How you like that brandy? Drink it all up!! Good for you!"

Jule laughed her loudest! "You all right Ma! Well—I'll take the bottle—get ready for Artie! Gosh what did Sister Johnson put in that stuff? Got an awful kick! I feel kinder funny already!"

"Yeah, Jule? Have some more! Here—!!"

"Say—Ma! You're sposed to be a deaconess too, ain't you! Heh—Heh! Well—Good night!"

She went out, leaving Ma's door open. She went along the hall singing.

"Oh the dog jumped a rabbit.
Run him for one sol—id mile!
And the rabbit set down! ...
The rabbit set down!
And hollered like a nat-chul chile!"

Ma called after her. "Say Jule? Ain't that the piece where the rabbit run the dog? Ain't it?"

"Aw no, Ma! Ain't no rabbit never run no dog! You all right, Ma, but you ain't no jazz baby!'

"No! Well—I jes thought the rabbit might run the dawg this once!"

"We'll see you in the mornin', Ma!"

Ma should hear her humming around her room. She heard her open a drawer—close it. She heard Jule yawn. She heard her move a chair. She heard Jule yawning—yawning. Then she heard her lie down on the bed.

Ma listened.

There was no more humming.

There was no more yawning.

Ma listened.

There could not be any more humming. There could not be any more yawning—yawn-ing—yawning.

Ma emptied the rest of the sleeping medicine in the glass.

Then she pulled the carpet back so that she could see the little square of light from the kitchen—where Pa and Margaret and Vernice were—where they all were.

Then she drank her share.

She wanted sleep. The fire slept.

It was out.

She could have peace now.   [*The Crisis* 46.12 (December 1939): 360–362, 376–377]

PLANTATION STAIN

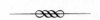

by Corinne Dean

"Oh it's going to be terrible," exclaimed Doña María in a quavering voice.

"What's going to be terrible?" Concha asked dully.

"You were in town all day yesterday and you didn't learn a thing," reproached Concha's mother.

"But I went to Doña Juana's to get my measurements taken for an Easter dress."

Doña María's mouth dropped open in sheer disgust. Was there any more propitious occasion on which to get the gossip than while trying on a dress in a household composed of three women and a precocious twelve-year old girl? It was always humiliating to Doña María that her best gossip came through the kitchen and not through the parlor.

"You *do* know that next Tuesday is Mardi Gras," said Doña María sarcastically.

"Well?" questioned Concha, unperturbed.

"Well, aren't you interested in who is going to be queen of the Mardi Gras?"

"No, I'm not," replied Concha so flatly that I could see Doña María's hair rise and bristle in indignation.

"Who is going to be queen?" I asked rushing gallantly into the breach.

"That's just it. No one knows yet," answered Doña María desperately anxious to talk about the matter. "Let's go out on the veranda." She glared at Concha. "It's a pleasure to talk to some one alive."

I could have told her that Concha was very much alive, that at eighteen Concha was in love with the wrong man from society's viewpoint but the right man from her soul's viewpoint that this socio-soulistic conflict so occupied Concha's every conscious moment until she heard nothing, saw nothing, and above all, thought nothing but how "this dreadful tragedy" as she called it "would all end." I could have also told Doña María that Concha didn't get her measurements taken yesterday—at least not by Doña Juana.

Doña María, whose maiden name was Marie MacDonald, toddled out to the porch way ahead of me. She was English, she insisted, mixed with a wee bit of Scotch. She grew weary explaining to one and all that she was not Irish. The Irish spelled it McDonald. Her girth and manner, plus the fact her English accent was full bodied and guttural, caused her to be considered a transplanted German. Too, she always spoke with more thought than form— so she couldn't have been English.

Doña María's rocker was already straining at the rounds by the time I got to the porch. Shaking a couple of surprised lizards out of a siesta, I sat down adjacent to Doña María and turned on her a gaze bursting with polite curiosity, although like Concha I really didn't give a damn who was going to be queen.

Not that I'm indifferent to gossip, but it is impossible to be curious about "foreign" gossip whether at home or abroad. One must be definitely within the web, a part and parcel of its intricate pattern to feel any pull when one of the lines breaks down. Later on, after a stay of four or five months in Puerto Rico, I became as much a part of the gossip web as the rich widower, Don Luís Gova, whose wealthy but homely bride disappeared and was never seen again—six weeks after marrying the poor but personable Don Luís. People disappear in the United States, but no one disappears on a tropical island thirty by one hundred miles. There just isn't room and any attempt to do so causes never ending speculation and gossip.

"Now this is the difficulty," Doña María began, "Alicia wants to be queen again."

"Alicia who?" I asked.

"Alicia Morales, of course," she answered slightly exasperated, forgetting I had been on the island only one month, and had met six Alicias. "The one with the big black eyes and olive skin." I thought: "Most Puerto Ricans leave big black eyes and olive colored skin." I said: "Oh, yes, the banker's daughter."

Doña María carried on: "You know he owns half of Humacao, and that's not all he—"

"Has a mortgage on the other half," I ventured.

"Exactly. Well he thinks his every wish is law, and so if Alicia wants to be queen again—the matter is settled." At this point her voice dropped to an awesome whisper. "The town is in revolt."

"What are they going to do?" I asked.

"The Mardi Gras committee had a meeting yesterday but the meeting almost ended in a fight. Those working for or almost for Don Alfredo were a little timid about openly saying they wouldn't have his daughter queen again. The landowners and property owners were reticent in proportion to their mortgages."

"But why the near fight?" I asked.

"Well they put up several candidates saying they wouldn't be dictated to, they would vote for a choice of their own. Even Concha was a candidate, just think. When the voting was over Alicia was elected. Then each one accused the other of being the double crosser and you can imagine the rest."

"But why did they vote for her if they didn't want her?"

"They were afraid Don Alfredo would find out. Each one voted to save his own skin hoping the others would take the risk of insulting Don Alfredo."

"Wasn't the voting by secret ballot?" I asked.

"By ballot, but not so secret. Those collecting the ballots have a way of flipping the ballots and seeing what you write. The result was although Alicia was elected the majority shouted it was impossible, there was some dirty work, etc., the weak-kneed and the informers were for letting the vote stand."

"What did they decide?"

"They didn't decide. They voted and re-voted all day each time electing Alicia. Finally they split into two camps those who were for letting the vote stand and those who would go on voting forever until the vote came out right.

"About six o'clock Don Alfredo must have got tired of waiting for the returns, because he went down to the meeting and made a speech. Whoever informed him did a good job of reporting because Don Alfredo was able to review the day's events as if he were reading from the minutes. He said there was no need for such turmoil. He was always willing to compromise. (They cheered and clapped.) Alicia was rich, but not selfish. (More clapping.) She knew her father owned this and owned that but she wasn't greedy. He recalled her generous gifts (mostly to teachers about to fail her). She would not be queen, he'd see to that. Their choice was his choice.

"The committee was almost in tears by this time. He then asked curtly who was chairman of the meeting. All breathed relief at not having to stand up—except Don Ignacio. He was the chairman. He was equal to the occasion, however. He lauded Don Alfredo's generosity, Don Afredo's wife's generosity and in particular Don Alfredo's daughter's generosity. He concluded these eulogies by asking, nay beseeching, in behalf of the committee, Don Alfredo to designate, in view of Alicia's magnanimous withdrawal, a second choice. Certainly Don Alfredo's idea of the second most beautiful and queenly girl in all of Humacao (six blocks square) would flatter and honor the one chosen."

"What happened? I asked.

"Don Alfredo named his daughter-in-law and then went home."

"So it's all settled," I said, getting ready to rise.

"No, just the contrary. No one said anything until Don Alfredo had been royally escorted to the door. Then pandemonium broke loose."

"Don't they like his daughter-in-law?" I asked. She seems gracious and charming."

"She is—but!"

"But what?"

"She's an American!!!"

I knew this was intended to be a bombshell so I looked as shocked as if I had just sat down on an electric eel. Not knowing what to say I repeated: "She's an American!!!"—in the same tone of voice that I would use had I looked into the sky and felt I saw reason to exclaim: "Why it's a flying whale!!!"

Don't misunderstand me," Doña María hastened to add, "All of Humacao loves her. But she *can't* be queen. *Never* has the island had a foreigner for queen. Don Alfredo knew that. The committee was aghast."

"What did they decide?"

"They didn't decide."

"Again!"

"Everybody talked at once until two A.M. Then they went home. They have been in session all morning."

"Any news?"

"I don't know yet."

"But it's one o'clock now. They must be all talking at once again. Maybe the meeting is over. Shall I go to the plaza and find out?"

With her eyes moist with infinite gratitude for my good intentions Doña María replied: "No, thanks. It isn't necessary. The meeting can't be over yet. Aida hasn't come back with the morning marketing yet."

"Won't the food spoil before she gets back?" I hinted.

"I ordered nothing but staples today. Besides Aida is a good servant and so I kind of gave her the day off. She works hard and needs—."

The hue and cry of "Extra!" "Extra!" by two little brownies interrupted her tender remarks about Aida. Doña María would have leaped to her feet had not her bulk and the backward tilt of the rocker prevented her gaining any such instant momentum.

"An extra?" I questioned. "I didn't know there was even a newspaper in Humacao, to have an extra."

"There isn't," she replied simply.

"All newspapers are extras. This is surely about the controversy. Hold him while I get some money."

Life wouldn't have been worth living if I hadn't held him. Mustering one half of my Spanish vocabulary I yelled: Muchacho, aquí," and kept it up until the "extra" was safely in my hand.

Then a strange thing happened. The other lad came over and thrust another extra into my hand and the more I tried to tell him in my U.S.A. Spanish that I already had one the more he shook his head negatively insisting all the time that I keep the extra "extra." He waited for Doña María to come out and pay him. She came out very soon, took both papers, paid both boys and sat down to read both papers, at the same time if possible, like a gluttonous little boy who keeps his eyes riveted on the ice cream while eating the turkey.

Poor me, I hadn't realized that there couldn't be an extra without a counter-extra. That would be like having a revolution in South America without a counter-revolution!

"Oh! Oh! Oh! This is going to be terrible."

"How do things stand now?" I asked.

"Look!" and she thrust one of the extras into my hand.

I tried to get the full import of the article, but my Spanish was too limited. I noticed the title of the extra was "Mancha de Piantación" meaning "Plantation Stain." The extra seemed to be trying to convey the information that the whole island knew Don Alfredo's family tree was blighted by the plantation stain, and therefore he should cease to be the dictator of the town's most important social event the Mardi Gras ball, even though he was the town's richest man.

"What do they mean by plantation stain?" I asked.

"Oh, everyone knows the gossip about Don Alfredo's grandmother. "You've never heard?"

"No, I haven't."

"Well, you know the family claims she's crazy and so they keep her practically locked up in one of their country houses."

"Oh," I broke in, a dim light dawning. "Plantation stain means—insanity."

"No! No! She is as sane as you or I."

By this time I wasn't so sure about my sanity or that of anyone else, but I acknowledged the compliment with a nod. "They don't like her, much," I suggested.

"They're crazy about her. They visit her all the time, *but* they forbid anyone outside the family, to visit her, by claiming she's 'violent.' Of course they forbid her to visit them or anyone else."

"Well, what's the matter with her then?"

Doña María leaned over and whispered: "She's black! Black as coal. And every time the town reminds Don Alfredo he has some Negro blood—called the plantation stain—he forecloses his mortgages. Oh, it's going to be terrible!"

As an anticlimax Aida came hurrying down the road almost breaking into a run as she neared the gate. Not daring to withhold any information as long as she was within earshot of Doña María she shouted, "She ees elected!"

"Who?" shouted back Doña María in unison with the neighbors who had stuck their heads out the windows at the first sound of Aida's voice.

"Alicia!" said Aida simply.   [*The Crisis* 47.1 (January 1940): 16, 18]

PATCH QUILT

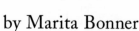

by Marita Bonner

Sara unrolled a piece of damp clothes from the basket beneath her ironing board and shook it out.

"Another one of them ruffled dresses for Mrs. Brown's Sally. I 'clare I can't iron it today," Sara spoke aloud to herself.

She looked at the clock. Twelve o'clock. She should have known that by the sunshine though it was hard to tell time by the sun in March.

Jim ought to be coming any moment now. Jim ought to be coming home from his new job.

"First time in near three years that Jim'll bring home a pay envelope on Saturday. Shore glad the government made them put some of the colored relief men on the new road job along with the white!" Sara had a habit of talking aloud whenever she was alone. She made a half-hearted swoop with her old-fashioned sad-iron over one ruffle before her on the board.

A whistle blew somewhere.

Sara held her iron up from the board and listened. Then walking swiftly to the rusty iron stove that glowed red hot beneath a burden of six irons, she released the one she held in her hand.

"Shame to waste this fire and these clothes all damped just right to iron but I gotta git ready to make market."

She took the board down from its position between two chairs, tossed the dress back into the basket and went into the bedroom.

"I'm going to get me some of the things I been wanting to eat these three years." Sara planned happily as she put on a clean cotton house dress and her only pair of silk stockings.

"Jim's bringing twelve dollars and I got four or five up in the closet. Guess we'll have chicken and yeller yams and greens and ice-cream—if the freezer is still any good—and two kinds of cake for Sunday dinner! Got to celebrate!"

She broke off talking to herself to listen again. Jim ought to be coming into the house right now. Only took fifteen minutes to get home if he took the short cut.

"Guess he gone down town to git his hair cut! Git all prettied up," Sara decided finally.

She went to the cupboard in the kitchen, took down an old tea-pot and drew out four dirty crumpled one dollar bills.

"We can take the ten dollars rent out of Jim's money. I'm going!" she decided recklessly.

She snapped her pocket-book together, unlatched the door and stepped out.

Her house, like all the other houses in the colored district on that hill, stood below the level of the street.

Sara puffed a little as she climbed over the ditch where last night's rain had left a little water.

"Wished they'd let that new road come this side of town," she panted aloud as she came up on the street.

She began to pick the driest spots in the mud to walk through for there were not side-walks.

"Hi, Sara! Looks like spring's most here!" a voice called.

Sara halted and looked around. A tall, dark colored woman of indeterminate age leaned over the gate of a yard across the road.

"Aw, hi, Miss Susie!" Sara greeted her. She drew nearer to the woman. "I'm 'bout to go to town to make market."

"Jim home yet?"

"Naw, but I can't wait for him to get home! I got right smart buying to do."

"Y'all having company tomorrer?"

Sara drew herself up proudly.

"Naw! Je's Jim and me but I 'clare I feel like eatin' a good dinner like I used to when times was good! I want ice cream and two kinds of cake!"

The other woman did not answer. Instead she looked off toward the top of the hill.

A white cottage stood there.

"Wonder how Miss Drake is?" Miss Susie said after a pause.

Sara looked surprised. "She sick?"

"Naw—! I jes' wondered how she was!"

There was another silence. Sara stirred restlessly and said, "Well—! I'll be gettin' along!"

The other woman did not speak again nor did she look at her.

Sara walked off, down the hill.

Once she looked back. Miss Susie still stood as she had left her, staring down the road after Sara.

"What ails Miss Susie? What she say that 'bout Miss Drake for? She ain't no company of Miss Drake! Jes' said that so's I wouldn't git to tell her what I'se having for dinner! How is Miss Drake!!"

Her mind went back to the house at the crest of the hill, too.

Nobody was Miss Drake's "company." She lived alone with her two children, Sandy and Marie, and earned her living by sewing for white families of the little southern town of Redmond.

"She sews so much for white folks, she thinks she's white too!" was the common belief among the Negroes of the town. "Always stayin' to herself! Keeping that girl and boy cooped up all the time."

"That gal ain't home all the time! She off somewhere passing, workin' in a white store," town gossip proclaimed.

"How anybody going to pass in Redmond where everybody knows everybody else here!" others countered.

Sara thought of all this as she pushed on down the hill toward the shopping district.

She paused once near a clump of bushes to rest.

The shrubbery shook suddenly and a tawny, freckled-face boy in his teens clambered out.

Sara recognized Sandy Drake by the reddish hair.

"Howdy, Miss Sara!" the boy muttered.

"How are you, Sandy! How's your ma and your sister?"

The boy flushed and stuttered something. Sara could not understand him. She tried another tack.

"How they makin' out with the new road? I see you come 'cross the hill from that away? Ain't they knocked off for the day yet?"

Sandy reddened still more. "Yas'm—er—I guess so! I dunno. Ma sent me out to meet sister."

He plunged on up the hill abruptly.

Sara stared after him. "What ails that little fool? Big as any man and can't talk straight so you can get any sense out of it!"

She watched the boy out of sight and quickening her pace set off down the hill until she reached the base where the colored section ended and Market street—the main street—began.

She crossed Market street, lost herself in the midst of the mud and chicken crates, the side-walk vendors and hawkers, the muddy automobiles and crowds of poor whites and Negroes that made Saturday the most exciting day of the week in that town.

With a sort of giddy triumph Sara acquired her chicken and her yellow yams, her fat back and greens, lemons, sugar, flour and vanilla.

At the end of an hour she found herself outside the Five-and-Ten at the far end of the market, trying to juggle her packages so the oysters would not spill and with but twenty cents in her purse.

"Guess I'll git me an ice-pick! That other thing is enough to try the devil!"

Ten minutes later, with the ice-pick and a pound of pink jaw breakers added to her pack, Sara started back up the hill.

She was heavy with packages—and not one cent was left to her.

She was tired but she was happy. She crunched the candy noisily.

A broad black woman hung across the fence at the first house she reached.

"Hi, Sara!" She called in greeting as Sara came abreast her gate. "Looks like you been doin' right smart buyin'?"

Sara choked hastily over a large piece of candy to make room for a complete answer. "Yas. I been jes' makin' a little market! Spent every bit of fo' dollars for just this one meal, though!" she broke off to giggle and watch the effect of her statement.

The other woman let her eyes sweep up and down Sara's figure.

Then she gazed up the hill toward the top and back down and said, "I hear that one of them travelin' buses done fell over on the new road!"

Startled, Sara forgot to giggle.

"Ain't nobody hurt!" she managed to ask. "You know, Jim's workin' over there."

The other woman shook her head doubtfully. "I ain't heard that. I jes' heard 'bout the bus! Say! Whyn't you cut across the back lots and see?"

Sara shot off without saying a goodbye and left the other gazing with veiled eyes after her.

Anxiety and the uneven ground of the field brought a breathless Sara upon the highway.

A cross-country bus lay on its side in a ditch, a group of people, apparently passengers, and mostly white, stood clumped disconsolately around their bags piled in the road. All the machinery used for excavating the road stood idle. No laborers were in sight.

Uncle Eph, a deaf Negro who claimed to be one hundred and ten, sat on a rock nearby cleaning a red lantern.

Sara approached him.

"Who got hurt!" she screamed, pointing to the bus.

"Ain't nobody hurt!" Answered Eph mildly.

Relief loosed Sara's giggles again. "That Annie May Jones had me thinkin' all y'all was kilt out here on the job!" she cried.

Eph rubbed his lamp. "I gotta git these things ready for the night. I keeps the lights on this here job at night."

"So Jim told me. Is Jim gone home?"

Eph scrubbed the lamp in his hand and sat it down on the ground. He did not answer this time.

"I reckon Jim's gone on home!" Sarah screamed again.

Uncle Eph sat back suddenly, shook his rag out and looked Sara directly in the face.

"Go on up to the tool shed!" he said loudly. "Go on up there!"

Sara gaped at him amazed. "Guess the poor soul don' know what I ast him!" She hesitated an instant, thrust her hand in her bag of candy and set two pieces down beside Eph. Then she started off up the hill toward the shed.

The door of the shed was open. Sara peered into the semi-darkness there. She saw nobody and was about to turn back when a sound came from behind the door.

She thrust her head inside, peered around the door.

Something green waved in her face and she heard a low murmuring. "You kin have it all honey. I'm crazy 'bout you!"

It was Jim's voice—Sara's eyes grew accustomed to the gloom. There was Jim's back, and staring with pale stricken fright across Jim's shoulder was Marie Drake. In her hand she clutched a bill.

Sara's bundles hurtled to the ground. Sara's hands snatched up the new ice-pick. Sara lunged and struck and lunged and struck again.

Then she ran screaming and crying aloud back into the sunshine.

Right outside the door she ran straight into the arms of Uncle Eph.

"I hadn't ought to a tol' you, honey! I hadn't ought to a tol' you, but I couldn't stand no more to see this deceivin' goin' on!"

The bus driver came striding up the hill.

"What's the matter here?" he demanded with that bustling flimsy authority assumed by cheap whites when they want to impress Negroes.

"She busted her eggs and her flour," Uncle Eph replied laconically. "See?"

He pointed to the ground. The driver glanced indifferently, grunted and turning on his heel, strode back to his own troubles.

When he was out of hearing, Eph pushed open the door wide. He saw the ice pick on the ground. He saw the blood on the ice pick.

"Y'all?" Eph shouted.

There was no reply. Eph drew Sara in, closed the door and struck a match to a candle.

Jim lay across the girl, Marie. Blood was streaming from one of her eyes and she lay staring in terror. In her hands she still held the money.

"You ain't dead! Ain't no use pertendin'," Uncle Eph ordered, "Git up."

"He's bleeding to death on me!" screamed the girl hysterically and began to cry.

"Shet up! Want all them folks from the bus come here and take you to the lock-up?" Eph cried.

Eph knelt beside Jim—rolled him over a little. He beckoned to Sara who leaned, hands clutched at her throat against the door.

"Ain't dead! Neck cut on the side. I'll git some water and we'll lug him 'cross the fields to Dr. Butler."

Eph stood up, yanked the door open back to its hinges. He pointed to Marie and shouted loudly as if she too were deaf, "Git on out of here! Tell your ma its best to keep young ones like you tied in their own yard!"

And that is how it happened that Marie Drake dropped out of sight.

"She gone North to school"—some people said. "Passin'!!"

But Sandy and his mother knew that Marie sat at home with her left eye closed forever and a deep ugly scar marring her left cheek.

Shame made a wall around the house on top of the hill.

And that is how it happened that Jim Brown had to lay off working—"cause a pick fell on his arm"—a useless arm hanging limp, a tendon cut at the shoulder.

Spring passed, the job on the road ended, but the tendon did not heal. Jim sat listless on the porch and gazed back toward the hills that hid the highway. Sometimes he looked up toward the top of the hill.

He did not say anything. He did not even offer to go fishing any more.

"—And when he did go fishin', that gal was right along with him. He used to come home with scarcely no fish!"

—Like patches in a quilt, Sara could piece the whole story clearly now.

The neighbors had known that day when she went shopping for chicken and oysters, lemonade and a new ice pick. They had known all this.

That is why they had looked at her so. And she thought it was envy.

And from those fishing trips, Jim used to come back absent minded, suddenly irritable, with little red patches—that were made by the imprint of a mouth coated with lip stick.— Sara knew now—on his shirt ... "berries done that!" he had lied.

"You ought to get right smart insurance from Uncle Sam if that pick fell on him!" the neighborhood declared to Sara.

Sara did not answer. She had to work harder to make ends meet.

Only she and Jim and Marie knew about the ice pick.

And shame, humiliation, and despair froze them to silence.

Uncle Eph knew, of course, but he never told.

Sometimes he felt sorry because he had been the one who had sent Sara to the tool shed. But he always comforted himself with the thought that he had fed the chicken to his cat.

He could not eat delicacies that had been meant for a feast of rejoicing—and dropped for a maiming—and a slaughter of hopes.   [*The Crisis* 47.3 (March 1940): 71–72, 92]

SUNDAY

by Lucille Boehm

Outside the window the yard was slaty-green, like it had sunk under water. And the pressure of steamy dampness lay everywhere, and seemed heavy as water pressure on an ocean bed. Anna breathed thickly beneath her sheet. She rolled over to her right hip, flopped down on her stomach. Parallel rows of stitches spread out before her closed eyes. Neat, tiny, even stitches. Little tracks of them. And some tracks criss-crossed others at miniature junctions. Shiny silk stitches on stiff felt. Her hot fingers weaved in and out under the sheet. In, out, in, out, in—and the third finger pushed mightily and the thumb and fore-finger pulled fiercely. Half waking, she felt the old thawing ache at the tip of her spine. The cramp in her bent shoulders, the tautness of her straining neck. And her fingers weaved under the sheet and burned like they were flayed.

Suddenly a thought wrenched her from sleep. She sat up straight in bed and stared through the window. Today was Sunday. She kicked down the sheet, trampled it with her toes. Today was Sunday! Her tight muscles gave like springs and she bolted from the couch. Tugged a suspended string to light the feeble red bulb in the dark closet-room. The light cast a dreary pinkish veil over her eyes. She blinked, dragged the sheet and unused quilt from the heap they made at the foot of the couch. Tucked them under the lumpy cushions with one sliding sweep of her hand on either side.

"You up, Anna?" There was a clashing of pots and plates from the kitchen.

Anna stepped over a heap of dirty clothes strewn on the floor. She brushed a pair of bedroom slippers and a torn cotton dog from the stuffed arm-chair onto the heap, and then deftly kicked the whole tangled mess under the couch.

"You cleanin' up in there, Anna?" came from the kitchen.

"Yeah," said Anna. She opened a home-made wooden cabinet and rummaged through the sparse garments hanging from the rack. Finally she selected a washed-looking georgette blouse with faded candy stripes and glass buttons.

"Be done in a minute," she yelled to the next room. She stepped into a crepe skirt, and the white of her slip gleamed through two splits in the seam. Shrugging her shoulders in the sleeves of the striped blouse, she shuffled through the gathered yellow cheesecloth that served as a summer curtain.

A rust-speckled coffee pot was percolating on the stove. Anna lifted it off and brought it down with a clang on the porcelain-top table. Seized a cup from the shelf, its handle in the crook of her forefinger, and yanked a saucer from under a pile of chattering cups. "Sh!" said her mother. Anna poured the coffee quickly and gulped it standing.

"Why'nt you sit down, rest your feet?" asked her mother, shoving a low stool toward the table.

"That ain't no rest. I been doin' that all week. Sit an' sit an' sit in a place that's so hot you can't hardly breathe. I ain't goin' sit still one minute today."

Anna dumped her coffee grounds into the sink and dangled the cup by its handle under the faucet. She felt that her mother was watching her carefully, and her guts hardened for what she knew was coming.

"What you mean you ain't gon' set today?"

Line shadows deepened firmly about Anna's mouth. And the tiny pockmarks bit deeper into her square, brown chin.

"Roy gonna take me to the beach."

Each word was a hard little pellet as she spat it from between her teeth.

Worry muddied her mother's eyes behind their rimless glasses. Worry that wavered uncertainly between fear and fury. Each week was a tide driving her relentlessly against the unpaid bills. Beating her like waves beat a battered ruin against a rock. Week after week the worry drove her. There would be three dollars from Buster's part-time job at the riding stable. And there would be two-fifty for cleaning the corset shop. Five-fifty. And Anna says she prepared a dozen hats every day down-town. That brings it to fourteen-fifty. Anna's mother fished a stubby pencil from her house-dress pocket and squatted down behind the stove to mark figures in tiny perpendicular rows on the wall. If Anna can finish another dozen bodies today there will be sixteen-thirty altogether: forty cents for coal, and thirty-five cents for ice, and maybe the salt bag on the gas meter will keep this month s bill down to about nine-tyeight cents, and seven nineteen for food and six seventy-five for rent, and she can lock out the electric man if he comes around this week.

Anna's mother stood up, fearfully calm. She thrust a strand of hair behind her ear— black hair thickly peppered with grey, like a nappy tweed.

"Ain't you gon' do them hats you brung home?" she asked quietly.

Anna shook her head, and her lips were clamped like a scar.

"How you think I'm gon' pay tomorrow's rent if you don't gimme that buck fifty you owe me?"

Anna struggled insolently and turned her back. "I don't owe you no buck fifty." She ripped a page from Saturday's *News*, crumpled it, struck the faucet mouth with it until a few drops made it damp and then used it industriously to wipe the glass cabinet doors.

Her mother stood watching her from the middle of the floor, hands on her hips, squat and still as a tree stump. Fear lapped over her in little waves. And her throat pulsed quickly and beat hot blood down her neck and through her shoulders. Every week. Every week. She shivered.

"Yes you do." she said thinly, "you sure do owe me a buck fifty. The rent cost me almos' seven dollars every week, an' you lives here just like everyone else—"

"Will you cut jivin' my ear off!" Anna boosted her skirt and mounted the stool so she could reach the top of the cabinet with her soggy ball of paper. She made wide arcs on the glass and her shoulders moved freely, gladly breaking the huddled cramp that jailed her body all week. Today's short sip of freedom was wrung from the parching drought of endless work-days.

"You'd never a got that job if it wasn't for me!" Her mother's voice was thinning to a blade-sharp wail.

"Well if you give me that job, Ma'am you can take it right back. It stinks. That Miss Alice—she pay all the white girls by the week. I'm the on'y one get paid by the dozen. An' she don't ask *them* to take no homework! That Miss Alice!—If she say anythin' to me boy I cuss her out so fast—"

Anna made broad circles on the cabinet door and her arm swung luxuriously.

Today Anna. Tomorrow the rent man. Seems like you can never be with folks. Always against them. Always quarreling. Even with the ones you love. Anna's mother was quivering as she advanced toward the stool. She kicked it with the side of her slippered foot. And when she spoke there were barbs in her voice.

"You come down off here," she warned, "come right down off here now. I don't hafta take no stuff outa you! You come down an' finish up them hats!"

"I'll come down when I'm good an' ready," blurted Anna, but she wisely chose to be ready as soon as she spoke, and stepped off the stool at once. "Me an' Roy an' the whole Acme Hipsters Gang is goin' to Orchard Beach. We gonna cut up, boy!" She stretched upward, pushing the ache from her back through the stiff joints of her arms and out to the tips of her bruised fingers. "If you think I'm gonna sit around makin' hats all day on a Sunday you're crazy!"

She moved toward the bedroom. Little Aaron scooted before her and she shoved him roughly out of the way. Aaaaa!" he bawled. "Whyn't you stop worryin' that child, Anna!" screamed her mother. The last layer of restraint was peeling from her raw, helpless rage. "I've a good mind to lick you, old as you is!"

Anna was in the dull-red hole of a bed-room, squinting before the mirror. She patted light powder over her face, dusting her skin to a pale sugar-brown. She heard her mother rustling through the cheese-cloth and stiffened slightly without looking. "Did you hear what I said!" the older woman shrilled, her voice sharp as a sudden cough. She walked swiftly to Anna and desperately she snatched the puff from her daughter's hand. "Don't bother fluffin' up so. You gon' set right here 'til you finish them hats!" Without a word Anna reached forward and tore the puff through her mother's fingers. Feather! pieces floated down and clung to her blouse. Her mother struck her on the ear with the back of her hand. Both of them stood stunned. Then Anna pushed her way out of the room and rushed through the hallway to the stoop. Roy was sitting on the railings outside.

"Where the hell you been so long?' he demanded.

"C'mon, Roy. Sorry I couldn't fix up no lunch. C'mon. Let's go quick." She pulled him by the hand.

"You wait a minute!" It was her mother, flying wildly down the hall. "Roy, don't you take her out to no beach. She got work to do!"

"C'mon, Roy, quick," Anna tugged his hand.

"Don't worry, we ain't goin' to no beach, Mrs. Rawson. My feet wouldn't carry me as far as the subway station."

"All right," her yellow face softened, "You get Anna back here in fifteen minutes."

"What you mean we ain't goin' to the beach!" cried Anna.

Roy steered her down the block. "Do you know where I was at six o crock this morning? Tossin' crates around a stock-room. An' I been tossin' crates around all week an' baby I'm tired."

"You promised me we was goin'. The whole gang is goin'!" Anna's voice quavered.

"No good, baby," said Roy.

"Well where you goin' now?" whinnied Anna.

"Down by the river where it's cool. I'm gonna lay me down an' take life easy."

"Oh," scorned Anna, "well *I* ain't goin' down by no river!"

"Yes you are," Roy pressed her arm 'til she squealed.

They hurried down the grey street, dark under a squalid sky. And in their nostrils were the thick smells of smoke and squalor. Past the Rescue Mission. Past Delphine's Beauty Parlor. Past the drab poker-face of the candy store. Past the boarded-up houses with their gaping black holes of windows where the boards had been chopped away. Across the avenue and over the ash-covered lot. Down the lane between the squat chromium-polishing plant and the big stone power house with its six towering stacks—six massive pillars ejaculating smoke. Into the poultry yard where the snaky train tracks met the long tin sheds over the chicken crates.

Anna sulked at the concentrated stencil of packed fowl. "*Phew!*" The cry strained through her nose as she pinched her nostrils together.

Everywhere were hung rotographed card-board signs: "THROW DEAD CHICKENS IN CANS." Roy chuckled.

"Find me a can, baby," he said, "I wanna throw away this little dead chick I got on my hands."

His humor sand-papered Anna's mood.

Whyn't you park in the slaughter house?" she muttered.

Roy laughed loudly. They passed under the great concrete highway with its broad black iron cross-beams like giant ribs beneath the roaring bloodstream of traffic. Before them lay the docks, and to the left, the empty shell of the old pier jutted into the river. The planks of the docks were warped and moist in the heat. The green water moved beneath, a translucent skin over big, flexing muscles.

Roy lay down on the soft rotten boards with a groan. He spread out his arms, palms up, and the skin of his palms was spiraled into hard little screws. Moisture widened the pores of his fine oval chin, turning them into tiny black wells. Drops glistened in the soft hairs over his lip. And he lay flat along the ground, sucked down by a weariness more powerful than gravity.

Anna stood over him. She shuffled her feet restively. "Hey! Roy!' she kicked him smartly under the ribs. "Don't you go fall asleep on me!" He was numbed by fatigue, paralyzed and could not move. His lids closed and he smiled faintly.

"Hey let's go for a walk, Roy."

Once he lay down on a Sunday, the strange wonderful strength that carried him through seventy hours of crate hauling all week suddenly crumpled and left him helpless. He had no *will* to lie on the dock under the sultry smoky sky. Will and strength drained from him. Only overwhelming weariness remained.

"Let's go," whined Anna, tired of standing in one spot. She longed to be free of the ache that imprisoned her body. "I been sittin' over them hats all week. Just sittin'! Can't move nothin' but your hands."

"See these dogs?" Roy wiggled his toes under his dirt-grey sneakers. "Baby, they is *beat*."

Anna paced around his spread-eagled form. "That's right." Roy encouraged her, "I'll lay here an' you can walk around me." She came to quick halt.

"Oh you're mean" she said. "I ain't gon' stand here watch you snore!"

"Don't he like that chippy." Roy smiled up at the deep scowling groove in her chin.

"*Good-by!*" she said, and walked away quickly, hoping he would follow. A few yards further on she turned. He was lying motionless with closed eyes. She came back slowly and he felt her presence above him.

"You know baby," he began, his eyes still closed, "It's funny ain't it? Me hustlin' so damn hard all week I can't move a finger, an' you workin' so damn hard you just wanna jump around like crazy."

"Why'nt you come after me before?" she asked peevishly.

"Anna, you an' ten like you couldn't budge me right now."

"Well, this time I'm goin' and I *mean* it," she backed away.

"I ast you stay. That's all I can do." He lay close to the dock, and soot from the river-smoke coated his face. He lay dark and still as a plank on the dock, dark as the coal-colored streets he came from, and the smouldering laughter of the community burned deep into him, and the bitter wearies of the community lay heavily on him and weariness was re-building a great angry strength within him.

"I'm goin'," warned Anna. His silence was a challenge. She turned, caught a sob in her throat. Then suddenly she thought she would burst if she didn't run, cast off the thick pressure of dampness, throw off the stifling pressure of sitting by the steam-iron table in the shop all week, and sitting and sitting. She ran across the street under the concrete highway. Raced along the poultry sheds. Tore past the power-house, over the ash lot, across the avenue and up to the stoop of her house. A light drizzle sprinkled her face and arms. Black clouds like great cinders moved swiftly against the steely back-drop of the fog.

When Anna pushed open the kitchen door her mother looked up from the stove. "Your hats an' needles an' thread an' everything is waitin' right here," she indicated the porcelain-top table.

Anna said nothing. She moved sullenly to the table and dropped onto a stool. She cut a felt body around on the faint chalk mark and double-threaded her needle. From outside came the soft swish of fine rain. "That'll keep up a good long time," said her mother. Anna jabbed the needle in, out, in, out into the resisting felt and then stabbed it through with her thimble finger and yanked it out between thumb and forefinger. In, out, in out, in, out. And the parallel tracks of stitches appeared once more. And the old ache returned to her neck and spread like fire down her spine. And thread sliced her hands and her fingers burned like they were flayed.

She bent nearly double over the hats, rushing to get out the dozen before evening. And as her face leaned close to one of the neat little tracks a small dark blot spread slowly in its path. Then another, then another. Wet, angry, blood-colored blots on the bright red felt.

[*The Crisis* 47.5 (May 1940): 141–142, 154]

HORNS AND TAILS

by Corinne Dean

"Gor a' mighty, Massa," exclaimed Hezekiah, "Horns? What?! An' tail too?!! Gor a' mighty!!!"

Hezekiah's big round eyes became bigger and bigger until the whites were so bulging and full they made his eyes look like two little moons which had somehow got suspended in the middle of his midnight black face. In an effort to clarify his thinking, he scratched his head first with one hand and then with the other. He would have scratched his head with both hands at the same time, so great was his astonishment, but he had to keep one hand free for digging into his flesh whenever the home spun cloth of his new shirt irritated his skin beyond endurance. The new shirt scratched all parts indiscriminately and without favor so that, between Hezekiah's arm flying and his horror struck expression, he resembled a tight rope walker who was headed for a fall and knew it.

In the midst of his acrobatics he was thinking: Mus' be mah haid is quair. Maybe hit don' hear right, no mo.' Or could be Massa Daniel is jus' a foolin' me. Ah'll axe 'im agin, fo' sho.'

"Ah you sho' Massa? Positif?"

Ryan's crafty eyes twinkled as he replied firmly: "I'm positive, Hezekiah. I saw 'um myself."

"Gor a' mighty, Massa, Gor a' mighty," was all the pop-eyed Hezekiah could say.

Unable to figure it all he stared intently, for sometime, at a non-committal lilac bush, but finding in its bland foliage no solution to his problem, he at last started walking slowly away, still scratching his head and practically dancing in his new shirt. He kept repeating over and over, in an ever fainter voice his eternal "Gor a' mighty."

It was an obsession with Ryan to let his slaves get almost out of sight and then call them back for some real or fancied need. He said they were lazy anyhow and needed the extra steps to keep them fit for their 16 hour workday. Besides this unadulterated perverseness, he had another reason this time. He wanted his first coating of propaganda to soak in before applying the second coating. With his shifty eyes fixed on Hezekiah, he let the youngster get almost to the corner of the house before calling, in as casual a tone as possible:

"Oh Hezekiah. Come heah."

Hezekiah came back as fast as he could considering how the weight of his meditations was boring him down.

"Yes, Massa?"

"By the way, if you see any of them Yankees who look as if they don't have no horns and tails, don't let that fool yuh. The Confederates have shot 'um off, that's all, but they're devils just the same. Lemme know if you see one, and I'll kill him before he can do you any harm. Them Yankee devils are fond of cuttin' up little boys into pieces, and once they see you they'll come back to get you, if they don't get you the first time."

So thoroughly alarmed was Hezekiah that his tongue stuck in his throat as he tried to reply. He stuttered: "D—D—Don't marry Massa. Ef—ef—ef Ah seed one of 'um c—c—coming foh me, Ah—Ah—Ah'd tell you, sho.'"

Ryan laughed good-naturedly and waved the boy on his way. The next time Hezekiah got almost to the corner of the house, he broke into a run.

"Good," said Ryan rubbing his hairy red hands together. "He's goin' to tell the rest of the little darkies. At last I'll catch up with that Damn Yankee."

Gleefully Ryan pictured to himself little Negro slaves stampeding his veranda, in a double effort to get out of the way of the Yankees, and to get the Yankees wiped out of existence.

His soaring flight into fancy was abruptly leveled off by old Sam saying: "Hyar's yoh mail, Massa."

Instead of taking the letters Ryan turned on Sam a vicious look of fury and frustration. He was so angry he could have beaten Sam. Ryan's eyes blazed as bitter thoughts, like a nasty medicine that wouldn't stay down, welled up in his mind. Two years ago I would have beaten Sam—he thought—but today the Damn Yankees have spoiled everything, including the niggers. God, when will the good old days come back when you can even afford to beat a nigger to death if you want to.

In spite of the Yankees, Ryan could still have beaten Sam had he wanted to, but it wouldn't have done any good and it wouldn't have been profitable. It wouldn't have erased from Sam's old eyes that glint of secret malice, nor from his behavior that subtle resistance which Ryan felt but could not put his finger on; but it would have created, and this was of vital importance, a shortage of help because Sam was sure to be or "pretend to be" sick after a beating.

Ryan hadn't wanted Sam to know what he told Hezekiah. Sam couldn't be trusted. Hadn't Sam insisted he couldn't read although one day Ryan had caught him red handed teaching a group of youngsters their A, B, C's? Sam had insisted he knew only his A, B, C's and not all of them. He also pretended he didn't know it was a crime to teach the slaves "anything." Added to this, was Ryan's innate distrust of anyone who handled his mail. Consequently he not only distrusted, but actually hated Sam because it was he (albeit at Ryan's orders) who brought the mail with its increasingly distasteful contents. Ryan hated the mail and therefore he hated the man who brought it.

The letters were always the same—nauseating. Yet Ryan read them with that same kind of sickening fascination with which one stares at the bloody and maimed victims of a terrible accident.

As Ryan did not take the mail, Sam remained motionless patiently holding letters at arm's length. His indifferent expression as if he didn't care whether Ryan ever took the letters or not infuriated Ryan. Ryan's face was ominous and foreboding for Sam as he said:

"Always sneaking around, Hey Sam?"

"No, Massa. You no hyeahred me," Sam explained. "Ah sade twice 'Masse hyeah's yoh mail,' and—"

"Stop lying," snarled Ryan as he snatched the letters out of the old Negro's hand.

Sam shuffled away on his unsteady legs. As he opened the porch door Ryan called out: "Come heah!"

Sam wheeled his old bones around and returned.

"Yes, Massa."

"Bring me some whiskey."

Sam wheeled himself around again, and started to execute the order.

"Don't take all day," snapped Ryan. "God a' mighty, get a move on you."

"Yass, suh," replied Sam wheeling himself around and about again.

After Sam brought the whiskey Ryan took a drink, a big drink, to brace himself for the ordeal of reading the mail. He ripped open all the letters at once as if to save time once the gruesome work was begun. Hurriedly he skimmed through the first letter—no use to read it all—damn Yankees, damn niggers. He skimmed through some others, afterwards crushing them in his big clammy hands and throwing them on the veranda as if each one were the body of some Yankee. Then, when all had been read, he sat with his eyes shut, in moody and bitter silence. He seemed as crushed as the poor battered letters lying at his feet.

Phrase after phrase from the letters flashed and burned through his mind—"down here there have been very alarming disturbances of the blacks; on more than one plantation the assistance of the authorities has been called in to overcome the open resistance of the blacks" ... "last night a house was set on fire; last week 2 houses—our troubles thicken indeed when treachery comes from that dark quarter." ... "We have found out a deep laid plot among the

Negroes of our neighborhood and from what we can find out from our Negroes, it is general all over the country—we hear some startling facts. They have gone far enough in the plot to divide out our estates, mules, lands and household furniture" ... "by a private letter from Upper Georgia we learn that an insurrectionary plot has been discovered among the Negroes in the vicinity of Dalton and Marietta." Ryan squirmed in his chair as other excerpts weaved incoherently in and out of his brain like a bad dream—"no general insurrection has taken place though several revolts have been attempted, two quite recently, and in these cases whole families were murdered before the slaves were subdued"—"The Negroes are the source of the greatest trouble. Many persons have lost them all."

Civil war at large—and at home: sabotage, rebellion, conspiracy and insurrection; while hanging over all was the constant threat of desertion by some of the remaining, if not all of the remaining Negroes from the plantation. Crops rotting in the fields for want of hands to gather them! Once or twice Ryan even thought of working himself but the thought was so repugnant to him he vigorously pushed it aside. Even in the best of times, Ryan recalled, the cotton had never really paid. The crop in the field was always mortgaged. To make the cotton pay he needed more cotton acreage; if he got more acreage he would need more slaves; to get more money for more slaves he needed more cotton acreage; to get more cotton he needed more slaves. Like little snakes chasing each other's tails, the cotton slave-cotton idea ran around in circles in Ryan's brain.

He didn't know how long he had been sitting there. Must have been at least two hours for here was that sneaking Sam back again saying:

Miss Essie say tuh tell you she a waitin' foh you to come to dinnah."

Damn Sam,—thought Ryan—when the war is over and the Yankees have all been killed off, and things allowed to return to normal, the first thing I am going to do is lynch Sam. I need him to help with the crops or I'd lynch him now. Angrily Ryan gathered up his crumpled letters before getting to his feet and starting for the door with long irregular strides.

In the parlor, his worried wife was looking at but not seeing some old daguerrotypes. Spying the letters in Ryan's hand, she said with false gayety: "Good news?"

Pre-occupied, engrossed in his thoughts Ryan strode past her into the dining room.

Ryan never read nor discussed any letters, lately. His silence was agonizing to her. No news was bad news, in this case. The tension that gripped every slave-owner was evident in Ryan's sullen face, his taut, harsh mouth. What made her feel so frustrated was the fact she didn't really know what was in the letters, although she surmised. She felt if the good-for-nothing slaves would only work diligently (for nothing) Ryan's troubles would be over. But no, just to be contrary, they either ran away or if they remained ate up more than they earned. How they ate! When she thought of all the money poor dear Daniel could have had if he hadn't had to feed and clothe the slaves, she could have cried. It was all their fault. How she hated them. Now, if she could only read. It was all the fault of the poor white trash that she couldn't read. If they hadn't insisted on attending the only school where poor aristocratic children could get an education, the proud aristocratic families, such as hers, wouldn't have taken their children out of the school rather than see them contaminated with the poor whites.

As a result Essie Mather Ryan had grown up in proud ignorance while the children of the poor whites had grown up in humble literacy.[*]

She'd give a good deal to know the exact contents of those letters. Wistfully she followed Ryan into the dining room, where attempts to draw him out were futile. The meal was eaten in a penetrating silence broken only when Sam entered to say:

Eastern Shore of Maryland

"A lettah from Massa Whipple."

Ryan scowled at Sam who seemed doomed to be the emissary of missives distasteful to Ryan. Whipple was a professional slave "middle man," buying and selling slaves for profit and as such he was held in the greatest contempt by the Virginia plantation owners such as Ryan. But Whipple got about, he heard things, Ryan needed him now. Gingerly, Ryan took the letter from Sam.

The note was brief: "His name is Crawford. Will take you there tonight after supper."

Ryan bolted from the table as if an electric current had gone through his body.

"Sam" he shouted, "Get my boots ready. I'm going hunting later on."

Then he went to his room where poor Essie Mather Ryan could hear him pacing up and down. She went upstairs too. He took no notice of her as he cleaned and fingered his gun.

From time to time Ryan would mutter to himself: "If I can kill only one of those damn Yankees I'll die happy. So Crawford's his name. I'll teach him to cause desertion among my niggers. I'll get him."

Suddenly he looked up. "Sam, damn it, what are you doing here?"

"Pardon, Massa, but you say to get yoh boots. Well heayah they is."

"Later, later. I didn't say now," shouted Ryan.

Sam practically dropped the boots in the middle of the room, in his hurry to get out of the way, because it looked for a moment as though Ryan wasn't going to wait until the war was over but was going to blow the old Negro's brains out then and there.

"You sho' you ain't got no horns or tail mister,'" questioned Hezekiah. "Cause if you has Ah ain't goin' to hab nuttin' to do wif you."

Crawford burst out laughing although with each burst of laughter his wounded scalp seemed to expand and stretch, making his head ache. Still he couldn't stop laughing. Hezekiah was the newspaper and liaison "man" for the little group of runaways. He always had a lot of funny things to tell.

When Crawford could stop laughing he said:

"Now Hezekiah, you don't believe I got horns and a tail, do you?" and he unwound the bandage on his head in order to convince Hezekiah.

There were no horns, to be sure, but there were two funny red marks where horns might have been before they got shot off.

Hezekiah answered evasively: "Sam say you doesn't."

"Atta boy," said Crawford and he slapped Hezekiah on the back.

Poor Hezekiah jumped forward as if a pitchfork had been rammed between his shoulder blades. The group howled with laughter, all except wise, weather-beaten Martha. She saw nothing funny in the boy's doubts and fears. If he should falter through fear, all might be lost. She could tell by the way Hezekiah kept looking at Crawford's rear, that he, Hezekiah, expected to sight a tail or the remnants of a tail at any moment.

Martha stood up, took the clay pipe out of her mouth and said to Hezekiah by way of changing the conversation: "Go find Jeffuhson Davis, foh me an' bring him back. He's around hyah some whair."

But just then Jefferson Davis, the group's fat little pig, hove into sight under his own sturdy powers.

Ebenezer, who was cleaning his gun with ashes, looked up long enough to say reassuringly to Hezekiah: "Only devils have horns, son!"

"Dass what Ah knows," replied Hezekiah.

Martha tried again. She said in mock severity: "Hezekiah did you bring us de life-everlastin' foh de tea? De baby got de colic, you know. An' de paregoric? We ain't got no mo!"

"I fohget," said Hezekiah guiltily.

"Now devils—," began Ebenezer.

Martha drove her wedge: "An' de lily petals foh de fever stew; an' de palm o' christian leaves, an' de mutton tallow foh Angie's chess cole."

"I fohget," replied Hezekiah.

"You doan remembah nothin' tuhday," Martha reproached. Then, more kindly, she added: "Maybe cose yous' hongry. Come ober by de fire an' I'll gib you some hot yams. Did you see yoh little red bird tuhday?"

"I'se not hungry," said Hezekiah.

Martha was stumped. Anytime Hezekiah didn't want hot yams, things were serious. "Come over hyeah anyhow, Hezekiah. I wants to talk—to—." She stopped.

A dog had barked far away but not far enough away. At the sound, Hezekiah's smooth black skin turned ashy gray.

"I fohget, I fohget," Hezekiah started crying, in bitter resentment against himself for forgetting at a time when he wanted to be so dependable and man-like. "Sam say tuh tell you de soonuh you shake de lion's paw de bettuh. Don' know what he mean—but—"*

"Sam say dat?" interrupted Martha "My God!"

Collectively the camp jumped to its feet and began packing. Jefferson Davis was igno-miniously dumped into a bag along with some old rags. Guns, knives food, pans, blankets were hastily gathered together. As life hung on a slender thread of a few moments gained, the group stepped over and on a bewildered Hezekiah who sat on the ground weeping uncon-trollably as he realized now how important the message had been.

It all happened so suddenly. Like phantoms, the campers disappeared into thin air. Martha was the only one still there. She was shaking Hezekiah and saying over and over something about "It ain't so, it ain't so Hezekiah." Martha was crying too. Swiftly she put a crying baby in his lap. Hezekiah heard a far away voice saying: "No paregoric, can't put Brother tuh sleep, so can't take him wid me. Take good care ob de baby, Hezekiah, and carry him safely back. Goodbye and God bless you, Hezekiah."

All at once Hezekiah realized the camp was empty, empty with that heart-aching empti-ness of a place once filled with the voices of beloved friends. Forlornly he sat on the ground, his head in a whirl, his little body trembling with sobs. He held tight to the baby, though, who cried louder whenever Hezekiah's hot tears fell and spattered on his tiny head.

When Ryan, like a god of vengeance, stamped into the deserted camp, it was difficult to say who looked the most surprised, he or Hezekiah.

"God a' mighty, Hezekiah, what a' you doin' heah?!" Ryan exclaimed.

"I'se tendin' de baby," said Hezekiah meekly as if it were the most natural thing in the world for him to be 'tendin' the baby" in the middle of a woods. He held "Brother" in front of him as if the babe were some sort of defense which could protect him from the wrath of Ryan.

"Put that brat down," ordered Ryan, "and come here and tell me have you seen any Yan-kees around here."

Ryan was more interested in (reeking) vengeance on Crawford than in retrieving thou-sands of dollars worth of runaway slaves. His main objective was to "get" Crawford "for lead-ing his darkies astray." It never occurred to Ryan to admit that there were Negroes running away every day who had never heard of Crawford.

*Shake the British lion's paw: Get to Canada

Hezekiah stood up and also stood his "defense" up, though he still held on tight to the baby, with one hand. Hezekiah's predicament made his moon-eyes enormous and fixed. He couldn't betray Crawford without betraying the rest of the group. Besides he liked Crawford—if it weren't for that horns and tail business. Yet if Crawford were going to come back and cut—? Hezekiah stared straight ahead of him as his befuddled mind refused to give him an answer.

"God a' mighty answer me," demanded Ryan impatiently, "I ask you a question and you go into a trance."

Suddenly, like a ray of sunlight striking through a cloud, Martha's words, as if he were really hearing them for the first time, cut across Hezekiah's fears and doubts: "It ain't so, Hezekiah, it ain't so."

Hezekiah took a deep breath and said: "Gor a' mighty, Massa, no, Ah ain't seed none, foh if I'd seed one you wouldn't kotch dis darkey heah 'cause you done tole me dem Yankees got horns and tails an' is debbils, an' I'se afeared ob debbils. If I'd a seed one a' cumin, foh me, I'd a died sho.'"

"Doggone my luck," sputtered Ryan.   [*The Crisis* 47.7 (July 1940): 202–204, 210]

GIRL, COLORED

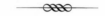

by Marian Minus

Girl, colored, to assist with housework and baby; must be reliable; $20 per month. German girl considered. Clark, 1112 Highdale Rd., Long Island City.   Advt.

The subway wormed its way through the tunnel that lay below the frenzy and filth of urban streets into the dripping tube that arched its back beneath the river. The air that came in through the half-opened windows was moist and musty, and Carrie's wide brown nostrils flared in sullen offense. She watched the thoughtful contortions of her face reflected in the mirror of the train window, her timid eyes large and staring.

Carrie had come out of the South, the red clay clinging to her misshapen heels, made migrant by the disintegration of a crumbling age. She had been unconscious of the transmission of idea and attitude from age to age until its outworn mechanism and wild momentum had forced her outside the terminals of habit and sour acceptance.

German girl considered. Fear was filling a place which not even thought had filled before.

The train converged on light, and roared upward onto high steel trestles. No longer able to see her face in the window, Carrie gave her attention to the neat brown paper bundle in her lap. Her thin fingers with their big knuckles smoothed out the wrinkles in the package. It held her stiffly starched white work dress, a pair of comfortable shoes, and a thick beef sandwich. Even if she got the job, she might not be provided with lunch. Her memory of fainting from hunger on the first day of her last job, six months before, was bitter-sharp.

As she left the train, Carrie hunched her shoulders in sudden fear that she would soon be retracing her steps. She hugged her parcel close to her breast.

"Number ten's over there," she said softly, gaining the street, "so number two must be down there a way."

She walked with a tread that was firmer than the resolution in her heart in the direction of her reasoning. For six months she had answered advertisements. She had related the necessary details of her life to prospective "madams," and she had returned beaten and cynical to her basement room.

She went through a gate and up a gravel path to a small brick house. Her nervous hands played with a dull knocker until sound was forced from the beat of brass on wood. A pale blond woman opened the door. Wisps of inoffensive hair strayed from the leather thongs of a dozen curlers set at variance on her head.

"Yes?" The woman's voice was spuriously cheerful.

"I come about the job," said Carrie.

The woman opened the door wider. "Come in."

Carrie followed her into an untidy living room.

"We'll go into the kitchen," the woman said, pointing ahead.

Carrie's eyes flickered professionally about the room and her nose lifted on its wide base. They walked through to the kitchen, and she saw the table cluttered with unwashed dishes.

The woman waved her to a seat. "Sit down," she said briefly.

Carrie found a chair and settled on its edge, resting her package on her knees.

"My name is Clark," the woman said. "Mrs. Cado P. Clark."

"I'm Carrie Johnson," Carrie said quickly. She did not have the inclination or energy for a prolonged interview.

"Have you references?" Mrs. Clark asked.

"Yes." A flash of anger that started somewhere deep within her lighted Carrie's eyes. She resented being asked for information before being given any.

"I'll want to see them later," said Mrs. Clark.

Carrie gave her prospective employer an impatient glance. They measured each other in momentary silence. Carrie was the first to speak.

"You want somebody to help with the housework and the baby." she asked. "At twenty a month?"

"Yes, I do," Mrs. Clark answered. "I want a reliable person. Someone I can put utter trust in."

Carrie did not speak. She smiled wryly and dropped her eyes.

"Have you had much experience?" Mrs. Clark asked. "Have you had to take much responsibility, I mean?"

Carrie shrugged weary shoulders. "I reckon so," she answered shortly. "I been on jobs where I had to do everything under the sun and I did it. Guess that's being reliable."

Mrs. Clark gave her a sharp look. She murmured unintelligibly.

"Ain't that the right answer to your question?" Carrie parried maliciously.

"Right answer?" Mrs. Clark inquired. "You mean you're trying to give me the answers you think you ought to give, instead of just telling the truth."

Carrie shrugged again. "I guess I didn't make myself clear," she said in simulated apology.

Mrs. Clark's face brightened. She took a deep breath.

"I want someone to clean, help with the cooking, look after the baby, and do general things about the house," she explained.

"'Bout how long would the hours be?" Carrie asked.

Mrs. Clark calculated quickly. "Well, my husband gets up at seven. He takes breakfast about seven-thirty then he goes to his office. I've been getting his breakfast, but if I get a girl, that'll be changed, of course."

"Oh, certainly." Carrie said with emphasis. "You'll get up 'bout nine then and have your breakfast, won't you, if you get a girl?"

"Yes," Mrs. Hark said eagerly. Then she looked hard at Carrie. She bit her lip and patted the curlers on her head. Carrie snorted audibly.

"Of course, if it'll be too much work for you," Mrs. Clark said waspishly, "I can get a German girl to do it."

The back of Carrie's resentful resistance was broken. She rolled her eyes about the kitchen, seeking some tangible evidence of the competitor whose spirit held nebulous hands at her throat.

"You say you can get a German girl?" she asked uneasily.

"Yes." Mrs. Clark pulled hard at her lip with her even teeth.

Carrie was silent. She did not think for a moment that Mrs. Clark had not already interviewed the omnipresent German girl.

"It's very simple," Mrs. Clark went on. "You see, there are quite a few impoverished refugees in this country now. They can't become public charges so they are very eager to work."

Carrie nodded dumbly. She did not trust herself to speak.

"I think it's wonderful the way they look for work right away after landing in the United States," Mrs. Clark continued, warming to her fantasy. "I've already talked to one of the refugees."

"What'd she say?" Carrie turned miserable eyes on her tormentor.

Mrs. Clark cleared her throat. "She said she'd let me know."

"She didn't think it was too much work for five dollars a week?" Carrie asked in a low voice.

Mrs. Clark looked taken aback. "Why," she stammered, "no."

"I was just wondering."

Carrie looked at the dishes on the table. She saw the smear of childish fingers around the woodwork. She remembered the mussed living-room.

"I don't see how her decision affects you," Mrs. Clark said slyly.

There was an unexpected hint of hardness in her voice that alarmed Carrie. For the first time she wondered if the German girl were not a bogey set up to frighten her by this wily woman. She shook her head and decided to take no chances.

"What about the baby?" she asked, her voice respectful.

"He's no trouble at all," Mrs. Clark said indulgently. "He's only four."

Carrie nodded wearily. "What would you expect me to do exactly?"

"After breakfast," Mrs. Clark elaborated, "there'd be the cleaning. I would expect you to do the marketing. I have a light lunch. In the afternoons you could rinse out a few pieces and do a bit of ironing. Dinner is usually about six-thirty. So you see you could have some free time between lunch and dinner if you got your other duties finished up. Of course, you'd have to take the baby out in the afternoons. After dinner your evenings would be free. Sometimes there is mending to be done. That would take one or two of your evenings a week."

Her recital finished, she waited for Carrie to speak. Carrie's throat was dry. She did not trust herself to do more than croak if she managed to get her mouth open.

"Would you give a day off a week?" she ventured finally.

"Oh, not a whole day," Mrs. Clark said quickly. "Just one afternoon a week. One day a month would be satisfactory."

"Oh." Carrie lifted her shoulders in a weary hunch. "There ain't much I could do with a day off every week nohow," she said philosophically, "if I ain't gonna be making but twenty a month."

There was a sighing silence into which Carrie's spent breath and Mrs. Clark's anxiety issued like desperate winds.

"Would I have a nice room?" Carrie asked after the pause.

Mrs. Clark rose, victorious, then sat down again. "Before we go that far," she said, "I'd like to see your references."

Carrie pulled a thin packet of letters from her purse. She passed them over silently.

"They're very flattering," Mrs. Clark said when she had finished reading.

"They ain't flattering," Carrie retorted. "They're the gospel truth. I worked hard for every word wrote on that paper."

Mrs. Clark rose hastily. "Your room's this way," she said.

They left the kitchen, and Carrie followed her upstairs to a little, boxlike room. It was bare except for a bed and one chair.

"The last place I worked had a radio," Carrie said unreasonably.

"It did?" Mrs. Clark asked in surprise. She straightened her shoulders. "I don't approve of servants having too many advantages."

"I b'lieves you," Carrie said shortly. She walked around the room "The floors ain't bad," she volunteered meaninglessly.

"It's a very nice room," Mrs. Clark said defensively. "It could be home."

Carrie looked at her searchingly. "Madam," she said with dignity, "one little room like this couldn't never be home 'less it was in the house of your loved ones."

"There's a table down in the basement," Mrs. Clark said, ignoring Carrie's remark, "that could be brought up here."

"What about a bureau to keep my clothes in?" Carrie asked. She walked to a closet in one corner of the room. "This ain't got no shelf space," she said, looking in, "for me to use."

"You'd have to use your suitcase."

Carrie sighed. The woman knew that she needed the job, and that she would like it. She was too weary to gamble on finding pleasure in upsetting all of Mrs. Clark's calculations by refusing to stay. She could not face the thought of taking the long, fruitless ride back to Harlem.

"You satisfied with my references?" she asked fearfully.

"Your references are satisfactory," Mrs. Clark said, enigmatically stressing the second word.

"You mean you got some doubts about me personally?" Carrie asked meekly.

"Well," Mrs. Clark informed her, "you understand that I must satisfy myself on every score. After all, you'll be coming into constant and close contact with my child."

"Did the German girl satisfy you?" Carrie asked, almost whispering.

Mrs. Clark nodded slowly. "They really work well," she said. "They don't ask for anything but the chance to make an honest living."

"I think I'd like it here," Carrie said quickly, hating her haste. "If it's all right with you, we could call it settled."

"All right," Mrs. Clark said indifferently. Carrie's released breath rushed through her trembling lips. "I think we can call it arranged. Can you begin working immediately?"

Carrie's face broke into a reluctant smile. She was working again.

"Right away," she said. "But I'll have to go up to Harlem tonight after dinner and pick up my belongings."

"You can't go tonight," Mrs. Clark said coldly. "My husband and I are going out after dinner and you'll have to stay with the baby."

"Oh."

Mrs. Clark read the disappointment on Carrie's face. She breathed deeply and smiled inscrutably.

"I know it's difficult for you to make quick adjustments," she said sweetly. "Perhaps I should hire the German girl after all. They don't have any ties in this country. They have fewer arrangements to make than you, for instance."

"That's all right, ma'am," Carrie said quickly. "I can 'tend to it tomorrow night just as easy." [*The Crisis* 47.9 (September 1940): 284, 297, 301]

JOE CHARLES KING

〜∞〜

by Vera L. Williams

There is a common belief among people who have never suffered privation, that those who have are naturally in a lower class than themselves; that they are ignorant and that there is little use in doing anything for them or about them.

Having taught in an underprivileged neighborhood of Negro families for fifteen years, I have grown to resent this feeling in white people. Still more do I resent it in my own people. We should certainly know better. Almost all Negroes of prominence who have reached the goal of successful living, have at some time in their journey along life's way, rubbed elbows with poverty. And yet, some of us are actually snobs with each other.

In this neighborhood where I have taught for fifteen years, there are bootleggers, sporting houses, dives bearing French names, and most all kinds of mentionable evils. The streets are narrow and poorly lighted. Officers of the law come through occasionally to be served at the bootleg joints and go on their way. There are some families who live here because of the cheap rent. Their children are as promising and as sweet as the children of our more fortunate people. It really seems to me that they are smarter. Certainly, Joe Charles King was the brightest youngster I have ever seen.

I became acquainted with the King family through their little son, Joe Charles. One morning the door of my room opened quite suddenly and a little round-faced boy came in. He wore blue wash shorts and a white knitted sweater. He was very clean and very cute. He looked like nothing so much as a little black pixie. His eyes had an impish slant and his engaging grin exposed a set of pearly first teeth, still intact. I smiled at him.

"Who sent you in here?" I asked.

"Nobody. I just came. This is a school, ain't it?"

"Yes it is," I told him. "Did you see a lady with a blue dress on as you came in?"

"I saw the lady with the blue dress on," he said. "She was writing."

"Did she tell you to come in here?" I persisted.

"No, I just came myself. Ain't you the teacher?"

"Yes, I am," I said and drew out an entrance blank. "What is your name?"

"Joe Charles King," was the answer.

"How old are you, Joe Charles?"

"I am five. I will be six February 22."

"What is your father's name?"

"Charles King."

"Joe Charles, Sr.?" I asked.

"No. My name is Joe Charles. His name is just Charles. My mother's name is Lillian," he finished.

"Do you know the number of your house, Joe Charles?"

"Yes. It is 1505 Pearl street."

From the very first Joe Charles intrigued me. He had answered all my questions. He could talk quite plainly. Most of our youngsters could not answer these questions. A great many who could, used "r" for "w" and "t" for "c" and it was difficult to decipher what they were saying. One little fellow said his name was "Dunior," his baby effort at saying "Junior."

"Who came to school with you, Joe Charles?" I asked then. He came close then and said in a confidential whisper, "Nobody. I slipped off." Immune by now to surprises, I said, "Slipped off from whom?"

"My grandmother. She doesn't know where I am." We found out that he had slipped off. The floor principal sent his grandmother word that he was with us and that we would take care of him for the day. Such enthusiasm for school, we felt, should not be dampened. He was too young to come and no one had sent him. But each day he returned. He would cry silently when we prepared to send him home. So each day, Mrs. Bell relented and let him stay.

He was very much interested in learning. He wanted to learn. He also wanted to tell a lot of news. I learned from him, that his mother worked at the laundry, and that his father drove a coal truck. He knew many useful and interesting things. When we had an amateur program, he recited without error, *The Twenty-third Psalm*.

"How did you learn it?" I asked.

"My mother reads it to me every night."

Every day Joe Charles did something interesting or amusing. He learned to read readily, but found writing difficult. One day as he labored over his writing, Hawthorn, a mischievous rascal, leaned over and erased his effort. "Mrs. Winn, make Horse Corn stop erasing my writing," he said. Needless to say, that is the name Hawthorn had to wear thereafter.

One day a little sandy-haired, brown girl went on a crying jag during story hour. Knowing from experience that Delores would stop sooner if completely ignored, I went calmly on with the adventures of *The Three Bears*. Having a profound respect for tears, Joe Charles went to her, and placed his hand on her head and said coaxingly, "Little, bittie girl, won't you please stop crying and listen to the story?" Amazingly she did.

On February 22 he was greatly excited. His suppressed happiness made him nervous. He asked several times what time it was. Finally, I asked him why he wanted to know. He said,

"When I get home today, my mother will be there already. It's my birthday."

"Then I shall have to give you six spanks," I told him.

"But I won't be six until seven o'clock tonight," he said.

One day in spring he came to school dressed up. He was dressed in a blue wool suit. His shirt was white as could be and his oxfords shined with greatest care. He was always clean, but today he was resplendent. But his little pixie eyes slanted dolorously, and he was very quiet.

"Joe Charles, you look so nice," I told him.

"Yes'm. I am going to a funeral," he said.

"Whose funeral?" I wanted to know.

"My grandmother's. She is dead. They are going to have her funeral today." He came up close to my chair and laid his head on my shoulder. I saw that he was crying. I put my arm comfortingly around him.

After that I wondered who took care of him while his mother worked. He came to school as usual, never missing a day. I had been to his home only one time. I had not met either of his parents, however. I sent them a note asking them to come to the school. But his mother replied by note that both she and her husband worked and could not come. I asked Joe Charles who sent him to school on time each day and who cooked his breakfast.

"I do," he said.

"What do you cook?" I asked him.

"An egg apiece," he said. He had long ago told me about "Lillian," the baby sister who was four years old by this time.

"Why do you cook? Doesn't your mother—?"

"She cooks the oatmeal," he explained, "and leaves it in hot water. When I get up I cook the eggs. I help my sister to dress. We go to the day home then. I come to school at eleven. When I get out I go back to the day home. At five o'clock we go home." I decided to go there early one morning on my way to school. I wanted to meet his mother.

Accordingly, one morning I went through Pearl street. It is a wide, though unattractive street. The 1500 block belonged, apparently, to one man. He had cut the wide lots up into narrow ones and had built two rows of three-room houses, all exactly alike. Each had a tiny door yard in front.

I reached 1505. In the small space before the front door, flowers were blooming. Purple and yellow iris grew along the fence and a circular bed of nasturtiums flourished at one side of the walk. They made the little house look cool and inviting. I knocked at the door.

"Come in," called Joe Charles' voice. I went in. His voice had sounded from the back. "Come on in the kitchen, whoever you are," it further instructed. I obeyed. I followed the sound through two doors. I came upon Joe Charles in the last room. He was down on his knees, lighting an oil range.

My glance swept around me. It was a dainty kitchen. It was clean. White curtains, bordered with red checked material, were tied back at the high, narrow window. The floor covering was a congoleum rug, patterned in black and white. A white table, with a steel top stood in the center of the floor. On the table was a blue bowl, containing two eggs. At each end of the table was a little bowl, decorated with ducks. Beside each little bowl a spoon was placed.

Seated at one end of the table was a little, fat brown girl. Her hair made a soft, hazy halo about her dimpled face.

Her little blue dress was open at the neck. Her small feet were bare, but a pair of sandals of minute size, were sitting side by side beneath her chair. Joe Charles said, "NOW," with the air of one who has just accomplished a task. I noticed that the blue flame of the burner he had been lighting, now emerged from the top. He rose and turned toward me with a casual greeting, as though there was nothing unusual in my early visit.

"I am getting breakfast," he explained, and added with evident pride "This is my sister." Her brown eyes were direct and admiring. "Are you Mrs. Winn?" she asked.

"Yes, I am. And you must be Lillian," I told her.

"Did Joe Charles tell you my name?" she asked.

"He told me all about you," I said.

"May I come to school with you today?" she wanted to know. I hedged quickly.

"Not today," I said. "But I will ask Mrs. Bell if you may come soon."

I filled both bowls with oatmeal from the double boiler. Joe Charles secured a bottle of milk and poured milk over each steaming mound. He sprinkled sugar on it and they ate while I scrambled the two eggs. I buttoned the little brown girl's dress and fastened the small sandals on her pretty feet. Somehow, I wanted to cry as I did these things. I thought of the little mother, who must work in the laundry or there might be no milk and cereal. I thought of the father who worked all week for only eight dollars. And these two poor babies were left alone to care for themselves.

My thoughts seemed to conjure the father out of nowhere for I heard his footsteps and his call. He was in the kitchen before I could rise from my knees, where I had knelt to put on the baby sandals. He was as much surprised as I was embarrassed. I explained that I came thus early to see Mrs. King and had helped the children get breakfast. He smiled. He was very young. His clean, brown khaki suit showed, as yet, no traces of coal. His teeth were even and beautiful. He spoke correctly and charmingly:

"You will have to come some Thursday. Lillian has a half day off then. Why didn't you tell her, Joe Charles?"

"She didn't ask me," mumbled Joe Charles into his bowl.

"He didn't know I was coming," I said. "Aren't you afraid to let him light fires, and to leave them alone like—" He held up his hand to silence me.

"Of course we are," he said simply. "But we don't tell him. We tell Charles he is big enough to be careful. We teach him he must take care of his sister. He really is very careful. I always come by with my first load of coal to see about them. I usually snatch long enough to get them away and wash the dishes. Lillian likes things clean."

"It is really wonderful the way you manage," I said. Between us we had washed the dishes and I prepared to leave. He caught me at the gate.

"If you come back Thursday, don't mention about lighting fires. Lillian will just worry and—what else can we do?" he finished. I could see the anxiety in his lean, brown face.

"Of course, I won't," I told him. "I shouldn't have said so to you. Joe Charles is such a little man. I know he will always be careful. He is unusual, you know. I think he is splendid." He was relieved, and proud of my praise of his son, who was so like him. I hurried away to school, thinking of the hard lessons of the poor. Here, I knew, were four wonderful persons, working together and loving each other with unselfish devotion.

[*The Crisis* 47.11 (November 1940): 347, 364, 366]

"BEHOLD I STAND …"

by Violet C. Haywood

Deciding that the late afternoon sun gave enough light, Mrs. Simms gazed with satisfaction at the image of herself in the big mirror. Inspecting her straight, well-shaped nose closely, she saw the need for a bit more powder. A few final pats and pulls here and there and she was ready. She glanced at her watch. Um—m, time enough to make the meeting with a few minutes to spare. She walked lightly from the room, a well-groomed, graceful creature with finespun, bright hair and surprisingly dark blue eyes. A typical Nordic beauty she was.

As she walked toward the kitchen she fished in her expensive bag for her car keys.

"Lillian," she said to her small wrinkled, colored cook, "I shall dine out today, so don't bother to fix anything. Mr. Simms won't be in either."

She had already started away when Lillian's "Yessum" came. Indeed she scarcely heard the reply. Her mind was so busy with the speech she was going to make in a few minutes before the Women's Club. She had composed this speech with very little difficulty because she felt so strongly on the subject. Why certain parts of it made tears come to her own eyes.

"It is our Christian duty," in her mind she went over the closing sentences "to open our arms to these poor homeless innocents of war-torn Europe. Children are the flowers in this great world. We must not let them know terror and pain, and hunger. We *must* not sit idly by, letting it be as nothing to us. They stand, even as the Master, at our door and knock. In the name of humanity we must hear and open to them.

"Good, very good," she thought happily as she unlocked the car. She was about to slide under the steering wheel when a piercing scream halted her. Lillian had heard, too, and was running toward the alley in back of the house. Mrs. Simms ran after her.

When she got there Lillian had off one of her surprisingly large shoes, and was beating away at a big dog. Mrs. Simms saw that the dog was holding fast to a ragged little object. It was a boy.

"Leggo, *leggo*, I tell you!" Lillian hammered away with all the strength of her frail body.

"What—what *is* it?" Mrs. Simms was plainly distressed.

Finally a hard blow on the head brought a yelp of pain from the dog. He bounded away swiftly and was soon out of sight.

"You hurt, honey?" Lillian helped the boy to rise.

"Naw!!" he flashed a watery smile at her. "I guess he jess skait me." He gathered his tattered rags about him, lapping the over-large trousers in front with a big safety pin. His hands trembled, in spite of his brave words, and his black little face was still ashen.

"What was you doin' when he got after you, boy? What's your name, anyway?" asked Lillian.

"Tenny" the boy answered the latter part of the question. When he said no more Mrs. Simms repeated Lillian's question.

"What were you doing, Tenny, when the dog got after you?"

Tenny hung his head and replied only by scuffing his toe back and forth on the cement.

"Can't you talk, boy, when folks asts you a question?" Lillian was not famed for her patience. She seized Tenny by the arm and shook him slightly, more in impatience than in anger.

"I—I was gittin' sumpin' t' eat." Tenny's answer was so low as to be almost indistinguishable. His face was sullen.

"Eatin'? Eatin' what?" Mrs. Simms and Lillian asked the same question, only Mrs. Simms said "eating."

Tenny pointed a grimy finger. They looked where he pointed, then gazed at each other in horror.

"You—you were eating—out of—*that?*"

"Yes." There was defiance in Tenny's voice now.

"But that's—why that's—*garbage*!" Mrs. Simms seemed scarcely able to bring herself to say the word.

"It had some good in it. It always do." Tenny looked at her, daring her to deny this. They stood looking at one another: Mrs. Simms, as if at the rarest creature her eyes had ever beheld, Tenny, stubbornly determined not to drop his eyes first. Neither heard Lillian's breathed exclamation.

"My Gawd."

"I wasn't hurtin' nuthin or nobody. Jess trying to get sumpin' t'eat."

"But why don't you go home and eat? Why your mother should be ashamed to—"

"Don't you talk about my ma!"

"I wasn't talking about her child. I just wondered why she'd let you *do* like this."

"She's ... dead."

"Oh!—and your father?"

She had her answer by the swift pain in those dark eyes.

"But there must be agencies—*something, someone*—"

"I ain't going to no damn orphanage." He spat out the words with such intensity that Mrs. Simms almost jumped.

"But have you no home? No one? Where do you stay nights?"

Tenny's eyes became crafty.

"Oh—places," he replied easily.

Mrs. Simms heard the bells of the tower chime out the hour. She glanced at her watch with a start. Heavens, the meeting! She looked at the thin, ragged creature before her. Should she? But he was too dirty—dirtier than she had ever seen anyone. Too dirty to go in her kitchen.

"Here, boy. Here's a quarter. Lillian, I—you—" she floundered hopelessly. Then straightening her shoulders she said firmly, "I've got to go to a meeting!" Turning she hastily walked away, in a hurried effort to escape the foolish turmoil in her breast.

She got into her beautiful car, pressing the gas so hard that she literally leaped away. Into her mind, unbidden came the words of the speech, which no longer seemed so good to her.

"They stand, even as our dear Savior, at our doors and knock. In the name of humanity, we must open to them." [*The Crisis* 47.12 (December 1940): 384]

GRAZING IN GOOD PASTURES

by Margaret Williams

Handsome young David Woods made a mistake when he fell in love with a bright-skinned gal. At least all of Coonville thought so. He was fair to rue the day he brought home a woman like that. A farmer had no more use with a light-eyed wife than a monkey had with a side-saddle. Why her hair was too yellow and straight and her skin too fair for her to hoe in the field. That would mean that David must hire all his work.

That was what all of Coonville was saying when young David brought his bride home to the little farm in the pines down in East Texas. He had found her in Dallas. Being city-bred and practically white, she would have ideas, of course, that would soon ruin any hard-working man. That was to be expected.

But Rubye was determined to prove to the settlement that no matter how bright was her skin she could make a farmer a good wife.

She had a good education, better than that of any of the white folks around there. Before she had left she had gathered all the information she could about farming in East Texas. Her fancy had been struck when she learned that roses was one of the main crops.

"I love roses!" she told David. "Roses teach us that everything must have a purpose for coming to this earth. A rose's duty is to be beautiful and to smell sweet. He starts out being beautiful, and the older he grows the sweeter is his expression. I'm going to love growing roses. I'll cross them. I bet I find one no one else has ever found."

David's expression was non-committal. No doubt, though, he was wondering how he could break the news to her easy-like that the farm was for cotton and corn. That was all that had ever been raised on it.

"Why, when business gets good, we'll even get a tractor to work the roses. I read that people have acres and acres of roses down there."

"I'se afraid, honey, we can't never have no tractor. The stumps is so bad. We have to use a hand plow so we can pull up from around the stumps."

"We can get the stumps out."

"Too hard a work, honey."

"Nothing is going to be too hard now, David. We're going to progress. In a year you won't know the place."

"Don't expect too much."

But Rubye had expected more than she found. Just a two-roomed log cabin with one lone pine at the back. The stumpy field surrounded the house. The dump ground for gen-eration was to the right of the low front porch in a sand hollow. She tried hard to hide her disappointment when she climbed out of the model T in front of the fallen-down abode.

"Why, it can be made so pretty. Trees surrounded the farm. Those trees yours?" She pointed to the distant wood.

"Sure, honey. A creek runs through the entire place. And them woods is sho' full of hogs."

"I hope you don't mean those funny-looking skinny long-nosed things resembling the hog we saw always running across the road?"

"Them is the piny-woods rooter. They make the best lean bacon."

"That'll be all right for the present until we get our roses started. Then I'll make a pretty park in the wood, with bridges winding across the creek. I am somewhat of a landscaper myself."

"Uh-huh. 'cuse me. I see Evvy, my hired boy," said David, as his black eyes shifted bewilderedly from his wife's pretty face.

He strode on off to have a chat with his hired hand at the barn, which was to the left of the cabin. Rubye wanted her husband to carry her across the threshold, and so she sat down on the edge of the porch to wait for his return. She could see that the hired-hand was only about sixteen and of a skin the color of good liver. She heard him say to her husband:

"All of Coonville is sayin' you sho' is grazin' in good pastures; and I see yo is."

"Yeah. But she may find country life disappointin'," replied David.

"Most city womens gits crazy notions when they come to the country. Jest put her off,

Pa says iffen she does. That's what Pa always done. Oncet Ma went to town and seen some wallpaper and takened a notion to paper the cabin. She even went as fur as to borrow the catalog and see how much buildin' paper was. Pa agreed, but kept puttin' her off givin' her the money. Finally Ma give up the idea and the bare walls done her jest as much good."

* * *

The next morning David wanted to get the cotton in the ground, but Rubye told him that he must first plow up an acre in one corner so that she could start on her roses.

"That can rest, honey. Jest as soon as I git this cotton in the ground. It might rain. Yo know we gots to eat."

So he was taking Evvy's advice!

"My roses will bring more money."

"I don't know roses, but I do cotton."

"That is why so many people remain in the same rut: afraid to try the new. You'll see if you'll only do as I say."

"Jest as soon as I gits the cotton in the ground, honey. Besides I don't wants yo in the field alone. A black runner might attact yo."

"A black runner? What's that?"

"A snake here in East Texas. It ain't poisonous, but the male snake attacts womens or girls and den she don't git help he'll injure her fur life. I had to cut one off my cousin oncet."

"You're just trying to scare me. Besides I can watch out and carry my hoe."

Then she tried putting her arms about her husband's neck. He always softened under her kisses. But he pulled her back, no doubt realizing he might give over if he once let her touch him.

"Please," she begged.

He just shook his head and promised as he started toward the barn.

Rubye let him hitch up. When he came by in front of the cabin on the way to the field, she ran out to beg him again. He only waved his hand to her and told Pete to get hisself on down the trail before he skinned his head.

Rubye stood there and watched him. She didn't know that David could be so stubborn. Her pride was hurt.

"All right," she told herself, "I'll show him. I'll show all of Coonville. They think—they think—I don't care what they think. It is what I think that counts."

As Rubye hadn't yet felt the effects of coming from a high altitude to this low altitude, she found the shovel and walked down to the acre she had picked out and began spading it up.

All morning she worked, so long in fact that she forgot to see about getting dinner. When she saw David coming in for lunch, she wiped the perspiration from her brow, and fled for the cabin where she found a pile of dirty dishes. The sound of bacon frying on the wood stove was the only hope for a dinner when her husband came in.

A half-hour later she sat him down to bacon, gravy, and cold biscuits. He said not a word of complaint, but ate in a strained silence.

That night it was the same thing, and the following day. The third morning he said:

"I see I ain goin' to git any dinner if I don't plow up that land. Yo stay here and I'll git that done."

Rubye was thankful. Already she was beginning to feel tired and without energy to lift a shovel. But she didn't mention the fact to her husband. Really they had little to say to each other.

That day Rubye forced herself to sweep the house, wash the dishes, and to cook. Between work she fell down on the bed and sighed what time she was not sleeping.

Finally her husband had the acre plowed, and still Rubye did not feel like setting out her roses she had placed in a dirt box under the big pine tree. About five that afternoon she went out under the tree and looked at them. That tired feeling had her gripped so hard that she only sat down on a rusty bucket and groaned.

"This sun is so hot. Is this the reason these people never have flower yards nor paper their walls? But I won't give up. I'll keep on and on and show them. I'll whip myself to it."

The next morning Rubye dragged out to the rose field and managed to set out two rows of bushes. She was so tired when she came in to cook dinner that she sobbed as she fixed a fire and made up bread.

After dinner she dragged herself again to the field, but spent most of the time on her knees or sitting down, groaning from aching muscles and from that terrible feeling of depression.

Time dragged on. Though their days were strained, their nights were filled with love, for after all they were young and very much in love. They would lie awake and kiss and forget about the cotton field and the rose garden and listen to the cry of the whippoorwill or to the silly talk of the hoot owl.

"Listen, honey," David would say, as he held his wife in his arms, "can you make out what he's sayin'?"

> Rubber boot
> shoe boot
> chicken soup
> so good.

Then they would kiss good-night and sigh. And she would go to sleep with her small fist doubled up in his big palm.

One year passed. Rubye had become accustomed to the low altitude, but she had never regained the feeling for a desire to progress. Still she stubbornly fought with the rose idea. She wanted to show David and all of Coonville that she knew what she was talking about. She would stand by a rose bush and gaze down upon its pretty bloom, trying hard to feel something beautiful for the flower.

"It's this hot sun pouring down upon this red sand which does something to people," she would sigh.

At last fall came, the time for the county fair at Pinecrest. Both the colored and the white were welcome. The biggest stalk of cotton, the finest ear of corn, the best pickle, and the sweetest tasting jar of jelly were to be brought there. Everyone was guessing that David's wife would not be represented because she did not belong to the Home Cooking Club. She never canned. In fact she never stayed in the house long enough for her to cook David a decent meal.

Rubye knew what they were saying about her. The white folks, of course, would have nothing to do with her even though they did take time off to have their say. A drop of nigger blood was nigger to white folks in Texas. They never stopped to weigh one's soul. The colored folks treated her nice, but they openly showed her that they felt sorry for David. He should have married a dark brown-skinned gal from the south, someone who would have made a hand in the field. Then all of that extra hiring could be saved.

"He wouldn't of lost his cotton in the east field if she'd throwed in there with him," she heard one woman tell another.

What David thought the young man kept to himself. He had grown depressingly silent.

He and his wife hardly spoke a word a day now. Even at night they forgot to listen to the hoot owl say his silly ditty.

That last day before the fair opened Rubye tried to draw her husband into conversation as she took the noon meal from the stove to the small pine table across the room.

"Tomorrow, David, the fair starts. Aren't you going to take something?"

He shook his head. She could see tears in his eyes. He was undergoing some terrible emotion, she saw. Was he sorry he had married her?

"I've crossed three different roses and have discovered the prettiest rose I ever saw in my life. It is sort of an orange rose. The bush grows about four feet tall, and the blooms are as big as a saucer. I am taking that."

She started to tell him about her black rose, but he didn't seem to be listening, and so she retorted:

"I know all of Coonville is feeling sorry for you, and I can see you are even sorry for yourself now. If I don't make good with my roses this year, I'll quit and go home."

Still David did not reply.

"And this is the last word I'll say to you until I find out tomorrow."

David's black eyes held resentment for his wife.

"I darsent say a word or I'll git my head skinned."

"How can you say that! I only try to show you the sensible side of things, and you act like a child, believing all of Coonville rather than me."

"The onliest way we have of knowin' a thing is to take it from experience."

"Then we would never progress. There is always someone to start things first."

"Then why in the devil did it have to be my wife! Yo color is enough to make folks take notice to yo. Why couldn't yo have been like others of our race? Why did yo have to try and show us a lot of white folks' notions?"

Rubye rose from the table. It was all so useless. Well, she would go on with her roses this fall, and then leave David. She could never make him happy. They were as different as a pea and a bean. But why did that ache in her heart grow worse upon considering such a thing as leaving him? He had stopped loving her; he thought her a failure as a wife.

Just as she left the kitchen, her husband said:

"Don't expect me to carry you in to town tomorrow. I got work in the field to do. No money to hire hands with."

David had long ago sold his model T. Their first year had been a crop failure, due to so much rains. There had not been enough hands to chop out the grass. And he had to use the team in the field.

* * *

It was five miles in to Pinecrest, but Rubye did not let this stop her. She got up at three in the morning, hastily cooked up some bread for David, and fried meat. She left his breakfast on the stove and then lit the lantern. She did not want a bite herself, for she felt sort of weak and tired.

She closed the door behind her, and went straight to the rose field to cut her orange roses. Not until she was nearly there did she remember that she had not got her hoe. Well, surely the black-runner would not be out at night.

When she reached her prize roses, she let out a pitiful gasp. She could hardly believe her eyes. All the leaves had fallen off during the night. Or had they been plucked? She sank down beside them, broken-hearted, weeping:

"I can't believe it! He wouldn't have done such a horrible thing to me. But the leaves were too firm to have dropped off. Oh, he knew if I failed, I would leave. That's it! He wants me to leave. He really wants me to leave."

She sat there in the dew for at least twenty minutes, sobbing out her heart. Suddenly she became aware of a long black thing beside her. A black-runner! Before she could rise the snake was across her lap. She grabbed out at it, every drop of her blood seeming to have turned to ice. As she tugged and struggled to get up, the snake only wound himself tighter about her, drawing her back to the ground.

"David! Oh, my God! David!"

But he was at the house. He could not hear her. Still she emitted one scream after another. Then she heard:

"Comin'!"

And she fainted.

When she came to, she was lying on the bed in the fireplace room. David was bathing her face.

"He didn't git time to hurt yo, honey," he was saying. "I killed him with my knife first. I cut him off yo. Yo is just scared, not hurt."

Rubye suddenly sat up.

"No, I'm not hurt. Just scared. Please leave me alone so I can rest."

She had remembered how he had destroyed her prize roses that night. She did not want him even in the room with her ever again.

David gave her a funny look, but obeyed and left. Soon she saw him hitching up and going out to the field.

"He actually thinks more of his cotton than he does of me. He's got to get that precious white stuff out of the field before a rain."

Rubye was not to be beaten. She remembered her black roses. Though the black rose had before been grown, she knew it had not in this section. She rose and hastily dressed.

It was noon before Rubye reached the fair grounds. She was thankful to find that she was in time to enter her roses. In fact hers were the only ones at the fair. She learned that a man from the A. and M. was to judge the plants. She waited with bated breath. Maybe he would appreciate her roses. No one in Coonville did.

* * *

As she waited there on the hard bench, she realized that she had not had a bite to eat that day. Still she was not hungry. She felt sort of sick at her stomach. Cold chills ran up and down her spine. Then hot flashes passed over her. She thought it was due to her scare. She prayed that she could stand it until her plants were judged.

It was four that afternoon before the man came to judge her plants. Rubye had held on somehow, but she hardly realized what was going on until a man said:

"Whose roses are these? By George, I never saw such roses! I've seen the black ones before, but not such large specimens. Judging by the stalk they must grow six feet tall."

Rubye rose.

"They're from David Woods' farm out in Coonville Community. He—he raised them." The man turned to the young woman.

"You representing him?"

"I am his wife."

"How did he do it, lady?"

"I—he is keeping that a secret. He hopes to sell cuttings. He also has found the orange rose. And some of the biggest pink and yellow ones you ever saw."

"That's a damn' lie!" said a voice behind them.

Rubye turned and saw David stumbling up, his black eyes filled with both resentment and anger.

"She done it by herself. I raise cotton and corn."

"Well, she's done something, man. She'll win five hundred dollars for just this black rose. And I can fill as many orders for her orange rose as she can supply. Probably some of these others, too.

David looked at his wife in time to catch her as she fell in a faint.

When Rubye came to, David had the doctor with her. She was at the Pinecrest Hospital. David was sitting beside her crying.

"Why are you crying?" Rubye asked her husband. "Am I that bad off? Or is it because I am not going to die?"

"Mrs. Woods, you have the malaria fever. Nothing to worry about. I'll have you fixed up before long. I'd better be going now. See that she takes her medicine, young man." Then the doctor picked up his case.

"Yes, suh."

As soon as the doctor had left the room, David looked sorrowfully at his wife and said:

"Honey, I wish yo'd take a gun and kill me."

"We'll forget all about it, David."

"No, we won't until yo understand it was the cotton I was so stubborn about, not that I didn't love yo. Folks first thought I was grazin' in good pastures when I brung yo home, and then soon they got to sayin' I wasn't. I wanted to win out, win by myself, even if yo wouldn't help. But yo won without my help. I'm a fool!"

"If you are, you are the sweetest one I ever saw. David, you can't drive me off now that I know you love me. That is all that matters to my heart. Tonight take me home and let's listen to the hoot owl quarreling again."

"Sho' will. He says somethin' new now, honey. I heard him last night."

> Work done
> no done
> night come
> go home.

[*The Crisis* 48.2 (February 1941): 42–43, 59]

ONE TRUE LOVE

by Marita Bonner

When Nora came through the swinging doors between the kitchen and the dining room with the roast, she was just a butter-colored maid with the hair on the "riney" side hurrying to get through dinner so she could go to the show with the janitor's helper, Sam Smith.

By the time Nora had served dessert, though, she had forgotten the show, forgotten Sam—forgotten everything but this: she was going to be a lawyer!

"They" had had company to dinner. ("They" in Nora's family were a Mr. and Mrs. This is not their story—so they are merely "They").

Company came often enough, but this time everything had been different.

"We are having a noted lawyer to dinner tonight, Nora" Mrs. had said.

Nora had expected a bay window, side-chop whiskers and a boom-boom voice.

When she backed through the door with the roast she saw sitting at the table in the guest's place, a woman. She had been beautifully but simply dressed in black velvet: her hair was cut short, worn brushed up in curls: every inch of her had been smart and lovely.

"This must be the lawyer's wife. Maybe be couldn't git here!"

But then "they" began talking. "Is your law practice as heavy as it was two years ago or do you devote more time to lecturing?" he asked.

"We hear you've been pleading at the Supreme Court!" 'she' cut in.

Nora nearly gaped.

This was the lawyer!

All through dinner she noted how nicely the lawyer ate, how pleasant her voice was when she spoke—how direct her eyes were when she looked at you.

"I'm going to get in some kind of school and be a lawyer, too!" Nora declared to the dishes as she washed them.

A knock at the back door cut into her thoughts.

Nora opened it and Sam bristled in.

"Why ain't you through? It's quarter to nine!"

"Whyn't you say good-evenin' and ask me how I feel?" Nora shot back at him. "You always act so ignorant!"

"What you got to talk so mean to me for? Ain't you glad to see me?"

"Can't say that I am if you always going to act so ignorant and degrading!"

"De—who?? S'matter with you, Nora?"

"Nuthin' cept I'm tired and I'm not going to be bothered going to no show tonight!"

"Well who—!" Sam staggered back from the choice of two words to follow his who: "cares" and "wants" decided he did not want to use either. "Well, good night, then!" he finished instead. "Maybe Sadie Jones would like to see a show!"

"Maybe so! She's your kind! Two ignorants together!" Nora flashed back at Sam.

"And maybe I don't need to come back here no more! I won't be seeing you!"

Nora did not even turn around to close the door after Sam. He had to close it himself.

Now Sam was a runty, bowlegged dark brown janitor's helper with a shiny scalp on which his hair grew in kinked patches.

That is what Sam was to the world.

And Sam was just that to Nora, too.

But to Sam, Nora was elegant and beautiful and more desirable than anything ever had been to anyone at anytime.

His, "Maybe I don't need to come back here no more!" frightened him.

Nora forgot it.

He had said it on Wednesday.

He stayed awake all Wednesday night, all Thursday night—all Friday night—hearing himself say over and over again: "Maybe I don't need to come back here no more!"

Suppose Nora thought he really meant just that!

Suppose Nora would never see him any more!

By Saturday morning, his eyes were so red it upset your stomach just to look at him.

"You ain't taking to drink, is you Sam?" the head janitor asked. "Cause if you is, then I needs another helper 'stead of you!"

"Naw I ain't drinking! Don't feel good!"

"Take a good physic! Do something! You look right bad—!"

Sam had said "Maybe I won't be seeing you any more" on Wednesday.

So Saturday night he bought a box of flour water and cocoa chocolates and came and knocked humbly on Nora's back door.

"Want to go to the show?" he asked anxiously as Nora opened the door. "They got that 'Kiss in the Dark' down to the Dream World."

"I don't mind," Nora answered mildly. "I have a lot of things to talk over with you!"

Sam's heart turned completely over. "You mean we—going to get—you going to give up working here and we going to get married? That guy keeps telling me he'll rent them two rooms on Rommy Street for twenty dollars and Levack's got some swell new furniture real cheap!"

Sam was breathless.

Nora was not listening to him. She knew vaguely that Sam was talking so she merely waited until his voice ceased before she began to tell him what was in her mind.

"I've enrolled in the night classes at the City College! I'm taking law!"

"You taking law! How come you taking law?"

"I mean I'm going to study to be a lawyer!"

"You ain't! When we going to get married?"

"I been telling you never! I got to get some education first anyhow!"

"Aw you don't need no education! You know enough to get along with me!"

"Aw Sam ! Wait'll I get my hat on!"

As they walked toward the town center, Nora gossiped a bit, "They" surely was having a terrible fuss tonight! She really cussed and damned him off the boards!"

"Yeah? What's the trouble?"

"Oh, she went down town and tried to buy up the stores and he got to hollering but she out-cussed him! I don't see why they don't get along lovely! Everything so lovely in their home and he and she both educated."

"What make you talk so much 'bout this education business now? That ain't what makes a man and woman git on together!"

"Aw Sam you so ignorant! If you are educated you know how to do everything just right all the time."

"Everything like gettin' along with a husband? Naw! You got to love folks! A guy really got to love a girl so he kin pass by the beer gardens and the hot mamas and the sheeny what wants him to lay a dollar on a suit and a watch and a diamond and a God knows-what-all— and bring the pay check home to her so they kin go in on it together!"

"Aw pay checks ain't everything!"

"And edjucation ain't everything! You got to love folks more than books!"

"And more than money!"

"Yeah! You got to love folks more than everything to git along and live fifty years with 'em!"

"Who said anything 'bout staying married fifty years?"

"Me!" Sam retorted stoutly. "My grandma did and I'm going to too!"

"You ain't going to do nothing your grandmother didn't do! That's ignorant!"

They reached the theater and no conclusion to the argument, so they went in.

Nora kicked off her shoes and munched chocolates and lived the picture. She felt comfortable and happy in a remote way that there was somebody with whom she could talk and argue good-naturedly—someone who knew enough to pass you his handkerchief at the cry parts.

She was glad—dimly—about all this.

What gave her feelings a real edge was that Monday night she was going to her first class at City College to study law.

City College was not particularly glad to receive Nora.

They endured a few colored students there but they had always been men—men whose background of preparation made professors and students of the lesser type, keep their sneers under cover.

But after it was seen that Nora got her superlatives mixed and "busted" when she should have "broken" and "hadn't ought to" come out when she meant "should not have"—quite a few sneers came out in the open.

People like to place you and your desires and tastes where they think your particular color and hirsute growth belong. They do not like to feel that Something-greater-than—themselves can give you the feel for the ermine and satin of living, the air for silver services and a distinct love of beaux that sets you quietly aloof—truly poised beyond the rough wood of living.

If they are above you—culturally—sometimes they shower sneers down at you, forgetting all the while that the thick coats of culture which surround them began once with one coat—thinly applied—sometime—somewhere—on their own family tree.

If they are below you—culturally—they try to stone you to death—sneer at you until you reach the point where you gladly smother all your ideas and ideals and crawl into a protective shell of sameness so that the mediocre mob will let you alone.

Nora had a touch of this something that made her struggle to get beyond a stove, a sink, a broom and a dust-mop and some one else's kitchen.

She worked hard at her books. She stayed up late to struggle with books full of pages that she had to read ten times over to even begin to get a glimmer of sense from them.

Professors demand more than a glimmer of information. They want things presented as they are and a bit more grafted on to it to show you are really getting an education.

Came the mid-year exams.

Nora snapped at Sam—burnt two steaks and had to buy a third one out of her own pocket one night—trying to untangle torts and contracts. Haggard with overwork and bewildered with subjects for which no preparatory steps had ever been laid in her, Nora flunked all her examinations.

Sam came one Sunday night to carry her over to the colored section of town for a special celebration.

Nora met him at the back door and began to cry.

"They flunked me, Sam! I didn't pass! No need to go celebrating."

"You mean those old fools didn't give you no good mark? Much studyin' and stewin' and strivin' and worryin' and stayin' up nights as you did? S'matter with them folks? I bet if I'se to go down there they'd pass you or sumpin!"

Nora's anger flared: "Why you always have to talk so ignorant, Sam? You can't do nothing! I didn't know enough to pass, that's all."

"Taint no need to bellow at me all the time! I'clare you got to feelin' right important since you got your feet inside of that City College! Good enough for you! You bound to fail! You too bigotty!"

"You get out of here! You no kind of friend! Rejoicing at my downfall!"

"Wouldn't fall down—if you's a married me 'stead of learnin' law all the time!"

"Don't need your love! I can lean on law and be a lawyer too if I wants too, Mr. Sam Smith!"

"Well go on leaning on your busted crutch, then!"

"Aw go on home Sam! My head's achin fit to bust!"

Sam backed out in a huff.

When he came back the next night and knocked at the door no one answered.

The kitchen was dark.

"Gone to bed! Still mad! Let her stay mad!" Sam growled as he left.

The next night he came again and no one opened the door.

Sam did not come back for two whole days.

When he knocked at the door a strange colored woman opened it.

"Where's Nora?" Sam gasped in surprise.

"Nora? Oh you mean the maid what was here? Oh she sick!"

"Sick?" Sam shouted and bounded into the kitchen. "Where she at? Whyn't nobody tell me?"

"Who you anyhow?"

"I'm the man what's going to marry huh! Marry Nora! Where she at?"

"Well don't yell so and don't come running in here that-a-way! She ain't here! She in some hospital. Wait'll I ask the lady."

When the woman came back to the kitchen Sam was already running down the back stairs!

"She got pneu-monyer in the City Hospital," the woman called down the stairs after him. "And you might have shut the door if you couldn't wait."

Sam tore up the gangway between the buildings and hired the biggest taxi lurking in front of the apartment house where they worked.

"Steppin' out for a big night, Boy?" the driver jibed as he pushed down the meter.

"I'm going to City Hospital to get my wife—what is going to be—. Got to bring her home and take care of her!"

It took a while to find Nora. She was in a public ward somewhere and since pneumonia cases were coming in at that particular season faster than the registrar could list them, no one could locate her for a full half hour.

Beads of real agony dropped from Sam's face when the nurse showed him the elevators.

He found the ward.

And he found a white screen around Nora's bed.

He could not believe this gray-faced woman who lay panting—panting was Nora. Her nostrils flared wide—too wide. Her teeth stuck deep in her lower lip and her eyes stared straight at nothing.

If "they" had said a little more—if someone had said that they would pay for Nora—she would not have been shoved aside and forgotten in a public ward.

Sam raced frantically back to the hall where the night nurse sat.

"Could Nora Jones be put in one of these here rooms to herself? I got every bit of four hundred dollars! Couldn't nobody set by her?"

The nurse glanced at a paper on her desk.

"She can't be moved right now! Perhaps—if she's better tomorrow—maybe—!"

You could tell all this meant that nothing nobody could do would help Nora anymore.

Sam went back to the bed and sat behind the white screen. He laid his head beside Nora's and cried.

His love must have reached her somewhere.

Nora's eyes focused on him for a second. "Sam—! Sam—" he could hardly hear her. "I've got I—I've got I—!"

It sounded as if she said "law" her breath rasped so and her lower jaw seemed to fall away from the work.

Sam wiped his eyes and grabbed her hand.

"I know Nora! I know you got that old law to lean on! Ef you could of just want something I could a helped you git! Just get well! I'll help you get that law!"

Nora tried to shake her head.

Couldn't he understand?

She had waited and waited to tell Sam that down deep somewhere where she had been lost in pain for so long—there was nothing about books and what they gave you. The only thing she had remembered had been that there was someone who loved her enough to love her even when she was snappish and cross—who came back again and again—no matter what.

And she was glad!

So glad she wanted to tell Sam that' she loved him—had love enough for the two rooms he wanted on Rommy Street and enough to try to understand how his grandmother came to stay married fifty years.

Right now Nora was too tired to try to tell him again.

She closed her eyes.

But she closed her eyes carrying with her the love that was in Sam's eyes.

She thought she smiled.

The doctor said the death agony had set her face at that angle.

He wondered too, why that little colored man just sat by that empty bed crying so long. The nurses wanted to prepare the bed for another case.

And Sam sat crying—wishing he had been elegant and wonderful enough to match the wonder in Nora—trying to take something out into his empty world from an empty bed.

[*The Crisis* 48.2 (February 1941): 46–47, 58–59]

BOYZIE

by Lucille Boehm

Boyzie rubbed the shoulder of his yellow suede jacket, where a furrow had been dug into it by the sharp edge of the grocery box. A jab-toothed ache sawed the flesh beneath the furrow. Fourteen hours toting groceries around the streets, stupidly, through the thick fog of white faces. Tired, dull-minded not even feeling, by the time the sky clogged up heavy with evening. All day he was a lump of black earth, nothing in him alive but the ache biting his shoulder, gnawing at the muscle of his raised right arm.

Homeward now, he walked fast up Eighth Avenue. Boyzie came out of the day's long numbness stinging raw and raging like a frost-bitten toe. In the thaw he wanted to jump like pop-corn, or laugh violently, or grip something yielding in his hands and throttle it! And he wanted more than all this. He wanted a meaning for himself apart from hauling groceries.

He swung east at a Hundred and Twenty-first street. A mean wind slapped around the corner. The block ahead was long and black. There was a big sprawling apartment with a "NO LOITERING" sign, a vacant lot orange with a blaze two kids were nursing, rows of furnished flats facing each other stiffly. Boyzie shoved his face forward against the wind. His skin was porous as dark soil. Deep grooves were cut like scars under his eyes. His big mouth scowled broadly over strong, stubby teeth. He hunched up under the rubbed-looking collar of his jacked and punched his fists hard into his pockets and strode head-on into the jabbing wind.

Home was a one room furnished flat off Seventh Avenue. The narrow stairway led to a long hall with two one-family rooms on either side. Boyzie climbed the stairs and walked into the darkness at the west end of the hall. He felt his way along walls that were lined with bare wire, like springs ripped out of a bed. Then his hand touched the hard stubble of a frosted glass door. He pushed into the flat.

He found the string to the electric bulb and yanked it. The kitchen-bedroom was washed in a sick yellow light. His mother way lying on the faded brown studio couch in the corner. Must have just got home from the laundry. She lay face to the wall, belly down. Her worn black shoes had budded and swelled like old potatoes from the constant pressure of her feet. Her damp blue uniform was caught under her thighs, showing where the coarse stockings were rolled and knotted at the knees. One big arm hung straight at the side, crinkling the pale, stiff elbow-skin, and the pink palm faced upward. Part of her face could be seen over her right shoulder. The black flesh was rubbery and thick, bloated with weariness. And her whole body, massive and steaming like a tired dray-horse, lay ragged, limp as the wash that was strung across the room.

Boyzie looked at her. Vaguely he wondered when the steam would explode that was throttled in that great, choked engine! Then he sighed softly, heavily, "Aaaa shucks!" and went to the window. Tugged at the rattling frame until finally it gave, admitting a wet draught that sliced him coldly through the ribs. He dragged in a sooty platter, covered by a soup-plate and slammed the window sharply. The platter skidded like ice between his fingers. He held it on the thin ledge with his body and pushed away the soup-plate. A strip of salt pork, not much longer than his middle finger, had frozen and stuck to the china. Boyzie picked it off with his nails. A small sliver stuck to the platter, tearing from the strip. He dangled the frayed pork under his nose, sniffed it and cursed.

"This all?" he asked, turning to his mother. The blue lump on the bed was silent. "Hey!" called Boyzie. He stood facing the couch, wanting to pound the stillness out of his mother's body. His fists tightened. "Where' my supper, Ma!" Sleep was a great cumulous cloud around her. Boyzie gave the pork a lean look of contempt. "You call this mess a supper?" he shouted. His mother barely stirred.

It maddened him to be hungry and alone like this. All day he was alone and hungry. All day the things he felt and thought hardened inside him like a zygospore, weathering the bleakness of the white faces. And now when he wanted to be alive again—to feel and think and talk and eat—there was only cold salt pork, and silence.

"Goddamn—" Boyzie dropped the pork back onto the platter and slammed it hard against the window frame. He fished a nickel and three cents out of his back pocket. Then he flung off his suede jacket and began to undress ...

He smoothed his hands backward over his hair to rub in the "Conkolline" when he was dressed. And he looked down at himself. Long yellow shoes, high-belted green pants—like full-blown carpet-sweepers on top and pegged close to hug the ankles—a blur coat that hung snugly to the mid-thigh, a pointed white collar and colored handkerchief. Boyzie put on his broad felt hat. Then slowly he took his new overcoat off the clothes rack. Held it away at arm's length. It was tan camel's hair, smooth, raglan cut. He stroked it with the tips of his fingers. Soft and warm—he touched the lining. Glossy!

Luxuriously Boyzie slipped his arms into the sleeves. A thirty-four buck coat! It took him four months to pay for it out of a year's savings. Two dollars down and two a week— cutting out lunches and carfare, sweating at the grocery store for eight fifty on Saturdays with Ma draining away the money like a leak in a straw. A year and fourteen weeks—and two more payments to go! But it was the first new overcoat he had ever owned. It was worth it.

He buttoned the coat and walked out of the flat. Stepped across the hall and rapped with his knuckles on the door opposite. "Benny!" he blasted a whistle through his fingers. "Benny, hey!"

The door opened and Mrs. Benjamin's spare-lipped face peered through the crack. When she saw Boyzie her look thinned to water and she whisked the door shut in his face. He sat down at the door and sang in a loud, uneven voice,

"*Sly Mongoo,' you aught ta be ashaim'* ..." as he ran downstairs.

Benny and the boys were waiting for him in front of O'Keef's Bar and Grill. They were standing around a little fire, rubbing their hands.

"Hi y', boyzie. We goin' to that Church jump tonight?" asked Skeebee.

"Sure, boy, we gon' gorilla that place!" Boyzie said, and the others laughed. "C'mon," he turned down a side street.

"Fred ain't here yet," called Benny.

"So whut? He know where it's at." Boyzie shouted without looking back.

A few of the boys poked their toes into the fire to scatter it, trampled the sparks under their heels. Then they sauntered down the block after Boyzie, their hands in their pockets....

St Mark's Baptist Church held its functions in the basement of an old brown-stone three-story house. Two large windows faced the street, and you could look down into the big ugly hall with its dirty floor boards, its splintery benches lining the walls, its holy pictures, its brown sermon stand and high, scarred piano at the back. Tonight there were strips of green and yellow crepe paper hanging from the lights, and the bulbs were bandaged in pale orange remnants.

The Young People's Society was giving a dance. It was Reverend Brice's idea. He needed another thirty dollars so he could get heat turned on in the congregation house for the winter.

The Reverend was at the door, watching the intake of admission money. He was a towering man with a cavernous voice buried deep in his big, broad body. He was mild and bald and gentle. It was rumored that he was a Red because he had helped organize a local tenant's union. The church patrons grumbled and funds for the congregation had begun to thin. So Reverend Brice's face was intent on the admission's table, and his forehead was crinkled like charred paper.

Boyzie's gang looked in through the street windows. Couples were dancing in the subdued orange light and punch was being served on folding tables beside the sermon stand. Then the boys rushed down the steps and in past the open iron grill. They mobbed the admission's table. Three church boys moved between the table and the door. "Twenty-five cents each, please," said one of them, eyeing the gang uncertainly.

Boyzie was at the front. He stuck out his chest and pushed himself up against the youth who had spoken. And he talked hard.

"Listen, Johnny, come down off that jive, will you? Me an' my friends here we ain't lookin' for no trouble, see."

The boy was somewhat cowed. "Well all *we're* looking for is a quarter each. Can you pay?" he asked.

"What ch' you mean can we pay! Sure we can pay. Only you gotta show us somethin' worth two bits aroun' here."

Boyzie was shoving insolently against the three boys who stood in his way. His gang pressed close behind him. Some of the dancer's had stopped to watch. For a moment the two groups strained against one another in silence.

Then there was a shattering crash of glass and a large tin can hurtled through one of the street windows. Two of the church boys made for the window. Benny scurried back from the street to join the gang and the outsiders shoved their way into the hall amid the general confusion.

Reverend Brice was sore. "Who done that?" he demanded. He rounded up the boys who were supposed to watch the door. "Harry, why don't you get those ruffians out here!" he scolded.

Hank was laughing it off. "We don't wanna raise no sand in here, Rev'end Brice," he said. "You know once they in, they're awful hard to get out."

Boyzie's gang had already mingled with the crowd. People had begun dancing again. This was a push-over!

Jimmy Lunceford was on the piccolo. A fast jump number. The drum was beating out a riff, agitated, imperative. And the quick beat filled Boyzie like food for which he had hungered. Replenished the hot energy that stirred his knees and thighs and shoulders. "Come on, babe, let's you an' me jump," he commanded a little chippie in a green sweater, standing near the door. Recklessly he flung off his overcoat, threw it over the back of a wooden bench. He pulled the girl by the hand toward the open dance space.

The clarinet had taken it up from the drum in a weird, high, irregular corkscrew of sound. It screamed with anguish, it laughed hysterically, it gasped. Boyzie began to dance with restraint, pawing the ground smartly, impatiently, like a thoroughbred. Through scowling, parted lips he grunted "*Hoy! Hoy! Hoy!* ..." in time to the music. Then he fell away from his partner and sent her out, letting his left leg slide backward on the inside of the heel. He tattooed the floor rapidly with his foot. He was up again, rocking a little from side to side. His knees flashed out and quivered together while his partner came in. And all the while his body held rigidly to a single axis, from head to heels. It was as though he was strung lengthwise on an invisible, unbending pole that moved with him about the room. The music passed through him steadily like food through the gut—wave on wave, rhythmic and muscular. And he held his body erect: disciplined to the unseen pole ... head high, as if answering an insult. It was proud, defiant dancing.

As the band was beginning to jam, the record stopped suddenly. There was a surprised silence in the room. Boyzie's keen agitation unraveled like a tightly twisted cord suddenly loosened. He freed his partner's hand and stepped back. "Say what the Hell!" he muttered, looking around.

Reverend Brice was standing in the center of the hall, waving his big palms in the air. He looked like an outraged genii, but his voice was controlled and low.

"Now—just a minute, folks. Everybody just—be quiet a minute." The words rolled softly like purring drums. "Now—most of us in here is good friends, see. An' we are aimin' to keep peace in here with all our outside guests ... so just make yourself welcome." He smiled suddenly and broadly, and then his face was grave. "But there is a few young boys who came in here uninvited an' busted up one of our windows, which is goin' to cost us a good sum of money to repair. Now we don't—"

"*Who* busted a window!" blurted Boyzie indignantly.

The Reverend went on. "We don't aim to have uninvited guests in our midst. So until these young gentlemen leave, you will kindly leave off playing the piccolo." There was a pause. "Now we'll just wait." He folded his arms and stood still in the middle of the floor, waiting.

The crowd shifted uncomfortably. A few of the girls giggled. People stared at Boyzie's gang. Skeebee leaned indifferently against the sermon stand. Benny was moving nervously across the room. Boyzie plumped down on a chair, tilted it back and planted his feet firmly on one of the serving tables.

"I'm gon' break up this joint!" Benny said suddenly. He walked to a table and with the back of his hand swept a tea-cup off the edge. There was a ringing slap as it hit the floor, the purple punch spraying wildly. The handle splintered and the cup settled, shuddering.

A tall yellow lad made for Benny and shoved him sideways toward the front door. Instantly Boyzie sputtered up from his chair, sizzling like a drop of water on a hot stove. "Think you somebody, huh, big boy?" he shouted, and he lunged at the tall fellow, catching one long leg behind the crook of his knee. The youth stumbled forward and Boyzie's gang scrambled on top of him.

Some of the church boys came to the rescue with chairs. The young girls escaped silently through the other door. Two of them disappeared into the bathroom. A large round table was upset, hurtling thick water glasses and ash trays to the floor. Bodies and chairs intermingled with creaking, thudding noises. Reverend Brice stepped into the tangle aghast, and was flung backward. The tide of struggling bodies carried Boyzie toward the door. Angrily he tried to pummel his way back into the room. A fist caught him sharply behind the ear and left the pain singing in his skull. Boyzie fished his knife out of a pocket, tried to switch it open. The blade was rusty and stuck. He scratched it fiercely, tore it open with his fingernails. Then swiftly he turned and backed wildly and struck the scruff of a brown neck as it flashed by—not knowing whose it was. The blade went deeper than he had intended. He had to give a quick yank to get it out. From somewhere came a gasp, strained inward through clenched teeth, and there was a low, short moan. Something heavy stumbled against him.

Suddenly Boyzie was scared. The blade was rusty and the neck was a bad place to cut deep. You could kill a guy that way. He didn't look, was afraid to see what he had done. The scare mounted to his throat, shivered down into his knees. He listened carefully to his knees. He listened carefully to the painful singing in his ear, not sure if it was a siren from the street that he heard. In horror he shook free of the thing that was sagging against him. Fear made little explosions inside him, turning over the engine of his stomach the way gas turns the engine of a car, and the impact sent his legs speeding toward the door. He jammed the open knife into his pocket, bolted up the stairs, three at a time. Raced up the side street to Eighth Avenue.

Boyzie sprinted fiercely up the avenue. People watched him. He felt that he was being chased by someone and dared not look. Fear was a motor purring in his temples, in his neck, in the hollow of his belly. Fear was an electric current rushing in waves over the wires of his nerves. His whole body was awakened and whetted by fear.

And there was a peculiar joy in this. For during the long, hard work-day his senses had been stifled in the sweat of his aching body. Now there was no part of him that did not tinge with live sensation! All day he had been as empty of purpose as a gourd, drained hollow of life for someone else's use. And now suddenly every nerve, every muscle and fiber in him was taut with purpose. Escape! In long bounds Boyzie fled up the avenue, ignited by the strange, exultant fear.

On the corner of One Hundred and Sixteenth Street there was a mounted policeman. Boyzie saw him and skidded down to a rapid walk. The cop was an invisible bit in his mouth, dragging back at the scare pulsing and rearing inside him. He noticed another cop standing on the next corner. He would have to keep walking.

The dampness that had gathered at the nape of his neck was chilled by the night air. It sent a shuddering thrill through his shoulders. He shrugged up under the light coat of his suit. Suddenly a terrible realization loomed up like a fist at the end of a great arm and punched him square in the face. He had left his new overcoat at the dance! His tight insides slackened sickly. For a moment he stood still, shutting his eyes against the overwhelming thought. Desperately, he pinched the bridge of his nose between his fingers. No—couldn't have left it! He never took off his coat when he tried to gorilla his way into a place. But helplessly he remembered how he had tossed the coat on a bench to dance with a little chick. Jesus Christ almighty! It was back there now: he could even go and get it.

Boyzie looked quickly in the direction of One Hundred and Fifteenth street. Painful considerations jolting him. How about the neck he had slashed? The church people could get hold of him for that. Maybe it was serious. And if it was one of his own boys ... Goddamn, he hadn't thought about that! He'd be all washed up with them. They'd gang up on him some night and give him a good going over! Still—how would they know who had done it? But maybe they're sore anyway. Maybe they think he ran out on them.

A sudden question swept over him. Why had he run away? Nobody would have known who had knifed who in that jamboree. Other people might have taken out knives. If he had only stayed, even if that kid really was hurt bad, how could they have pinned it on him? But now he had beat it and his gang would be sore. And if someone ratted on him he'd look suspicious because he had left so quick. The cop might have noticed him running, besides.

Boyzie looked around briefly and began walking uptown again. His mind was overstuffed with jumbled thoughts. He tried to clear himself. Whut's got into you, Boyzie? You knocked a couple a guys around before. He probably ain't hurt bad. An' if he is, what ch' you care? Nobody gonna know who done it in free-for-all. Maybe you just run out 'cause you don't like no tangle....

At a Hundred and Twenty-first street he turned up toward Seventh. He was unsatisfied, desolate. All the electricity of the scare had been yanked out of him like a plug. The little fangs in the raw-wet wind bit through the thin weave of his suit. Dampness slid up his sleeves to the hind-arms. He tried not to think of his lost coat, tried to forget the tiny pringling mounds that the chilly air had raised on his skin. All at once a violent shudder shook him. He stumbled over an ash-can top. "Damn!" He kicked the round tin viciously, trampled it with his heel, wishing it was alive and could feel pain.

The long block was rosy-grey in the mist. The wind was thick with drizzle and the pavement had begun to glimmer. The row of furnished flats was dark, silent except for dance music from a couple of radios, muzzled in airshafts to the rear. Most of the lights were out, and the tired lives behind those blinded windows were snatched back into an endless, meaningless routine of sleep and work.

When Boyzie climbed the steps of his stoop, he saw himself meeting the gang sometime on the street corner, or in front of O'Keef's Bar and Grill. The thought stung in his chest. His teeth clamped the fleshy lining of his under-lip and he pushed into the dim hallway. The hollow brown-wood stairs groaned under his feet.

The door of the flat had been left open for him. He felt his way into the room. Then he stood still, frowning, studying the darkness. The dreary pinkish light from the window fell in patches on his mother's broad shoulders and hips. She was still lying where he had left her, on the studio couch he was supposed to share with his older brother Tom. Bernice and Marguerite lay on the wide, bony-looking bed in the opposite corner, their bodies pinned together against the wall to leave room for the mother. Tom wasn't home yet.

Boyzie groped uncertainly toward the studio couch. Three feet from the window the room was buried in blackness, but the smells proclaimed its squalor like loud voices. The strong washed smell of his mother's body, faintly bitter like over-soaked coffee grounds. The stale smell of dust. The rank, greasy garbage smell. The sweet stickiness of the two girls clinging together under the hot bed-clothes, their necks and faces moist with cold cream. And there was the chalky smell of must that gets into old wood. From the smells Boyzie could see the spotted garbage bag that his mother had been too tired to empty—soggy, alive with the quick, sensitive bodies of roaches. He could see the damp, rumpled sheets of the bed three people shared at night, the soft rotten floor boards, the dank bowl of the sink, gun-grey where the white paint had peeled.

His mind took in the room like a mouth takes moldy food, chewing on it reluctantly, letting it flip-flop over and over—hating to swallow it, yet hating to keep the nasty taste alive. At last Boyzie spat the ugly room from his mind. He lay down lengthwise along the edge of the bed where the girls were sleeping. Crimped up his knees and raised he elbows high. He locked his brain tightly against thoughts; contracted his belly to force out the explosive misery that was bottled there.

And now it was only emptiness that crowded him. Emptiness filled him so full that it burst from him in the thickness of his weighted breathing.

[*The Crisis* 48.11 (November 1941): 344–346]

ON SATURDAY THE SIREN
SOUNDS AT NOON

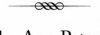

by Ann Petry

At five minutes of twelve on Saturday there was only a handful of people waiting for the 241st Street train. Most of them were at the far end of the wooden platform where they could look down the street and soak up some of the winter sun at the same time.

A Negro in faded blue overalls leaned against a post at the upper end of the station. He was on his way to work in the Bronx. He had decided to change trains above ground so he could get a breath of fresh air. In one hand he carried a worn metal lunch box.

As he waited for the train, he shifted his weight from one foot to the other. He watched the way the sun shone on the metal tracks—they gleamed as far as he could see in the distance.

The train's worn 'em shiny, he thought idly. Train's run up and down 'em so many times they're shined up like a spittoon. He tried to force his thoughts to the weather. Spittoons. Why'd I have to think about something like that?

He worked in a hotel bar room once as a porter. It was his job to keep all the brass shining. The door knobs and the rails around the bar and the spittoons. When he left the job he took one of the spittoons home with him. He used to keep it shined up so that it reflected everything in his room. Sometimes he'd put it on the window sill and it would reflect in miniature the church across the street.

He'd think about Spring—it was on the way. He could feel it in the air. There was a softness that hadn't been there before. Wish the train would hurry up and come, he thought. He turned his back on the tracks to avoid looking at the way they shone. He stared at the posters on the walls of the platform. After a few minutes he turned away impatiently. The pictures were filled with the shine of metal, too. A silver punch bowl in a coca-cola ad and brass candlesticks that fairly jumped off a table. A family was sitting around the table. They were eating.

He covered his eyes with his hands. That would shut it out until he got hold of himself. And it did. But he thought he felt something soft clinging to his hands and he started trembling.

Then the siren went off. He jumped nearly a foot when it first sounded. That old air raid alarm, he thought contemptuously—always putting it off on Saturdays. Yet it made him uneasy. He'd always been underground in the subway when it sounded. Or in Harlem where the street noises dulled the sound of its wail.

Why, that thing must be right on top of this station, he thought. It started as a low, weird moan. Then it gained in volume. Then it added a higher screaming note, and a little later a low, louder blast. It was everywhere around him, plucking at him, pounding at his ears. It was inside of him. It was his heart and it was beating faster and harder and faster and harder. He bent forwards because it was making a pounding pressure against his chest. It was hitting him in the stomach.

He covered his ears with his hands. The lunch box dangling from one hand nudged against his body. He jumped away from it, his nerves raw, ready to scream. He opened his eyes and saw that it was the lunch box that had prodded him and he let it drop to the wooden floor.

It's almost as though I can smell that sound, he told himself. It's the smell and the sound of death—cops and ambulances and fire trucks—

A shudder ran through him. Fire. It was Monday that he'd gone to work extra early. Lilly Belle was still asleep. He remembered how he'd frowned down at her before he left. Even sleeping she was untidy and bedraggled.

The kids were asleep in the front room. He'd stared at them for a brief moment. He remembered having told Lilly Belle the night before, "Just one more time I come home and find you ain't here and these kids by themselves, and I'll kill you—"

All she'd said was, "I'm gain' to have me some fun—"

Whyn't they shut that thing off, he thought. I'll be deaf. I can't stand it. It's breaking my ear drums. If only there were some folks near here. He looked towards the other end of the platform. He'd walk down that way and stand near those people. That might help a little bit.

The siren pinioned him where he was when he took the first step. He'd straightened up and it hit him all over so that he doubled up again like a jack knife.

The sound throbbed in the air around him. It'll stop pretty soon, he thought. It's got to. But it grew louder. He couldn't see the tracks any more. When he looked again they were pulsating to the sound and his ear drums were keeping time to the tracks.

"God in Heaven," he moaned, "make it stop." And then in alarm, "I can't even hear my own voice. My voice is gone."

If I could stop thinking about fire—fire—fire. Standing there with the sound of the siren around him, he could see himself coming home on Monday afternoon. It was just about three o'clock. He could see himself come out of the subway and start walking down Lenox Avenue, past the bakery on the corner. He stopped and bought a big bag of oranges from the push cart on the corner. Eloise, the little one, liked oranges. They were kind of heavy in his arms.

He went in the butcher store near 133rd Street. He got some hamburger to cook for dinner. It seemed to him that the butcher looked at him queerly and he could see himself walking along puzzling about it.

Then he turned into 133rd Street. Funny. Standing here with this noise tearing inside him, he could see himself as clearly as though by some miracle he'd been transformed into another person. The bag of oranges, the packages of meat—the meat was soft, and he could feel it cold through the paper wrapping, and the oranges were hard and knobby. And his lunchbox was empty and it was swinging light from his hand.

There he was turning the corner, going down his own street. There were little knots of people talking. They nodded at him. Sarah Lee who ran the beauty shop—funny she'd be out in the street gossiping this time of day. And Mrs. Smith who had the hand laundry. Why, they were all there. He turned and looked back at them. They turned their eyes away from him quickly when he looked at them.

He could see himself approaching the stoop at 219. Cora, the janitress, was leaning against the railing, her fat hips spilling over the top. She was talking to the priest from the church across the way. He felt excitement stir inside him. The priest's hands were bandaged and there was blood on the bandages.

The woman next door was standing on the lower step. She saw him first and she nudged Cora.

"Oh—" Cora stopped talking.

The silence alarmed him. "What's the matter?" he asked.

"There was a fire," Cora said.

He could see himself running up the dark narrow stairs. Even the hall was filled with the smell of dead smoke. The door of his apartment sagged on its hinges. He stepped inside and stood perfectly still, gasping for breath. There was nothing left but charred wood and ashes. The walls were gutted and blackened. That had been the radio, and there was a piece of what had been a chair. He walked into the bedroom. The bed was a twisted mass of metal. The spittoon had melted down. It was a black rim with a shapeless mass under it. Everywhere was the acrid, choking smell of burned wood.

He turned to find Cora watching him.

"The children—" he said, "and Lilly Belle—"

"Lilly Belle's all right," she said coldly. "The kids are at Harlem Hospital. They're all right. Lilly Belle wasn't home."

He could see himself run blindly down the stairs. He ran to the corner and in exciting agony to the Harlem Hospital. All the way to the hospital his feet kept saying, "Wasn't home." "Wasn't home." "Wasn't home."

They let him see the kids at the hospital. They were covered with clean white bandages, lying in narrow white cots.

First time they've ever been really clean, he thought bitterly. A crisp, starched nurse told him that they'd be all right.

"Where's the little one?" he asked. "Where's Eloise?"

The nurse's eyes widened. "Why, she's dead," she stammered.

"Where is she?"

He could see himself leaning over the small body in the morgue. He still had the oranges and the meat and the empty lunchbox in his arms. When he went back to the ward, Lilly Belle was there with the kids.

She was dressed in black. Black shoes and stockings and a long black veil that billowed around her when she moved. He was thinking about her black clothes so that he only half-heard her as she told him she'd just gone around the corner that morning, and that she'd expected to come right back.

"But I ran into Alice—and when I came back," she licked her lips as though they were suddenly dry.

He could see himself going to work. The next day and all the other days after that. Going to the hospital every day. Living in an apartment across the hall. The neighbors brought in furniture for them. He could hear the neighbors trying to console him.

He could see himself that very morning. He'd slept late because on Saturdays he went to work later than on other days. When he woke up he heard voices. And as he listened they came clear to his ears like a victrola record or the radio.

Cora was talking. "You ain't never been no damn good. And if you don't quit runnin' to that bar with that dressed up monkey and stayin' away from here all day long, I'm goin' to tell that poor fool you're married to where you were when your kid burned up in here." She said it fast as though she wanted to get it out before Lilly Belle could stop her. "You walkin' around in mournin' and everybody but him knows you locked them kids in here that day. They was locked in—"

Lilly Belle said something he couldn't hear. He heard Cora's heavy footsteps cross the kitchen. And then the door slammed.

He got out of bed very quietly. He could see himself as he walked barefooted across the room. The black veil was hanging over a chair. He ran it through his fingers. The soft stuff clung and caught on the rough places on his hands as though it were alive.

Lilly Belle was in the kitchen reading a newspaper. Her dark hands were silhouetted against its pink outside sheets. Her hair wasn't combed and she had her feet stuck in a pair of run-over mules. She barely glanced at him and then went on reading the paper.

He watched himself knot the black veil tightly around her throat. He pulled it harder and harder. Her lean body twitched two or three times and then it was very still. Standing there he could feel again the cold hard knot that formed inside him when he saw that she was dead.

If the siren would only stop. It was vibrating inside him—all the soft tissues in his stomach and in his lungs were moaning and shrieking with agony. The station trembled as the train approached. As it drew nearer and nearer the siren took on a new note—a louder sharper, sobbing sound. It was talking. "Locked in. They were locked in." "Smoke poisoning. Third degree burns." "Eloise? Why, she's dead." "My son, don't grieve. It will probably change your wife." "You know, they say the priest's hands were all bloody where he tried to break down the door." "My son, my son—"

The train was coasting towards the station. It was coming nearer and nearer. It seemed to be jumping up and down on the track. And as it thundered in, it took up the siren's moan. "They were locked in. They were locked in."

Just as it reached the edge of the platform, he jumped. The wheels ground his body into the gleaming silver of the tracks.

The air was filled with noise—the sound of the train and the wobble of the siren as it died away to a low moan. Even after the train stopped, there was a thin echo of the siren in the air. [*The Crisis* 50.12 (December 1943): 368–369]

HEART AGAINST THE WIND

by Gwendolyn Williams

No part of the day is more beautiful than the twilight with its faint tinge of gold left by the sun as it disappeared beyond the horizon. It brings a quietness that rests the very soul; it distills a gentleness upon the world that is the magic of dancing stars and another new moon.

Lys sat at her desk by the window and gazed raptly at the evening sky. It would be dark in another hour; then that lovely pale sky would become inky so that the stars would be as specks of glistening metal and the moon would be all silvery in her flight across the heavens. It would be dark, and she'd be alone again. Alone for how many more nights?

Lys's expression changed, and her eyes fell on the letter she had just written Stephen. Stephen! How glad she would be when he came home again. How different she hoped the word "home" would be then....

> Dearest Stephen
>
> How's everything with you? Where are you? Don't tell me; I know. You're far off in a strange land where you will see many wonderful things probably both beautiful and horrid, and I won't be there to share them all with you. You're sorry, aren't you? I wish I were there beside you wading through the mud or whatever it is you wade through at any time.
>
> I didn't write to say that though. I am writing to make an announcement; we are going to have a baby. I waited this long to tell you, because I had to be absolutely certain. And, Stephen, forgive me for being so cruel, but I don't want it. Doesn't that sound bad! You are shocked; I can see the sad shame for me creep into your eyes; then I see you catch your head with your hands as you number the reasons why I should be one of the happiest women in the world. Of course, I picture the whole thing.
>
> So much has happened to change me! You long to know why I don't want our child. First of all he has no heritage. Stephen, a heritage is more than an innate quality—it's a birthright. He has no birthright, he's a little black boy. He can be anything. A doctor, lawyer, business man, or even an actor or a preacher. He might be a teacher or pull people's teeth without giving them gas. But there are other things; those possibilities must run parallel with hate, prejudice, and any outrage that might occur. If all the unkindness in existence could be erased—
>
> Secondly, he has no country. No, don't take that literally. I suppose what I mean is does his country want him. His ancestor died with the scars of chains and whips upon them, but that was yesterday, and yesterday is dead. Today is important, Stephen. Through the years black men have proved themselves to the country, but the country ... to be honest, the people of the country have never thanked them for their faithfulness.

The oration at Gettysburg has lived through the ages as a masterpiece; yet those words delivered so hopefully have not had much meaning for the step-citizens of our country. Shall we listen to our son recite them some day? Of course! And he shall weep over their futility?

He shall grow up observing the fourth of July. Truly, we will never tell him that independence is a reality for some and a lie for others. No! We shall hang out the proud flag and pledge allegiance to it. Independence is freedom, so maybe by the time he is eighteen he will be free. A black boy's freedom is measured out by teaspoonfuls.

He shall swear by his constitutional rights. He can lick any man who dares him to board a trolley or demands that he sit in the back of a train. He shall spit in the face of fear and want; he shall worship as he chooses whom he chooses, and he shall say what he pleases to say and to the right people. I'm laughing, Stephen.

Gettysburg, July the Fourth, and constitutional rights are ashes. The people who read them have made them so. They have degraded the words associated with them so that they are destroyed surely as if lighted by a match. There was no speech, no declaration; the bill of rights is a hoax. Because it does not work both ways.

Stephen, why are you fighting? It boils down to the fact that you are on a foreign soil to free the enslaved peoples of a foreign land while at home they step in the faces of your brothers. A man can be murdered for no other reason than he is black. We are slaves of a modern age. Who will free us this time that there is no Lincoln and no states seceding from the Union? And we won't stoop to violence because we are a few. And we acknowledge the good privileges we have been permitted.

What difference does it make about the color of a man's skin? A man's a man in spite of that—with ambition, passion, and blood flowing in his veins. All men have a head with hair upon it until neglect or age eats away the roots; and eyes, a nose, a mouth; also every normal body is a trunk with the correct appendages attached. All men have that whether they are white, black, brown, red or foreign. Strip one at random and prove it for yourself.

And women. A woman is subject to the same dangers when she conceives a child and again when she is in labor in spite of her color. The babe in her womb is recipient of the same opportunities to be perfect or afflicted.

All men spring from the same source. Sure, and all men die. There is evidence that no man is superior to another; if he were, his progeny would inherit the earth, and he would be as God with life everlasting.

Oh, Stephen! I would rather destroy this child and go to hell than to deliver it into a world like this where those who cry democracy and are so prolix in their love of freedom are reeking with hypocrisy. He will have friends, our son, but he will also have foes. And, Stephen, could he fight them.

I'd rather he never know the anguish of being black, nor the pride—nor the injustice of being an unsung hero.

Tears stole down Lys's cheeks. She crushed the paper; it dropped short of the wastebasket and made a slight thud on the floor. There it lay until the wind, blowing in the open window, chased it into a corner.

Lys sighed. She lifted another mail form from the box, dipped her pen in the ink. She studied the blank paper for a while. She must write against the thoughts of her heart. Stephen had enough to go through without her writing a lot of foolishness over there to him.

But things were in such a muddle that they didn't even make horse sense. One way you looked at it, it was downright funny; here we are trying to help fight a war and promote a victory for freedom. How do you spell it! What does it mean! There are those who know; and still there are those who believe it is the state of being the boss of everything and everybody this side of tan. It's a lust for power, any kind of power, over the step-citizens of this country. It's the talking against Nazis, fascists, and all the other ists, isms, et cetera.

It will be, as it has been, a shame if a country whose people have sworn by Liberty fails to sponsor a fair play program after this great world struggle. How will they curb the laughter if they help to win a struggle for the freedoms of other peoples and changes its spots in the very places where they should not have been for bigger spots.

We all ought to begin now to count the differences that color established in some circles. If we did, Lys wondered, would we be honest enough to apologize for the instances where the prejudices were silly.

She began to laugh. It was absurd to realize that a country of such distinguished folks should sponsor a promulgation so like the one it was striving to liquidate. Democracy is an example of a serpent which gorged itself on a supposed prey and didn't find out till too late that it was eating its own tail.

Lives have been forfeited, liberty has been raped, and happiness has been pursued into the gutter.

Lys twisted a button and the room flooded with light, with the light came a fresh point of view, Stephen's point of view. We men will fight for what we have now, that's more than we have had before; it's worth something, but maybe we won't be wrong in expecting some more of that which we honestly deserve.

And there was Stephen, and all black people, in the room.

Her pen touched the paper.

> Dearest Stephen,
>   We are going to be the proud parents, within this year, of a very special citizen. Don't worry about me, everything is going swell.
>   I've waited so long to tell you because I had to get me straightened out on a few points which you can well guess.
>   All the folks say howdy and send best wishes for your continued safety...
>   Love, love, love,
>   Lys.   [*The Crisis* 51.1 (January 1944): 18, 26]

"WHATSOEVER THINGS ARE LOVELY"

by Florence McDowell

Saturday afternoon was on Seventh avenue. Lavinia Randall recognized the signs. Down on Eighth avenue she had done her marketing just as a shower was ending. Then, with her yams and corn-meal and pork-chops and coffee and okra, she had hurried through the narrow cross-street that was cluttered with children and crap-games. On Seventh avenue it was easier to move and breathe. And perhaps there she could find a clue or catch an idea for what she must soon be doing.

Surely there was more beauty on Seventh avenue than on any other street in Harlem. Where else could one feel the space that let her spread out inside? Where else could one see trees marching up the center? Her biology teacher had told her that they were Chinese plane trees. Lavinia liked the balls that hung like toy fruit or grace-notes after the leaves had given up, and she liked the rich brown and gray bark with its undergarment of cream and yellow.

If she were walking on Morningside avenue, she could get close to such trees and sniff the bitter, teasing odor of the bark while it was still wet from the rain. Now the leaves were new with May. Those Seventh avenue plane trees did bring something to Harlem—more than could have been foreseen when they were planted.

On this day there were always more people sauntering or loitering in clusters. The usual swarm was in front of the movie theatre. Barber shops and beauty parlors had plenty of customers. Lavinia had once written a theme on "kinks." It seemed queer that while hair was being uncurled down here, kinks should be crimped and set and baked just above Morningside Park—all at the same time, on Saturday afternoon.

She shied away from the pale, unwholesome man, like a potato-sprout, who was trying to sell "reefers" and from a pack of women and girls whose blatant slacks and suspenders matched their insolence and their insinuations.

It was a relief to look at some men in uniform. They knew how to carry themselves, these young Negroes, and there was dignity in their faces. Some day she'd like to marry a man like that and have four children. One would sing like Marian Anderson, one would be a doctor, one would build houses entirely unlike Harlem houses, and one would be a policeman who couldn't even think of letting graft come near him.

Here was a man dealing out handbills. She knew what they would contain—bait for the kind of Negroes who are so sick of all that is that they are ready to risk anything that isn't.

There, one block east, was the church that always made her look up. The steeple insisted that there was something above it. And, sure enough, although most of the sky was still clouded, over that steeple was a scrap of blue in which a gull was a white airplane.

Too soon she must turn off into her own dirty block. On the corner was the gang of slouching hoodlums who could snatch a handbag when they were not shooting craps—or making trouble in some other way. Only night before last they had beaten up a soldier who was walking through the block. He was still in the hospital with a fractured skull. One of the ruffians had said, "We ain' a goin' the have any eh them uniform squares a comin' aroun' here, 'cause if they do, then the girls they won' pay us no mind."

Stoops, steps, and pavement were covered with children of all sizes. Boys were playing "stick ball," and she had to dodge as she passed. Here were garbage cans still unemptied and piles of refuse that must wait until the unsoiled portions of the city could be regroomed.

Before going into her house, she would do what had been proved helpful. Tucking her bags under her arm, she took from her pocket a handkerchief and held it over her face. Never could she get used to the smell of that hallway and those stairs—a smell that was made up of so many bad smells that one tried not to inhale or think. She always went very fast up the steep steps and down the dark little corridor that led to her home.

Inside that door she would find cleanliness that had been won and kept, but at what a price! When they had first tried to reconcile themselves to that flat, they had agreed that they would stay only until they could get out of debt. That was just after her father had broken his leg, when her mother's wages in the millinery shop were all they had, for the slim insurance could not last long. Now that her father was back in his job on night shift, her mother was in the hospital mending after an operation. Lavinia had thought that she should seek work and gain her diploma in evening school, but both parents had said that since she was a senior, she must go on. They would wiggle through somehow, and some day they would be out of debt and away from smells. They had seen the model flats (*Paradise Found* they should be called). Some day...!

She would slip in quietly for her father was still sleeping. About four she would give him his dinner. Early that morning she had cleaned the bedroom so that it would be ready for him, and later she had cleaned the kitchen and the room that was living-room and din-ing-room for the family and bedroom for her. Tomorrow her mother would be coming home, and she would find things as she had left them, as decent as soap and water and disinfectants could make them.

But there was something to be done at once, and she must turn to her task. She must sit by the window and try to discover what she was almost sure was not there to be discovered.

She had been glad to remain in school for several reasons, but one of the weightiest was Miss Palmer, her English teacher. Miss Palmer was young and invigorating, with black hair that she didn't try to kink. Her blue eyes had lashes that were like black petals, and her skin was like the inside of the seashell that Lavinia had picked up on her one excursion to the sea. Miss Palmer rode horseback and played tennis when she could get away from English papers. Air from out-of-doors seemed to come in with her, to be a part of her. Being in her class meant more than learning punctuation and grammar or any facts. One felt that this person really lived, that she had roots through which she could draw what was needed for herself and others. And she gave it. She made Lavinia feel that life could be interesting and rewarding, even for a Negro girl in Harlem.

Miss Palmer had commended Lavinia's work and had told her that she had ability in writing. Several of her poems would be in the school magazine, and one of her stories was to be entered in a national contest for high school pupils. Some day she might write what many would read.

That night after that revelation, Lavinia had forgotten that her bed-spring sagged and squeaked and that neighbors were swearing and fighting. She had sat up in the bed and had written down in her notebook lines and thoughts that gurgled up. Seeing the light through the cracks about the door, her mother had come in with, "What's the matter, Honey? Can't you sleep?"

Lavinia had hesitated. Then she repeated Miss Palmer's words. The wonderful thing about having a real mother is that she can be told what one couldn't tell other people without sounding conceited. This mother had hugged her girl and had said, "Lavinia, if you can truly write some day, I'll be the proudest woman that ever tried to put a hat on anybody's head." They had laughed together, and then her mother had said, "Let's sing a little bit—just low—so we won't bother anyone. Then we can get to sleep. Don't forget that morning's just around the corner." And they had sung very softly "Goin' Home."

Now at her window she was trying to see what Miss Palmer had asked the class to see—something beautiful. "'Whatsoever things are lovely'—write about them." That was the assignment. But the lovely things were to be observed from one's own window. "No, this is not an exercise in truth-telling," Miss Palmer had explained, "but you will do better work if you stick to what you really see." And Lavinia would play the game if she could.

From their rear apartment she was gazing into the long, cramped area. If it were winter, there might be some hope, for when snow fell like popcorn, even that sordid spot had its brief moment of transfiguration.

She was looking out upon windows and fire-escapes that were jammed with everything that ought not to be in a window or on a fire-escape; mops, milk bottles, wads of clothing, beer-bottles, pails, tin cans, empty flower-crocks, dish-pans, cartons, old newspapers, brooms, shoes, pillows, police dogs, spoiled bedding, jars of food, an old mattress that told too much— the catalog might equal one of Walt Whitman's. Strutting back and forth were clothes-lines drooping under dejected garments that could furnish another weary review. All were limp, for they had been in two showers. The second was just ceasing. How could anyone wish clothing or bedding to be out in the rain?

Below on what should have been grass or cement, were mounds of rubbish and filth in which rats grew hardy and nourished fleas. Three live cats and one dead one were visible. Once a dead man had lain there for a whole morning. A list of what was down there would rival the recipe for the witches' brew in "Macbeth." Yes, and more was coming, for another installment of garbage was being thrown down. If only an ailanthus tree, the patron saint of city courtyards, had braved this wretched hole! But there was none. Where was loveliness? Could Miss Palmer or St. Paul, with his shining words, find it here?

And the sounds! Although the neighbors were not in evidence, their voices were. Voices that might have been like velvet, the heritage of the race, had lost their native quality and were shrill and raucous. Nagging, screaming and cursing, they banged against her ears, while dogs barked and babies cried. Enough of that!

Her father had told her that pitying oneself was like eating poison, but she did feel sorry for herself. Why did she have to live in such a place? Why did such squalor have to be? Why couldn't that area be cleaned up and kept clean? Why couldn't people who liked cleanliness and beauty live with flowers and sunshine and quiet? She was honestly trying to find one thing that was not unattractive or repellant, and she was losing.

She was about to give up. This would mean failure on Monday, but she couldn't help it. Then something happened.

The disgusting mattress was on the fire-escape across from Lavinia. In front of it protruded a piece of sheet iron that she had not noticed. Kerosene had been used liberally, and the iron had caught and retained some of it.

The kerosene was there because of a diseased mattress, but now it was associating with water brought by the showers and with the mystery of light rays. The result was a miracle—colors! There they were: clear violet and indigo; strange greens; gingerbread yellow and coppery orange; and, instead of triumphant red, purple and a darkened rose-violet. No, there were not the rainbow colors of the sky as Lavinia had once seen them, free, keen, and joyous. Here were deeper, mingled tones, for water and light had come down to earth.

[*The Crisis* 51.5 (May 1944): 160, 172]

At My Table

by Teresa O'Hiser

From far across the tideflats the noon whistles blew; the midday hum of traffic increased in the streets below. The pharmacist in the drug department set out her can of cinnamon. Before going to lunch she would burn the spice to clear the air of the heavy smell of sickness and poverty—of wrong diets, old clothes, unplumbed houses.

The clinic was almost emptied; only five remained of the "Thursday Morning Club"—as the nurses called the long rows of the anxious and the listless awaiting their "shots." Few other patients came on Thursday morning, and those who did sat apart, out of sight, beyond the turn n the long L-shaped waiting room. Not necessarily from squeamishness, but because the girl at the desk indicated, as she did now, "You may wait there, Mr. Clayton."

Mr. Clayton waited, his hand white-bandaged, only the long, curving flexible thumb, dark on top and white underneath, showing. He was a young Negro with deep-set eyes brilliantly dark, yet soft, and a full-featured gentle face. His brown shoes new-shined, his overalls clean and pale at the knees, he sat in the furthermost corner, his feet close together, like a man ready to be photographed. He held his bandaged hand carefully, and stared at the three pictures on the finger-smudged, off-white walls. Two were old-fashioned prints. One, lovers in Grecian attire at dalliance beside a reed-filled pond; the other, a misty Orpheus leading an equally misty Eurydice up out of the Land of the Shades. The third picture the boy looked at longest—a world-loved portrait hanging close to the door of the doctor's office. It worried him that the frame hung crookedly, but he was too shy to straighten it and sat where he was.

When an interne, white-clad, with a dark sharp face hurried into the drug department, the pharmacist whirled from her work among the labeled bottles. She was a plump, dark-haired girl.

"Oh, it's you, Dr. Friedman," she said. "Here's the capsules you wanted. Mildest we've got." She twinkled then, her cheeks dimpling. "And many happy returns on your birthday, child-prodigy, interne at twenty-two!"

He tweaked her nose, peered around the cubby-hole counter window to be sure that they were alone. Then seeing the boy in the far corner, he smiled and asked, "Wounded on the home front, buddy?"

The boy nodded. "First day on the job. Ah hurt the tip of mah finger and then later ah burned it—now ah've got a felon."

"A felon's about the most painful hurt there is. You seem to be a pretty good soldier."

"Not last night I wasn't. Last night ah nearly climbed the wall with pain. But no ah'm telling myself the pain is exquisite—simply exquisite!" The boy grinned, showing his white teeth back to the last molars—teeth as white as the unironed shirt he wore.

The interne laughed. "I've got a patient upstairs I'll have to tell that to!" Three hospital bells sounded, and he grabbed the little white box from the pharmacist. "That's the old coot now, I'll bet!"

Alone once more the boy got up and paced the floor, holding his bandaged hand and waving it with pain. Catching the curious eyes of the young pharmacist as she passed by her counter window, he sat down on a wicker settee close to the office door.

The door was lightly ajar and a voice sounded distinctly from the office within—a new patient giving an old case history.

"I know I shoulda come before," the man finished lamely. "But you know how them things are—the more serious, the more you put it off...."

The doctor's pen went on scratching. The patient scraped his throat. He hitched his chair. When he spoke his voice was high and ingratiating.

"We sure all enjoyed your talk, Doc, at the Union Meeting last Friday. I heard some of the guys talking about it afterward. "Yet, socialized medicine's all right, I say. Socialized everything's all right—as long as it don't go too far—"

The doctor's pen went on scratching. Wearly he asked, "and what do *you* think's too far?"

"Why—why—well, f'rinstance, we had a colored guy come into our union meeting— electrical union I belong to. The business agent, in a quiet way, so's not to attract too much attention, takes the dinge by the arm, and talkin' to him low, edges him out of the room.

Up pops one of them radical guys, rushes out, asks the dinge, "Say, buddy, what'er they tryin' to do to you anyway?"

"'I don't know,' the Negro says, 'seems the white folks don't want me to sit in their meeting. I paid my membership—I pay my dues.' And then that radical guy, you know the type, thin-faced, glasses, looks more like he oughto be in a college room than being just an electrician's helper, he rushed back in and says, maddern' any soap box agitator I ever heard, 'What's the matter with you guys I'd like to know! He's good enough to eat with. I see you sitting around and eating your lunch with him over there in the yard. I see you patting him on the back, laughing at his jokes. Why isn't he good enough to sit in here?'"

"We all look down our noses embarrassed as hell. Because it's true, doc, that particular dinge's likable as heck. But you know yourself, Doc, you've got to draw the line somewhere."

"Yes, Hitler draws it...." The doctor's pen scratched on.

"I don't know anything about him and the niggers ... don't think they've got them in Germany...."

"The Jews, I believe, he considers outside the white race...."

"W-e-ll, I'm not sticking up for Hitler by a long shot, but it seems to me he's got something there. We've got too many Jews in this country doing damage in the high places. Why, Morgan's father was a German Jew—Du Pont a Jew, and Roosevelt's name is really Rosenveld!"

"You're sure of all that? You know it sounds a little like Nazi propaganda you're so free with."

The man sputtered. He scraped his chair. "But ... but you can find that in the library."

"Did *you* find that in the library?"

"No—but—well, anyway I ain't really got anything against the Jews personally—"

"Against the Negroes?"

"I come from Missouri, Doc. Maybe you ain't never lived in the south and seen niggers like I've seen 'em. Got to be kept in their place. Filthy and dirty, niggers are. No, Siree, one ain't ever goin' to sit with me at my table!"

"Did you ever have a 'nigger' serve you food at your table?"

"Sure, on a train—"

"A filthy, dirty nigger?"

"Well, I guess they ain't all filthy and dirty. There's niggers and niggers. The educated ones is all right, but too many of them ain't educated."

A chair scraped again, feet moved. "Well, I guess I've done a lot of talkin', Doc," the worker said lustily, "but you can take my word for it I'm workin' like the very devil, swing-shift, seven days a week—Sundays, holidays and all, buildin' ships to beat hell out of Hitler!"

"The door to the left across the hall for your shot. I don't think the nurse has left yet," the doctor said. "No, this other door out."

The young Negro sat with his bandaged hand between his knees. He slowly raised his eyes from the pair of broken shoes, with knotted shoestrings, shuffling through the doorway, from the bagging trousers, the stomach that hung out over the belt, straining the buttons of the greasy blue shirt. The man's face, heavy with pink, hanging down flesh, was unshaven, his nose pocked with blackheads. His red-rimmed eyes were blue and watery. He had teeth only on one side....

[*The Crisis* 52.1 (January 1945): 13, 29]

OLAF AND HIS GIRL FRIEND

by Ann Petry

This is Olaf's story. I don't pretend to know all of it. I saw parts of it that happened on the dock in Bridgetown, Barbados. And I saw the ending of the story in New York. The rest of it I had to piece together from the things that Olaf's friends told me. As a result I think I'm the only person who actually knows why a pretty little West Indian dancer disappeared very suddenly from the New York nightclub where she sang calypso songs and danced *la conga* and the *beguine*. She was beginning to make the place famous. And she vanished.

It's only if you know Olaf's story that you can understand her disappearance. He was a great big black guy who worked on the docks in Bridgetown. Some two hundred and twenty pounds of muscle and six feet of height. I liked to watch him work. The way his muscles rippled under his skin as he lifted boxes and bags fascinated me. They were those long, smooth muscles you find in perfectly trained athletes.

When the sun shone on him it caught high lights in his skin, so that he looked like an ebony man. I soon discovered that there was a slender native girl who found him even more interesting to watch than I did. I only wanted to paint him against the green water of Carlisle bay. She wanted to marry him.

Her name was Belle Rose. She had that sinuous kind of grace that suggests the born dancer. When she walked she swayed a little as though she were keeping time to a rumba that played somewhere inside her head.

She used to show up at noon time, two or three days a week. She'd sit by him while he ate his lunch. They talked and laughed about nothing at all. His great laugh would boom out the length of the dock and the other dock hands would grin because they couldn't help it.

"Olaf's girl's here," they said.

She couldn't have been more than seventeen years old. The dock boys used to look at her out of the corner of their eyes and flash their white teeth at her but it seemed to be pretty well accepted that she was Olaf's girl.

It was nearly a month before thing's started going wrong. One day I heard a lot of noise at one end of the dock. I welcomed the interruption for I'd been trying to paint the bay and I was filled with a sense of despair of ever getting that incredible green on canvas. So I left my easel to investigate.

Olaf's girl was standing sort of huddled up. All the laughter gone out of her. She was holding her face as though it hurt. A short, stumpy, dark brown woman was facing Olaf a little way off from the girl.

The woman was neatly dressed even to the inevitable umbrella that the upper class island women carry and she looked for all the world like a bantam rooster. She had one hand on her hip and with the other hand she was gesticulating with the raised umbrella while she berated Olaf in a high, shrill voice.

"I tell you I won't have you seeing her. She's too good for your kind. Belle Rose will marry a teacher," she shook the umbrella under his very nose.

He looked like an abashed great dane. But he stood his ground.

"I do no harm. I love her. I want to marry her."

And that set the old girl off again. "Marry her? You?" she choked on the words. "You think you'll marry her? I'll have you locked up. I'll—" she was overcome with sheer rage.

"I'm honest. I love her. I think she's beautiful. I wouldn't harm her," he pleaded.

She shook her head violently and went off muttering that Belle Rose's father had been a school teacher and Belle Rose wasn't going to marry any dock hand. Her umbrella was still quivering as she hurried away holding the girl firmly by the arm.

She turned around when she was half the length of the dock. "Besides you're a coward. Everybody knows you're scared of the water. Belle Rose will never marry a coward."

Olaf followed them. I don't know how that particular episode ended. But I was curious about him and questioned the dock hands. They told me his father had been a sailor and his grandfather before him. Olaf should have been a sailor but his mother brought him up to be afraid of the water. It seems his father went down with a ship during a violent storm.

Shortly after I learned about Olaf's fear of the sea, he slipped on the dock and went head first into the bay. He managed to stay afloat until the boys fished him out but he was obviously half dead from fright. It was a week before he came back to work.

"You all right, mahn?" the boys asked.

Olaf nodded and kept any feeling he had about it to himself.

It was only because he loved Belle Rose that he came back to work. I overheard them talking about it. They were sitting on the edge of the dock. It seemed to me they were the most paintable pair I'd ever seen. He was stripped to the waist because he'd been working. His wide, cream colored straw hat and faded blue dungarees were a perfect foil for the starched white of her dress and the brilliant red of the turban wound so deftly around her head.

"And we'll have a house not too near the sea," she said in a very soft voice.

"Yes. Not too near the sea," was his answer. "It'll be just near enough to watch the sun on the water in the bay."

"Olaf, you don't like this job. Do you?" she asked.

"Only for you. I like it for you. It means we can get married soon. That's why I came back to work."

I walked away and I asked the boys what became of Olaf's girl friend's aunt. Had she decided they could get married after all? The boys looked sheepish.

"They will have big wedding. Olaf goes every Sunday now to call on Belle Rose. All dressed up in scissors tail coat. With stiff collar. Olaf takes the aunt plantains every Sunday. I don't think she change her mind. Olaf just too big. And she got no man to deal with him," was the answer.

The boys were right in one respect. The marriage banns were posted. But it wasn't to be the big church wedding Belle Rose's aunt had set her heart on. Olaf threatened to elope unless it was a small wedding. And auntie gave in gracefully. I wondered about that. She seemed a domineering kind of old girl to agree to a small wedding when she wanted a large one. The more I thought about it the queerer it seemed that she should have consented to any kind of wedding.

The dock crew quits about five o'clock in Bridgetown. The day I discovered that the girl's aunt had no intentions of allowing any kind of marriage, a big American merchant ship had been loaded with fruit. She was due to sail at seven o'clock. On that particular day Belle Rose's aunt set Olaf on an errand that took him half way across the island.

I went down to watch the passengers clamber aboard the launch. There were a lot of native women at the dock. They were seeing a couple of passengers off. You could hear their goodbyes and messages half way across the bay.

I stared in amazement. It was Belle Rose and her aunt who were going away. The aunt all officious and confidential at the same time. Ordering Belle Rose to do this and did she have that and where was the small bag. She was fairly bursting with importance.

"My boy in New York sent me the money. The passage fare for both of us," she explained loudly for the benefit of a late comer.

"Belle Rose, do you think you'll like it?" asked one of the younger women.

The aunt didn't give the girl time to answer. "Of course she will," she said firmly. "She's never been off the island. She wants to see the world a bit. Don't you, dear?"

Belle Rose nodded. "Yes, I do. But I wish I could have said good-bye to Olaf. And I did want to stay near him," her voice was wistful.

"You can write to him. You'll see him soon. After all he can come and see you, you know," and with that she hurried the girl into the steamer's launch. She leaned over to whisper to an older woman, "You know it aren't as though he were fit for her," and then turned her attention back to the girl and their bags.

I stood on the deck until the ship had become a mere speck in the distance. New York was a long ways away. A dock hand could hardly hope to get there in a life time. And though the old woman had counted on that, she deliberately sold that girl the idea that New York was some place just around the corner and practically suggested that Olaf could commute back and forth to see her.

I felt like calling the ship back. Because if ever a man loved a woman that man was Olaf and the woman was Belle Rose. He stopped laughing after he discovered the girl was gone. He got very quiet. It wasn't that he brooded or was sullen. He was just quiet and he worked with a grim determination.

When he got letters from her he seemed to come alive again. And I could tell when ever he'd received one. Then the letters stopped coming. I asked him about it. "Have you heard from your girl?"

"No. Not lately. I don't understand it," he said.

A whole year crept around. A year that brought the war a little closer to us. A year in which his letters kept coming back marked, "Moved. Left no address." A year in which the native women came down to the dock to look coyly at Olaf. They walked past him and flirted with him. He ignored them.

I found out later that Belle Rose never received the letters that he wrote her. Auntie saw to that. Finally she intercepted the letters that Belle Rose wrote to him. And then, of course, they moved and auntie gave the post office no forwarding address.

One day out of a clear sky, Olaf signed up on a ship. Olaf who was so afraid of the sea that when he looked out over the bay his eyes would go dead and blank. Loaf who worked with one eye on the sky when the storms came up suddenly. He signed on one of those gray, raffish looking ships that were forever limping into port and disgorging crews of unshaven, desperate looking men. Olaf, who hated the sea, signed on a merchant ship.

It was a long time before I found out how it happened. It seems that he got a message. These day s people talk about the underground of the little people in the conquered countries of Europe. But there's always been an underground that could send a message half way round the world.

It happened in Olaf's case. The message travelled in the mouths of ship's stewards and mess boys. It took a good six months for Olaf to get it.

The first boat with the message on it left New York and went to Liverpool. And then to northern Africa. She bummed half way around the world—speaking from one port to another carrying guns and men and God knows what. And Olaf's message. And everywhere she went the message was transferred to other ships and other men.

The steward on a boat that lumbered back and forth across the Atlantic helped relay it—"tell Olaf"—. The message went to India and the messmen on an English ship learned about it.

Finally it got to Olaf. It was a little, excitable man with just two hours leave who delivered it to him on the dock.

"Belle Rose is dancing in New York in a place that is not good. Not by 'alf. Elmer and Franklin and Stoner sent back word to you. They work in that same place. She dances. And it is not a good dance."

The word had come such a long way and had been such a long time getting to its destination that the little man was breathless from the sheer weight of it. He'd learned it from two sailors in an infamous house on the edge of the water front in Liverpool. His beard fairly quivered with the excitement of it.

"Did you hear me, Olaf?" he asked sharply as though his voice would bring a reaction. "It is not a good dance."

Olaf stared out at the sea. It was a long time before he spoke. "I heard. Yes," he said slowly. "I heard. I will take care of it."

And he walked off the dock and signed up on the same ship that had brought the little man with the message. Just like that. The man who was afraid of the sea signed up on a ship.

I learned afterwards that he worked in the ship's galley—washing dishes and helping with the cooking. He was very quiet. His quietness permeated the stuffy bunk rooms. It made the men uneasy even when they were shooting craps or singing, or just talking.

He was always in the bunk when he wasn't working. He lay there staring up at the ceiling with an unwinking gaze.

"S'matter with the big guy?" the mate asked nervously. "Guys like that bring bad luck."

"Just quiet," was the usual apologetic answer of the little man who was responsible for Olaf's being aboard.

Olaf hadn't even bothered to find out what port they were heading for. When they docked on a cold, wet night he asked a question for the first time. "New York?"

"This England, mahn," was the answer. "Liverpool."

But they headed for New York on the return trip. If Olaf thought about the danger of the queer, crazy voyage he didn't show it. He was on deck hours before the boat docked, peering into the dark. He would start his search now. At once. In a few minutes.

He asked a black man on the dock, "You know a girl named Belle Rose?"

The man shook his head. "Bud, there's a lot of women here. All kinds of people. You won't find no woman that way. What she look like?" And then he added, "Where does she live?"

"Like—like—" Olaf fumbled for words, his throat working, "like the sun. She's so high," he indicated a spot on his chest. "She's warm like the sun—" his voice broke. "I don't know where she lives."

The man stared at him. "What's your name? Where you from?"

"The Islands. Barbados. To the South. My name is Olaf," and then his voice grew soft as he said again, "Her name is Belle Rose." He seemed to linger over her name.

"Naw," the man returned to his work, "you won't find her, Bud, just knowin' her name."

They were in port just two hours and they were gone again. But the underground had the message. "Olaf from Barbados is looking for Belle Rose."

The dock worker told a friend and the story went into the kitchens, and the freight elevators of great hotels. Doormen knew it and cooks and waiters. It travelled all the way from the water front to Harlem. People who'd never heard of Belle Rose knew that a man named Olaf was looking for her.

The cook in a nightclub told three West Indian drummers who were part of the floor show. Elmer, Franklin and Stoner looked at each other and gesticulated despairingly when they heard it. A message started back to Olaf. It took a long time. Olaf saw the edge of Africa and a port in Australia and Liverpool again before the message reached him.

His silence had grown ominous, portentous. The men never spoke to him. They left him alone—completely alone. They shivered a little when they looked at him.

One of the crew picked the message up in Liverpool and brought it to him. "The name of the place where Belle Rose dances is the Conga."

Olaf went to the mate when he heard it and asked when they'd dock in New York again. The mate stared at him, "I don't know. I never know where we're goin' until we're under way. You got some reason for wantin' to go to New York?"

"Yes. I have to find a girl there," Olaf looked past the man as he spoke.

"You? A girl?" the mate couldn't conceal his amazement. "I didn't know you were interested in girls."

But Olaf had turned away to watch the ship being loaded. They left Liverpool that same night. It was a bad voyage. Stormy and cold. With high seas.

They docked in New York early on a cold bitter morning. They were paid off for the Atlantic voyage and given two days shore leave. The crew disappeared like magic. Only Olaf was left behind.

He asked a policeman on the dock, "Where do black people lie in this place?" he gestured toward the city.

"You better take a taxi, boy. Tell the driver you want the YMCA on 135th Street between Lenox and Seventh Avenue. In Harlem."

The man wrote it down for him on the back of an envelope. Olaf looked at the paper frequently while the cab crawled through a city that looked half dead. It was shrouded in gray. It was cold. There were no lights in the buildings and few people on the streets. They snaked their way between tall buildings, over cobble-stoned streets, long miles of highway that ran for awhile along the edge of the river. It was getting lighter and he became aware that all the people on the streets through which they were passing were dark.

He relaxed a little. He was getting near the end of his long journey. "All this place—is all this place New York?" he indicated the sidewalk.

The driver studied him in the mirror and nodded, "Yeah. All of it's New York. Where you from?"

"Barbados," Olaf said simply. He was wondering what could have happened to Belle Rose in the Place. And where would he find her?

It was the first thing he asked the man behind the wicket when he paid for his room at the 'Y.'

"I wouldn't know anybody with a name like that," the man said coldly.

"Where is the place called the Conga?" Olaf asked.

"I never heard of it," the man shoved a receipt towards him. "Take the elevator to the fifth floor. Your room is number 563. Next please."

But the elevator man had heard about the Conga. He told Olaf how to get there. Even told him that eleven o'clock at night was the best time to visit it.

Olaf sat in his room—waiting. He was like a man that had been running in a cross country race and realizes suddenly that the finish line is just a little ways ahead because he can see it.

At eleven o'clock he was in a taxi, on his way to the Conga. The taxi went swiftly.

It was the expression in his eyes that made the doorman at the place try to stop him from going in. He tried to block his way and Olaf brushed him aside, lightly, effortlessly, as though he'd been a fly.

Once inside he was a little confused. There was smoke, and the lights were dim. People were laughing and talking; their voices blurred and loud from liquor. He walked to a table right at the edge of the space used for dancing. A protesting waiter hurried towards him, pointed at the reserved sign on the table. Olaf looked at him and put the sign on the floor. The waiter backed away and didn't return.

I recognized him when he sat down. He folded his arms on the table and sat there perfectly indifferent to the looks and the whispered conversations around him.

I used to go up to the Conga rather often. Barney, the guy who runs it was a friend of mine. He told me a long time ago that all the dance lovers in town were flocking into his place because of young West Indian girl who did some extraordinary dancing. Barney knew I'd lived in the Islands and he thought I'd be interested.

I was more than interested for the girl, of course, was Belle Rose. After the first visit I became a regular customer because I figured that sooner or later Olaf would show up. I wanted to be there when he arrived. The gods were kind to me. As I said before, I saw him when he came in and sat down.

He'd completely lost that friendly look he'd had. He was a dangerous man. It was in his eyes, in the way he carried his head. It was in his tightly closed mouth. A mouth that looked as though laughter were a stranger that had never passed that way. All of the humor had gone out of him. He was like an elastic band that had been stretched too far.

The lights went down and the three West Indian drummers came in—Elmer, and Franklin and Stoner. They filed in carrying the native drums that they played. Drums made of hollowed logs with hide stretched across them. They sat astride them the way the natives do—and drummed.

I couldn't swear to it that they'd actually seen Olaf. After all if you play in one of those places long enough, I imagine you get to know the tricks of lighting and you can see everybody in the place. And yet I don't know. Mebee they had some kind of umpteenth sense. Perhaps they felt some difference in the atmosphere.

When they stared to drum it was—well, different. The tempo was faster and there was something subtly alarming about it. It ran through the audience. Men tapped ashes off their cigarettes—and there wasn't any ash there. Women shivered from a draft that didn't exist. The waiters moved ash trays and bottles for no reason at all. The headwaiter kept shooting his shirt cuffs and fingering around the edge of his collar.

Belle Rose came on suddenly. One moment she wasn't there. And the next moment she was bowing to the audience. I wonder if I can make you see her. Half of New York used to go to that dinky little club just to watch her dance. She was a deep reddish brown color and very slender. Her eyes were magnificent. They were black and very large and a curious lack of expression. There's an old obeah woman in Barbados with those same strange eyes.

I think I said that Barney Jones was a showman. He'd gotten her up so that she looked ·like some gorgeous tropical bird—all life, and color and motion.

She danced in her bare feet. There was a gold anklet around one ankle and a high gold collar around her neck that almost touched her ear lobes. The dress she wore was made of calico and it had a bustle in the back so that every time she moved the red calico flirted with her audience. She had on what looked to be yards of ruffled petticoats. They were starched so stiffly that the dress stood out and the white ruffling showed from underneath the dress. A towering red turban covered her hair completely. There were flowers and fruit and wheat stuck in the turban.

She sang a calypso number first. Something about marrying a woman uglier than you. The nightclub was very quiet. Somebody knocked over a glass and giggled in a high, hysterical fashion. There was a queer stillness afterwards.

I looked at Olaf. He wasn't moving at all. He was staring at Belle Rose. His hands were flat on the table. He looked as though he might spring at any moment. The reflection from the spotlight shone on the beads of sweat on his forehead.

And I thought of that other time when I used to see him, laughing on the dock at Bridgetown with the sun shining on him. Now he was in a nightclub in a cold, alien city watching the girl he had intended to marry. He'd come a long, long way.

The applause that greeted that first number of hers was terrific. She bowed and said, "I weel now do for you the obeahwoman."

Olaf stiffened. His eyes narrowed. The drums started again. And this time I tell you they talked as plainly as though they were alive. Human. They talked danger. They talked hate. They snarled and they sent a chill down my spine. The back of my neck felt cold and I found I was clutching my glass so tightly that my hand hurt.

Belle Rose crouched and walked forward and started singing. It was an incantation to some far off evil gods. It didn't belong in New York. It didn't belong in any nightclub that has ever existed anywhere under the sun.

"Ah, you get your man," and then the drums. Boom. Boom. "Ah, you want a lover." Boom. Boom. Boom-de-de-boom. "Ah, I see the speer-et." And the drums again. Louder.

And she walked towards Olaf. She was standing directly in front of him. Hands outstretched. Eyes half shut. Swaying. She stopped singing and the drums kept up their message; their repeated, nerve racking message. The faces of the drummers were perfectly expressionless. Only their eyes were alive—glittering. Eyes that seemed to have a separate life from their faces.

Belle Rose went on dancing. It's a dance I've never seen done before in a nightclub. It was the devil dance—a dance that's used to exorcise an evil spirit. I don't know exactly what effect it had on Olaf. I could only conjecture. I knew he'd been on boats and ships for months trying to reach New York. The West Indian drummers told me.

He'd been tasting the salt air of the sea. Seeing nothing but water. Gone to sleep at night hearing it slap against the ship. Listened to it cascade over the decks when the seas were high. Even in port it was always there, moving against the sides of the ship.

And he hated the sea. He was afraid of it. He must have gone through hell during those months. Always that craven gnawing fear in the pit of his stomach. Always surrounded by the sea that he loathed.

And then he sees Belle Rose. She's completely unaware of him and more beautiful than ever. With artificial red on her lips and a caste mark between her eyes.

I said Barney was a showman. I suppose he thought it made the girl more exotic. As a final touch he's had a caste mark pointed on her forehead. It was done with something shiny. It may only have been a bit of tinsel—but it caught the light and glowed every time she moved.

I heard Olaf growl deep in his throat when he saw it. He'd been completely silent before. He stood up. All muscle. All brawn. All dangerous, lonely, desperate strength. He walked over the railing. Just stepped over it as though it wasn't there. And confronted her. He had a knife in his hand. I could swear, now, to this day, that he meant to kill her.

She kept right on dancing. She moved nearer to him. I say again that he meant to kill her. And I say, too, that she knew it. And she reached back into that ancient, complicated African past that belonged to both of them and invoked all the gods she knew or that she'd ever heard of.

The drums stopped. Everything had stopped. There wasn't so much as a glass clinking or the sound of a cork pulled. It seemed to me that I had stopped breathing and that no one in the place was breathing. She began to sing in a high, shrill voice. I couldn't understand any of the words. It was the same kind of chant that a witch doctor uses when he casts a spell; the same one that the conjure women use and the obeah women.

Her voice stopped suddenly. They must have stared at each other for all of five minutes. The knife slipped out of his hand. Clinked on the floor. Suddenly he reached out and grabbed her and shook her like a dog would shake a kitten. She didn't say anything. Neither did he. And then she was in his arms and he was kissing her and putting his very heart into it.

They walked hand and hand the length of the room and out through the street door. A sigh ran round the tables.

I think Barney, the guy who owns the joint, came to first. He ran after them. And I followed him. When I reached the street he was standing at the curb raving, frothing at the mouth as he watched his biggest drawing card disappear up the street in a taxi. I could just see the red tail light turn the corner.

"That black baboon," Barney fumed. "Where in the hell did he come from?"

I started laughing and that seemed to infuriate him even more. Finally I said, "Barbados. Where Belle Rose came from. It took a long time for him to find her but I'll guarantee New York will never see her again."

I was right. She disappeared. With Olaf. I worried Elmer and Franklin and Stoner until I finally heard that they were back in Bridgetown.

You can have your choice as to why Olaf didn't kill her that night in the Conga. I like to think that when he got that close to her he remembered that he loved her and that he'd gone through hell to find her. And all he wanted was to hold her tight in his arms. After all she was very beautiful.

On the other hand, though Belle Rose's father may have been a school teacher, her grandmother was an obeah woman.

[*The Crisis* 52.5 (May 1945): 135–137, 147]

THE BLACK STREAK

by Octavia B. Wynbush

"And you won't go, mother?"

Lucia Manton leaned eagerly forward from the cushions on the long, rust-colored divan and stared hard and expectantly at the slight, brown-haired woman standing across the room, framed in the exquisite lace curtains through which the late afternoon sun, streaming in, illuminated the woman's lovely profile.

The beautifully cared-for hand grasping one edge of the curtain tightened; the face turned more resolutely toward the window as Marianna Manton shook her sleekly-groomed head a determined no.

"Mother, you're wrong, so very wrong!"

Springing from the divan, Lucia moved in graceful slenderness across the thickly padded Oriental rug, and stood beside her mother. Gently the girl covered the hand on the curtain with her own.

"Don't try to persuade me!"

Marianna's hand slid down from the curtain, found its mate, and twined with it tightly. She turned her face fully to the window. Through a blur of quick tears, her eyes fixed on what hung before her.

Drawing back the curtain, Lucia stepped closer to her mother, then let the curtain fall into place, so that they were both framed within its folds. Her eyes, too, rested on the emblem hanging in the window.

For two years it had hung there, a blue star, bravely saying, "He will come back some day." A month ago yesterday, it had changed to gold.

"Grant would want you to go, mother."

The last slanting rays of the sun, gold-sparkling her brown hair, caught the frown that wrinkled Marianna's high, fair forehead; scintillated the icy fire that flared quickly in her gray eyes, and splashed more deeply the sudden red which encarmined her cheeks.

"Don't say that!" she rasped.

Lucia sighed. A more tactful daughter would have known how to handle this difficult mother. But Lucia had never been known for tact.

"You know he would, mother."

There was no gentle, tactful persuasion in the girl's tone. Her words rang with a passionateness which, although controlled, was plainly evident.

Marianna's brow straightened; the icy fire flickered out before astonishment, and the crimson faded from her cheeks. Really, this could not be her daughter, Lucia, speaking in such a tone to her. Tactless, Lucia always had been, but quiet and deferentially worshipful, at all times; always seeing eye to eye with her parents—after a little persuasion.

Disengaging her hands from her daughter's Marianna pushed aside the curtains and, with all the stateliness her five feet four inches could command, she stalked across the dim room to the long, wide mahogany desk that occupied much of the center floor space. Flicking on the fluorescent desk lamp, she slipped into the desk chair, and began nervously thumbing through a neat pile of typed manuscript.

Slowly Lucia followed her mother. Perching herself on the opposite side of the desk, she rested one foot on the floor and began swinging the other deliberately back and forth. What she had to say did not come readily, and her mother was giving her no co-operation whatever.

"You see, mother, it's getting awfully awkward for me."

"And why should it be getting awkward for you?" petulantly snapped Marianna, as she snatched a disarranged sheet of the manuscript back into place. She did not, however, look up at Lucia.

"Well, the kids at school are saying things."

"What things?"

"Oh—things. Innuendoes, I guess you'd call them, if older, more refined people said them, but the kids at High aren't very old and they're not very refined. They just crash things down on your head—like—like—"

"Yes?"

This time Marianna looked up, as Lucia's sentence faded into the stillness of the room.

"I didn't mean to go at it like this, mother, but today one of the girls at the table where I sat in the cafeteria spoke up and said that she thought it a shame when the whole world is fighting for democracy that some people right here in Homeville were so darn color-crazy they couldn't forgive a black girl for marrying into their family, even—even—after her husband had been killed."

"She said that to you?" Marianna's voice seemed thin and far away.

"Not *to* me, mother, but *at* me. When I got up and left, she pretended that she didn't know I was at the table, but everybody there knew better. Everybody knew she meant us, because—because Sylphania's the only—dark girl, and Grant's the only—"

Lucia's voice choked, and her sentence remained suspended.

With one delicate hand, Marianna waved the incident away—completely away. As her hand moved in the graceful arc of the gesture, it passed through the light cast by the desk lamp. How beautiful my hand is, thought Marianna, gazing for an enraptured second at that member, and how fair. How very transparent it is, in this light.

"Don't let those ignorant children at High worry you, Lucia. I'm sorry that you have to be thrown with them, but it's your father's idea, not mine, that you go to public school. If I had my way, you'd be in a good boarding school."

Leaning forward, Marianna lifted her pen from its bronze stand, and held it tentatively over the first page of the manuscript.

"Now, run along like a good, dear child. I must finish proofing my speech. You know, I have to deliver it before the Interracial committee tomorrow night."

Lucia smiled—a sour, comprehending smile. Such an old dodge! Didn't her mother know that she couldn't work it forever on a sixteen-year-old miss? And, too, the speech had been proofed three days ago, and she, Lucia, had helped with the proofing.

"I'm not going, mother, until we talk this thing through."

Marianna stretched out her hand to put the pen back into place. Her eyes fixed on Lucia, she missed the stand twice before the pen was safely lodged. If ten years could miraculously disappear, she would put this fractious youngster across her knee, and settle the argument with a well-placed slipper.

"Just what is there to talk about? I've said my say."

"After all, mother, Sylphania is Grant's wife, and Grant's your son, and my brother. I say *is*, because, to me, his being dead doesn't change the relationship. And Sylphania's still his wife."

A bitter smile writhed the corners of Marianna's mouth. She would never forget the resentment which had run through her deepest grief like a discordant note; resentment over the fact that it was through a telephone message from the father of her son's wife that she had learned of the boy's death. The circumstance had served to impress the one fact that she was trying so hard to erase. That Grant had married this black girl. Marianna propped her elbows on the desk, twined her fingers together, and pressed them against her forehead.

Slowly Lucia moved a hand over the highly-waxed surface of the desk. As her hand came within the glow of the light, she involuntarily compared it with her mother's hands, twined so tightly together. Marianna's hands were alabaster; Lucia's a warm ivory with the soft patina of age.

"You shouldn't hate Silly and her people, mother, just because they're black."

"I don't hate them. It's—it's just—"

Marianna's voice trailed off. Her hands gestured vaguely.

Lucia swung herself down from the desk and faced her mother. The sudden movement forced Marianna to look up.

How like her father the girl looks now, thought the mother. The way her hair grows in a widow's peak from her slightly rounding forehead, with its vertical wrinkle; the black eyes aflame with inward lightning; the slightly flaring nostrils quivering with emotional stress; the firm, slightly square chin thrust out just now in unfamiliar defiance, makes her look more like her father than ever.

"Look, mother!" Lucia's little fist beat the desk. "All that was good in your day—I guess—when you were growing up, I mean. Color must have been about all there was to make a distinction, wasn't there? I'm just guessing, you know. I mean—it must have been that the people who had the best chance got it because of color—Oh, I don't know what made it that way here, in Homeville."

Lucia paused, hoping that her mother would help her, but Marianna merely regarded the girl with hard, unfriendly eyes.

Lucia stumbled on, "I recall hearing Aunt Carlotta boast, when I was little, that all the 'elite' could trace their ancestry back to some of the best—white folks—in the state. That must be why we considered ourselves so much better than the dark colored people—being able to wear the bar sinister."

"Lucia, I never thought I would live to hear my own daughter talk in such a vulgar manner!"

"I'm not being vulgar. I'm just talking the way everything is done nowadays. Straight and plain. I think it's downright shameful the way this family has behaved to Silly and her folks. When the whole world's talking about democracy."

"Democracy! If democracy means I have to wallow with all sorts of people because I am unfortunate enough to have, somewhere, a black ancestor—"

"Being nice to Silly's folks is not wallowing, mother! They're respectable and well-thought-of."

"Silly! Such a common, made-up name. Her real name is bad enough, but a nick-name like Silly!"

"Grant liked it. In fact, he gave it to her."

Lucia's voice lowered to its usual cultivated pitch; her lips trembled, as she added, "and he would have adored Grant, junior, I'm sure."

Marianna looked sharply at Lucia. "Have you seen—the baby?" she demanded.

"Only at a distance. I've never been to the house, because you told me not to go."

Marianna nodded, a smugly complacent nod. Lucia was still her obedient, unquestioning child.

"The day I saw Sylphania," Lucia went on, "she was coming down Main street, with the baby in her arms. When she got sight of me she turned into Rosewell's store. I feel sure she did so just to avoid meeting me. And now, the baby is sick."

Marianna stirred uncomfortably. Lucia was back where she had started. It was the news of the baby's illness, conveyed to her by one of her high school friends, which had begun this argument.

"It's nothing serious, I'm sure," Marianna said. "All babies get sick some time."

"Helen said he's pretty sick, mother. Even if he weren't sick, we ought to go call on his mother, especially since he's all we've got to remind us of Grant. It's the only decent thing to do, don't you think?"

The jangling of the telephone bell in the hall cut off any reply that Marianna might have made.

"Answer it, please, Lucia. Katie doesn't like to be interrupted when dinner is so nearly ready, and I'm quite fatigued, myself."

Marianna's face took on that peaked, exhausted look which usually brought her family to her feet.

Lucia slipped swiftly into the hall. Marianna sighed and sat back in her chair. Closing her eyes, she gave herself over to her thoughts.

Words of her quadroon mother came floating back over the still years. "Keep 'em on their own side of the fence, girls. If you once let the bars down, you can't put 'em back up again. You can't rub a black streak out, and we don't want any more great-grandmother Janes in this family."

Great-grandmother Jane, the bête noir of the family; great-grandfather Hugh's black African wife. Marianna had never seen her, but she had often shuddered at the vivid description given by her own mother. Every generation, since great-grandmother Jane's day, had feared the black streak that might, at any time, show up in some child.

Sister Carlotta had borne no children, because of her mortal fear of the streak. Toni, brother John's third child, possessing the most beautiful features and the loveliest hair that had ever been known in the family, was a constant problem to the others. She could never accompany her parents, or her brothers and sisters on any of their excursions to theatres, restaurants, or other places where a dark skin would not be countenanced. Lucia, herself, had barely escaped. There had been no more children for Marianna after Lucia. The risk was too great. And Sylphania, Grant's widow, had brothers. Lucia must be protected. The bars must be kept up.

"Mother, you haven't heard a word that I've said!"

With a quick jerk of her shoulder muscles, Marianna returned to consciousness of her surroundings.

"What is it?" She queried, looking up.

"The telephone, mother."

"Oh, yes." Marianna started to rise. "Who wants me?"

"Nobody? Then why interrupt me?"

"Helen just telephoned to say that the baby died a few minutes ago."

Frozen into a half-sitting, half-standing position, Marianna stared at Lucia, down whose cheeks a rivulet of tears were coursing.

"Surely you'll go now, mother?"

Keep the bars up—once they are down—the black streak—Sylphania's brothers—Grant gone—Lucia lone left.

"No!"

"Mother!"

With an angry twirl of her short skirt, Lucia swung around and started for the hall door. Marianna sprang up.

"Lucia!" she cried, amazement, anger and authority struggling for mastery in her voice. "Lucia, come back here!"

The answer came in a furious stamp of running feet n the hall stairway, and the faint sound of an upstairs doors being slammed.

Marianna walked swiftly to the hall door, looked up the stairway, and opened her mouth to call out. However, her habitual restraint, her distaste for scenes and the thought that Katie, in the kitchen would know that something was unusually wrong with this well-conducted household overmastered her impulse. A step or two more took her to the foot of the stairs. Tentatively she placed her hand on the newel post, stood undecided a moment longer, then, turning slowly, walked back into the living room and sank down in the chair before her desk.

"She'll throw herself on her bed, have a good cry, and be herself again by the time Katie serves dinner." Marianna spoke aloud, in the manner of one who is trying to convince herself by the sound of her own voice. She rested her elbows on her desk once more, twined her fingers, and pressed her forehead against them.

In her heart there was a strange mix-up of emotions. She was sorry and she was glad. Sorry because her son, Grant, had married a black woman. Sorry because Grant was dead. Sorry for the grief of the black woman for her dead baby. Of course, she was sorry for that; but glad, darkly glad, that the baby who, she had heard, was very brown, would no longer hold a claim upon the Manton family. Lucia—

Running footsteps descending the stairs broke in upon Marianna's thoughts. Lucia had recovered quickly, too quickly. Marianna raised her head. The hall light was on. Lucia, hatted and coated, drawing on her gloves, flashed past.

Quickly Marianna got to her feet.

"Lucia!" she called, knocking against the side of the desk in her haste to reach the hall. "Lucia!"

Marianna stood painting in the hall, staring at her daughter, who was turning the door knob.

"Where are you going, Lucia?"

"Out, mother! Definitely, out!"

Lucia wrenched the door open as she spoke, letting in the sharp, tangy autumn air.

"Where? Tell me!"

Marianna was at the door, grasping Lucia's hand, as it held the knob.

The girl turned her face to her mother. Dark lightnings quivered and flashed in Lucia's black eyes.

"It seems to me, mother, that a woman of your intelligence could answer that question with very little trouble."

It was but for a moment. The clashing of wills in the looks that were exchanged. In that moment a battle was fought and won. Marianna knew that never again would Lucia give unthinking obedience to her mother.

Slowly her hand dropped; slowly she turned and walked back into the living rom. As she crossed the threshold, the outer door slammed decisively shut. Marianna crossed to the window. By the light of the street lamp directly in front of the gate, she watched Lucia's quickly retreating figure until it vanished from her sight.

Sighing, Marianna walked back to her desk and sat down. For a long while she slumped there, eyes closed, brows drawn in a black frown. Her fingers, thrashing about on the desk, finally touched the manuscript. Opening her eyes, Marianna drew the first sheet toward her. The speech. It wouldn't hurt to go through it again. A reading would help quiet her nerves.

Page by page she re-read the manuscript. Little by little the frown erased itself from her brows, and her lips relaxed their grim tautness. When she reached the last page, her face was clear and complacent.

"This," she murmured, "is a perfect ending. The best I've ever written."

In a half-whisper, she read the concluding paragraph aloud: "And finally, there can be no real peace, no successful realization of democracy until all people, everywhere, learn to look beneath the accidents of birth, creed and color, and find the man in God's own likeness hidden there."

[*The Crisis* 52.10 (October 1945): 286–287, 301]

LIKE A WINDING SHEET

by Anne Petry

He had planned to get up before Mae did and surprise her by fixing breakfast. Instead he went back to sleep and she got out of bed so quietly he didn't know she wasn't there beside him until he woke up and heard the queer soft gurgle of water running out of the sink in the bathroom.

He knew he ought to get up but instead he put his arms across his forehead to shut the afternoon sunlight out of his eyes, pulled his legs up close to his body, testing them to see if the ache was still in them.

Mae had finished in the bathroom. He could tell because she never closed the door when she was in there and now the sweet smell of talcum powder was drifting down the hall and into the bedroom. Then he heard her coming down the hall.

"Hi, babe," she said affectionately.

"Hmm," he grunted, and moved his arms away from his head, opened one eye.

"It's a nice morning."

"Yeah," he rolled over and the sheet twisted around him, outlining his thighs, his chest. "You mean afternoon, don't ya?"

Mae looked at the twisted sheet and giggled. "Looks like a winding sheet," she said. "A shroud—" Laughter tangled with her words and she had to pause for a moment before she could continue. "You look like a huckleberry—in a winding sheet—"

"That's no way to talk. Early in the day like this," he protested.

He looked at his arms silhouetted against the white of the sheets. They were inky black by contrast and he had to smile in spite of himself and he lay there smiling and savoring the sweet sound of Mae's giggling.

"Early?" She pointed a finger at the alarm clock on the table near the bed, and giggled again. "It's almost four o'clock. And if you don't spring up out of there you're going to be late again."

"What do you mean 'again'?"

"Twice last week. Three times the week before. And once the week before and—"

"I can't get used to sleeping in the day time," he said fretfully. He pushed his legs out from under the covers experimentally. Some of the ache had gone out of them but they weren't really rested yet. "It's too light for good sleeping. And all that standing beats the hell out of my legs."

"After two years you oughtta be used to it," Mae said.

He watched her as she fixed her hair, powdered her face, slipping into a pair of blue denim overalls. She moved quickly and yet she didn't seem to hurry.

"You look like you'd had plenty of sleep," he said lazily. He had to get up but he kept putting the moment off, not wanting to move, yet he didn't dare let his legs go completely limp because if he did he'd go back to sleep. It was getting later and later, but the thought of putting his weight on his legs kept him lying there.

When he finally got up he had to hurry and he gulped his breakfast so fast that he wondered if his stomach could possibly use food thrown at it at such a rate of speed. He was still wondering about it as he and Mae were putting their coats on in the hall.

Mae paused to look at the calendar. "It's the thirteenth," she said. Then a faint excitement in her voice. "Why, it's Friday the thirteenth." She had one arm in her coat sleeve and she held it there while she stared at the calendar. "I oughtta stay home," she said. "I shouldn't go otta the house."

"Aw don't be a fool," he said. "To-day's payday. And payday is a good luck day everywhere, any way you look at it." And as she stood hesitating he said, "Aw, come on."

And he was late for work again because they spent fifteen minutes arguing before he could convince her she ought to go to work just the same. He had to talk persuasively, urging her gently and it took time. But he couldn't bring himself to talk to her roughly or threaten to strike her like a lot of men might have done. He wasn't made that way.

So when he reached the plant he was late and he had to wait to punch the time clock because the day shift workers were streaming out in long lines, in groups and bunches that impeded his progress.

Even now just starting his work-day his legs ached. He had to force himself to struggle past the out-going workers, punch the time clock, and get the little cart he pushed around all night because he kept toying with the idea of going home and getting back in bed.

He pushed the cart out on the concrete floor, thinking that if this was his plant he'd make a lot of changes in it. There were too many standing up jobs for one thing. He'd figure out some way most of 'em could be done sitting down and he'd put a lot more benches around. And this job he had—this job that forced him to walk ten hours a night, pushing this little cart, well, he'd turn it into a sittin-down job. One of those little trucks they used around railroad stations would be good for a job like this. Guys sat on a seat and the thing moved easily, taking up little room and turning in hardly any space at all, like on a dime.

He pushed the cart near the foreman. He never could remember to refer to her as the forelady even in his mind. It was funny to have a woman for a boss in a plant like this one.

She was sore about something. He could tell by the way her face was red and her eyes were half shut until they were slits. Probably been out late and didn't get enough sleep. He avoided looking at her and hurried a little, head down, as he passed her though he couldn't resist stealing a glance at her out of the corner of his eyes. He saw the edge of the light colored slacks she wore and the tip end of a big tan shoe.

"Hey, Johnson!" the woman said.

The machines had started full blast. The whirr and the grinding made the building shake, made it impossible to hear conversations. The men and women at the machines talked to each other but looking at them from just a little distance away they appeared to be simply moving their lips because you couldn't hear what they were saying. Yet the woman's voice cut across the machine sounds—harsh, angry.

He turned his head slowly. "Good Evenin', Mrs. Scott," he said and waited.

"You're late again."

"That's right. My legs were bothering me."

The woman's face grew redder, angrier looking. "Half this shift comes in late," she said. "And you're the worst one of all. You're always late. Whatsa matter with ya?"

"It's my leg," he said. "Somehow they don't ever get rested. I don't seem to get used to sleeping days. And I just can't get started."

"Excuses. You guys always got excuses," her anger grew and spread. "Every guy comes in here late always has an excuse. His wife's sick or has grandmother died or somebody in the family had to go to the hospital," she paused, drew a deep breath. "And the niggers are the worse. I don't care what's wrong with your legs. You get in here on time. I'm sick of you niggers—"

"You got the right to get mad," he interrupted softly. "You got the right to cuss me four ways to Sunday but I ain't letting nobody call me a nigger."

He stepped closer to her. His fists were doubled. His lips were drawn back in a thin narrow line. A vein in his forehead stood out swollen, thick.

And the woman backed away from him, not hurriedly, but slowly—two, three steps back.

"Aw, forget it," she said. "I didn't mean nothing by it. It slipped out. It was a accident." The red of her face deepened until the small blood vessels in her cheeks were purple. "Go on and get to work," she urged. And she took three more slow backward steps.

He stood motionless for a moment and then turned away from the red lipstick on her mouth made him remember that the foreman was a woman. And he couldn't bring himself to hit a woman. He felt a curious tingling in his fingers and he looked down at his hands. They were clenched tight, hard, ready to smash some of those small purple veins in her face.

He pushed the cart ahead of him, walking slowly. When he turned his head, she was staring in his direction, mopping her forehead with a dark blue handkerchief. Their eyes met and then they both looked away.

He didn't glance in her direction again but moved past the long work benches, carefully collecting the finished parts, going slowly and steadily up and down, back and forth the length of the building and as he walked he forced himself to swallow his anger, get rid of it.

And he succeeded so that he was able to think about what had happened without getting upset about it. An hour went by but the tension stayed in his hands. They were clenched and knotted on the handles of the cart as though ready to aim a blow.

And he thought he should have hit her anyway, smacked her hard in the face, felt the soft flesh of her face give under the hardness of his hands. He tried to make his hands relax by offering them a description of what it would have been like to strike her because he had the queer feeling that his hands were not exactly a part of him any more—they had developed a separate life of their own over which he had no control. So he dwelt on the pleasure his hands would have felt—both of them cracking at her, first one and then the other. If he had done that his hands would have felt good now—relaxed, rested.

And he decided that even if he'd lost his job for it he should have let her have it and it would have been a long time, maybe the rest of her life before she called anybody else a nigger.

The only trouble was he couldn't hit a woman. A woman couldn't hit back the same way a man did. But it would have been a deeply satisfying thing to have cracked her narrow lips wide open with just one blow, beautifully timed and with all his weight in back of it. That way he would have gotten rid of all the energy and tension his anger had created in him. He kept remembering how his heart had started pumping blood so fast he had felt it tingle even in the tips of his fingers.

With the approach of night fatigue nibbled at him. The corners of his mouth dropped, the frown between his eyes deepened, his shoulders sagged, but his hands stayed tight and tense. As the hours dragged by he noticed that the women workers had started to snap and snarl at each other. He couldn't hear what they said because of the sound of the machines but he could see the quick lip movements that sent words tumbling from the sides of their mouths. They gestured irritably with their hands and scowled as their mouths moved.

Their violent jerky motions told him that it was getting close on to quitting time but somehow he felt that the night still stretched ahead of him, composed of endless hours of steady walking on his aching legs. When the whistle finally blew he went on pushing the cart, unable to believe that it had sounded. The whirring of the machines died away to a murmur and he knew then that he'd really heard the whistle. He stood still for a moment filled with a relief that made him sigh.

Then he moved briskly, putting the cart in the store room, hurrying to take his place in the line forming before the paymaster. That was another thing he'd change, he thought. He'd have the pay envelopes handed to the people right at their benches so there wouldn't be ten or fifteen minutes lost waiting for the pay. He always got home about fifteen minutes late on payday. They did it better in the plant where Mae worked, brought the money right to them at their benches.

He stuck his pay envelope in his pants pocket and followed the line of workers heading for the subway in a slow moving stream. He glanced up at the sky. It was a nice night, the sky looked packed full to running over with stars. And he thought if he and Mae would go right to bed when they got home from work they'd catch a few hours of darkness for sleeping. But they never did. They fooled around—cooking and eating and listening to the radio and he always stayed in a big chair in the living room and went almost but not quite to sleep and when they finally got to bed it was five or six in the morning and daylight was already seeping around the edges of the sky.

He walked slowly, putting off the moment when he would have to plunge into the crowd hurrying toward the subway. It was a long ride to Harlem and to-night the thought of it appalled him. He paused outside an all-night restaurant to kill time, so that some of the first rush of workers would be gone when he reached the subway.

The lights in the restaurant were brilliant, enticing. There was life and motion inside. And as he looked through the window he thought that everything within range of his eyes gleamed—the long imitation marble counter, the tall stools, the white porcelain topped tables and especially the big metal coffee urn right near the window. Steam issued from its top and a gas flame flickered under it—a lively, dancing blue flame.

A lot of workers from his shift—men and women—were lining up near the coffee urn. He watched them walk to the porcelain topped tables carrying steaming cups of coffee and he saw that just the smell of the coffee lessened the fatigue lines in their faces. After the first sip their faces softened, they smiled, they began to talk and laugh.

On a sudden impulse he shoved the door open and joined the line in front of the coffee urn. The line moved slowly. And as he stood there the smell of the coffee, the sound of the laughter and of the voices helped dull the sharp ache in his legs.

He didn't pay any attention to the girl who was serving the coffee at the urn. He kept looking at the cups in the hands of the men who had been ahead of him. Each time a man stepped out of line with one of the thick white cups the fragrant steam got in his nostrils. He saw that they walked carefully so as not to spill a single drop. There was froth of bubbles at the top of each cup and the thought about how he would let the bubbles break against his lips before he actually took a big deep swallow.

Then it was his turn. "A cup of coffee," he said, just as he had heard the others say.

The girl looked past him, put her hands up to her head and gently lifted her hair away from the back of her neck, tossing her head back a little. "No more coffee for awhile," she said.

He wasn't certain he'd heard her correctly and he said, "What?" blankly.

"No more coffee for awhile," she repeated.

There was silence behind him and then uneasy movement. He thought someone would say something, ask why or protest, but there was only silence and then a faint shuffling sound as though the men standing behind him had simultaneously shifted their weight from one foot to the other.

He looked at her without saying anything. He felt his hands begin to tingle and the tingling went all the way down to his finger tips so that he glanced down at them. They were clenched tight, hard, into fists. Then he looked at the girl again. What he wanted to do was hit her so hard that the scarlet lipstick on her mouth would smear and spread over her nose, her chin, out toward her cheeks; so hard that she would never toss her head again and refuse a man a cup of coffee because he was black.

He estimated the distance across the counter and reached forward, balancing his weight on the balls of his feet, ready to let the blow go. And then his hands fell back down to his sides because he forced himself to lower them, to unclench them, and make them dangle loose. The effort took his breath away because his hands fought against him. But he couldn't hit her. He couldn't even now bring himself to hit a woman, not even this one who had refused him a cup of coffee with a toss of her head. He kept seeing the gesture with which she had lifted the length of her blond hair from the back of her neck as expressive of her contempt for him.

When he went out the door he didn't look back. If he had he would have seen the flickering blue flame under the shiny coffee urn being extinguished. The line of men who had stood behind him lingered a moment to watch the people drinking coffee at the tables and then they left just as he had without having had the coffee they wanted so badly. The girl behind the counter poured water in the urn and swabbed it out and as she waited for the water to run out she lifted her hair gently from the back of her neck and tossed her head before she began making a fresh pot of coffee.

But he walked away without a backward look, his head down, his hands in his pockets, raging at himself and whatever it was inside of that had forced him to stand quiet and still when he wanted to strike out.

The subway was crowded and he had to stand. He tried grasping an overhead strap and his hands were too tense to grip it. So he moved near the train door and stood there swaying back and forth with the rocking of the train. The roar of the train beat inside his head, making it ache and throb, and the pain in his legs clawed up in to his groin so that he seemed to be bursting with pain and he told himself that it was due to all that anger-born energy that had piled up in him and not been used and so it had spread through him like a poison—from his feet and legs all the way up to his head.

Mae was in the house before he was. He knew she was home before he put the key in the door of the apartment. The radio was going. She had it tuned up loud and she was singing along with it.

"Hello, Babe," she called out as soon as he opened the door.

He tried to say "hello" and it came out half a grunt and half sigh.

"You sure sound cheerful," she said.

She was in the bedroom and he went and leaned against the door jamb. The denim overalls she wore to work were carefully draped over the back of a chair by the bed. She was standing in front of the dresser, tying the sash of a yellow housecoat around her waist and chewing gum vigorously as she admired her reflection in the mirror over the dresser.

"What sa matter?" she said. "You get bawled out by the boss or somep'n?"

"Just tired," he said slowly. "For God's sake do you have to crack that gum like that?"

"You don't have to lissen to me," she said complacently. She patted a curl in place near the side of her head and then lifted her hair away from the back of her neck, ducking her head forward and then back.

He winced away from the gesture. "What you got to be always fooling with your hair for?" he protested.

"Say, what's the matter with you, anyway?" she turned away from the mirror to face him, put her hands on her lips. "You ain't been in the house two minutes and you're picking on me."

He didn't answer her because her eyes were angry and he didn't want to quarrel with her. They'd been married too long and got along too well and so he walked all the way into the room and sat down in the chair by the bed and stretched his legs out in front of him, putting his weight on the heels of his shoes, leaning way back in the chair, not saying anything.

"Lissen," she said sharply. "I've got to wear those overalls again tomorrow. You're going to get them all wrinkled up leaning against them like that."

He didn't move. He was too tired and his legs were throbbing now that he had sat down. Besides the overalls were already wrinkled and dirty, he thought. They couldn't help but be for she'd worn them all week. He leaned further back in the chair.

"Come on, get up," she ordered.

"Oh, what the hell," he said wearily and got up from the chair. "I'd just as soon live in a subway. There'd be just as much place to sit down."

He saw that her sense of humor was struggling with her anger. But her sense of humor won because she giggled.

"Aw, come on and eat," she said. There was a coaxing note in her voice. "You're nothing but a old hungry nigger trying to act tough and—" she paused to giggle and then continued, "You—"

He had always found her giggling pleasant and deliberately said things that might amuse her and then waited, listening for her delicate sound to emerge from her throat. This time he didn't even hear the giggle. He didn't let her finish what she was saying. She was standing close to him and that funny tingling started in his finger tips, went fast up his arms and sent his fist shooting straight for her face.

There was the smacking sound of soft flesh being struck by a hard object and it wasn't until she screamed that he realized he had hit her in the mouth—so hard that the dark red lipstick had blurred and spread over her full lips, reaching up toward the tip of her nose, down toward her chin, out toward her cheeks.

[*The Crisis* 52.11 (November 1945): 317–318, 331]

IT'S NEVER TOO EARLY: A TRILOGY

by Thelma Thurston Gorham

As soon as she returned to Bungalow A, following the kindergarten recess, Judy Carlisle sensed something wrong with the little doll house in which she and her small charges took such inordinate pride. The dolls were seated, in prim array, around the tea-table: three or four distinctly oriental-looking ones, a Mexican señorita, a colorful Tyrolean lass and several run-of-the-mill blondes and brunettes of unmistakable American manufacture and origin. Then, as automatically as she had sensed the wrongness, Judy knew what it was. There was one empty chair in the tea-table circle. Where was Suzanne with the long-lashed eyelids that covered life-like brown eyes when she slept? Suzanne, with the coarse, black curls who cried, "Ma-ma," when she was laid down? Beautiful, sepia-tinted Suzanne was not in the circle of precisely-propped dolls.

"Where's Suzanne?"

To her question there was a tense, disquieting silence. Usually every kindergartener tried to answer at once; but this time none of the children uttered a word. Stretched on their mats, most of them appeared asleep.

Judy repeated the question: "Where's Suzanne, Shirley's doll? Has anyone seen her?"

On a mat near the blackboards, a little Negro girl sat up and the teacher saw that she was clutching a doll, pressing it tightly against her body, as if to protect it from some great danger.

"Oh, Shirley, you have Suzanne." There was relief in the teacher's voice. "Why did you take her away from the doll house? Your mother said we could keep her until the end of the week. You've wrapped her up as if you are going to take her home."

"I am." Shirley made the statement in a defiant, half-whisper, never loosening her grip on the doll.

"Why? We're going to have the doll's tea party and you wouldn't want Suzanne to miss that, would you?"

Shirley only clutched her doll closer and shook her head.

"What's the matter, then? Won't you tell me?" And stooping down, the teacher knelt beside the little girl and put her arms about the tense, hunched little shoulders.

She was close enough to catch the words that came, reluctantly, from Shirley's lips: "Neddy said Suzanne is a nigger baby. He said a nigger baby had no business at a tea party with white dolls."

"That's what Neddy said!" Almond-eyed Dickie LinYing, pretending deep sleep on the mat beside Shirley had heard, too, and was corroborating the statement. Now the room was suddenly normal again, and the uneasy silence was gone. Judy Carlisle stood up, looked at Neddy, but said nothing to him. Neddy was a new pupil in the kindergarten. He was from the South and his first day in the school had been difficult. He had run away twice because he wanted to sit next to "no one but white children."

Judy was thinking fast, talking a little between her racing thoughts: "We'll keep Suzanne here just the same until the end of the week," she told Shirley, "because on Friday we're going to do something extra special, and we'll need Suzanne. We'll also need Carmen Rodriguez's new dolly and if Rose Shapiro can bring the doll that her uncle sent her from Palestine, it will be wonderful." She allowed the roomful of children to forego the afternoon nap as plans were made for "something extra special."

After the kindergarten had gone home, Judy waited for her two friends, Beth Carnegie of the sewing department and Nina Coleman, geography teacher. "Girls," she announced with preamble, "I've got a little job for you. A rush job. I want flags of all the United Nations and I need some fairly authentic national costumes for some dolls—Spanish, Russian, Polish and Swedish."

Laughingly her friends consented to pitch in and help out. "But what's up?" Nina wanted to know. "Is the peace conference meeting in bungalow A?"

"No," Judy replied, "the kindergarten is going to have a festival of dolls of all nations—while I try to teach a few lessons in tolerance." She rubbed her chin thoughtfully and added, "It's never too early to teach tolerance, you know."

II

It was a beautiful morning. One of those mornings when everyone feels glad to be alive. The air was sharp with spicy fragrance of a freshly-cut geranium hedge, children and dogs cavorted across the cool, green lawns, somewhere a sweet-voiced bird wooed its mate, and bright, warm rays of sunshine were dispersing the morning mist. Peggy Carroll felt good, happy, glad to be alive. Head proudly uplifted, she pushed the pram as if it were a richly brocaded carriage with platinum wheels and the little brown baby therein, a royal prince wrapped in an ermine robe. On the way to do her marketing, with enough red points to have steak for dinner, a song on her lips, her eyes following the clouds of mist on the distant hills, Peggy did not hear or see the grimy-faced little white boy until he bumped against the baby carriage.

Still smiling, she looked down at the youngster, red-haired, snaggle-toothed, snub-nosed face generously sprinkled with freckles. He was about six years old. "Whose baby you got there?" he inquired, sidling up to the buggy in a friendly fashion. Then he looked into the buggy. "Why, gee!" There was no hostility, only a grave disappointment in the exclamation. "It's a little nigger baby!"

The boy's words had the effect of suddenly taking all of the sunshine out of the day and enclosing the lovely morning in an ugly, gray sheath. Coming to a jolting stop, standing still, Peggy felt her face become hot all over. She could not speak; but she thought if the boy were older she would have slapped his face.

With feet that no longer skimmed lightly over the ground, eyes scarcely seeing the little brown baby in the pram, she started on her way again. The little white boy was walking in the same direction, slightly ahead of the carriage. Now and then he looked back at the baby. Something in that blithe, backward glance made Peggy suddenly push the buggy a little faster in order to overtake the boy. Deliberately she blocked the child's path.

"Look, my little boy has a new tooth," she invited the youngster's attention. The six-year-old looked and grinned appreciatively.

"His name is Lawrence," Peggy went on matter-of-factly. "Lawrence David Carroll."

"My name is Bobby," the little white boy volunteered. "And I know a boy at school named Lawrence."

"Really, how large is he?" Peggy asked, continuing to make conversation.

"Oh, he's a big boy. 'bout my size, I guess," was his answer. "We call him Larry. Do you ever call your little baby—your little boy Larry."

"Yeah. I 'spect so, too. Larry sounds more friendly, more—more pal-like than Lawrence." The boy walked slowly, keeping pace with the carriage, grinning in a friendly fashion at the baby, smiling shyly at Peggy. At the corner, he put out a grimy-hand and shyly touched the buggy. "This is as far as I can go," he declared regretfully. I just wanted to walk this far with Larry. Now I gotta go back. Good-bye. 'Bye Larry."

"Goodbye," Peggy called back to him. A song as on her lips again, a lilt in her step; and as suddenly as it had come the cold, gray sheath was gone, allowing the world to be bright and warm again. It was a beautiful morning and it was so good to be alive!

III

Caucasian Social Registerite Amy Rhodes knew that sooner or later it would happen. That one day her small daughter, Elise, would come home from the exclusive Briar Brook school with a problem that had nothing to do with reading, writing or arithmetic. Having seen Elise's erstwhile bosom friends of the third grade pass the house well ahead of her own offspring and now watching the latter's downcast, slow approach, she knew this was it. Whatever it was, it had happened.

Obviously Elise had been holding back her tears; but when she saw her mother she gave up. "Oh, Mommy!" Burying her face in Amy's lap, she let out all of the pent-up hurt and frustration. "I don't like Briar Brook anymore. I don't want to go there."

Amy had been thinking of trying one of the new progressive schools; but she didn't mention it. She wanted to know why Briar Brook was no longer desirable to her child and between tears she learned the reason. "The girls play a game...."

"What kind of a game, Darling?"

"We were playing it on the way home, coming across the playground. We were going over and under obstacles and the last one through was a—nigger baby." The last two words came out in a rush of breath as if Elise felt that having to say them she'd get it over as quickly as possible.

Amy had been trying to prepare herself for something like this; but she was still unready. "You mean a little Negro baby."

"No. I meant what I said. They said it that way, only worse. Doris said, 'The last one through is a nasty, dirty, little old nigger baby.'"

"Well?" Amy prodded her daughter on, knowing there was more to come.

"I said that word was an insult and a white person could be one as well as a colored person. I told the kids that and—"

Elise's eyes sought a spot on the floor and warm color suffused her neck and face.

"And what, Darling?" Amy felt that this final answer would be the key to Elise's unhappy state of mind. "After you told them that, what did they say?"

"Doris said she heard her mother say that you had colored—Negro friends and that you were teaching me to be a Negro-lover."

"Only she didn't' say 'Negro-lover' like that, did she?"

"No, she said it the other way, the insulting way; and she said that if they found out that I was one they wouldn't play with me."

"Would you mind their not playing with you?" Amy had tried hard to inculcate in her child not just the lukewarm virtues of tolerance but the warmth and sincerity of appreciation and love in her dealings with persons who were different from her ideas or appearance. Since the day that a chance lecture in anthropology had opened her eyes to fallacies of her own early training, Amy (reared according to the most popular traditions of race supremacy) had learned the hard way to derive real happiness from her associations with people of all groups. She had tried hard—perhaps too hard—to pass on that new-found heritage of happiness and understanding to Elise. Some day she had hoped it would pay salutary dividends; but she had known that along the way the going would have its rough spots. This was one of them. "Would you mind it terribly if they didn't play with you?" she repeated.

"Not terribly much. But then I'd be like Myrtle Margolis. She's Jewish and she gets so lonely at times."

The knowledge that her offspring had passed at least one test with flying colors gave Amy a glow of pride tinged with humility. Nevertheless she asked, "How do you know how Myrtle feels?"

"I play with her and she tells me how she feels when they say mean things to her."

"Now you're afraid they'll say mean things to you, too; and call you names, aren't you? Afraid they'll call you names like 'Negro-lover' and 'Jew-lover,' maybe? Aren't you?"

Again seeking the elusive spot on the floor, Elise managed a muffled "Yes."

Just that morning, Amy had learned of a new progressive school where children were taught the truth about so-called racial differences and even allowed to work out their own suggestions and solutions in practical democracy. It would be a bit expensive, but it would be worth it. Only, she hadn't wanted to transfer Elise in the middle of the term. And now—

Amy drew the tear-stained face upward until the reluctant blue eyes were obliged to look squarely into her own. "Remember the story of the 'Fraidy Cat?' Remember the times when you were small how you tried so hard not to be like that old 'Fraidy Cat'? You aren't going to be like him now, are you?"

The blue eyes were meeting the challenge, losing their look of frustration, mirroring something bright and courageous. "No! I won't be like that 'Fraidy Cat'!" She said it with spirit. "I'll take my new book to school and read it on the way home tomorrow. The one with all the photographs, about the little colored girl. I think, maybe, Doris and the rest of the girls could learn something from that book. And Doris is nosey, she'll want to look at it and I'll let her. I won't be a meanie."

"That's right," Amy agreed.

Bouncing off her mother's lap to find the book, Elise paused: "But do you know one thing, Mommy? I feel sorry for Doris. Really I do."

What now, Amy wondered as she asked the inevitable question.

"Oh, for several reasons. But mostly because she doesn't have a mommy like you."

In a swift, engulfing moment, Amy knew how Elise felt when she had "that good-all-over feeling." It was wonderful—to know that though there would be other rough spots, Elise was acquiring the means of getting past them with a minimum of hurt and heartache.

[*The Crisis* 53.3 (March 1946): 82–83, 93]

THEY KNOW NOT WHAT THEY DO

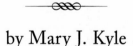

by Mary J. Kyle

I went to Jed Peterson to get the whole miserable story and found him sitting in the dingy living room of his big stone house. As I entered he looked at me with watery blue eyes, then motioned toward a shabby chair. The room gave me a smothery feeling with its drawn shades and tight shut windows. I wanted to step over to the casements, snap the shade clear to the top, and fling windows wide open. The man must have read my mind.

"Ain't never going to look out that window again," he mumbled, and shivered a little. In that split second I felt sorry for Jed Peterson and all his kind, thinking to hide from reality and shame behind drawn shades and closed windows. And then, remembering the events of the night before, my pity for the old man was gone; hot anger flared within me.

"You were an eye-witness, weren't you, Mr. Peterson!" I asked curtly. His pale eyes searched my face taking in every line and feature before he parried my question with another.

"You're one of them, ain't you?" I wondered what would happen should I deny my racial connections. Would the story be any different if Jed Peterson thought I was not "one of them," as he so crudely put it? I spoke up.

"Yes. I'm a Negro, but don't pull any punches on my account. Give it to me straight."

He seemed to shrink into his baggy blue suit as he ran a trembling hand through his straw colored hair. "I'd have to begin from the beginning so's you'd understand," he said. "It's kind of a long tale so maybe—" He looked hopefully from me to the door and I knew he wanted me to go away and stop prodding him. Ignoring his veiled hint I said,

"I've plenty of time to listen. Just take your time and tell me the whole story."

He began with the usual trite phrase, "I like colored folks, all right. Haven't a thing against them, you understand. Why, the porter down to the store is one of my best friends. George would do anything for me—" I started to ask if he was sure the porter's name was George. Instead, I urged:

"Sorry to interrupt you, Mr. Peterson, but please get to the point." He raised startled eyes to mine, then stared at the worn red carpet.

"Well, I just wanted you to understand that what happened wasn't exactly my fault, because I like you people all right." I swallowed hard. This job promised to be almost more than I could take. But I'd come to get a story and I was going to get it, even if it made me sick at my stomach. The man continued, "That old house had been for sale a long time. Guess it was too ramshackle for most folks to bother with. We were all getting kind of disgusted with the place, being so run down and all. Not that this is such a swell neighborhood or anything like that."

I could certainly agree with him on that point. It was one of those "has-been" sections of the city, rubbing shoulders on one side with swank Lake Avenue while the fringes of the Negro ghetto brushed lightly against its heels. It certainly wasn't a "swell neighborhood." Jed Peterson read my thoughts.

I bit my lips to keep back the angry words that pressed against them. "Go on, please, Mr. Peterson." My voice was so low I could hardly hear myself speak.

"Well," he continued, "when the 'for sale' sign came down we naturally wondered who had bought such a dump. Living right across the street, like I do, I could see some one moving around in there at night. But during the day not a soul came near the place. It was kind of mysterious and interesting. Len Williams, who lives next door, came over one night to get a ring side seat, you might say. All we could see was the shadows of two people moving behind the drawn shades. Len whispered something in my ear but I didn't believe what he said. Such a thing just couldn't happen right under our noses. Even if the neighborhood was seedy it wouldn't have got that bad."

Jed Peterson looked at me to see how I was taking this, but I kept my eyes on my note book. The page was still blank.

"Well," Jed went on, "I guess Len must have told other folks what he thought because they began to get restless. Finally Len went to the real estate office to find out who bought the place. All the neighbors got together in my house to hear what he had to say. Len just shook his head.

"'Guess we're barking up the wrong tree this time,' Len told us. 'Some Mr. Simmons laid out cash money for that shack. A big red headed fellow.'

"We all drew a deep breath then and didn't think more about it till the folks moved in." Jed Peterson paused again and looked at me.

"Listen, Mr. Peterson," I said. "Just tell the story straight through without stopping. Tell it as if you were living it again. As if I weren't here." My patience was wearing a bit thin. He hesitated a moment, then cleared his throat and plunged into the tale, words tumbling over each other, as if he were eager to get the thing out of his system, once and for all. This is Jed's story:

Well, in a day or so, the furniture came and a little yellowish woman directed the men where to put it. There was nothing fancy about the stuff, you know. Just plain nice tables and chairs and things like that. Only the stove was new, all white and shiny in the bright sunshine. Once it slipped a little as the men lifted it off the truck and the woman put out her hand to steady it. Just before the van drove off the men handed down a little leather rocking chair. A kid's chair. The woman picked it up and carried it into the house. Not another soul came around till long after dark. Then all you could see was shapes moving just like before.

The next morning the yellowish woman came out leading a dark brown kid by the hand. Every curtain in the block did a regular devil-dance as the folks watched those two go up the street toward the school. Shortly after, a big black man came out of the house and walked up to the car line. Len Williams had been right. The new family was ni—, I mean, colored! The folks just about went crazy. My house, being right on the scene of the crime, so to speak, was a sort of meeting place for the whole neighborhood. Len spoke his piece about getting rid of them and then Cliff Edman added his two cents' worth. Cliff's from Georgia so he had some very unhealthy ideas. The way he talked made the skin on my back tighten up like a piece of dried leather. Why, he actually wanted to lynch those folks. And some of the tales he told—whew. They sure weren't pretty. When I did manage to get a word in I told him that, after all, this was Minnesota, not Georgia, and we'd have to do things different. But it was Len who thought up what to do. His plan sounded easy bit it didn't work.

A bunch of us got together and went over to the Negro's house that night, Len being the spokesman. When we got inside I was surprised how clean the place smelled, considering. Like it had been scrubbed with plenty of strong yellow soap and hot water. The wood work and floors looked cracked and thirsty for want of paint and you could see the places where the scrub brush had bit into the soft old boards. The black man stood in the middle of the tiny living room, the top of his cropped head almost touching the dangling light bulb. He towered over all of us and I felt kind of funny when his sharp black eyes flicked across our faces like a whip-lash. Len pulled himself together and said,

"Now you—" The man interrupted him and his words were clipped short as he spoke.

"The name's Charles Trent." You could almost feel an icy wind blow through the place his tone was so cold. His wife and child were crouched over in a corner of the sofa watching every move. Len Williams talked on.

"Now you tell us what you paid for this house and we'll buy you out. That's fair enough, isn't it?"

Trent's eyes snapped, and he answered Len real defiant like.

"I don't want your money. My boss bought this place for me and I'm paying him back. Besides," his voice seemed to come up out of his stomach and slapped against our ears. "We like it here. It's near the school, got a nice yard for my little girl, and when I get it fixed up—"

Len exploded then. He didn't like that nig—, I mean Man's attitude. "You may like it here but we don't like having you. Understand! If you know what's good for you you'll take a couple hundred more than you paid for the place and get out. That's if you've got any sense in that kinky head of yours."

I thought for a minute Trent was going to blow a fuse. The muscles in his jaws worked up and down in tight little jerks, and he clenched and unclenched his bony hands till the knuckles stood out like knobs. Finally, he got himself together and ripped the ragged words out of his thick lips: "You're the one who'd better 'get' and get quick!"

I could feel the folks tighten up like fiddle strings. Cliff muttered something about "if this was only Georgia." But it wasn't Georgia. It was just a nice town in Minnesota, so what could you do? We got out. One of the men in the bunch turned and spit back through the window and it trickled down and dripped on the sill. Trent and his wife hadn't moved till then, but at that nasty trick he snapped the shade down in our faces.

The next day the kid walked to school alone, the woman watching from the doorway. You could tell the little girl had been cautioned the way she looked straight ahead and held herself so stiff. Even when a stone whizzed through the air and grazed her arm she kept right on, only rubbing the sore spot with the thin brown hand. It was really kind of pitiful, even if she was a ni—, I mean a colored kid.

Well, the days went by and our cash offer jumped till it was up to $5000, nearly twice what the house was worth. Trent still refused. His spunk was sort of impressive, but darned uncomfortable. I felt like I was sitting on the lid of a box of dynamite, knowing all the while that the lid would blow sky high if the fuse was ever lighted. It sure made me sweat. And, you guessed it, Cliff Edman lit the fuse that blew the whole thing to kingdom come.

He got us all together one night and talked a lot about this being a white man's country, and keeping niggers in their places. Then he told some hair raising tales about what they did to uppity blacks in the South. It was enough to take the curl out of your hair to hear him. After that he showed us the cross he'd made. Just a couple of rough boards nailed together, but I didn't like the looks of it. You know how it is. You read about stuff like that but you never figure to get mixed up in a mess like that. Not in this neck of the woods, any how. I kind of suggested we raise our offer to ten thousand if we had to. It sure was worth that price to me to get back to peaceful living again. Not that the colored folks were rowdy or dirty, understand. It was just the idea of them living right in our front doors, so to speak. We just couldn't take that, you know.

Well, Cliff said we'd wasted enough time and no darky was worth that much money, and he'd get rid of them slick as grease in no time flat. He took the cross outside, us trailing behind him like a herd of sheep, and doused it good with kerosene. Someone said, "We don't want no rough stuff," and Cliff laughed a little.

"Just going to scare hell out of 'em," he said. "They'll be gone coons before another night rolls around." He laughed some more. "You Northerners got to learn the quick way to handle niggers."

I didn't like the whole "set-up" but tagged right along with the rest of the gang. After the lights had been out in the Trent house more than an hour, Cliff carried the cross over and stood it right smack in front of the place, near the windows. The earth was soft and squashy like it is in the spring, and a couple of hard whacks drove the wood down in the ground. Seeing the curtains puff in and out of the windows made me notice the screens were off. Then I remembered Trent taking them down to paint the trim. Before I could think more about it flames shot up and around the wooden cross and it stood there, burning hot and bright in the darkness. It wasn't a pretty sight. I closed my eyes to shut out the picture. Then it happened! Like I said the curtains were puffing in and out like little white sails. One edge of the scrim lace whipped through the fire. The next thing we knew the flames were lapping at the window still, up the other curtains, around inside the dry wood, burning like the flames of hell. You won't believe it, but the crowd cheered. That's right. The hideous yell ripped the quiet night to shreds. You've heard of mob hysteria, or something like that. Maybe we all had it. My own throat was raw from shouting, and darned if I know what I was yelling about.

Well, the old place was so dried out inside that the whole downstairs was a blazing furnace in a few minutes. It was really pretty awful. The wail of the fire siren snapped us out of whatever it was we had, and I thought of Trent and his family. Looking up at the high window I saw them all standing real still, outlined against the light from the fire, watching us. Then they rushed to the back of the house and scrambled out on the porch roof. From there it was an easy matter for Trent to drop to the ground, hold up his arms for the kid, then help his wife down. The kid's head was bandaged and she looked like a funny little figure from a Hindu fairy tale in the flickering red light. I wondered for a minute what could have happened to her, then figured maybe one of the rocks had hit too hard, since the kids were always pegging at her. There was a sort of puzzled look mixed up with sadness in her big black eyes as she watched the fire and murmured, "My chair, mama—please, my rocking chair." My mind tumbled back across the days and I could see that woman lifting the little leather rocker from the sidewalk and carrying it into the house. For all I knew it might have been that kid's only toy. I didn't feel very good, thinking about it. Then I remembered that shiny new stove and I looked at the woman. Honestly, her face was as pasty as it will be the day she dies. Not a speck of color in it. She kept pressing her hands hard against her mouth to hold back the whimpering sobs that burbled out.

Then I saw the man and my stomach drew up in a hard knot. Stripped to the waist, he was, and the muscles of his big chest rippled and bulged with every tormented breath he took. There was agony in his black eyes. Yes sir, that's the only word that describes Charley Trent's eyes. Agonized. I wish to God I could forget.

In a little while that blazing inferno was nothing but a blackened, soggy mess. Not a whole stick of furniture left in the place. Someone asked Trent if the stuff was insured. It nearly finished me up when I saw big tears spill out of his eye-sockets and slide down the deep hollows on each side of his mouth. He shook his head slowly from side to side, swaying like a huge tree that had been axed in the vitals. It's awful to see a strong man's weakness. Even though he was black there was something horrible about his—helplessness is the only word I can think of. When he spoke the words were raw and sore. Over and over he moaned, "The dirty trash. The low-down, dirty trash." Not much to say was it! But it sure was a mouthful. I left there and crawled in this hunk of stone and I been here ever since.

Jed Peterson had finished his story. Finished the telling of it, but, looking at his shrunken figure and nervous hands, I knew he'd be a long time getting over the nasty business. I turned away from him and fumbled with my note book. The pages were still blank. Jed's tale was so old I needed no notes to refresh my memory. The only original twist was the locale. Otherwise, it was monotonously the same hopeless account of man's inhumanity to man. I felt drained and empty as I started toward the door.

"Thank you, Mr. Peterson, for the details," I said. "And I do think you'd feel better if you let in God's sunshine and fresh air." I tried to smile. He shook his head violently.

"Oh, no!" he answered. "It'll be a long day in June before I open them curtains. What I don't see won't hurt me, you know." He lifted himself out of his chair and approached the door, running his hands nervously through his hair and across his watery eyes. "You might put in that story that what happened wasn't exactly our fault, you know. If those ni—, I mean, if those colored folks had stayed in their part of town—well, what I'm trying to say is, if they hadn't come right up to our front door, so to speak. Not that I got anything against them, you understand. You make your people know how much most of us like colored folks. Why, the porter down at the store—"   [*The Crisis* 54.3 (March 1947): 78–79, 94]

GHETTO SOUNDS

―⊗⊗⊗―

by Hazel James

The children cry every night. Beginning at first dusk. As the shadows lengthen; as darkness descends, their pitiful wails echo, rebound, fill the air. The dirge commences, a singsong. It rises, swells, until it becomes one endless soul-stirring, heart-tearing sound. The mournful chant saturates the atmosphere; seeps into the soul, burning, searing. The soul cries out in unbearable agony, "My God, no!"

If the heart could separate them, these wailing, sorrowful cries, it would quickly distinguish those sobs of naked hunger—those passionate pleas for bread. And milk. Night after night, they fall into fitful slumber, only to awaken, screaming from the unmerciful attacks of hunger, empty bellies contracting in anguish; small throats dry for the taste of cooling, soothing milk. There is no milk! There is no bread! No bread; no milk for the starving children! Their cries, weak, spasmodic, suffuse the air; sear the soul. And tear the heartstrings!

(We had a little baby, a pretty little baby. She was chubby, bright-eyed. We loved our baby, our pretty little baby. We kissed her and squeezed her. We held her and loved her. And lost her! We watched our baby crushed by the hands of hunger; smothered by the kiss of poverty. We had no milk for our baby. No milk! No bread! There was no milk in this land for our baby! O, what shall we feed our pretty little baby? How can we keep our baby alive?

(We'll pilfer garbage buried deep in dark alleys. We'll stand on street corners and beg for bread. We'll sell our bodies, our tender, young bodies. We'll give up our bodies for the price of one loaf. Bread of Heaven, bread of Heaven, feed our baby! Feed her 'til she wants no more!

No one bought our tender, young bodies. No one heeded our plea for one loaf. Heaven ignored our tears and our pleadings. No bread, no milk could be found for our child! Our baby succumbed in the embrace of hunger. She cried. And died!)

The children cry every night. Beginning at first dusk. Neglected, deserted, abandoned, their wails wrench the heart, set the brain afire. The lonely pathos of all ages lies wrapped in their lament. No mamas! No papas! No loving hands to wipe the tears away. No cooing voice to chase the goblins. Poor frightened little souls, screaming in agony for crumbs of love! And assurance! Outstretched arms, baby arms, lift, reach, plead, hold me! Parched hearts, baby hearts, pine, sigh, cry, love me!

(Poor wretched little baby! Unloved! Deserted! Your mummy didn't' want you! Your mummy wouldn't keep you! Your mummy didn't love you! She wrapped you, your mummy did, in a dirty receiving blanket and laid you on the steps of the church. On the church steps she laid you where aspiring saints tread, head held high, robes pulled tightly about self-righteous bodies. Poor, abandoned baby! Trembling from the touch of cold, manicured fingers: frightened by stares of icy eyes. Scream, baby! Scream for fear! They'll take you, those hands, and put you in pens of stone as animals. They'll feed you and diaper you and make you fat. Like a bloated little pig! Scream! They'll place you in numbered pens with countless other bloated waifs. They'll herd you and drive you and teach you. And give you no love! Scream, baby, scream! Cry to the Lord to free you; to let you die! Scream!!!)

The children cry every night. Beginning at first dusk. As shadows lengthen; as darkness descends, their pitiful wails echo, rebound, fill the air. Plaintive utterances of hurt pour forth, diluting louder whines and groans of discomfort filtering through the clamor, piercing the breast; freezing the soul. The shrieks are coated with fever, shrouded in delirium. The cries penetrate the brain, curdle the soul. Wasted bodies writhe in pain, tumble, twist, pulsate. Deformed bodies broken by fists; lashed by ships! Pitiful, torn bodies! Swollen tongues! Blackened eyes! Nerveless fingers dripping gore!

(Hush, little twisted, broken baby! Hush! Your screams have started the wheels once more. Those infernal, grinding wheels! Churning! Turning! Grind, grind, grind! They're melding! Meshing! Crunching! Crashing! Terrifying, relentless wheels! Hush! Shut up, twisted little whimpering baby! You know what the wheels do to me. You know what horrible things they whisper to my brain! They scream, spank him! Twist his skinny little arms! Bury your fist in his little jelly-belly! Burn his toes! Hold the match close! Closer! This little piggy went to market.... Stop screaming, little twisted baby! Stop! You'll frighten me and I'll go 'way and leave you. That's what I'll do! I'll run away, far away where I can't hear you shriek and yell and yell and shriek.... I'll take my needle and my packet of powder and go 'way. Aha! Have a little prick before I go. A little prick for you before I go. That'll do it! A little prick here.... A little prick there! A prick, prick, prick, prick, everywhere! Sleep, little pin-cushion. Sleep!)

The children cry every night. Beginning at first dusk. As shadows lengthen, as darkness descends, their pitiful wails echo, rebound, fill the air. The dirge commences, a sing-song....

[*The Crisis* 82.1 (January 1975): 28]

Touch Me!

———— ∞∞∞ ————

by Hazel James

I am old. The relentless waves of Time have bruised my body; eroded my bones. Skin that was once firm and elastic has shriveled beneath many summers of flaming suns; has become withered from the caress of icy winds of many winters. My steps are now measured and faltering—from my bed to the wheelchair are agonizing miles. I grope blindly for the glass of water there on the table beside my bed. My hand touches instead the plastic bowl of plastic flowers and bitterness rises in my heart. Two years ago this past Mother's Day, they sent them. Two long years ago!

The children whom I birthed, nurtured, loved, have wandered away. In their quest for happiness, they've forgotten me! The faded flowers in the faded bowl are mute reminders of their forgetfulness. They no longer remember tender kisses that soothed the hurt away. They don't remember strong, loving arms shielding young bodies from danger. Endless day on endless day I sit, surrounded by those who are also forsaken while the faded flowers remind me I'm at the mercy of strangers.

Poker-faced, stern, these strangers minister to my physical needs. Impersonally, they perform those acts necessary for my survival. To them, I'm not a person. Only a number! Number 54 is tendered medication. Number 54 is bathed, dressed assisted into her wheelchair. Number 54 is brought her tray. And forgotten!

I am old and ill. I don't complain of the ravages of disease on my emaciated frame. That's the penalty one must pay for living too long. I seek no sympathy for the excruciating pains that have taken permanent residence within me. The aged must expect such. However, my body could bear its infirmities so much more cheerfully if it were occasionally embraced by warm arms of love; it if were pressed, now and then, in affection. And understanding. And compassion. I don't ask much. Not daily attention. Not hourly companionship. Just, touch me!

Touch me, so I'll know I'm still a segment of this vitally alive, pulsating world of human beings and not an inanimate number lying here staring daily at a plastic bowl of plastic flowers. As you give me medication, allow your sturdy fingers to press my trembling ones in reassurance. Such as act will bring back sweet memories of other days; of other hands, clinging, clasping baby hands; hands raised in supplication; pleading for love. Your act will unroll the scroll of Time and, once again, I'll feel tiny arms about my neck, squeezing, clinging. Touch me!

I know you grow weary of endless complaints and the inane monologues of oldsters like me. You hear so many in the course of your day! We don't mean to complain. We only do so that you'll realize we are alive. And lonely. Look at us! When you do, you don't really see us, do you? You can't discern the utter loneliness, the heart-wrenching loneliness, lurking behind hooded, rheumy eyes. Nor do you see the silent pleading in the trembling hands extended to you.

The endless monologues you hear are not senseless ramblings of disoriented minds. They're the heartcries of forsaken souls begging for remembrance. Only the flicker of an eyelash; the remotest trace of a smile! They're wails of love-starved beings, pleading for a crumb of affection. Look at me!

Look at me and you'll see yourself a few years from now. Your youth, too, will have vanished, stolen by merciless Time. Steps that are quick and sure now will falter, hesitate, slowed by too many mountains climbed; too many rivers crossed. Your hands, too, will reach for love and understanding. They, like mine, will grasp a plastic bowl of plastic flowers. As you sit alone in your wheelchair, your arms, too, will ache for small bodies against your bosom. Your lips will burn for the feel of wet, sticky kisses; for childish pledges of undying love. And, you'll need someone to touch you.

Touch me! The miracle of physical contact will remove the thick crust of disappointment and disillusionment from a heart battered by unkind years. Number 54 will become a person again; a grateful old woman, alive—and thankful! She'll soar beyond her aches and pains; she'll forget plastic flowers in a plastic bowl, and face her day in peace. Trembling hands will grasp each such moment greedily, never letting go. This old, pain-torn body will be revitalized with hope and purpose for when the heart is happy, the soul sings. You'll see! Just touch me!

[*The Crisis* 82.10 (December 1975): 422]

THE LIONS AND THE RABBITS: A FABLE

by Mary Carter Smith

Once there were some rabbits who had lived in a beautiful land as long as anyone could remember. They were brown rabbits. Yet they were not all alike. Some were darker than ivory, others had fur that glistened like black satin. Some were covered by coarse fuzzy fur, some had short beaded fur, still others had fur that was curly.

They lived as families do. There were years of peace and sometimes, as happens among all animals, there would be quarrels. When a quarrel become too intense for words there would be war between one rabbit family and another. But when the war was over, each family would go back to its own part of the land, to its own home.

One day some different animals landed on the shores of the land of rabbits. They were strong gray lions. They were strong because they had strange weapons that breathed fire. The rabbits fought them. But what chance has a rabbit with its small teeth and claws, even with the wooden sticks they used as weapons, against lions with murder in their eyes, smoking sticks in their front paws, and the blessings of their God?

The lives of the rabbits were never the same after that. Some of the rabbit families ran far, far into the bush. The lions captured many of the rabbits and forced them to do all the kinds of work the lions thought demeaning. The rabbits could no longer choose where they would live. The lions claimed the land belonged to them. The rabbits could only live where the lions allowed them to live.

The rabbits could not understand the lust of the lions for the shining gold and the hard diamonds that could be found, even on top of the earth and in the streams of the land. The lions rejoiced when they saw the gold and the diamonds. They could not eat them, yet, somehow, possessing the gold and diamonds made the lions leap for joy. They were greedy for more. Many other lions came with strange machines. They dug up the trees and made deep holes in the earth. The male rabbits were made to leave their families and go down into the deep holes and bring up the gold and the diamonds. Sometimes it was very cold in the deep, deep mines. At other times it was so hot that the rabbits could hardly breathe. But work they must. In the evenings when they were brought up to the top of the earth they had to stay in the cages the lions had built for them. The rabbits missed the tender food they used to eat. They missed their families. But what they missed most was their freedom. The lions beat and abused them whenever they liked. Many rabbits died. Then the lions went out and forced other rabbits to leave the lands where they had lived for thousands of years and come to the City of Gold the lions had built and work in the mines.

The rabbits who worked in the mines had always danced for joy. Now, once a week, the lions would have the rabbits come out and dance for the visiting lions who would come to watch them. At first, some of the visitors would throw juicy carrots to the rabbits as they watched them dance. But the leaders of the lions had signs put up: DO NOT FEED THE RABBITS.

Secretly, when they could, the rabbits gathered together to plan ways to defeat the lions.

But the gray lions with hearts of gray steel broke up their meetings and killed or jailed their leaders.

Finally, one young rabbit whose eyes and mind had not yet been dulled by forced labor, hunger, and beatings decided to try to find the Chief of Rabbits who lived in a faraway place. The little rabbit's journey was long and arduous. But he was helped by other rabbits who knew from the drums that sent messages the lions could not understand that he was coming. They hid him when the lions were about. They shared what food they had with him. After many days the young rabbit reached the kraal of the Chief of Rabbits, a kraal so well hidden that the lions with all of their power could not find it.

Little Rabbit bowed in respect to the old chief Rabbit. Then he told him what was happening to their land and to their people. Chief Rabbit sighed and told Little Rabbit he already knew what was happening and that they could depend upon no others to save them. All over the world other animals, too, knew what was happening in the City of Gold and the Land of Diamonds. Some spoke righteous words against the lions. But most of the other animals wanted to trade what they had for the gold and diamonds of the lions and would do nothing to help the rabbits.

Chief Rabbit knew one sure solution to their problem; one each rabbit must choose to accept or to reject. Little Rabbit wanted to know what the solution was that would end the nightmare their lives had become. Chief Rabbit told him. With tear-filled eyes Little Rabbit left the Royal Kraal. As he traveled the miles back to the poor land the lions had selected for his family the little rabbit told every other rabbit he met the message given him by the chief. The drums carried the message onward. Soon every rabbit in the beautiful land had heard. Secretly, the rabbits spoke one to the other and it was decided to accept the solution offered by the Chief Rabbit.

A date was set. On the night before, the rabbits in the prisons, in the mines, on the farms, on the locations, in the towns, and in the villages, gathered the food they had and brought the clearest water they could find. After pouring a libation in memory of their ancestors, the rabbits ate, danced, and talked of their love for each other. Then certain groups went out to perfect their part of the plan. The last thing the adult rabbits did that night was to kiss the children goodbye for a while. Then they fed them food mixed with a deadly but tasteless herb.

The next morning there was pandemonium amongst the gray lions. Not one rabbit came to work. There was a sudden stillness in the air. No lion babies were fed. No lion's food was cooked. No lion's garbage was collected. The streets were not swept. The clothes were not washed. The lion women were too upset to remember their daily target practice. All of the lions were very much upset. When no rabbit would work in the gold and diamond mines, the anger of the lions knew no bounds. They went to the cages where the rabbits slept. The rabbits were there. But not a rabbit moved. The lions raised their clubs and their firesticks. The small rabbits swarmed over them biting with all their strength before they were killed. Then the smoke began to rise from the most treasured building of the lions, the many buildings that, in various ways, supplied the money the lions worshipped. The rabbits who had carried slow-burning sticks in their mouths perished in the fires they ignited. Other rabbits simply would not open their mouths to eat or to drink. To these, the lions pleaded. They promised them some of the freedom for which the rabbits were now dying. It was too late. The rabbits had already decided. They died slowly with dignity.

Soon the City of Gold and the Land of Diamonds was filled with the stench of death and the fires of vengeance.

Weeks before The Day of Reckoning each tribe had sent one family to live in the Royal

Kraal. There the nucleus of the race of rabbits lives; believing someday a just Presence will enable them to return to their homes.

Each rabbit that died passed to The Land of Forever. There they greeted the newcomers, communed with the ancestors, and are living with joy.

As for the lions, the last I heard they were struggling midst the total confusion their sick minds had brought upon them.

MORAL: Strength and kindness do not often walk hand in hand.

[*The Crisis* 85.3 (March 1978): 104–105]

INDEX

Abyssinian Church 239

Africa 1, 4, 6, 9–11, 15, 49, 83, 106, 126–131, 135, 142, 156, 181, 427–428, 431, 436

Aidoo, Ama Ata 6

Anderson, Marion 420

angels 32, 62, 72, 77–78, 92, 106–107, 109, 124–126, 128, 138, 187, 214, 255, 275, 282, 284

Arkansas 11, 347–348

art 2–5, 16, 19, 94, 96–97, 108, 165, 167, 187–188, 236–237, 291, 420; *see also* artist

artist 3, 5, 7, 9, 11, 14, 19, 71, 94, 166, 192; *see also* art

Athens 109

Aunt Jemima 335

Baltimore 20, 136, 243, 246

Baptist 18, 58, 123, 187, 189, 221, 409

Baton Rouge 21, 313

beauty 4, 8, 14–16, 21, 52, 90, 92–94, 96, 99–100, 105, 118, 131, 135

Bible 18, 43, 59, 72, 92, 188, 296, 312

Boston 11, 22, 124, 169, 192

Bronx 413

Browning, Robert 134, 149, 271

California 13, 22, 23, 258

Camden 68

Caribbean 206

Caucasian 23, 330, 445

Chicago 8, 14, 20, 23, 124, 242, 256, 294–295, 297–298, 350, 354

children 7–12, 14, 17, 19–20, 24–26, 38, 47, 51–53, 57, 58, 60, 62, 64, 66, 70, 73–74, 77–79, 81–83, 86–87, 91–92, 94–95, 96, 98, 101, 103, 107, 109, 111–112, 115, 117, 124, 126–127, 135, 137, 142, 144, 147, 149, 152–154, 158–159, 163–164, 167–168, 173, 178–180, 182, 184, 188–189, 191, 192, 198–201, 211–214, 216–220, 222, 223, 225–227, 229–231, 234–236, 243, 248–250, 253, 254, 256, 260, 274–275, 277–278, 280, 286, 289–290, 292–293, 297, 301–302, 304, 306–307

China 23, 205, 223, 419

Christian 18, 32, 77, 188–189, 225–226, 281, 283, 286, 364–365, 386, 395

Christmas 20, 28, 31, 33–34, 39, 41, 59–63, 79–81, 227–229, 276–277, 279, 291, 301–305, 339–340, 342–344, 354–355

church 9–10, 18, 42, 58, 72, 76–77, 111–112, 123, 135, 137, 160, 163, 184–185, 187, 190, 221–222, 225–227, 238–239, 263, 277–278, 280, 283–

285, 287, 302, 305, 311, 324, 355–356, 360–361, 365, 409–412, 414–415, 420, 426, 452; *see also* ministers; preaching

Civil War 136, 294, 384

clinics 138, 328, 422

colleges 5, 7–8, 11–13, 17, 20, 27, 59, 77, 93, 127, 192, 225, 234, 257, 276, 334, 404–405, 424

colored 1–4, 7–9, 12–15, 17–19, 23–27, 29–33, 37–39, 44–46, 48–50, 54, 62–63, 66–69, 71–72, 82, 85, 89–90, 92, 87–101, 103–107, 109, 111, 114, 124, 135–137, 140, 144, 160–161, 164–165, 168–171, 173, 175–176, 181, 184, 187, 189, 197–198, 203, 213–214, 244, 246–248, 250, 253, 255, 259, 265, 267, 274, 296, 298, 330, 331–332, 334–335, 338, 341, 346–347, 351, 353–354, 357, 361, 369, 373–374, 381, 387, 395, 399, 402, 405–406, 409, 420, 423, 426, 432, 439, 446–451; *see also* Negro

deacons 58, 225–226, 280–281, 285, 360, 361, 366, 368

Delaware 32, 136, 244

Detroit 13, 295

devil 79, 99, 142, 170, 214, 222, 248, 280–281, 310–311, 364, 374, 382, 385, 400, 424, 431, 449

doctors 18, 43, 62, 112–117, 137, 144, 154, 166, 173, 180, 182–184, 216–220, 236, 238, 308, 328, 355, 360–365, 402, 407, 417, 420, 423–424, 432

Dover 21, 243, 246–247

Du Bois, W.E.B. 1–13, 16–23

Egypt 201

engineers 33, 48, 50, 70, 89–90, 137, 244

England 11–13, 17, 20, 65, 68, 69, 97, 128, 136, 186, 188, 232, 235, 256, 350–352, 369, 421, 428

Episcopalianism 18, 135

Europe 5, 69, 74, 135, 395, 427

factories 17, 248, 260–261

farmers 17, 67, 127, 133, 135, 176, 187, 266, 268, 282, 396–397

Fauset, Jessie 4–5, 9, 11, 23, 41, 64, 84, 91, 132

France 11, 13, 24–26, 35, 39, 65–73, 97–98, 101, 105, 110–112, 117, 135, 162, 188, 195, 201, 204, 264, 391

gardeners 144, 346

gardens 28, 35, 38, 42, 72, 81, 105, 114, 130, 147, 153, 171, 188–190, 207–209, 211, 221, 239, 272–